The
STORM
of HEAVEN

Tor Books by Thomas Harlan

The
STORM
of HEAVEN

Book Three of
The Oath of Empire

Thomas Harlan

TOR®
fantasy

A TOM DOHERTY ASSOCIATES BOOK
NEW YORK

This is a work of fiction. All the characters and events portrayed in this book are either products of the author's imagination or are used fictitiously.

THE STORM OF HEAVEN

Copyright © 2001 by Thomas Harlan

Edited by Beth Meacham

A Tor Book
Published by Tom Doherty Associates, LLC
175 Fifth Avenue
New York, NY 10010

www.tor.com

Tor® is a registered trademark of Tom Doherty Associates, LLC.

ISBN: 0-812-59011-2
Library of Congress Catalog Card Number: 2001021952

First edition: June 2001
First mass market edition: July 2002

Printed in the United States of America

0 9 8 7 6 5 4 3 2 1

For the Three Lions,
who did their very best to help
but mostly lay around and dreamt
of mice and sun-warmed beds

Many thanks must go to Dr. Allison Futrell, Dr. Jeanne Rheames Zimmerman, Jeanne Hasman, Colin Dunnigan, and Melissa "Queen Bee" Giffords for their help with various translations, arcane questions, and other historical quibbling. A lasting debt to Hergé, Uderzo, and Goscinny must also be acknowledged. All resulting errors, of course, are the author's.

NOTES ON
NOMENCLATURE

The Roman mile is approximately nine-tenths of
an English mile.
A league is approximately three Roman miles in
distance.

MAPS

The Roman Empire
The Levantine Coast
Jerusalem
Constantinople
Roma Mater
The Plain of Mars

OATH OF EMPIRE ON THE WORLD WIDE WEB
http://www.throneworld.com/oathofempire

THE WESTERN ROMAN EMPIRE

Partial WESTERN and EASTERN
ROMAN EMPIRES
624 AD

The Levantine Coast (624 AD)

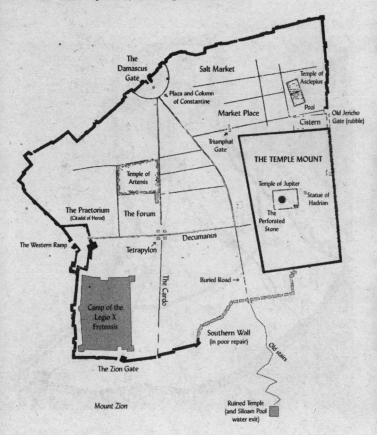

Jerusalem (Aelia Capitolina, Hierosolyma) in 624 AD

The Damascus Gate

Salt Market

Temple of Asclepius

Plaza and Column of Constantine

Market Place

Pool

Cistern

Old Jericho Gate (rubble)

Triumphal Gate

THE TEMPLE MOUNT

Temple of Jupiter

Temple of Artemis

Statue of Hadrian

The Perforated Stone

The Praetorium
(Citadel of Herod)

The Forum

The Western Ramp

Decumanus

Tetrapylon

The Cardo

Buried Road →

Camp of the Legio X Fretensis

Southern Wall
(in poor repair)

Old stairs

The Zion Gate

Mount Zion

Ruined Temple
(and Siloam Pool water exit)

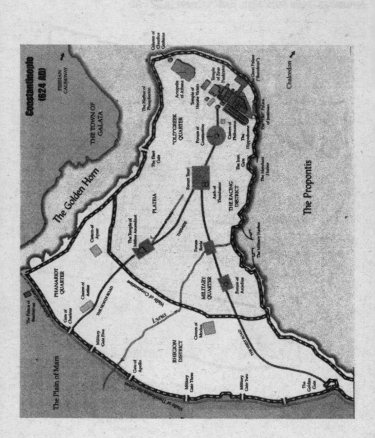

Constantinople (624 AD)

PERSIAN CAUSEWAY

THE TOWN OF GALATA

The Golden Horn

The Plain of Mars

PHANARIOT QUARTER

The Palace of Botianeum

Gate of Charisius

THE SECOND ROAD

Cistern of Aetius

Cistern of Aspar

The Temple of Militia Abundant

PLATEIA

Forum Tauri

The Fourth Gate

"OLD GREEK" QUARTER

The Harbor of Phosphorion

Acropolis of Athena

Temple of Athena

Temple of Zeus

Temple of Hecate Victrix

Cistern of Philoxenus

Porticus of Constantine

Forum of Constantine

The Great Palace (Boukoleon?)

The "Old" Palace of Justinian

The Hippodrome

Military Gate Five

Lycus

Cistern of Mocius

RHEGION DISTRICT

Cistern of Modestus

Gate of Apollo

THE THIRD ROAD

Military Gate Three

Military Gate Two

THE WALL OF THEODOSIUS the Great

The Golden Gate

MILITARY QUARTER

Region of Arcadius

Forum Bovis

THE RACING DISTRICT

Arch of Theodosius

Forum Tauri

Emissary Tract

The Town Gate

The Military Harbor

The Merchant Harbor

The Propontis

Chalcedon

Columns of Claudius Gothicus

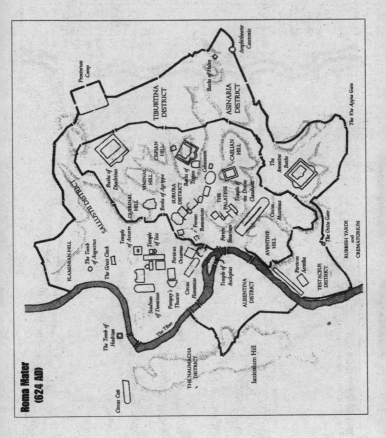

Roma Mater
(624 AD)

Circus Gaii

The Tiber

The Temple of Hadrian

FLAMINIAN HILL

The Tomb of Augustus

The Great Clock

Temple of Astarte

Temple of Isis

Porticus Octaviae

Stadium of Domitian

Pompey's Theater

Circus Flamminus

Temple of Aesclapius

SALUSTIAN DISTRICT

Baths of Diocletian

QUIRINAL HILL

VIMINAL HILL

Baths of Agrippa

Baths of Constantine

CISPIAN HILL

SUBURA DISTRICT

Baths of Trajan

Forum Romanum

THE PALATINE

Forum Boarium

TIBURTINA DISTRICT

Baths of Helen

Coliseum

CAELIAN HILL

Temple of the Divine Claudius

ASINARIA DISTRICT

Amphitheater Castrense

The Via Appia Gate

The Antonine Baths

Praetorian Camp

Circus Maximus

AVENTINE HILL

ALSIENTINA DISTRICT

Porticus Aemilia

TESTACEUS DISTRICT

The Ostia Gate

RUBBISH YARDS and CREMATORIUM

THE NAUMACHIA DISTRICT

Janiculum Hill

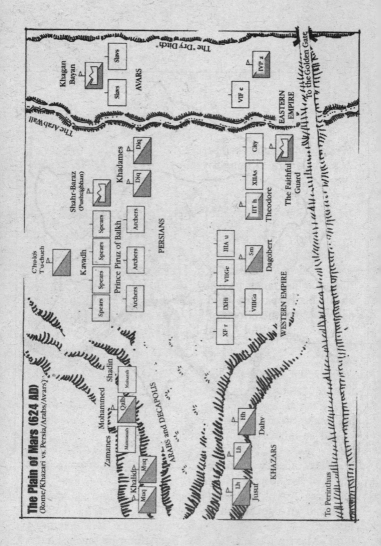

The Plain of Mars (624 AD)
(Rome/Khazari vs. Persia/Arabs/Avars)

The Dry Ditch

Khagan Bayan — Slavs / Slavs — AVARS

IVP a

VIP e

EASTERN EMPIRE

The Arab Wall

Diq / Diq — Khadames

Shahr-Baraz (Pushtigbhan)

City

Theodore — XIIAs — IIT h

Kavadh — Spears / Spears / Spears / Spears / Spears — Archers / Archers / Archers

Prince Piruz of Balkh — PERSIANS

Cholos Tu-chueh

The Faithful Guard

IIIA u

Dagobert — Sm — VIIIGe

IXHh / VIIIGa

XF r — WESTERN EMPIRE

Zamanes — Mohammed — Shadin

Mansarah

Qalb

Mansub

Khalid — Muq / Muq

ARABS and DECAPOLIS

Hh — Dahv

Lh

Jusuf — Lh — KHAZARS

To Perinthus

To the Golden Gate

DRAMATIS PERSONAE

THE ROMANS AND THEIR ALLIES

GALEN, Augustus ("emperor") and God of the Western Roman Empire. A thin, driven man; the eldest of the three Atreus brothers, sons of the Latin Roman governor of Narbonensis (southern France). Formerly a Legion commander on the German frontier, and Emperor of the West for seven years.

HERACLIUS, Avtokrator ("emperor") of the Eastern Empire. A tall, blond man of Armenian descent, the young Emperor has fallen prey to a debilitating sickness which swells his limbs with fluid and has driven him into madness. Despite the efforts of his wife, Martina, and the captain of the Faithful Guard, Rufio, each day brings him closer to death.

AURELIAN, Caesar ("prince") of the Western Empire. The middle Atreus brother, a cheerful, burly redheaded man with a talent for engineering, constructing mechanical toys and horse breeding. Galen's heir while the Emperor's son is still an infant.

MAXIAN, Caesar ("prince") of the Western Empire. A priest of the Temple of Asclepius the Healer, youngest of the three Atreus brothers. Gifted with the rare ability to heal and an unexpected and dangerous talent for necromancy. Not yet grown into his full power as a thaumaturge, Maxian has lost his way. Everything he touches has turned to ash, veering into disaster.

THEODORE, Great Prince of the Eastern Empire. Heraclius' younger brother, a proud, willful and aggressive man. Though he loves and obeys his elder brother, he cannot stand the Empress Martina, his niece, or his brother's— in his view—incestuous and impious marriage.

HELENA, wife of Galen, Empress of Rome. An inveterate writer and socialite, the sharp-tongued Empress is the last of an ancient house and a throwback to the Empire's days of glory. The sole person in the Empire feared by Emperor Galen—and for good reason! Confidante, co-conspirator and friend of the Duchess de'Orelio. Mother of Theodosius, Galen's infant son.

ANASTASIA DE'ORELIO, Duchess of Parma, former minister of the Western Office of Barbarians. Widow of the elderly Duke of Parma, a semiretired spymaster for Emperor Galen, and secret priestess and agent of the forbidden cult of Artemis the Hunter. Orphaned as a child by Visigothic pirates and sold as a slave, Anastasia was taken in by the Thiran priestesses of Artemis and has risen high in their councils as "Queen of Day."

BETIA, the Duchess's Maid. Young Gaulish novitiate of the cult of Artemis. Anastasia's eyes and ears in Rome.

KRISTA, a former maid of the Duchess de'Orelio. One of the Duchess's heirs and agents, along with Thyatis, Krista was Prince Maxian's lover before choosing to stand with the Duchess and the Empire against him. Murdered by the Prince atop Vesuvius, her body is now in Maxian's possession.

THYATIS JULIA CLODIA, agent of the Office of Barbarians. Adopted daughter of Duchess Anastasia, her heir, novitiate of the cult of Artemis and centurion in the Roman Legion. She served, for five years, as the Duchess's primary *sicarius,* or "assassin." The eldest daughter of the ancient and (sometimes) respected Clodian gens in Rome. A distant descendant of Mark Antony, via his marriage to the daughter of Clodius Pulcher, an enemy of Julius Caesar during the last days of the Republic.

NICHOLAS OF ROSKILDE, agent of the Office of Barbarians. A Latin child purchased as a slave by the Stormlords of the Dannmark, Nicholas returned to the Empire as a mercenary and freelance agent for the Eastern Empire's secret service. He now has his first command, leading a cohort of Roman engineers in the troublesome and desolate province of Judea.

VLADIMIR, a wandering K'shapâcara (or "nightwalker"), agent of the Office of Barbarians. A cheerful barbarian exile from the Walach tribes in highland Carpathia, forced into the Empire by the vicious expansion of the Draculis tribes. Glad to have found good friends in Nicholas and Dwyrin, but disconsolate at being sent into the desert.

DWYRIN MACDONALD, Hibernian-born thaumaturge in the service of Rome. A young, cheerful lad with little experience and tremendous potential as a firecaster. Despite many misadventures and thumps on the head, Dwyrin is glad to be back in the desert. He likes the heat.

GAIUS JULIUS CAESAR, formerly dictator of Rome. Revivified by Maxian's power, the cunning, lecherous, brilliant ancient now serves as Prince Maxian's spymaster and adviser. Imbued with new life, he intends to take advantage of every grain of time passing through his fingers.

ALEXANDROS, descendant of Zeus Thundershield, last of the Agead kings of Macedon. Like Gaius Julius, the youthful king has received new life from Maxian's hand. Though still brilliant, rash and headstrong by turns, the weight of centuries has taught the Conqueror a tiny fragment of caution. And now, there is a new Persia to defeat . . .

THE CAT-EYED QUEEN, an ancient sorceress of uncertain antecedents. Mysterious ruler of the K'shapâcara tribes dwelling in the human cities of the Eastern Empire.

THE PERSIANS

SHAHR-BARAZ, shahanshah ("king of kings") of Persia. A former farmer, rebel and lately general of the armies of Persia. Known as the "Royal Boar" for his vigor, enormous mustaches and relentless headlong success on the battlefield. The Boar previously served Chrosoes Anushirwan, but with the great king's death, he has reluctantly taken the throne of Persia, declaring himself the protector of the Twin Radiances, the princesses' Azarmidukht and Purandokht. In their name, he rules a weakened and divided Persia.

KHADAMES, a Persian general. An old friend and subordinate of Shahr-Baraz, Khadames serves both the King of Kings and his brother, Prince Rustam—otherwise known as the sorcerer Dahak—as aide and chief of staff. Weary, and worn down by the enormous effort of the sorcerer's vast plans, Khadames continues to labor in the service of a beloved Persia.

DAHAK (RUSTAM APARVIZ), a sorcerer. The younger brother of the dead Shahanshah Chrosoes, Rustam has trafficked with dark, inhuman powers. In this way he has gathered many servants both fair and foul to his service. Through his powers, Rustam intends to see Persia restored and Rome destroyed.

C'HU-LO, yabghu of the T'u-chüeh (Western Huns). First among Dahak's lieutenants, the T'u-chüeh khan has fallen far since the days when he ruled an empire stretching from the Rha (the Volga) to the Chinese frontier. Now he commands a small but growing army of expatriate kinsmen and is the voice of Dahak in the wilderness.

PIRUZ, Prince of Balkh. Greatest of the Aryan feudal lords along the northern frontier of Persia, Piruz—a young, aggressive noble—seeks no lesser prize than the hand of Princess Purandokht, and by that means, his sons on the throne of Persia.

THE SAHABA

ZENOBIA VI SEPTIMA, queen of Palmyra, lineal descendant of Emperor Aurelian and Zenobia the First. Though her great desert city has been destroyed and the Queen herself struck down by the might of Persia, Zenobia lives on in the memories and thoughts of her kinsmen and allies. The heart and soul of the Decapolis—the Greek and Nabatean cities of the Middle East.

ODENATHUS, Prince of Palmyra, the Queen's nephew. A Legion-trained thaumaturge, the young prince now commands the armies of Palmyra-in-Exile as Queen Zoë's second-in-command. Close friend of Khalid al'Walid and many of the Arab captains.

ZOË, Queen of Palmyra, Zenobia's niece. Heir to the Palmyrene throne and a powerful thaumaturge in her own right. Like Odenathus, she was trained by Rome, and fought in the great war against Persia. The leader of the revolt of the Decapolis and the Arabs against the tyranny of the Eastern Empire. In her, most of all, the memory of Zenobia burns bright.

KHALID AL'WALID ("the Eagle"). Dashing and handsome, the young Eagle commands the Sahaba scouts. Accompanied always by his silent companion, Patik, the Al'Walid intends nothing less than to become a famed general.

JALAL, a Tanukh bowman. Former mercenary, now risen to command the Arab *qalb,* or heavy horse. One of the few surviving companions of Mohammed who fought at the siege of Palmyra.

SHADIN, a Tanukh swordsman. Like his old friend Jalal, a former mercenary. Commander of the Arab *muqadamma* or "center." He too served under Mohammed at Palmyra.

URI BEN-SARID, captain of the Mekkan Jews. Boyhood friend of Mohammed, and the leader of the various Jewish contingents in the army of the Sahaba.

MOHAMMED AL'QURAYSH, a merchant of Mekkah. After a long life of wandering on the fringes of the Empire, unable to find his destiny, Mohammed fell into the company of an Egyptian priest and into the crucible of war. Embattled and trapped in the destruction of Palmyra, Mohammed encountered true evil made flesh. Soon after, distraught at the death of his beloved wife, Khadijah, he attempted to end his own life. Instead, a voice entered him and gave him new purpose and direction. Guided by the voice from the clear air, Mohammed set forth to punish the treachery of the Eastern Emperor Heraclius, precipitating a new war.

THE KHAZARS

JUSUF, tarkhan of the armies of Khazaria, Shirin's uncle. A lean, laconic horseman who has variously served as

Thyatis' second, Anastasia's lover and commander of the Khazar armies. In his youth, he spent time as a hostage in the Avar *hring* and the T'u-chüeh court of the reviled *kha-gan* Shih-Kuei. Widely traveled and an expert with horse, bow and lance.

DAHVOS, kagan of the Khazar nation, Shirin's uncle. The youthful son of the late kagan Zeibil Sahul. Now the weight of his responsibilities press upon him, and he must choose whether the Khazar realm will continue to stand against Persia and beside Rome, or if they will strike their own path.

What Has Gone Before

In the year 622, the Eastern Roman Empire was close to destruction, the capital of Constantinople besieged by the Avars in the West and Persia in the East. As told in *The Shadow of Ararat,* the Emperor of the East, Heraclius, and of the West, Galen Atreus, launched a daring attack into the heart of their Persian enemy. The half-mad Persian shahanshah Chrosoes was taken unawares, and after great battles, he was defeated and his empire given as a wedding gift to the Eastern prince Theodore. At the same time, while the two ancient powers strove to overthrow each other, two critical events transpired. First, in Rome, the young prince Maxian Atreus discovered an ancient thaumaturgic pattern—the Oath—constricting the lives and dreams of the Roman people. Aided by the Nabatean wizard and Persian spy Abdmachus, Prince Maxian embarked on an audacious quest to find the sorcerous power he needed to break down the lattices of the Oath and free the Roman people from their invisible slavery. Second, while the Prince exhumed and revivified Gaius Julius Caesar as a source of thaumaturgic power, a young Roman mage, Dwyrin MacDonald, was swept up in the chaos of the Eastern war.

Attempting to find and save his pupil, Dwyrin's teacher Ahmet left the ancient School of Pthames on the Nile and struck out into the Roman Levant. By chance, in the ancient, rock-bound city of Petra, Ahmet encountered an unexpected friend in the Mekkan pottery merchant Mohammed. Together, the teacher and the merchant found themselves in the service of Zenobia, Queen of Palmyra. At the urging of the Eastern emperor Heraclius, Zenobia and the princes of the Decapolis and Petra gathered an army to resist the advance of the Persian army, under the command of the Great Prince Shahin, into Syria. Unaware of Heraclius' intention to see the independent cities of the Decapolis destroyed while diverting Chrosoe's attention, Zenobia clashed with the Persians, was defeated and then besieged in Palmyra itself. Despite furious resistance, the City of Palms fell to the monstrous power of the sorcerer Dahak. Zenobia and Ahmet perished, and Mohammed escaped with only a small band of his followers through sheer luck.

While Persia collapsed, the Roman agent Thyatis, accompanied by the Khazar tarkhan Jusuf, entered the capital of Ctesiphon and stole away with mad Chrosoes' second wife, the Empress Shirin, Jusuf's niece. Though she was supposed to deliver the Empress to Galen, Thyatis chose instead to disguise her escape and flee south, making a circuitous and eventful return to the Empire via southern Arabia, the East African coast and the black kingdoms of Meröe and Axum. A dangerous decision, not only for the terrible peril of the voyage, but to thwart the desires of her Emperor . . .

Not far away, in the ruined Imperial city of Dastagird, Prince Maxian found the last piece of his puzzle—a crypt holding the stolen, hidden remains of Alexander the Great. As he did with Gaius Julius Caesar, the Prince revivified the Macedonian and felt his power was at last sufficient to break the Oath strangling the Roman people.

In the year 623, as told in *The Gate of Fire,* the Roman armies of East and West returned home, and both nations rejoiced, thinking the long struggle against Persia and the Avar khaganate had at last come to an end. Great plans were laid, both by Heraclius and Galen, and many legionaries rested their weary feet. Yet, all was not well, either within the Empire or without. Heraclius' attempt to return home in triumph was spoiled by a sudden and unexpected illness. Galen's return was more joyful, for he found his wife, Helena, had borne him, at last, a son.

In Arabia the merchant Mohammed reached Mekkah to find his beloved wife, Khadijah, cold in the ground. Devastated, Mohammed climbed a nearby mountain and attempted to end his own life. As he stood poised between death and life, between the earth and sky, a power entered Mohammed, speaking to him from the clear air. The voice urged him to strive against the dark powers threatening mankind. Heeding this voice, Mohammed—after a brutal struggle in the city of his birth—set out with an army of his companions, the Sahaba, to bring the treacherous Emperor Heraclius to justice. To his surprise, he found many allies eager to overthrow the tyranny of the Eastern Empire. First, the rascal Khalid al'Walid, then the lords of Petra and Jerash and finally the exiled Queen of Palmyra, Zoë. With their aid, Mohammed raised the tribes and the cities of the Decapolis to war against Rome. Heraclius' treachery would be repaid with blood and fire.

Indeed, even in Persia the enemies of Rome did not lie quiet. The sorcerer Dahak escaped from the Roman victories with an army and he made his way to the ancient, remote fortress of Damawand, high in the mountains of Tabaristan. There, in a shrine once held holy by the priests of Ahura-Madza, the sorcerer began to muster a great power—not only of arms and men, but of darkness. Deep within the fortress lay a door of stone, behind which unguessed inhuman powers waited. Risking his life and the earth itself, Dahak opened the stone door to capture the power of the ancients. By these means, he shed the last of his humanity and became a true master of the hidden world. Flushed with strength, the sorcerer made his way to ancient Ecbatana and there—with the aid of his servant, Arad—placed the great general Shahr-Baraz on the throne of Persia. Now, a reckoning would come with Rome, and Persia's lost glory would be reclaimed.

In Rome itself, events rushed to a devastating conclusion. Prince Maxian, endowed with the strength of Julius Caesar and Alexander's legends, strove again to overthrow the power of the Oath. Unable to sacrifice his brother Galen, the young prince failed, nearly killing himself and wounding his companion Krista. Fleeing to the safety of his mother's ancestral estate on the slopes of Mount Vesuvius, Maxian struggled with his conscience. Unwilling to wait for his decision, Krista fled, bringing news of the Prince's whereabouts and fatal plans to the Duchess de'Orelio—the Western Empire's spymaster and secret priestess of the Thiran Order of Artemis the Hunter. Her position reinforced by the return of Thyatis, Anastasia ordered the Prince murdered.

Thyatis, Krista and their companions found the Prince on the summit of Vesuvius and, after a deadly battle, failed to kill him. The Prince, mortally wounded, opened himself to the power in the mountain, bringing himself back from death and inciting the somnolent volcano to a staggering eruption, which destroyed the cities of Baiae, Herculaneum and Pompeii. Maxian escaped aboard his iron dragon, while Thyatis chose to plunge from the flying craft into the burning wasteland rather than become his servant. Only the two survived, all else having perished in the cataclysm. Far away, in Persia, Dahak became aware of the Prince and his growing power, realizing a rival was emerging to contest his control of the world of men. . . .

THE PORT OF KORINTHOS,
31 B.C.

)H(

T he sea gleamed like spoiled glass, a flat murky green. Smoke from the town hung in the air, drifting slowly along the beach in thin gray wisps. The Queen, her pale shoulders covered by a rose-colored drape, stood in the surf. Tiny waves lapped around her feet, making silver bangles lift and fall with the water. The sea was as warm as a tepidarium pool.

"No man has ever set foot on the island." The Matron's tone was harsh.

"This is my *son*," said the Queen, her voice urgent. "I need your help."

Sweat beaded on the Greek woman's face, even in the shade of a wide parasol that her servants had lodged in the sand. The Matron stood on the polished plank deck of a small galley, riding low in the water a dozen yards away. Despite the Queen's entreaties, the gray, stiff-backed woman had refused to leave the ship and come ashore.

"We give shelter to women, grown and child, but never to men."

The Queen winced, for the harsh snap of the older woman's voice carried well over the water. There was no wind to break up the sound, or drown it with the crash of surf on the rocky shore.

"He is your get, you must care for him. This is the rule of the Order, as it has been from the beginning."

The Matron turned, flipping the edge of her woolen cloak, black and marked with white checks, over her shoulder. The Queen flinched, feeling the rebuke in her bones. She turned, staring back up the beach to the awnings and pavilions of her camp. The bright colors of the pennants and the cloth that shaded her son and the waiting servants seemed dull and grimy in this still, hot air.

"Have I not given enough?" Despite her best effort, the Queen's voice cracked and rose, shrill and carrying. "Must I give up my son for your faith? He is all that remains of our dream—his father murdered, his patrimony stolen. Hide him for me . . . just for a few months, perhaps a year!"

The women in the galley's rowing deck, responding to the shrill whistle of a flute, raised their long leaf-bladed oars as one. The Matron's figure descended from the platform and paced, slowly, to the foredeck of the vessel. She did not turn or look back, and the angle of her head was canted towards the horizon. A single bank of oars dipped into the water, and the galley turned, swinging easily in the calm sea.

The flute trilled, and the ship slipped across the water, gaining speed with each flashing plunge of the oars.

The Queen felt great weariness crash down upon her, pressing on her shoulders with thick, gnarled fingers. She swayed a little, feeling the sand beneath her feet slip, but then righted herself. Her right hand clutched at a diadem around her neck, slim white fingers covering a golden disk filled with an eight-rayed star.

It would not do, she thought, *to be carried up from the baleful shore by my servants.*

The Queen walked in darkness, her head bent in weariness. A bare gleam of firelight from the bonfires by the ships touched a curl of hair. Now her feet were bare, the wet slippers long discarded, ruined by the salty water. At the very edge of the firelight she stopped and turned, staring out at the gloomy sea. It lay flat and still, windless, as it had done for days, stranding her fat-bellied troop ships in the port.

"Your son is beautiful, daughter. I see him standing by the fire, light gleaming on his limbs."

The Queen stiffened, feeling the air grow chill. She raised her head sharply, nostrils flaring at the languid voice in the darkness. There was a woman, there in the shadow, just beyond the edge of the light. A rustle of cloth and a flash of white caught the Queen's eye as a hood was drawn back.

"Who . . . ? I know you." The Queen's voice turned brittle and hard. "Why are you here?"

Laughter drifted, dying leaves in the fall, cascading down on chill autumn air. "You need me, Pharaoh, to save your son and your dream."

A hand came out of the darkness, thin and elegant, with long, tapering nails. Their surface winked in the dim firelight, glossy and black. Thin gold bracelets jingled a little as the woman stepped closer. The Queen raised her own hand sharply, though the imperious gesture seemed futile against the presence in the darkness. "I will not give him to you. I did not summon you. Go away."

The figure stopped and paused, and the Queen sensed a lean head turning in the night, considering her. A faint wind began to rise, brushing the Queen's curls and softly fluttering the silk draped around her shoulders. Pale red caught in the eye of the figure, gleaming with the bare echo of one of the bonfires.

"Then he will die, spitted on the blades of your enemies, or strangled in some cold cell. Is this your desire? To see your son placed on a pyre of scented wood? To see the flames leap up around his beautiful face?"

The Queen shuddered, feeling her gown cold as a shroud under her fingers.

"Give him to me," hissed the darkness, "and he will grow strong and powerful. He will learn many arts lost to the race of men . . . everything that you dreamed for him will come true. . . ."

"No!" The Queen ran. Sand sprayed away from her feet,

but the cold breath on her neck gave her feet wings.

Behind her, far from the firelight, a figure moved, gathering its consorts. Silently, on padded feet, they went away in the night. The pale woman turned on the height above the town, looking down upon the dim lights in the windows and the torches burning on the steps of the temples.

"So did old Pelias run," the woman mused, amusement stealing over her. "When his daughters came singing, bearing a cauldron of ruddy, red iron . . ." She settled her cloak on thin shoulders and turned her face to the stars in the dark sky, smiling.

▣0-0-0-0-0-0-0-0-0-0-0-0-0-0-0-0-0-0-0-0▣

THE YARMUK PLATEAU, SOUTHERN SYRIA COELE,
624 A.D.

)(

T his is it! Form up by ranks, you lot!"
Colonna, centurion of the Third Cyrene, wiped his face with a dirty white cloth wound around his helmet. The sun had risen only moments ago, wallowing up huge and pale orange in the eastern sky, but the air was already hot. The Roman tried to spit but his mouth was too dry. Around him, legionaries staggered to their feet, strapping on belts and pulling on rivet-studded helms.

Dust puffed into the sky, forming a slow-moving, yellowish cloud over the stirring army. Orders had come before dawn, and Colonna, at least, had seen his men fed before the chill of night fell away. Thousands of soldiers shuffled into formation on dry grass and stony ground. Mindful of the flags of his *banda* commander, Colonna walked along the line of his men. He kept his face grim and impassive, but in his heart he sighed, seeing painfully young faces squinting out from under metal helmets.

A fresh army; those were the words that the Imperial Prince Theodore had used when they had first landed at the great port of Caesarea Maritima, down on the Judean coast. *One destined for victory and glory.*

"You men, listen close." Colonna stopped, settling a hard glare on his face. He scowled at the legionaries in his squad and paced slowly back down the line. They were fit enough, with kit barely a year old and clean weapons. Their ranks were trim; his hobnailed boot had been on their backsides enough in the last month. The baby fat was gone, burned away in the Syrian sun as the Imperial Army marched endlessly, searching for the enemy.

"This is the day. No more running up hill and down valley, trying to bring these bastards to heel. This is the day they stand and fight."

Colonna half turned, shading watery-blue eyes with a sunburned hand. He looked east, squinting in the glare of the morning sun. The land was open and uneven, marked with tumbled hills of black rock and shallow washes filled with scrawny trees. A slight slope descended from the Imperial camp, down toward a dry watercourse. Beyond that an equally gentle slope rose up, thick with tufted grass and scattered fist-sized stones. There, anchored by a high tor of crumbling black rock on the left, and by the edge of the plateau on the right, massed the enemy. A lone outcropping of dark stone rose up just behind the enemy's right wing.

The centurion pointed, one cracked finger stabbing at the foe.

"Look, lads." His voice was soft and some of the men bent forward to hear him. "There they are, this *rabble* that we have chased about, these *bandits* that the Prince rails against. Do you see them?"

None of the men turned to look. Colonna had a quick reward for rash action!

"Arrayed in ranks, four divisions, with flags and banners and horns. Half our number, if that . . . Do you see them?

They stand ready for battle. We are still knocking the sleep from our eyes yet they are already in battle line. . . ."

The *ouragos* sighed, settling the lorica of overlapping iron scales on his shoulders, blunt fingertips brushing over his sword, his bow case, the edge of his layered oaken shield. The scutum's painted leather cover was freshly oiled and he hoped it would not crack in the heat of battle. There would be a struggle today.

A deep note sounded in the air, the drone of a bucina in the hands of one of the signalers.

"Squad, face forward!" Colonna tugged the cheek plates of his helmet down and tightened them snug under his chin in one motion. "Ready at the walk!"

All around the centurion, the Roman army was in motion, shaking out into line of battle, men jogging slowly forward in great square blocks. Cavalry thundered past, raising more dust. The horsemen wore long striped robes and chainmail glinted beneath. Thin lances lay across the shoulders of the horses. Within a moment, the Ghassanid auxiliaries were gone, trotting down the slope, angling towards the left.

Colonna looked sideways, seeing the flags of his banda commander rise and fall. He raised a hand and chopped it towards the enemy. "Forward!"

"Lord of the Wasteland, O power that raises the wind and moves the stars in their courses, strength that brings the crop from barren ground, I submit myself to your will. You have spoken from the clear air, and I have listened. Now, our enemy is before us; now our strength will test his. In your hands, I leave victory or defeat. I am your servant, fill me with your desire."

The man bent his seamed forehead to a plain rug laid down on the rocky soil. For a moment he rested there, feeling the peace of early morning. He put from his mind the rising sound of men and horses and metal clattering against metal. He closed his ears to shouted commands and hooves thudding on the ground. In his mind he cradled the silence of the predawn air, when he walked alone among the sleeping men, feeling the wind rising in the east, rushing over the land, fleeing the coming sun.

In a single smooth movement he rose, drawing up the rug with a thick, scarred hand. He blinked, unseeing, and minded only the business of brushing dirt and grass stems from the woven fabric in his hand. When he was done, he smoothed down his beard, ruefully fingering thick tendrils of white creeping among the black. His body still felt young and strong, thick with muscle and hardened by long years of travel on the fringes of the Empire, but his beard was that of an elder, a chieftain. . . .

Fool! he chided himself. *You* are *a chieftain now, a king.* . . .

"Lord Mohammed?" The voice was low, but the man smiled at its soft, husky quality and the carrying power hiding within. He turned, raising a bushy eyebrow in question. "Yes, Lady Zoë?"

The young woman matched his gaze, dark brown eyes narrowing in suspicion. For a moment she considered him and he could tell that his good humor had put her on edge. Then she plunged ahead, pushing aside her fear that he was mocking her. "You rise each morning to greet the sun, praying to your god?"

Mohammed nodded, stowing the rug behind the saddle on his flea-bitten gray mare. "I do."

"What do you say?"

Frowning, Mohammed turned and looked around, seeing that a large number of his Tanukh were loitering near, just out of earshot. The men, seeing that he glanced their way, feigned indifference, bending to their tasks. Some were speaking softly with their horses, hands moving slowly on glossy brown necks, or checking over weapons and armor. Nearly all were garbed in long desert robes of white and tan laid over green coats. Some, like the massive Jalal, had wrapped their helmets with twined cloth. They had come a long way from the ragged, hungry band of men fleeing with Mohammed out of dying Palmyra. Strength and purpose were apparent in the surety of their movements, in their quiet voices.

"I say that which is in my heart, Zoë."

The young Palmyrene woman frowned, her patrician nose wrinkling. Unconsciously, she brushed a curling tendril of rich dark hair back from her cheek. Inwardly, Mohammed sighed to see her tuck it back into the folds of cloth cushioning her curving steel helmet. Like his companions, the Sahaba, she was armed with a long, straight cavalry sword and clad in armor of iron rings sewn to a leather backing. Like them, she would fight today, pitting her strength against the enemy.

Such a maiden should not carry anger like a cracked water urn, he thought sadly.

"Does this god hear you?"

"The Lord of the Empty Places hears all things, Zoë. He fills the world."

"Does he . . ." Zoë paused, her eyes troubled, lips pressed into a line. "Does he answer?"

Mohammed nodded, his rugged face suddenly lighting from within with a smile. Fine white teeth flashed in the thicket of his dark beard and he saw her relax minutely. "He does, my friend."

Mohammed pressed the flat of his hand against the center of Zoë's chest. The thick iron rings were still a little cold from the night air. "Here, in true silence, you can hear the voice from the clear air. Take a little time each day and listen. If you can still your own thoughts, if you can calm your heart and put your fears aside, you will hear it. It sings, calling like a dove. . . ."

Zoë blushed, her fingers darting towards his hand, then away, falling stiff to her side. Mohammed quelled his smile and took his hand away.

"Come, there will be battle today." He strode up the hill, mindful of the loose black rock covering the slope. Tents waited, just beyond the crest, and a banner fluttered above them, a green field marked by a crescent moon and a sword.

"It is a strong position," Jalal growled. The stocky Tanukh commander had plaited his hair into four long braids, and two of them hung down nearly to the surface of the map table. His knuckles, glassy with scars, rested on the table like the roots of ancient trees.

"It is a trap," the younger man said, lean and fine-boned like a hunting bird, with a deep-hooded robe of rich cloth thrown back from broad shoulders. "Look at the ground! Bounded on one side by cliffs that plunge a hundred feet or more to the bed of the Wadi Ruqqad. On the other, there is a swath of ground so broken and rough that our camels can barely pass, much less these soft-hooved Roman horses. Behind their camp is *another* ravine crossed by a single bridge. He has put his neck in a noose!"

"All that means, O most noble Lord Khalid, is that we must confront the enemy head-on, across a frontage *he* has the men to cover, while we do not."

Khalid shook his head in dismay and made a show of rising from his camp chair. He flicked his robes into order and smoothed dark blue silk down over a fine Persian mail shirt. The young man glanced sidelong at the older Tanukh and stifled a smile. "I wonder, Lord Jalal, why it is, if the Roman position is so strong, that we are the ones outside and they are the ones inside. They outnumber us, conservatively, by four to one. They have better arms and armor and far more cavalry. Their heavy horse, these cataphracts, these mounted armored bowmen, are rightly feared throughout the world. Did they not crush the might of the Persian empire just two years ago?"

Jalal bridled at the sneering tone in Khalid's voice and his eyes narrowed. The young commander grinned back at him, silently daring the older man to violence.

The door to the tent parted and Mohammed entered,

with Zoë hard on his heels. Jalal stood back from the table, relieved, and made a sharp nod in greeting. "Lord Mohammed, good morning."

Mohammed ignored the tension in the air and looked idly from man to man. Khalid bowed in greeting and reclaimed his seat. Jalal also stepped away from the folding wooden table, taking his place with the other Tanukh on the opposite side. Mohammed marked the way in which the other men—the lieutenants and chieftains and petty kings—arranged themselves into familiar groups by clan and nation.

"Good morning," he said to the assembled men.

The table was covered with tattered papyrus scrolls. Mohammed leaned over the maps, pushing some aside. Luckily, his travels as a caravan master had taken him along the Roman roads tying the Empire together. He had crossed this highland plain before, coming up from the coast and heading for Damascus. Thick fingers smoothed his beard as he considered the sketch maps Khalid's scouts had devised.

"Al'Walid," he said, after a time, "you count the enemy numbers at forty-five thousand."

Khalid leaned forward, his dark eyes bright. He nodded sharply. "Yes, lord. The better parts of five legions face us, bolstered by auxiliaries and mercenaries of various sorts. My men have been in and out of their camps several times, garbed as their local scouts. I am sure of their strength, down to the count of horses lamed and the men sick from bad water or the sun."

Mohammed nodded and turned back to the papers and the table. After a long pause, he looked up, his gaze searching the faces of the men in the tent. The air was growing hot as the day advanced and the sun mounted into the sky. Soon it would be fierce indeed, particularly on the plain below the hill, where the wind was blocked by the rising land.

"Our number," he said, musing, as if to himself, "is half

that. Perhaps a little more . . . Have any new contingents joined us in the night?"

"No," said a stoutly built man of middle height with a thick, curly black beard ornamented with small glittering jewels. Like many of his fellows, he wore Roman-style armor and carried a legionary's helmet under one arm. Despite his young age, he squinted nearsightedly in the dim light of the tent. "One of the local clans came in last night. Fifty or sixty men with bows and small shields at most."

Mohammed nodded. "Thank you, Lord Zamanes. Our strength is complete, then."

The King of Jerash and Bostra ducked his head and stood back, finding his place amongst the captains of the regiments drawn from the old Hellenic cities of the Decapolis. Zamanes was not comfortable with Mohammed, not since the Tanukh had started talking about the things that they had seen at the Ka'ba, or on the High Place in Petra. Still, the young prince had thrown his lot in with the southerners. It was far too late to crawl back to his old allegiance now.

Mohammed considered them, these rebels. He was sure of the core of his army; the Sahaba—Jalal and Shadin and the rest of the Tanukh—that had made the haj from Palmyra, his own kinsmen from Mekkah and the lands about the dry city. The Sarid tribesmen had long been his ally, and their chieftain, the rascal Uri, had been his friend from youth. Even the Yemenite fighters with Khalid's captured fleet were familiar to him—the Quraysh and the Bani Hashim had traded with them for centuries.

Too, he knew the Palmyrenes. He understood Zoë. He could feel the furious anger burning in her heart, the overwhelming desire for vengeance that had broken her ties to the Legion. She was an eager hawk, straining against the hood, desperate to fly shrieking at the enemy. Her, he kept close by. Her talent and power had to be guided, or they would bring disaster.

Her cousin, young Odenathus, Mohammed thought he

understood him as well. He followed his queen, Zoë, and his loyalty was to the dream that his beloved city might be rebuilt. Like her, he would fight, but the Quraysh lord thought the young prince could be trusted to keep his head. His men, they would follow their queen. They were a small band, now no more than a few thousand exiles, but Mohammed trusted them near as much as his own Tanukh.

But these city-dwelling Romans that formed the majority of his army . . . Mohammed studied their faces openly, for he was not given to slyness or guile. Zamanes seemed a solid-enough fellow, but their loyalty had been to the Empire for so long! For centuries Roman rule had held the Levantine coast, the Decapolis and the great cities of Syria in its withered gray hand. Now they had risen up, outraged by the treachery of the Eastern Emperor, Heraclius. Frightened and stunned by the destruction of glorious Palmyra. Angered by the new census and the threat of heavy taxes to repay the cost of the long war against Persia. But would they stand, when the battle reached its pitch and men were dying in droves all around them?

"Khalid, you say that the Romans will come forth?"

"Yes, lord. My spies in their camp brought me news only hours ago . . . the Imperial Prince Theodore intends to crush us, today, in a single blow."

"Tiamat's dugs, you fool, what are you doing?"

The Imperial Prince Theodore, younger brother of the reigning avtokrator of the Eastern Roman Empire, the commander of the Legions currently in Judea and Syria Coele, turned in his saddle. A furious Armenian pulled up in a cloud of dust and gravel at his side. Theodore motioned slightly and one of his servants jogged up to the side of his stallion and whisked yellow-brown grains of sand from the Prince's cloak with a long-handled duster made of hawk-tail feathers. Behind the arrival, a cordon of tall men in red cloaks closed like a lake swallowing a sling-stone.

"General Vahan. You have left your post on the left wing? Is there a problem you could not resolve on your own?"

The Imperial Prince inclined his head, still smiling faintly, watching with amusement as the burly, thick-bodied Armenian princeling sputtered in rage, his weathered face turning red under a heavy black beard. Theodore and his escort of Egyptian body-servants and slaves, red-cloaked Faithful with long blond hair in plaits and axes gleaming in the morning sun, stood at ease across the crest of a low hill near the center of the Roman line. The forest of spears and colorful umbrellas and a windscreen of mauve-dyed linen sewn to iron strakes drew the eye from miles away.

From this low height, the Prince could cast his eyes right, shaded by a shining white parasol of waxed linen, and see rectangular blocks of his legionaries stretching away, two or three miles, to the edge of the plateau. To the left, past where a shallow streambed curved under the shoulder of a hill, there was a sloping open plain filled with slowly moving clouds of dust that marked the presence of Roman and Armenian cataphracts.

The cavalry and the left wing were Vahan's responsibility. The Armenian brought his roan mare up, wither to wither, with Theodore's black, glossy mount. The Prince laid a gentling hand on his horse's shoulder. The presence of the mare was beginning to excite the stallion. Both horses were fitted with barding: the Prince's an elaborately decorated chanfron of heavy felt reinforced with bands of iron, Vahan's of simpler hardened leather, stained by travel and use.

"Lord Prince . . ." Vahan swallowed another curse and blinked sweat from his eyes. Like his kinsmen on the plain below, he was clad in a heavy woolen doublet under lamellar armor of overlapping iron bands. Sweat seeped from the edges of his armor, turning the heavy leather laces black with moisture. Theodore wondered if the man could fight a full day in such heavy gear and not expire of thirst.

The Prince raised a finger and gestured. One of the servants hurried up. The cream-colored ceramic jug in her hand was beaded with water droplets, forced from the cool interior by the heat of the day. "Drink, Lord Vahan. You are not used to this lowland heat. Please . . . indulge yourself."

"No," Vahan said abruptly, ignoring the outraged glances of Theodore's aides. "You are sending the infantry ahead too soon. You must have them hold their position on this side of the wadi until my light horse deploys to screen their advance. A swift charge from my cataphracts will shatter the bandits; why spend your legionaries so fruitlessly?"

Theodore turned his attention back to the plain. The blocks of legionaries on the right-hand side of the hill were shaking themselves out into a long line of battle. As each cohort advanced over the uneven ground, they tended to separate and clump, following the path of least resistance. Despite this, Theodore could faintly hear the stentorian bellowing of the centurions, keeping their knock-kneed, imbecile charges in order. The first detachments were jogging up the slope beyond the dry streambed.

"It will take time for the infantry to cross the creek, Vahan. Your horsemen are swift . . . they can easily make up the difference. You have your task, in any case. Drive off their camelry on the left. I will not send your heavy horsemen up that hill."

Vahan ground a fist into his high-cantled saddle. It was old-fashioned, with four jutting corners and a flimsy-looking belly strap. He gestured, stabbing out with a thick finger. "Lord Prince, you haven't fought these bandits! See, there, before the mass of their army? Lines of horsemen already advance at a trot—those men are javelineers, Lord Prince. They will take great delight in striking down your legionaries from a distance. They will have a height advantage, to give the flight of their javelins greater weight."

Theodore nodded absently, watching with professional interest as the legionaries crossed the streambed, keeping a steady pace, keeping even spacing among the cohorts. Looking down like this, seeing the whole of the battle spread out before him like a map, he felt a fleeting giddiness. Couriers and riders stood close to hand, just behind him on the crest of the hill, fleet horses waiting. His orders could fly on those hooves to any point of the battle line in moments. . . .

"Lord Prince!"

Theodore shook his head slightly and turned back to the Armenian. "Yes?"

"Pray, signal your men to halt their advance until they can be supported!"

"Oh," Theodore said airily, "they are. Watch and you will see." Then he said, crossly, "You should not have left your command. Such things set a poor example for your troops."

Mohammed squatted atop a splintered black boulder, hands resting easily on the tops of his thighs. Tan-and-white robes fell around his boots, pooling on the cracked rock. He was very still, letting a sluggish breeze flow over him. The sky was clear, though horses curveting in the valley below him raised clouds of pale yellow dust. Some of it was beginning to hang in the air. In a few hours, a thick pall would lie across the whole battle. There, below, several thousand of his riders were darting towards the slow-moving Roman advance.

"Do they think this is a game?" Zoë's voice growled up from below. She was sitting at the base of the boulder, in a tiny scrap of shade, her sword, sheathed, over her long legs. A white veil draped her face, revealing only dark, brooding eyes. "Seeing how close they can come to the enemy? Flaunting their riding skill with a shot from full gallop, standing in the saddle?"

"Some do," Mohammed said, voice still and quiet. "See how their shot falls amongst the enemy? Like rain falling in the dust."

"Will it become a deluge?" Anticipation sparked in Zoë's voice and Mohammed could hear stiff linen robes rustling on the stones.

"No," Mohammed said, "not yet. Khalid wishes to test their discipline."

"Huh." The sound was filled with grievance. "He is a reckless boy. It is unwise to trust him with such authority."

Mohammed tasted the air, the tip of his tongue appearing briefly between his lips. There was a brittle taste. He continued to watch.

"You are jealous, I think," he said after a moment. "Your cousin is quite taken with our young Eagle—on some days they seem inseparable. Khalid is an . . . attractive man, in many ways."

Zoë just hissed in disgust, settling back against the crumbling rock. "Men are fools."

Colonna avoided a pale gray stone jutting from the slope. His hobnailed sandals slapped on the dry ground, adding more dust to the cloud thickening around him. "Advance! Step left! Advance! Step left!"

The centurion's throat was already hoarse as he shouted over the rattle and din of his men advancing, shields held up before them. He moved, five paces behind the men in the third rank of his detachment. This was slow work, tramping up the long incline, ducking away from arrows whistling out of the sky. Luckily, they were still at long range for the light bows these tribesmen used. The men in the first and second ranks were already slowing, not just from the fatigue of humping sixty pounds of armor, shield and weapon, but from the steady tension caused by the snap of shafts striking the ground around them. Some men had four or five arrows studding their shields.

Colonna, even in the rear rank, was grateful that the enemy hadn't really come at them in force. Not yet. He looked over his shoulder, towards the low hill where the Lord Prince stood. Dust smeared across the sky, making it difficult to see. He could make out swatches of bright color and gleaming metal. The sun, full in the sky, burned on his neck. Soon his armor would be too hot to touch. He guessed, in the pale yellow murk, that most of the army had crossed the streambed.

"Advance! Step left!" He was still shouting, automatically. Shaking his head, he wrenched his attention back to the men. Some of them had drifted to the right, behind the shelter of their fellow's shields. More arrows whistled out of the sky.

"Accursed dogs!" Colonna, groaning a little, picked up his pace and lashed at the backs of the men in front of him with a long stick. "Keep left, keep left!"

An arrow flashed past his face, black fletching only inches away, and the centurion swore bitterly. *I don't want to die here, not on some damned rocky hillside in some pox-ridden flea bite of a province. . . .*

There was a thundering sound and he raised himself up, looking over the shoulders of his men. The ranks of the bandits had parted, making avenues through their line. Robed horsemen charged down the hillside, helms glittering in the morning sun. The sky darkened with arrows.

"Do you feel that?" Mohammed's voice was very faint. "Stand ready."

Zoë looked up, craning her neck to try and catch a glimpse of the Arab on the boulder above her. It was no use and she stood, slinging saber and sheath over her shoulder in one fluid movement. She put a hand, gloved in leather, covered with tightly sewn rings of Damascene steel, on the corroded black stone. The Quraysh was still squatting there, forearms on his knees, but now his eyes were closed.

The back of Zoë's neck started to tingle and she turned slowly, dark brown eyes narrowing to study the valley below. There was something in the air, a familiar-tasting sound and an unheard touch . . .

The Queen of Palmyra's eyes widened and her fine-boned features, dark with the sun, twisted into a snarl of rage. The sensation trembling in the unseen world was all too familiar.

Sorcery. The Legion thaumaturges are putting forth their strength.

Theodore urged his stallion forward, out from under the cool shade of the parasols, and squinted, watching the far slope with interest. Behind him and to one side, Vahan was cursing continuously and with ill-disguised heat. The Prince shook his head in delight, hiding a grin behind his hand. "Vahan, you've fought these desert rats before?"

"Aye, Lord Prince, many times. Your legionnaires won't catch them . . . they'll take a dreadful punishment from javelins and swift, stabbing attacks by those lancers. When your men rush them, they will gallop away. If your men stand fast, they will swelter in this heat, endlessly, while the bandits pick at them with bows from a dis—"

"Good," the Prince interrupted. "Then I don't need to explain. If we had time and leisure, I would bid you stay, and watch the battle as it unfolds." The Prince's voice changed in timbre, becoming cold and commanding. "But you, sir, are absent from your command. Get yourself back to the left flank and get your lancers and cataphracts sorted out! In a little while, the enemy will be fully engaged along our front, yet our superior numbers will allow us to spill round his left. That is your task, Vahan, get to it!"

Theodore motioned with his head to the nearest of the Faithful and the Armenian found a pair of blond giants at his elbows. They grinned. Vahan swore under his breath and reined his horse around. The Scandians stepped back, long axes across their shoulders.

"They will not stand to face us today, Lord Prince," Vahan barked. "Why should they? The desert is their sanctuary. . . ."

Why indeed? Theodore had pondered the issue for weeks, while his forces mustered on the plateau. He had chosen his camp carefully. There was good water year-round. Below the cliffs to the south ran the main road to Damascus. Other roads converged from the north. Here on the heights above the Sea of Galilee was the turning point of the entire defense of Judea and southern Syria. The Prince was sure he wanted battle, his full strength gathered. Did the bandits? *They seem to, having come out in force, in full array, to face me.*

"Boleslav, attend me!"

The captain of the Faithful stomped up, a single-bladed ax slung carelessly over one mighty shoulder. The Northman was nearly six and a half feet tall and built like a mountain. Even the steadily growing heat did not seem to touch him. *"Ja?"*

Theodore leaned from his horse, his mouth close to the Northman's conical helmet. "Have word sent to the thaumaturges. Tell them to begin their working."

Boleslav nodded, thick neck sliding like the gearing of a water mill. *"Ja, altjarl."*

Zoë jogged down the slope, riding boots sliding among the stones and scrub. A single plait of her hair bounced on the back of her armor. The sleeves of her robe were tied up to keep her arms free. Mohammed remained on the boulder, high above the line of battle. Regiments of her clansmen squatted at the base of the hillock, banners furled and kaftans pulled over their faces. The men of Palmyra respected the sun. Water skins passed along the lines of men.

She came to a halt, senses filled with a slowly rising hum of sorcery building in the valley. "Do you feel it?"

Odenathus nodded in greeting and acknowledgment. "I do," he said. His long face, darkened like hers by the sun, was pensive. "They're not messing about today."

Zoë shaded her eyes and stared across the swale at the Roman camp. There, among the stunted trees and tamarisk, she could make out the rectangle of a Legion marching camp and, just outside the palisade, a circle of staves and withes marking the tents of the thaumaturges.

"There must be at least twenty battle masters," Odenathus continued, his voice steady. "Plus the usual apprentices and journeymen. Almost double the usual complement to a Legion force of this size." The Palmyrene's face was grim and his hands moved restlessly on the hilt of his sword.

"Yes," Zoë said, distracted, "they must have borrowed from the other legions, maybe the ones in Persia. The Prince wants to make a big show. . . ."

Closing her eyes, Zoë settled her mind, letting the heat and the dry wind and the sound of flies recede. It was difficult. The air was charged with anticipation and fear. Odenathus was worried and she could smell the fear-tang in his sweat. Her own armor was heavy and the bindings bit into her skin. She breathed out slowly, measuring the intake of air to the beat of her heart. She knelt, the pommel of her sword pressed against her forehead. The sensation helped her focus, let her mind block out the *sensi* constantly flooding her sight, hearing, taste and touch.

Faintly, she felt Odenathus kneel beside her, and the whisper of his thought.

Zoë let the image of a wheel form in her mind. This came of its own accord, from long practice, and with it, as the wheel spun and brightened and grew larger, she felt the last distractions of the physical world fall away. An old friend called this the Entrance of Hermes, and once told her, as they sat beside a high mountain stream, road-weary feet cooling in the chill blue-white water, that he imagined it as the eye of Horus, coming up out of unguessable depths. First, he had said, it was a single bright mote in an abyss of darkness. But then, as it rushed closer, it became larger and brighter. At last, as it came very close, it was enormous, bigger than a house, a burning eye trailing sparks. Once it rushed over you, once it consumed you in cold fire, you had passed the first entrance to the hidden world.

Zoë invoked the image of a wheel of fire, but the effect was the same. When it whirled over her, her mind was freed of the physicality of the senses. Her hidden sight opened and she beheld the valley in its true form.

For a moment, before asserting a pattern of symbolism fitting her waking mind, she beheld a shining void, filled with millions of hurrying lights. The streambed below was a slow blue surge coiling and twisting across a ghostly landscape. Thousands of men moving on the slope were sparkling motes. The horses thudding across the dusty ground, delicate traceries of living fire. Arrayed across the enemy camp was a shining wall of gold. Symbols danced across its surface, forming out of the rainbow shimmer, then disappearing again. Her perception shied away from the abyss of the sky, for the blue vault and thin white clouds were gone, leaving only an infinite depth filled with a haze of burning spheres.

Sweat beaded on her forehead and she summoned up a second image, the first in a swift succession of patterns. This was the second entrance, where the adept, the sorcerer, brought forth from his hidden mind a series of symbols and patterns that allowed the manipulation and perception of the hidden world without going mad.

That raw sky, the unfettered vision of the truth of the world, was too much for the human mind. Even in the brief instant Zoë stared into the abyss of light, she had felt the core of her being begin to dissolve, losing the unique identity that made her Zoë, Queen of Palmyra.

A flower box unfolded before her, expanding into a constantly growing pattern of planes and forms. Each facet gleamed with a single pure color, bright enough to hurt the eye. At the heart, where the wheel of fire spun and hissed, a shining trapezohedron emerged. The people of her city, though they were born and bred of the desert, thought of themselves as Greeks. "The heir of Athens," they called fair Palmyra under the reign of the first Zenobia. Poets and sages, mathematicians and astrologers flocked to her golden court.

Zoë's teachers were mathematicians, geometricists. They instilled their own symbology in her. The trapezohedron tore, then reknit, becoming a dodecahedron. Now her mind settled and familiar reality asserted itself. The hills had shape and solidity; Odenathus, still at her side, now seemed a mortal man, not a thing of fire. But the golden wall remained and the sky was filled with the tracery of power and intent.

"The thaumaturges are attacking?" Zoë was startled. The Eastern Empire prided itself on the strength of its wizards, but their skill had always been turned to defense.

"They have learned from the Western mages," Odenathus rasped. "We must work quickly."

Zoë rose, her mind finding her cousin's thought waiting. They had been trained in a swift, harsh school, under the tutelage of the Legion during the Persian war. Now the circle closed. Zoë extended her will and meshed with Odenathus. Together they turned to face the valley. Power from the rocks and stone, from the air, from water buried deep underground, flowed into them. Their own matrices and hidden shapes began to build.

Here they come, Odenathus thought, and flame boiled out of the golden wall, licking across the ranks of Arab and Decapolis troops. Zoë knew that the men could see nothing, maybe only feel unease, a sour taste in the air. She put forth her strength, lashing out with a deep blue arc of light that hewed into the red fire. The tendril of power recoiled, flickering back into the safety of the shield wavering beyond the streambed.

Thunder grumbled in a clear sky, and the Arab soldiers, still waiting in the hot sun, looked up in surprise.

"Allau Akbar!" The sky rang with the massed cry of four thousand throats.

Colonna felt the earth shake as the Arab cavalry hurtled towards the front rank of the legionaries. In the instant before the shock of contact, the centurion bellowed *Ground* and *Lock shields!* The first line of soldiers went down on one knee and grounded their rectangular shields. The second rank stepped up, shields held high, spears a thicket of iron. The Arab chargers slewed aside at the last moment, the desert-men turning in their saddles to fling javelins at a dozen paces. The entire charge slid sideways along the Roman front, the riders howling a battle cry as they hurled into the closely packed Romans.

The heavy darts pincushioned the shields, some tearing straight through the heavy laminate. Some of the legionaries in the front ranks fell, their throats pierced, gushing bright red blood onto the ground.

"Loose!" Colonna screamed.

Behind the first four ranks of Romans, two lines of men cocked their shoulders and flung their javelins. The heavy wooden shafts, capped with triangular iron heads, whipped through the air and tore into the ranks of the Arabs as they wheeled away. Dozens of riders fell, light leather and mail armor pierced by the heavy bolts. More horses screamed and bucked, or fell heavily onto the sandy ground.

Colonna hissed in triumph. "Halt fire and re-form!"

"Advance!" The Romans untangled their shields and shook out their line, orderlies dragging the dead and wounded away from the front rank. Men from the second and third ranks stepped up, their shields filling the gaps. The legion advanced a pace at a time.

The Arab horsemen withdrew in a cloud of dust, robes flapping in the wind of their passage. Gravel spattered on the faces of the shields, making a sound like rain on a roof of wooden shingles. The legionaries pressed up the hill at a steady pace. Dust settled out of the air, coating their faces. The swirl of javelineers faded back, while other riders in black robes with green flashing swept in. These men had long bows made from cane. Single arrows snapped through the air. Colonna ducked aside again and cursed, realizing that the screening force was shooting for officers.

"O, Lord of the Wasteland, fill me with your strength."

Mohammed ignored the battle spreading up the slope below him. Six months before, he would have been a-horse, riding hard along the line, directing his squadrons and regiments into battle. Clan standards would have fluttered at his shoulder. Messengers would have been rushing up to him, looking for orders, carrying word from the flanks. Today, Khalid and Jalal bore that burden. He could feel the shape of the battle, though, and there was a trill of fear in his heart.

The Romans advanced steadily, hobnailed sandals eating up the long slope a pace at a time. Their numbers overlapped the Arab line, too, and soon the right flank might be overwhelmed. He was not worried about his left wing, anchored against the cliffs lining the edge of the plateau. Horses thundered past, making black pebbles on the top of the boulder quiver and dance. Mohammed pressed his hands against the decaying lava, feeling the strength in the earth.

"We go forth against your enemies. Our faith is strong and we abide by the laws that you have laid down to govern the lives of men."

He sang to himself, reciting the prayers that had come to him while he had lain exposed on the summit of An'Nour. The voice from the clear air had spoken, showing him the movement of the stars in their courses, revealing the passage of cranes and ravens in the sky. Now it steadied his mind as he opened himself to the shining power that filled the world.

"We submit ourselves to your will, O Lord of the World. Give us strength."

Grains of sand and dust spattered against the back of Mohammed's cloak. Blood seeped from beneath his fingernails as they dug into the ancient, corroded rock.

Sweat poured from Zoë's face and neck, soaking the doublet and cotton shirt under her armor. Her mind was far away from her body, struggling in the unseen world. Her eyes stared, sightless, across a broad valley filled with a vast cloud of dust. Fire burned openly in the sky, hidden powers revealed as they strove in the air above the knots of men grappling on the desert floor.

Together, as they had been trained, Zoë and Odenathus invoked a wheel of burning white and sent it, spinning, into the midst of half-seen forms rushing forth from the wall of gold. Lightning rippled into the dust cloud where the powers met, and the two Palmyrenes staggered, their faces flushed with heat, at the impact. Barely a hundred yards away, the lines of the Decapolis infantry were locked in a din of combat with the Legion.

Zoë, risking the loss of her connection to Odenathus, dropped out of their battle meld.

The rebel city-dwellers were being pushed back, phalanx bulging between their line and the Ben-Sarid tribesmen on the right. A wedge of Roman helmets was in the gap, their swords and spears flashing with blood. The city-dwellers were fighting hard, but they were not professionals. Luckily, the citizens of the Decapolis were blessed with good, heavy armor and new weapons. Zoë wiped sweat from her eyes. She looked around, seeing the block of Palmyrene exiles still holding their position, making a hedge of steel and iron around the two sorcerers.

"Hadad!" It took a moment to summon enough spit to make her voice work. The commander of the Palmyrene swordsmen jerked around, his face pale with worry.

"My lady!" Hadad scurried over to her, his pale, thin

face barely visible in the heavy visored iron helmet strapped to his head. Like most of the men gathered on the slope, he was wearing scaled armor under a surcoat of white and gold, and had a long sword at his side and a round shield slung over his shoulder. "I feared to wake you, but the Gerasans are falling back; we should move you to safety!"

"No," Zoë rasped, dark eyes fierce. "Attack now, leave us. Push back the Romans—otherwise the line will break."

Hadad shook his head violently. "No," he said, "Lord Mohammed directed us to protect you. If you fall, it will go poorly indeed."

Zoë spat on the ground, seeing blood in the sputum. She met the man's eyes squarely and he flinched. "Attack now, or I'll cut you down where you stand. The line must not break."

She unclenched her hand, joints throbbing. The day seemed overlaid by a gray haze. *Fatigue,* she thought dully. *Odenathus and I aren't enough to stop them.*

Hadad disappeared, and distantly, through the roaring in her ears, she could hear men shouting. She pushed the sound away, descending into the unseen world again. Power flowed to her, rushing to meet her purpose.

"Odd . . ." Theodore was still on his horse, though hours had passed since the sun had risen. His brother, Heraclius, might have the red cloak and boots, but he could no longer match his younger brother for stamina and strength. "They are standing and fighting."

"They are brave men," Boleslav growled. The captain of the Faithful remained on the hilltop, keeping a close eye on his charge throughout the day. Theodore grinned at the big Northman, knowing that the Faithful were growing restless, seeing the day decided by others when their own axes had yet to taste blood. "They fight like cornered wolves."

The other Faithful, hearing a snatch of the conversation, grunted in assent.

"That is what is odd," Theodore mused. "The rabble of the desert are *not* brave. They are like the wind, like jackals, feckless, coming and going . . . yet here, on this day, they stand and fight. I do not understand it. Still, if they want to die on our spears, let them!"

Boleslav turned his shaggy blond head to one of his undercaptains and rumbled some command. The other man nodded sharply and jogged off down the hill, leaping lightly from boulder to boulder. Theodore raised a questioning eyebrow.

Boleslav shrugged, saying, "They shout something as they fight. I send Firdik to hear it."

Theodore nodded absently, one gloved hand stroking his short-cropped beard. Like his brother, he was mostly blond, but his beard came in red. He thought that the Faithful counted him as one of their own. He surely bore more resemblance to them than to the dark-complected Greeks and Anatolians Heraclius ruled.

For now, the Lord Prince thought idly. *Brother is sick and may not last the year. . . .*

"Ah!" Theodore thrust the thought away and stood in the saddle, feet held securely by the Sarmatian-style stirrups that he had adopted for his own troops. The insufferable Western Emperor Galen might be a sanctimonious, overbred fool, but he could pick good mercenaries. Theodore had learned a great deal from watching the Western Legion during the war against Persia. The Lord Prince did not intend to waste his knowledge.

The thin line of Arabic camelry on the far left wing gave way in the face of a massed charge by Vahan's Armenians. The bandits fell back in haste. Some dismounted and shot with their bows from behind their ungainly mounts. All that stood on the enemy's wing was a camp of lashed-together wagons and carts at the base of one of the tumbled lava cones. Theodore smiled, seeing the opportunity open for Vahan to turn and roll up the entire enemy line. "Well done!"

Dust plumed from the dry ground and the Armenian general reined in his horse. Around him, his kinsmen crowded with their armored horses, sun glaring from their armor. It was burning hot in the neck-to-toe suits of iron. An arrow spiraled out of the sky and glanced from his breastplate. The cheap iron tip shattered, but the Armenian only grunted. The bandits had scattered before his charge, but they were still lurking about, sniping with their bows.

"Get those bastards away from that camp! Wheel to the right," he shouted, voice booming from the helmet. He chopped his hand towards the slopes of the hill. The legionaries were still grinding forward, toiling up the slope. His bannermen heard him, and their tall flags dipped and swayed, indicating the direction of movement. It would take a bit to rein in all his men. Some had ignored orders and were nosing about the camp, doubtless out for a bit of loot.

Cataphracts milled around, trying to redress their lines. Some of the men unshipped long horse bows and were shooting at the Arabs hiding behind their camels and in the circle of wagons in the pass between the big hill and its lesser cousin. The ground was getting rough, littered with head-sized stones and larger boulders. Crossing the wadi had been difficult, but now the ground was worsening.

"Advance at a walk!" Vahan turned his own horse and lumbered up the slope towards the cone-shaped hill. "In good range, shoot, then close with sword and mace."

The Armenians, still scattered across the swale between the two hills, began to drift to the right, following the wail of their trumpets and the signal flags. Vahan motioned to one of his lieutenants, a cousin, who commanded his light horse.

"Vargir, screen that camp and keep the camelmen off

our flank. That bastard prince will get his victory, I suppose, but it will be hard going up this hill."

The man nodded, pushing a blue-felt cap back on his head. Like the other horsemen in his band, he wore a leather jerkin reinforced with iron rings, and was armed mainly with a horse bow and a stabbing sword. "As you say, lord."

Vahan turned away, ignoring the motion of the scouts as they peeled off from his main force. The ground was worsening, and the Arabs had turned the end of their line. Now they faced him at an angle, with crowds of men with spears and brightly painted shields among the boulders and rocks. He swore, but urged his horse forward. At least he was facing out of the sun.

"Run!" Odenathus tugged hard at Zoë's arm, then scooped her up in one motion. Despite her weight and his own burden of armor and fatigue, the young Palmyrene prince sprinted away from the outcropping of rock. The infantry screening them from the battle had been swallowed up in the racket of steel and iron downslope. Despite the addition of Hadad's fighters, the Decapolis troops had been forced back again. Boys carrying amphorae hurried along the line, bringing water to groups of men that were resting just out of the battle. A constant stream of wounded staggered up the slope from the rear of the rebel line.

The ground was littered with the bodies of those who had failed to flee.

The air over the outcropping convulsed, distorting like heat rising over a campfire. For an instant, the clouds in the sky behind the distortion could be seen reflected a thousand times, faceted like the surface of a jewel. Odenathus threw himself to the ground, covering his cousin's body with his own, and clapped his hands over his ears.

The ground where they had stood spasmed violently and then burst into a whirl of violet fire. Men in the rear ranks of the Decapolis regiments screamed in fear and then burst into flame. A huge *boom* echoed across the battlefield and splinters of rock rained down on the two Palmyrenes as they cowered on the ground.

"So much," Odenathus croaked, wiping blood out of his eyes, "for our battle sorcery."

He could barely move. His limbs cramped painfully. The two of them had held the Roman thaumaturges at bay for almost five hours. Despite the agony in his muscles, he hooked his cousin's arm in his and began dragging himself across the ground, away from the outcropping.

"We are Your servants, O most mighty and merciful Lord. Your will is our will."

Mohammed stood, cloak flapping in a stiff breeze blowing up from the east. His face was grim and set, for he saw now, having opened his eyes at last, that his army had been ground back against the base of the hill. The right flank had been bent back perpendicular to the main line of battle. Where the camelry had been driven back, the last of the Decapolis reserves had shored up the line, fighting amongst jagged black boulders. The slope there was getting steep, which let the infantry gain an advantage over the Roman cavalry for the moment. Even from this distance, he could pick out individual men fighting, struggling in the mass of melee, their shields and swords streaked with blood. A steady stream of the wounded spilled away from the back of the line. The Romans were pressing hard against their foe.

But still, the Arabs fought on, falling back slowly. Their spears and swords were still sharp and the ground where the battle passed was littered with the dead and wounded, with shattered armor and broken shields. Beyond the fighting, the Arab encampment was surrounded by a swirl of Roman auxiliaries exchanging bow shot with defenders crouched behind wagons and carts. Most of those in the camp would be women or servants or older men who could no longer stand in the main line of battle.

A woman of the people, Mohammed thought, *who knows the drawing of a bow, is blessed.*

The sun was beginning to fall to the west, but the full heat of midday was strong on the land. The sky had faded from blue to dusty white. The heat shimmer from the valley floor was thick, distorting sight and confusing distance.

Too, forces worked in the air. Green flame stabbed out of the sky, lighting amongst a troop of Arab cavalry rushing to shore up the right wing of his army. Horses screamed and men died, wrapped in a fire that burned flesh and armor alike. Mohammed snarled in rage, seeing the power of his enemies at play among his troops, unfettered.

He squinted, but could not make out the banners of the Palmyrene regiment that he had set to defend Queen Zoë and her cousin. *If they are dead* . . . He halted the thought. Khadijah was dead, too, and his family left far behind. There was a power that called to him, that directed his thoughts and his actions. There was no need to wail at fate.

His hand came to rest on the hilt of his saber. The men and women of his city forged this blade. He could feel their faith trembling under his hand. The sword carried the sense of the black stone resting in the shrine of the Ka'ba, in the most holy place of his people. When he touched the ebon metal, he felt the presence that dwelt in the empty places.

"O Lord of the Heavens, most gracious and most merciful, put forth Your strength . . ."

Sunlight winked on armor and lance tips, there behind the conical hill rising behind the embattled camp off to the north. Green and white pennons snapped in the rising wind.

Cornicens blew, ringing clear in the air. Colonna ignored them, though they sounded the call to stand down and reform the line. The man in front of him, a man in halfarmor and a sharp conical helmet wrapped in white linen, was busy hewing at his shield. The man's curved sword bit into the edge of the big rectangular scutum and Colonna felt the blow slam against his arm. Other men were struggling all around them. The Roman line had splintered on the rough slope, losing cohesion. Luckily, the enemy was exhausted and unable to exploit the opportunity. He stabbed, hard, with his gladius and the Arab skipped aside.

The sword whipped around again and Colonna managed to drag the shield into the stroke. Splinters flaked from the back of the panel, stabbing at his eye. He cursed, hacking blindly at the enemy. Suddenly there was a gurgling cry and a clatter as the saber fell to the stones. Colonna blinked, seeing another legionarie wrenching his sword from the Arab's side.

"My thanks," the centurion rasped. The legionary, his face gaunt with weariness, nodded dully. Dried gore caked the man's hauberk and his arms were seeping blood from a dozen cuts.

The cornicens blew again and Colonna shook his head, wiping blood out of his eyes. Sweat leaked from his armor, mixing with the dust caking his legs. *I've got to get the lads back in line.*

"Form up! Fourth of the Sixth of the Third, form on me!"

Other legionaries stumbled towards him. The Third had suffered today, going uphill against these bandits. Unexpectedly, the enemy had been better armed and armored than the Romans. Too many of the new lads were lacking quality gear. They had been mustered too quickly. Their own cavalry trotted past and Colonna stared at them in surprise. These men were fresh, with their tunics clean and weapons dry. Upslope, the Arabs were falling back again, their lines tattered and disjointed, but they still stood firm amongst the black rocks. A column of fresh infantry came marching up the hill and Colonna ordered his men to stand aside. *That bastard of a prince isn't going to let up, is he? Good for him!*

· · ·

Theodore took a moment to dismount and refresh himself in the shade of one of the pavilions. One of the servants brought him a porcelain bowl of water to lave his face and a clean towel. Things were well in hand on the field below. It might be time to deliver the final stroke.

"Lord Prince?"

Theodore turned at the voice, grinning, for he owed much to the tired-sounding man standing beside the tent. He finished drying his hands and then gestured for a chair to be brought immediately. Servants scurried off to find something suitable. "Master Demosthenes! You are most welcome! Please, sit."

The thaumaturge slumped into a camp chair. Theodore motioned for wine and something to eat. Demosthenes was exhausted, his long face graven with weariness. His beard, usually neatly trimmed and brushed, was tangled with sweat and dust. Dark smudges colored his eyes and there was the mark of bruising and a burn on his right hand.

Wine arrived, in a silver ewer, and Theodore poured it himself. The thaumaturge put the cup to his lips and drank greedily, though his hands were shaking. "That was hard work, today." Demosthenes' voice was a harsh whisper. Theodore leaned close to hear him. "Their sorcerers were young and strong. Well trained in the art."

"How many were there?" Theodore had begged, borrowed and stolen every thaumaturge he could lay his hands on for this campaign, stripping the entire eastern half of the Empire, including the garrisons in upper Mesopotamia. It might be *traditional* for the thaumaturges to be parceled out, one or two to each legion for siege work and to block the sendings of the enemy, but Theodore had bigger plans in mind. He had seen the power the Western Empire brought to bear with a massed group of mages. The powers of the Persian priests were legendary . . . why not match them, strength for strength?

"Not many," the thaumaturge said, some strength re-

turning to his voice, "but they stood only on defense, while
we must make do with attack. It is draining work, trying
to twist the world that way. Still, we overcame them . . ."
He paused, and Theodore could see that the man was sift-
ing memory, trying to find a pattern in the day's chaos.

"Why," Demosthenes said, surprise in his voice, "I believe there were only two! But skilled, my lord, and well
used to one another . . . perhaps brother and sister. Great
strength can be had that way, if the minds can find a common join."

The Lord Prince stood, grinning from ear to ear. "But
not enough to carry the day, master wizard!"

Not enough. The Prince swung around, his step light.
He looked west, checking the sun. There were still hours
of light left. Enough time to smash the Arab army into the
dust.

"Send word to the mage's encampment," he called to a
courier rider that was standing close by; "tell them their
work is done for the day. Tell them to rest, to recover their
strength."

"All day we wait, sitting and getting fat." The Tanukh's
voice was low, but it carried to where Khalid was sitting
on his horse, half shaded, half covered by the overhanging
branches of a thorn tree. The young commander feigned
deafness, brilliant eyes focused on the clouds of dust rising
beyond the pass and the two dark hills.

"The city men, they are being heaped with glory. Soon
they will rest in soft paradise, their every whim catered to
by white-limbed maidens with long, rich hair . . ." Shadin
had been dwelling overmuch on this topic throughout the
long, endless, day. ". . . each a virgin and willing, even
eager, to learn from a man's hand. Soft-spoken, too, and
demure, with downcast eyes."

Khalid ignored him. The big Persian, Patik, waited quietly behind him, squatting in the shade of a thorn tree. The

rest of the men were resting in whatever shade they could find, or moving quietly among the horses.

Beyond the little pass, the battle had moved away to the left, though there was still some fighting around the encampment. Khalid ignored that. The wagons were empty, the carts overturned. The camp followers were within, it was true, along with some men wounded earlier in the campaign. The Romans were more interested in the mass of Arab and Decapolis troops now fighting on the shoulders of the hill where Mohammed's banner and tents stood. He squinted, watching a singular figure, dressed in white and brown, standing on the height.

The Romans can see him, too, Khalid mused, his thoughts disguised behind a carefully bland face. *But will they know what they see? Can they feel him, their sorcerers?*

"These men of the city, they are dying with the word of god on their lips. They will find Paradise." Shadin was still holding forth to the men of his squad, most of whom were trying to sleep, upon the world that awaited them after death. "They will find two cool gardens planted with shady trees, each watered by a flowing spring. Every tree, for I have heard it from his lips myself, will bear every kind of fruit, each in pairs."

Distantly, horns blew and Khalid sat up a little straighter. His eyes swerved to the hilltop. The lone figure remained, standing on the dark boulder, wind blowing its robes out like a flag. The young man looked back to the pass, eyes narrowing. He could see a great flock of banners and pennons moving, as if a mass of mounted men were coming up out of the streambed.

Khalid hissed in delight. Behind him, Patik's cold gray eyes flickered open and the Persian diquan stood. His lamellar armor of overlapping iron plates rippled like a snakeskin. Gentling his horse, the easterner mounted. The other men, roused by the movement, looked to their own horses. Shadin, interrupted in the middle of a long and detailed description of the "dark-eyed houris," scrambled to his feet.

Khalid ignored them all, his full attention focused on the hilltop. He ignored the sky darkening behind them.

Light flashed there, from metal turning across the path of the sun, across the mile or more of scrub and twisted thornbush. Khalid felt something like a physical shock as the tiny figure on the boulder turned and looked at him.

"Mount up!" Khalid's voice carried, strong and clear, across the rocky hillside. Hundreds of men scrambled for their horses, armor jingling in the hot afternoon air. Ahead of them, scouts raised their heads, preparing to rise and run alongside. "Paradise is waiting!"

"This is the last act," Theodore said to the cluster of courier riders waiting beside his pavilion. They were very young, these scions of the great houses. For many, this was their first campaign. As had generations before them, they would run errands and messages for the cataphracts, for the nobles who commanded the armies of the Eastern Empire, even—as now—for the Lord Prince himself. Someday these boys would carry the lance, bow and sword of the cataphract themselves.

Theodore smiled genially, seeing their tense, determined faces. "We have held back our full strength throughout the day, waiting for the enemy to weaken. Now he has been driven back onto his camps, or onto that hillock yonder, where his tents lie. Go down into the valley and carry word to the centurions that the exhausted men are to fall back, while fresh troops take their place."

He clapped his hands sharply in dismissal and turned away. The boys scrambled for their ponies. "Boleslav!"

"Ja, altjarl?"

"We move, too. Have the servants break camp. I wish to see the end of this myself."

There was laughter amongst the Faithful, for their axes were hungry. It was boring, sitting on the hilltop. Red cloaks moved swiftly as Theodore swung into the saddle of his stallion. By the time he spurred the horse onto the trail leading down to the valley floor, a cordon of great-thewed Northmen surrounded him. The Prince laughed as he walked the stallion down the slope, the Northmen running at his stirrups. The wind of his passage dispelled a little of the day's heat. It was good to feel the air on his face.

Colonna stepped off the roadway, motioning for the men behind him to do the same. He had wrapped a cloth around his face to keep the dust off. The road they followed was barely a track. It meandered down from between the two dark hills and crossed a deep ravine lying behind the Roman camp. A rider had found Colonna and his detachment sitting in the shade of some stunted trees lining the little streambed. The boy directed them back to the main camp, beyond the hill and beyond the ravine. The centurion shrugged and rousted his men.

Now the road was crowded with wounded men as they approached the bridge.

It wasn't much to look at, this bridge, only a single arch of stone over the narrow slot of the ravine, but it was still standing. Men and horses and wagons carrying those too wounded to walk were backed up on the near side of the crossing. There was only room enough for a single wagon to cross at a time. The ravine, steep sided and choked with brush, was impossible to cross.

"Make way! Make way!" A rider on a well-lathered horse trotted up behind Colonna and his men. A troop of men in heavy armor, their helmets held on their saddle-bows, followed. They looked weary and hot and Colonna could see from the make of their armor and saddles that they were not regular Legion troopers.

Only the Eastern Empire maintained a predominately cavalry Legion with their noble cataphracts. *These men must be mercenaries,* thought Colonna, *probably Armeni-*

ans by the look of their beaded tack and bridle. He heard they were brave fighters, but touchy.

"You, centurion!" One of the men, blessed with a thick dark beard, was pointing a stubby finger at Colonna. "Your men are wounded?"

"No," Colonna said, rising to his feet. It felt good just to sit for a moment, but officers rarely thought about things like that, leastways not when centurions were lolling about. "We're fit. A rider from the Lord Prince told us and our mates to fall back and let the reserves take over."

"Good," the man barked, and Colonna saw the rider's breastplate had been gilded before someone tried to stave it in with a mace. "You've charge of the bridge crossing. Get this herd of addled sheep sorted out and the road open!"

Colonna started to salute, but the black-bearded man had already curveted his horse around in a half-circle and ridden off, his escort in tow. Some of the legionaries were coughing and waving their hands to dispel the dust.

"Let's go," Colonna growled, wedging the helmet back on his head. "Now we're *vigiles*."

"You there," he shouted at the first of the drovers crowding the road with a wagon. "Get that rattletrap off the road!"

Behind him, the rest of his detachment fanned out, spears in hand, trying to get the walking wounded and stray farmers all onto one side of the roadway.

Theodore let the stallion take its head and pick up to a run as they approached the dry streambed lying between his day camp and the battle. The horse leapt the sandy wash with ease and the Lord Prince laughed, feeling the power coursing in the magnificent beast. The Faithful had fallen behind, crashing through the thickets lining the dead stream. Theodore reined around to let them catch up.

Boleslav jogged up, his thick, trunklike legs seemingly tireless.

Theodore opened his mouth to speak, but stopped, hearing a great shout rise up behind him.

Allau Akbar!

The Prince turned in the saddle, staring up the slope, as the Faithful re-established their cordon around him. There, under the eaves of the rocky hill, was sudden, violent motion. The Prince raised an eyebrow, seeing the massed ranks of his army stagger back as the Arab bandits, trapped on the higher ground, suddenly charged pell-mell down the slope.

Allau Akbar!

The sound echoed from the hills, raising a chill on Theodore's arms. It seemed the cry of tens of thousands of men, not the bare handful struggling with the front ranks of his own army. The sun was beginning to fall behind the hills and Theodore shaded his eyes with a hand.

"Boleslav, where are my couriers and runners?"

The north-man grunted, his own deep gray eyes searching the slope for any foes that might have broken through the main line of battle. "None have yet returned, altjarl. Soon they will, I think."

Theodore grunted in disgust. The din of battle was rising sharply. These bandits had acquired unexpected fervor. "Then we shall have to find them. Forward!"

Mohammed stood, though the wind picked up again, plucking at his robes with sharp fingers. Thistles bounced past, driven by the gusts. Under his feet, on the slope below the outcropping, the men of the Decapolis, stiffened by the Ben-Sarid and the Yemenites, had thrown themselves into the Roman lines with terrible energy. The enemy, still forming up for a second round of battle, had been taken off-guard. Two wedges of Decapolis heavy infantry had hacked their way into the Legion ranks. Behind them the Yemenis were filling the air with arrows, firing up at an angle to let the shafts plunge into the Romans massed downslope.

They have proven themselves, Mohammed thought. The city men had paid a terrible price throughout the long day, taking the brunt of the Roman attack on their shoulders. Now they should be on their last legs, exhausted and bled white by the struggle. Despite this, they attacked ferociously, regardless of their casualties. The storm of their war cry echoed up around the boulder like the beat of a drum. Twenty thousand throats, crying out to the heavens.

"Now His strength comes," Mohammed whispered, leaning into the wind. Sand and gravel whipped at him, but he ignored the cuts on his hands and the dull roar that had been building out of the east in the last hour. "Now, you men that lay your hearts down before Him, who take His guidance and law into your own houses, know that He will succor you. He, the Compassionate and Merciful One, will hold you in the palm of His hand."

Mohammed's eyes closed, shutting out the vision of men dying, sliding in their own blood, their bodies pierced by the short-hafted spears of the Romans, on the slope below. The attack faltered as the Romans re-formed their lines, and now it was failing as the flanks of the wedges were attacked by hundreds of legionaries.

A voice came from the clear air and it rolled like thunder.

Khalid rose up in his stirrups, sword held high and forward, gleaming as the polished blade caught the westering sun. He howled, and his men howled behind him, a thousand riders on fleet-footed horses. The drumming of their hooves made the ground jump. Rabbits and birds fled before them, startled from their day nests.

Allau Akbar!

The ring of wagons swelled in Khalid's vision and the ground flashed past under the hooves of his mare. Before them, he saw the Ghassanid archers break away, fleeing before the weight of his charge. Behind him, and on either side, a flowing line of charging horses unfolded, filling the shallow pass. Some of the men, the Bedu, raised their voices in a long, ululating scream, and Khalid joined them. He and his personal guard, Patik among them, galloped past the wagons. No one tried to stop them, though the women and old men among the wagons cheered as they hurtled past.

Khalid flashed them a brilliant smile but then turned his attention to the roadway he could make out down the slope. It was crowded with men walking, and more wagons, and beyond all that, there was the dark slash of a ravine cutting across the plateau and a bridge.

The rest of the Arab reserve flowed past the wagons on the uphill side, with Shadin in the lead, his thick hand gripping the hilt of a long, hand-and-a-half sword. The drumming of hooves almost drowned out the war cries of the Tanukh and the Palmyrene knights, but those men raised their voices all the more. Shadin's thoughts flickered, momentarily, to his sword-brother Jalal, who had held the command of the center of the Arab line at dawn. *Do you still live, my brother?*

It didn't matter now, for the lead edge of the Arab charge, six thousand men strong, was about to slam into the rear cohorts of the Roman left wing. Shadin raised his voice in a scream of rage that echoed back from the empty sky. *Allau Akbar!*

Theodore and his bodyguards reached the standards of the tribune commanding the left wing of the Roman force as the sky began to darken. The Lord Prince was hurrying the man through the usual pleasantries, trying to find out where Vahan had gone, when Boleslav suddenly shouted in fear. Theodore's head snapped up in alarm; he had never heard such a cry from one of the Faithful.

The eastern half of the sky was gone, swallowed into a towering wall of darkness. The sky above turned a sickly yellow, boiling and seething with angry motion. Sodiumyellow lightning rippled through the depths of the black cloud, illuminating a rushing storm front from within. For an instant, the Lord Prince was aware that a terrible silence had settled on the field of battle. Men all around him looked up in awe and terror, seeing only the outline of the outcropping and a single white figure that stood on the summit, hands raised. There was no wind, no sound, not even the rattle of metal on stone.

"All-father, receive our souls on bright wings."

The Faithful broke the silence with their song, raised in a hundred basso throats. Theodore stared around wildly, seeing that the Northmen had raised their axes in defiance to the dreadful sky rushing towards them.

"All-father, hear us, send your winged messengers to bind our wounds, to lift us up from the field of battle. Valhalla is waiting, the golden hall on a green hill. All-father, hear us!"

Then the song was drowned by the awesome roar of the wind and the world vanished in a howling storm of blinding sand and grit and Theodore's horse bucked in fear and he was falling.

Zoë cowered in the lee of a slab of cracked blackish rock. Odenathus crowded in beside her, his cloak stretched over both of them. The sky screamed and raged and she could hear, somehow, through the tumult the sound of Mohammed's voice tolling like a temple bell. Sand lashed at their shelter, spilling through the cracks between the stone and the cloak. The fabric was stretched taut by the pressure of the wind. Her cousin moaned in fear, feeling the power that was unleashed in the sky above them.

I knew he was strong, Zoë wailed to herself, palms pressed over her ears, trying to shut out the hammering noise. It was useless; the roaring sound was in the ground as well as the sky. It filled the hidden world. *I didn't know what that meant!*

The earth shook under her and she screamed in fear.

Mohammed stood on the boulder, staring down into the valley. The wind died around him, leaving a quiet space in the maelstrom. Not more that a dozen yards away, the storm raged, tearing out brush by its roots, whirling away tents and wagons. Eddies of dust and sand and grit curled around an invisible sphere, rushing past like the current of a river. Here, where he stood, listening to the sky, there was only a quiet whisper of movement in the air. Tiny grains of sand pattered down where the storm met the quiet, making little cones on the ground.

You must act, O man, but I will guide you.

A voice was speaking from the clear air, here in the heart of the storm. Outside, beyond this sanctuary, the wind ripped and howled, shifting the stones of the hill in their foundations. Darkness covered more than the sky now as the sandstorm flowed across the desert, cracking trees and lashing men as they lay huddled on the ground.

Some men still moved in the storm. Khalid and his riders were galloping down the road towards the bridge across the Wadi Ruqqad. Mohammed could see them, in the queer yellow-green light filling the quiet sphere. He knew that they would reach the span and seize it from the Romans, stunned by the storm. On the slope below him, where the men of the Decapolis had watered the ground with their blood throughout the long day, his followers could stand in the wind. The Roman army had already splintered, in fear and surprise, and Shadin and Jalal were meeting amid the carnage, their faces striped with blood.

You must strike to the sea. Swiftly. Swiftly.

Mohammed nodded. The voice from the clear air rarely gave him counsel, but in this thing he was already determined. He fingered a medallion hanging around his neck. It had come to him by a messenger's hand, while he and his men had been encamped at the old Nabatean capital of Petra. It was from his wife's sister. It was an old coin, struck in the mint of Mekkah in his father's time. On the obverse was stamped the image of a ship.

Mohammed stared out, into the storm, at the ruin below him. Across the valley, between curtains of hurtling dust, he could see lightning stabbing in the murk. The Quraysh shook his head slowly, feeling the ripple of power even at this distance. The Roman thaumaturges could feel the will in the storm and sought to meet it with their own.

Foolish.

Mohammed knew the strength of the lord of the empty places, of the wasteland. Was it not the strength of the whole world itself? Of all that existed, or had ever existed?

How can men seek to overturn that?

The lightning faded and died, muted and swallowed by the roiling yellow-brown sky. Intermittent red and viridian flashes continued for a little while, but then they too ceased.

The Quraysh turned away, pulling a scarf over his face. This work was done.

Wind shrieked and hissed, lashing Colonna with a stinging hail of sand and gravel. Bits of wood, splintered from the leaning trees, flew through the air like tiny javelins. The centurion was crouched in the lee of a wagon, close by the bridge abutment. Some of his men had climbed down the steep sides of the ravine, seeking shelter from the storm.

What a fine day, the centurion thought, head bent to his knees, hiding his face from the gale threatening to rip the flesh from his bones. *All our work undone by a freakish storm, a khamsin, out of the deep desert.*

Most of the men trying to cross the bridge had gone to ground when the thundering black wall had come roaring out of the east, but Colonna's detachment had tried to keep order on the span itself, shoving the remaining wagons across with main strength. Then the storm had hit, smashing them to the ground, tearing shields from men's backs. Carrying young Domus Aureus shrieking in fear, right off the bridge itself to fling him into the ravine.

The color of the air changed, deepening from a sickly yellow to a darker, more ominous shade. Colonna felt the wind shift too, and then suddenly it slacked off. Shaking dust and sand from his shaven head, the centurion staggered up and lurched out onto the road.

"Form up!" he started to call out to his men, then felt the echo of hooves on the ground.

Colonna turned sharply, his gladius sticking as it rasped out of a sheath clogged with red grit.

A horseman loomed out of the darkness, robes billowing in a following wind. Colonna started to shout, started to bring up his sword to block the lance tip flickering in the air.

Too late, he thought, feeling the point punch through his shoulder. The metal scales of his armor rang, screeching as they crumpled under the impact. Colonna gasped, feeling his arm go numb. Blood spattered across his vision and then he was lying, arms and legs askew, in the spiny brush by the side of the road. A river of horsemen rushed past, their faces covered with scarves, their long robes flying around them.

More screams filtered through the air. The storm continued.

A fine rain of sand began to fall out of the air. Colonna blinked, trying to keep it out of his eyes. It was very dark.

〔◎〕-〔0〕-〔0〕-〔0〕-〔0〕-〔0〕-〔0〕-〔0〕-〔0〕-〔0〕-〔0〕-〔0〕-〔0〕-〔0〕-〔0〕-〔0〕-〔0〕-〔0〕-〔0〕-〔0〕-〔◎〕

THE WASTELAND, EAST OF THE BAY OF NEAPOLIS

〕€〔

The land lay gray under a sullen brown sky. A lone figure moved in the devastation, crawling slowly along the side of a military road. Dirty white flakes drifted on hot, sluggish air. Foot-high drifts of ash buried the road.

The figure was twisted and bent, one arm dragging uselessly in the powdery grit. Gasping in pain each time she moved, the woman crawled onward. The dim ochre disk of the sun was touching the western horizon before she stopped, overcome with exhaustion. The woman's rich red-gold hair had once been plaited into a single thick braid hanging down her back. Now the half-burned remains were matted and foul. Soot streaked her face and back, where a charred tunic clung to her flesh. Her arms, chest and legs were dark with ground-in pine needles.

She shuddered, wracked by a smoky cough. She lay on the stunted, burned grass, resting. Even lying perfectly still was torment. Her abused body was near death. Blood leaked slowly from dozens of cuts. There was a sound, muffled but distinct. The faint chuckling of water over rocks.

The woman raised her head, flinching from pain grinding like crushed glass in the nerves of her shoulders and neck. She could see the road dipping down ahead of her, and burned trees thick in a streambed.

Gritting her teeth, she dragged herself up onto the road. The smooth, carefully fitted stones drove cinders and tiny crescent-shaped flakes of volcanic glass into her good arm. With the tiny rise in height, she could see an arched bridge abutment ahead. She gasped, consumed by fierce, all-encompassing thirst. Dragging herself forward, she inched towards the bridge and the stream.

A dark pall hid the light of the stars. Even the moon was only a faint blur. The woman woke, shuddering with cold. Sharp rocks dug into her flesh. Her head lay in running water. Her nose and mouth were above the sluggish flow. She blinked, trying to focus on something in the darkness. There was nothing.

A sour, sulfurous taste filled her mouth and she tried to spit. Even that much effort brought a blinding wash of pain. Faint sparks flooded her vision. After a time they passed. Turning her head a little, she filled her mouth with water from the stream. It was strong-tasting and gritty, but it was water. She drank slowly. There was a vague memory of doing this before. Full, she leaned back, letting the current lap against her. She felt a chill seeping into her, but there was nothing she could do. Weariness overcame her.

A moon, bobbing and yellow, flickered over the edge of the bridge. The woman felt light touch her face and her gray-green eyes opened. The moon came closer and she heard the clatter of rocks knocking into one another.

The woman blinked and turned her head away from the moonlight. It was bright and hurt her eyes. What remained of her hair was floating in the current like a net, clogged with burned leaves and twigs.

"Otho! Look, another corpse in the stream."

The sound reverberated in the woman's skull. She tried to move her hand, to cover her face.

"Fool Celt, it's alive. See, the arm moved."

Metal clinked on stone and there was a splashing. The current changed, blocked, and the woman closed her eyes. The moon was close now, huge and burning. She could smell pitch and wax and the chalky odor of sweating men. Something touched her useless arm and she cried out.

Muted gray striped the woman's face. Her hair had been brushed back and covered a thin white pillow. The caked-on blood and soot were gone, revealing ugly bruises covering her face and neck. A cut above her eye was shiny with ointment. She lay on a narrow bed built into a wall.

The room rocked with an even rhythm. Bands of light, falling from a window set high above her, slowly moved across her body. Sometimes they faded away entirely and she lay in soft, dim quiet. From time to time she heard the braying of donkeys. But it was faint and muted by distance and the walls of red cedar surrounding her. Soft woolen blankets covered her. One arm lay atop the coverlet, bound in strips of cloth and held straight by wooden slats.

She snored softly. Occasionally she would stir and moan, but her mind was far from the world. A man sat with her, watching her quietly while she slept. He was elderly, with a polished bald head, a long white mustache and a prominent, skewed nose. His deep-set eyes watched her gently. His hands were thick with calluses and corded with muscle. Under his shirt, his body was lean and hard, without even the memory of fat.

The wagon rolled on, through the wasteland, leaving tracks in the ash that drifted across the Via Appia like snow.

The woman woke suddenly. She saw a dim ceiling, partially lit by candlelight. She drew breath and smelled beeswax and tallow and cedar wood and fresh linen. It smelled like home. Memories of pain warned her not to move her head, but her gray-green eyes wandered.

A bald man was sitting across from her, tusklike mustaches half lit by a candle.

"Salve," the man said. "I am Vitellix."

"Hello," the woman croaked. She stopped, her tongue feeling huge in her mouth. She was ravenously hungry and very thirsty. Everything tasted like sulfur. "Water, please."

The man nodded, his smooth round head bobbing in the light, and leaned close, a cup in his hands. The woman tasted copper on her lips as he tipped it for her. The water was cool and fresh. It felt heavenly on her tongue.

He stopped her before she drank too much. She lay back, relieved, on the pillow.

"Thank you," she said.

The man nodded his head gravely and sat back against the wall. She slept.

When she woke again the room had stopped rocking and sunlight slanted through the window. It was quiet and still in the little room. Outside she could hear the rattle of wood on wood and an odd *hup-hup-hup* sound. The pain had receded a little, letting her move her head and look around the room. The walls, which had seemed plain by candlelight, were joined planks. The wood was painted, in its upper courses, with scenes of bears and men and horses. The figures seemed to be part of a celebration or procession. Some wore masks while others went naked bearing standards before them. On the ceiling the gods looked down, their faces peering from blue-and-white-painted clouds. A golden-rayed sun surrounded the window.

"Hello?" The woman frowned; was this her voice? It was weak and harsh. What had happened to her? It should be clear and strong, ringing with command.

The door folded out of the wall. Bright sunlight and the smell of crushed green grass and damp oak trees spilled in. A head appeared; a girl with tousled brown hair, her nose wrinkling like a field mouse's. The woman in the bed tried to get up, but her right arm betrayed her and she fell back with a hiss.

"Poppa! She's awake again." The mouse-girl disappeared.

After a moment, the man from her night-dream entered. His skin was slick and glistening with sweat. A short linen kilt clung to his thighs.

"How do you feel?" His voice was muffled by a towel as he wiped his face.

"You . . . you are Vitellix? I remember you, speaking to me in the night."

He smiled, strong teeth very white in the dimness.

"Yes," he said, "I am Vitellix. What is your name?"

"I am . . ." The woman paused, feeling a huge, dull pressure in her head. "I . . . I don't remember."

As soon as she spoke, the pressure eased and a trickle of relief flooded through her. She sighed, gesturing weakly at her immobilized arm. "I don't remember what happened. Can you tell me?"

Vitellix closed the door and there was a muffled complaint from outside. "My boys found you in a stream. You were badly hurt, burned and covered with blood. Your arm was broken and your legs had been badly sprained. You'd taken a chill, too, but they carried you up to our camp. It took a long time to clean your wounds. Many leaves, bits of stone, pine needles and twigs had been ground into your skin. Your clothes were only rags. I've tended many hurts, but you taxed my skill!"

"Yes . . ." The woman captured a fragment of memory, of fire and a door silhouetted against the flames. "There was something burning . . . a house?"

Vitellix made a sharp, barking sound, neither laughter nor disgust.

"Everything burned, lass. That bridge was within the devastation of Vesuvius. Do you remember where you were before you were injured?"

The woman stared back at him with wide eyes. For a moment there was a look on her face, a moment of comprehension, then her eyes clouded and she shook her head. "No . . . What happened to the mountain?"

Vitellix' face turned grim and he looked away. In his hands, the towel twisted as he clenched his fists. "I have seen Vesuvius many times in our travels. We often camped on its wooded flank, buying our dinner from the farmers or vintners. The mountain slopes were rich—the finest wines, the richest cheese, the fattest calf—all came from the bounty of Vesuvius. There were fine cities on its shoulders, too. Pompeii, Herculaneum, Baiae."

The man's face paled as memory took hold.

"A week ago, now, in the night, the mountain shook off its slumber and woke. We were miles away to the south, camped on the road coming up from Croton. It was an odd night of rushing wind and clouds, yet there was no rain. Thunder shook the air and lightning spiked from cloud to cloud. A storm gathered on the height, crowning the mountain with a diadem of cold fire.

"I climbed onto the roof of the wagon. I could see over the trees of the orchard lining the road. The mountain was still and dark, silhouetted against the clouds. Then . . . then there was a light, just a spark on the summit. It seemed that the thunderheads gathered, lighting the upper slopes with the flicker of lightning. Then the glow began, a fierce red light, radiating from the very top."

The woman felt a creeping chill, even under the heavy blankets.

"Then there was a flash, a brilliant light. It lit the olive trees and shone in my face like the sun rising. I turned away and then there was a sound, like a great shout that rushed over us. Horrible wind followed and it threw me off the roof of the wagon, but I landed square."

Vitellix' voice dropped, becoming almost a whisper.

"Then ruddy, red fire filled the sky. The glow rushed down the mountainside, faster than a galloping horse. Burning stones fell hissing from the sky and the air turned foul. We hid beneath a bridge, there in the countryside above Nuceria, for three days. Sometimes the earth shook like a wet dog, heaving and bucking. Praise Lugh, the bridge did not fall around our ears!"

He sighed and picked up the towel again.

"When the rain of fire stopped, we moved north again, along the highway. Everything was covered with ash. It falls like snow, though it has slacked off. Until we found you, we thought sure that only the dead and ghosts lived under the shadow of the mountain."

The woman coughed, feeling a harsh, grating pain in her lungs.

"Did you see . . ." She stopped, took a breath and then said: "Did you see where I might have come from? Was there a house, a town, anything?"

Vitellix shook his head slowly. "If there was, lass, it is gone now. All the land around Vesuvius is dead. I'm sorry, but if your family lay nearby, we could not find them."

))C((

A gleam of pale blue light caught the priest's eye. Tarsus turned, hands clasped on his staff of office. Something flickered and burned at the center of the plaza, casting long shadows on the arches and windows of the surrounding buildings. The stoutly built priest frowned. Sometimes criminals and outcasts tried to creep into the sacred precincts and steal from the pilgrims sleeping on the grounds. He hefted his staff, taking confidence from the weighty bronze snake coiled around its length.

Determined, he strode forward through cool, damp air filled with the quiet echo of running water. "You, there by the spring pool! Stand and show yourself!"

Someone was hunched down in the darkness by the outflow pipe. The blue glow disappeared, but Tarsus could make out a figure turning towards him. The priest grimaced and summoned a pale white light from his staff.

"Gods of Olympus!" Tarsus froze in shock. A haggard face stared back at him, marked by pain and weariness. A thick, irregular beard clouded a once-patrician visage. Though much changed, he knew the man. "Prince Maxian?"

Tarsus had never seen such a transformation in one of his students. The baby fat of youth had sloughed away from sharp cheekbones; lively intelligent eyes had grown haunted; the healthy, tan skin of youth had turned sallow. The Emperor of the West's cheerful, handsome little brother was changed almost beyond recognition. A dim, strange radiance flickered around the Prince like a half-seen shadow. Tarsus stepped back, grimacing. The air around the Prince was repellent.

"By the gods, lad, what happened to you?"

Maxian leaned heavily on the smooth marble lining the spring box.

"Tarsus? You are still alive?"

"Yes," said the priest. "Though you look on the verge of death yourself."

"Help me." Maxian's voice was low and tinged with panic. "You must help me bring her back."

The Prince motioned weakly. Something lay in the shadows at the top of the steps.

Ah! Tarsus thought. *That explains the smell.*

The priest knelt next to the corpse. The body was not too far gone. Whatever hot flame had licked over it—he reached down and gently turned the skull, feeling the jellylike resistance of muscle attaching the shoulder to the neck—had done so recently. The charred skin was brittle and stiff under his fingers. Long experience and repeated exposure let him put aside horror while he made a swift, thorough examination.

"Ah, my friend, she is long gone." Tarsus sighed. "The ferryman has taken her coin and rowed her across the black river."

"Not so, not so!" The Prince's voice was urgent in the darkness. "If you help me, I can restore her. I beg you, take us to the chambers of healing. With your skill to guide my hand, I know that I can save her."

"Lord Prince, this is foolishness. We are both men blessed with the gods' power, but no one may call back the souls of the dead. That is in the hands of the gods, not of mortals."

Maxian stopped as if struck. Then he straightened and loomed over the priest, his handsome face clouding with anger.

"I have summoned men back from the dead," Maxian said bitterly. "Twice I have stood over tumbled bone and scraps of dusty flesh. Twice I have raised lightning and fire to fill those bodies—one dead a thousand years!—with the quickness of life. Breath and sight and lively limbs have sprung forth from the dust. I *know* that it can be done. My strength is great enough."

Tarsus stepped back, uneasy. Unconsciously, his mind began to weave a pattern of subtle defense. When he spoke again, the compassion in his voice was gone.

"What have you done, Lord Prince? What words have you spoken over a fresh-turned grave?"

Maxian ignored the warning in the older man's voice, eyes brightening. He began to speak, his voice coming from a great distance, reciting from memory: *"O Furies and horrors of hell! Dread Chaos, eager to destroy countless worlds! O Ruler of the underworld, who suffers for endless centuries—"*

"Cease!" Tarsus moved, his staff lashing out to strike the face of the man before him. The blow rocked Maxian backward, leaving a deep cut on his cheek. "Such words are never to be spoken in this sacred place!"

Tarsus trembled with anger. There were secrets known to his fellow priests that should never see the light of day. There were pale-eyed creatures haunting the night, whispering at the windows of learned men. The thought that one of his best students—though not the most studious!—had turned down such an evil path filled him with despair. "Where did you learn such foulness?"

Maxian, stunned, touched the wound. Under his fingers, the cut faded, torn skin knitting closed. Blood rushed to his face, restoring circulation to the area. He looked up and Tarsus stepped back, shocked by the fury in the Prince's expression. In the hidden world, a glittering white shield of interlocking geometric forms shimmered between the two men.

"I sought them out." Maxian's visage cleared, anger draining away like spilling water. Great weariness replaced the fury. "A man helped me. He had learned those words as an apprentice in the East. Tarsus, I have done some questionable things, but I beg you, help me make them right. This girl . . ." his hand fluttered towards the corpse, ". . . she trusted me and died. I have salved her wounds before, even mortal ones! With your skill, I can bring her back from beyond the black river."

Tarsus shook his head. The stillness of the courtyard, the quiet susurration of the sleeping penitents, the empty night sky, all pressed upon him. He could feel the Prince's entreaty like a physical pressure, urging him to accept. It was the role and the practice of the priests of Asklepios to help those who needed aid. Here was a man in deadly trouble . . .

Should I refuse? He was my student!

Tarsus sighed. "Follow me. Bring the . . . girl. We will speak inside."

The priest spilled thick wine into a cup. Water followed. His little room lay on the western side of the temple complex. One side abutted a channel of fitted stones guiding a stream along the edge of the plaza. The priest pushed the cup into Maxian's hands.

"Drink."

Though he felt a great desire for wine himself, Tarsus did not drink. The corpse of the girl was laid out on a table between them. Wooden cabinets, filled with murky bottles, covered the walls. The worktable was smooth, polished granite. When necessary, Tarsus had performed surgeries on the table. Tonight, however, the bone saw and hammer would not be required. This body was beyond even the considerable power of the high priests.

"What happened to the girl?"

Maxian looked up, his pale, thin face flushed with wine. In the warm light of the oil lamps, he seemed very young, as young as when he had first come to the temple. It had been hard to come from a noble's household, to cross the length of the Empire and enter such a renowned school.

Luckily, the boy had only been a governor's son when he had first set foot in the Asklepion, not the Emperor's brother! Tarsus sat, keen eyes surveying his student. Maxian looked much older. His hair was tangled and matted with burrs. The priest guessed he had not eaten or slept in days. An odd air surrounded the Prince, like half-heard whispering.

"She . . . I didn't know what was happening. I . . ."

Maxian stopped, his eyes distant. Troubled thoughts moved in the Prince, plainly etched on his face. The innocence of youth had fled, leaving a grim and troubled man. "Tarsus, I killed this girl."

The flat statement hung in the air.

"Yes," the Prince said, hand making a nervous, sharp motion. "She came at me with a . . . a weapon. There was an invisible fire around me and it consumed her like a moth in a candle. I was distracted—everything was burning, even the sky. By the time I could bend my will upon her, she was dead."

"Did you strike her down?" Tarsus' voice was quiet and patient.

The Prince shook his head. "I was beset. Enemies surrounded me. I had raised a sign of fire against their arrows and spears. She—Krista—ran up. I thought she was in the city. I turned and she threw herself into my arms. The sign burned her. It was very quick."

Maxian looked away, face pale. Tarsus continued to watch and wait.

When the Prince had mastered himself, he began speaking again.

"I fled to safety. I tried to restore her as I had done with the others. She came! She walked on the iron floor, she answered, she could move . . ."

Tarsus nodded, his heart filled with familiar sadness.

Does each of us face this moment? Has any priest of the god not found himself at these crossroads?

"But," the priest said softly, "there was no spirit in her

eyes. No spark. No laughter. All the semblance of life, but nothing of the living woman."

Maxian turned, stricken. "Yes! That is exactly . . ." His voice ran down, seeing the pity and sorrow in the older priest's face. "What does it mean?"

Tarsus sighed and reached for the wine jar himself. The little ritual of pouring and mixing took only a moment. It steadied him and let him put the past away, in dim memory, where such things belonged. The wine was sharp and bitter on his tongue. Tarsus welcomed the discomfort.

"When you left us, my friend, you were a journeyman. In truth, barely more than an apprentice. Many thought—*I* thought—that you had gone as far as you could in the mysteries of our order. It seemed inevitable, with your brother's struggle for the Purple, that you would be drawn into the civil war at his side. Your skills would never be given the chance to reach their full potential. Perhaps your brother would fail, and you and he would die at the hands of the victor."

Tarsus emptied the cup, then met the young man's eyes directly.

"There are many secrets not revealed to apprentices. There are rituals not taught to journeymen. Some lessons can only be learned by hard experience—these things make a master. This summoning of life to dead limbs is one of the things that we do not teach. It is forbidden."

Maxian's face creased with anger. "Why? Isn't the purpose of our order to save and safeguard life? Why swear our holy oath? If the dead can live, what joy we could bring to the world!"

Tarsus remained still, quiet and patient. After a moment, the Prince sat down.

"The spark of life is the province of the gods. Do you remember your first lessons? Do you remember the tale of our revered founder, holy Asklepios himself?"

Maxian frowned. His early days in the school were a blur. He hated the endless drill and practice. The other students had ignored him, leaving him desperately lonely. The skills themselves, the binding of wounds, the closing of flesh, the banishment of disease and righting imbalanced humors, those things came swiftly to him. He remembered that his tutors had praised his quick instinct and native skill. But the reading and copying? He had put all that from his mind long ago.

"Master Tarsus, I remember the school was founded by some prince who barked a shin on Mount Pindos. He claimed drinking from the spring cured him and he gave money to start a sanctuary. But of Asclepius himself, the 'best of the physicians'? No . . . I don't remember."

Tarsus hid a sigh. *All the best lessons are forgotten!*

"Asklepios," he said, "was the half-human son of Apollo the Archer. He was the first physician. In his hands lay the cure for the world's hurts. There was no disease, no wound he could not defeat. He went abroad in the land, in old Achaia across the waters, tending to the sick and to the lame. One day he came upon a woman grieving by the side of the path. At her side, under a stained and mended cloth, lay the body of her husband. Asklepios turned his powers upon the man. In the corpse he found darkness and the echo of the Styx. But the light in Asklepios was so strong, his power so great, he could restore the dead to life."

Maxian's eyes gleamed and the discarded wine cup jiggled and danced on the tabletop. Tarsus stopped, feeling power build in the air like the tense humidity before a thunderstorm. He raised a hand, summoning calm and quiet. The cup, teetering on the edge of the wooden table, spun to a halt and then lay still.

"There is more. The man stood up, hale and filled with life. With great joy, both husband and wife returned home. Asklepios, pleased, continued on his journey. But above, on high Olympus, Zeus, father of the gods, looked down in anger. Here was a man—yes, half god, but still mortal—who took the privilege of life and death upon himself. Here was a man who mocked the ferryman and the guardians of the underworld. In this, the order of the world was set awry and Zeus, foremost guardian of the pattern of things, struck him down forthwith.

"Asklepios was slain on the road, riven by a lightning stroke from the fist of thunder-shielded Zeus."

Maxian cursed and sprang up from his chair, his face dark with anger. "This is a tale for children! There are no gods, no power that moves the storm cloud or the sun. Any man with the sight can see the pattern of the world, its warp and weft. Each priest may call thunder and storm, cast lightning. We make our own destiny, find our own path. I have beaten death before, I shall do so again! If you help me, I know that we can succeed. I have the power to my hand; I but need your skill, noble Tarsus, to guide me."

Tarsus shook his head, his face marked by old and bitter pain. "You *are* a child, to believe this. This is beyond you. Her soul, her *ka* has fled into the darkness beyond the river. You are not a god, you cannot make a new soul from common clay. You may summon life to cold limbs, but you cannot make her *live* again. She is gone."

Maxian snarled, clenching his hand into a fist, and Tarsus felt, for the first time, the enormous strength in the Prince. The room flickered, the walls becoming insubstantial, the light of the lamps dying. A sound rose from the stones, the voices of tens of thousands crying out in fear. Tarsus leapt to his feet, his mind filled with a vision of burning cloud covering the sky. His shield of Athena, once so perfect and white, rippled and fragmented. The power flooding forth from the Prince beat against him.

It touched the body, seeping into skin and bone.

The corpse convulsed, rattling like dried peas in a gourd. Tarsus cried out, but the stones creaking and groaning all around him drowned the sound. The cabinets shattered violently. Where each splinter fell, roots grew out with dizzying speed. They writhed like pale worms on the floor.

From them saplings grew. The body on the table suddenly lay still, smooth white flesh covering the bone and rich dark hair spilling down from the skull.

The Prince lowered his hand and the room snapped back into focus. The roaring and the lamentations stopped. Tarsus gaped, imprisoned by a stand of young pines filling the room. The branches dug into his sides, pinioning his hands and legs.

A woman, live and whole, lay on the tabletop, her breast rising and falling as she breathed.

"Rise, my love," the Prince said. He did not seem tired, but his eyes were haunted.

The body sat up, rich, dark brown eyes open. Tarsus saw that she was comely and well made. Her flesh, recently so tormented and ravaged, was ripe with youth. She came up upon her knees, then stood, her head brushing against the curling vines and flowers crowding against the roof.

Tarsus shook his head, seeing the blank look on her face and the stillness that lay behind her eyes. *It is ever so . . .*

"Lad, your strength has grown far past any master of the order. But look upon her! Where is her heart? Her spirit? Those things come from the gods, they are beyond us. You will never make her as she was before. Those eyes will never sparkle with mischief or look upon you with delight."

"But . . ." Maxian turned, his face intent, "I *have* done it. Two men, long dead, I raised up. They are filled with life! By the gods, sometimes they show too much liveliness! Why them? Why them and not her, she who is worth far more to me?"

Tarsus pushed back one of the branches, easing himself out of the close grip of the dwarf trees. The room filled with a heady aroma of crushed pine needles. "I know not. Who were they? Were they friends, newly fallen?"

"No," barked Maxian in abrupt surprise. "Not friends! I

struggled against an invisible enemy. I needed power. A man, now dead, advised me to seek a lever long enough to move the world. I did. I found them both, still moldering in their tombs. But they were long gone to dust."

"Who are these men?" Tarsus put his hands on Maxian's shoulders. "Were they masters of the art? Could they have hidden their spirit away, holding it back from death, from poor, grim Charon?"

Maxian laughed again and took his teacher's hands in his own. Something like true humor was in his face. Fond memories of his time as an apprentice to the dour and proper Tarsus fluttered at the edge of his thought. The older priest had seemed so harsh and unyielding when first they met. Could he have forseen the genuine warmth and friendship that would grow between them?

"Masters of the art? Not those two rogues! Abdmachus advised me that some men, in death, become powerful by their memory. The greater their legend, the vaster the power that they might contain. Did I need all that strength for my long battle? I did! So I sought out two of the greatest men that have yet lived."

Tarsus felt a cold chill grip his heart.

"I woke him from a cold bed, this Gaius Julius Caesar." Maxian's voice was filled with a near hysterical gaiety. "But he was not enough! Oh no, master, he was not quite strong enough to let me shake the earth. I needed a greater legend, someone who would dwarf that old Republican tyrant as the sun blinds the moon. It was a long, dangerous task, but I found him too, hidden beneath the sand. Locks and wards and guardians ringed him about, but they could not hold me back. He, too, the golden-hair, the living god, this Alexander, son of Olympia, best of the Greeks, master of the Persians, I woke, my hand on his shoulder, letting him rise up and walk under the sun!"

"No . . ." Tarsus breathed, staggered by the words. "Not that butcher, the parricide, the drunken thug, the kin slayer!"

"Yes," Maxian snapped. "Both of them, the scheming, duplicitous pair, I filled with life and thought. By my will, they walk this earth, a merry pair of rogues. I needed them, and by the gods, they did not fail me. All that I asked, they gave."

Tarsus grasped the edge of the table, his mind busy with this revelation. Maxian stood staring glumly at the girl. She looked down at him, quiet and motionless. He smiled wanly. She remained quiescent, watching him with flat, dead eyes.

"What were they like, these men you raised from the cold ground?"

Maxian shrugged, saying, "As you would expect. Alexander is young and vigorous, eager, charming, always rushing to the front, delighted in new things. He craves battle and adventure. He cannot sit still, but who could gainsay him? Any man would love him.

"The other? Old Gaius? He is gray and sly, the politician's politician. His mind is subtle and filled with tricks. He seems an affable old fellow, the country farmer or the senator on holiday, but his heart is as black as any Parthian chief's. Do not turn your back on him, or leave anything in his care! They are, I suppose, just as you would expect."

"Yes," Tarsus said slowly, ". . . but they are strong, they have power."

"Indeed! In the hidden world, they burn like bright stars." Maxian held out his hand to the girl. She took it, her arm moving smoothly and mechanically. The Prince frowned and the trees that blocked the door writhed back, leaving a passage. "Krista, go and find yourself clothing, then return here."

Without a word, the young woman walked out, her bare feet rustling in the pine needles on the floor. Maxian turned back to the older priest.

"A man lies dead, as an old friend once said, but his memory lives. Men swear by him—*Praise Caesar!*—or worship at his tomb. Each time such a devotion is made, some tiny spark accrues to his memory, this dead legend. Over centuries, if he is well loved, then great strength may be in him. But—is this not rich?—*he lies in the grave!* The man may not use this strength, but that which raises him up? Oh, then this power may be tapped . . . Alexander is like the sun! Do you know, they still fear him, worship him, in far India? Barely a year was he among them, the sudden, unexpected invader, and still, *still* they know him. And Gaius? He does not burn so bright, yet he is cunning and served me well."

The thought of attack, of striking out at the young man, crossed Tarsus' mind. His oaths forbade him, though the enormity of what his pupil had done seemed adequate excuse. A swift blow with a dagger, into the brain, into the heart of thought and motion, might slay him.

But how can this be, if he speaks truly? Could he have brought back these legends as living men?

"Where are they now?"

Maxian shrugged, turning away. "I don't know. I sent them away from me, from my mother's house at Ottaviano. I told them to trouble me no more."

"Ottaviano?" Tarsus' voice was sharp as new fear blossomed. "When were you there?"

Maxian shrugged, avoiding the priest's eyes. "Some time ago . . . a week, perhaps two . . ."

Tarsus turned gray. Now he knew what curled and drifted around the Prince. It was the stench of mass death, of entire cities consumed by fire, by choking gas and burning stone.

"You were at Vesuvius." His voice was flat with horror. "You were there when the mountain burst. The girl—she was burned in the explosion? How close were you?"

Maxian smiled sickly and Tarsus could see guilt and shame in his face.

"We were," he whispered, "on the crown of the mountain. Men came to kill me. My brother sent them. I saw his face in my mind, when the red-haired woman had the knife at my throat. My own brother sent hired men to hunt me down. Is this possible? Can you believe it?"

Tarsus backed away, edging for the door with his hand. Now he could make out the screams of the dying, faint as the sound of dolphins beneath azure waves. The aura around the Prince was so plain and clear, so violent with the taste of dying, fled souls, that the older priest shuddered in reaction.

Here is the source of this unexpected strength. He has drunk deep of the dying, gaining their power like one of the K'shapákara of legend! By the gods, what a horror!

"Get out," Tarsus snarled, face flushed with disgust. "You are a monster, an abomination! How could you come here, to the sacred precincts themselves! You have violated every oath, every binding, every restriction of our order!"

Maxian blanched at the vehemence of his old master's words.

"What have I done?" the Prince cried in despair. "Defended myself, kept my own life? Do you shout at the fox, or the dog, that kills for its supper? What of the man beset by brigands—do you chastise him if he lays about him with a stave?"

"No," Tarsus bit out, "I do not. But you have drunk deep of the souls of the dying and the dead, growing fat on their suffering and pain. You are a ghoul, a corpse feeder."

The Prince's eyes widened in astonishment.

"Do you hear them?" Tarsus felt bile rise in his throat. "Can you feel them, the shadows of the dead? They are in you! I can feel them, smell them, hear their lamentations—"

"But I did not mean to drink them up!" Maxian's face burned with shame. "It happened—I was at the helm of the engine—the cities were aflame below me and all those souls, all released at once, rushed into me. I could not stop them!"

Tarsus shook his head in disgust and turned away. "Go

away from this place," he said. "If you come here again, we will strike you down, if we can. Get out."

The Prince, feeling a great emptiness in his chest, watched in bewildered pain as the older priest hurried away up the stairs. With each step, he felt the air grow cold and loss mount.

"But . . . what about . . ." Maxian stared around the little room, surprised to see the crowded trees and vines. He looked at his hands, then at the room again. One of the vines was beginning to bloom, sending out small white flowers with pale orange pistils.

How can my power be so great, yet fail?

Rousing himself enough to move, he climbed out of the room, stepping over the thick roots that crowded around the door, and stumbled up the stairway.

The moon was still bright, throwing deep shadows under the porticoes of the temple. Tarsus watched, his entire body stiff with tension, as the Prince crossed the square. His conscience raged at him, demanding that he lash out at the monster creeping away in the night.

I should raise an alarm, light the night with fire, summon lightning and storm to rage against him.

Remaining still and utterly quiet, Tarsus waited until the Prince had disappeared up the steps. Then he moved quickly along the line of columns that bounded the plaza, reaching the entryway. He looked out into the night, and saw at the far end of the colonnaded road the dim flicker of that fey blue light. The Prince was gone.

Tarsus breathed easier, leaning on his staff.

O praise you gods, that gave me some small common sense! He is so strong, so filled with vile power, reeking of the abattoir. . . . He would overmaster us in a sudden duel, each priest woken from a deep and dreaming sleep!

The priest, his heart still thudding with fear, turned from the gate and hurried away. The elders and the council of the temples had to be informed. They must do something, and quickly, before more innocents were consumed. Plans would have to be laid, friends summoned. Hopefully, the boy would not go far. Tarsus hurried down the steps, his sandals making a quick *slap-slap* sound on the pavement.

⊡[O]-[O]-[O]-[O]-[O]-[O]-[O]-[O]-[O]-[O]-[O]-[O]-[O]-[O]-[O]-[O]-[O]-[O]-[O]-[O]-[O]-[O]⊡

THE BUCOLEON PALACE, CONSTANTINOPLE, CAPITAL OF
THE EASTERN EMPIRE

)⊫(

Dim yellow candlelight illuminated a smooth wooden wall. The close-grained surface was carved with rows of curling flowers and vines. Fat-tailed sheep, heads low, alternated with stiff figures of hunters and farmers, frozen in the field or at the hunt. A thick Serican carpet hung from the wall, covering most of the panel.

It creaked and moved, sliding open, revealing darkness. A hand came into view, stubby fingered and webbed with scars and old cuts. A man followed, stocky, broad shouldered, with lank dark hair and the ghost of a beard on his chin. His eyes were narrow and cautious, surveying the room carefully before he set foot within. He moved with the ease of long practice, his feet bare, avoiding those tiles that might creak or make a noise. Behind him, equally quietly, came a taller man, younger, with long blond hair tied back in a single plait behind his head.

Set into the far wall of the room was a sleeping platform draped with silk and linen. A figure lay there, asleep, though the sound of breathing was labored and thick with a watery cough. The dark-haired man approached softly, his nose wrinkling at the thick smell that hung in the chamber. He was used to the stench of the battlefield, the raw-sewage smell of corpses bloated in the sun, the buzz of

the flies. This seemed worse, for the man in the bed was
still alive.

*Is this the punishment of the gods? Are these whispers
in the Hippodrome true?*

Rufio, captain of the Faithful, the red-cloaked barbarian
guardsmen of the Emperor of the Eastern Roman Empire,
knelt on the woolen covers, his face pensive. Here, in the
darkness, where there was no one to see, not even Sviod,
who shared this secret, he let some of the worry show in
his face. The man in the bed, his master, the Emperor
Heraclius, avtokrator of the Greeks, was dying. He was
not dying of a spear thrust taken on some battlefield, or
even of old age, with his grandchildren about him. He was
not dying facing his enemies, the men of the Legions at
his back. The Emperor was not dying the death Rufio desired.

This was a cold and lonely death, suffered in silence
and isolation. A slow, wasting disease ate away at the Emperor from within.

This, they said in the markets and the streets of great
Constantinople, *is what comes of flaunting the laws of the
gods, of flying in the face of decency!*

The illness had come suddenly, striking the Emperor
down as he returned in triumph from the eastern frontier.
Peace had been forced upon the ancient empire of the Persians. The mad king Chrosoes had been cut down, his capital of Ctesiphon burned to rubble. Vast sums in coin and
bullion had been taken from the golden palaces, from the
rich houses of the nobles and the merchants. The vaunted
Persian army, which had previously besieged Constantinople itself, had been smashed at the Kerenos River. The
great nobles that formed the backbone of the Persian state
squabbled amongst themselves. Chrosoes had left no living
male heirs. Rome, at last, after a thousand years of conflict,
was triumphant.

It was the Emperor himself who was failing. Some decay had come upon him as the army had marched up out

of the plains of Syria into the high Taurus Mountains. His flesh swelled, distending with clear, noisome fluid. His limbs betrayed him, failing to support his weight. Skin bulged and grew thin and transparent, strained by the water that accumulated in his flesh.

And the smell . . . always the smell.

Rufio grimaced again but put these thoughts aside. There was delicate and careful work to be done. He focused his mind, blocking out the rasping breath of the man lying before him. First, with a delicate hand, lighter than a feather, he opened the Emperor's lips. A bubbling sound rose from the throat. Rufio reached behind him and felt Sviod press a small glass vial into his hand. It was closed with a cork and Rufio thumbed it out with care. It made a popping sound and he palmed the stopper. A fresh smell of juniper and pine cut into the thick air. Rufio kept his mind on the task.

With the swelling of the flesh, the Emperor had conceived a terrible fear of any kind of liquid. He would not drink, seeing that his flesh pouched and distended with bile. In his extremity, for he was tormented by thirst, he would sometimes take small sips of wine. He would take no medicine or potion offered by the Imperial physicians or the priests of Asklepios. Even the master of their order, summoned up from their sanctuary at Pergamon, had been unable to halt the disease.

After that sour incident, the Emperor had banned any priest or sage from his side. He had never trusted them and now held deep hatred for their kind. Rufio, who had seen men laid open by the blow of an ax restored by the powers of the ancient order, did not think this was wise.

But Rufio was not the Emperor. Indeed, he was oathsworn to execute the Emperor's orders instantly, as were all of the Faithful. On that day, when the Emperor had screamed insults at the old, white-haired priest, if he had been ordered, Rufio would have cut the elder down. This was the burden laid upon him, to serve at the right hand of the Lord of All Men, Augustus Romanorum.

Yet, in all this, Heraclius had never ordered Rufio to cease trying to save him.

So, here in the darkness, in secret, the soldier crouched in the bed of the Emperor, urging single drops of aromatic fluid from the glass vial, letting them fall one by one into the Emperor's slack mouth. This was a distillate of juniper berries and parsley seeds, made by Sviod in a hidden room in the barracks of the old palace. Rufio had served with the northern barbarians who formed the bulk of the Faithful Guard for many years and he trusted this one, this blond youth, more than most.

Besides, he thought bitterly, *this is his grandmother's recipe! Why not trust the Empire and my own neck to the wisdom of a woman likely dead and moldering a thousand miles away?*

The glass vial was empty, the last drop trickling down the Emperor's throat. Rufio let out a thin, controlled breath and began to ease his way off the bed. In such tainted air, Rufio's nocturnal visits would be considered treason, and more than one captain of the Faithful had ended his days in the small Courtyard of the Ax, his sightless eyes staring up at the sun. The Faithful Guard had sworn an oath to the Emperor, not to their captain.

"It is done," said Rufio softly, rearranging the bed-clothes to cover up the dents his knees had left in the sheets. "Let us go."

Sviod was already at the panel and it closed softly after them, sliding flush against the wall. Behind them, in the dark room, the Emperor stirred, moaning in pain. His guilt and fear tormented him, even in sleep.

Another sliding panel revealed another room, and Rufio stepped out into a well-lit space filled with fine oil lamps. The chamber was slightly smaller than the Emperor's bed-chamber, but it was vastly better smelling, with the scent of rose and jasmine touching the air. He took a deep breath, hoping to clear the reek from his lungs. Tall, narrow windows let in cool, northern light by day and were shrouded with tapestries by night. Stacks of papyrus scrolls and parchment books buried the sleeping couch set into the wall. A large acerwood table dominated the room. It too was covered with papers and tablets and maps. More boxes of wicker and wooden slats covered the floor, containing Imperial tax records and audit reports. Behind it, curled up in a large wing-backed chair, her feet tucked under her, sat a young woman with long, tousled brown hair.

"It went well?" She looked up at the sound Rufio made, crossing to the table. Her light green eyes were smudged with exhaustion and worry. He nodded and put his hands on the back of the chair.

"No one saw us, Empress. Sviod is disposing of the evidence."

Rufio had parted from the Scandian in one of the tunnels that bored through the heart of the Bucoleon. Sviod had found a rubbish pit in the upper city, hard by the street of glassmakers. The bottle, washed out with springwater and then broken, would be cast away there, lost amongst a million fellow shards of glass. Rufio hoped that he was not marked by any of the spies that thronged the city.

"Is he any better?"

Rufio roused himself from his thoughts and met the woman's eyes. Her face was fixed and calm, like a mask. He knew that she had tried to put the pain of her husband's decline and his rejection of her aside. She carried a heavy burden well, but it was beginning to tell. The pert, open features and the ready smile that had endeared her first to her uncle and then to the palace staff were shrouded by exhaustion.

"Empress, I cannot tell. He was in pain, suffering from evil dreams. Sviod says that his uncles, when they suffered this ailment—"

Martina raised a hand.

"I know," she said, her voice weary. "They drink gallons of this concoction of their granddames. And it takes a week or more to show an effect." She put down the Anatolikon tax record she had been reviewing and rubbed her eyes with the palms of her hands. "While we, in this hornet's nest, are forced to get by with a drop or two a *day,* should we be so lucky. It might take months, should he live so long, to cure him."

Rufio nodded in resigned agreement. It was a tricky situation. The Empress sighed and stood, stretching her arms over her head. Rufio looked away quickly. Martina, as was her wont after "retiring" for the evening, was wearing a soft plum-colored tunic that barely reached her knees and fleece slippers. At first it had troubled Rufio even to be in her presence; it was a crime to be alone with her, much less while her husband was sick abed two floors and a hundred feet away. Now, since he had compounded that crime with treason and conspiracy, he just tried to ignore that she was a pretty young woman.

"Should I leave?" Martina faced him, hands on her hips, watching him with a serious expression on her face. "I am sure, for the black looks that Bonus gives me during temple services, that the high priest of Zeus Pankrator would gladly countenance my divorce. Within a day I could be safely away, within a week I could be home in Africa. Within the month, if need be, I could be in Mother Rome. I know a woman there, she could help me."

Rufio shook his head slowly, though what she said was true.

"And your son, what would you do with him?"

Martina pursed her lips and looked away, her gaze straying to the crib in the corner of the room. In it, sleeping deeply—at least for this little while!—was her son by Heraclius. Little Heracleonas had come into the world early and roughly, in a tent in the mountains of Armenia, but had seemed a hale child. Now, nearly a year later, he was troubled by vague illness. A priest of Asklepios came every two or three days and looked upon the child, but it seemed that nothing could be done to make him strong. He could not even walk yet.

Like my husband, brooded Martina. *Hidden powers move against us, denying us happiness.*

"I do not know," she said, turning back to Rufio. "One of my stepsons has already died by odd circumstance, and the other, poor Constantius, fears to be seen with me. If I flee, taking Heracleonas, he may die before I can find refuge. What will happen to Constantius then? While his father lives, while I am here and my son is alive, he is safe from the attentions of these parasites."

Martina glared at Rufio, who spread his hands, showing his agreement. She bit at her nail, then picked up one of the long quill pens that lay on the countertop. She needed something in her hands.

"If I go, then Theodore will return. Papers will surely appear, making him the heir, the regent of his invalid brother. He will be Emperor, if not in name, then in fact."

Rufio watched the Empress carefully, for she had begun to change under the pressure of her situation. When she had first been brought from Africa to live in the house of her uncle, to be tutored in art and literature, she had been quiet and demure. Compliant, even. Far more interested in the doings of books and painting, of sculpture and the theater, than the tawdry business of who stood closest to the Emperor. The guard captain sighed quietly. Heraclius and his niece had married out of love. Such things were not done, particularly among the nobility. Certainly never the Emperor!

Yet, he insisted. Even his closest allies argued against the match . . . and now, here we are.

Martina had shed her compliance, her naivete, in the harsh training yard of the palace. Life in the Bucoleon was simple—if the Emperor smiled upon you, then you prospered. For this moment, while Heraclius lay between life and death, everything was out of balance. While he lived,

Martina could continue to exist, even when the great lords and priests were dead set against her. Once he died . . .

"I will not let that fool replace my husband." Martina's voice was hard.

Then too, there was a deep and abiding hatred between the Empress and her other uncle, Prince Theodore. Rufio did not know where it had sprung from, but from the first day that the little girl had been in the palace, that tension had existed between them. Only the love that both parties shared for Heraclius had kept peace in the house. Now that they dealt directly with each other, the dislike had deepened. Rufio was well aware that Theodore held no love for him either. Should the Prince become regent, he would be lucky to escape with a head on his shoulders.

Martina smiled coldly, her fingers smoothing the quill down on the pen.

"Captain, we will persevere. Tell your young Scandian to make more of his potion. I will find a way to see that my husband takes more of it rather than less."

Rufio nodded and rose, hearing a tone of dismissal in her voice.

Very Empresslike, he thought to himself, pleased.

"Wait." Martina sat again at the desk, turning one of the lamps so that it gave her better light. A cup of red ink sat close at her hand. She dipped the quill and then, with a quick motion, scribed a signature on the scroll in front of her. "These papers are ready—place them on the *logothete* of the treasury's desk before you go to sleep."

Rufio grimaced, but he took the papers. They were neatly lettered, and not by any scribe in the palace. Those fellows needed coin as badly as any did, and were notorious for making extra copies of interesting things that passed over their writing desks.

Three crimes against the state in the passage of one day, he thought glumly to himself. *My record improves.*

Without looking at the fresh signatures, he placed the drafted laws into leather slipcovers and bound them up with a special dark red twine. Martina bent close, her head almost touching his own, and dripped wax onto the knots. Her small, creamy-white hand stamped down hard with the sigil. Rufio tried not to breathe, but the heady aroma of the Empress's hair, perfume and hot wax filled his nostrils.

"Done," she said smartly, tucking a strand of hair back behind one ear. There was a smudge of ink on her cheek. "Good night, Rufio. I will return the ink and the binding twine to their *proper* places."

Rufio did not answer her smile or the wicked gleam in her eye. The patricians who held the esteemed and noble offices of the Keeper of the Imperial Inkstand and the Holder of the Legal Binding were corrupt and venal men. It pleased the Empress that she, or her servants, could make free with their signs of office in the depth of night. It made Rufio nervous, for those men already held Martina in contempt. Slighting them in this way only bred more ill will.

He bowed and went out through the panel in the wall.

Behind him, Martina stood at the crib, one slim hand brushing the sleeping face of her child. She was terribly lonely, bereft of husband and family, but she dared not keep Rufio with her long. His discovery with her, particularly without a proper escort, would mean his death and her disgrace. This galled her, for she knew from the histories that previous empresses had entertained whole troops of gladiators, grooms, foreign princes, even chariot drivers and street sweepers in their chambers. But then the Empire had been at peace, or their husbands had countenanced such behavior in the interests of public image.

Or they were powers in their own right.

Moodily, she stared out the window. The moon was high enough to illuminate the crowded maze of buildings, some new, some decrepit, which made up the palace.

I am in a not particularly well kept up cage, she thought, not for the first time. *I need an advantage, an ally, something to hold back these jackals and wild dogs . . . I need a friend.*

)(

"H ello, Helena."

Late-spring rains had come to Rome, washing the marble and plaster buildings clean. The ash and grit drifting down out of the sky were gone. For the first time in months the air seemed clean and clear, and a spring sun shone down, making the temples on the Capitoline Hill glow with a blaze of color. Even the Tiber, that notorious muddy stream choked with the city's filth and the outwash of a hundred Latin farms, was running high and swift against its banks. With another week of rains like this, it might even begin to flow clear.

"Hello, Anastasia. May I sit?"

At the center of the river, on the Tiber Island, there was a verdant garden on the grounds of the Temple of Asclepius. From its benches, under graceful willows, one could sit and watch the parade of humanity surging back and forth across the Pons Aemillius, the oldest stone bridge in the city. Today, there were flocks of ducks under the bridge and a funeral procession crossing it. The rattle of drums and the wailing of the professional mourners carried across the water. Despite the tumult, in the garden there was a sense of peace and tranquillity. The priests of the temple lavished care upon the plantings, for the masters of their order held that the sound of running water and the smell of fresh and growing things were the best care that could be provided.

Helena sat brushing away a few narrow leaves fallen from the willows shrouding the bench. As befitted a lady of the city, she was wearing a conservative dress and tunic, with a light lace scarf covering the sleek line of her hair. In defiance of usual fashion, her hair fell only to her shoulders. Like many in the city, she wore somber colors and very little jewelry. The extent of the devastation in the south, where ancient Vesuvius had erupted only months before, had touched everyone. Of course, with the resources at her command, the bracelets on her left arm had come from distant Taprobane and blazed with rubies set in electrum. Sitting, she sighed gently, leaning on one hand.

A breeze sighed through the willows and quaking aspen that filled the garden behind them. It was a beautiful sound, like falling water, and it moved Helena's heart to thoughts of peace. This was a rare thing, for she was a woman of considerable and vehement conviction. Her husband often marveled at her restlessness, when he had time to notice it. Emperors tended to be distracted.

Her companion was silent, her head bowed, her face obscured by a dark, soot-colored cloth. Helena could barely make out a pair of folded hands in the woman's lap. Her bare fingertips peeked forth from heavy sleeves. Helena frowned, her fine white forehead creasing in vexation. Anastasia's fingernails were unpainted and in dreadful need of a manicure.

"Anastasia, you are not well."

The dark shape on the bench gave a choked snort, which Helena took to be the beginnings of a laugh. Helena waited, wondering if her old friend would say anything, but a turn of the glass passed and there was only silence between them.

"I wonder," said Helena at last, picking restlessly at the edge of her shawl, "if you would care to have dinner with us in our apartments. Just the three of us. Perhaps tomorrow? If, of course, your social schedule is not too full."

Anastasia did not reply for some time and Helena was beginning to grow angry when the woman in the dark cloth said, "You must have something new to show me. A wig of black Indian hair? A tiger pup? A brace of pygmies? Some new contraption of Aurelian's?"

The voice of the other woman was old and bitter and cold. Helena swallowed the heated words that had been close to flying from her mouth. She turned, fully facing her companion, and reached out with a gentle hand. Anastasia did not resist the touch and Helena carefully drew aside the veil that shrouded the older woman's head.

"Oh, my friend . . ." Helena's voice trailed off. She laid aside the cowl, draping it on Anastasia's shoulders. "You, my dear," she continued in a stronger voice, "must entertain my hairdresser. Whoever has charge of your hair now is addled!"

Anastasia still did not smile, though there was a faint wrinkling around her eyes. Seeing her friend for the first time in weeks, Helena despaired. Rumors were rife, amongst the ministers and notables of the city, that the notorious Duchess of Parma, Anastasia de'Orelio, the wealthiest woman in the Western Empire, had at last laid aside her interest in the world.

Can it be? they whispered in the baths, while they thought no one could hear. *Can the violet-eyed goddess have turned her back on us at last? Will the glorious Villa of Swans lie empty and cold? Where will the grand parties be, the decadent bacchanals? The social season is ruined!*

Helena had sat, these past weeks, holding court in her own salon, worrying. The patrician wives of Rome were in an uproar as no one knew what the truth of the matter was.

Is she abroad? Some of the women were sure that the Duchess had taken some barbarian king for her lover and lay in his dusky arms in far Hesperidia. *Is she, praise Caesar, dead?* Others, who had felt the whip of her tongue and the dagger of her intellect, prayed that she might have fallen among the dead of Vesuvius, asphyxiated on the docks of Herculaneum with half of the idlers in Rome. *Who,* lamented a few, *will tweak the noses of the corrupt,*

*self-serving men who clog the Senate chambers like so
many pigs in the trough?*

Helena worried for her friend, who had vanished from
the public stage, and for the Empire. Helena was one of
the few people in her husband's confidence who knew the
full scope of the Duchess's influence and power. The common herd of senators and tribunes knew her only as a
scandalous society matron. Anastasia, a young widow, had
inherited more than her husband's estates and title upon
his untimely death. For the last seven years she had been
the Emperor's spymaster as well. The old Duke had chosen
well, taking her as his wife. He had been a canny old goat,
keeping his head and fortune in the midst of the War of
the Three Pretenders. Helena had never met him, but she
could see the memory of him living on in Anastasia.

Galen Atreus was a good emperor and a good husband,
but he did not have the passion for intrigue which could
make him a *great* emperor. In this respect, as Helena was
fond of reminding her dear husband when he grumbled
and muttered about "women of power" and "that damned,
know-it-all Duchess," she made a perfect match. Galen
was an exceptional administrator, daring general, notably
honest and beloved of the Legions. Anastasia filled in the
sly and devious and underhanded traits he lacked.

But the former Anastasia was elegant, refined and impeccably dressed. Helena had learned nearly everything
that she knew of the art of public appearance—the use of
artful paints, of proper clothing and jewelry, the wry re-
mark, the cutting rejoinder—from the Duchess. Anastasia
had been the most well-presented woman Helena had ever
known.

The Anastasia she now beheld, draped in stained linen
and this grimy stole, had left her rose chalk and white lead
behind. The haggard eyes were not disguised, her once
glorious hair a tangled, snarled, tar-colored mess. The un-
kempt fingernails were only the beginning. The Duchess's
skin, once the marvel of the baths, was dry and patchy,

her voluptuous figure well hidden by baggy cloth. There was even a slight smell around her. Helena repressed a shudder and swallowed.

"Dear . . . what afflicts you? Whom do you mourn?"

Anastasia shook her head minutely, but the burst of pain was so clear in her eyes that Helena knew she had come upon just a thread of the truth. The Empress took her friend's hand, surprised by the chill touch. It seemed the claw of some dead thing, some bog creature crept out to take the form of the living. Unthinking, she took the hand in both of hers.

"It was the eruption?"

There was a minute flicker in the dead eyes. Helena took a breath and decided to press the issue. Her husband needed help—the little men in the offices and ministries were beginning to encroach on the privileges and authorities the Duchess had once held. Soon all of the power Anastasia and her husband had built up, all of the networks of contacts, the favors, the closely held secrets, would fade away. Men without her personal honor, her sense of responsibility to the state, her loyalty to Emperor Galen, would flow into those places. Those men, Helena did not trust to advise her husband. So, she must trespass in the personal affairs of a friend.

"Do you *know* they are dead? Have their bodies been exhumed from the ash?"

Anastasia's eyes flickered open and her pale lips twisted in a grimace.

"No . . ."

"Then there is some hope, however small, they may still live." Helena pressed the Duchess's hand tight, willing some of her warmth, some echo of the glorious day, into the cold flesh.

"No. They are all dead." Anastasia's eyes dropped.

"How can you say this?" Helena snapped, notoriously short temper struggling with concern for Anastasia. "Surely they were in Baiae, or Oplontis, where many have survived, but are lost in the vast crowd of refugees thrown out of house and home."

Now Anastasia did laugh, a sound filled with despair.

"Dear Helena," she said, her voice hoarse from disuse. "I know that you mean well, but those that I mourn were at the very crown of the mountain. *I am sure of it.* By all accounts a full mile of the peak is gone, torn away by the anger of the gods."

Helena made a sour face. If this were true, then there was no hope. She straightened her spine, brushed her hair back and met the Duchess's eyes once more.

"Then," she said stiffly, "you must leave off this malingering and return to decent public life. More, you must resume your accustomed duties in the Imperial service."

Anastasia managed a crooked half-grin. "You sound like one of those letters of yours, when you're trying to convince me to give up my debauched lifestyle."

Helena smiled back, pleased that she had roused her friend to some semblance of life.

"But," said Anastasia, the momentary spark fading, "I cannot be your husband's spymaster. I have lost my taste for that game. He will find another—there are always men eager to work in secret, in the name of the Emperor." She made a dismissive motion with her hand, but even that was obviously an effort.

"No!" blurted Helena, squeezing the Duchess's hand. "He needs *you,* not one of these lackwits that infest the halls of the Palatine, maundering on about conspiracies and informers! It would take someone years to rebuild your organization—Galen has too many enemies to take such a risk."

Anastasia stood, brushing a hanging branch of silver willow away from her head. A servant, a young blond girl, appeared as if from thin air. Helena was taken aback for a moment. She had not noticed the slave at all. The girl was dressed in mournful brown and black as well, matching her mistress.

"Good-bye, Helena. Tell Galen that I appreciate his concern, but I will leave the city soon. There are only dead memories here."

With that, while Helena grasped for something to say, the two women departed, their steps slow. For a moment, Helena could see them, the girl helping the older woman, two stooped crows with brown wings, and then they passed into the trees and were gone.

Hades take this despair that grips us all! Helena was enraged by the passivity suffocating the populace. The eruption of Vesuvius was a calamity and a disaster, true, but half the people in Rome, even in the Imperial government, even her husband, seemed to think it was the end of the world. It was past her comprehension. Many people seemed lifeless, or directionless, now that the first frantic burst of activity had passed. Bread and olives and salted meat went south in wagons, people with little more than the clothes on their back came north. Crowds of refugees gathered in the public forums, listless, barely capable of feeding themselves.

Even Galen and his younger brother Aurelian were gripped by the same malaise.

"We will see about that," she snorted, rising and gathering up her skirts so that the mud in the garden did not soil the edges. "If everyone is going to droop about like ugly boys at the feast-day dance, then I shall have to see about it myself."

THE PLAINS OF SCYTHIA, SOMEWHERE EAST OF TANAÏS

Smoke curled up over the rooftops of Itil, merging with a twilit sky. A lean-faced rider cantered over the long wooden bridge crossing the Rha as the first stars of evening began to appear in the east. The river was low and slow moving, and moss clung to the pilings of the span. Jusuf clucked his tongue at that—someone should have rousted the boys out to scrape the thick, wooden poles down and put new copper plates on them. He came to a gate of stone, thirty feet high, that loomed at the eastern end of the bridge and reined in. Lamps burned under the eaves of the tower, and guardsmen were already coming forth to meet him.

"*Salve, viator,*" called the first, his voice a basso rumble. Jusuf leaned forward on his saddle, an expression of surprise on his face.

"By the one god, Basir, you wound me with such ugly speech! Where is the glad greeting for a lost son, home at last?"

The guard captain drew up short, his head turned to one side in surprise. Jusuf grinned, seeing the curious expression on the man's face. The uneasy light of the lanterns and torches made it difficult to see in this gloom, but still . . . Basir stepped closer, his hand ready on his saber.

"Ay! What is this? Some beggar comes creeping in at dusk, hoping to pass the gate without paying?" Basir's voice rose as he spoke and he strode forward. A smile grew on his face, half hidden by a mighty beard and the cowl of his helmet. "Some young fool riding at night, not knowing mist devils and *surâpa* lie in wait for the unwary?"

Jusuf swung down easily, though the first days on his horse after the long sea voyage from Rome to Tanaïs had been rough going. He clasped hands with the old soldier and then crushed him into a fierce embrace.

"Ha! I saw nothing save some drunkards blinding themselves with lanterns by a gate!"

Basir met his hug and then stepped away, holding Jusuf's head in his hands.

"Oh, lad, you've grown old in these past years . . . look at you, such a neatly trimmed beard, such short hair!

They'll not let you into the council of warriors now, not with this down on your chin." Basir rubbed Jusuf's cheekbones and the back of his head.

"What did you do? Get it all burned off?"

Jusuf shrugged and scratched behind his ear.

"It's nothing, Uncle. They have different ways down in Rumish lands. It's better to blend with the forest . . ."

". . . than stand out for the lion." Basir nodded in appreciation, then he grinned and a sparkle came into his eye.

"Ho, now, what is this?"

Jusuf looked down, puzzled, and then blushed as Basir's thick fingers tugged a swatch of deep red cloth from beneath his jerkin. The other guardsmen, who had held back while the two met, came up in a cheerful, loud mob. Seeing the rich cloth, they whistled.

"Thunder! That's a fine silk tunic, Persian red, too!"

"What's her name? Say, she's pretty! Miss, will you have a drink with me?"

Jusuf snarled and made to draw his blade. The guardsmen jumped back, laughing, then closed around him, pounding him on the back and shoulders. Basir stepped back, letting the younger men greet the Prince. He smoothed his mustaches out, grinning fit to burst.

In a moment, when everyone had said hello, Jusuf shouldered his way to the older man's side.

"How's your back?" Basir put a trunklike arm around his nephew's shoulder, guiding him through the gate and into the city. Jusuf gave him a look.

"After that punishment? It's fine. How stand things here in the city?"

Basir sighed, his good humor gone. He stopped, standing in the shadow of the tower. The peaked shingled roofs of Itil rose up on either side of the street, making blocky shadows against the night. Small lamps hung before many of the houses, illuminating carved and painted doors. The street itself, as befitted the capital of a powerful nation, was surfaced with felled logs, planed smooth. In the spring and the fall even they would not keep the thick black mud of Scythia from oozing up and fouling the street, but it was better than nothing.

Jusuf took the lead of his horses from one of the guards, who clapped him on the shoulder again before returning to his post.

"Things are not well," he ventured, leaning towards the older man.

"No, no," said Basir gruffly, his voice catching. "There is no trouble, no strife amongst the people. There is . . . great sadness. I did not . . . no one expected Sahul to fall, to die far away, on some foreign field."

Jusuf bent his head to meet his uncle's, forehead to forehead, his own hands holding the older man.

"He died in battle, gloriously. Without him, without the lancers he led, the day would have gone ill for us. Persia and its mad king would have triumphed. The southerners would besiege Itil even now and the Rumish would have been put under the yoke."

Basir wiped his eye, looking away.

"I miss my brother, lad. He was a fine man. Sometimes, when the learned men chant . . . I think I can hear his voice, in the chorus."

Jusuf nodded. "Sahul had a fine voice, Uncle. But the length of his years came to an end."

"I know." Basir straightened and the old gruffness came back into his voice. "Each man must mark his own time on the cord. He chose ten lively years when the noose was on him, and so it was. Come, enough of this maudlin talk. You almost missed it, but the first feast of the *strava* is tonight."

"I'm not too late?" Jusuf blurted, his face lighting up. "I was sure the funeral would be long done by now. . . . Is Dahvos in the city?"

"He is," barked Basir, his humor entirely restored. "Come, I will ride with you to the citadel. Many old friends are there, raising their cups to the memory of our king. That young scamp, too!"

A great wash of heat and noise rolled out the doors of the citadel as Jusuf walked in, his head high in delight, letting the thunder of the revels crash against him. Basir was at his side, urging him on, but the Prince halted just within the massive double doors, surveying the crowd. The great hall, the feasting hall, was a round building a hundred feet wide. It had a high domed roof, supported by long spars of pine that curved to meet at a central oculus. Smoke billowed there, thrown up by four great roasting fires that lay in stone-lined pits at the center of the room. Long rows of benches surrounded the room, thronged with men and women. The walls, paneled with polished beechwood, were covered with trophies. Jusuf looked upon them and knew, remembered in his heart, all of the stories, all of the tales told by the campfire, all of the songs that carried the meaning and the history of his people through these relics.

The great hall of Itil was a hall of memories and mighty deeds. Jusuf smiled, content in himself, and knew that his people were a great people. Tonight, in grief and loss, they feasted and raised their voices to the heavens in song. With Basir going before him, he entered the chamber with the cowl of his cloak half turned up. They moved among the throng, seeing the warriors and chieftains of the people in their scaled mail and brocaded shirts, hair hanging long in braids and plaits. Tonight every man had entered without his helm, leaving them in racks by the door. Tonight the god looked down through the wide hole in the roof, seeing each man, marking his face, counting the deeds of his life. They were not dead, these men of the People, and they took joy in it.

It was not the way of the Khazar people to lament the passing of their king in dour mourning. Tonight, each house in the city would blaze with light, every candle and lantern lit. Each family gathered, even as the sprawling, rambunctious house of Asena crowded the hall of feasting. In each house, no matter how poor, cups were raised and the elders would give forth the tale of their fathers' deeds. Children sat at every hearth, listening, their eyes bright. In the shadows, where the red gleam of the fires lit their cheeks, mothers would sit, holding their youngest, telling the *true* tale of what had happened when Great-grandfather Avrahan did battle with the boar in the canebrake.

In the great hall, in the house of Asena, there was no throne of gold that set the king above all other men, there was no crown of ruby fire and emerald marking their leader. But there was a chair, a single carved seat, with wood so dark with age it gleamed in the firelight like oil, which had come out of the east with the people on the great journey. This chair had been placed here by the first Khazar to look upon the black waters of the Rha and it marked the place where his first yurt had been raised. It was old—the singers could tell its tale, but it was a long one and better suited for winter nights.

Tonight the chair stood empty.

Jusuf paused, his hand on the shoulder of a cousin. That empty place, so obvious in this crowded, boisterous hall, struck at him. Basir halted too and bowed his head. Young men and women, not yet come of age, flooded past them, dressed in white and gold, their hair twined with bright blue flowers. They were dancing, making a great circuit of the hall, their faces flushed with exertion.

Before the empty seat, a plate of silver was laid, filled with meat and cheese and bread. A cup sat beside it, topped with wine.

Jusuf could not speak, his throat constricted, for he saw the memory of his uncle before him.

Sahul was shorter and stouter than other men, with streaks of gray in his sandy-blond hair, and watchful, watery-blue eyes. He was strong, with powerful shoulders that could lift a foundered horse. He rarely spoke, but his voice in song was a marvel. He lifted a young boy who had fallen from a pony and broken his leg. His eyes were compassionate and warm and the boy stifled his tears, for it did no honor to the People to be weak. He stood, his short beard ruffling in the wind, on a platform of cut logs, watching the army of the Roman emperors parade before him.

At either side of the empty chair, the great chiefs of the People sat. Here was old Yakov, his barrel chest straining at a brocaded shirt, his wise old wife, Rahel, at his side. There were the chiefs of the northern clans, there the clan-lords of the fishermen who plied the waters of the salty sea. Their clothes were rich, their jewels bright, for the People prospered in their kingdom.

He smiled in darkness, grinning at Jusuf through slow-falling dust. A tomb rose around them, vaulted arches lost in the gloom. Between them, a woman, her face intent, drew in the dust. She was clad in armor, fiery hair tucked up in a bun at the back of her head. Jusuf protested, but Sahul shook his head. They would follow the plan of the Roman huntress.

At the left hand of the empty chair, a young man sat, his hair a cascade of red-gold curls, his beard rich and carefully combed. Seeing him, alive, Jusuf smiled. The young man seemed strong, with powerful arms and the broad shoulders of his father. He wore a dark shirt of silk embroidered with flowers and ivy. A bracelet of silver was on his wrist. He bent his head low, laughing with a young woman at his side. Her hair was a dark, rich brown, like the wings of a kestrel. She was wearing green and gold. Over the din of the crowd, what they shared could not be heard a foot away.

Before the chair, beside the plate, a riding whip lay, waiting for a skilled hand to take it up.

Hooves thundered, shaking the earth, as the People wheeled, their horses surging under them. Sahul rose up in his stirrups, his face clear under the crown of his helm. He raised his voice, calling out to the riders. As one, they

*followed him, shouting his name. As one, they swept to-
wards the lines of the Persians. Forty thousand of the People rushed forward.*

Basir bulled ahead through the crowd, pushing his way
through a flock of priests who were arguing amongst themselves, debating the words of the book. Jusuf followed,
slowly, remembering.

*The shock of contact shuddered through the mass of
armored men. Horses screamed and men cried out in agony. Wood splintered on shields, maces rose and fell. The
sky was dark with arrows. Sahul was at the center, his
sword a bright blur in the air. A Persian champion
stormed forward, armor glittering in the sun. Sahul took
the first blow on his blade, then—swift!—stabbed, trans-
fixing the man's eyeslit. Red blood gouted, staining the
metal.*

The young man with golden hair rose, his face breaking
into a smile. Jusuf pushed through the crowd the last few
feet, feeling the fierce, strong grip of his brother on his
arm.

"Jusuf!" Dahvos was shouting, grinning, clasping his
brother to him. Jusuf wrapped his arms around his little
brother, feeling the warmth of his body, the strength in his
arms. Tears were wet on his face, but he did not care.

"Hello, Dahvos. You live, I see."

*Sahul coughed blood onto the ground, feeling the earth
under his hands shake with the thunder of hooves. Somewhere on the field of battle, a cavalry charge was going
home. He staggered up, a long knife in his hand. His helmet was missing, smashed off by the blow of a Persian
war mace. Blood streamed into his eyes. Horses and men
rushed by him in the swirl of battle. His horse was gone,
as was the small round shield that had been strapped to
his upper arm.*

*A Persian in half-armor spurred towards him, cutting
overhand with a long, straight sword. Sahul ducked aside,
slashing at the horse's legs. He missed, but the tip of the*

Persian sword caught in his shoulder. The diquan *disappeared into the fray. Sahul jumped at the next horse that thundered by, but missed the saddle horn and was knocked down hard. Gasping for breath, he caught a glimpse of a spear flashing in the sun, then there was a stunning blow to his stomach.*

Jusuf shouted, seeing him fall, then furiously attacked, trying to cut his way to the King's side. The spear rose up, thin red blood sluicing off the leaf-shaped blade. Jusuf's saber cut into the Persian's neck. Then he stood over the body lying on the ground.

A cry went up in the hall, and Dahvos led it, springing up onto the feasting table.

"Look you, see who comes among us! See my brother, he is safe a-home!"

The hall quieted for a moment, then Dahvos dragged Jusuf up onto the table. A plate of roasted grouse went flying, but Dahvos raised his brother's arm high.

"See the prodigal returned! Now, there may be feasting and celebration!"

The roof shook with the cheer that rose, and Jusuf blushed red, seeing the bright and smiling faces of his people all around him, their cups raised to him. A skirl of pipes and drums cut through the tumult and Dahvos shouted in delight.

"Ho, my brother, join me!"

Jusuf laughed too, and between them they danced the Rider's Homecoming on the tabletops. Before long, the whole of the building shook with the chanting and the thunder of tables rattling.

"Wait just a moment," said Aunt Rebekah, raising a small brown hand. Jusuf, as was befitting a son of the house, paused in his story. "You've said a great deal about all these doings with tunnels and tombs and battles, but you've not said anything about my girl."

Jusuf repressed a smile, for he could see desperate worry

in his aunt's small, bright eyes. Rebekah was the youngest of his father's wives, the last taken by old Cis. The dynastic business of the house of Asena, with each kagan having, perhaps, more than one wife, was complicated. To make things simpler, each mother was referred to as "Aunt"; each brother of a different mother, "Uncle." Sahul and Basir were the sons of Gea, who had died when Jusuf was very young. She had fallen into the Rha while hunting for winter geese that had frozen to the ice. Nami was the mother of Jusuf and Dahvos, while young Rebekah had only borne one living child before Cis had been killed in an ambush by the Bulgars.

"Ah, our wayward sister, she of the shining face and long hair, that impudent brat, Shirin."

Rebekah, who had been quite a beauty herself in her youth, glared hard at Jusuf.

"Yes, my little bird! Now, quit your lovesick maundering on about the white thighs of this Roman woman and tell me—did you get word of her down there in the southlands? Is she well? I have heard from this braggart"—now Rebekah clouted Dahvos on the head, and sharply too—"that her husband, the boy Khusro, is dead. What has become of her?"

Jusuf raised an eyebrow at Dahvos in surprise. Rebekah was very angry and quite beside herself with worry. Then Jusuf clapped a hand against his forehead in dismay.

"Aunt, forgive me! I forgot that Dahvos went *north* with the army! He has not heard of all that transpired in Ctesiphon . . . no one has!"

Jusuf stood. The inner circle of the family had gathered to hear of his journey and the latest news from Rhomanoi lands. They sat in a companionable circle in the comfort of one of the old yurts in the citadel. It was piled thick with rugs and lit by small lanterns. He bowed deeply to all of them, knowing beautiful young Shirin was the best loved of all the children. The thought that she might be friendless and alone, even dead or captive, must have weighed heavy on them.

"Listen, then, and I will tell you what happened. But fear not, Rebekah, when last I saw your daughter, she was getting into a longboat—yes, like a coracle, but made of fitted planks—in the middle of the ocean! She was safe and happy."

"Humph!" Rebekah said, her eyes bare slits, still glowering. "And those children of hers by that southland prince who got his head knocked in? What of them?"

Jusuf hid a grin, for Rebekah doted on all children, hers most of all.

"They are well—though I have seen them more recently. They are in, if you can believe it, mighty Rome herself! Staying with a dear friend, in a palace, with ornamental pools and gardens and their own servants. . . ."

Rebekah settled back, apparently mollified that her grandchildren were being lavished with the proper care. Jusuf took up the tale of himself and the Roman woman, Thyatis, in the streets of the Persian capital, Ctesiphon, itself.

". . . and so I come home again, with the favor of the Emperor of the Romans and this news."

Jusuf sighed and drank deep from a cup of *kumis* that was at his side. His voice was hoarse from speaking through the night and into the dawn, relating all that he had seen and done. Like many of his people who had trained under the regime of the *ozan* priests, his memory was prodigious.

Seeing that he was done, his aunts nodded to one another and rose, stiffly, to file out of the yurt. They would take themselves to the steam baths by the river and discuss this matter among themselves. The men, being men, would just fall asleep somewhere. Jusuf wondered, as he rose and stretched, if his old rooms were still his.

Probably not, he groused silently; *someone will have*

thrown all my things in a basket and put them away. Probably Rahel! The very old woman, the wife of Great-uncle Yakov, was fond of cleaning up other people's business. Jusuf wondered if he would ever find his belongings. Probably not.

"Well," drawled Dahvos, rubbing his eyes in exhaustion. "I see you skipped lightly over certain matters between you and this *duchess* while you were in Rome. But no matter, you can tell me the details later, after we've slept! I am glad Shirin is safe and happy."

Jusuf nodded, smiling. "How is it," he asked, "that she is able to find the finest match? This is twice now."

Dahvos nodded, but his face was shadowed with concern. "Yes . . . but we clasped hands with Chrosoes, too, and called him brother. He seemed a mighty king and faithful friend as well. You see how he ended!"

"He is dead?" Jusuf caught Dahvos' eye. He had not seen the king of kings fall. "This is not a rumor, circulated by the Romans to make trouble among the *diquans*? You are sure of it? What of Kavadh-Siroes, the Crown Prince?"

The younger man nodded, a shock of his long hair falling in front of his face.

"I am," he said, "the news spread like fire in dry grass. The Eastern Emperor Heraclius paraded Chrosoes' corpse before the whole of the city. No one has come forth to gainsay it. And that youth, Kavadh-Siroes? He is dead, too, and they say that the Western Emperor Galen killed the boy himself while Heraclius watched."

Frowning, Jusuf ducked under the low door and came out into the dim morning light. This corner of the citadel was planted with trees and brushy vines. Piles of cut wood and lattices of drying sable furs lay against the fieldstone walls. The skins on the yurt had good company. Dahvos followed and stood blinking, watching him.

"What is it? I see your thoughts; they are dark as carrion crows."

Jusuf shook his head and raised a hand.

"I was thinking of little Avrahan . . . Shirin's son, her son by Chrosoes." Jusuf turned, his face dark with worry.

Dahvos met his gaze, his limpid blue eyes puzzled. But then understanding flickered in them and he put a finger to his lips.

"Say it not, my brother . . ."

"Chrosoes' son," grated Jusuf. "His surviving eldest son. Our nephew, the silly little rabbit, is by blood Shahanshah of Persia, the rightful king of kings."

Dahvos made a sign to ward off ill luck. "But he is safe, and far from harm, and by your words, *no one knows he is alive!*"

"Rebekah knows," Jusuf said sharply, "and she can count who begat who as well as anyone. You've heard her in her cups—*My father ruled from the Chin capital to the Rhomanoi frontier, from the ice in the north to Persia in the south . . .*"

Shaking his head, Dahvos turned away, his nose in the air.

"Come on, I smell breakfast cooking. All those things can wait."

The gelding sprinted, hooves flashing over the grass, its head stretched out, legs pumping. Jusuf leaned low, his face split by a wild grin. The land rushed past as the young horse let on full speed. The Khazar let the wind flow, rejoicing in the feeling of the horse running under him.

"Hey-yup!" Dahvos, astride a black-and-white horse, galloped a dozen feet away. His long hair whipped in the air behind him as the two horses, going all out, reached the turn. A spear thrust into the earth blurred past, a kerchief snapping atop it. Jusuf urged his mount close around the marker, putting the heaving shoulder of the roan into his brother's path.

Dahvos let out another yell, his horsewhip snapping behind him. The black-and-white jolted forward, swerving to the outside. Jusuf and the roan were away, in the straight, and now the horse really started to run. Head down, letting the air whip over him, Jusuf urged the horse on. The wooden fence of the *aǧil* grew closer. The course from the corral by the river, up the hill, around to the spear and back again was two full Roman miles. Both horses burst up over the ridge overlooking the river. Below them, as they thundered down the slope, were the long docks of Itil, crowded with river barges and shallow-draft ships plying the waters of the Mare Caspium. On this side, the east, there were great stockyards built for the cattle cull. Now they were empty, filled only with weeds and short-grass.

The slope down to the aǧil was not too steep, just enough to let them build up a fierce speed as they came down into the final stretch along the riverbank. Scattered yellow flowers went past and Jusuf let out a yell as his roan began to pull away on the flat. Dahvos cracked his riding whip again, trying to get another length of speed out of the black-and-white.

It was not enough. Jusuf and the roan thundered into the corral in a cloud of dust. Whooping with joy, Jusuf swung down, catching the horse's bridle.

Dahvos cantered up, his black-and-white blowing and running with sweat. Two of the boys set to watch the horses ran up with towels and leather buckets of water. The younger Khazar swung down as well, catching a thrown rag. The sky was very blue and cloudless. Summer heat was beginning to come on, and soon it would be blisteringly hot. Jusuf stepped into the shade of a tent that was put up next to the aǧil by the watch-boys. There was *kumis* and wine and tea inside. He took up a cup and filled it with the tea, a strong green blend that came out of Tashkent on the caravan trade.

"A fine horse," he said to his brother as Dahvos entered the tent and flopped down.

"Indeed! What will you give me for it?" Dahvos grinned, but Jusuf shook his head.

"Nothing, wretch! It is fast in the sprint, but it was

blowing hard at the end—no good for a long chase . . . pretty, though."

"True enough."

In the corral, the boys walked the horses until their heaving flanks and pounding hearts calmed. Jusuf squinted, seeing a rider approaching from the city, cantering up the path along the riverbank. He stepped out into the sun again, waving. The messenger arrived moments later, his young, beardless face grave.

"The lord Basir said to bring this to the Prince," said the lad, handing down a leather pouch. It was sealed with a clasp showing a doubled star. During the rule of the T'u-chüeh, a courier service had been established among all of the cities of that far-flung realm. Even after throwing off their yoke, the Khazars maintained the innovation. Old Cis and Sahul had spent a goodly sum establishing regular way posts throughout the Khazar realm where fresh horses and fodder could be found. Only government business went by dispatch rider, but when it did, it flew.

Jusuf snapped open the clasp and pulled out a sheet of parchment. It was covered with crabbed writing, in the Greek style favored among the merchant houses of Constantinople. Dahvos, peering over his brother's shoulder, made a groaning sound.

"Greek! The lord of heaven bless us, what a dreadful language . . . even the Persian yodeling is easier to learn."

"Quiet," Jusuf said absently, his attention focused on the letters. Dahvos' Greek was quite good, but Jusuf had enough of the written language to make out what was on the paper. It came from one of Anastasia's agents in the Eastern capital, relayed through from Tyre on the coast of Phoenicia. The Prince, reading, smiled grimly at the first fruit of the promises made to him by Emperor Galen and the Duchess in their last meeting. Though relations between the two Roman Empires had been good for the last fifty years or so, before that there had been intermittent warfare and continuing economic struggle between the two states. Galen was a farsighted man; it was not beyond him—and certainly not beyond the Duchess—to establish an alliance with the Khazar nation to counterbalance a resurgent Eastern Empire.

Jusuf let out a long hiss of dismay as he reached the end of the page.

"What is it?" Dahvos felt the change in his brother's demeanor. The cheerful good humor of the afternoon had fallen away.

"There has been a battle," Jusuf said, beginning to read the letter again. "The Imperial Army of the Great Prince Theodore has been decisively defeated at a place called Yarmuk in Roman Syria. The cities of the Decapolis rose up in revolt over taxation, then were joined by the Nabateans and some unknown number of Arab and Palmyrene mercenaries. Theodore cornered them at this place and then lost badly in a stand-up fight. Forty thousand Roman troops were bested by half their number. Theodore has fallen back to Damascus, but his army has scattered."

Dahvos whistled, considering the professionalism of the Roman army, its skill, the power and weapons at its command. Even under poor generals, a Roman army could usually thrash twice its number in provincial levies, tribesmen and barbarian sell-swords.

"What happened?"

Jusuf read the last sentence again, shook his head and then put the paper back in the dispatch pouch.

"Sorcery. The Petrans whistled up a sandstorm to plow over the Romans, breaking their morale. Then a flank charge by Arab lancers cracked them wide open."

Dahvos shook his head in admiration. He had served alongside the Romans in their common war with Persia and he knew them to be brave fighters. Still, he had crossed paths with Prince Theodore too and the thought of the man forced to flee, his dreams of empire in ruin, brought a faint smile to Dahvos' face.

"What does this mean?"

Jusuf considered, staring off into the bright blue sky over the river and the towers of the city. Itil was a wooden city, but the Khazars and their Slav craftsmen were fond of curlicues and ornaments. Nearly every house had a carved roofline, wild with fantastic creatures and stylized, interlocking plants. The temples of the god in the city were brightly painted, too. Thin pillars of smoke marked the cook fires, forges and workshops in the city.

"It means more war, dear brother. Despite our victory over the Persians, the Eastern Empire is very weak. Heraclius was counting on a time of peace, with his enemies humbled, for him to restore trade and commerce and those border provinces ruined by Chrosoes' war. Now he will not get it. Too, his policies in the Decapolis have lost him two valuable allies—Petra and Palmyra—as well as the riches of the Indian and Serican trade."

Dahvos scratched his nose, watching his brother.

"Will they need our help?"

Jusuf turned, puzzled. "Our help? Why would they ask for that? Even this disaster is only a local setback. Heraclius will return his main army from Constantinople and suppress the revolt. Without some kind of patron—some great power—these rebels have little chance. In the old days, this would be a grievous situation, for the Persians would already be invading. But Persia . . ."

"Is in ruins," sighed Dahvos. "I guess there will be no letters begging our help then, no embassies heavy with gold and gifts."

Jusuf laughed. "You have become quite mercenary, little brother! Has Sahul taught you this lesson? What did you hope to gain—*more* glory, more feats of arms to swell your *engorged* legend?"

Dahvos, unexpectedly, blushed and turned away. Jusuf cocked his head, even more puzzled.

"What . . . You *were* hoping to extort something from the Romans! What is it?"

Intrigued, Jusuf stepped around his brother and stared hard at him, hands on his hips.

"Tell me. Come, we're brothers. If you have set yourself on something, tell me and I will help you get it."

In answer, Dahvos reached into his shirt and took out a small enameled gold locket. Jusuf had seen such things before, in the markets of Van and Chersonesos. Inside would be an engraving, or a cameo of . . . *a woman*?

"May I?" Dahvos still refused to meet his eyes, but he handed the locket over. Jusuf, his fingers gentle, worked the little clasp and opened it. Within, set in ivory, was a tiny painting, a miniature, of a young Greek woman with dark brown hair and a thoughtful, pensive face. She seemed very young. Jusuf looked up, meeting his brother's eyes with a questioning expression.

"And the young lady is?"

Dahvos muttered something, looking down at his feet. Jusuf coughed and then smiled when his brother looked up.

"Sorry, I couldn't hear you."

Dahvos scratched the back of his head, then said, "Her name is Epiphania."

"A good name. A good Greek name, a good *Roman* name. Did she give you this token?"

Dahvos shook his head, finally standing up straight and sighing. "No, Sahul gave it to me, the night before Kerenos River. He said I should keep it for him. He said . . . he said that Emperor Heraclius was offering her in marriage to seal the alliance between the Eastern Empire and our realm. Sahul thought she was a little young for him . . ."

Jusuf made a clucking sound, thinking on his uncle's thoughtful nature and eye for the long ride, rather than the sprint. He turned the cameo over in his hands. It was magnificently made, the product, no doubt, of one of the Imperial workshops in Constantinople itself.

"A relative of the Emperor's? A niece?"

Swallowing, Dahvos shook his head. "No, she's his daughter from his first marriage."

Now Jusuf whistled and raised an eyebrow at his brother. "You've no lack of ambition behind that charming blond face, do you?"

Dahvos blushed again.

"You will be the next kagan, so much I know from the elders," continued Jusuf, his tone serious. "You have yet to take a wife. The daughter of the Eastern Emperor would be a bold victory, if you could secure her. A strong alliance with a powerful ally and a bond with her family, who, if memory serves, are rich and well connected within the Empire. Even greater glory than *kagan* of the Khazars might be within your reach—or if not yours, then your son's."

Nodding, Dahvos met his brother's eyes. "But Sahul is dead," he said, voicing Jusuf's question as well. "There is no formal treaty, no nuptial arrangements. Everything was private between Heraclius and our uncle. Now, we might have to start over . . ."

Jusuf waited. It was clear that Dahvos had given this a great deal of thought.

"I thought," continued the younger man, after a strained pause, "that we might strike the same bargain again, if the moment arose. With this war in the Levant, I hoped—"

"It is not impossible," Jusuf said, interrupting, "for such a thing to come to pass. But it will take some doing, and hard riding, to be in the right place at the right time."

Spreading his hands in question, Dahvos returned the raised eyebrow. Jusuf laughed.

"Have you taken note, dear brother, of the way the young men of the People hang on your every word? How they plague us for tales of our adventures in the Persian campaign? Do you think that they have neglected to notice the fine jewels, the gold, the cloth, the *loot* that your troops were laden with on their return?"

Jusuf, smirking, laughed again and put his hand on his

brother's shoulder. "Consider, if you will, what will transpire if you let it be known that you intend to take an army to the aid of the Eastern Empire in their war against these rebels. Why, it would not surprise me if more than a few young fellows, barely come into their beards, might follow you. Even some veterans might agree to come, just to keep the youngsters out of trouble."

"You are wise, brother." Dahvos bowed, but he was still worried. "But where do we go?"

Jusuf wagged a finger, saying, "Not the Levant, if that is what you are thinking. No, for this matter, we must go to Constantinople. The Emperor will muster any response to this disaster from there. He is a man that believes in central control. He will want, particularly now that his brother has failed him, to make sure that things are done right. Besides, the Eastern Empire possesses a large fleet. Let us put it to work."

Understanding dawned in Dahvos' eyes. He knew the lands about the Khazar realm as well as any man. "Chersonesos? Or Tanaïs? We could barge everyone up the Rha to the Khazarim Way, ride the portage road, then down past Sarkel on riverboats. That would be fastest. We could be to Tanaïs in a month, Chersonesos in two, even if we had to ride overland from the mouth of the Don."

"You have the right of it, brother." Jusuf was pleased, both with the initiative of his brother and the prospect of returning to Roman lands. There was a dark-haired woman that he found he missed, even here, amongst his people. Constantinople was still far from Rome, but it was closer than Itil! Something occurred to him, and he caught Dahvos' shoulder.

"One thing, if you do not take it amiss. Don't fall in love with this woman, pretty as she is, until you've actually made her acquaintance."

A VILLA OUTSIDE ROME

)H(

The woman turned her head, revealing glassy scars on her neck. Gently, Ila ran a straight razor down the side of her head, shaving away the last tufts of red-gold hair. Her eyes distant, the woman bent her head down obediently, letting the mousy-haired girl shave the nape of her neck. When she was done, Ila laved the woman's head with scented oil.

"There, dear, now it'll grow out even." Ila wiped her hands on an old cloth, then tucked her own ragged mop of hair behind her ears and squatted on the ground. Her quick hands arranged the razors and combs of bone and bronze strigil. The tools fit into a neat leather carrying case. The woman watched, distant and uninterested.

The wagons stood in a stand of quince trees, a hundred yards from the nearest road. The baldheaded master, Vitellix, had made an arrangement with the local estate manager. He said, as he left that morning, they would stay a few days. It was cool and shady in the orchard. Goats and sheep wandered under them, cropping the grass short and clearing out the weeds. The woman, now bald, her pate shining with oil, sat on a three-legged stool on the grass.

The side of the wagon was not ornamented, showing weather-beaten gray wood and peeling paint. Nothing suggested the delicate carving and amusing paintings ornamenting the interior.

"What's your name?"

"I don't remember," the woman said in her smoke-hoarsened voice. "What is your name?"

Ila smiled, showing crooked teeth in her nut-brown face.

She was young, perhaps only fifteen. "Silly! I've told you before. I am Ila. I ride the horses."

"Of course," the woman said, but her eyes were vague. Sometimes, when she tried to remember what had happened before she woke up in the wagon, her fists could clench until the nails scored her flesh.

"You must have a name," Ila mused, brown eyes squinting up as she thought. "Perhaps we should name you Lump or Mossy."

The woman frowned at the girl's laughter. "I do not want to be named Lump or Mossy. You are a mean girl."

Ila laughed, seeing a spark of life in the woman's eyes.

"But all you do is sit!" Ila put her hands on her waist, bending close. "Like a stone, or a loaf of bread fresh from the oven . . . so, you shall be called Lump."

The woman stood angrily, but her body swayed and there was a rushing sound in her ears. "Oh. This feels strange."

"It is called standing up," said Ila, her voice filled with mousy laughter. "Sometimes, when people are not pretending to be stones in a streambed, they try it."

The woman tried to turn, one hand splayed against the wall of the wagon. Her eyes narrowed and she glared at the girl.

"I . . . can . . . stand," she said weakly. Her legs were trembling, but the dizziness passed. The world seemed different from her higher vantage point. She saw that the mouse-girl was quite short-bodied and deeply tanned. "I am not a *lump*."

"Yes, you are," Ila said, skipping back on the grass, hands clasped behind her back. "You're just a little taller than most lumps! You can't even walk or stand without a wagon holding you up. You're lucky it's a friendly wagon or it would let you fall down."

The fury in the woman's eyes burned a little brighter and she pushed away from the wagon. Her legs felt gelid and weak and she took three quick steps, trying to get her balance. Ila drifted away, laughing and covering her mouth with a hand. The woman stopped, taking a half-step, regaining her balance. One of her legs, still bandaged, was throbbing furiously. Blood pounded in her head.

"I can stand," she bit out, though her arms were wobbling as she tried to stay upright. "And walk."

"Can you?" Ila stepped in quickly and poked the woman in the chest. The woman's left arm made a weak movement to block Ila's hand, but it was far too slow. She fell backwards and struck the ground hard. Breath chuffed out of her and a blinding pain jolted up her spine.

"See?" Ila's voice came out of the haze, "a *lump.*"

The woman staggered up, her face turning red with effort. The pain in her legs and her arm faded, replaced by a burning sensation. She lunged for the girl. Ila stepped aside, clapping in delight. The woman, unable to stop herself, ran into the side of the wagon. Soaked with sweat and panting, the woman clung to the rough wood. Tears streamed down her face.

"Leave me alone . . ." she managed to choke out. Despite a furious effort, she slipped down to the ground, limbs trembling.

"That is not necessary," Vitellix said, stepping out from behind the wagon. "Otho, Franco, help her up, back to the chair."

The woman groaned as the two brothers appeared and gently lifted her up. Their muscles rippled hard and distinct under smooth brown flesh. They carried her to the chair and placed her in it without breathing heavily or even feeling the effort. Vitellix crouched down beside her.

"You are still weak," he said gently, strong, thick fingers probing the line of her bandaged leg. She barely hissed when he kneaded her shin and squeezed her toes. "But you are healing quickly. You were very strong before you fell. I think that you will be strong again, but you must try."

"How . . . how can you be so sure?" Vitellix met the woman's eyes, seeing pain and confusion in sea-gray depths. Sometimes her eyes were green or even blue, depending on the light of the day. He smiled gently at her, rolling back her eyelids with a practiced thumb.

"It is my business," he said simply. Vitellix nodded at the people standing behind him, watching. "They are my business—I look after them, train them, tend their hurts. Sometimes, if the gods are smiling, I find us paying employment!"

The others laughed. Tentatively, the mouse-girl crept up to the woman's side, taking her hand. "Please, mistress, don't be angry. Papa thought you should walk today."

The woman turned her head, though it cost what little energy she had regained to do so.

"I can walk," she whispered.

"Yes, you can." Ila kissed her forehead. "Soon you will run."

Vitellix stood, satisfied with what he had seen.

"Yes," he said, bronzed face creasing with a smile. "But you still need a name. Something auspicious . . ."

"Epona," said a man standing amongst the others. Like Otho and Franco, he was short-bodied, but in perfect proportion. His blond hair was cropped close to his head, making him seem sleek and quick. His smooth body, barely covered by a leather belt and a short woolen kilt, was hard with muscle. "May she run like the Huntress, graceful and swift as a red mare, with a steady hand and eye."

"Well spoken," Vitellix said, laying a forefinger alongside his nose. "I think Dummonus has the right of it. But we are not in Gaul in these days, no. Such foreign-sounding words may fall ill on the ears of the patricians. I think we shall call our foundling Diana, for did not my sons find her among the oak groves, by moonlight?"

Otho and Franco beamed at this, for they had been away from the wagons without permission. Now it seemed the goddess of the wilderness guided their feet.

"Diana," the woman said, face pensive. "That is not my name."

Ila, still holding her hand, squeezed it in affection. "Do you remember?"

The woman shook her head, feeling the warmth of the girl's fingers. Her own were very cold. "No . . . but it is a good name. I will take it up, until I find my own again."

"Good," said Vitellix, voice sharp and businesslike. "Now there may be proper introductions. Stand forward, you sacred band!"

Diana looked up, her face clear of anguish for the moment. She had seen many of the troupe pass by while she lay in the wagon. Most of the time, Ila brought her food or helped her to the privy, but others had put their heads in the door, too, greeting her. They seemed friendly.

"I am Vitellix. I am the master of this little troupe. We perform for the pleasure of the gods, the fathers of the city, the priests, or anyone else that can pay for our supper. I am from Narbo, in the southern reaches of Gaul. My craft is laughter and the ridiculous."

He bent his head to her, taking her hand and kissing it in greeting. "Well met, Diana."

She smiled, for he had always shown her great courtesy and care. "Greetings, Vitellix."

The master stood aside and Dummonus stepped forward, his handsome face grave and composed. His features were those of a statue, perfectly chiseled. His blond hair was very pale, almost white, and his eyebrows were quick strokes of light on his tanned skin.

"Greetings, lady. I am Dummonus. My craft is flight, may it please you. I also own some small skill with throwing and hurling."

He too bowed, though he did not press his lips to Diana's hand.

"Well met, Dummonus. Did you say that you flew?"

He nodded soberly. "I will show you, when there is time." Then, he stepped away.

Ila was next, blushing. "You know me . . . I'm just Ila, the horse girl. I ride the gray and the gold. Plus, well, I feed them too, and curry and comb them and put ribbons in their hair . . . that's all."

She made to sit, but Diana caught her other hand. "Pleased to meet you, Ila. I am Diana."

"Well met," Ila said, blushing at the welcome in the woman's eyes. Then she sat down, hiding behind Diana's chair.

Across from her, Otho and Franco glanced at each other. Then Otho made a half-bow to his brother.

"Please, I insist."

"No," said Franco, returning the bow. "After you."

"I couldn't. Please, you must introduce yourself!"

"But I cannot, not until you do the lady honor!"

"Impossible! You, who are so much more than I, the very weight of a man, must go first."

"Your honor does me honor, but your largess is so large, I cannot go before it."

Diana laughed, seeing them banter, and both men, alike as twins, with lithe, supple bodies, turned to her as one. They grinned, showing fine white teeth, and then, without looking at the other, they sprang forward, hands turning on the ground. With explosive quickness they bounced up into the air, crossing one under the other, and were—in the blink of an eye—kneeling before Diana on the grass, their faces flushed.

Diana put a hand to her mouth, impressed. "But who is who? You've switched places!"

"I am Otho," said the one on the right, bowing his head. "Greetings, Diana. May you grow strong again among us."

"And I am Franco," said the other, grinning up at her through a mop of black curls. "Greetings, lady!"

"Well met, then, the both of you." Diana inclined her head, holding out her hands, one to each. They kissed them and sprang straight up, from their kneeling stance, to make a pair of cartwheels back to their original positions. Ila clapped and even Vitellix seemed amused.

"This is our number," said the master, hooking his thumbs into his belt. "Now six, with you among us. But listen, for I have news."

The others and Diana, exhausted from speaking, turned their attention to Vitellix.

"I have just come from the house of our benefactor, the *noble* Lucius Cornelius Balbus. He is a *vigorous* supporter of the games and the theater and he has said to me, just this morning as we sat in his garden drinking a middling Campanian wine, that a great series of *munera,* of holy games, is in the offing in glorious Rome."

Diana saw the faces of the others light up with joy, but she herself felt nothing.

"Yes, this is great and good fortune. It seems that the noble and just Emperor Galen has seen fit to issue a proclamation that within the month a schedule will be posted for games to honor and propitiate the dead of Vesuvius. All expect—particularly *dear* Lucius Cornelius—that they will be the greatest games ever seen in the city of Rome."

Vitellix paused, his head bent. For an instant, Diana thought the man was praying, but when he looked up again, there was a beatific smile on his face.

"These games and celebrations," he continued, "will not merely be the usual to and fro of gladiators and chariot races. No, they will be of a full scope and grandeur not seen since the days of the blessed Emperor Trajan."

"There will be feats of strength and agility?" Franco and Otho spoke as one.

"Yes, so it is said," Vitellix answered.

"Dazzling displays of skill, even from horseback?" Ila's voice was soft from behind the chair.

"I have heard it," Vitellix said.

"Perhaps, if the gods smile," Dummonus ventured, his placid face marked, at last, by some small apprehension, "even the art of flight might be displayed?"

"Even so," Vitellix said, letting out a great breath. "It is well known that the Emperor, bless his name, has little time for the games. He regards them as 'wasteful' and 'a useless diversion,' but he is a pious man and knows that the spirits of the recent dead—of which there are so many!—must be appeased. Their names, their honor, must be upheld. My *good* friend Lucius Cornelius assures me that these games will encompass every ancient art—the days when some staged battle in the Flavian is sufficient are gone. All the spirits of the dead will look down upon Rome and see it bright with flowers, alive with song and dance, filled with festivals."

"But!" Vitellix clapped his hands sharply, his eyes becoming hard. "We must be ready! To practice, lazy children! Go!"

Diana remained sitting, for she was past exhaustion, as the others scattered off amongst the wagons and trees of the grove. Only Dummonus remained for a moment, loitering in the dappled shadow of the branches, watching her. Then, he too left.

Diana grunted, arms straining as she pressed her palms against the lacquered side of the wagon. Her legs, bare under a borrowed kilt, were tense with effort.

"Strength in the body does not come from the arms," Vitellix mused as he pressed down on the small of her back with his fists. "It does not spring from the chest, or from the biceps."

Diana gasped, feeling the man bring his full weight to bear on her. At his command, she was keeping her elbows at an angle. Sweat beaded her face and ran down her chest.

"Strength does not come from the legs," he continued, "or from the heart."

The pressure continued to build and now Diana's legs were trembling. Memory fluttered, pressing and pecking at her, trying to make itself known. She was very near her limit.

"Strength is balance." Vitellix suddenly eased off, for

the sensation under his fingers had told him that the woman was about to collapse. "It springs like Athena, from the legs, from the arms, from the heart, from the chest—"

"Strength," Diana said suddenly, her voice hollow with weariness, "comes from the mind."

Vitellix raised an eyebrow, looking absurdly pleased with himself.

"Who told you that?" he asked sharply.

Diana began to answer, but then puzzlement clouded her features.

"I don't know . . ."

A dark-haired woman stood half in light, half in darkness. Her long hair fell to the ground, a spreading pool of ink on ancient blue tile. Only her small hands were visible. She was holding herself up on one hand, palm flat. Slowly, with great patience, she raised herself up, her legs standing out, almost at right angles from her body, onto only her fingertips.

"What do you remember?" Vitellix leaned close, his face intent, his eyes searching her face. "What do you see?"

Diana turned away, blushing in embarrassment. "Nothing, no one. A dream."

Vitellix sighed, hiding his disappointment. He sat beside the wagon. As before, they were in the grove, in the afternoon, letting the heat of the day pass while they exercised under the spreading trees. Diana squatted down, rubbing her face with a woolen towel. Her hair was growing back as a red fuzz.

"You have been trained before," he said after a moment of contemplation. He rubbed the side of his nose, watching her. "Your body remembers, even if your mind does not. I could see you were strong when the boys dragged you out of the stream. Anyone else would have perished."

Diana looked up, sea-green eyes gleaming in the dappled sunlight. "Was I a sacred performer, like you? Did I travel in a painted wagon?"

Vitellix shook his head sadly. "No. I know the names and faces of every performer in Italia. You are not among them. Too, you're Roman. Most of the sacred performers are Gauls or Spaniards. Many of us come from the Narbonensis. This is a traditional profession among our people."

"What am I, then?"

"Give me your hands," he said. He took them gently, thumbs tracing out ridges of hard muscle and callus. Without speaking he ran his fingers along the hard, flat planes of her forearms and biceps. As he did so his face darkened with memory.

"What is it?" Diana cocked her head, watching him like a marsh bird. "What do they say?"

The Gaul's face turned sad, fingertips tracing a puckered white scar that curled across her shoulder and upper arm. He sighed and squeezed her hands, putting them together.

"It is not for me to reveal," he said at last. "The gods have given you a second chance, taking away your old life, granting you a new one. Let us leave it at that. I will not ask you any more questions."

Diana stood, her body moving easily at last. The terrible weakness that had plagued her was beginning to fade. At a distance, the sound of Franco and Otho practicing came through the trees: grunts and the *slap-slap* of their feet on hard-packed earth. She frowned questioningly at Vitellix, though his usually open face was closed and guarded.

"This is a change! Usually you are pestering me, wanting to know if I remember anything at all, even the color of my mother's eyes!"

"I know," he said, lips pursing. "I remembered something . . . I have been impolite and vexing, I am sure. What went before is in another life, Diana. This one is trouble enough without rousing old ghosts."

Diana frowned again. *Men! First they want something, then they don't!*

"Then," she said with asperity, "will you answer some of *my* questions?"

"Surely," he said, mouth quirking into a half-smile. "I should be vexed in turn."

"Huh! I don't know about that. . . . It seems there is trouble with this Emperor Galen. Otho and Franco are constantly arguing about him."

"Yes," Vitellix said, shaking his head in dismay. "He is a just ruler, but he does not understand what the games mean to the people of the city. They say that he is pious, that he makes the proper sacrifices to the gods, but that he does not believe in them. It tempts the gods to flaunt their will . . . what will the spirits of the dead do, if they do not receive their offerings?"

"So, the people are troubled by this delay?"

Vitellix nodded his head in assent. "Rumors are rife in the city, saying the Emperor does not care, that he has turned his back on the dead."

Diana grimaced, saying, "That does not seem wise . . ."

"No," Vitellix sighed, "it is *not* wise, even if we gain a few more days to practice and train."

"What happens next, then? Do we go to Rome and take part in these games? Where will we perform?"

Vitellix laughed, a strained sound. Diana suddenly realized that he was very worried.

"Were it so simple . . . here is how these things are done, my innocent! When the great games, the *munera,* are declared, the Emperor usually sponsors them himself. He, having other duties as well, then hires an *editore* to actually compose, arrange, cost and execute these performances. Of course, he must bear the cost as well, which can be vast. The editoré, in turn, arranges with the *bestiarii* for wild beasts and exotic slaves, with the *lanistae* for gladiators and dancing girls, with the directors of the theater troupes, with those that deal in dwarves and freaks, with the purveyors of musicians, of acrobats, of Spanish dancers . . . it is an enormous business, employing thousands of professionals and slaves."

Vitellix sighed, leaning back against the wagon. "And our small troupe merely the least of players . . . yet, if these games are as great as rumored, even we will find a place."

"Our employment is not assured, then?" Diana was troubled. She had been clothed, fed, bathed, nursed back to health by Vitellix and his family. She had no money, no way to repay them for their kindness. "What will we do?"

"Our employment is more likely if we can gain the attention of someone with the ear of an editore or one of the sponsors. I have arranged, again through the most *notable* Lucius Cornelius, for an appearance in a regional festival in the town of Narni, which is not far off. I hope that it will be attended by certain agents of the Ludus Magnus or the Flavian in Rome. They may find some worth in our skill."

Diana nodded, flexing her arms. In a few weeks she might be strong again. "What can I do to help?"

Vitellix considered her. He had been wondering the same thing. A thought occurred to him. "Perhaps . . . perhaps you will have the strength and eye for the wire."

AELIA CAPITOLINA, THE ROMAN PROVINCE OF JUDEA

It was cold on the hilltop, making every breath a cloud of frost. Odenathus squinted at the eastern horizon, urging the sun to rise and bring him warmth. A steep-sided, boulder-strewn valley separated him from the city of Aelia Capitolina. Lights gleamed on the walls, illuminating guardposts and fortified towers.

Odenathus had been sent forward with the scouts to observe the lay of the land. The Palmyrene snorted to himself. Jalal had sent him. This had caused vigorous discussion between the burly Tanukh soldier and the whippet-thin Lord Uri, who vied with Jalal for command. Each man was *sure* that Lord Mohammed had placed him in charge of the expedition. Even sending scouts forward required a vehement and prolonged discussion of the options. For reasons best known to himself, Lord Uri was dead set on being the captor of this hilltown.

Mohammed may be infallible when the voice from the clear air speaks through him, Odenathus thought, cold hands stuffed into his armpits, *but he is still just a man when he speaks with his own voice.* The Palmyrene youth was pretty sure that Mohammed had intended for the two men to work together. They certainly behaved themselves when he was about. Odenathus shook his head in dismay and wonder. *Like two boys with only one toy between them!*

Rock clicked on rock and Odenathus turned, seeing that one of the Sahaba was clambering across the cracked and weatherworn boulders.

"Sir? We've checked the hill and the nearest huts. Everything seems empty. No Romans about, anyway."

Odenathus raised an eyebrow at the boy and received a shrug in return. "Not even a goat or a watch goose?"

The boy, his face mostly shrouded by the dark cloth of his *kaffiyeh*, shook his head.

"They must know we are coming, then. Send a rider back to the camp and tell our . . . commanders that there won't be any surprise attack for this place."

In the wake of the victory at Yarmuk, the Arab army had split in two. The main body, with two-thirds or more of the men, under the direct command of Mohammed, had pressed on to the coast, aiming to capture the great port of Caesarea Maritima. At the same time, a second effort had been sent south, towards the town that controlled the highlands of Judea. Odenathus had been attached to this expedition as their sorcerous support, even though that meant breaking up the team that he and Zoë made.

Somehow, Odenathus thought with a smile, *Mohammed will make up that lack.*

The Palmyrene didn't know how the Arab chieftain had attracted the attention of a *"power"* but it was clear beyond doubt that he had. Looking upon him in the hidden world was almost impossible. He shone like a cloth hung over the sun. Conversations with the Mekkans in the army revealed that the man had never received any kind of training in the arts. Something had found him, though, and entered the world through him. Odenathus shivered, but not from the cold. There were things in the universe that were vaster than the human mind could imagine.

Odenathus had been taught, both by his tutors as a youth, then later in the Legion, that these *"powers"* were hostile to man. They were beyond the pale, weak gods with human faces that the people worshiped. They were more than the tiny spirits and servitors a man could call up and control. These things, unnamed by any sane man, were to Odenathus as he was to the least of the insects. Trafficking with them meant madness and annihilation.

I pray that the lord Mohammed has not been found by one of the Ancient Ones. If he had, Odenathus knew, then it was very likely the world in which he walked, breathing the chill air of a summer night finally breaking into dawn, would be destroyed. *An elephant brushes against an anthill with one ponderous foot, smashing it into the ground. The ants, milling about, rushing here and there, are reduced to a stain. The elephant, continuing on its own business, fails to notice.*

The sun at last rose, washing the olive trees on the mountain with golden light. Odenathus held his hands up in the air, greeting the sun. Around him, the Sahaba were kneeling, making their prayers. Soon the heat of the day would build and it would be blindingly hot. He turned, watching the rosy light slowly paint the tops of the walls and the roofs of the buildings in the city. It seemed quiet and still. Soon the cocks would be crowing and the priests ringing the summoning bar. It seemed clear that the city was held by the Romans, by a garrison, and they knew the Sahaba were coming.

Today, if Jalal and Uri could quit arguing about who was in command of the expedition and the order of march, they would lay siege to the place.

"Um . . . Nicholas?"

Three men were crouched in the shadow of a gate postern. The gate was a deep-set opening in the eastern wall of the praetorium of Aelia Capitolina. It was the main gate from the city—a crowded, ramshackle affair of tiny streets, overhanging roofs, close-set tenements and shops—into the fortress maintained by the Roman government to administer the province of Judea. The praetorium was built on the foundations of an older citadel that had once been partially demolished to make way for an extensive palace that had lined the western wall of the city. As a result, it rose up on an artificial hill of debris, looking down over the rooftops of the city. Too, Aelia Capitolina was built on three hills with a streambed between them. The praetorian rose on a spur of the southwestern hill, while to the northeast, on a broad, flat platform, there was a massive temple complex.

Like most things in the city, the original structures on the temple mount had been torn down by the Romans and rebuilt. Between the fortress and the temple lay the body of the city, creased by the streambed, which had long ago vanished under pavement and buildings and centuries of rubble.

"Yes, Vladimir? You're having some second thoughts?"

Due to the confined nature of the city and the fact that the southwestern wall faced directly onto a rather steep slope which was unsuitable for building, the plaza before the gate of the Praetorium was far smaller than the Roman city planners had desired. There was barely thirty feet between the brooding overhang of the gate tower and the nearest building. Too, the narrow alleyways that snaked between the buildings, twisting and turning, plunging down flights of steps or climbing steeply, were very dark. In some places, even the noon sun did not illuminate the courtyards. The Roman planners, particularly the engineers attached to the old Tenth Legion, had expressed some reservations about the security of the praetorium, given that it would be easy for a hostile force to hide in the alleys, only a short sprint from the gate.

"Second thoughts? No, my friend, nothing like that. I just wonder . . ."

As it happened, the alleys fronting on the plaza were crowded with Roman engineers. Though not technically hostile, their presence would have caused some consternation amongst the inhabitants of the praetorium. These men, armored in the overlapping plates of their *lorica segmentata,* dark red cloaks bundled around them, spears and short, stabbing swords at the ready, helmets tied securely under their chins, were waiting for the gate to open.

The three men in the shadow of the gate overhang were their commander and two close companions.

"Wonder what?" Nicholas whispered crossly. The last three days of frenzied activity had not been without some discussion amongst Nicholas and his staff. If the Walach had concerns, he should have brought them up. The barbarian, his thick black hair clouding his face, scratched the back of his head. Nicholas turned slightly, so that he could see Vladimir's eyes.

"Well . . . we're about to seize the residence of the civil governor of the province with Imperial troops. This is the same governor, appointed by the Emperor, who has struck a deal with the largest clan in these parts to see that order is maintained and the taxes are collected. If this Albanian is thrown in the jug, they'll be pissed."

Nicholas nodded, mauve eyes in shadow. Though the sky was brightening, it was still quite dark down in the brick and plaster ravines of the city.

"That's so," he said in a whisper.

"Doesn't it strike you as reckless to pick a fight with half the province and the governor when we received news not more than three days ago that the Great Prince Theodore has been routed by a rabble of desert bandits and unhappy farmers? Isn't it a little *unwise* to do this when the city may be under siege within days?"

Spreading his hands, Nicholas shrugged.

"Sometimes, Vlad, you've got to take the bull by the horns and leap. This pustule of an Albanian is a thief and corrupt as a Persian clerk. He's driven the *other* half of the province to the edge of revolt with his tax policy, and I do not trust him to hold the city against these raiders. If we make him disappear, then I think the rest of the citizens will fight. If he stays . . ."

The third member of the little group stirred, putting a finger to his lips.

"Quiet," breathed the young man, his red hair tied up behind his head. "I feel someone coming."

Nicholas froze and Vladimir became so still that he seemed to fade into the bricks behind him. The young Hibernian settled back behind the heavy bulk of the Walach, whose shoulders dwarfed his. Nicholas, his face settled and calm, slowly drew his blade from its sheath. The metal gleamed in the poor light, showing a rippled, watery surface. The sword was of the hand-and-a-half style favored by the northern barbarians, with hilts wrapped in grooved leather and wire. Nicholas brushed lank brown hair out of his face and took the blade in both hands, tensing for action.

Brunhilde quivered in his grip, smelling blood.

Beyond the heavy pine door, bound with iron bands and held by a pair of bolts sunk into the rock of the tower on either side, there was a rattling sound. The voices of men came, muffled by the thick wood. Metal squealed, sliding along a stone groove. Then the door opened, pushed by two of the governor's guardsmen.

For an instant, Nicholas looked upon them, seeing a pair of Illyrians with stubbled faces and corselets of round iron rings. Their swords were slung over their shoulders in wooden scabbards held up by a leather strap. Neither was wearing a helmet, though one man had a pointed *spangenhelm* hung from his waist belt. Both were grunting, their strength matched against the rust and grime in the hinges that kept the door from swinging freely.

Nicholas' jaw clenched and he moved, Brunhilde whipping past at shoulder level as he drove her with the full power of his upper body. The Scandian blade sunk into the first man's unprotected neck, parting the skin and muscle like soft bread. Blood spurted, fouling the clean length of the blade, and Nicholas stepped into the doorway, wrenching the sword free. The first man was falling, unable to make a sound with his throat torn away, as Nicholas reversed direction with Brunhilde's wedge-shaped point and ran it through the open mouth of the second man. The soldier's eyes bulged and droplets of blood from his cheek spattered his face. Bone ground and popped, then Brunhilde was on guard again. Nicholas, letting the blade keen softly, strode over the bodies. He was in the courtyard.

Behind him, Vladimir sidled into the chamber of the tower, crouching low. An odd light burned in his eyes as he loped past the two bodies, still twitching on the cobblestones. In the gateway, Dwyrin raised his hand and whistled sharply.

The Roman engineers darted across the plaza, their rectangular shields held up at an angle. No one expected the garrison of the praetorium to be awake and armed at this hour, but it never hurt anyone to be thorough. The engineers that Nicholas commanded believed that more than most, since lax attention to detail on their part could kill hundreds. They reached the gateway without incident and poured through.

Dwyrin watched them go. When the last of the men had filed inside, taking up their positions at the gate to prevent any disturbance, he entered the gatehouse himself. There was little place for him in the swift, bloody business that Nicholas intended, so he climbed the long flight of stairs to the observation deck on the top of the main building of the fortress. He went quickly, being young and limber. Two years of service in the Thaumaturgic Corps of the Eastern Empire had cut the fat from his teenage body, leaving wiry muscle. His hair, long and red, trailed behind his head in a thicket of braids. Despite his obvious outlander appearance, he wore the red cloak, strapped boots and tunic of a Roman soldier.

The sun was full over the horizon when he reached the top of the stairs and he stepped out into bright golden sunlight. He squinted, shading his face with a hand. Life in the desert suited him, even when he had been in the wizards' school in Egypt. That was surprising, considering how green, foggy and wet Hibernia was, but his memories of his homeland were growing fainter with each day. After three months in the Judean capital, the barren hills and dusty olive groves on the mountains seemed homey and familiar.

Yawning a little, he leaned against a battlement. Like the rest of the city, the citadel was built of quarried limestone blocks fitted with cement. It made everything a yellowish-white color, matching the mountains and valleys. From a distance, if the sun did not strike on the gilded roofs of the Temple of Jupiter on the other hill, it could be hard to distinguish the city from the hill. The local tribesmen tended to wear pale white, tan and cream robes, too, which made *them* match the ground. It always seemed dusty, even when it was not.

Dwyrin stared off to the east, worrying. Two years ago, when he had been sent by the school to satisfy the Imperial levy, he had been drafted into a thaumaturgic *manus,* or "five," with three other youths. During the war with Persia, Eric had died, drowning in frigid waters before the gate of a besieged city. Last year the other two, Zoë and Odenathus, had left Imperial service after they had learned that the Eastern Emperor had betrayed their home city, Palmyra. That rich and glorious city had been destroyed. Dwyrin had parted from them amid bitter anger and hatred. He had stayed with the Legions, while they had vanished into the desert.

Sometimes couriers came to the city bringing news from other Roman outposts. When they did, Dwyrin stayed close to Nicholas' office, hoping that he might hear some rumor or news of his friends. He hoped that they had not been killed or captured by slavers. The provinces across the Jordan River, to the east, had risen up in revolt. War engulfed the whole region.

Dwyrin straightened suddenly, disturbed from his thoughts by the wink of sunlight on metal. There, on the height of the mountain that rose on the eastern side of the city, something was shining. He squinted, trying to make it out, then laughed aloud. He had learned more than a few tricks while training in the Legion.

Time to earn my pay, he thought as he raised his hands.

Entering the hidden world was easy now; hardly a moment's concentration and thought was required to see the solid surfaces and forms of the world of physicality melt away. He turned aside from the abyss of full sight, letting his mind discern the patterns of the city and the hills amid the fury and chaos of the true world. A sorcerer could lose himself in the vast depths that opened before him. Some apprentices entered the hidden world and never returned, their bodies withering as the mind failed and the heart ceased. There were depths in the sky that did not bear investigation.

The Hibernian turned his attention to the swiftest of the motes that flooded the space around him, letting his thoughts bring into focus the tiny photons that made up the wash of light that fell over him, warming his face and lighting the stones. It was difficult, for the training he had received told him to ignore the minute, flickering ether that filled the sky. But now he needed to gather them, folding them towards his eyes, letting a transparent disk form before him. His raised hands marked its edge, letting the disk de-form and flex, making a convex surface.

Turning towards the distant hill, he let the disk expand and capture the photons that had reflected from the shining metal there and touched his eye. They flooded against his face, making it slightly warmer. Dwyrin, trying not to squint, let his mind restore regular vision and sight.

The far hilltop sprang into view, seemingly as through he stood only yards away, floating in the air, looking up at the men clustered there amid the olive trees. One of them turned, his head coming up, dark eyes narrowing in suspicion.

"Ay!" Dwyrin jumped back and the invisible disk spun out of control and fragmented, scattering light across the white stones of the tower roof. The Hibernian youth was sweating, his face hot and burning. He blinked furiously, almost blinded.

Despite this, he staggered towards the top of the stairs, letting his hands find the way along the battlement.

Nicholas, armored arms crossed over his heavy scale breastplate, squinted at the Armenian.

"You don't have a problem, then, serving under my banner?"

The Armenian, a long-mustached rascal named Nezam, grinned and made a weighing motion with his right hand. Nicholas nodded, not surprised. As long as the highland mercenaries that Nezam commanded were paid, in coin of a full weight, they would be loyal. Luckily for Nicholas, who had not come with any great store of gold, the lock rooms under the citadel held part of the tax revenue that the governor had been collecting. A troop of stonemasons from the engineers' cohort was guarding them right now, with Vladimir along as insurance.

"I no care who sits in praetor's chair," said the Armenian, his musical accent making the Greek sing. "We will fight or watch, no matter to us."

"Good," said Nicholas in his equally poor Greek. "Divide your men into groups of five. They will go with the engineers to secure the town and the gates."

Turning to the other two men in the room, Nicholas raised an eyebrow.

"Sextus, Frontius—see that your men and these barbarians are at each gate in the city. No one comes in or goes out until I've talked with the city senate and the other ne'er-do-wells that thrive in this place."

The lead surveyor and the master draftsman nodded. Each looked a little uncomfortable in their armor, but it was clean and it fit. Their role in the Legions might not be to fight on the front line, shields interlocked, but they were Roman soldiers. Nicholas sighed to himself, wishing he had the cohort of Eastern veterans he had been promised when he arrived in Judea.

But that is bootless, he reminded himself. The troops he had expected had gone off on some bandit-chasing expedition in the north, leaving him with a stranded Western Empire siege and road-building cohort. At least they had tools and equipment and some idea of what to do with a sword. The late governor, who had fallen down a flight of stairs when Nicholas and Vladimir had dragged him out of a rubbish shaft for questioning, had not done much with the local militia or the city garrison. Most of those billets were empty, the presumed soldiers having been cashiered out or died. Of course, the records of the garrison still showed them on the rolls. It was an old trick.

The problem was, Nicholas needed those men even to police the city, much less hold four miles of double-ramparted wall against whatever army had thrashed Prince

Theodore and eight legions of Eastern troops. Which led him back here, to this cramped office in the citadel, where he was buying off the five hundred Armenians that the late, lamented governor had imported for his own protection. There was no doubt that the Armenians could fight—they were professionals—but what if the gold ran out, what then?

"Sir, what about our survey?" Neither Frontius nor Sextus had left the room.

Nicholas took a deep breath and put his hands on the tabletop. "The survey . . . will have to wait until the city is secured."

Neither man moved, staring at Nicholas with sad eyes. Frontius, with his permanent squint, looked particularly disturbing.

Gods! They're worse than a pair of Locrian hounds!

When Nicholas and his troops had entered the city, there had been an argument between Sextus and the local magistrate about the aqueducts. The Western officer, long accustomed to the massive public works of Rome, had held forth over a flagon of weak wheat beer that the Judean provinces were sorely lacking in proper waterworks. The magistrate, an Illyrian émigré who had lived in Aelia Capitolina for thirty years, disagreed with some heated words. Luckily, the dispute had not been resolved by fisticuffs but rather by a trip into the basement of the tavern.

There in the ancient stone floor was a round stone lid with a heavy iron ring. With the help of those engineers that could still stand up, a great deal of rope and a pulley, Sextus was suspended head-first over the hole and then, with a racket of shouted commands and laughter, lowered into the mysterious chamber. Nicholas had been watching from the top of the stairs, trying to keep his hair from catching fire in the lantern. A grain passed, then another, then there was some more shouting and the engineer was pulled up, choking and coughing from the smoke of the lantern he had in his hand.

"It's incredible!" The engineer had that look, like a boy really seeing a girl for the first time. He was dripping water and looking like a half-drowned rat but he was smiling. "It's enormous!"

Apparently the tavern stood atop a vast underground cistern. The ancient builders of the city, plagued by war and raids from neighboring tribes, had built their water system underground. The hilltop was riddled with caverns and tunnels and buried springs. The soft limestone was easy to cut, allowing the stonemasons of old to quarry out great vaulted chambers and pools. This discovery had transported Frontius and Sextus into a veritable frenzy of excitement. With them, bound in a waxed leather cover, was a thick book of parchment. It was a matter of cohort pride that they possessed a copy of Vitruvius' *De Architectura*. It rode in one of the special wagons in a locked iron box.

Like their ancient idol, the two engineers were working on a survey of all modern waterworks, siegecraft, buildings and construction materials. The thought of adding the expertise of the ancient Judeans—consolidated and revised, of course, by these two stalwarts—quite distracted them from the tasks that Nicholas had set them.

The centurion had then suffered at length as the engineers had pressed him to let them conduct a full survey of everything in the city, above and below ground. Nicholas had refused, and was still refusing. The gates, the walls, the ramparts—everything was in disrepair after years of neglect. He had work teams supplemented with local workers out from sunrise to sunset, shoring up walls, repairing gates, clearing the old ditch that ran along the exposed northern wall. Nicholas guessed that perhaps only half of the work that needed to be done to restore the defenses of the city was done.

"But, sir! We could do it on off hours."

Nicholas raised his hand sharply and was about to bark some severe words when there was a rattling of boots in the corridor outside.

Dwyrin was at the door, panting, his face sunburned. "They're here!"

"Who?" snapped Nicholas, but he could guess as well as the two engineers.

"The Arabs—I just saw their advance party on the mountain to the east."

Sextus and Frontius were gone, their armor banging off the jamb of the door. Nezem, having stood well aside while the two Romans dashed out, followed more sedately, hand on the pommel of his sword. Nicholas was about to follow them when he caught the look on the boy's face. He pulled up hard and caught Dwyrin's eye.

"What is it?"

"Nothing, sir—"

Nicholas grimaced and seized the young sorcerer by the throat, jamming him up against the wall. Breath *oof*ed out of Dwyrin's lungs and his eyes bulged.

"I've no time to dally about," snarled Nicholas, his face close to Dwyrin's. "Tell me what you saw."

He released his fist and the Hibernian slumped down, gasping for breath. While he recovered, Nicholas' face, which had grown quite grim, softened a little.

"Sorry, lad," he said, setting the boy upright. "Everything counts now, though."

Dwyrin nodded, his face red with shame. Withholding information from your commanding officer in time of war was an offense punishable by running the gauntlet. The Hibernian had seen men dragged from the end of that corridor of fists and staves, their faces ruined masses of blood and broken bone. The Legion had great hopes that all of its soldiers would live to reach their twenty-six-year retirement and collect the *honesta missó*. Nothing in that hope kept the Legion officers from enforcing a brutal and strict discipline on their troops.

"I saw a man with the scouts on the mountain; I know him. He was my five-mate in the Persian campaign. His name is Odenathus, a Palmyrene noble. He and his cousin

Zoë left us at Antioch, when the *auxillia* mustered out."

Nicholas' eyes narrowed. The boy had told him a little of what had happened in Antioch when his comrades had taken their discharge from the Legion. "A sorcerer? Like you? How strong is he?"

Dwyrin started to speak, then stopped. A pensive, thoughtful look came over him. The thought of who in the manus was better or worse had seemed very simple when they were fighting as one. Dwyrin was the youngest and the least experienced, therefore Odenathus must be far stronger than he. But was that still true? Dwyrin had grown in the past months, freed from the strictures of having to fight in the battle-meld with the two others. He lacked many skills, but this was a siege. His fire-calling talent, which now hovered ever-eager for release, might be the difference between victory and death.

"He's not like me, centurion. He made a solid second for our manus and he's good at deception and defense, but he can't call fire or lightning well. I can master him if we come to blows . . . I think."

The Scandian nodded, his mind turning the situation over, viewing it from more than one angle. There was something disturbing here, but what was it? *Ah.*

"Take yourself to the northern wall, lad. Find cover near the main gate, but don't show yourself. These fellows may be rash and try and rush us. If they do, I want you to surprise them."

Dwyrin nodded, still rubbing his throat, and jogged off. Nicholas, alone in the governor's office, brooded.

The Palmyrenes are with these bandits. Theirs was a rich city, with many ships and warehouses and great trade. Their agents and factors were in every city on the Levantine coast, even here. This is no rabble that comes against us. . . .

Then he laughed, bits and pieces of rumor and fragmentary news falling into place. It was not a laugh of pleasure or joy, but rather of the knowledgeable man who sees what others have not.

Prince Theodore had been soundly defeated in the north, on the Syrian heights, on the road between the port of Caesarea Maritima and Damascus. Such success at arms had not been achieved by rabble. It was well known from merchants and travelers fleeing along the roads from the east that the Greek cities of the Decapolis—Bostra, Jerash and so on—had risen in revolt. Now the Palmyrenes and these Arab bandits were involved. A rebel army was here, well south of the line between Damascus and the port. This was no longer a provincial dispute over taxes. This was a war between the Empire and a new pan-Levantine state.

That collection of events meant that the entire Imperial frontier from Damascus to Aelana had collapsed. It was likely that any survivors of Theodore's army would fall back to the north, towards Tyre, or to the sea. Worse, at the center of the Decapolis was the massive Legion camp of Lejjun, which he could only assume had fallen into the hands of the rebels. That meant they had gained arms, armor, siege equipment, supplies, wagons. It meant his position, cut off here in this vile little town on a poky hill, was completely untenable.

Cursing, Nicholas strode out of the room. He would not wait to discuss matters with the town senate, he would root them out of their homes *right now* while there was still a little time.

"Look, the walls are empty. Do you see any watchmen? No."

Uri, lord of the Sarid clan of Mekkah, pointed with his riding staff at the crumbling yellow walls of the city. He was astride a spirited bronze-colored gelding, his left hand wrapped in the reins. His kaffiyeh was cinched around his high forehead with a twisted cord threaded with the colors of his tribe. Like all of the Sahaba, he had a flash of green in his headdress.

Jalal, riding just ahead of Odenathus in the van of the army, grunted. The old soldier's eyes were watching the wall very carefully. His bow, sweeping horn and bone with a half-bent top arm, was laid across his saddle with a flight arrow set to the string. The Tanukh had spent thirty years wandering the fringes of the Roman and Persian empires, taking his pay from any lord needing a strong bow and a stout arm in the line of battle. He had never commanded before the lord Mohammed had placed him over the left wing of the army of the Sahaba. Now he knew why all generals were such bastards! Still, he would not trade the command of the *maimanah* for anything.

"What is this?" Uri was continued to berate the Tanukh captain, his voice sharp. "Why—a scaffold where someone is trying to *repair* the gate! I think, my friend, that you worry too much about this place. It is old and decrepit, barely worth your time."

Odenathus, who had been aware of a quiet watching sensation since the lead elements of the Sahaba had come up onto the ridge that ran down from the city walls and off to the west, nudged his mare with a knee. She ambled out of the line of march, letting him have a clear view of the gate and the walls. It was true they were in poor shape. Some of the embrasures on the battlements were missing, leaving gaps. The gate itself was closed, but scaffolds and piles of cut stone littered the area around it. Odenathus smiled a little, imagining the panic that must have set in among the workers when the first Sahaba lancers had ridden into view.

There was no one on the walls, though, and he had a good idea of what that meant.

"You'd put your head in the noose on a lark?" Jalal's voice was deep and rolled like rocks falling down a hillside. Somehow it fit here, in this desolate country. "You've a hankering to take your men over the wall first, do you?"

Odenathus squinted at the wall. He was sure the defenders were crouched down behind the stone teeth, wait-

ing for the Sahaba to come into range of their bows and
slings. He was listening to Jalal and Uri with only half an
ear. They had been bickering for so long that it had become part of the background noise. Rubbing his face, he
began to concentrate, letting his mind slip through the entrance of Hermes and into the whirling void waiting beyond.

"You think the Ben-Sarid have no stomach for a little
blood? Shall we have a wager, then?"

Odenathus let his sight expand, seeing the hidden cracks
and shifted foundations under the gate. The land had settled a little, tilting the stones and splintering the plaster off
the old Roman brickwork. It would not take much to bring
down the whole structure. He put forth a subtle pressure,
letting his will infiltrate the stone courses.

Distantly, Jalal barked in laughter, waving for the Sahaba to stop. A cornicen shrilled and the wings of the army
began to fold out into the rocky plain before the city. Men
and horses moved at an easy trot, kicking up a flat cloud
of dust. Off to the left, the ground fell away towards a
valley under a hill covered with olive orchards and the
humped shapes of tombs. To the right, the ground rose a
bit, irregular and cut by walls of piled fieldstone. Small
gardens crouched between them. Odenathus concentrated,
negotiating the ancient wards and spells that had once protected the gate.

They were very old and fallen into disrepair. Centuries
ago they had been violently broken and only poorly repaired. In them, the Palmyrene could suddenly feel a little
of the history of the city—a long struggle of capture and
recapture, of repeated destruction and slow, painful re-
building. Blood soaked the stone and brick, but there was
dust too and the taste of long neglect.

At the fringe of his vision in the waking world, a troop
of the Sarid galloped forward, their lances glittering in the
midday sun. Despite his bold words, Uri was not leading
them. He looked on, still sitting at Jalal's shoulder, still

arguing. They had moved into the shade afforded by an old Roman triumphal gateway that stood, alone, a few hundred yards from the gate of the city.

Odenathus felt something in the air, a change in pressure, a sharp spike in the gradient of power in the land around him. Reflexively his hand ran through the mnemonic to call a pattern into waking memory. In the hidden world, the glittering blue sphere of the Shield of Athena sprang up, surrounding himself and the two arguing captains.

The earth shook, booming like a drum slammed by a heavy hand. The Sarid lancers, who had just come within a spear's throw of the gate, vanished in an eruption of sand, blazing limestone dust and red-orange flame. Burning horses catapulted through the air, their riders enveloped in white fire. Odenathus' mare reared, screaming. The two captains shouted in fear, their arms raised to shield their faces. Within seconds steaming ash, burning skulls and scorched limbs rained out of the air from a spreading black cloud. It drifted away from the gate.

Odenathus tried to rise. The mare had run away, her reins trailing on the dusty ground. The shield remained intact, though it was wavering in time with the thudding of his heart. Both Jalal and Shadin had managed to remain mounted and they were hiding behind the ancient gateway.

"Get away," Odenathus shouted. "It might be trapped."

It seemed the defenders had prepared a hidden ward under the ground, waiting for the Arabs to ride up the road to the gate. His brow furrowed with effort, he put forth his strength again, sending his will forth, probing for the enemy. In the ether the blast area flickered and gleamed with violence, making the patterns around it shimmer and twist like light in a rising pillar of heat.

There was a figure on the rampart, Odenathus could feel him, almost see him like a burning brand. The enemy was strong. Gritting his teeth, for he had never tried to strike at an enemy without Zoë at his side, their minds and powers amplified by the battle-meld, he chopped his hand at the distant wall. The air around him chilled and the nearest statuary on the triumphal gate splintered and cracked. Power leached from the dead ground and the sky and the roiling motion of atoms in the air. A cyan burst flared against the gate.

The enemy sorcerer's shield rippled as the blow struck, radiating heat and light like a rainbow. Odenathus swayed to his feet.

The enemy flexed his strength and Odenathus' shield fractured like pane of glass struck by a hammer. Crying out, he was blown fifty feet down the road by the shock of contact. The air where he had been standing boiled and burned with a fierce blue-white light. The triumphal gate, licked by the roaring flame, cracked and shattered. Black smoke billowed out of the sandstone. Then half of it crumbled, in a roar of tormented stone and wood, to the ground. Bits of brick and facing pattered down around Odenathus in the sand.

The Arab army streamed away from the city at a full gallop, men shouting in anger and dismay.

The Palmyrene raised his head, feeling the world spin around him. His cloak was on fire, sending up a curl of bitter white smoke. At the last moment, he had managed to invoke a second shield. This had saved him. The enemy was very, very strong. Weakly, Odenathus threw off the smoldering cloth. His face and hands stung from the light.

"Oh," he gasped. "You've grown mighty, old friend."

The fire signature was far too clear, for Odenathus had seen it before, in the training camps and practice fields of the Legion.

Jalal jogged past, on foot, shouting something at the youth lying in the dirt. The burly soldier had Uri slung over one shoulder like a side of beef. The horses were disappearing in a cloud of dust. Odenathus' ears were still ringing and he couldn't hear.

)⊂(

"Pustulating, corrupt, wine-soaked, illegitimate wretches!"
Martina, Empress of the Eastern Empire, walked
quickly, her face dark with rage. The corridor she passed
through was dark and stained by mold. In the vast sprawl
of the Bucoleon, there were areas damaged by earthquake
or fire that had never been rebuilt. Each new emperor
tended to add a new hall or courtyard rather than refur-
bishing the old. Her sandals, heeled with wood, made a
sharp *clack-clack* on the ancient tiles. In places the tessellated floor had decayed into gravel or even dirt. At the
moment, Martina noticed neither that nor the increasing
darkness as the hallway tended downwards, following the
slope of the hill towards the Military Harbor.

"Degenerate freaks, wombed from some diseased
whore! Lower than the scum on the sewers, they are . . ."

Her fists clenched in time with her words, and blood
seeped from the cuts that her fingernails made in her
palms. The Empress negotiated a series of decaying marble
steps without incident. Her feet knew the path she followed, even if her mind was wholly involved in a violent
fantasy in which she choked the breath from certain men
with her own hands.

Her morning had been, as most were in this unsettled
time, filled with a slow procession of those seeking her
favor. She had been in her salon, seated, with servants
around her to bring a cool drink or a fan, if she desired.
Lady Penneos had been by her side, discussing some matter involving her grandson. Many of the nobles in the city

reviled the Empress in secret, or whispered behind their hands if she appeared at the theater, but still more sought advantage for their children or their children's children. The woman hoped that Martina could find a position for her grandson in the palace. It was a tedious business, this bartering of favors and implied gifts.

Martina was quite on edge already, dealing with the irritating woman, wishing she could return to her books and scrolls in the workroom. She had begun doodling a history of the great Constantine the Founder when she had first arrived in the capital. It was far more interesting to chronicle his heroic efforts than to listen to Lady Penneos.

Then Rufio had entered, unexpected and uninvited, his face a cold mask. Martina had frozen herself, flooded with fear, seeing him in his dark armor in the airy, light space of her salon.

"Most noble and gracious lady, some humble servants beg your illustrious presence."

Martina had risen, her eyes searching his face, finding nothing. Rufio's eyes, which of late had seemed sympathetic and even warm, were like chips of flint. Out of the corner of her vision, she suddenly realized that more guardsmen were waiting outside the archway that led into her rooms.

She had bent her head towards Rufio, her voice low and tight with distress.

"My husband?"

He had shaken his head minutely. The tightness in her chest and stomach eased.

"Please, most noble lady, come with me. The logothetes of the ministries seek your guidance."

Her feet, unerring, led her down a broad ramp of stairs puddled with slowly dripping water. Walls of brick loomed over her head in heavy barrel vaults. There were small, high windows, but years of dust and soot from the cookfires of the city had obscured them, cutting off even that source of light. The long hallway echoed with the sound of her shoes. Bats and birds, disturbed by her passage, fluttered near the ceiling. The Empress, ignoring the mud clinging to her slippers, marched down the hall, her voice ringing back from the peeling frescoes.

"Oh, to gouge their eyes out! To feel their fat, doughy flesh under my hand . . . to tear out their lying, duplicitous, soft tongues! Lowest of the low, schemers, wretched connivers, peddlers, mountebanks, fools with overbred hands and feet!"

She came to a door, half ajar and shrouded with cobwebs and the trailing bits of a tapestry that had long ago fallen into mildewed fragments. It was an unremarkable door, save that candlelight spilled around it, lighting up a pale stretch of blocky tile. Given the depth of her anger, however, Martina did not notice the illumination. Furious, both with herself, with the *logothetes* and the ministers, with Rufio and with the gods themselves, she slammed the door open. It made a terrible screech and then bounced on its hinges.

"Cursed, vile worms! Things that gnaw in the earth, disturbing the cursed dead! Oh! I would . . . excuse me. I didn't know anyone was here."

As it had always been, the room was dark and filled with shadows. The tall racks of scroll cases, the shelving bent with heavy leather-bound books, the familiar musty odor of decaying paper were all as they had been. Even the archaic-style oil lamps that hung down from long brass chains still protruded out of the gloom. In place of the long wooden table, however, there was now a . . . well, a *thing* and a startled-looking young man.

A priest, actually. Barely more than a boy. Perhaps only sixteen years old.

Martina smiled, a sort of sickly smile. She unclenched her fists and gently closed the door.

The boy was staring at her with wide eyes in a round,

moon-shaped face. He was also hiding, half behind the table, with a heavy ivory scroll case in his hands, raised in protection.

"My name is Martina," she snapped, then paused, collecting herself. "Who are you?"

The boy flinched at the tone in her voice, slipping lower until only his eyes watched her from just above the tabletop.

Martina stepped forward, striding around the table. Her dress, now stained with algae and black, pitchy mud along the hem, rustled as she bent down next to the boy. Her tousled brown hair, which had come completely free of its pins and ribbons, spilled down around her face. She grasped the collar of his tunic and dragged him to his feet. No one could say that the Empress was a brawny woman, but when she was mad . . .

"I'm . . ." The boy gulped. "My name is Alexos. Please, milady, don't . . . do anything violent."

Martina released him and grinned guiltily.

"Sorry! You're just . . . I expected the library to be empty."

Alexos ducked his head and made some kind of a sign with his hand.

"Your pardon, milady. I was set here to, ah, well, watch the *telecast*. No one said there would be any visitors. And, really, there haven't been. You're the first," he finished brightly, trying to smile. Martina narrowed her eyes, watching him slowly sidle away along the length of the table.

Her voice rose slightly; "Young man." He stopped. "I apologize for startling you."

"Oh," he said, standing very still. "It's no problem, really."

"But," she said, raising a slim white finger smudged with ink. "I have had a troubling day. I don't want to talk to anyone, or see anyone, for quite some time. So—you should go and find a temple somewhere and pray."

When she was done, she settled a particularly steely glare that she had learned from her mother on him. The boy blanched, his hand rising to his throat, but at the same time he did not move.

"Milady, I have been given careful orders by the Emperor not to leave this device unattended. A message could come at any time! It is my sworn duty, and I will not set it aside."

With that, his chin rose and he took a step forward. Saying *Emperor* had filled him with resolve. Martina stepped forward too, her lip curling in a snarl.

"I've no time for priestly duty, boy. I am the *Empress* of the Roman Empire and I want *some peace and quiet!*" Her shriek rang hollowly off the brass lamps and the walls of dusty books. The priest did not move, even though the Empress's face, contorted by anger, was only a finger's width from his own.

"No," he said with a quiet dignity, looking down a little at her. "I will not leave my post. If you want peace and quiet, I believe that there are some tombs at the end of the passage. At least, it smells like there are."

Martina hissed and spun around, striding quickly to the end of the table. This interview was going much the same way that her morning conversation with the ministers and logothetes had gone.

Rufio had ushered her into a long, narrow room clouded with smoke. The walls, hung with soot-stained tapestries, seemed very close. Martina kept her face impassive, calmly surveying the men seated around the fringe of the chamber. She did not sit, though there was a plain wooden chair set in the middle of a cleared space. Rufio was close behind her, with two of his Faithful blocking the door. The guardsmen were very large, with chests like barrels and arms like tree trunks. If she put her mind to it, Martina knew that she could summon forth their names. Her memory was exceptional. At the moment, she was occupied with suppressing mild revulsion.

The men in the room, those that had summoned her, were sweating slightly. She could smell their chalky odor, even through the thin, bitter-tasting smoke that filled the room.

"Good morning, noble lords," she said in an even and refined voice. It was her Empress voice, which she had cultivated for discussions with country cousins and drunken ambassadors. The court had not regained the tremendous sense of ritual and ceremony that had marked some of the old emperors. Things had been in far too dire straits for that. Martina, from her reading, had hopes of restoring certain customs, particularly those that kept the Empress from having to deal with slobbering barbarians and slimy little men like these.

"Glorious Empress, you honor us with your presence. Pray, take your ease."

This was the smallest of them, Colos, if she matched name to face correctly. He had been recently promoted to logothete of the civic works. Behind her placid expression, Martina tensed. There had been some business with the previous minister . . . something involving Theodore. A fragment of a conversation swam back up into her memory. Yes, the old minister had been forcibly retired at the behest of the Prince. That red-bearded oaf had suggested a replacement, too. It seemed odd, in retrospect, that a powerful minister should be so easily brushed aside—but if his own ministry had already offered up a replacement?

Martina smiled, a thin stretching of her lips, and she met the bureaucrat's eyes directly with her own. The man's smile became waxy and fixed, then he averted his gaze.

"I would not waste the precious time of such noble men by taking my ease. You summon me in haste, without formal invitation, without speaking first to my husband. There must be some crisis."

The ministers glared openly at her now, their hands

twitching a little on their brocaded robes. The matter of the Emperor's health, as far as Martina knew, was never openly broached. A simple fiction maintained in the palace—the Emperor? He was fine, just . . . somewhere else today. The bureaucracy continued to run as it had always done, just without the Emperor. The prospect of openly discussing why the Emperor might not have been available to give permission was skirting very close to the cancer that ate at the palace.

"Most noble Empress," said a deep, gravelly voice from the back of the room. "A concern has been raised by some loyal but deeply worried men."

Martina felt a chill steal over her. A figure, mostly shrouded in the dim smoky recesses of the room, moved an arm into a puddle of candlelight. Her left eyelid twitched and even with Rufio standing behind her, solid and heavy in his armor, she felt exposed. The arm was pale and thick with fat. Rings of silver and gold bit into thick, sausagelike fingers. The figure leaned a little forward, revealing a placid face marked by slabs of fat and small, brilliantly dark eyes.

"We beg a moment of your time, gracious lady. It is a small matter, just the accounting of some wax, some twine and perhaps a little ink."

The logothete of the Imperial tombs smiled, his small, round teeth gleaming in the candlelight. The other ministers seemed to recede into the walls, becoming small and insignificant. Martina felt her hackles rise, and a wash of goose pimples rippled along her arms. The heavy brocade and silk of her dress failed to keep her warm.

"Master Nidus, I am surprised to see you come out in the light of day." Martina pitched her voice to match the chill in the room. "But you intrigue me. You speak of twine and wax. These are simple items, easily acquired in the marketplace. Surely any servant can be sent to fetch them."

She felt Rufio stiffen, but she ignored him and the outraged looks on the faces of the Keeper of the Imperial Inkstand and the Holder of the Legal Binding. Both of those men were turning a shade of purple she normally associated with aubergine ripe on the vine.

Nidus laughed, his thick jowls bouncing a little. His voice was dry and slithery, like snakeskin.

"Glorious Empress, we would not trouble you, I would not trouble *myself,* save that there is unease in the community of the palace. There is dissent, if I may be so bold, among our little family."

Martina remained standing, her hands folded at her waist. The chill remained and deepened. She heard the threat in the rumbling voice. The master of the tombs and crypts was not to be trifled with. Hadn't this one survived four emperors? She felt the anger and the hatred in the other men like heat radiating from a hot griddle. Inwardly, she heard Rufio's cautioning voice urging her to leave the writs and edicts alone, to let them sit.

I can't! Things have to get done! The Empire is only running on inertia now. . . .

"Dissent? Does this twine, this ink, trouble someone? Are their responsibilities too heavy? Do they wish, perhaps, another position—something less taxing?"

Martina turned slowly, her face creased by a cold smile. One by one, she met the eyes of the men sitting in the room. Most of them looked away or could not meet her gaze at all. In the end, there was only Nidus, sitting half in the darkness, half in the faint, shadowy light. Many of the logothetes had been born in the palace. Some had never set foot beyond its walls. Some of them were freed slaves. None of them would last long outside, in the vigorous cacophony of the streets. The tomb master, he was of a different stripe. His position came from the priesthoods. Some said that the role of Custodian of the Tombs predated the great Constantine himself. Even before the Eastern capital had been raised up, there had been an ancient Greek city, Byzantium, on these hills.

Some of the tombs were older yet.

"When a family is troubled," said Nidus, his rasping voice growing deep, "the pater must keep order. The gods tell us this in ancient tales. A strong father ensures peace and goodwill. Some of the children . . ." the corpulent man paused, the thick folds of skin around his eyes wrinkling, ". . . in such a family may grow distressed, even angry, if they think that the *rightful* usages and rights of the father are being usurped by another."

Martina raised an eyebrow, impressed the fat old man would speak so forthrightly. Her estimation of him rose a notch, even as her heart sank. There was no legal basis for any of this; Heraclius had failed to appoint a regent before his illness. A pure power struggle in the palace, in the city, would ensue if the matter became public. She felt a little faint but remained standing and composed. Only Rufio's presence steadied her, that and the faint thought that she could order him—*and he would obey*—to strike all these men down.

"Without a harmonious family," she said, her voice clear by an effort of will, "there is chaos and ill luck for all. Every member of the family should remember that they have a role to play, a place in the familia to fulfill. The gods are pleased if they look down and see a hearth in order, where the proper sacrifices have been made."

A muscle spasmed in her jaw but eased after a moment's pause. She met Nidus' eyes and some flicker of respect passed between them. The deal was offered, accepted and sealed in that look. She unclasped her hands, raising a finger and motioning to Rufio.

"I must pay my respects to my husband now, lest I show him disrespect. I assure you, master of the tombs, that *everyone* in the household, no matter how mean and low, or how high, will follow their honorable duty. Everyone may rest assured, and sleep easily, knowing that everything is in its proper place."

With that, and a chill glance at the logothetes of the

inkstand and the binding, she turned and swept out of the room. Behind her, there was a thin, dry chuckle from the back of the room.

Martina stopped, putting her hand on the end of the worktable. She looked over her shoulder, smoldering at this *boy* that thwarted her. He seemed very young and scared, but despite that he refused to leave. She sighed, suddenly tired. There was—well, there had been—a large leather-backed chair pushed into one of the corners of the library. Now, feeling drained and exhausted, she stumbled to it and sat down. The boy let out a breath in relief.

"What are you doing here? What's this device?"

Martina closed her eyes, letting herself relax into the chair. Like everything in this ancient place, it was moldy and redolent of age. It still fit her shoulders, though, as an old friend should. An age ago, when a very young girl had first been brought to the palace in the company of her uncles and their retainers, she had found this chair. Old age seeped from it; the cracked arms and the splintered back all pointed to hundreds of years of sitting in this abandoned room. The palace, with its servants and rituals and the fear that permeated its walls, was no place for an impressionable young woman. Particularly when she had no friends. All she had had, in fact, was the ability to read and to write, and an unquenchable curiosity. Those had been evil days, with a young emperor on an uneasy throne. Enemies on all sides had beset Heraclius. The Avars raided even to the western gates of the city. The Persians waged unrelenting war in the east. Everywhere, there was disaster.

Martina had longed for her childhood home in Roman Africa, where there was some small peace. But her parents were dead and she had been sent to live with her uncles. In those days, with even Constantinople on the verge of daily revolt, she had spent her time far from people, rooting about in the basements and attics of the palace.

One day, sneezing with dust and guided only by the

light of a stolen lamp, she had found this library. All of the scrolls and books were very old, the newest being at least a hundred years old. Apparently this part of the palace had been abandoned after a great fire and riots in the Hippodrome. There was a book from that time, filled with lies and rumor and innuendo, and Martina had found it so obviously biased that she had never finished it. It was here somewhere, leaning neglected on a shelf. While her uncles struggled with the priests and the nobles and the barbarians, she had closeted herself here each day, her small brown head bent over one moth-eaten scroll after another. In the cool, comforting darkness there were no snippy ladies-in-waiting, no uncles that hated her. Even the fear that gripped every adult in the palace was easy to ignore.

Looking back, Martina knew that the Empire had been at the very edge of destruction. The acid panic that ate at every adult, making them angry and sharp and mean to a young girl, had not been her fault. It was something outside of them, and her. Even now, when the palace was gripped by this new crisis, it was a thousand times brighter than in those terrible days.

Despite exhaustion, anger roused itself in her again. Now, without so much as asking, someone had invaded her sanctuary, pushed all of the tables around, piled the books willy-nilly and put this *thing* in the middle of the reading room. She raised her head and pointed a long, well-manicured finger.

"You haven't answered me, young man. What is that?"

Alexos had remained standing behind the table, his mouth thinned to a harsh line. When Martina pointed, he did not turn aside to look. He was well aware of the mechanism that sat at the center of the room on a block of smooth travertine marble. It was his charge and purpose. He was quite familiar with every groove, every plane, every inch of the device.

"You cannot order me, miss. I have the Emperor's charge to watch here and you do not. If you do not leave,

I will summon the Faithful Guardsmen and they will take you away."

His voice softened. "You should leave now. You'll get in trouble otherwise."

Martina stared at him in amazement but stifled a laugh. *He is so serious!* "Alexos, you don't get out much, do you?"

"No," he said slowly, his plump face tensing. "I've my duty here."

"Do you sleep here, too?" Martina looked around, wondering if there was a pallet or cot or something behind one of the scroll racks.

"Yes," he said. "The kitchen staff supervisor sends me meals."

"Where did you live before you came here? In one of the temples?"

"You should go." Alexos turned away from her, still clutching the ivory scroll case to his chest. "I won't answer any of your questions."

Martina sat up, her hands on the smooth curve of the chair wings. The boy was embarrassed. There was a pang in her heart—she knew that feeling far too well. "I'm sorry. I didn't mean to pry."

He remained facing away, though it seemed that the line of his head had changed, risen. Martina brushed her hair, still in a tangle, back behind her ears and over her shoulders.

"Alexos? I meant no insult. You should know, if you have not been about in the palace, if you have not gone upstairs and seen the great halls and the jeweled court-yards, that I am the wife of the Emperor Heraclius. I am Martina, Augusta Romana, mother of the infant prince and heir, Heracleonas."

Alexos' head came up and he turned, staring at her with undisguised curiosity. "You're the Empress? You're just a little girl! You don't look . . ."

"Look what?" Martina cocked her head, her voice filled

with venom, her eyes slits. "Like a monstrous, unnatural creature or someone cursed by the gods? Can you still speak with me, or will you turn aside, passing on the opposite side of the chamber? Will you pretend not to see me, lest the taint of my scandal touch your holy robe?"

"Wait!" Alexos raised his hand, halting her words. "I have no quarrel with you, Empress. The matter of your marriage is for the gods to judge, not I."

Martina's rage subsided somewhat. The boy's face was so open and guileless that she believed him. It was refreshing to find a priest that did not get that sick, shocked look on his face when introduced to her. Many of the temples refused her admittance, too, unless she took the Faithful with her.

Fools. It's not as if the gods don't lie with their sisters. . . .

"May I stay, then? I doubt that my husband would mind, seeing that he confides so much in me."

Alexos paused, considering, and Martina sighed, seeing that he had missed the sarcasm in her words. The brief flare of her anger was gone. She was sure that many of the common people did not care that she and Heraclius were married. They had their own concerns. The high priests, now, they had their own agendas and plots to pursue. To them it was a point of weakness to pick at. Her eyes had adjusted to the light, allowing her to see the mysterious device clearly. She stood, brushing down her skirts, and approached it.

"You may stay," said Alexos in a formal tone. "But you must be careful . . . this is an ancient and supremely valuable artifact. It must not be touched!"

Martina looked at him sideways, her lips pursed. "You mean, no one knows quite how it works and you're afraid of breaking it?"

Alexos shrugged and raised his hands, palms up. "That is so . . . but it does work!"

"Can you show me?" Martina smiled at the boy, dimpling.

"Ah . . . maybe. It's a little tricky. . . ."

"Oh," said Martina, looking sad. "You don't know how?"

"I know how." Alexos stepped to the other side of the device, his hands resting lightly on the green stone block. "It has a mind of its own, though. Sometimes it will show things you don't want to see."

"It can show you things?" Martina's interest suddenly perked. "What did you call it? A . . . *telecast?* A far-sender?"

"Yes," said Alexos, but his mind was elsewhere. His head bent and his forehead furrowed in concentration. "I . . . can . . . make it spin. . . ."

Martina stepped back sharply, her hand rising to shield her face. A sullen blue glow began to fill the room.

On the top of the block lay a bronze disk, formed of many concentric rings. Each ring was tarnished with age and graven with thousands of tiny, spiked characters. They were indistinct, some almost rubbed away by time. From the ancient bronze, radiance seeped like water oozing through a porous stone. It spilled out and, as Martina watched in amazement, it began to fill upwards, describing an irregular sphere.

A hum began, first very low, making her spine and bones tremble, then rising. With it, the rings of metal began to rustle and shift. First the innermost ring rattled, making a tinny sound, then it rose into the air. The other rings, first slowly and then faster, rose as well. As they drifted up into the air, they began to spin around a common center. At the same time, whirling sparks of brown and white and gold replaced the blue light. Now the hum was a buzz, and the books and ancient, suspended lamps rattled. The room brightened.

Martina turned her head away, shielding her eyes. Her teeth hurt, echoing the shriek of the spinning metal.

"There!" Alexos sounded exhausted. Martina opened her eyes, relieved that the blinding light had dimmed, illuminating the room with a wavering blue light like sunlight reflecting off the ocean. It washed and rippled over the arching stone walls and the surfaces of the books. The Empress laughed in delight—it was like being in Poseidon's realm under the dark sea! Then she turned and her eyes grew wide at last, seeing what shimmered and gleamed before her. The rings of bronze were gone, replaced by a shining blue-white globe.

It is the world, a sphere, round and complete, she breathed to herself, stunned. *Pythagoras was right!* "Oh, Alexos . . . it is the most beautiful thing I've ever seen."

The boy-priest grinned, his round face lighting up at her praise. The strain of maintaining the telecast at speed was telling on him, drawing sweat from his forehead, but the look in the Empress's face was worth it.

"Oh . . ." She leaned closer, her button nose only inches from the minute white clouds that were curling over the tiny African shore. "I can see Lepcis Magna! I can see the forum and the amphitheater! I can see my . . . house."

She stopped, covering her mouth with her hand. Alexos squinted, wondering if she was crying. Something seemed to be in her eye, anyway. Sometimes the telecast shifted the vision that it displayed without warning, disorienting the viewer.

"Can you show me something I want to see? Something up close?"

Alexos gulped, feeling the full force of her personality. Her eyes seemed particularly large and green. He had not realized, while he was yelling at her, how attractive she was. He gulped again.

"Like . . . like what?"

Her tongue ran over her lips. She smiled. "Like, a person, a person here in the city. Can you do that?"

THE CAPITOLINE HILL, ROMA MATER

)℃(

H mm . . . Your city seems afflicted with disquiet."
Two men stood in the northern portico of the
temple of Jupiter Optimus et Maximus. Each wore expensive robes, padded hoods thrown back now that they were
under the shelter of the temple roof. The sun was setting
in a huge, swollen orange fireball. It wallowed down
through air thick with smoke and ash, banding deeper red
as it slid down towards the horizon. It had been a bad day
in the city, close and hot, without any kind of wind or
breeze. At some unguessable height the winds had shifted,
bringing a slow-falling cloud of dust and ash to settle over
the city. A light patina of gray marked both men's robes.
Here, on the height, looking out over the massed rooftops
of Rome, there was not even the hint of a breeze.

Despite this, the temple was empty, abandoned. The sacrificial fires on the altar guttered low in the dim red light.
One of the men, the blond, was grinning a wolf's grin,
looking out over the city. It seemed desolate, for few lights
had been lit against the coming night. The sky was washed
bloodred and the marble and concrete temple buildings
glowed murky vermilion. This man took a petty joy from
it, seeing a vision of destruction spread before him.

"It is not my city," said the other man in a querulous
voice. "Not anymore. It is a poor night to be abroad in the
streets."

"Nonsense, Gaius, it is the best of nights. Listen, do you
hear that sound?"

The older man, a tall fellow with a balding head and a

close-cut fringe of white hair, bent his long face, listening. There was a murmur growing in the still air, coming up from the streets below the Capitoline. Hearing it, he tensed, for it sparked dark memories of his youth. Men were shouting in the streets, crying out in rage. Women were shouting too, and some were screaming.

"A riot," said Gaius Julius, tugging the cloak closer around his shoulders. "A poor day, indeed, though it must please you, Alexandros, to see Rome come to this."

The younger man smiled, his face shining with delight. "The city means little to me, Gaius. What you built has surpassed my empire, true, and excelled in many respects. But I do not waste time with the past—the future intrigues me. A night such as this, with wild chaos in the air? That whets my appetite, as it should yours."

The youth put his hand on the older man's shoulder, leaning close.

"In nights such as this, when the common people huddle in their homes, the lights dark, hoping to live to the morning, that is when strong men can steal destiny."

Gaius made a half-smile and put his hand over Alexandros'.

"Perhaps."

The noise from the streets, still unseen below the encircling platform and wall of the Capitoline, suddenly rose. Metal rattled and there was a deeper, hoarser shouting. Gaius' head rose, and he stiffened, recognizing the sound. He made to leave the shelter of the portico, drawing the hood over his head. Then he stopped. He knew what he would see.

"Yes," Alexandros said as he descended the broad marble steps, "let us look upon your beloved Rome."

Gaius peered out one of the embrasures, gripped by a peculiar old fear. In his youth the city had been wracked by violence and intrigue. Armed gangs had roamed the streets, attacking the partisans of other political factions. Some of those gangs had been in his pay. Many had not.

In those days, it had been wise to travel among a crowd of guards and servants. Now, with the city gripped by this morbid fear, he and Alexandros traveled alone.

"Ah! The Emperor moves at last." Alexandros had pulled himself up into the next embrasure and was sitting, looking down into the street below with interest.

A great mass of people, their faces pale, white ovals in this darkening red murk, was surging along the avenue. An inchoate noise rose up from them, equal parts anger and fear. Two cohorts of armored legionaries blocked their way, making a wall of shields and iron from side to side. The soldiers had not drawn their swords or hefted javelins to their shoulders, but rather were armed with staves of hickory.

The lead edge of the mob paused as it turned the corner into the street. Some of the men and women in the front stopped or tried to turn around. The pressure of those behind them was relentless and they were pushed aside, crying out as they were crushed against the stone walls or knocked down. Some struggled up, their arms pressing against the bodies of those that continued to flood into the street.

"Foolish." Gaius Julius sneered at the soldiers below, drawing his cloak up. Ash drifting out of the sky settled amongst his thinning hair. "Let these poor fools into the Forum! Are they not citizens? Then give them some bread and cheese and a ration of wine. Let them eat and drink—"

Alexandros laughed, standing up, his arms on the worn teeth of the battlement.

"The Emperor's patience grows short, my friend. His soldiers feel it and they are angry, too."

Gaius Julius turned away, his face dark in the shadow of the hood. Behind him, the crowd had begun to yell and run, charging forward, heedlessly, towards the lines of soldiers. There was a rattling clang as the first rank of men locked shields and braced for the shock of the oncoming mob. The hickory staves were raised up to shoulder height like a thicket of wands. The old Roman strode away, down the walkway behind the battlement. He had seen such things before—he had *done* such things before—and it gave him no pleasure. Alexandros watched for a moment longer, his face lit by the ruddy light of lanterns hung before the gate. The mob gave forth a deep, growling sound, then there was a crashing sound and the whipping sound of cane on flesh.

Men and women, their faces cut and bloody, began to scream.

Alexandros grinned, his nostrils flaring, and then he jumped down from the wall and followed Gaius, whistling.

"Have you thought upon the matter of the Prince?" Alexandros followed the older man easily, though the streets were very dark and narrow. Gaius Julius seemed to have a destination in mind and the young Macedonian did not think it was a brothel or inn. *A pity,* he thought, *some diversion would be fine on this wicked night.*

"What do you mean? We have parted his company—cast aside like broken toys. He is about his own business, doubtless reconciling with his noble brother."

Alexandros raised an eyebrow at the bitterness in the Roman's voice. "Do you miss him?"

"I do not," Gaius snapped, turning into a narrow lane barely wide enough for a single man to pass. "I am beloved of this new life, dear Greek, and while he is away from us he may fall to harm. And then where will we be? Dust again. If he were near, then we could take steps to see that he remains whole and alive."

"Well thought," Alexandros allowed, who experienced the same gut-gnawing fear. It only *seemed* that they were free agents, released from their thrall to the Prince and his will. In truth, they were still his pawns, merely set aside for a time like abandoned toys. "I wonder, though, about some things only half heard in conversation between you and he. You have been with him longest in this mad effort of his . . . perhaps you can set my mind at ease."

Gaius Julius stopped. They had come to a small, round plaza, half choked with garbage and offal. Streets led off it, showing black mouths in the dim light. People slept on the cobblestones or sat, nursing an amphora of wine. Gaius turned left, entering a lane that rose sharply up the side of a hill. "Your mind never rests, dear Greek. I cannot see how I might allay it."

"You can, perhaps," said Alexandros, easily matching the Roman's pace. "Consider how little we know of the Prince and his intent; he is the scion of the Imperial house, yet he has escaped the burden of rule because he has a talent."

"He is a priest, a healer, a man of respected power and ability," Gaius interjected gruffly.

"Indeed," Alexandros replied. "He discovers that all Rome, all this Empire, is bound by the strictures of an Oath laid down in the time of your adopted son, Augustus. He finds that your dear son, aided by this lamentable Egyptian, Khamûn, has enforced his social rules and mores with this Oath, binding the people and the Empire."

The Macedonian paused, waiting for Gaius Julius to respond to the jibe. The Roman kept walking silently. Alexandros shrugged to himself and continued.

"Something happens . . . a friend, a shipwright, is killed by this hidden power. The Prince, outraged, takes up an effort to break the power of what he calls a curse. At first, he labors alone but finds that he cannot overcome it, he cannot understand it without help. He seeks assistance."

Gaius paused. They had come to the crest of a hill. The lane turned sharply right. Behind and below them, Alexandros could now make out the jumble of sloping roofs that marked the Forum and, rising above them, on the right, the shining wall of the Capitoline and the massive shape of the temple of Jupiter Optimus et Maximus. The Roman turned to Alexandros, only the tip of his long nose showing in the shadow of the hood.

"He finds," growled Gaius Julius, "the little Nabatean spy and wizard, Abdmachus."

"Yes," said Alexandros, his voice rising, "he finds a *Persian agent* to help him. A man sent into the Empire thirty years before to wait and to watch. He finds a man, perhaps the *only* man in the city who knows whereof he speaks. Does it not strike you a little strange that these two should come together in this matter?"

"Perhaps," allowed Gaius Julius, one long, thin hand rubbing the side of his chin. "You don't believe it was coincidence? You think that the twice-dead Abdmachus had been looking for a man like the Prince, a Roman sorcerer who stumbled upon the same secret yet lived? That he guided the Prince to him by some unknown means?"

"I think," said Alexandros, flexing his arms, "that Abdmachus was a subtle man. In comparison, I do not think that our dear Prince is subtle at all. Consider . . . traditionally the Persian magi are accounted great wizards. They are a powerful arm of the state, they stand at the right hand of the king of kings. Now, in battle, they wield powerful magics. More than one barbarian army has fled before them, riven with lightning and ghastly apparitions. But against their great enemy, Rome? They are well nigh powerless. This Oath defeats them, thwarts their skill, turns their sendings back upon them. The armies of Persia must match themselves, man to man, against Rome. Abdmachus himself, apparently a wizard of considerable skill, must move carefully and quietly on his mission lest he be destroyed."

Gaius Julius smiled, for his old mind, long enamored with intrigue and hidden plots, was turning hungrily upon the problem. "You think that Abdmachus had been waiting all that time for a weapon to appear. Some scrap of information, some man, some mechanism, which would allow him to break the power of the Oath. A chink in the armor of Rome . . . what better opportunity than this callow, inexperienced boy?"

Alexandros grinned, his eyes sparkling in the darkness.

"Ah, at last you begin to wake, old turtle. Yes—I think that Abdmachus influenced the mind of the Prince. I think that he led the Prince to you and then to me, each time promising the boy greater power to fight his enemy. That boy is a great power, he has enormous strength . . . but skill? Abdmachus was old and wily, a man well versed in the arts."

Gaius Julius began walking again, but now his steps were those of a man in deep thought. "He pressed the boy, then, to follow this insane goal. He was quiet and a dutiful servant . . . he hoped that the boy would break the power of the Oath, perhaps even dying in the process. Then Rome would be stripped of its great defense, even while locked in a bitter struggle against Persia."

"Yes, but then the Prince turned on him too soon. You had some little to do with that, I think."

Gaius Julius chuckled, a grim, cheerless sound. "I did. That cat Alais and I, we sought to influence the boy ourselves. We thought the Persian a threat to our little diumvirate. So, he was slain and made one of the lifeless. Like us, but less so, it seems. That is odd, too. You and I, we are veritably flush with thought and will and purpose, but he—he seemed far less, only a shadow of what he had been."

"It *is* odd." Alexandros sighed. "There was a book, in the library we so carefully gathered, that spoke on this subject." The Macedonian scratched the back of his head, brow furrowed as he pillaged his memory. "I have it—the *Pert Em Hru*—the book of coming forth by day. It speaks of the means and methods of anointing, preserving and summoning forth the dead. It was part of that rag bag of scrolls and parchments we stole from the biblios."

He frowned, his face troubled.

" 'The "uneasy dead" do not come forth whole,' " he quoted from memory. " 'They lack the essential spirits and humors that drive the living. They are incomplete, for the ka of the body has already fled. The guides and guardians have passed them through the Golden Fields and into the Twelve Hours. . . .' Then there is a long passage describing the underworld and the judges. I left off reading there, for I had seen those portions of the text before."

Gaius Julius raised an eyebrow. A trace of envy showed in his face. "You read the hieroglyphs of the Egyptians? I remember those scrolls, a muddy mass of pictures and scribbling . . . how came you by that skill?"

A peculiar look crossed Alexandros' face. "We are an anomaly, then, dear Roman. Our will is strong and we have purpose. By some act of the gods, we have escaped the land of the dead and can sing and see the world with living eyes. But this is a little matter—Abdmachus is now wholly dead, annihilated in the destruction of your house in the hills. Where is the Prince, then? Is he free of the old man's influence? Has he taken this task into his heart? What drives the Prince now?"

"Who can say?" Gaius Julius stopped, one hand on the edge of his cloak. "We might know more if we had taken all of the books rather than a pittance. Ah, we should have, my friend. What a rich collection they were!"

Alexandros nodded in agreement. The robbery of the Imperial library had stricken Alexandros with fear—it was an affront to the very gods!—but once he had begun to catalog and examine the trove, his unease had faded. Many books long thought lost had been among that collection. Coupled with the loot that had been dragged from the wreck of the Bygar Dracul's house in Constantinople, the Prince had amassed a fine collection.

"I grieve as well, my friend. Our lives proclaim that the Prince lived through the destruction of Vesuvius, but the books and tome and parchments? They may all be gone, burned in the ghastly wreck. Still, we have what we have. Our quiet friends will have to bear with us and our loss."

"Indeed."

They had come to the top of the hill, where a street of

blank walls pierced by small, narrow doors faced them. Alexandros looked around, marking that the street was swept clean and the plastered walls were free from graffiti. A district of the well-to-do, then.

"Is this our destination?"

Gaius nodded, pacing along the street in the darkness. Pools of light spilled from the doorways, where oil lamps hung. At the fourth one he stopped, his head bent towards the inlaid tile decorating the sides of the door alcove.

"This is the house of Gregorius Auricus, also known as Magnus."

Alexandros frowned, puzzling through the Roman names and this barbarous Latin tongue.

"Gregorius the Great?"

"Yes," laughed Gaius, "he is accounted the richest man in Rome and a good friend of the Emperor Galen and his family."

Now Alexandros raised an eyebrow. Given the crimes that they had committed in the service of the Prince, it was quite likely that the Emperor—should he have the two of them in his hand—would see their new lives swiftly ended. *That is what I would do*, thought the Macedonian. *A ruler should never allow other men that have tasted kingship loose in his state.*

Gaius' eyes twinkled and he put a finger alongside his nose.

"The Prince mentioned the name to me and said that Gregorius had offered him 'help if there was no one Imperial to turn to.' If I understood the boy correctly, this Gregorius is a patron of the Goths and other barbarian allies of the Empire. He is a fellow with access to gold, to armed men, to ships, to all of the sinews of power."

Alexandros grinned at that, feeling his blood quicken. Though he had grown up amid the vipers of his father's court—enmeshed in his mother's intrigues—he preferred the presence and action of open war.

"That would make him a valuable friend," Alexandros

said, smoothing back the tongue of hair that always fell across his forehead. "Have you already arranged a meeting?"

"I have," said Gaius Julius, pinning a golden brooch to his cloak and stepping to the door. "I believe that the man needs some assistance that we may provide, to our mutual benefit."

Alexandros put a hand on Gaius' shoulder, halting the older man.

"To what end?" His voice was serious. "You have not said much of these goals of yours since we have come to the city. For myself, I have watched and waited, bettering my skill in this rough tongue of yours, observing the customs and practices of your people. But you have been quiet and withdrawn, thinking, I judge, of what you will do now."

Gaius nodded, still looking to the door.

"This is so," he said in a low voice. "When I was young, I was plagued by dreams and desires that filled my days and nights. They drove me to wild, frantic efforts. I pursued power, women, men . . . anything that would make me great. It was a grim time, filled with chaos and civil war. I sought to bring order out of that foment. I found success, but then I was empty. I tried to emulate you, dear Greek, by conquering the world, but I was cut down ere I could undertake that campaign."

"And now?" Alexandros was watching him closely, seeing the twitch of muscles in the older man's neck. "Do you desire the world?"

"No," said Gaius Julius, shaking his head. "That thirst has left me. But I want this life, strange as it is, to continue. I find it impossible to relinquish this sweet draught that is set before me again. To that end, I must protect our young Prince, exalt his state, enrich his domains, stymie his enemies, throw down those that would oppose him."

Laughing softly, Alexandros said, "My thoughts entire, sprung whole from your orator's mouth. You think that this man can help us, help our *beloved* Prince?"

"Yes."

"And after that? Have you given thought to the future? What will you do when the inevitable comes, as I believe it must, and the Prince sets aside his brother and claims the Purple himself?"

Gaius Julius turned at last and met the Macedonian's eyes directly. "I have not given that thought wings. This now, this moment, is enough. Once, when I was young, I gave great thought to the future. I made plans for the course of my children and my children's children." He sighed. "But then, where were they? I had none . . . a waste. See how wretched Octavian seized the role? Oh, that cloak he donned, taking my name and power for his own. Cur."

Alexandros shook his head in feigned dismay. "Oh, so true, a crawling whelp that crept up and stole your glory while you slept . . . and did what you could not, built a new state, this very Empire, from the ashes of your crumbling Republic. One of our dear quiet friends relates the tale of it—this youth Octavian was a fine ruler. He endowed a realm that has maintained to this very day. I bow before him, for he has built well."

"*Pfaugh!*" Gaius Julius spit on the pavement. "I read that fop Suetonius, too. He kisses the feet of a man dead for centuries! Pitiful. Oh, you are right, my nephew did well with the ashes he gathered, but I still resent him. Leave me some bile for my old age!"

"You have no bile," Alexandros laughed. "You are the very corpse of a man."

"Enough, stripling. Your flesh is cold, too. Let us enter and see what advantage may be gained by clever words and a smiling face, for we have little else to offer."

Alexandros stood back, letting the Roman strike the door with his fist, summoning the watchman. He was a little troubled, for he had read the histories of Suetonius and the Annals very closely, seeking to understand the rise of this Octavian to power. A brief passage was trying to raise itself to his attention . . . *Ah.*

Gaius Julius had fathered only daughters on his Roman wives, of which he had plenty. But he had made a son, a single boy, Ptolemy Caesarion, with Royal Egypt. A boy who lived to manhood. *Doesn't he remember? Was the boy unsuitable for the Roman people to see as his descendant? A small mystery* . . .

"Gaius Julius and companion," intoned a servant as they entered the sitting room.

A robust man with expensive, refined tastes was sitting in a wide-backed chair. A mane of fine white hair swept behind his head, framing an ancient, calm face. A broad table covered with sheets of parchment, inkstands, tally boards, quill knives, alabaster cups and silver platters stood before him. The man looked up, serious eyes flicking over the two of them. The man returned his attention to the matters before him.

"One moment, if you will," he said as he put some papers in order. When he was done, he stood slowly, showing the weight of considerable age. "Welcome to my house, Gaius Julius. I am Gregorius Auricus. Please, sit and take some refreshment."

Alexandros followed the older Roman in taking a chair beside the great desk. He was not pleased to be left out of the conversation, but considered the situation and silently acceded to Gaius' will in this thing. It was not the time to dispute the approach, not when one was at grips with the enemy.

"You are most generous, sir." Gaius sat, his face and motions indicating pleased acceptance. "I hope that we do not disturb your work. We can easily return at another time, if that is convenient."

Gregorius waved a hand, settling back into his chair. "It is no matter. You are a welcome guest and diversion from these other matters."

Alexandros hid a smile, keeping his face composed. It was quite early in the evening, well before the usual hour for social visits. Too, it was past the time when a senator would entertain his established clients and employees. Gaius Julius had managed to finagle an interview between other appointments. The Macedonian wondered what it had cost.

"Your letter said that you were recommended by a common friend, that you could offer me expertise that I had need of in these troubled times." Gregorius indicated a folded letter on the tabletop. "It does not say who recommended you, sir, nor what need of mine you fill."

"Noble sir," said Gaius Julius in a straightforward blunt voice, "I've come about the matter of your private efforts to relieve the suffering of those afflicted by the explosion of Vesuvius. A man well known on the Palatine, indeed, one that might even call it home, said that I should find you and offer you my services."

"Private effort?" Gregorius squinted at the older man, his lips pursed. "There is no private effort under way—though I do spend a great deal of my time aiding and assisting the Imperial government in its own efforts to find housing for the displaced and provide them with food and drink and clothing."

"Your efforts are well known, sir. Your name and your generosity are well spoken of in the city. I do not speak of the efforts made to see to the basic needs of those unfortunates that have been driven to seek shelter in the welcoming arms of Mother Rome. Another need, one more pressing, must be met and I am sure that you are the man to see it done."

Gregorius looked pained and raised his hand sharply. "Please, sir, you are my guest, but my weariness is great. Speak plainly and set aside the devices of the orator."

Gaius Julius restrained a smile and nodded earnestly. "As you say, sir. I will be blunt. Sir, the theaters are closed, the amphitheaters locked up, the circus itself desolate and dark. Can there be any greater calamity than this? How will the people know that the Emperor loves them and shares their loss if he does not go among them, attending the theater, opening the races? How can they set aside their fears if they are not given diversions?"

Alexandros was slightly puzzled by this tack in the conversation, but he saw that their host understood Gaius Julius' intent. The senator sighed and picked up a quill pen from the desktop, testing its point with his thumb in a nervous gesture.

"This troubles me too. I have argued with him, more than once, about this very thing. The princeps Galen is adamant that the resources of the state will not be wasted on 'frivolity' and 'shadow play' when there are roads to be cleared, cities to be dug out of the ash, grain and oil imported in vast quantities at the expense of the state."

"These are necessary things, sir." Gaius Julius' voice dropped a tone. "But what do the people say, sitting in their homes when the sky is dark with portent? The Emperor must not forget that the people of the city must feel his love, they must see he cares, they must hear his voice and behold his face. He cannot hide on the Palatine, buried in the affairs of state, lest the love of the city be lost to him."

"I know," said Gregorius curtly. "I am not the only adviser who has urged him to reopen the theaters and the Flavian and the circus. He refuses."

Gaius Julius nodded to himself, by which Alexandros assumed that he knew this already, having nosed it out of the wine shops and baths of the city.

"Sir, what of these funeral games, these *munera*, that have been so long rumored? Will he wait, too, before giving the countless dead their due? Will he let the shades and *manes* throng the countryside, all unshriven and restless?"

"There is some news of this, which I have recently heard." Gregorius grimaced. "Galen issued edicts a month

ago saying that there would be a great series of games—
with gladiators, wild beasts and all—to commemorate the
dead of Pompeii, Herculaneum and Baiae. Yet no date was
set, no festival declared in their honor. Each day he is
pressed for details or a date, yet he demurs. I fear that he
will not appoint an *editore* to see to this matter, seeking
to handle it himself."

"And his attention is ever elsewhere," said Gaius Julius
softly. "There are many demands upon the Emperor's time,
many threats to the Empire. *Someone* must ensure the
plebe in the street has bread and wine and oil to fill his
stomach. In the face of such a catastrophe, some small
details might be lost."

"So they have been," said Gregorius, showing great
weariness in his face. "Every man in the Imperial service
carries a backbreaking load in these times. The relief effort
is staggering."

"Not all men are so employed, noble sir." Gaius Julius'
voice was firm. "I stand before you, willing to lend hand
and thought to the task—but I beg you, sir, that you do
not set me to this matter of the public relief. Let me do as
the tribunes and aediles and magistrates did in ancient
times; let me arrange such performances of the theater,
such games and wild animal hunts in the amphitheater, as
are deemed needful to restore the spirit of the people."

Gregorius sighed and put the pen away. "The Emperor
will never release funds for such a thing. I have already
related he plans a great series of games."

"This is so," said Gaius quickly, before the senator could
continue. "But *you* could spare some coin for some trivial
amusements for the citizens, while we wait for the funeral
games. You have placed your fortune in the service of the
people before—you hired ships to carry corn and wheat
and wine into the city when civil war wracked the state
and the people were starving. Rome needs you, sir."

The senator seemed suddenly to come awake. Alexandros, watching the two men, thought their host saw his guest for the first time in that moment.

"No senator can undertake to sponsor games, festivals, theater performances or triumphs without the express permission of the Emperor himself. No senator," Gregorius said in a sharp tone, "has ever been allowed to do such a thing since the reign of Divine Augustus himself."

"Indeed," said Gaius Julius, "the noble Agrippa undertook a lavish and prolonged series of games in the time of his aedileship. If memory serves, and if Cassius Dio speaks truly, Agrippa 'rained upon the heads of the people tokens that were good for money in one case, in another clothes, or yet again something else.' But Agrippa was the close confidante of Augustus, and surely undertook such things with the full knowledge and support of the Emperor. Sir, the people lament and are fearful. This is such a small thing, perhaps it could be done."

Gregorius shook his head, though his face showed disputed thoughts. He did not speak.

"Sir," said Gaius Julius after a moment, "I have some experience in these matters. I have recently returned from the East, from Persia, and am no longer in Imperial service. Let me lend my arm, my hand, my eye to resolve this. Let me set in motion an effort to restore the normal pattern of life for the Roman people. Perhaps the Emperor will let one of the theaters, not even the Marcellan or the Pompeian, reopen on selected days for the performance of . . . of classical tragedies, or the *Aeneid,* so that the people— who are tormented by omens on all sides, by the unnatural nature of the sky, by these stenches and fumes—may see life continues, and the flow of the city may resume its accustomed course."

The senator was thoughtful now and considered the words carefully. Alexandros hid a smile. He knew something of Gaius Julius' experience in these matters, knowing by all accounts the elderly Roman was a master of stagecraft and planning. Alexandros had arranged some spectacles himself, in his breathing life, and he guessed his friend and companion had already prepared all that would transpire. All it needed was coin and some veneer of Imperial permission.

"Just one theater would not tax my coffers over-much . . ." Gregorius began. "No pantomimes or farces, of course, but instead reliable, older works, reminding the people of the ancient heroes and the traditions of the city."

"Even so," said Gaius Julius, his voice painfully earnest. "Nothing filled with spectacle or trickery, no mechanical elephants, no forests rising from the floor of the theater, no brawling gladiators. But it will be enough, sir, to guide the thoughts of the people away from all this death and destruction. Let them think of life again, and look to the future. Let them think kindly of the Emperor, and of you, whose generosity and concern for the people is so well known."

Gregorius rose, pacing to the window. He drew aside a heavy drape, revealing a window looking down off the hill, across the sprawling mass of tenements and the bulk of the Forum. There, framed in the window, lit by hundreds of distant torches and lamps, was the Palatine. The Imperial palaces gleamed watery red in the night. Ash was still falling, tainting the air.

"I meet with the Emperor in the morning," the senator said. "I will offer him this gesture and I will use, with your permission, your words. It may move him. I know he feels the wounds of the people deeply. Some gesture to them, to reassure the citizens, may warm his heart to this endeavor."

Unseen by the man, Gaius Julius turned to Alexandros for an instant, his face split by a huge grin, his eyes sparkling with triumph. Then he schooled his face to concern and faint hope as the senator turned around again.

"Which theater do you suggest? The Balbus, perhaps? It is small and the entrances could be easily controlled by the urban cohorts."

Gaius Julius rose, taking a wax tablet and stylus out of his robe, and joined the senator at the large table. "My very thought, sir. We would not want a riot! That would be a poor omen indeed."

Dawn was near, shading the dark sky with a muted violet glow, when they left the house of Gregorius Aricus. A chill had settled in the air and the smell of the river seemed sharp. Alexandros, inured to the cold, walked briskly, his hood thrown back, letting the dew bead on his skin. Gaius Julius walked at his side, radiating satisfaction.

"You are well pleased," the Macedonian said as they crossed the empty plaza at the heart of the Forum. Their lodgings, an apartment secured by Gaius Julius during their previous time in the city, were on the edge of the Aventine Hill. The rooms were small but out of the way, and their comings and goings would not be easily noticed. "This business of the theaters and races seems overly indirect. Of course, you may siphon off large sums of coin to finance other schemes by these means, but—"

Gaius Julius laughed suddenly, pulling back his own hood. They had crossed the expanse of the Forum and were passing by the pillared front of the temple of Castor and Pollux. Within, flames burned on the altars, illuminating the massive statues with a flickering light.

"My dear Greek, there is *nothing* indirect about the theater and the circus in Rome! Haven't you paid attention to Suetonius? I know you have, for I saw you grimace and exclaim aloud over the doings of my nephew's successors. Did you mark the fate of dour Tiberius?"

Alexandros nodded slowly. Of the emperors following the Divine Augustus, only the "glorious" Germanicus had died in bed. It seemed, from the vantage of history, that only the enormous impetus imparted by the long-lived and wily Augustus had carried the Empire through Tiberius' foul humor, Germanicus' too-short reign, Claudius' fumbling and Nero's profligate insanity to the able Vespasian.

"Yes, he died friendless and alone, murdered upon his return from that island."

"Do you remember why he had lost the affection of the people and the senate? Why he was murdered? Why the reign of Germanicus, 'he of the highest quality of body and mind,' was so welcomed?"

Alexandros pulled up short, vexed, and stared at Gaius Julius.

"Because Tiberius could not stand to attend the theater, the races and the other public amusements? That is madness!"

"Perhaps," said Gaius, putting his arm around the younger man's shoulder. "But this is Rome and here there is a special and intimate relationship between the people and the Emperor. There is a balance, a harmony, in the city between the least citizen and the most exalted. The theater, the circus and the Colosseum are at the heart of it."

Gaius Julius stopped and pointed up at the towering shapes of the Imperial palaces to their left. "There sits the Emperor in his gilded cage, surrounded by ceremony and guards and the weight of dreadful privilege. The common man, the citizen, rarely sees him. He is remote and distant. The senate, which by ancient tradition should represent the tribes and the citizens, is a useless social club. It has been this way for centuries. Even the fiction of voting for tribunes is long discarded. The Emperor's will is absolute, but he is *not* a tyrant."

They resumed walking, following the covered arcade down into the markets by the river.

"How does he escape becoming an isolated god, as so many of the kings in the east do? Why, my friend, through the theater, through the circuses, through the wild-animal hunts. In these things, the Emperor appears in person, the focus of all attention. Every man and woman and child can see his face, see him laugh or cry or curse if his favorite driver fails in the turn. In the theater, the common people may address the Emperor with their own voices. Do you see what that brings?"

Alexandros nodded, for he had sustained much the same relationship with his hoplites.

"A grievance aired," he mused, "is a grievance halved."

"Just so," grinned Gaius Julius. "You will see, my friend, that the weariness of this Emperor Galen, his distaste for these frivolities, will deliver the heart of Rome to me."

He paused, running a hand over his bald pate.

"I have some talent for swaying the allegiance and favor of the people, I must say."

THE SEVERAN PALACE, ROMA MATER

Long drapes, rich with gold thread, luffed slightly in the faint night breeze. The room was dim, lit only by a pair of beeswax candles. A man was lying on the quilts, still in his tunic and toga from the day. One sandal was on the floor, the other still on his foot. He pressed the heels of his hands against his eyes, trying to dispel a throbbing headache. A door opened in one of the painted walls, casting flickering shadows on naiads and swimming dolphins. For the moment that it was open, the piercing wail of a crying child stabbed into the room. The man on the bed twitched as if struck by a spear, then sat up, his thin face tense.

The woman that had entered made a sharp motion with her hand. "Galen, lie down, there's nothing to be done by *you*."

The Emperor of the Western Empire, Augustus and god of the Romans, master of Italy and Gaul and Germania, lay back down, relieved. He turned his head, watching his wife sit at her side table, carefully brushing her neat, short hair. Even with a screaming child in the next room and all the despair and unease in the city, she remained well kept and elegant.

"What makes him cry like that?"

Helena cast him a look over her shoulder, eyebrows hard over her dark brown eyes. "Do you care? If you knew, would you order the matter resolved? Issue an edict to quiet him?"

Galen sighed. Helena was as tired and worn as anyone. Her pregnancy had been hard, though she had delivered a strong boy, if the volume of his wailing was any indication. In the decade since they had married, he a young tribune from the provinces, she the daughter of an ancient patrician house, she had struggled with numerous ailments. Once he had feared that bearing a child would kill her outright, but her stubborn will seemed to have overcome that obstacle.

"Is he all right?"

"Yes," she said, putting down the brush and letting her face soften a little. "The nurse says that he is colicky. She says that it will pass as he grows older. She's giving him some smelly infusion, catnip, I think."

Galen let his eyes close. The soft sound of the comb continued for a moment, then stopped. Turning his head, he let one eye open. Helena leaned close to the small silver mirror set on a three-legged stand on her table. She was wiping powder from around her eyes with a soft rag dipped in oil. The Emperor smiled and rolled over, his hands under his head so that he could watch her. Before they had come to Rome, she had never bothered with makeup. Now removing it was a nightly ritual, a colophon to the weary day.

"The boy could be raised by the servants, in Catania, perhaps."

Helena stopped and put down the rag. She turned, her

eyes narrow and her lips compressed into a thin line. Galen frowned at her reaction.

"I will raise my son. If you wish us to leave so that you might sleep easy at night, we can certainly do so." The Empress's voice was very cold. Galen sat up and swung his legs off the bed.

"A suggestion only, my love. I do not want you to go, or him either. As you say, the colic will pass."

"Then don't talk like a fool," she snapped, turning back to her mirror. Sitting up, he could see part of her face in the silver. The lines of anger faded and she dipped her hands in a porcelain ewer filled with rose-scented water. After laving her face, she took a towel from the table and patted herself dry.

"How went things today?"

Galen smiled to himself as he removed his remaining sandal. Somewhere in the palace, there were slaves specially trained to remove his shoes, and his tunic, and the toga. There were probably slaves who were supposed to brush the Empress's hair and remove her makeup, too. Galen had spent too many years in the field lugging his own kit and tending to his own business to allow them into the tiny, besieged sanctuary of the Imperial apartments. The palaces on the hill were enormous, but they also held a vast army of servants, clerks, ministers and other hangers-on. Nearly everyone in the city shared a room with someone. The addition of the refugees from the south only made things worse. The thought of a private space was almost unheard of, but—by the gods!—he *was* the Emperor. If he could have a room to himself and his wife, then he would.

"It is very difficult. Everyone is still recovering from the shock of the disaster, I think. It's almost impossible to get things done. The provision of food to Campania is a particular problem."

"I heard," said Helena, sniffing with distaste. "I have received an inordinate number of letters from various and sundry distant relations, all begging for corn tokens." She slid under the covers of the bed, wriggling her toes down into the quilts.

Galen turned his body, making a space for her to fit against him under the covers. She was warm and soft and smelled of roses and coriander. He buried his face in her neck.

"It's the harbors at Misenum and Baiae," he said, his voice muffled. "Moving so much grain and salt pork and bread and wine and oil is impossible over the roads between here and there. Most of the bridges are damaged and the highways themselves are crowded with refugees or looters or troops sent in to restore order. It will be months before you could travel overland in safety."

Helena sighed and curled her husband's forearms to her chest, kissing his fingers. The candles had gone out, leaving them alone in the nest of the bed, in the dimness. "The harbors are still closed?"

He nodded, holding her tightly against him. "The work of dredging them clear of wrecks and sunken ships will take weeks, too. The work crews are moving at a snail's pace . . . it's the same malaise which afflicts everyone here."

She turned her head, shifting so that she could see his face. Even in the darkness, there was still a little light from the windows. The height of the Palatine was studded with towers and temples, all illuminated by great torches and lanterns. Here, at least, it was never fully dark.

"How do you feel?"

"Tired. Exhausted. There is this weight, which is so enormous. . . . Aurelian is a dutiful brother, and he is putting in the same long hours, but he does not have the breadth of vision, the understanding of the problems, to resolve things on his own."

Helena nodded and put the tip of her finger on his nose. "You need help," she said. "Like you had before the disaster."

Galen raised an eyebrow, looking down at the serious, small face of his wife. The smell of her hair tickled his nose, but he was not too distracted to notice the tone in her voice. He felt his weariness increase—must he politic and bargain in his own bed, too?

"Are you lobbying again? I have made up my mind. The Duchess is a broken woman; the loss of those men and her daughters was too much for her. The loss of my trust worse. I will not place her in charge of the Office of Barbarians again. She has proved far too dangerous to myself and our family."

Helena frowned, watching his face. The curious events of the days immediately before the eruption of Vesuvius and the annihilation of the Atreus estate at Ottaviano had only been discussed obliquely in passing between them. The Empress knew Anastasia had sent men into the south, to deal with some trouble. She had not heard "some daughters" were involved. Helena ransacked her memory—there was nothing to indicate the old Duke had gotten her with child. Though, doubtless, the ancient goat had tried!

"Daughters?" Helena tried to keep feral curiosity out of her voice. "I didn't know she had any daughters."

Galen hissed and tried to hide his head in the pillows. "Let us talk of it another time."

"I think not," she said with a sharp tone in her voice. "You're killing yourself with work and worry. You've not even been out of the palace to ride, or hunt, or walk among the people in the Forum in weeks. Now, the Duchess, who has been our dear friend, is near dead herself of grief. Both of you drive me to tears! Do you say daughters of hers, *adopted* daughters, I assume, were killed in the eruption?"

"Yes," Galen growled from under a pillow. "Let us sleep!"

"No," she said, snatching the pillow away and flinging it across the room. "I would like to hear about this business *now*." She sat up, shift falling from one white shoulder. Though she constantly reminded Galen to go outside, to see the sun, to walk in the wind and rain, to find some exercise and play, she rarely did any such thing herself. Indeed, among her peers in the nobility of the city, her naturally pale skin and lustrous hair were a source of envy.

Galen scowled and rummaged around in the sheets for another pillow. She clouted him across the side of the head with hers. It was heavy with goose down and made a satisfying *thump*.

"Ow! You are in a mood. I thought you wanted me to get more sleep."

"You can sleep later," she said, "when I'm satisfied."

"Oh," he said, grabbing for her leg and catching her by the ankle. "I thought you wanted to talk!" Grinning, he began dragging her towards him. Helena squealed in fury and hit him with the pillow again, hard. Galen rolled over, laughing.

"You're impossible," she spit at him, brushing hair out of her eyes. "Tell me what happened."

"All right." Galen sat up, his brief laughter gone. Helena, who had been about to ask a pointed question, stopped, for her husband's face was suddenly very old. For the first time in weeks, she saw the full, crushing burden he carried reflected in his eyes. She had a momentary feeling that a door, long held closed, was suddenly open.

"Oh, my love . . ." She crawled to him and took his head in her hands. "You've the same look in your eyes as she does." Helena kissed his forehead, then their lips met and he was holding her very tight. Salt stung her eyes and she blinked his tears away. Her Emperor was on the verge of crying and she cradled his head in her arms.

"Tell me," she said softly, her lips brushing his ear.

Some time later, when he had finished, Helena held him close, rocking back and forth. He still refused to cry, but her own face was wet with salt.

"Our dear friend sent men to kill your little brother?" It seemed impossible, even insane.

"Yes." Galen's voice was a faint shadow of its usual commanding baritone.

"And, they all died when the mountain exploded?"

"Yes."

Helena sat quietly for a time after that, thinking. Galen drowsed in her arms. The moon rose, cutting a pale, white shadow on the floor of the room. In the flavorless light the patterns of mosaics and tiles turned strange and unrecognizable. Then the moon passed the angle where it could shine in the window and everything became dark again.

"Little Maxian," she said at last. "He truly had these powers, he could raise the dead, heal all hurts?"

"Yes," Galen said, voice filled with sleep. Much of the brittle tension which had marked him of late has gone. "He commanded powerful servants and forbidden powers. Or so the Duchess said."

Helena's forehead furrowed in thought. Her lips pursed for a moment, then she smoothed back her husband's lank, dark hair. "Love, your brother had a machine that *flew*?" The thought of it filled her with terrible envy.

"Yes, so the Duchess's servants reported. Something surely carried him to my camp on the shores of the Mare Caspium with unmatched speed, then back again."

"Ah-huh. Do you think he still lives?"

"No." Galen's voice was filled with heavy grief. He was not the kind of man to part easily from his brothers, for their bond had been very strong. Other emperors, as Helena well knew from the histories, had been quick to hate and fear their siblings, to murder them with the noose, with poison, with a suffocating pillow. Galen enjoyed the most precious gift any emperor had ever held in his hand—the love and trust of his family. "He is dead. There . . . there was a moment, as Aurelian, the Duchess and I stood in Phillip the Arab's dining chamber. I saw him, the piglet, he was covered with blood, a blade in his chest. I saw fire and flame and he was dying, dark blood bubbling from his mouth. His eyes were filled with fury. Then I saw the life go out of them, and the vision was gone. He is surely dead."

Helena sighed and kissed his forehead, feeling the heat of his body on hers. He seemed very old and tired, exhausted by the long struggle. To know this; then to hear, day after day, the count of the dead from the south. Messengers came each morning, bearing reports from the tribunes and consuls who had charge of the relief effort. Mass graves lined the roads into Baiae and Misenum. Thousands of slaves worked, bent over shovels and hoes, burying the dead. The cities of Pompeii and Herculaneum had become tombs of their own, buried by the smoking black rock that flowed down from Hades-cursed Vesuvius. Galen must feel the grief of every family that had lost a son, a daughter, a father, as his own loss.

"There is no body, my love. Perhaps it is impossible to think of, but I know *you* would have contrived escape from this thing—with these powers, with a machine that flies, you would have escaped. Could your brother do less?"

"Don't say such things . . . our little piglet is dead, by my hand. I will not think of it."

"By your hand?" Helena's voice rose, her fingernails digging into his shoulder. "You did not put the knife into his breast—that was Anastasia's doing. That was business of the state, not you."

Galen turned to her, his eyes fierce. "I *am* the state. Must needs he die, then I am the one with the sword in my hand. I accept my responsibility—do not try to sway me with your words."

Helena flinched away, feeling the coldness of his rebuke. It was painful and it reminded her she had once sworn to never meddle in these affairs, to keep to her books, her poetry, her letters. It was sin enough in the eyes of many patricians she was accounted an able playwright. *There are two rooms in our house, the state and the family,* she thought. *Now I have stepped into his room, uninvited.*

She wished she had stayed in Catania, at the summer

villa. Then all of this would be far away and out of her control. She wouldn't even be worrying about it, save to lament over the tragedies reported to her in letters. The words on her lips would not issue forth, cutting at her own love of his family like a shearing knife.

"Husband, please! If Maxian lives, then he is your dreadful enemy now. He will know who sent those men against him. You must take all care and seek him out, find him. You must protect yourself. Set hounds upon his trail."

Galen raised a hand, his eyes flashing with disgust. "I have said, wife, that I will *not* employ the Duchess again!"

"But—"

A sharp rapping at the door interrupted them both. Galen cursed luridly and swung out the bed. He was naked, but he scooped up the semicircular toga from a chair where he had thrown it and cast it about his shoulders.

"Yes," he barked, approaching the door. "What is it?"

"A message, my lord." The voice was that of one of the guardsmen who sat outside the doors of the apartments during the night. Galen halted, suddenly suspicious. "It has come in great haste by dispatch rider from Portus, sir, with the seal of the Alexandrine prefect."

Galen put his hand on the door, given pause by the odd tone in the man's voice.

If there are assassins without, he thought, *then there is little reason to make me open the door. They could break it down, having overcome my guards.*

The panel swung wide under his hand and the guardsman, a very young German with a stubbly reddish beard and two braids on either side of his face, bowed deeply. The message packet was thrust into his hands. Galen smiled, seeing the embarrassment on the boy's face.

"You've done well, Rufus. Resume your station."

Galen shut the door, wondering what had driven the prefect—an able man whom he had put in place only last year—to send such an urgent message. He thumbed open the packet, breaking a double wax seal. There was a single sheet of fine-quality papyrus inside, covered with slanted writing. Galen squinted at it. The light was very poor.

"Here," said Helena, holding up one of the candles. She had drawn a cloak around herself and the candle hissed and spit, but it illuminated the message. "What does it say?"

"The usual blather about praising me, my divine rule, my genius . . . then, 'Word has come from Tyre on the Phoenician coast of a great disaster that has befallen the Eastern Prince Theodore, blessed be his name,' and so on. . . . Here it is, some details: 'The various and diverse states of the Decapolis have risen in revolt, claiming tyranny and misplaced faith between the Emperor Heraclius and themselves. By this means a great army has come out of the desert, laying low Theodore and his many men. This army, unchecked by the gods or Roman arms, now advances upon Tyre and Damascus.' Then he says he fears that Egypt may be next. He begs me that men and ships be sent to reinforce him."

Galen turned the paper over, his face grim, but there was nothing on the back.

"What will you do? Will Heraclius ask for your aid?"

The Emperor ran a hand through his hair, momentarily brushing the lank bangs out of his eyes. "He may not ask . . . he stripped the cities of the Decapolis of men to fight the southern Persian army the year before last. Most of them were reported scattered or slain at Emesa. I wonder . . ."

Galen's face, which had reverted to its usual grim mask while he considered this news, suddenly brightened and something like a smile came upon it for the first time in months.

"By the blessed gods, we can *see* what transpires in the East. If Hermes, god of messengers, wills it, we may even have converse with my brother emperor concerning this matter."

"Are you mad?" Helena watched in surprise as Galen

pulled his tunic, still stained with sweat from the long day, over his head. "How will you accomplish that? It's impossible."

"Not at all, my love." Galen grinned, his teeth white in the candlelight. For an instant, he looked like nothing so much as a mischievous boy with a terribly huge secret. "There's something I've not shown you yet. Come, put on your slippers."

The telecast flickered and hissed, bronze rings humming with power. An acolyte of the temple of Mars Ultor, his face tense with effort, knelt beside the granite block, his whole concentration focused on the slowly spinning discs before him. Green fire licked along the edges of the rune-carved metal bands. Now they rose into the air, whirling ever faster. The light grew, flooding across the ceiling and the walls like the rising sun.

Helena hid behind her husband, her eyes wide, watching with fearful anticipation as the buzzing, whirling contraption formed a globe of flickering bronze above the ancient slab.

"This one was found in Spain, buried under an old temple near the Pillars of Hercules. Eventually it came here, part of some lot of odds and ends. Aurelian found it in the market and bought it for a minor sum. You know him, he loves every kind of machine and gadget—he drafted some of the thaumaturges from the Imperial academy to figure it out."

The rising, shrill whine suddenly stopped and a swirling, milky globe of blue and brown and green swam in the air before them. Helena's eyes widened even more and her fingers dug into her husband's shoulder, cutting into the fine linen of his toga.

"That's . . ."

"Yes," he said, laughing. There was a great feeling of relief in his chest, seeing that *something* in this cold, gray world yielded to his will. "It is glorious, isn't it? Lad, show us Constantinople and the matching sphere."

"There is another?" Helena tried to keep surprise from her voice but failed. This was far more than she expected. How could she relate this? Who could she tell? *No one, I warrant,* she thought in disgust. *State secrets! Ah, but what a fine story in one of my letters it would make!*

"Yes . . ." Galen's attention was diverted by the fluctuation of the sphere. The glassy blue-white world disappeared, flickering, and then there was a face hanging in the air. A young woman with tousled brown hair and enormous eyes stared out at them, her face frozen with surprise. A gloomy, dark room loomed behind her, interrupted only by the face of an overweight young man in one corner of the scene.

"Empress Martina?" Galen was startled, his voice rising in surprise. "What are you doing at the *telecast?*"

The girl in the sphere gulped, staring out at them. "Emperor Galen? I'm sorry, I wasn't trying to look upon you! Alexos, you fat cow, you've bothered the Western Emperor! I'm sure that some suitably fitting punishment can be contrived—"

"My lady," interjected Galen, stepping towards the sphere before he stopped himself. It wasn't as if he could reach through the buzzing globe of witch light to touch her. "Please, I've just had word of Prince Theodore's defeat in the desert—I had hoped to speak with my brother emperor about the matter. Is he nearby?"

Martina's face passed through surprise, shock and then resigned fear. "Lord Galen, I've heard nothing from Theodore for weeks, but my husband is not nearby. I fear . . . I fear he will not speak with you, nor with anyone at the moment."

Helena jabbed her husband in the back, then whispered urgently in his ear. He raised a hand and nodded, acknowledging her.

"Martina, have you heard, in the palace, in Constantinople, that Theodore's army in the Levant has been destroyed? The Prince has been killed?"

The Eastern Empress's face paled, then furious anger burned through the shock and her eyes flashed. "Killed? Not by my eyes! That wretched, horse-loving traitor! I assure you, Lord Galen, that we've heard nothing of any failure on his part here. Oh no, only reports of victory over some towns and estates in the back of beyond! Miserable peasant . . ."

Galen tried to catch the Greek woman's eyes, but she was shouting at the priest behind her. "Lady Martina! Stop shouting at the boy, you'll disturb his concentration. You say that Theodore is alive?"

"Yes," she said, throwing a slipper at the young priest. "Letters arrived from him this week."

Galen digested this news, then said, "Pray tell me, is Heraclius there? Can you send a messenger for him? It is most urgent."

The Eastern Empress turned back and shook her head. Helena thought that the girl looked like she was going to cry. "I can't! He won't see *anyone,* even me. He's been terribly sick, Lord Galen, since he left Antioch. He hides in his rooms and won't come out. Everyone is terrified!"

Galen cursed, striking the granite block with the flat of his hand. "Martina, listen. If Theodore has sent no word of his loss, then none of the regional commanders can prepare . . . these rebels may overwhelm the whole of the Levantine coast, even threatening Antioch or Tarsus, before anyone can stop them. If Heraclius is ill, you must take steps to alert the fleet and all of the garrison commands. Can this be done?"

Martina bit at her hand, swaying a little. "Perhaps! I don't know . . . no one here will listen to me. I was trying to get things done, but the ministers have banded together against me. I have no power to order the fleet to sea, or anything . . ."

Helena stepped out from behind her husband, drawing

Martina's attention. The girl seemed to take heart from her appearance. Helena leaned close to the whirling, glowing sphere and smiled gently.

"Martina, dear, you mustn't listen to those old men. Can you trust your bodyguards, the . . . the Faithful Men, the Varangians?"

A smile flickered across the brown-haired girl's face and she nodded. "Yes, Empress! Rufio and the Northmen are still here. They are helping me."

"Good. Write letters to each of the garrison commanders—Rufio will know who they are—and have the Faithful carry them for you, in secret. Do this straightaway! Then, after you've seen the messengers away, tell these logothetes and ministers what you have learned."

Martina nodded, taking a writing tablet out of her cloak. "I will. I will, right away."

The two women's eyes met in the burning radiance of the telecast, and Helena saw the girl smile, taking heart from her. Then the buzzing slowed and the vision passed, the bronze rings rattling slowly down onto the granite block. Helena turned away, feeling a flush of heat on her face. It felt good, here in the cold room where the device was stored.

Galen was watching her, his thin face marked by a long-familiar half-smile. "It's not enough, then," he said, "to boss *one* emperor around?"

Helena sniffed and flipped the hood of her cloak up, saying, "Isn't it time for bed?"

THE TEMPLE OF ASKLEPIOS, BELOW PERGAMON

)━(

Tarsus, priest of the temple and initiate of the mysteries of Apollo and his mortal son, Asklepios, drank deep from a curved red cup. Wine spilled at the edge of his mouth and dribbled through his beard. The liquid stained his tunic, but he was past caring. He set the *kylix* down on the common table.

". . . and then he was gone." Tarsus wiped his mouth. "Leaving my cell filled with writhing life and this . . . girl . . . behind."

The priest motioned to the still, silent figure of the young woman that stood against the wall of the common room. She breathed, her chest rising and falling. She could hear, for she obeyed commands that were addressed to her. She seemed, to all examination, to be in perfect health. But her rich, dark brown eyes stared straight ahead, acknowledging nothing.

"It is not a living girl," rumbled the eldest of those seated around the table. Demetrios was a veritable bear of a man with a carefully clipped white beard and massive shoulders. "It has no spirit, no *ka,* to give it life."

The other priests nodded solemnly. This sad matter had occurred many times before in the annals of their order. It was lamentable, but the ancients were clear on what must be done.

"Yes, it must be destroyed before a malign spirit enters the body." Demetrios put aside his own cup, signaling to the others that it was time to discuss hard business. Tarsus nodded as well, though he was loath to give up the sweet grape. His nerves were still frayed. The depth to which his old student had fallen embarrassed and frightened him.

"Tarsus, you did well in this. Had you angered him, or incited his wrath, we might all be dead. From the words you report, there is madness in the boy. He has trespassed into forbidden knowledge and become consumed by it."

The other priests murmured in assent. Tarsus could see the depth of the shock and horror on their faces as he had related the Prince's words. It had taken some time, for chills and uncontrollable trembling had seized him when he relived those moments in his cell.

"Master," ventured Tarsus, though he wondered if such things should be spoken aloud, "can it be true, what he said about the Conqueror and the first Caesar?"

Demetrios' eyebrows bunched and a grave look stole over him. Thinking, he cracked his knuckles. "Such a thing has never occurred before . . . the matter of the death of a man is well known. The girl's state shows well what happens if the *body* is revived. But without the ka? No. If what he says is true, something more must have transpired."

Tarsus licked his lips, for there was a horrible fear building in his heart. "What . . . what if the boy could bring their spirits back from beyond the Black River?"

The other priests hissed in surprise and not a few turned pale. "Impossible!"

Demetrios turned, glaring at the priest who had spoken out of turn. "Nothing is impossible, Epicharmus. But Hades does not yield his harvest lightly. Only gods have dared such a thing and succeeded, as the old tales tell." Demetrios turned back to Tarsus.

"Is the boy a god?"

Tarsus shook his head. He did not know. "He was tired, master, and giddy with exhaustion. He did not *seem* a god! The young man that I trained, here in these very precincts, was no god. He bled when cut, he slept, he shit. . . ."

Demetrios frowned again, his forehead dark like a thunderstorm. "It is said that some men, heroes, have gone into the underworld and stolen back souls from Hades' cold domain. The gods guided those men. Such a thing has not happened in millennia. . . . Would we not feel it, if the gods walked among men once more?"

The eldest priest rose and turned, bowing before the figure of Apollo that stood in a niche at the end of the dining hall. The cold marble stared back at him with shining abalone eyes, one hand raised. The stone did not speak, and the other priests rose, white robes rustling, and bowed as well. Then Demetrios sat again, his huge hands on the tabletop.

"Something has happened which we do not understand," said the eldest in a pedantic, lecturing voice. "This is puzzling, yet it may be explained if we discover more of the matter. We do know, however, that a member of our order has become a danger to every living being in the Empire. We must send a messenger immediately to Constantinople to warn the Emperor and our brothers there of what has transpired."

Tarsus felt his stomach heave. This would reflect very badly on the order. Demetrios had thought of that too.

"He will not be pleased with us." The high priest's voice was leaden. "There have been rumors—some of which you have doubtless heard—that the Emperor is sick. This is true. It is also true that our brothers in the capital, despite great efforts, have failed to cure him of this malady. We have been banned from the Imperial presence. It may transpire, if our enemies among the other priesthoods take advantage of our position, that we will be banned from the capital."

Some of the priests in the room had not heard this news and cried out in dismay. Demetrios silenced them with a black glare. He pointed at two of the younger acolytes with a blunt finger.

"Take this body away and prepare it for cremation. When the sun rises, it will go back to the gods on a pillar of fire and smoke. Tarsus, you must prepare yourself for a journey. The Western Emperor must also know of this, and hear our apology from reliable lips. Emperor Galen knows you, has broken bread with you in his very house. You will take ship to Rome as soon as a ship can be hired. I will compose a letter to carry to him."

Demetrios rose and the other priests followed. The two acolytes took the girl by her hands and led her out of the dining hall. Tarsus, despite the admonition, tarried, watching the high priest with a sick look on his face. When the others were gone, Demetrios raised an eyebrow. "Yes?"

"Master . . . what if the boy *can* bring the dead back to life, but not with their original spirit? What if he can make something like the ka from whole cloth? We do not know what the ka is, or how it manifests itself in a newborn child, but what if this stripling has divined that secret?"

Demetrios shook his head sharply. "Impossible. That is the realm of the gods alone. Some things are beyond the reach of man."

Then the high priest went out, the slap of his sandals very loud in the quiet room. Tarsus followed, heart heavy and his mind a chaos of horrible thoughts.

The smell of resin and oil filled the yard, making the girl's nostrils flare. She stood quietly beside a pyre of pine logs, watching the two acolytes drag the last bough into place. They were sweating, not used to such heavy work. Distantly, a bell was ringing, summoning them to supper.

"You stay here," said the eldest of the boys. The girl did not react. The sound of their feet receded down the passageway.

Night filled the courtyard and then the stars emerged from the black firmament. They twinkled in the thick air, obscured by a thin haze of cooking smoke rising from the city. The girl remained motionless, though her legs began to tremble with fatigue. The moon idled up in the east.

After a time, there was the patter of small, soft feet on the rectangular red tiles. A tiny dark shape padded up to the girl. In the moonlight, yellow eyes winked and a small red mouth opened in a yawn.

"Mrrrow!" the little black cat said imperiously.

Without looking back, the little cat darted down the porch and into the darkness. The girl stirred and followed, her bare feet silent on the tile.

Beyond the temple, the girl climbed a grassy hillside in the moonlight, heading north.

THE GARDENS OF THE BUCOLEON, CONSTANTINOPLE

M artina moved one of her stones, closing off a diagonal. She smiled and leaned back among the cushions in her chair. Her opponent, one of the maids, scrunched her face up, leaning over the round board. The girl was very close to losing, but Martina did not care. It was a fine day, the bright blue sky filled with fluffy white clouds. The usual cold wind from the north had gentled to a breeze, stirring the willows and pines that were planted in the garden. The Empress took her ease on a wooden platform built among flowering bushes and shady trees at the eastern end of the palace grounds. The platform was on a bit of a hill, though Martina knew that it was really the crumbling foundations of an old dining hall. Some Emperor had covered it with dirt and set his gardeners to shape it into a fine, grassy outcropping. The platform itself held a fine view of the Propontis and the distant shore of Chalcedon and Asia. Striped awnings of cloth shaded her from the direct sun.

Things had markedly improved of late, now that she and that dear boy Alexos had reached an equitable arrangement. The girl placed one of her stones. Without looking,

Martina placed one of her own and idly reversed four of her opponent's.

"Oooh! Mistress, you are too clever."

Martina smiled, feeling the soft touch of the wind in her hair. She took great comfort from the secrets that the telecast yielded up to her. She knew the full depth of the confusion and terror that gripped the Imperial government. Indeed, she had even ventured to look in upon the Master of the Tombs in his dusty, dank lair at the base of the hill. He was just a man, albeit a man with expensive and refined tastes. These secrets, even unused, calmed her heart and gave her what she desired most greedily—knowledge of her enemies. Now they seemed small and petty. In truth, she did not even feel the need to move against them.

Let them cower in their precious offices and piddle themselves!

"Arsinoë, you are too hard on yourself. You're not looking ahead. See, what will happen if I place this stone here?"

Martina bent over the board, her fingers moving quickly amongst the stones, showing the Axumite girl what would happen in the next five moves. It was a child's game, but it served to while the time away. Rufio would come soon, bringing her the latest news of her husband's condition. At the thought, the Empress felt a little dread enter her again. Heraclius' health did not seem to be improving, despite nightly doses of the Northmen's medicine.

I wonder if it will truly work, she thought, biting her thumb. *If it does not, then there will be a struggle over Heraclius' sons. . . . Praise Hera that his first wife is safely dead!*

Seeing that she had been overtaken by a foul mood, the maids quietly departed, leaving Martina alone on the platform. Their mistress had only very recently paid any attention to them at all, emerging after a year of seclusion in her apartments to be seen in the palace itself. The weight of opprobrium that fell upon her from the nobles, the temple priests and the ministers was heavy. She was prone to fierce rages if bothered while she was brooding. Arsinoë, her liquid brown eyes troubled, was the last to leave, carefully drawing the curtains of the awning closed. Then she descended the hill to a bench where the roses were in bloom and sat, waiting for her mistress to call for her.

Martina roused herself from ugly thoughts and stood, strolling to the side of the platform facing the sea. She bit her lip, looking out on the blue waters. At the urging and good advice of the Western Empress, she had sent out messengers to the *drungaros* of the fleet and the governors of all the provinces, warning them of Theodore's defeat. A new army would have to be assembled as well, to reclaim the lost provinces. She had received no word back yet, and she wondered if the men in those distant cities and towns would believe the messengers.

She had refrained, for the moment, from issuing the rescript under Heraclius' seal. Instead, she had ordered Rufio to compose and sign the letters. They did not carry orders, after all, just news and a warning. She hoped that it would rouse the provincial leaders to action. Still worried, she patted at her hair. It was coiled and curled up on her head in a Western style. The maids had proclaimed it lovely, after they had finished tormenting her with their hot iron rods and combs. At least it was different from the usual tangle.

The priest Alexos thought it beautiful too, but he was only a boy. She sniffed at the thought of him. Still, he seemed quite taken with her when she visited him in the old library. Since discovering the telecast, Martina had been careful to visit the priest every day, taking him his food. He was lonely, mewed up in that moldy basement, and seemed to take great consolation from her visits.

And he does show me the most interesting things!

"My lady?"

Martina stifled a start of surprise and turned slowly, her

fists clenched. Then she sighed out loud in relief. It was only Rufio, come up from the little trail that led up to the platform from the seaward side. He bowed as he stepped up onto the wooden deck, ducking under the low overhang.

"What news, dear Rufio?" Martina stepped to her chair and made to sit, but he made a halting motion.

"I've just heard," he said, his voice clipped and quick. "Prince Theodore has entered the city. He came by a swift galley from Rhodes. Seeking, I warrant, to outrace the news of his defeat." Rufio grinned. There was no love lost between the Prince and the captain of the Faithful.

"What will he do?" Martina gathered up her skirts and kicked off the light silk slippers that Arsinoë and the others had forced upon her. "He must seek audience with my husband, trying to explain his failure."

"My very thought," Rufio said. "Your maids are on the other side of the hill; we may depart unobserved and, later, you may return the same way."

"So secretive, Rufio! What do you intend?" Martina put her hand on his shoulder, feeling the thick ridges of muscle under his tunic. She smiled up at him. He did not smile back.

"There are secret ways, my lady. One of them may let you hear what is said between the brothers. I will have to be in attendance myself."

For a moment, Martina's heart thudded in fear, wondering if the guard captain had also discovered the secret of the hidden library and its treasure.

No, she scolded herself, *Alexos would have told me if the Faithful knew.* . . . "Lead on, then, and show me these secret ways."

Martina knelt in darkness, her eye pressed to a round oculus cut into the wall of the tunnel. The air pressed around her, musty with age and dust. The oculus cut through a foot or more of brick and was covered on the far side by painted cloth behind a carved stone screen. To the unknowing eye, the wall of the Emperor's audience chamber seemed solid marble.

The sound of boots on stone echoed through the oculus and Martina tried to calm her heart. She was afraid of discovery, though only the treachery of Rufio could reveal her. Gritting her teeth, she forced down the fear.

"Dearest brother, my heart is glad to see you at last."

That was Theodore. Martina wondered how he looked. She could see no more than light and shadow through the oculus. He sounded as hale, hearty and prideful as ever. In the darkness, her mouth tightened in a snarl. His hair was probably perfect and his armor immaculate.

"I have not . . . seen you . . . in some time, brother."

Martina bit her thumb to keep from crying out. This was the voice of her husband, but it was a dreadful, watery croak, not the rich, commanding voice of memory. Rufio had reported no change in his physical condition in recent days, but it sounded like he was at the edge of death itself.

"Brother, you set me to punish the rebellion in lesser Syria! It has taken some time, I must report. However, things are close to a conclusion, so I have returned, fearing for your health."

Another croaking sound came, like that of some monstrous amphibian from the Nile swamps. Martina covered her ears, trying to blot out the horrible sound.

Rufio's jaw clenched tight. His dark eyes, slits beneath the visor of his helmet, glinted as he watched the reaction of the *great* prince. Theodore, stepping forward to declaim before his brother, halted, his face ashen at the cold laughter. Rufio glanced down out of the corner of his eye.

The Faithful had carried the Emperor into the sitting room on a reclining wicker chair. It was well padded with the finest silk and light, downy cushions. The Emperor lay in it, his naked body covered by an opaque dark-red drape. Only his hands and face were exposed. Rufio knew, from the muffled cries the Emperor made when they covered him up, even the gossamer weight of the linen was a cruel torment. Of course, one could make out the distorted outline of the Emperor's body through the covering, and see the thick gray fingers lying on the cushions. Even the Emperor's face was dreadful to look upon. It had not puffed up with the foul clear fluid that tormented his limbs, but it had grown ancient and withered, fever-bright eyes staring out of gray flesh.

"You . . . amuse me . . . brother." Heraclius, with a great effort, moved one of his fingers.

Behind the Great Prince, four of the Faithful Guard entered the chamber and closed the doors behind them. Theodore heard them, heard the door close, but he did not turn. Rufio noted that the Great Prince's left eye had developed a tic, but the man's face was impassive.

"I am glad, brother, to bring you some small joy. But I do not know *how* I amuse."

"You . . . know. You . . . dissemble poorly. Rufio."

The Emperor coughed. Yellow phlegm dotted the dark red cloth on his chest. When the Emperor's breathing had resumed, Rufio squared his shoulders, still facing straight ahead, and said:

"Theodore, son of Heraclius the Elder, brother of the Avtokrator of the Romans and the Greeks, you were charged with the suppression of illegal and immoral revolt and unrest in the provinces of Syria, Judea and Nabatea. Entrusted to you for this matter were eight legions of Imperial soldiers as well as numerous auxiliaries, mercenaries and other specialist cohorts. The Emperor has learned, from loyal and conscientious servants who love the state and the Emperor as their own father, that you have failed in this. Your army has been broken and scattered. Many towns have fallen to these rebels, and more are under siege. Further, you have ignored the able advice of those set to counsel you in war and in peace, and you have abandoned the field of battle to the enemy."

Theodore's face, normally a handsome tan, turned

white. He spared an instant of sheer hatred for Rufio, then bent on one knee to the floor, prostrating himself before his brother. Sweat beaded on his neck and forehead. "Brother, these are lies! I assure you that the army remains whole, though we have suffered some small reverses. I hurried back to the capital to seek your advice and assistance in how to bring these troubling matters to a swift conclusion. Certain persons, disloyal to our brotherly love, have exaggerated and falsified these claims!"

Heraclius moved another finger, then lay still.

Rufio nodded to the two guardsmen standing closest to the Prince. With ill-concealed grins, the two Scandians stepped forward and dragged the Prince to his feet. Theodore snarled at their touch, then shook off their hands. Heraclius watched him from beneath lidded eyes.

"You . . . crawl before me . . . hoping that I will make good your . . . failure."

Theodore made to speak again, but Rufio raised his left hand. It was clad in a mailed glove. The Prince's eyes were drawn to the bright metal. The guard captain shook his head slightly. Theodore closed his mouth with a snap. Behind the Prince, a guard lowered his stabbing sword.

"I . . . will not," the Emperor continued, his voice a bubbling, watery rasp. "You have . . . shown yourself . . . unworthy of the trust I have . . . shown you. Heraclius loves . . . his brother Theodore. But the . . . Empire . . . cannot support . . . your largess of folly."

Rufio saw that the Emperor was exhausted. He took a half-step forward and drew a parchment from the belt at his waist. Carefully, with slow and studied motions, he unfolded the paper. All this time, Theodore was staring at his brother in horror, unable to speak.

"Theodore, son of Heraclius the Elder," Rufio said, "you are stripped of your posts, that of consul of the East, of tribune, of commander of the armies of the Levantine coast. Those estates and properties that you hold in the name of the Emperor are taken from you. Until further notice you will remain within the grounds of your residence here in the city and await the Emperor's pleasure."

Rufio closed the paper with a snap and returned it to his belt.

Theodore stepped back, brilliant fury apparent in his face and the line of his body. "I am a loyal and devoted servant of the Empire, and you, my brother. I will obey your orders and remain within my residence here in the city."

He bowed and Rufio was forced to acknowledge the man's presence of mind. An unwary outburst, perhaps laced by threats, would have allowed the captain of the Faithful to strike the man down. Treason was a chancy thing, and Rufio would have taken even a taint of it to rid himself of an enemy as volatile and dangerous as the Prince.

Theodore stood, smiled tightly at the guard captain and then turned on his heel.

Rufio nodded to the guards at the door and they parted, allowing the Prince to pass between them. The door swung open and Theodore strode out, his head high. The Faithful watched him pass, their faces marked by respect and hidden laughter. Rufio knew what they were thinking—no one liked the Prince, but he bore himself like a man and a warrior, even on what must be a black day for his ambition.

"Rufio . . ." The guard captain knelt beside his Emperor. Heraclius' voice was faint with exhaustion. "Close . . . close the shutters. The sun is too . . . bright."

"Of course, my lord."

Rufio stood and motioned for the Faithful to come and lift the chair. There were no shutters in the room, nor any windows. The Emperor had mistaken an oil lamp for the sun. Sviod and the others bore him away, hopefully already asleep. For a moment, the Greek stood thinking, then he heard a faint, muffled cough from the nearby wall.

Ah, he thought and then hurried away through the dim

corridors. It was a roundabout way to retrieve the Empress from her hiding place.

Martina sneezed, then batted Arsinoë's hand away when the maid tried to dab her nose with a cloth. "Silly girl, I can do that myself."

The Empress snatched the cloth from the Axumite's hand and sneezed again. She would clean her own nose! Arsinoë fluttered around for a moment, trying to be helpful, then Martina pointed stiffly at the rose bower and the bench where the rest of the maids were sitting. To Rufio's eye, they seemed quite glum.

"Get to your sewing," Martina snapped. "If I need help walking or something, I'll call you!"

Rufio watched the maid scurry down the hill. When he was sure that the girl was safely out of earshot, he turned back to the Empress. She was looking quite doleful, with cobwebs in her hair and smudges of dust and grime on her hands. Luckily, she often looked like this after hours of poring over ancient tomes and scrolls.

"You heard," he said, "what the Emperor intends for his brother."

"Yes," replied Martina in a surly voice. "The great ass will loll about his town house here, entertaining his sly friends and plotting against me and the Emperor. By the gods, he should be banished to some small island without food or water, inhabited by fierce dogs tearing at his vitals!"

Rufio raised an eyebrow, then waited until the Empress had simmered down to a low boil.

"The Emperor is growing stronger, I think. A month ago, he could not have managed such a long discussion. I have some hope that he will recover from this affliction. Until then, you must be patient."

"I am patient," Martina snapped. She dragged cobwebs from her hair, scowling, with an ivory comb. "Can you place him under close arrest? Prevent anyone from seeing him?"

Rufio shook his head. The authority of the Faithful did not extend out of the palace. "The Emperor would have to declare such a thing. Shall I put the matter to him?"

Martina considered, her hands toying with the comb. "Perhaps . . . if a moment comes when a suggestion would be favorably received. My husband holds a great love for his brother. Even with this debacle in Syria! If we press him too hard he will become stubborn. I will keep an eye on the Prince myself, to make sure that he does not cause any trouble."

The guard captain did not react, though he wondered at the Empress's strange confidence. Rufio excused himself and descended the grassy hill. Behind him, the Empress was still combing her hair and muttering. *If it is not one thing,* he worried, *it's another. What is she up to?*

※ ※ ※

THE TOWN OF NARNI, EAST OF ROME
ON THE LATIN PLAIN

)※(

Diana stood, half-shadowed, in an alcove high on the sidewall of the theater. Torches sputtered on the rank of balconies below her, casting a bright, flickering light across the arches and balustrades of the monumental backdrop. The *scaenae* rose three stories high, each floor fronted by columns, embrasures and recessed alcoves. Below this wall there was a long, rectangular stage of smooth wooden planks over a brick superstructure. In front of the stage were a low wall and then the half-circle of an orchestra pit.

Night was falling, leaving the sky a deep purple black,

streaked with long, thin clouds glowing like fresh ingots in the light of the fading sun. A long day of celebration was winding down. As Diana watched, a troupe of tragic actors in brightly colored robes and enormous wooden masks were vacating the stage. The four men, having taken their bows to desultory applause from the crowd, were exiting through the stage passage directly beneath her.

Curious to see them, she leaned out over the thirty-foot drop. One hand was wrapped in a stay line for the canvas sunshade. From her current vantage, Diana couldn't see the bustling temporary village behind the amphitheater, but she knew that a crowd of buskers, sweetmeat sellers, priests, acolytes, prostitutes, citizens and merchants were busy there.

The actors disappeared into the passage. Diana swung back into the alcove, feeling the play of her muscles. She was feeling healthy for the first time in weeks. Vitellix had been working her hard, making her run, jump, climb, crawl and work out on the wire. It seemed rushed, but she had not protested. They fed, clothed and cared for her. If she could repay them in this way, then she would. Today, clad in the tight white *strophium* and short kilt of the flyer, she felt light and strong.

Diana grinned happily, watching the few people in the audience stretch and yawn. The tragedians had executed a lamentably long and poorly done version of Pomponius Secundus' *Aeneas*. From the snickering comments of the theater workers handling the lamps and cables, she gathered that the actors were local amateurs. Little Ila said the play itself was poorly regarded. Diana didn't care, really, she was too excited about finally testing herself on the wire.

Vitellix walked out onto the stage below, followed by Ila holding a tall pole wrapped in leather bindings, and then Otho and Franco. The troupe master was wearing a loose, dark shirt bundled at the waist and tight-fitting hose. His long, white mustaches were waxed in smooth, swoop-

ing tusks. He descended a set of steps at the center of the
stage. Ila, who would not be performing tonight, was wearing a fantastic mask of feathers and colored cloth. She
stopped at the center of the stage and slid the pole into a
round hole cut into the stage. Then she knelt, thin, little
hands gripping the leather-wrapped staff. Otho and Franco,
taking deliberate steps, walked out at an angle from the
pole, forming a triangle with Vitellix at its head.

"For the edification, amusement and pleasure of those
attending these sacred games, I present the Mani Lughi
from ancient and noble Narbonensis. We beg your indulgence in the performance of our sacred duty."

Vitellix was standing on the orator's stone in the orchestra pit of the theater. His voice echoed and rattled from
the high arches behind the top row of seats, fifty feet above
him and three hundred feet away. Most of the audience
ignored him. Despite the high hopes of the whole troupe,
Vitellix had only managed to secure them a brief appearance sandwiched in between the tragedians and the main
act of the day, a famous pantomime named Nurnius, who
had come from Rome itself. Diana had never seen a pantomime herself—or none that her troubled memory allowed—and the others were excited at the prospect of
seeing a master in action.

Vitellix, as was the custom of his troupe, bowed to the
audience, then turned smartly and bowed to the stage and
the statues of the gods on the upper tier of the backdrop.
Under his breath, he recited a prayer that Diana had half
heard once before. This time, she caught none of the
words, which were in an unfamiliar, barbarian tongue.

I am not from Narbonensis, she thought, absurdly
pleased with the discovery.

"Begin!" Vitellix shouted and then ran up the stairs, his
thick, powerful legs pumping hard. Like a bolt, he shot up
onto the stage, took two running strides and sprang up into
the air. Diana, even though she had seen the old man practice before, held her breath as he twisted in midair and

seized the pole with both hands. It twisted under his momentum, bending into a graceful curve. As it bent, Vitellix let his legs, held tightly together, ride up into the sky, pointing to the heavens. The pole completed its arc, brushing the stage floor, and Vitellix, with a powerful flex of his shoulders, flipped off of it to land upright and facing the audience.

He bowed, smiling. In the audience, one small girl, sitting beside her parents, clapped for a moment. Then her mother gave her a look and she put her hands in her lap. In the alcove, Diana felt like clapping too, but knew it was not time for such approbation.

That must wait, she remembered, *until all of the sacrifices are complete.*

While the stage master made his exit, Otho and Franco paced to opposite ends of the stage. Ila remained kneeling on the wooden floor. The flexible pole had sprung back upright. Otho bowed to Franco, indicating that he should go first.

Franco bowed in return, indicating that, no, his brother should precede him.

Otho shook his head angrily, waving for the other man to proceed. Franco did not.

Otho scowled and looked to the audience for guidance. Save for the little girl, they were ignoring him. A vendor moved through the sparse crowd with a tray of roasted glazed duck. Some of the people shouted at the man to get his attention. He was doing a fine business this evening amongst those too drunk to leave the amphitheater to reach one of the food stalls. Otho shrugged, then wagged an admonishing finger at his brother. Franco turned his back and gazed up at the stars.

Otho stamped his foot, then made an exasperated motion and ostentatiously clapped his hands together as if to remove dust. Franco spied a nightjar flitting amongst the torches overhead and began to follow it back down the stage, head turned up and walking backwards.

His brother, seemingly moved beyond outrage, suddenly sprinted forward, bare torso gleaming in the light of the torches. Franco stopped suddenly as the nightjar disappeared into the darkness beyond the lights. Otho barreled forward, slamming into the staff with his right shoulder. As before, the pole bent and he flowed into the motion, suddenly bent forward at full length, body held parallel to the floor, his outstretched fingers mere inches from his brother's head.

The little girl in the audience made a muffled gasp.

Franco put a hand to his chin, puzzled, and stepped away.

The pole rebounded, flinging Otho sharply backwards. The acrobat flipped up at the same time, letting the snap of the pole flip him head over heels. Otho sailed through the air and lighted, still holding onto the upper part of the pole, back where he had started, facing his brother, who had turned around.

Franco stamped his foot and made an angry gesture. Otho released the bent pole, sneering, and turned his back. The tip of the pole whistled through the air, arcing sharply at Franco. Just as it reached the end of its swing, Franco snatched it out of the air, took a firm grip, and sprang upwards with all the strength in his powerful legs.

Otho, feigning indifference, planted his feet and put his hands on his head, fingers intertwined, palms up.

Franco flew up with the pole, swinging his feet into line with the swift arc. The pole was thrumming with tension as it whipped him overhead and then down. Franco's feet landed solidly in Otho's palms and the twin took the blow with a sagging squat. Then Otho surged up, his muscles rippling, sweat slick on his body, and flung his brother skyward.

Franco reversed his vault, his grip spreading on the pole as he flew through the air. This time, the pole bent in a sharper half-circle, guided by the placement of his hands, and Franco landed lightly on the pine boards. He released the pole and it shivered upright. As soon as the vibration settled, Ila lifted the pole from the recess in the floor and undid a length of cloth wrapped around the base.

Springing up in a somersault, she let the long banner snap out and then made a quick figure eight in the air. The cloth snapped and fluttered, making a swift green and gold sign in the air. This done, she ran off the stage to the right, with Otho and Franco behind her, their arms swinging stiff in long arcs at their side.

In the alcove, high above the stage, Diana felt her limbs tremble in anticipation. Her skin seemed hot and everything acquired a preternatural clarity. She began taking deep, slow breaths, nostrils flaring. Her chest flexed with each breath. Reaching up, she took hold of the wooden rungs of the ladder leading up to the top of the backdrop. She swarmed up, breathing steady and even, and stepped out onto the roof of the theater. At the other end of the rooftop Otho was waiting for her with the flying wire, sweating from his swift climb up the opposite ladder.

Diana paced forward, aware that the audience below could see her as a white figure silhouetted against the dark sky. Otho crouched down, letting the roof hide him in shadow. He held up the wooden handle of the wire, tightly wrapped with leather, for her.

Remember to let it slack as you set down.

She nodded to herself, hearing Dummonus' voice in her mind. The Gaul had drilled her on the art of landing from the wire a thousand times. She wondered, again, what she had done in her forgotten life. Whatever it had been, she had gained enormous upper-torso and arm strength to go with wire-fine scars crisscrossing her arms and chest. Dummonus had been impressed. His art required tremendous strength and body control. Now, she could repay Vitellix for a little of his hospitality.

The wire in Otho's hand was a heavy cord of tightly woven silk. Of all of the things in the troupe's wagons, the flying wire was the only thing locked away in an iron chest with a heavy cruciform lock. The value of the fabric was far more than the wagons, mules, props and baggage. Diana sighted down the length of the backdrop. Sixty feet of sloping tile roof and wooden walkway separated her from the far end of the stage. Down below, Vitellix, Franco, Ila and Dummonus were hooking a finely woven sisal net to the walls of the theater.

Otho, watching them finish, clapped his hand on the wooden walkway, and she sprinted down the length of the rooftop.

The wire was waiting, swinging from a contraption Dummonus had hooked into place on the central hub of the awning cables. One end of the flying wire was attached to the ring by a swiveling joint. The other was held tight in Otho's hand, his whole body straining against the weight of the line.

Diana hit the end of the rooftop at a dead run, right hand slapped into the wooden handle. Otho rolled away. She soared off the end of the backdrop and swung her legs out stiff behind her. Her right arm burned with the effort of keeping herself at right angles to the rope. Her left jutted straight out. Momentum swept her out and down, in a great arc, over the startled heads of the audience.

Faces flashed past, mouths wide, and Diana heard only the excited cries of a little girl jumping up and down in the stands below. It was a giddy sensation, swooping through the air, freed of the chains of the earth. Above and behind her, the ball joint whined as it spun. The cables and oculus ring groaned as her weight and centrifugal force torqued the assembly.

The swing of the wire brought her back towards the backdrop with dizzying speed. She brought her knees up a little and touched down, springing from column to column. The people in the audience gasped, seeing her running along the face of a vertical wall. The little girl shrieked with delight and her mother stared, slack jawed.

Diana kicked off the last column and into a turn. This

time, as she soared over the heads of the audience, she was very close, only a dozen feet away. She swung into line with the rope, bringing her legs up, stiff and close together. Her momentum shifted and her speed picked up. Coming out of the fly-by over the consular seats, she twisted sideways, breaking her momentum, slacking the rope. For a single moment, the wire went neutral in her hand and she alighted with a heavy *smack* of bare feet on stone in the round alcove on the third floor of the backdrop.

She turned, the wire still in her hand, and bowed deeply to the audience. Her arm was in agony and sweat was pouring off her body. She felt exalted and giddy, the world perfectly clear and distinct. The little girl was clapping her hands together as she jumped up and down.

Diana looked down and smiled, then bowed again and stepped away, out of the light. The audience suddenly found its voice, chattering and exclaiming in delight. Joyful sounds rose up in the wide bowl of the amphitheater.

Diana sat on the ground in the camp, arms stretched over Otho and Franco's knees. They were slowly massaging her muscles from fingertip to shoulder blade with scented oil and camphor. The art took a fierce toll on the arms and upper body of an aerialist, particularly when using the free wire. Some of the citizens attending the festival had sent the artists wine and roasted meat to show their appreciation. They had eaten well. Diana licked her lips, thinking of the fine lamb shank she had gnawed to the bone. The wine had been better than average, too, and she felt at peace with the world. Exhausted, but at peace. Having two men devoting their undivided attention to her didn't hurt either.

"... *still* the Emperor demurs on this matter of the games! It is past comprehension!"

Vitellix had spent the day making the rounds of the other performers' wagons, sharing a cup here and there with the actors, beast trainers, gladiators and fire eaters.

He seemed disheartened by what he had learned. Dummonus sat placidly, watching the older man declaim. Ila was curled up beside their fire, already asleep.

"Evil signs have been reported in Arretium and Ravenna. One of the bear trainers from the north told me that he had seen, *himself,* a sacrifice at the temple of Jupiter bleed black blood and worms. The skies remain dark and clouded with poisonous fumes and mists. In the southern lands, the earth shakes and rumbles with Poseidon's wrath."

The Gaul shook his head sadly, his old bald head gleaming in the firelight. "The Emperor is like unto a god, the bridge between man and the divine, yet he must not anger the king of the heavens! Worse, every *lanista* and *editore* in the Empire has kenned the profit to be made from these games when they *finally* occur! Our chances of securing a spot grow smaller with each day . . ."

"No one else," Dummonus said, "can boast of a tandem on the wire as we make."

Vitellix nodded, his face still glum. "There will be riots and unrest in the city soon, or so it is rumored. Perhaps the games will be canceled."

Dummonus smiled faintly. He and Vitellix had known each other for a long time. "I think not. This is Rome, remember? The citizens love their *panes et circi* more than the gods."

"True." Vitellix straightened up, drawing upon some inner strength. "I have to find us a patron, which is unlikely if we are touring the sticks. Tomorrow, friends, we shall make our way to Rome and see what we may see."

)(

The sound of waves crashing on rocks rolled out of the darkness. The shore was close, booming like a great drum, and the wave surge under the boat echoed each crash. Zoë was tied to the short-stepped mast of the second boat. Within an hour, the sun would rise, but now she was shivering in darkness, eyes closed in concentration. Around her, men labored on the sweeps, driving the boat downshore, with the wind whispering out of the right quarter.

The wind was supposed to die down by night. It had not. The sea had been rough when they had pushed the boats out into the surf at Krokodeilon. Two boats had keeled over in heavy waves, crushing many of their passengers, and then the rest had drowned in the rough water. There was no good harborage at Krokodeilon, only a steep beach and a landward wind.

The only good harbor was somewhere ahead. The roar of the sea led them on, for the Romans had built a vast breakwater out from the barren shore. When Zoë concentrated she could hear a wind bell sounding over the crash of the waves. A light, dull and green in the fog, gleamed and shifted in the sky.

"We're too close to the breakwater," Zoë called to the men on the steering oars. "Swing to sea." They struggled manfully to turn the boat away, across the rolling waves.

Zoë let herself relax into the ropes that bound her to the mast. She grimaced at the night, feeling the enormous strain of keeping the air cold. Fog boiled and writhed around the boats as they crabbed out to sea, trying to avoid the massive breakwater lurking in the landward darkness. By any right, the wind should have torn the fog from the wavetops and pushed it inland over the miles of sandy flat lying behind the harbor. Zoë couldn't stop the wind— it had been sweeping for hundreds of miles over the open water—but she could keep the air cold above the warm sea.

In any case, the wind was heavy from the southwest and that was exactly what she wanted. From that quarter, it blew directly into the anchorages on the outside of the breakwater, keeping the ships there battened down.

Veils of mist parted and something loomed out of the darkness. Zoë let some of her thought seep into sight and the darkness faded, replaced by the glittering shapes of the hidden world. A towering statue hove into view as the boat rode up on the crest of a wave. A man's face a dozen feet high jutted from the darkness. Behind him stood two more towering figures.

Supporting them, rising steeply from the massive bulk of the harbor entrance, was a slab of stone sixty feet high. The stone men faced the sea, heads turned to the west.

"Turn in, turn in!" Zoë suddenly remembered that the men on the oars could not see in the darkness. Off to the right, the green light flickered again, eighty feet above the water. In its muted gleam, another set of colossi were revealed. The entrance to the harbor was a hundred feet wide, filled with the boil and churn of the sea. Zoë breathed a prayer that she was riding a shallow-draft fishing boat. Her witch sight revealed jagged wrecks beneath the surging waters.

The lead boat, shrouded lanterns bobbing at the stern to guide the following ships, passed between the colossi. Then Zoë's boat was surging into the great sweep of the harbor. To her right, the watching gods passed away into the murk, their crowns of green fire swallowed by darkness. Zoë shuddered, chilled, and turned her attention to the pattern she was holding in the sea.

In a way, it was an easy matter to force her will in the hidden world upon the liquid gleam of the air, slowing down the flickering, gelid sparks that sped over the waters. As they slowed in their frantic dance, a vast and invisible swarm of minute bees, the temperature in the air dropped. At the same time, all that vigorous energy had to go somewhere, so she urged it into the rolling surface of the waves. Then the sea warmed, excited to infinitesimal motion. Where the chilling air and the turbid, warm sea met, mist boiled up. Zoë's forehead creased with effort. With the remaining six boats within the arms of the harbor, she could release her hold on the sea beyond the breakwater.

Like everything the Romans did, the harbor was massive. Even in the darkness, with her witch eyes stinging from the sea spray, Zoë could see a forest of masts lining the harbor wall. The Roman fleet was riding easy in harbor, sheltered from the wind that whined and moaned up out of the southwest. From Tyre in the north to Gazzah in the south, this was the only safe harbor for the Roman fleet. Fog and mist filled the four-mile-long basin, thickening up from the glassy waters. Zoë urged it to spill over the circular terrace filling the landward side of the harbor. There were more quays and piers there, crowded with ships. Heavy fog swallowed them, wrapping itself around their masts and flooding through the hatchways in their pine decks.

Zoë and her boat reached a small pier along the short, northern wall of the harbor breakwater. Towers loomed out of the mist, jutting from the breakwater at regular intervals.

Two of the Sahaba experienced with the merchant ships of the Al'Quraysh jumped from the front of the boat onto the pier. They lashed the boat to the stone mooring posts and then drew their swords. The side of the boat creaked against mossy stone, the sound muffled by the fog. They had seen no one yet, but everyone was sure that guards must be posted nearby. More sailors untied Zoë from the mast and helped her out of the boat. She felt weak. Even moving heat out of the air and into the water took a toll on her.

If Dwyrin were here, he'd have done it without a thought.

Zoë sighed as she staggered across the damp stones to the stairs that ran up from the dock to the ramparts of the harbor wall. She sat heavily, her legs trembling with the effort of walking. *But he's not and should I see him again, all ungainly ears and that damned red hair, it will be a cold business between us.*

"You must get to some cover, my lady."

Zoë looked up, raising her head from her hands. She had almost fallen asleep. The mist was falling over the town like slow rain, drenching the streets and rooftops with a thick dew. Blinking, she made out the face of the noble Khalid in the washed-out, gray light. He was leaning over her, his liquid brown eyes filled with concern.

Surely concerned, snarled Zoë to herself. *All his blessed plan depends on me and my skill. If I fail, he fails and his precious pride would fall hard.*

"Of course," she said, looking away, the corner of her mouth twitching.

Khalid grunted and leaned down, sliding his arm under hers and lifting her up. He was a lithe, pretty man, with long eyelashes and a mane of rich, dark hair. It reminded Zoë of her own, back in some sunlit summer day of her youth. He seemed untouched by the cruel business of war, still young and smiling, his white teeth gleaming in a sun-darkened face. Zoë lay stiff in his arms, but he affected not to notice and strode up the steps, blade rattling at his side. The column of bowmen followed him up the stairs.

Mist drifted over the ramparts of the seawall, spilling between the merlons like sea foam. Khalid paced to the gates of the tower of the colossi, his burden light in his arms. Zoë struggled to keep her eyes open, but the warmth of the man's flesh and the smell of some subtle perfume tugged her towards sleep. Even the cold air seemed banished by his presence.

A towering vault passed overhead and they were in a warm, flame-shot darkness. Men were talking in low tones and there was a sound of wooden furniture being dragged across a stone floor.

"Is the tower secure?" Khalid's voice rang from the ceiling, low and penetrating.

He stooped and slid Zoë into a chair facing the gate. Exhausted, Zoë folded her hands in her lap. Perhaps she could sleep for a moment. There was still a little time until she was needed again.

Thunder rattled, growling like a giant dog in the sky. Zoë's eyes flickered open.

The gates to the tower were open, showing her the town in the early dawn light. A barricade of benches, tables and barrels had been erected across the lower half of the doorway. Her chair had been moved up onto the last table so that she could see out over the harbor and the streets of the city. Zoë cursed. She *had* fallen asleep.

In the east, beyond the red rooftops and the shining bulk of the temple of Roma Mater, thunder rumbled and there was a bright white flash.

"Mohammed is coming," said a voice from behind her. It was Khalid, the hem of his cloak dripping seawater. His voice was smiling, but Zoë did not turn around to see the handsome face wreathed in triumph. "Do you hear the god of the wasteland speaking?"

Zoë almost laughed aloud, for her empty eyes were focused on the infinite distance between the harbor tower and the unseen gate of the city. Mohammed and his army were raging at the gate, swarming forward under a storm of arrows and heavy stones flung from siege machines the Sahaba had taken from the great Roman camp at Lejjun. On those walls, Roman soldiers hurled down stones and shot crossbow bolts and arrows into the white and tan horde that surged forward with ladders and rolling towers. Lightning rippled along the gates of Caesarea, but it was not the power which moved the wind and the sun that flared so brightly.

If that power had come, the entire nine-mile circuit of the wall would have shattered, bricks burning with lime-white fire. The brick-and-tile houses would have burst, blown down in dust and ash, before such a presence. The sky would have darkened and the sun grown faint.

"I hear a proud boy pretending to hear his father knocking on the gate of heaven."

Khalid hissed in anger, then jumped down from the table. Zoë caught his eye, her face cold and forbidding.

"The lord Mohammed," she said, "does not rely solely on the power of the voice from the clear air. He owns many powerful servants, all of whom do his bidding."

She smiled, but it was not a pleasant smile. This young man irritated her with his dashing looks and languid eyes. He always seemed to preen and strut, like a pampered hunting bird on the jess. His hood was invisible to most, that was all. She bit her lip to keep from laughing mockingly at him. The Queen whispered his secrets in Zoë's ear, but she withheld that knowledge from him. "Has the chain been raised?"

Khalid nodded, his nostrils flaring at the tone in her voice.

"Good," said Zoë, and she slumped back in the chair. Now she must exceed her night's effort. She folded her hands over her heart and settled her breathing.

Once more, her heart ached, wishing Dwyrin were here. This was his specialty.

Thinking of him, she called forth from her memory the sign of fire, as he had once shown her as they sat under a starlit sky, the air heavy with the smell of highland pines and burning resin. It had been cold and the air sharp. The stars bright and steady, without the flickering that they evinced in lowland climes. The sign trembled in her memory and she traced it, swiftly, in the hidden world.

Around her, in the room, the torches and lamps suddenly burst into violent flame, hissing and spitting. Sparks showered down, burning bright for a moment on the flagstones. Khalid cursed, shaking embers from his cloak.

"Outside," he shouted to the men in the room. They left quickly, climbing over the barricade.

Zoë, her face running with sweat, inverted the sign and drew greedily on the power in the air and the sea. Cold and wet she called to her, feeling her nerves burn with effort. The lamps and torches and the fire in the guardroom suddenly died. The air filled with the smell of the sea and ice. Unseen in the new darkness, she raised her hand.

All across the harbor, on every boat and barque, on the terraces and in the temples and whorehouses that crowded the edge of the docks, fire died. Lamps, candles, forges, lanterns, matches, flints all turned cold. In the temple of Roma, the priests had just lit the sacred flames, letting the finest oil burn blue white in a slender flame above the lamp dish. The high priest, stunned with horror, cried out as the fire flickered and died, leaving only a cold, dead feeling in the air.

In her chair, in the tower of Drusus, Zoë shuddered, sweating, feeling vast resistance slowly build against her. The inverted sign trembled in the hidden world and tried to right itself. But she dared not let fire bloom within the harbor, not with acres of ships riding at anchor. Ships of dried pine and tar and hempen rope, always eager to catch alight and burn fiercely right down to the water. The lord Mohammed had commanded the fleet be captured whole.

Mohammed walked along the harbor wall, his face smudged with soot. His cloak was ripped and spattered with dried blood. The Romans had fought hard here, on the rampart, trying to break through to the guardian towers flanking the harbor entrance. They had tried to break through the barrier in the seaway, but the chain-wrapped cordage had held. That had been some fierce business, fighting on the decks of the crowded galleys, keeping the Roman axmen from the chain.

Bodies sprawled on the bricks, caked with blood, heads bare, puddles of entrails and dried, sticky black fluid around them. These seemed to be citizens, clad only in bits of armor and their tunics. Their spears lay splintered on the stone walkway.

At the tower gate, the Sahaba were hauling the dead away and throwing them into the sea. The bodies fell, naked, and plunged with a sharp slap into the gray water. Their arms and armor, if they had any, were already stacked up along the platform.

Nothing shall be wasted, he had said to his commanders. *Our enemy shall arm us.*

The water at the base of the wall heaved, crowded with slick white bodies. Waves ground them against the harbor wall, leaving a bright red stain on the limestone. Gray shapes moved in the waters, serrated teeth digging into a thigh or torso, before pulling their cold feast down into the darkness. Mohammed looked away, silently chanting a prayer for the souls of those who had died in battle. At the gate, the Sahaba parted before him.

"Lord Mohammed, welcome." Khalid was just inside the door, holding a lantern. Despite its warm light, his face was drawn with weariness.

"Khalid, I am pleased to see that you are still alive."

The youth smiled, forefinger rising to trace a fresh cut along his cheek and the side of his head. Blood was caked around his ear and fouled his beard. "They tested us, but the merciful and beneficent Lord delivered us."

Mohammed shook his head. The young man was much taken, of late, with such aphorisms and sayings. The truth of the matter was the fearless strength of the Sahaba had held the tower and the seawall. Two hundred men had set forth in the boats, in the darkness. Mohammed looked around, his face heavy with sadness. Perhaps twenty remained, leaning exhausted against the wall of the tower. There were a few more down in the boats guarding the chain across the harbor mouth, sleeping, lulled by the rise and fall of the swell. Twice that many Romans lay dead, most of them just the citizens of the town, who had tried to fulfill their duty to Emperor and state.

Anger, bleak and hot like the anvil of the An'Nefud, welled up in Mohammed. For a moment, he felt sick and exhausted and tired and ready to set everything aside. Murdering clerks and cobblers in their nightshirts was not what he wanted. He put his hand, stained with gore, to his forehead. Where was the light that illuminated the world? Did it countenance this?

Listen, O man, listen to the sound of the world in the dawn time, when it was fresh and new.

Mohammed listened, hearing wind rustling in the leaves of the trees. It was a good sound. When, at last, he looked up, his exhaustion and weariness had dropped away. He saw with clear eyes once more. He stood straight again. "Where is the lady Zoë?"

Khalid gestured with a newly bandaged arm, pointing to a cot set against one wall of the octagonal room. Mohammed went there and knelt down, his face half in shadow from the nearest lantern. The girl was sleeping, deep in exhaustion, her face at peace. The Arab chieftain laid his hand on her forehead, feeling the warm heat in her skin. He smiled, his bristly white beard brushing her chin. She was snoring softly.

"Sleep, Zoë, and know that you did well."

She mumbled and turned her face to the wall. Mohammed tucked the ratty woolen cover around her before standing up. Shadin and Khalid were waiting, leaning on a table. Some of the other captains had entered and were speaking in low tones. Mohammed scratched his beard and joined them.

"Are the city and harbor ours?" He looked over them,

marking wounds and leaden arms, dead eyes and stained hands.

Khalid nodded, saying, "Yes, we hold the full circuit of the wall and the town."

Mohammed tapped a blunt finger on his nose. "How many ships were lost?"

The younger man grinned. It was his plan to seize the seaward towers, tying a noose around the Roman fleet, trapping it in the great marble harbor. Khalid guessed the Romans would try to burn the ships, if they thought the "desert bandits" might capture them.

"Not many, lord. Only sixteen."

"Just those nearest the town, then." Mohammed felt a constriction in his chest ease.

"Yes, lord. Mostly merchantmen, as far as I could see from the tower. Ships newly come to the port."

"And the others?"

Khalid motioned to one of his lieutenants, a tall, quiet Persian named Patik. The man dragged a leather case of parchments up onto the table and unsnapped the bronze latch. Like many of the brigands and ruffians who rode with the young Eagle, the Persian's background was unknown to Mohammed. Many men placed themselves in the custody of the Great and Merciful One. Their past was immaterial.

Khalid spread the papers out. Each sheet was covered with neatly lettered lines of text. "This is the harbor master's tally of ships in port and their condition. The fleet has been here for some time; four months at least, since they offloaded Prince Theodore and his army. Each ship is duly accounted for here. Bless these Romans, for they are fond of their records."

Mohammed made a half-smile. The boy was taking his time, taunting Shadin and the other, older Sahaba with his cunning. He let it pass, for it inspired the other commanders to greater effort.

."How many?" Mohammed let a tone of impatience creep into his voice.

"Two hundred and nineteen, lord. Most are triremes and heavier galleys. Many are those big, round-bellied transports, fitted to take horses, wagons, all manner of supplies."

Mohammed let out a long hiss of breath. He was relieved. He was pleased. A spear had placed itself in his hand, as the voice had foretold.

The Great and Merciful Lord will provide came a voice in his mind, speaking from the clear air. *See what bounty I have laid before you?*

"God is great," he said, smiling upon the faithful who had followed him into this place. "Prepare the fleet to sail. . Time is short, though luck has favored us."

The great gate on the road to Aelia Capitolina closed at last, as the final wagons rolled into the city. The last wagon was shrouded in dark cloth, drawn by fine black horses. In the gloom, even with the light of the torches at the gate to illuminate it, it seemed ethereal and indistinct.

The Persian, Patik, rode on the driver's board, his hands resting easy on the reins. The horses knew his will and went quietly, their heads low, their hooves ringing on the flagstones of the street. The mercenary was always gentle with them and showed long experience with all kinds of horses and riding animals. In the wagon a casket of wood and gold rode easily on a bower of pine boughs. The crushed needles sent up a sharp scent that masked the fetid smell of long-dead flesh. Patik did not notice the stench. He was oblivious to many inconsequential things.

He flipped the reins and the horses turned down one of the avenues that bisected the city. Moonlight followed the wagon but did not disturb its occupant.

The dead Queen entered the city, victorious.

)H(

Alexandros walked quickly along a colonnaded hall-way, passing gardens on his right. After a moment, he heard the chuckling sound of water falling. A fifty-foot-wide vault opened to his left. Fat-bellied pillars of red granite marked a set of wide, shallow steps leading up into the nymphaeum. The Macedonian turned and strode up into a room in the shape of a half-circle. As he did so, the temperature cooled noticeably.

Gaius Julius was sitting on the far side of the room, in a pool of sunlight slanting down through the half-dome overhead. The opening faced the south, allowing the sun to shine directly into the nymphaeum without exposing the room to the blustery elements. Behind the old Roman was a platform lined with statues of the gods, the fathers of the city and notable emperors.

At the center of the rear wall, flanked by heavy figures of Apollo and Zeus, was a three-story-high fountain. Water spilled from ranks of maeneads and porpoises at the top, falling in a hazy spray over tritons and naiads writhing around the central figure of Poseidon. The passage of so much water, over so many years, had left a thick crust of salt-white rime on the outer figures. Most of Poseidon's face had been worn away.

Alexandros laughed aloud as he approached Gaius Julius. The old Roman was sitting, his papers and books and correspondence spread out on a marble table in front of him, busily writing letters, his quill making a swift scratching sound on parchment. "You delight to tempt the fates, old man."

Gaius looked up, raising an eyebrow. Behind him, standing in the shadow of the nearest alcove, was a fifteen-foot-high statue of his living self. The artist must have been Greek, for the statue captured the visage and spirit of the old man perfectly.

"No one has noticed yet, my friend. I do not think that they will. Who would expect that the living would have traffic with the dead in the baths?"

Alexandros swung his leg over the corner of the table and sat, pushing aside some tally sheets. "Anyone with eyes . . . that is a very good likeness. Was it made when you were alive?"

Gaius Julius returned his attention to the letter he was writing.

"No," he said absently, "I understand it was made at the order of my *dear* son Octavian for funeral games he held in my name. It stood in the rostra of the Forum for a long time, but they moved it in here when these baths were built."

"Odd," Alexandros said, looking from face to face. "It is *very* good."

"I'm sure they used a death mask," Gaius said, inking his name to the bottom of the document. He blew on it gently, waiting until the ink dried. "Such things are often done, long after the fact." The old Roman looked up, smiling in memory. "Funeral games are usually given when convenient. I celebrated my fathers' . . . what, twenty years after he went into the cold ground? I think that is right. In any case, I had more hair when I was alive."

Alexandros laughed in delight, his voice booming harshly. The old Roman's vanity was undiminished by time. "I'm sure. Have you spoken with any of the Goths staying at the house of our benefactor?"

Gaius shook his head as he blotted the letter and then shook sand away. "No, have you?"

"Yes, I was just sparring with one of the younger ones. Ox-strong, nimble, completely lacking in subtlety. Your man was right to say that he could be found here today. They seem uneasy with their Imperial arrangements, or so this one says. Is there any truth to that?"

"I have no idea," said Gaius, pulling a fresh sheet of parchment out of a stack at his side. He began writing, still listening to Alexandros, in a strong, even hand. His letters were well formed and plain, without any flourishes or ornamentation. Alexandros cocked his head to one side, watching the older man write. Even upside down it was easy to read.

"You're in charge of the relief effort in . . . Nola? I thought you were avoiding Imperial service like the plague!"

Gaius stopped writing, put down his pen and looked up, frowning. "Do you usually read other people's letters? Isn't that rather rude?"

Alexandros shrugged, half-smiling. "I suppose. Are you?"

"Am I what?"

"In charge of the relief effort for Nola? Where *is* Nola?"

Gaius Julius sighed and pinched the bridge of his rather noble nose. "The strain on the Imperial resources," he said begrudgingly, "has grown sufficiently great that the Emperor has begun to sublet certain activities to certain senators. As it happens, the repair and reconstruction of bridges along the Via Appia—many of which were shaken down by the earthquake, or destroyed by falling meteors— are of utmost importance. It was entrusted to the esteemed and very reliable Gregorius, seeing as how he is a close, personal friend of the Emperor."

"I see," said Alexandros in a dry voice. "And Gregorius, who is hip deep in trying to arrange for sufficient food and water to reach the dispossessed in Campania, turned this other, simple matter over to you."

"Indeed," Gaius Julius smiled, "and I, the dutiful client,

gladly accepted. Now, consider, my fine Macedonian friend, what must happen if bridges and roads are to be repaired. Why, other contracts must be let out, to skilled craftsmen and masons and engineers. Contracts must be arranged to supply those work crews with food and lodging. Supplies, in great quantity, must be found, purchased, delivered to the work sites—"

"The scope of possible corruption," Alexandros interrupted, "is staggering. How much are you skimming off the top of this? It must be a princely sum."

Gaius Julius raised his hands, palms out, his face perfectly serious. "Alexandros! You wound me. I am not, in fact, skimming anything. In fact, I am taking great care that the subcontractors are worthy men, with good reputations, and that the work, though rushed, is of the highest quality. That is the purpose of this voluminous correspondence! I have spies in every work camp, reporting daily events to me, sniffing for shirking, corner cutting and substandard materials."

Alexandros stared at Gaius Julius as if he were a gorgon rising from the foaming sea. "What? Have you lost your mind? Didn't we just discuss the necessity of acquiring sufficient funds for our plans? What do you think you are doing?"

Gaius Julius smiled and it was the smile of a very satisfied fox, fresh from the hen coop. "Lad . . . you were not king of kings long enough! I am taking care this whole project is done swiftly and cheaply for three very serious reasons."

"Which are?" Alexandros was getting impatient. He brushed the wayward lock of hair from his eyes again.

"First, the Via Appia is the main highway from Rome to the great southern port of Brundisium. The appia is a crucial artery of local commerce throughout southern Italia. The highway is also a military road. I may be a politician but I am also a general, and the day may come when I need this road to be in good repair. Therefore, since I can, I will move heaven and earth to make sure that the work is of the finest quality."

The Macedonian nodded in agreement, though grudgingly.

"Second, this effort is an arrow to fling me into a position where I meet a vast number of men in the city who make things happen very quickly. It provides me with a respectable and visible position. I can enter into negotiations with anyone. I gain friends and influence at all levels of society by the judicious allocation of lucrative contracts. Everywhere I go, I am welcomed."

Alexandros gave the older Roman a disbelieving look.

"It is true, so do not make such a face at me. We cannot conquer Rome by knocking over the Altar of Peace and slaughtering half the population . . . let me finish!

"Finally, it provides me with a very public and respectable image as a man who can make things happen. An honest and aboveboard gentleman, I may note, who can deliver something very complicated on time and budget . . . without problems."

"Ahhhh . . ." Alexandros was smiling and he bowed to the Roman. "Because there is a larger, more complicated, vastly more expensive project waiting in the wings."

"Even so," Gaius Julius said, smirking. "The funeral games. Consider this." He held up a sheaf of parchments filled with notations. "These are the budgets of the road project. Perhaps ten to twelve million sesterces in total. Five or six thousand people working on ninety bridges. The work will be complete in no more than three months."

He reached over to another pile of papers and pulled a much thicker sheaf from the bottom. The rest of the tower of papers threatened to topple over, but Alexandros saved and stacked the pile neatly. Gaius Julius spread out the parchments.

"This is the initial plan I have drawn up for what I call the Vesuvian Games. They are modeled on the death celebrations of Augustus, my lamentable heir. He may have

been a lying weasel, but he could certainly put on a show.
. . . At first guess, I would say they will cost nearly a hundred and fifty million sesterces, take the effort of fifteen thousand people to stage and will last four weeks, after five months of backbreaking effort to prepare. Luckily, there are a large number of performers, gladiators, artists, actors and so on already in the city."

"I see," Alexandros said, "that you have the situation well in hand. There seems to be only one small detail remaining."

Gaius Julius looked a little glum, but a determined glitter shone in his eyes. "Yes . . . the Emperor must still approve the plan. I am confident, though. He will. He *has* to."

"Does he? Well, no matter. I'm sure you will be quite entertained."

Alexandros swung his leg off the table. He looked around the huge open space, admiring the wall paintings and the bright colors that outlined the honeycombed recesses in the half-dome of the ceiling. The falling water made the chamber cool and provided a pleasant background noise. Like the main hall of the baths, the nymphaeum was so large that the only other person, an old man reading a scroll, his feet up in the sunlight, was easily out of earshot.

"When these Goths leave the city, in a week or so, I am going with them."

Gaius Julius raised a thin white eyebrow. Since acquiring steady employment and a salary, he had substantially upgraded his appearance. No longer did he affect to be a rustic landowner, fresh from the countryside, but rather an elegantly attired patrician of the city. He spent more time in the barber's than one would expect, for a man with very little hair. "To Gothica? Why?"

"I hear echoes of the Macedon of my father in these men's words. A strong, vigorous nation, half-civilized, still young and filled with energy. They chafe, these Goths. I can feel it . . . they are a weapon waiting to be forged and quenched. You are well suited here, conniving and planning in the mazes of the city. I need an army. I need a *war.*"

"And in Gothica, you will find it, I am sure." There was a faint echo of regret and sadness in the older man's voice. "We must correspond, then, to see that each knows the other's mind and plans."

"I will write," Alexandros said, the corner of his mouth quirking up. He put his hand on Gaius Julius' shoulder and squeezed gently. "I will miss your company."

"Of course," said the old Roman, putting his own hand over the youth's. "It will seem strange without you here."

Alexandros bent down and kissed the bald crown of Gaius' head.

"I will return soon, and we will have our army."

A HILL ABOVE THE PLAIN OF SCAMANDER

Spiny brush crashed aside, long, wiry limbs bending. Branches tore at a sleeve of dark cloth and then a young man stepped out of the underbrush, face shining with sweat, pricked and bleeding from thorns. Wind whined in the oaks crowning the hill, rattling their stiff leaves. Climbing the rough slope, through tangled brush and over irregular stones, the air had been hot and stifling. Now, on the summit, in a stiff northern wind, the man was cold. He sat down heavily, exhausted, among tumbled, broken slabs littering the hilltop.

The hills spilled away below him, scattered olive and pine trees amid heaps of stone and thickets of dark gorse and thornberry. In the hazy distance a flat, rich plain spread out towards the sea. The man drew a tattered cloak around his shoulders, slumping down against a tilted stone slab. Warm from the sun, the weathered block shielded him from the wind. Settling among the grass he dozed, the long stems tickling his arms and face.

Slowly, as the sun fell towards the horizon, the slab was cast in shadowy relief, revealing ancient carvings of men and horses and chariots. The man continued to sleep, exhausted, his mind blessedly free from nightmares.

Maxian woke with a start, disoriented in the darkness. The slab at his back had turned cold as night advanced. Firelight flickered and gleamed on his face. His stomach growled.

"Are you lost?"

Maxian looked up sharply, away from the fire burning in the bottom of the little hollow. He did not remember starting a fire. The flames cast wavering orange-red light on the trunks of the trees and the shining, serrated leaves of the brush. Strips of mutton roasted over the coals. Thin trails of smoke drifted up, curling towards the dark sky.

The Prince could see a vast drift of stars in the space between the trees. The wind had died, leaving a great silence on the hill. It was very dark beyond the light of the embers. He rubbed his eyes, banishing stinging smoke. Across the fire, sitting easily on the ground, one arm back to support himself, was a boy.

"No." Maxian found his voice, rough and hoarse. "But I could not tell you where I am."

"An honest answer," the boy said, sitting up. He was a clean-limbed youth in a simple woolen tunic. His feet were bare and dark with soil. Light blond hair fell in ringlets behind his head. His face, easily seen in the light of the fire, was well proportioned. "Are you hungry?"

"I am," Maxian said gratefully. "I have not eaten in a long time."

"Here," said the boy, digging in the coals. He drew out

something sizzling and rich with a savory smell. It was a thighbone, heavy with roasted flesh, wrapped in bubbling fat. There was a wooden trencher beside the campfire and the boy flipped the meat onto it with a smooth, practiced motion. "It is seemly that this be yours, you a guest at my fire."

Maxian nodded gratefully and took the plate. Sizzling-hot fat popped and hissed as it drained away to the ground. The Prince tore at the meat with his teeth, feeling a rush of saliva flood his mouth at the glorious taste. For a time, he thought of nothing but filling his stomach. At last, sated by the rich meat, he laid back against the slab. His hands, thick with grease, he folded on his lap. A state of blissful contentment filled him.

The boy sat quietly for a time, occasionally casting bundles of aromatic leaves and herbs onto the fire. The smoke became a little thicker, carrying a heavy sweet smell.

"Why did you come here, to this place?" the boy said at last, playing with a cut branch. "It has a poor reputation."

Maxian stirred himself from the edge of sleep. For a moment he heard horns blowing and the booming roar of kettle drums. He listened, but the night was silent.

"My feet led me here," said the Prince. "I have been walking for many days. My mind is troubled."

The boy laughed, a musical sound. "This is a troubled place. Perhaps it called you. Tell me, what is your name?"

"I am Maxian Julius Atreus, a Latin and youngest son of Galen the Elder. What is yours, honorable host?"

"I am named Paiawon, son of Leto, but you should call me Pai, for my name sticks in some throats. Do you feel at ease here, lord? The house of Atreus was never welcome in this place—I should think that it would burn your feet to walk on these angry old stones."

Maxian shook his head in confusion.

"Pai, I don't understand . . . what is this place? Does someone live here? I see only wilderness."

The boy smiled and turned his head, looking out into the close darkness. "Whence comes your clan and house, Lord Maxian? Did they come over the dark sea in black-bellied ships?"

"No . . ." Maxian frowned at the boy. He was a puzzling creature. "We are old Roman stock, from Tarentum originally. I was born in Narbo in the Narbonensis, in southern Gaul."

"Ah," Paiawon said, idly jabbing at the coals with the leafy end of his cut branch. "Your clothes are in tatters, my lord, your arms and legs cut by thorns. Have you been in the wild long? What are you seeking?"

Maxian flinched from raw, violent memory. Images of his immediate past came to mind. "I am seeking peace," he said in a choked voice. "I have done evil things. I have lost my way."

Paiawon nodded, looking up at the night sky. "This is a place where evil things were done. Perhaps the gods guided you here, matching like to like."

Maxian stiffened, a flicker of anger roused in him. "There are no gods," he said sharply. Paiawon was looking at him with a calm expression, the cut branch tapping on the stones. "I am not evil."

"Can you be a good man yet do evil things?"

Maxian bit his lip. Horribly vivid memory filled his mind. The flames burning in the circle of stones seemed to echo the violence of an exploding mountain.

"If," said Paiawon, leaning forward, his face glowing in the warm firelight, "if you saw another man, someone whom you did not know, and heard the priests extol the roll of his acts, and these acts were the ones that you yourself have committed, would you call that man evil?"

"I . . . there were many reasons for these things! There were accidents, there were miscalculations! Some things . . . they seemed the right and proper thing to do at the time."

Paiawon laughed softly, then flicked his branch out of

the fire. It had begun to smoke. "Lord Maxian, is there evil in the world?"

"Yes," said Maxian after a moment. "Yes, there is."

"Are there gods above who set that which is evil from that which is good?"

"No, I do not believe so." Maxian's voice was firm and confident.

"Why do you feel there are no gods? Everyone else believes in them. Their temples are legion."

"I can see the true heart of the world." Maxian's face was stiff, his voice harsh. "I can bend the world to my will, call the storm and clouds. All these things that gods are said to drive, I can see their true natures . . . there are no mysteries, there is no place for the gods to hide."

Paiawon smiled gently, shaking the branch so that embers fell away from the leaves. Smoke beaded off, making whorls in the air.

"If this is so," said the boy, "then who says what is evil and what is good? Do men?"

"Yes." Maxian was fingering the hem of his cloak. It was shredded and thick with grime. "Our conscience tells us. Our morality tells us."

"Then, man, have you done evil?"

Maxian stared at the boy, with his harmonious features and his liquid, mellow voice, sitting across the fire. Memory was hot in him, bright with the pain and suffering that he had caused by his own hand.

Vesuvius burned, a hot cloud of deadly gas billowing out of the shattered cone.

Tens of thousands cried out in fear, perishing under a rain of burning ash and flaming meteors.

The body of a child writhed under his fingers, burning with black fire.

The old Persian's eyes were round in horror as Maxian's thumb seared his forehead with the mark of servitude.

Men, trying desperately to bring him down, incandesced to ash as he raised a radiant hand.

The high priest of the magi crumpled, felled by an angry burst of violet lightning.

A hot joy burned in Maxian's breast as he struck out at the ghost form of his brother.

"No, I am not evil!" Maxian was standing, the fire leaping up. Wind eddied in the bowl of the hill, stirring leaves and a cloud of dust. Debris swam in a cloud at the edge of firelight, sparkling and hazing the air. "I did . . . I did these things for the Senate and for the people of Rome. I am trying to save them from wretchedness and slavery. Their backs are breaking under the burden of the Oath! You've never seen their pale, barren, hopeless faces!"

"Was Krista wretched? Did her back bend under the weight of this power you have set yourself against? Did this Oath kill *her*?"

Maxian recoiled, his hand raised in a motion of warding. The boy continued to sit, staring up at him with guileless eyes. The Prince tried to speak but his tongue refused to move. He spit, clearing his mouth, and said: "How do you know her name? What are you?"

Pai pointed at the tilted stone with his cut branch. "When you were sleeping, you cried out, begging her for forgiveness." The leafy cluster moved, pointing at Maxian's chest. "Did you kill her? This woman whom you loved?"

Maxian slumped to the ground, fists clenched. "I did. It was . . . an accident. She leapt out of the darkness. My shield of fire was in full spate. She was destroyed. She . . . was trying to kill me."

Pai stood and placed the cut branch on the ground. He stepped around the fire, bare feet light on the ground. The boy bent close, his soft voice whispering in Maxian's ear. His fingers brushed aside the Prince's oily hair, exposing a glassy scar. "Why did she set herself against you? Didn't she love you? Didn't you love her?"

"I did," the Prince wailed, grinding his head against the ground. "I thought . . . I thought she loved me too. There were tears in her eyes when she . . . when she . . ."

Pai ran a thumb over the scar. "This wound would kill any mortal. How did you survive?"

"I called upon the mountain; it filled me with strength, more strength than I had ever commanded. It was a simple matter to close the wound, to repair shattered bone."

"Was there a cost for that? You traffic in the hidden world; does power come without cost?"

"No," Maxian gasped, trying to control his voice. He refused to break down, not in the face of this boy. "The power in the mountain demanded release . . . I gave it. I traded for my life."

"You traded the lives of twenty thousand men and women and children for your own."

Maxian could not answer.

"Do you see their faces when you sleep?" The boys' voice gentled, becoming barely audible. "Do you hear their cries for mercy, for salvation? Do you hear them choking on the poisonous air?"

"Yes." Maxian shuddered again. "Even when I am awake, I can hear them."

"Is this an evil thing?"

"Yes!" Maxian shouted at the earth, for he could not look up. "I have murdered so that I could live. It was an evil thing. I did it. I chose to live."

The boy stood, his face still smiling and calm.

"Yet, you say that you are not evil. You have murdered, kidnapped, lied, stolen, murdered again, violated temples and sacred places, trafficked with the dead, foresworn the gods, put your will upon others that they might do your bidding, sent thousands to a horrible death . . . and slain, with your own hand, one whom you loved. Are these not the acts of a madman, of someone consumed by evil?"

"I am not evil! I am . . . not. I cannot be! I am a healer, a priest of the god Asclepius, I am a good man!"

The boy shook his head sadly and turned away from the crying man. He knelt and picked up a wooden bow and its hooded case and slung them over his shoulder. He picked up the cut laurel branch and thrust it into his belt.

"If there are no gods to divide good from evil, then men must do so themselves. You must decide. Let your actions suit your words."

Paiawon stepped into the darkness, out of the firelight, and was gone.

The slowly whirling cloud of dust and leaves and twigs hissed to the ground. Maxian lay prostrate on the ground by the dying fire.

Dawn found the Prince sitting on the highest point of the hill. The air was brilliantly pure and everything was crisp and distinct. With the haze gone, he could pick out the white strand of the beach and then, a mile or more across the dark water, a farther shore. He remembered nothing after Pai's departure. Perhaps he had slept without dreams. He felt empty, like a jug poured out onto the ground. For the moment, in this quiet, soft dawn, he was at peace. Everything was still, both in the land and in his mind.

Am I evil or good? Can I find a way to repay the people for these crimes I have committed against them?

Would the Oath allow him to live? He had struck a powerful blow against it, this seemed clear. The pattern of the Oath, fixing the rhythm and motion of Roman life, had not allowed Vesuvius to erupt. The matrices had constrained the volcano, bottling up the slowly building power in the earth. The two forces had reached a balance point long ago. Only the sudden intervention of Maxian and his struggle for life on the summit had allowed that balance to tip. The result had been far more violent, the devastation more expansive, than if the matrices of the Oath had allowed nature to follow its course.

I should not have remained on the mountain. If I had

just left when I intended, none of this would have happened.

Maxian rubbed his hands together. It was cold. Soon the wind would come up and it would be chillier still on the hilltop, even in the hot sun. He *should* have gone back to his brother, *should* have explained everything and accepted whatever punishment Galen deemed sufficient. He *should* have laid aside his reckless task and accepted the way of things.

Can I still? Will the Oath allow me to live, a fly trapped in the amber of its invisible structures and forms? Can I find a way to coexist, when I have set myself against it for so long? Wait . . .

A thought blossomed in his mind, a simple, plain thought. His eyes widened. There was another way to resolve this, something so obvious it had escaped his attention.

Oh, blessed gods, I am truly an idiot!

A sick feeling washed over him. There had been so much suffering and death for *nothing.* Krista was dead, trying to keep him from further murder, for not so much as a copper. The solution to his problem was so obvious he must have been blind. . . .

"Wait," Maxian said aloud to the laurel trees and thick stands of grass at the foot of the stone he was sitting on. Some ravens in the nearest tree cawed back at him, fluttering their black wings. "What is this pressure?"

There *was* a pressure, subtle but distinct, against his will. In the hurly-burly of the day, as he went about his normal business, it would be unnoticeable. The Prince frowned, turning his attention inward. His eyes closed and his breathing deepened. He let his sight and vision in the hidden world unfold. With a great effort, for he had never done such a thing before, he stepped outside of himself. His body sat before him, eyes closed, legs crossed under him in the Persian style. The first zephyr of the day stirred his long hair. With great care, he allowed himself to become aware of his shape in the transparent world.

It was difficult, for his spirit burned like a star. It seemed that thousands of tiny points of light crowded in him, each flickering brilliantly. The dragon coil of his self burned brightest of all, surrounded by bright constellations. He let his thought roam, following the patterns that formed muscle and blood and heart.

There!

Not a lesion, not a scar, but a wraith of pale filaments that stirred and drifted at the core of his self. His thought approached and the pattern swelled in his true sight. It was beautiful and subtle and cunningly worked. It threaded into thought and memory and intent like a lover, curled close to the sleeping body of her partner.

What is this? The Prince marveled, for it was a work of art. Some master had built this, a feather-light pressure upon waking deed and desire. He reached out, touching it gently, letting it respond to him, letting it unfold like a swift-blooming flower to show itself.

Friend, it radiated, warm and inviting. *We are friends, you and I. What I will, you will. What I desire, you desire.* The pressure was so soft and faint, so gentle, that Maxian felt himself listening in joy. There was a great sense of rightness in the pattern, as if it were the only possible path that could be followed.

The shield of Rome, it whispered, *must be destroyed. It is foul, unconscionable, and abhorrent to free citizens. Let this lamia of the soul be cast down in ruin. See how it murders the sleeping, the innocent? See how it strangles the future in the crib? Here is a tyrant, a king, who rules the people in secret!*

Maxian recoiled with a jolt. The maker's touch burned in his mind. He knew the deft fingers and the agile will that had bound such a thing, crafted such an elegant pattern. The Prince felt sick. This was the touch of a dear friend.

Maxian was sleeping on a narrow cot, his head on a

thin pillow. The little storeroom was crowded with bags of
herbs and odd-smelling boxes. He was snoring, the thin
blanket pulled tight around him. Abdmachus stood in the
doorway, warming his hands with a copper lantern. The
old Nabatean looked down upon the young man intently.
The Persian agent's brow furrowed in concentration and
he raised a single finger, quickly tracing the glyph for
friend in the air before him. On the cot, Maxian moaned
a little and turned over, hiding his face.

"How is this? Am I a toy, a puppet, to the will of a
dead man?"

The Prince was filled with anger and despair. Here was
a subtle touch upon his mind, placed there by a man he
had counted as a friend. Maxian moved cautiously, his will
drawing strength from the array of floating stars that were
close at hand. Their power filled him and he struck.

The filaments, seized by his thought, shuddered,
screamed and then ripped free. With great determination,
he hunted them down, even the smallest thread, and ex-
cised them from his mind. These were cancers, he thought
with barely restrained anger. Not a great thing, but enough
to turn his path, nudging every step a fraction, until he
walked as the Persian magi wished, against his own people, against his brother, against the state that had raised
him and given him purpose.

Maxian returned to his waking mind and his body shook
for a moment. Then a brilliant wash of light spilled out
over the hilltop, making the stones and cracked columns
stand out, even in the morning sun. When it had passed,
the Prince stood, his face grim, on the summit. His tattered
cloak was clean and whole again, the glassy scar on the
side of his head vanished, his torn boots mended.

"Thank you, shepherd," he called out, over the tangled
brush and vines. "I will remember your words. I will strive
to erase the black stain on me with actions accounted good.
I have committed grave crimes against the people and the
state and my sworn oath as a physician. I will bend all my

effort to repairing this broken trust. I am going home."

With that, he climbed down from the boulder and began walking downhill towards the sea. As he clambered amongst fallen trees and stones, he sent forth a call, arrow swift, to the south. The crippled Engine was waiting for him offshore near Pergamum, hidden in shallow water. It was severely damaged but it could still fly.

Come, foal of iron, child of the Medusa, he called. *I need your swift wings and steel heart. I would be home and you my steed to carry me there.*

The Prince passed between two slender oaks and disappeared into a thicket of tamarisk.

[◎]-[◎]-[◎]-[◎]-[◎]-[◎]-[◎]-[◎]-[◎]-[◎]-[◎]-[◎]-[◎]-[◎]-[◎]-[◎]-[◎]-[◎]-[◎]

THE VILLA OF THE FAUNS, OUTSIDE ROMA

)=(

Ila woke in darkness, hearing a strange sound. She was curled up with a mended old quilt and a thin straw pillow. It was a small bed, really no more than a box bolted to the side of the wagon. Beneath were two cabinets filled with tent stakes, ropes, flags and boxes of carefully hoarded brass nails. Cautiously, she looked around, seeing nothing but darkness and a thin slat of moonlight at the edge of the door.

"Go away, bad ghosts," she whispered. Since the horrible night of the eruption, the *manes* and *lamiae* that crept and crawled in the countryside had been very restless. Sometimes, when the moon had set at night, she could hear them *tap-tap-tapp*ing on the doors or scratching at the windows. Ila made sure to keep inside, with her charms close at hand. It was worse, of course, if they were near a crossroads.

The sound came again, a hoarse moaning like a rabbit being steamed alive in a copper kettle.

Ila shuddered and burrowed under the covers, pulling the quilt over her mussed brown hair. She prayed fervently to the Many-Handed to make the sound go away, hoping that it was just one of the horses taken with the bloat or maybe Otho drunk, puking under the wagon.

Anything but a ghost!

This time the sound was sharp and abrupt, followed by a rattling sound. Ila poked her head out of the covers, pressing her ear to the wall of the wagon. There was a muffled sound—footsteps?—and the creak of a door. Now, that *did* sound like Otho. Perhaps he and Franco had been out too late and had gotten some bad wine. Then they had been vomiting behind the wagons. Ila shook her head. Those boys were going to get in big trouble.

She climbed down out of the box, dragging the quilt along, and pushed open the door. Across the way, dimly illuminated by the thin moon, she saw the door of Diana's wagon standing half open. Candlelight flickered inside.

"Oh, dear!" Ila scurried across the grass between the wagons and hopped up the steps to the doorway. The quilt trailed behind her like a big floppy tail, picking up leaves and stems. For the last two days, they had been camped on the hunting grounds of a rich senator whom Vitellix knew, near the city. The troupe master had been gone for quite some time, inquiring after the state of the games and who would be arranging them. It was very dull, waiting for him to come back. Ila was feeling skittish—she hadn't been able to show her riding tricks in Narni; the stage had been too small. Even teaching Diana to drive a chariot was dull—the redheaded woman's reflexes were too good . . . not so much as a crash to liven things up!

A small tallow candle lit Diana's wagon. Ila peered in, blinking in the light.

"Shhh." Ila's head jerked to one side, snub nose twitching. Dummonus was standing beside the bed. He was only half dressed, his broad chest smooth and bare, his hair mussed with sleep. His face, though, was as calm as ever, the placid perfection of a temple statue.

Diana moaned again, turning in the woolen covers. One arm rose, candlelight gleaming on the patchwork of fine white scars covering her forearms.

"Look out," she said in a perfectly normal voice. "No, Nikos. Look out."

Ila crept into the wagon and to the side of Diana's bed. The young woman was sweating heavily, tangled in her covers. Dummonus held her shoulders down. One of her arms was bruised from striking the wall of the wagon. Diana's eyes were wide open, staring sightlessly up at the ceiling. Ila gulped. Her friend's face was contorted by a horrible feral grimace.

"What is it?" Ila could barely whisper.

Dummonus shook his head slowly. Diana suddenly shuddered under his hands and he bore down. Her arms twitched and quivered, then her fingers curled around some invisible object as if she were crushing it. A deep growl issued from her chest. Then she suddenly became still again.

"I do not know, mouse. She woke me with a cry."

Ila's fingers crept out of the quilt and took Diana's hand.

"Oh, Dummonus. She's so cold!" Ila wrapped her thin hands around Diana's, trying to press some warmth back into them. "Is she remembering?"

"Yes," the aerialist said in his placid voice. "I think she is."

Ila crawled into the bed, dragging her quilt behind her. Diana moaned again, softly, and turned away from her towards the wall. Ila curled in behind her, dragging the blankets over the two of them. Ila wrapped her arm around Diana and closed her eyes. Diana's flesh was cold and chill to the touch, but her breathing eased. Dummonus waited a moment before snuffing out the candle.

Then he sat back down in the darkness to wait.

"Shirin?"

Morning sunlight shone in through the door of the wagon. Diana looked around, her eyes heavy with sleep. She frowned at the door. It should be closed. She tried to get up, but there was an unexpectedly heavy weight on her chest. There were three or four more quilts on her than she remembered and it was very warm in the bed. She fell back, still very sleepy.

Wasn't there someone here with me, sleeping, her head on my chest?

Sparrows called outside in the trees. There were voices too, the usual cheerful banter around the morning fire. Tin plates rattling and horses whickering. Otho whistling as he filled their feed bags. Everything was just as it should be.

"Oh, oh, goddess . . ." Diana felt a horrible pain in her chest. There was supposed to be someone here, right here, lying beside her. She put out her hand. There was warmth under the quilts, right where someone should have been. But no one was there. The pain got worse, choking her, and she struggled under the covers, trying to throw them back.

"Time for breakfast!" Ila climbed up into the wagon, her cheerful little face haloed by the morning sun. "Are you awake? Diana!"

Diana couldn't breathe. She was choking. Her left hand clawed at the wall. Ila was at her side in a blur of motion, her little round face close. Her eyes were huge with concern.

"Oh! Oh! Diana, you've got to breathe! Don't let the ghosts steal your breath!"

Diana made a choking sound and wrenched herself upright. Ila flew backwards, hitting the wall. The young woman rolled out of the bed onto the cold, hard floor and her stomach heaved. Nothing came out. She started to curl up, banging her head on the floor. Ila scrambled down off the bed and threw her arms around Diana's shoulders.

With all her might, she dragged back, trying to uncurl the woman. There was a gasping sound and then a groan. Diana collapsed.

Ila rolled aside, panting with effort. She was strong for a girl her age, but the raw power in the woman's shoulders and upper arms was more than she could overcome.

"Are you breathing?" Ila pushed at Diana's shoulders and rolled the woman over. Diana stared at her with dead eyes. She said nothing. Ila sat back against the wall and let out a huge sigh of relief. "You *are* breathing."

After a moment, Diana sat up, looking away from the girl. She stood and began to dress herself. Ila waited for a little while, but Diana refused to look at her. The mousy girl frowned and thought of saying what was on her mind, but decided not to.

"Vitellix came back," she said at last. "He says that there will be a choosing tonight, at the house of one of the senators. He has invitations for two of us. I think he wants you and me to go with him."

"Why?" Diana was still facing the wall and her voice sounded listless and drained.

"Because there aren't any other female aerialists, silly. And only one Ila, who can ride horses."

Diana turned a little, looking over her shoulder, eyes dark with anger. "Anyone can ride a horse."

"Not like me," Ila said with a sniff of disdain. "You should know that."

Diana glared at the girl, but her anger had already faded. She felt ill—empty and full at the same time. The world was filled with portents and hidden signs; even the beatific face of the girl seemed to hide something. Something foul.

"I will go," she said, her voice still flat. "I should have some use."

It was well after dark when they came to the house of the senator. The street was lined with bright torches and lanterns. Vitellix flipped the reins and clucked at the two high-stepping horses drawing the little chariot. Diana and Ila, wrapped in heavy floor-length cloaks, clung to the rails. Otho and Franco had built the chariot the winter before for a new act. Tonight, feeling they needed to make a suitable entrance, Vitellix decided to drive.

The senator's house was on the side of a broad hill, on a narrow street of blank walls and deeply recessed doorways. Tonight, with this party under way, the walls of the house were ornamented with hanging garlands and wreaths of holly and flowers. Guardsmen loitered around the doorway. Vitellix pulled up and dismounted with a flourish. Diana stepped down lightly after him, the hood of the cloak pulled well over her face. Ila hopped down afterwards and twitched her own hood forwards.

A servant ran up and Vitellix passed the boy a coin and the reins. The boy ducked his head, pocketed the coin before the guardsmen could see, then led the horses and the chariot away. The nearest of the guardsmen, his helmet crowned by stiff plumes of ostrich feathers, raised a hand as the three stepped into the entryway. "Invitation, citizen."

Vitellix proffered a stamped metal disk. The guardsman squinted at the token, his face mostly hidden by his helmet. Satisfied, he waved them inside. Ila crept past, hiding between Diana and Vitellix. The Gaul seemed quite at home in this place with its high white walls and evergreen wreaths. Diana seemed comfortable as well, though the guardsmen looked at her suspiciously as she passed. The doorway led into a hall of pillars and smooth, polished stone floors. More servants were waiting.

Vitellix waved them aside, politely refusing drink, food, a companion and a place to put his cloak. Diana drifted after him, her footfalls whisper soft on shining marble. The hall was formed by a series of domed vaults. The ceiling of each dome was filled with a painting of blue sky, complete with fleecy clouds, birds and—in the center of one— a glowing golden sun. Circular iron chandeliers hung from chains in each dome, crowded with candles. Ila followed

Vitellix, her hand on his belt, staring up in wonder.

In the massed candlelight the domes gleamed and shone, sparkling like the blue skin of a fish. Somehow the light of the candles was reflected back onto the crowd of people filling the hall. Vitellix moved among them smoothly, nodding to those he knew, speaking a few words to some. Diana and Ila, quiet and unobtrusive in their dark gray cloaks, followed silently. Diana, in particular, was unusually quiet. Ila wondered if Diana was really following, but whenever Ila turned to look she was still there.

The hallway opened into a pillared arcade surrounding a garden. There were even more people, all dressed in fine, elegant clothes. Ila peeked around Vitellix, marveling at a cluster of women with their hair braided up into high, sweeping cones. Jewels and filaments of gold were woven into their coiffure, shining and winking in the light of hundreds of lamps and torches.

A constant, steady noise filled the air. Servants in plain yellow tunics moved through the crowd, bearing platters of sweetmeats, candies, iced drinks, cleverly cut fruit, cheese and small stuffed owls glazed with honey. Ila clung tighter to Vitellix, and the man reached back and squeezed her shoulder.

"Only a bit more of this, mouse. Then we'll be someplace quiet."

They turned right and walked the length of the arcade. Slowly, as they moved away from the entrance hallway and the main part of the garden, the press of the crowd eased. Finally, at the corner of the garden, where the arcade turned, Ila could breathe again. It was darker here, with only half as many racks of candles and lamps. They passed doors into the kitchens, where dozens of cooks and servants were hurrying about in clouds of smoke and steam. Men loitered outside the doors, chewing on hunks of meat, leather flagons in the crooks of their arms.

"Ah, Dionysos!" Vitellix saw a man he knew among a crowd of tradesmen and actors sitting on long marble benches at the side of the arcade. Here, out of sight of the main crowd at the front of the house, the "regular people," as Vitellix called them, were sitting and eating their supper. The Gaul stopped at one of the benches and clasped forearms with a scrawny little Latin.

"Vitellix, you dirty Gaul, it's been a time since I last saw you!"

"And I, you, runt." Vitellix hooked his thumbs into his belt, smiling down at the tiny old man. "Are you well?"

"Oh, I could be," Dionysos replied in a sour voice. It matched his shrunken old face perfectly. "If this fool of an emperor—all praise him, Lord and God!—would get about his divine business!"

Vitellix sighed in sympathy and motioned for the two women to step into the shadow of the nearest pillar. They had eaten supper from a hamper before entering the city. Ila was a little disappointed. Now that there were owls to eat, she wanted one. Vitellix had forbidden them to eat or drink at the party. Ila hid behind Diana's broad shoulders, looking about with interest. The scrawny man and Vitellix were catching up, nattering on about old friends and boring business.

The house itself was far more interesting. Every flat surface on wall and ceiling was covered with clever paintings or carvings in stone. Hundreds of servants were in motion, both in the arcade and in the garden, moving tables, carrying food, hauling off guests already overcome by an excess of drink. It was quite early, but Ila supposed some of the guests had started imbibing in advance. The crowd was even more interesting, filled with an astonishing array of costumes. Most of them were designed to display as much of the wearer's portable wealth or physical charms as possible. Only a few of the men were dressed in what Ila had heard was the "proper" style in the city: a tunic covered by a wrapped woolen cloak, worn draped over one arm and one shoulder.

As she watched the ebb and flow of people, Ila realized

there were currents spiraling out from the somberly dressed men and women. Everyone else, she realized, gauged their worth in the slow, subtle dance of the party by their distance from these few men and women who did not need to draw attention to themselves.

"Diana?"

"Yes, mouse?"

"Do you know any of these people?"

"No, mouse. I'm not sure that I want to."

"Oh."

At least two hours passed while they waited in the arcade. The party got bigger and louder, with more people flowing out of the entranceway. The trees in the garden were hung with lanterns made from parchment and candles, casting a fairy light over the walkways and the ornamental pools. Servants continued to issue out in a steady stream from the kitchens, returning some time later with empty platters and amphorae. The tradesmen, having eaten quite well at their host's expense, drifted off to the rear entrance of the house, taking their leave.

Finally, only a small group of actors and other performers were left. Diana, who had finally begun to pay attention to the conversation and the faces around her, realized that these were the masters of the troupes in the city. The little bent man, Dionysos, had a whole menagerie of trained animals. Two of the other men specialized in importing wild beasts from the frontiers to be matched against men in the arena. The rest were actors, acrobats, jugglers, illusionists and men who supplied troops of singing boys to the festivities of the rich and the powerful. Vitellix sat among them in ease, apparently quite familiar with all of them and their business.

Diana swallowed, feeling an echo of the dreadful pain she had suffered in the morning. She reached down and took Ila's hand, clutching it tightly. The little mouse girl looked up and smiled, patting her hand. The moment passed, but it left her unsettled and wary. As before, the sensation grew on her that the world she saw was only a thin veneer over something else, something horrible.

"Gentlemen, welcome."

A man approached, silver hair neatly outlining a bald pate. He was dressed very conservatively in a toga and tunic of archaic cut and style but exceptionally fine fabric. Diana felt her skin creep, seeing his affable smile and open face. There were two other men with him: a blond youth with long wavy hair and a white-haired, older man in a very expensive silk toga over a sharply pressed linen tunic.

"I am Gaius Julius," said the personable man, bowing to the assembled actors and performers. "My most esteemed and noble patron, Gregorius Auricus, has charged me with selecting performers for a private theater performance in honor of the recent birth of the Emperor's son, Theodosius Augustus Atreus. This will bring you some joy, I am sure, for the recent dearth of performances in the theater, the amphitheater and the circus has been a burden to everyone."

The actors and performers laughed heartily at this, grinning in delight at the news.

Diana felt worse. Her mouth was dry. She blinked, trying to clear her vision. It seemed that she was looking out of herself and upon herself at the same time. Raising a hand to her face, she closed her eyes, blocking out the sound of the man's commanding, polished voice. The darkness lasted for only a moment, almost immediately replaced by a wavering, vague vision of Vitellix in front of her, amid the assembled actors, *licinae* and performers.

With a start, Diana realized that she was looking out of the eyes of one of the men standing behind Gaius Julius. She could make out, in this watery vision, his shoulder and the clasp on his cape. Indeed, she could see Vitellix, frowning, his eyes intent as he stared back at her.

The vision suddenly passed and she was leaning on a pillar, turned away from everyone else, her breath ragged.

She was sweating furiously and her hands were trembling. The world, even the smooth surface of the column, seemed very distant. There was a commotion behind her. With an effort, she turned around, supporting herself on Ila's shoulders. "Mouse, what happened?"

Ila pointed. The silver-haired man was kneeling over the body of his blond companion, face stiff with concern. "That man suddenly fell over. Lord Gaius says he sometimes has fainting spells."

A pair of servants, summoned by the raised hand of the elderly gentleman, hurried over and helped Gaius Julius raise the body of his friend. Under the direction of the older man, they carried him away into one of the rooms in the house. Gaius Julius looked after them, his face stricken with worry, but then he turned back.

"My pardon, my friends. This is quite unexpected. Please, let us go down into the theater and you may show me your specialties."

Diana fell in behind Vitellix, who let the others go first. His fellow *lanistae* were quite eager to make the acquaintance of this Lord Gaius, crowding around him, their hands on his arms, their faces bright with cheer. In comparison, Vitellix did not seem pleased and kept looking behind him.

"Master, is something wrong?" Ila tugged at the Gaul's sleeve.

"No . . . nothing I can put my finger on, mouse." Vitellix smiled and put his arm around her shoulder, but he seemed distracted. "There was just something odd about that young man who fell down. But perhaps it was just the spell coming on him."

Diana followed her friends down to the end of the arcade and carefully descended a flight of steps. She was still very dizzy. The double vision had not returned, but her limbs and body were distant from her mind.

"Master Vitellix?" She stopped, clinging to the head of a carved, rearing lion standing in a curved alcove. "Wait a moment."

"Is something wrong with you, too?" Vitellix stepped to her and took her head in his hands, peering into her eyes. "You didn't eat anything here, did you?"

"No," Ila piped up, "we just sat and waited for you. Poor Diana's not been feeling well today."

Vitellix frowned at both of them. "You didn't tell me? Both of you will have to perform tonight!"

"I can ride the wire," Diana said, gathering herself and pushing away from the wall. Her face was suddenly grim and determined. "I felt dizzy when the boy fell down. Perhaps it was something in the air, a bad humor or vapor."

Vitellix stepped away, letting her descend the stairs. He gave Ila a hard look and then followed. He did not seem pleased. Ila scurried afterwards, hoping that he was not too mad at her. She had not thought to tell him, amid the excitement that they would have an audition, of Diana's troubled sleep.

The stairs cut down through the lower stories of the villa and into a small Odeon-style theater cut from the hillside. The flight ended on the top steps of the small, half-round space. The lord Gaius was already seated on the bottom row of steps, watching a pair of jugglers on the little stage. Diana looked around, measuring the distance from the stage floor to the top of the backdrop: barely twenty feet. Vitellix had noticed the small size as well.

"Hmm . . . not enough space for the wire."

"Or for the horses," Ila muttered in disappointment. Her face fell.

"No matter," Vitellix said, thinking furiously. "Let's just sit and see what the others have to show."

With that, he led them down the steps and into seats two rows behind the lord Gaius, who was watching with great appreciation as the jugglers flung an assortment of razor-sharp knives and burning-pitch torches back and forth at high speed. Diana felt much better as soon as she sat down, with solid granite under her. The warm presence of Vitellix and Ila on either side was comforting. She shuddered, realizing that the man whose eyes she had so strangely borrowed had been very cold. Ila took her hand again and they sat, watching the jugglers.

After almost two hours, with night deep in the sky, the last of the actors departed the stage. Only Lord Gaius and the three of them were left in the empty, nearly dark amphitheater. The Roman turned, smiling and seemingly tireless.

"You are quite patient, good Vitellix. I apologize for making you wait."

Diana's lip twitched. The man exuded such a sense of camaraderie and good nature that she surely *wanted* to like him, to sit at his table and drink and dine late into the night, discussing all manner of things. Sitting so close to him gave her the slow rolling creeps. He seemed so sinister behind the falsely genial mask.

What is making me feel this way? Why does he seem so familiar?

"I'm sorry, Lord Gaius, I hadn't realized we had met." Vitellix seemed a little flustered that the Roman patrician knew his name. The man waved a hand negligently in the air.

"Oh, we've not met personally," he said, smiling again, this time at Diana and Ila. "But I have many men out and about, seeing those troupes and acts that are performing. You were most recently at Narni, I believe, with some stage tumbling and some . . . unexpected wire work."

Now Lord Gaius smiled directly at Diana and she felt a chill shock, as if she had plunged her face into icy water. The man looked at her in such a raw way that she could almost feel his desire like a physical touch. With great effort she kept her face calm and smiled slightly, meeting his eyes.

That brought a second shock, for there was something strange about them. Though surrounded by a patchwork of laugh lines and wrinkles, they seemed cold and flat, like the many-lidded eyes of a reptile. Then he looked away, back to Vitellix.

"My agents say that your troupe is part of a very ancient and well-respected temple, the *Ludus Solis*. Is this true?"

Vitellix nodded slowly, though to Diana's eye he became even more guarded than before. The Roman did not seem to notice the change.

"Delightful! I am both honored and pleased, then, to make your acquaintance. I have not had the pleasure, despite being in Gaul more than once, to observe your temple's ancient rites."

Vitellix cleared his throat, looking sideways at the Roman.

"Lord Gaius, our temple is no longer so well respected. Indeed, only our small band is left of the ancient cult. Our people are much reduced since the conquest of Gaul. Yet we strive to keep the traditions alive in this modern time."

Gaius Julius nodded, his face serious. "I understand, Vitellix," he said, touching the Gaul's arm lightly. "Many good and worthwhile things have fallen by the wayside. It seems many worthy traditions have been lost. Still, there must be hope for your temple if it has such skilled and beautiful acolytes."

Vitellix did not look aside at Diana, keeping his eyes on the Roman. "Is there some hope that we may find a place in your agenda for these games, then? You have not seen us perform—this theater is too small for our skills."

Gaius Julius made a dismissive gesture, indicating the seats and the backdrop and the villa with an airy wave. "This is no proper venue for the capabilities of your troupe, friend Vitellix! You need something grander, I know, with the proper machinery and some space in which to show your skill." Gaius smiled at Ila. "You cannot ride a horse in this place, young mistress! No, the likes of the Flavian are for your accomplishments."

Diana felt Ila begin to smile and then swallow her reaction, making a terrible grimace. She felt the same way.

It would be joyful indeed to show her skill, to fly in tandem with Dummonus high above a cheering crowd. The Flavian sat at the heart of Rome, the most magnificent amphitheater in the Empire. What performer did not dream of appearing there? It would certainly fill Vitellix' purse with coin.

"We would be honored and embarrassed by your generosity, Lord Gaius, if you would consider us for a role in your production." Vitellix bowed his head, graciously, as should a client to a noble patron. Gaius Julius stood, holding out his hands.

"Dear Vitellix, I have always wanted to see the *Ludus Solis* perform. It honors me that you would choose my small production for such a sacred act." He bowed as well, though not so deeply as had Vitellix. "One of my men will come to your camp tomorrow with a contract."

Vitellix bowed again, reclaimed his hands and started up the stairs. Ila was hard on his heels, her cloak pulled tight around her. Diana felt like running swiftly up the steep marble steps herself, but she refrained and followed at a normal pace.

"Lady?"

Diana did not intend to turn, but Gaius Julius caught her cloak in such a way, as she stepped up, that the cloth fell away from her head and shoulder. She turned, her face impassive, and looked down upon him. Gaius had stepped up as well, catching both hems of her cloak in his hands. He looked upon her with delight, the corners of his mouth turning up.

"You are as beautiful as they said. Would you stay a little while with me?"

"I am sorry, Lord Gaius," she said in a toneless voice, "I must go."

One eyelid flickered as he digested her refusal. Diana could feel the others watching from above. Vitellix' anger seemed palpable in the air, interwoven with the sharpness of Ila's fear. Gaius Julius smiled again.

"My dear, there is no reason to hurry. The night is still half formed, an infant! It would please me and gain much for your temple." He took her hand in his and she quailed inwardly. He was cold, too, like a stone. "Tarry a little and I will show some of the wonders of this house."

"I will not," she said, her voice rising minutely. She turned her hand from his grip with an easy motion. A flicker of anger crossed his face and he grabbed at her wrist. Without thinking, she slipped from his grasping hand and hooked his thumb with her fist, turning it over in one swift motion. Gaius Julius hissed in pain and found himself on his knees, arm bent behind his back. Diana pressed for a moment until he gasped aloud, then let go.

"My apologies, Lord Gaius, I almost slipped. Thank you for your hospitality."

Diana turned and strode up the steps, anger boiling in her like water in a steam kettle. When she came abreast of Vitellix and Ila, they were watching her with shocked eyes.

"Let's go, lass." Vitellix pushed her ahead of him and they left the theater at a quick walk. "Ay, so much for that soft life we wanted to lead, reaping the benefits of the heir's birthday celebration!"

"We'd not like being reaped ourselves," Ila whispered in a serious voice. "He was a bad man."

"Yes," said Vitellix, looking over his back as they entered the arcade. "I hope he is not too angry."

Gaius Julius picked himself up. He brushed some dust from his toga and then looked around. The theater was silent and dark, quite deserted. He sighed in relief. It had been a close business to remember to express pain. With interest he flexed his fingers. He had felt nothing of the woman's crushing grip.

Well, well, well . . . Alexandros was right.

"Oh, a fine thing that was," he said, shaking his head. "Just charge in like a bull in heat . . . that works wonders."

He sighed and drew the hood of the toga up over his head. Just the sight of her, tall and slim, self-contained and so utterly composed had fired desire in him. Before that moment, he had forgotten the flesh and its pleasures. Even his dalliance with Alexandros had been calculated. Gaius found himself at the top of the stairs, his feet urging him to hurry after her. He began to grin, thinking of the swift motion of the girl's hand. "I shouldn't want to face that one with . . ."

He paused, one hand on the arch of the doorway, his face transfixed with an inner vision. ". . . a blade in her hand."

A delicious twist to the game had sprung to mind, full formed and vigorous with a shock of short red-gold hair and burning gray eyes. With it, he felt a tremendous giddy rush of delight, better than conquering any woman or nation.

"O you blessed gods, you swift Huntress and mighty Apollo! Did you see her move? Her speed! These informants are too cautious, I think. I will reward that one, though. He shall have a fine seat in the circus and coin in plenty to spend!"

With that, humming a tune he had learned from one of Gregorius' musicians, the old Roman made his way up the steps, thinking of his plans for the coming funeral games and celebrations. He had seen many interesting things tonight and the procession of acts, of intervals, of men and women in his great show was beginning to come clear. In the garden, he took a moment to smooth his tunic and his hair. It would not do to look like he had tried to tumble a maid in the bullrushes.

I have to see her again, he mused to himself, *and I will. But not in such romantic settings as these.*

The chariot ride was much quieter this time and Vitellix drove with care, avoiding the delivery wagons crowding the streets after dark. Diana stood at his side, saying nothing, holding the rail with one hand and Ila with the other. After a time, they left the walls through the Tiburtina gate and were passing through the countryside surrounding the city.

"Vitellix? May I ask you a question?"

Diana's voice was barely audible over the rattle of iron-rimmed wheels on the hard surface of the road. The Gaul slowed the chariot, clucking at the horses. They were still at least a mile from their camp, rolling amid acres of vineyards and wheat fields bounded by stone walls.

"Of course." Diana heard the tension in his voice and softened the words she used.

"What god do we serve with these performances? I must be quite dense, not to have realized it before, but you are a priest, aren't you?"

Vitellix laughed and seemed to relax.

"I am," he said ruefully. "A high priest, even, of a forgotten and neglected cult. I am frankly surprised that this lord Gaius knew us at all. His agents must be well informed! But to your question—we serve Lugh the Many-Handed, the lord of the sun and creation and song. Ours was once, as the man averred, a rich and powerful temple in Narbonensis. The sacred games of the sun, the 'ludus solis,' were attended by thousands. No more . . . in the time of the Conquest there were over a thousand priests. Now there are just the four of us."

"And me!" Ila growled, hitting Vitellix with her fist. "And Diana! Girls can serve the Many-Handed too!"

"Yes." Vitellix laughed. "In the old days, women were not allowed in the ranks of the priests, but that has changed. Ila's mother was the first, but she died of the cough, and now there are the two of you. In truth, I think the god delights in all expressions of art. Ours is just harder to express than most."

"Thank you," said Diana, hugging Ila and Vitellix. "I feel better now, refusing that man's advances. The god will protect us if we serve him well."

"I suppose . . ." Vitellix' face was indistinct in the darkness, but Diana thought that he was worried. "We still need to eat and feed the horses, though."

"I have cost us a place in these games." Diana bowed her head. "I am sorry."

"That was too high a price to pay," Vitellix said, flipping the reins and getting the horses going again. "Tomorrow I will go into the city again and see if I can find another patron, one less, ah, devoted to the arts."

AELIA CAPITOLINA, ROMAN JUDEA

A hundred of the Sahaba sprinted forward, leaping over broken white gravel and crumbling fieldstone walls. Half the men carried ladders, the other half great wicker screens. The air above them filled with a hissing cloud of arrows. More of the Arabs shot from cover, aiming to keep the defender's heads down.

"*Allau Akbar!*" All along the mile-wide front, the fierce cry of the Sahaba roared from thousands of throats. The sun was rising, pale gold light brushing the city towers. More Sahaba poured out of shallow trenches. Hierosolyma sat atop a rocky hill. The fields along the northern wall were poor and thin.

Arrows splintered on the limestone battlements, forcing the Roman defenders to duck. The Sahaba charging across the barren swath before the wall ran all-out. If they could reach the base of the wall, there would be shelter from the stones and arrows of the defenders. At the central gate on the Damascus road, the Romans were shooting back with winch-driven crossbows and slings. A siege tower three stories high, clapped together from looted planks, rumbled down the road, pushed by four hundred Arab warriors. It swayed and jiggled, forcing the men in the top to cling for dear life. Roman arrows filled the air, pincushioning the wooden facing of the tower. Suddenly one of the Sahaba crouched down in the top coughed and there was a tinny ringing sound. He fell back among his fellows, the side of his helmet caved in by a lead bullet. A moment later they pitched him over the side of the tower, letting him fall with a crunch onto the rocky soil below.

In the shelter of the smashed triumphal arch, Odenathus sat cross-legged, his eyes barely slits. The trap that had incinerated a good quarter of the Ben-Sarid cavalry on the first day had seared the bricks, giving them an odd, glassy sheen, and knocked down part of the arch. A band of Jalal's troops squatted around him, restless eyes watching the hills and the road. Each man's spear was laid on the ground close to hand and they had arrows on the bow. The main body of the Sahaba army was fully engaged in this assault, so it paid to keep a weather eye out for sorties from the city.

The siege tower approached the wall, still shaking and rumbling on the stone-surfaced road. The huge wheels made an enormous racket. The front of the tower was thick with arrows and bolts. Some of the arrows had been dipped in pitch and were still burning. Though the face of the tower was draped with wet hides, parts of it were aflame, shrouding it in a haze of dirty white smoke. Archers in the top were firing back now, trying to hit their adversaries on the gate towers. Beside and behind the tower, more Sahaba crowded forward, wicker shields held up between themselves and the wall.

There was a snapping sound off to the right of the triumphal arch. One of the scorpions the Sahaba had captured at Lejjun let fly. The huge machine rocked back hard, dust spurting from its wheels. A long throwing arm of Lebanese cedar quivered in the air, bouncing against a restraining bar. The sixty-pound stone shrieked towards the walls. Sahaban engineers scurried around the machine, preparing to crank it back with great toothed wheels and load another stone.

The stone crashed into one of the square towers rising from the main length of the wall. Fine white dust billowed back from the impact and there was a ripping sound. The dust rose up in a cloud as the tower trembled. The hurled stone bounced on the ground at the base of the wall. Then a section of the stone flaked away, tumbling down into the ditch below. The tower remained. Romans staggered to their feet on the roof.

Odenathus turned back to watch the business on the road. The fighting tower was very close, only a dozen yards from the gate, and it was burning fiercely now, though the Sahaba continued to roll it forward, their efforts punctuated with repeated cheers.

"Allau Ak-*bar*! Allau Ak-*bar*!"

The lead edge of the tower crunched into the bastion flanking the gate. Smoke gouted up, clouding the air around the wooden tower and the wall. The Sahaba in the top raised a great shout and dropped a toothed wooden plankway onto the battlement. Romans crowded there, their mail glinting in the morning sun, swords already stabbing at the Arabs crowding out of the tower.

Odenathus tore his eyes away from the distant scene. He concentrated, reaching out slowly and carefully into the hidden world.

I should have done something by now! The Palmyrene was nervous. Jalal would be getting impatient, waiting with the main body of the Sahaba a mile away on the other side of the city. The northern wall of Hierosolyma ran from northeast to southwest. It turned southwards on the eastern side at the verge of the steep-sided Valley of Kidron. Similarly, to the southwest, it turned to follow a ridge that ran under the western flank of the city. Two main gates opened in the circuit of the wall—the northern, or Damascus, gate, and the western, or Joppa, gate. The western gate stood under the brooding flank of the Roman praetorium, a stout-looking citadel built directly into the wall. This was approached by a sloping road that ran under the wall itself, dropping from the ridge down into the Hinom Valley.

During the night, while the main body of the Sahaba made noise in the north, Jalal and two thousand of his best men had crept into the western valley to hide among the olive and lemon groves. Partially shielded by the ramp of the road, they were waiting for Roman attention to be focused in the north. In particular, the Roman wizards had to show themselves. Jalal intended to have his men scramble up a forty-foot stretch of rubble to reach the ramp, then cross thirty feet of open marble-surfaced road to the gate. It was an approach completely devoid of cover. Once there, they would have to storm the gate without the support of their one wizard, who was crouching on the other side of the city, waiting to engage the attention of their enemy.

The fighting on the wall by the siege tower grew sharper, with more Sahaba climbing out of the burning structure. The fighters had seized part of the wall. Ladders were going up all along the battlements, heaved up by eager hands, some men climbing the rickety rungs even before the ladders had touched down. Most of the men climbing the wall wore the clan signs of the ben-Sarid twisted into their armor or kaffiyeh. Odenathus closed his eyes.

The unseen world was furious with activity. Thousands of men running, fighting, dying, putting forth all their will to survive clouded it with dizzying waves of sparks and half-seen flames. Even the flow of power in the ground rippled and contorted, influenced by those struggling above. It made any kind of work very difficult. This complication usually limited sorcery in battle to defense or subtle effect.

Odenathus concentrated, focusing his will, and fixed his thought on the siege tower. He had spent the night placing simple patterns of defense on the wood. He had also etched a watching eye, squeezing his own tears into the cut wood. Now, with his intent upon it, that mirrored eye opened in the hidden world and he was there, atop the tower, wreathed in flame and smoke and shouting men.

The top of the wall was thick with men, pushing and shoving, shields locked, hewing at one another with axes and swords. Some of the Sahaba wielded spiked maces. A horrendous banging sound filled the air, mixed with the screams of the wounded. Before the heedless frenzy of the Ben-Sarid, the Romans fell back, yielding a thirty-foot section of rampart. Odenathus scanned the wall, looking for the telltale traces of a hidden pattern or the enemy himself.

There! On the nearest tower, a hundred feet away, a mage-ward swirled and reflected. In the shelter of the arch Odenathus made a motion with his hand, tracing the pattern of a shield mnemonic. His shadow counterpart on top of the siege tower duplicated the action. The glittering blue orb of the Shield of Athena sprang up around the fighting platform. Odenathus could feel the hidden world flex and de-form as the power on the wall tower became aware of him.

Time compressed, seeming to drag slowly, and Odenathus reached deep into the earth. There were hidden springs and rivers beneath the barren land, each a glowing blue current of power. He felt it rise, strengthening his shield, but it was slow work. The dim figure on the wall tower moved and the hidden world was filled with a violent reddish light.

Odenathus blinked, his eyes streaming with tears, and he fell backwards.

The siege tower blew apart in a shocking blast of light and fire. Burning men were thrown skyward, wreathed in blue-white fire and trailing smoke. The top of the wall was ripped by the blast, knocking men down. Shattered timbers torn from the superstructure of the tower scythed into the tightly packed ranks of the Sahaba. Men fell, pierced by rapierlike splinters. Others leapt screaming into the plaza behind the wall, their armor red-hot, cloaks smoldering and covered with tiny flames. All around the base of the tower, the Arabs surging forward to attack the wall lay in windrows, thrown down by the shock of the blast. Even the Romans were stunned.

The tower, stripped down to a skeleton of furiously burning logs, fell apart, pelting the men on the ground with red-hot embers and lengths of flaming wood. In the shelter of the archway, Odenathus staggered up, his right hand twisting in the air as he dragged at the power he had gathered around himself. A flickering electric-blue sphere leapt across the space between him and his enemy. There was a burst of light and a crazy display of reflections as the sphere smashed into the Roman shield. The facets darkened and flexed, then sprang back, burning even brighter.

The Palmyrene cursed, wiping his palms on his tunic. Smoke billowed up out of the ruined tower, blocking his view of the wall. Odenathus could feel the vibration of his enemy. It was far too familiar. He mouthed a curse.

Damn that boy! He gets stronger every time we cross swords. . . . Gods, Dwyrin, I don't want to hurt you!

A sharp boom echoed through the praetorium. Nicholas' head jerked up and he looked out the nearest window in surprise. It was narrow and barred with iron, but it showed the rooftops of the city and part of the northern wall. The centurion had been deep in conversation with Sextus Verus, the commander of the Roman engineers. Nicholas had begun to worry about the water supplies in the city. The siege was beginning to drag out and it seemed the "desert bandits" weren't going to leave. It might take months for a relieving Roman army to reach them.

"What was that?" Nicholas squinted out the slit of the window. A huge column of smoke rose from the northern gate, but the sound had been much closer. Sextus Verus was staring out the other window of the corner room.

"Centurion! It's the gate here! They're all over the ramp road!"

Nicholas cursed, interrupted by a second boom that made the pens and cups on the table shake. That one was close! Without looking back, the centurion leapt down the narrow flight of stone steps leading to the main floor. Sextus' boots rattled on the stairs behind him.

At the base of the staircase there was a common room, now filled with surprised-looking men and Vladimir, who was wiping his mouth. The Walach slept late. He spent the night prowling the wall outside the city, looking for unwary bandits and stray sheep. He was hungry most of the time, since all he wanted to eat was meat. Nicholas had put everyone on siege rations the very first day and directly controlled all of the grain in the city. They might be down to rats and dogs by the end, but they would not run out of food any sooner than absolutely necessary.

"Attack on the Joppa gate," Nicholas shouted as he ran across the room. "Signal the reserves!"

The men followed with a cry, snatching up weapons and shields. One of the boys that ran messages for the garrison sprinted back up the stairs, heading for the roof of the citadel. Some of the soldiers paused a moment to cram on a helmet, then the whole lot poured out of the main floor of the citadel and into the square. Other men, citizens, were running towards the gate as well, scrawny hands wrapped around makeshift spears or scythes. Some few had crude round shields and swords.

Aelia Capitolina was cursed with a polyglot population of locals, Syrians, Egyptians, Arabs, Roman settlers and vagrants. Hardly anyone could call it the city of their fathers. Despite fierce proscriptions, a number of odd religious cults remained active in the area, and many of their adherents had fled into the city with the approach of the Arab army. Luckily for Nicholas, a large number of legionaries had been settled here as part of an Imperial effort to "pacify" the province. Those men were old, but they still remembered how to be soldiers.

They and their sons held the northern wall. Many of the other denizens of the old city refused to fight at all, hiding in their homes behind locked and barricaded doors. Nicholas sometimes wished that he had the troops to root them out and expel them from the city, but he dared not fight a civic insurrection as well.

A violent crashing echoed out of the gatehouse as Nicholas skidded to a halt in the gloom under the gate. Sunlight suddenly flooded the dark chamber as the gate splintered open. The centurion cursed violently and slipped Brunhilde from her sheath with a singing rasp. The iron head of a large ram crashed through, throwing metal studs and heavy wood to the floor in a clatter. Nicholas caught a brief glimpse of the roadway outside the shattered door. It was thick with green turbans and round shields.

"Form shield wall!" Nicholas kicked debris away with his boots. He spared an instant to praise the Walküre for watching over him this day and reminding him on waking to kit out in full armor. Men surged in from the sunlight, leaping over the scattered wood. The ram retired, hauled back by a dozen brawny arms. Nicholas leapt forward, Brunhilde's hilts in both hands, and slashed the tip of her blade across the face of the first men swarming through the opening.

They were blinded for a moment, coming out of the sun and into the close darkness of the gatehouse. Unfortunately for Nicholas, it was a poorly designed structure, allowing the road to run straight into the city without so much as a dogleg or a second, interior gate.

The double-forged tip of the sword, razor sharp, sheared through the faces of the first three men, shattering bone and cartilage, spraying blood along its path in a flat hard arc. All three screamed horribly and toppled back. They fouled the men trying to push through the gate. Nicholas jumped in, ignoring the wounded men, and Brunhilde blurred down, shattering the helm of the next man with a ringing *clang*. The northern steel, birthed in Nebelungen forges, cut into the soft hand-forged iron like an adze into wood. The soldier convulsed, blood flooding out of his helmet. Nicholas wrenched the blade away, deforming the helmet and flinging it off into the crowd of men outside the gate.

Spears jabbed and there was suddenly a thicket of shields in front of him. Behind the green-turbaned soldiers, Nicholas caught sight of a thick-shouldered man shouting commands. The spearmen lurched forward as one, pressed by their comrades pouring up the slope outside. Nicholas skipped back, batting aside two spears snaking for his gut.

Then Vladimir was at his side, yowling his high-pitched war cry and swinging a heavy-bladed ax. It bit into the first shield and Nicholas tore his attention away. Another spear glanced from his breastplate and he twisted to one side. Brunhilde slashed down, splintering wood and hewing through two spear shafts. Another spear ground into his side and he gasped, feeling the point dig into the center of a mail link. Blood welled out, but Nicholas was past feeling any pain. Vladimir had retreated as well, fending off five or six spearmen with vicious sweeps of the ax.

"Shields, forward!" Sextus Verus' voice rang off the arched ceiling of the gatehouse.

Legionaries pushed past, their rectangular scutum covering them from ankle to chest. Nicholas felt them part, letting him fall back through them, and then there was an unholy racket as the Roman soldiers came to grips with the Arabs in the passage. Behind their interlocking wall of shields, the legionaries pushed in close, their short swords flickering in the space between the two lines of men.

More Arabs poured in, hacking overhand with their swords and trying to push forward with their spears. The Romans held in the passage, stabbing swords reaping a bloody harvest in the tight space. A second rank of Romans pushed past Nicholas, who squeezed back, his face slick with blood, to the square. He knew what would happen now. The legionaries would do their butcher's work in the gatehouse until the Arabs tired of dying. The critical moment had passed.

Vladimir was at his side, his bushy black beard thick with gore. The ax head was slick too.

"A nice wakeup." The Walach grinned. Nicholas could feel the eagerness in the man. "To the wall?"

"Yes," Nicholas said, pushing away from the cold stone. He needed to see what was happening in the city. Was this the only attack? There were barely enough Romans in the city to watch the whole length of the wall, much less repel multiple assaults.

Vladimir took the steps to the battlement three at a time, though Nicholas was beginning to shiver from the after-effects of the fight in the passage. When he got to the top of the stairs, he looked around in surprise. The sun was full in the sky and the white stones were already throwing back a shimmering heat. Cautiously, he peered around one of the merlons on the wall. The road below was swarming with men in desert robes, kaffiyeh twined with green cloth, swords and spears shining in the sun like a forest of silver. A sling-stone immediately spalled off the masonry and Nicholas ducked back, cursing.

"Archers!" he shouted down into the square. "Archers!"

A column of men with bows was running into the square even as he called out. Nicholas kept the reserve down at the center of the city, with boys squatting on the domed roof of the tetrapylon to watch for signals from the north gate, the praetorium, the temple of Jupiter or the tower at the Dung gate. At a full run, it took the lightly armored men of the reserves ten minutes to reach any portion of wall from the crossroads.

Vladimir howled down at the Arabs below the wall, shaking his ax at them. Someone below shot an arrow and the Walach jumped back, still grinning. "Pity the boy isn't here, he would slaughter them down there."

Nicholas waved the first archers coming up the stairs to the arrow ports. "There's only one of him, Vlad, and they attacked here after they fixed his position at the northern gate. You heard his thunder, just like I did."

Nicholas felt very tired. How long could they get by with this piecemeal defense?

The archers, mostly local kids with hunting bows and shepherds with slings, began shooting down into the press on the road. A cloud of arrows came hissing back, but the defenders had some advantage. A horn blew, clear and strong, and there were stentorian shouts from below. Nicholas risked another look over the wall. The Arabs were scrambling down the slope in a tan-and-green wave. A rear guard of men with shields backed away from the gate. Nicholas' eyes narrowed, seeing the thick-shouldered man in their midst, still shouting orders. They were withdrawing in good order, and swiftly too.

There's a commander, he thought, *mayhap even a general.*

The road below the walls emptied quickly and Nicholas spit a long series of curses when he saw they left it barren. No bodies, no fallen swords or spears. That was disheartening, since the citizens in the city were desperately short of armor and any kind of edged weapon. The loot from the abortive attack on the north gate had let him equip a good twenty men. There were forges inside the walls, and men skilled in making arms, but almost no iron stock to work from.

"Ah, Vlad . . . this is a real army. Where in Hel did it come from? Sextus! Where is that man?"

The centurion in charge of the engineers' cohort came up the steps. He was sweating. It didn't look like he had seen any combat, which was good because Nicholas had ordered him to stay out of any fighting. His technical skills were what they needed, not his sword arm.

"Yes, sir?"

Nicholas pointed with his chin to the gatehouse. "Fill in

the gateway. Levy the locals for workers, but get it done today."

The engineer raised an eyebrow, though the skeptical expression was mostly lost in the ragged bangs of his hair. "Entirely?"

Nicholas nodded.

"Will a facing wall with dirt behind it be enough, or should we try and brick the whole thing in?"

"Whatever you can get done today," Nicholas said, watching the enemy flit through the orchards in the valley below. "Then do the same thing for the northern gate. Block it all up. We're not going to be sallying forth in brave panoply anytime soon."

Sextus sighed and turned away, shoulders slumped with weariness. His work crews had already been stretched to the limit by the effort to get the wall itself in order. And now this?

No rest for the wicked, thought the engineer glumly.

Jalal strode through the Sahaba camp, face black with rage. Night was falling and the western sky was a sheet of plum and pale pink, striated with thin clouds. The campfires threw long shadows over rows of wounded men. Entire detachments had been wiped out today. A moaning, sobbing sound rose in cacophony around the general. At the entrance to the command tent, there was a cluster of guardsmen. Jalal seized the captain of the guard by his cloak and dragged him out into the twilight.

"See these men?" The guard captain, half choked, managed to nod. His hands clawed futilely at the bowman's thick wrists. "Take your men and cut the throat of every man badly burned. Now!"

Jalal threw the man to the ground, his face transfixed with rage. The guard captain stared up at him in horror. "Kill . . . kill them?"

"Yes," Jalal snarled, kicking the man in the side. "Unless you've a caravan of healer priests in tow, they will all die out here, slowly and in terrible pain. They have fallen in the service of the lord Mohammed and by all accounts they will make a swift passage to paradise. So, go!"

The man scrambled up, holding his throat. Jalal stared at him, terrible fury plain in his face, until the guard captain turned away, drawing his sword. Then the general entered the command tent. At one point the tent—acquired from the defeated Romans—had boasted a saffron-yellow awning. That had been cut into regular lengths and traded for fodder and grain for the pack animals that dragged the army wagons. Jalal did not believe in luxury as an end in itself.

At the center of the tent was a portable wooden table inlaid with an ivory mosaic showing the towns and cities of the Eastern Empire. Jalal had kept this particular piece of booty. Some expensive things were tools rather than distractions. Uri ben-Sarid, head low in exhaustion, armor and clothing caked with dust and blood, was standing on one side of the table. Most of his hair had been burned away and bandages swathed the side of his face. Opposite him, seated on a camp stool with his head in his hands, was the Palmyrene youth Odenathus.

Jalal snapped aside the cloth drape and stomped across the carpets to the table. Uri looked up at his entrance, then stepped back in alarm at the sight of his face. Without pausing, Jalal seized Odenathus by the collar of his mailed-iron shirt and dragged him to his feet.

"What—" Odenathus barely had time to make a noise before the big Sahaban smashed a thick, knotted fist into his face. There was a rude sound of crunching bone and Odenathus was flung down on the floor. Jalal kicked the three-legged chair away, sending it crashing into an iron-wood chest set against the wall.

"Useless child! Are you good for anything save getting good men killed?"

Uri had leapt around the table, intending to restrain Jalal, but now he stopped short and stared at the general in surprise. The Sahaba commander ignored the tribal chieftain, watching Odenathus clutch his broken nose. The Palmyrene had not cried out or fled.

"Our enemy," Odenathus said in a tight, controlled voice, "is stronger than I am. The best shield that I can build shatters before him if he puts forth his full effort." Blood seeped from under his hand, but Jalal saw that the youth's eyes were fixed calmly on him. Odenathus got his feet under him and stood.

"Then we will not play about with trying to *stop* his strongest *effort*," Jalal barked, voice ringing with sarcasm. "We will just *kill* him and be done with the matter."

"Kill him?" Odenathus' hand dropped in surprise, revealing a growing bruise and a crooked nose. "I can't kill him, he's my friend!"

Jalal's fist was lightning, smashing into the Palmyrene's stomach. Odenathus buckled, a great roaring sound in his ears, and tried to bring up a hand to protect his face. The Sahaban's trunklike leg crashed into his jaw and the Palmyrene was thrown back again, cracking his head against one of the supporting tent posts.

"We're not playing about here, you stupid child!" Jalal's voice rose into a howl. "Six hundred men were killed today because you couldn't stop your *dear beloved friend*!" Jalal grabbed Odenathus by the hair and dragged him to his feet. The youth could barely see or breathe. "I would kill you now to appease their spirits, if you weren't the only wizard I happen to have around!"

Odenathus sensed another fist coming at his face and, finally, anger sparked in his heart. He had spent the day wallowing in guilt, watching the litter bearers haul wounded men into the camp. The assault on the northern gate was a spectacular failure, with hundreds of men incinerated by Dwyrin's fire. The siege tower had been destroyed and the Sahaba who had reached the battlement had been hewn down. Odenathus had tried, again and again, to deflect the bolts, to hold a shield against Dwyrin's power, but it had been useless. His friend was too strong.

Jalal was still screaming at him and it was too much. Odenathus, despite the blinding pain in his face and head, let his thought settle and his will reach out into the hidden world.

The fist whipped through the air, aimed for the youth's ear, and then it stopped as if it had plunged into tar. Jalal goggled for a moment, seeing the air thicken around his outstretched arm. Odenathus' face wavered as if a fire stood between them, bloody and terribly grim.

"You may not hit me again," grated the young wizard and raised his hand.

The air rang like a great temple bar, drawing a cry of pain from Uri, and Jalal was hurled the length of the tent. His head, still encased in a heavy iron legionnaire's helmet, cracked against the main tent post, splintering the wood. The general gave forth a guttural grunt and sagged to the floor like a sack of millet. Odenathus stumbled forward, lips drawn back in a snarl. The map table sprang away from the distorted wall of air in front of him. Chairs and chests followed it a moment later, pressed aside by a gigantic invisible hand. Uri felt the power in the air wash over him, flinging him back into the cloth wall. Curlicues of pale white fire danced on the metal objects in the room and the Ben-Sarid lord felt his arms tingle as the hairs stood on end.

"This is your solution, to hit something until you feel better?" Odenathus laughed as he approached the supine form of the general. The body twitched, arms and legs limp, but now moved by the power that thickened the air and distorted the light. The Palmyrene clenched his fist and Jalal was blown through the back of the tent. The heavy cloth parted with a ripping sound and suddenly the entire back wall was gone, shredded away. The general sailed out into the darkness, flying over the heads of surprised soldiers and camp followers. A great wind rushed out, flattening their fires and blowing down tents.

"I will not kill my friend!"

Odenathus' voice raged like the storm winds out of the desert, cracking with anger and despair.

Jalal hit a supply wagon filled with huge pottery amphorae with a resounding crash. Wine and oil jetted out of the broken containers, leaving the general's legs sticking up out of the mess of crockery and broken wicker.

My friends. Odenathus spun around, his eyes wide with surprise. It was the familiar voice of Mohammed, but it echoed in his thoughts like his own. *We go, today, to war against a great nation. It is an empire that many of us have served in our lives. There are those among you who have friends, even relations, in the ranks of those we will fight.*

Odenathus stopped, shock-still, blood and tears leaking down his battered face. These were words that the lord Mohammed had addressed to the entire army when they had set forth from Petra to invade the northern Decapolis. The great camp at Lejjun had been their objective.

The day will come, as the Merciful and Compassionate One knows, when you will face someone dear to you in battle. They will be your enemy. They will strive against you, against the will of the power that moves the tide and the stars. When this occurs, you must put your faith and your heart in the hands of he who made men from clots of blood. All things begin with him and all things end with him. We strive against wickedness, and any man who falls in the service of the all-knowing and the all-seeing, he will find that paradise is his reward.

Odenathus shuddered. The boy, Dwyrin, his friend, was an enemy. Rome, the empire that he had once sworn to serve, was an enemy. There could be no quarter between them. He had given himself over to the service of the lord of the wasteland. Now the first hard choice had come.

The strange wind died down. Uri fell to the ground, as did a great deal of tent, crockery, tables and chairs. Odenathus knelt on the ground, his face contorted. He was trembling, trying not to cry out. He felt cold and empty, but something had become very clear to him.

I must kill Dwyrin or more of us will die.

Odenathus stuffed a cloth against his nose. It was still bleeding. He stood. Uri was watching him from the other side of the tent with wide eyes.

"Apologies, Lord Uri. I did not mean to harm anyone. That lummox is right, though."

The Ben-Sarid sheathed his dagger and stood up. His lean face was troubled. It had been a very hard day for the clan lord too, for his men had suffered grievously in the failed attack.

"What do you mean?" Uri sounded tired and exhausted.

"My mind has been clouded," Odenathus said and he realized that this was the literal truth. "I know this enemy wizard's capabilities as well as I know my own. I have no excuse for the losses your tribe has sustained. I owe your people a debt of blood. It will be repaid."

There was a clattering sound out in the darkness and a stentorian shouting. Odenathus grinned, his teeth white in the red wash that covered his face and beard. Jalal seemed to have recovered. "Once that blowing ox returns to the stable, I will tell you what we are going to do."

The streets of the city were narrow and overhung by ancient buildings, making them absolutely pitch black after dark. Dwyrin was only partially conscious of the gloom. His head hurt so much he wouldn't have noticed a slap. Guided by one of the local boys, he stumbled down a broad, flat flight of steps. Then they turned and passed through a maze of corridors and streets. The boy seemed to know where they were going, and Dwyrin followed along doggedly.

White sparks drifted in front of his eyes, clouding his vision. Curlicues of violet flame seemed to shimmer along his hands and arms if he looked down. Another sorcerer or thaumaturge might have been gibbering in fear now, watching in horror as the walls and bricks that surrounded him faded in and out of sight. Sometimes lighted rooms yawned before him, blurred by the indistinct vapor of walls and doors. He had overextended himself today, letting fire flow through him like a rain channel. It had eroded the symbolic mental barriers that kept his conscious mind from comprehending the true world.

Those same symbologies defined who he was in human terms. They gave him a name, a physical description, context for his thoughts and actions and they made him a unique entity. For most men, when those symbols ceased to define them, they went mad. Who could remain sane if he looked upon the face of chaos unveiled?

Once, Dwyrin had been stressed almost to the point of dissolution by the failure of these symbologies. He had survived. In the testing fire, he had become aware that there was a core pattern within the whirling dance of fire that described his physical body. There *was* a self, buried at the heart of his mobile shape. It was atomic, indivisible, but it was easily overlooked or forgotten. Something gave his pattern and form will and intent. This was what the teachers at the school named the *ka*, the indivisible spirit of man. Dwyrin had lived, clinging to that last, final uniqueness. From it, all things sprang. Many masters of the art never reached that point, blinded by their own pride and ego.

After an endless time filled with slowly writhing snake patterns that curled and squirmed under his feet, the boy led him into the citadel gatehouse. The room was warm and filled with firelight. Dwyrin stumbled into the edge of a table, cracking his thigh. Distantly, some part of his physical mind registered pain.

"Come on, lad, let me get an arm under . . ." Smell intruded, presenting an intelligible form where sight had failed. It was a warm, musky odor, thick with memories of the forest and newly turned earth and rotting logs.

"Vladimir?"

"Yes, lad," the Walach said, carrying him up the stairs. Dwyrin let his head fall against the man's chest. It was warm too, and soft with thick dark hair. Sound penetrated: the regular beating of a heart, the crack of a boot against a wooden door. Then there was softness: a blanket being turned over his weary body. Dwyrin tried to bring his vision under control.

"Is he all right?" That must be Nicholas. He sounded tired too, and concerned.

"His heart is strong," Vladimir answered, "but look at his eyes. Is he mad?"

"Lad?" Nicholas again. Dwyrin was aware of pressure and something closed. Ah, his eyelids. A hand was over them. Dwyrin could see the pattern of veins in it, pulsing with blood, and the twitch of muscles as it moved.

"I . . . hear . . . you." It was hard to make this body work. It moved so slowly. It was so cumbersome. "I . . . must sleep."

"Wine, perhaps?" Vladimir again and the sound of pottery rattling on the table.

"I've something better." Nicholas, voice receding. "Here." It was close again.

Something hot and bitter flooded his senses. Taste was still working properly. Something strong with alcohol. After a moment, Dwyrin felt a warm glow in his physical body, and the insane flight of the tiny brilliant lights that formed the air and the walls and the insides of his own eyelids suddenly dimmed. Welcome darkness flooded up, blotting out the true world.

The boy, lying on a Legion-issue cot in a nearly bare stone room in the citadel of the city, snored softly. His face, which had been a tense rictus, relaxed and the pale light seeping from his skin faded. Nicholas, his face slowly falling into shadow as the strange radiance died, breathed a sigh of relief.

"It's too hard on him," Vladimir said. "It wears on him. Look at him, Nick, he's like a ghost!"

"I know." Nicholas laid the back of his hand on the boys' forehead. It was very hot, the skin radiating heat like an iron stove. "But what can I do? Without him, those bandits would be over the wall in a day and *we* would all be dead."

Vladimir shook his head. He had no answer either.

SISCIA, MAGNA GOTHICA

)H(

Alexandros rode beside a swift river, sun shining in his golden hair. Along the bank, glossy-leaved willows drooped over the current. Great flocks of birds roosted in the trees, chattering like a storm cloud as he passed. The air was crisp and the Macedonian felt relieved to escape the dreary tomb of Rome.

The old Roman road turned through a break in the hedgerows and cut across a great field. Red flowers produced a riot of color against the dark hedge. Alexandros shouted, face lighting with joy when he saw horses browsing in the stubbly field. The herd, hundreds strong, drifted slowly across the side of a hill.

"They're beautiful," he called back to Ermanerich. "Do your people value horses?"

"Above all else," the Goth shouted back, light blue eyes twinkling. Ermanerich cantered up the hill. The Macedonian craned his neck, looking out over the valley. The horses had shied away, thundering down the far slope before turning and resuming their grazing. "What man can call himself a man without a horse?"

Alexandros nodded, feeling a subtle shock of recognition. Horses consumed fodder, effort and gold, but mounted men were the foundation of victory. Only Rome ignored this truth, relying on massed formations of heavily armored infantry.

But their lands are not well suited for horse herds, he reminded himself. *And they have been victorious for a long time.*

The Gothic prince pointed south, down the valley. A haze of gray wood smoke lay over the trees. "Our capital lies just there, friend Alexandros. You will see that it is a fine, modern city!"

Alexandros smiled to himself, hearing pride and insecurity mix like wine and water in his companion's voice. He had watched and listened, while they rode up out of Italia, crossed the snow-capped Alps and descended into the Pannonian basin. The Goths were a proud race, weaned on battle, and for a long time they had tested their strength against Rome, devastating the frontier. The greatest Roman defeat in modern history, at Adrianopolis, had been inflicted by Gothic arms.

A dark storm rushing out of the east had broken the death-struggle between the two nations. Ermanerich had labored through a long epic song to describe the war against the "ugly men." Tears had streaked his cheeks as he chanted the names of all the captains and heroes who had fallen at Olbia, where Attila had shattered the might of the Goths.

Trapped between the relentless Huns in the east and Rome in the west, the Goths had been forced to enter the Empire as penitents. At that time a Romanized Scythian named Flavius Aëtius had been Emperor of the West. Despite a dubious ancestry, Aëtius had, by constant and vigorous effort, restored the West and gladly accepted the Goths as a *foederata,* or "settled tribe." The description of the Gothic chiefs swearing fealty to the Western Emperor had raised the hackles on Alexandros' neck.

It was far too similar to the Legion oath Maxian had found in Khamûn's old book. Even the memory stirred unease in the Macedonian, knowing that each recitation of the story would bind the Gothic tribes ever closer in the service of the Empire. It had been enough, then, to stop the Huns, with Aëtius throwing back Attila's invasion of Gaul in a cataclysmic battle at Argentorate on the Rhenus. Extolling that victory, where the Goths had reclaimed their lost honor, occupied an entire evening. Again, Alexandros listened closely, picking out details of interest. The core of the Hunnish army, which crushed so many nations, was a host of heavily armored knights wielding a long, heavy spear called the *kontos*. Supported by masses of exemplary mounted archers, they had obliterated two Eastern Roman armies, as well as the Goths and Sarmatians, before breaking apart against Aëtius' Legions.

Since those heroic days, the Goths had held the Danuvius frontier from Carnuntum in the north to Sirmium in the south. From the evidence of his own eyes, Alexandros knew that it was a rich land, well watered and blessed with plentiful fields and easy-rolling hills. Under the tutelage of Roman engineers the Goths had reoccupied the fortresses along the river and repaired roads and bridges fallen into disuse during the Great Invasions. Even Siscia was relatively new, only sixty years old. The Goths were a strong, powerful people.

But they still knew, in their hearts, that Rome was the master. Alexandros could see it in Ermanerich's companions, a brash young lot, and in the boy himself. They *knew* they were strong, easily the equal of any Roman, yet this corrosive sense of inferiority bridled them. They were stepchildren of the Empire, and their hearts were filling with bile.

"This seems a rich land, Ermanerich. Is every man blessed with a fine horse?"

The Goths laughed and swirled around him, their faces bright. "That is so," they shouted, and two of the younger boys galloped down the hill towards the road. Ermanerich clucked at his horse and turned, following at a slower pace.

"Only the poorest men cannot ride. This land was empty

when we came and we have yet to fill it up. Though some try, I warrant!"

Alexandros responded with a grin. The Goths viewed large families as a right. In comparison to the Romans, they bred like rabbits. For the moment this meant more land fell under the plow every year and the towns along the river grew by leaps and bounds. It also meant there was still open land for horses. To Alexandros, Gothica promised everything he desired.

So many younger sons, filled with this desire for glory and honor won in battle . . . O Fates, I see your hand guiding me! I will sacrifice a white bull at your shrine, Ares, when I look upon dear Macedon again!

"Your people ride into battle, then." Alexandros let his horse turn onto the road. Poplars and beeches crowned the lane, making a dappled green tunnel. The smell of wood smoke filled the air, reminding the Macedonian they had not yet eaten a midday meal.

"No," Ermanerich scowled. "We fight on foot, behind our great shields, in line as the Romans direct. Some serve a-horse, scouting and covering the flanks of the army."

"You fight Roman-fashion?" Alexandros did not bother to disguise his surprise.

"Yes, the *reik* bids us do so and his advisers agree. It has always been this way."

"Why? Surely, if you and your cousins are any guide, you are fine horsemen!"

"Of course!" Ermanerich's sour mood lightened. "But that is not the Roman way. We follow the Emperor; his wisdom guides us and bids us fight in massed formations on foot, behind our round shields, axes and spears."

Alexandros frowned, but they were nearing the city, so he let the matter drop.

Siscia sat on the banks of the Savus, surrounded by a high wall of dressed stone studded with square towers. As they approached, Alexandros could see a gatehouse and towers flanking two gates, one set behind the other. A broad ditch ran at the base of the wall and a good hundred yards of space had been cleared out between the city and the forest. Oxen and kine grazed on the short grass filling the open meadow. To the left, a bastion rose on the bank of the river, easily double the width of one of the other towers. The Savus was thick with barges, skiffs and shallow-draft coasters.

They entered the gate, joining a steady stream of men and women in plain gray, brown or black homespun. Burly men with conical helmets and shirts of leaf-shaped mail under madder-dyed red cloaks eyed them as they passed into the shadow of the gate. Horsetail plumes hung down from their helmets and their faces were hard. Alexandros judged them to be veterans, not just city militia sent to police the gate. They were armed with long, plain-hilted swords in tooled-leather scabbards.

Within the walls, broad, regular streets, surfaced with fitted stone, marked the city. As in a Roman city, there were no wagons in evidence during the day, but there was a thick press of men on horses and every kind of citizen on foot. Two- and three-story wooden buildings lined the streets, most overhanging the avenues.

Despite the press in the streets the city did not seem festive. Many of the passersby flowing around Alexandros seemed tight-faced and quiet. Everyone moved with purpose. Occasional dashes of color revealed merchants or traders from the south.

Not a Greek city!

"Here is the house of my father," Ermanerich said, raising his voice over the mutter of the crowd. "You are our guest, so while you are with us, he will feed you and see that you have wine and beer in plenty to drown your thirst. Ho, Olotharix!"

Alexandros looked up as they rode through an arched doorway into a stableyard. The house was three stories high, with a sharply angled tile roof and red-painted wooden columns making a portico on one side of the yard. What seemed to be a stone barn sat to his right, where servants in plain white tunics came out to greet Ermanerich and his cousins. Alexandros slid down from the horse and patted its nose affectionately. It was no warhorse, but it had a pleasant disposition and hadn't complained all the way from Rome.

Two boys descended steps from the house, carrying flagons of wine and rounds of cheese. Ermanerich, having seen his own horse into the stable, joined Alexandros and motioned for his guest to join the boys on the portico.

"This is our custom, which came with us from the Salt Sea," he said, raising one of the flagons. With gusto, he drank deep, letting the wine spill red on the ground. This done, he tore a hunk of thick white cheese from the round and chewed it down.

Alexandros took the greeting cup himself and drained it dry. The wine was sweet and thick, hardly watered at all. It burned in his throat like an old friend and he ate the cheese with relish. It was heady with flavor, and sprinkled with tart seeds. It was light work to pretend hunger in front of these men.

"Greetings, Alexandros, son of Phillip, friend of the house of Theodoric!"

"Greetings, Ermanerich," the Macedonian replied, gripping the youth's arm with his own. "son of Theodoric, third of that name, *reik* of the Goths. Well met, I say, and I accept your welcome with a warm heart."

"Come inside," Ermanerich said, clapping his friend on the shoulder. "Later there will be a great feast and endless drinking, so my father wanted to meet you now, while he can still see your face."

Bales and boxes of goods occupied the portico, and women in dark tunics were working at looms set up under the eaves. These were tall wooden structures, fitted with copper and bronze guides, and the *clack-clack* of their shuttles filled the air. Ermanerich led Alexandros through a series of rooms occupied by women and children working at long plank tables. A great deal of industry, both to make and repair clothing and to devise ornamental brooches and clasps, seemed to be under way. Beyond these rooms was a second courtyard, this one larger and planted with fruit trees.

Alexandros, passing through the rooms, was struck by the degree of industry in the house of the King. Memories from his youth came to mind, and he again felt a shock of recognition. This was not the highly specialized environs of Rome, where every man devoted his life to one or perhaps two tasks. There, in that sprawling metropolis, the city functioned as a whole. Here, in this thriving city on the edge of the barbarian frontier, each household was responsible for the goods that they would use, wear or wield. Some specialized items, like swords or fired pottery, would be constructed at a dedicated building, but everything else was in each man's hand. This was the Pella of his youth, not the Babylon or Persepolis where he had ruled as a god-king.

Well, he thought as they walked up a short flight of steps into a high-ceilinged hall, *in every* woman's *hand, at least.*

The feasting hall was two stories high, with a balcony running around three of the four walls. The fourth wall faced the south and was pierced by high, narrow windows with sharply pointed tops. On a clear, sunny day like this, light flooded the southern end of the hall, illuminating a raised dais holding a long plank table and high-backed chairs. Other long tables ran the length of the hall, flanked by smooth-planed benches.

A white-haired man was sitting in the high seat, deep in conversation with two companions. Alexandros and Ermanerich approached slowly, giving the elders time to see and acknowledge their presence. The rest of the hall was empty at this hour. Alexandros breathed deep, savoring the smell of old smoke, wine, urine, fear, sweat and intrigue permeating the air, wood and long, rectangular tapestries hanging from the plastered walls.

This is Pella, he reminded himself, settling his face into a calm mask. *Here is a ruler like my father. I am not king here!*

Ermanerich knelt on one knee and Alexandros followed. Paying the lord of the house courtesy did honor to any man and cost nothing. Besides, in his youth, the Macedonian had ordered men slain for failing to render him due greeting.

"Ermanerich, you pup, stand and face me."

Theodoric's voice was gravelly and strong, though when the Gothic king rose Alexandros saw his cheeks were hollow with age and his eyes bright under bushy white eyebrows. Here was a chieftain who stood tall in his youth, his voice bellowing out over the battlefield, wheaten hair streaming behind him in the wind. Age had stolen his strength but not his great heart or the quick intelligence hiding behind the bushy white beard and the glowering nose.

Ermanerich stood, smiling, and clasped hands with the man and the woman who sat beside the reik. Alexandros waited to see how he would be introduced.

"My *new* aunt, Theodelinda," Ermanerich said, indicating the woman sitting at the reik's left hand. Alexandros inclined his head and the matron nodded back. Her deep blue eyes gleamed like the winter sea, and she was richly dressed, but not in Roman fashion. Instead of plain wool, her gowns were embroidered with a dizzying array of scenes and bright colors. Pale hair was tied back behind her head by a jeweled fillet of gold. Heavy rings were on her fingers.

"I am honored, Lady Theodelinda," Alexandros said.

"My *old* uncle, Geofric, who has lately wed, as you can see." There was subdued laughter in Ermanerich's voice, but neither guile nor hate. Alexandros took note of this. In time everything he learned here would be critical to his success. He made a half-bow to the elderly Geofric, recognizing him from the house of Gregorius Auricus in Rome. The uncle was a man of middling height, not yet bowed with age, with a raspy voice and a short-cropped brown beard.

Geofric raised an eyebrow and returned Alexandros' greeting. The Macedonian did not miss the moment of recognition in the man's eyes. *So, he knows me. Or has seen me before. Good.*

"Lord Geofric, well met."

"Father," Ermanerich said, turning to the reik, "this is Alexandros, who comes to us from Rome as a friend and ally. He hails from the East, from old Macedon."

"Welcome, Alexandros." The reik's voice settled into a low, rumbling boom. "Sit with my son, here, and tell us why you have come. My son thinks well of you, or so his letters say. He feels you do your venerable name honor."

Alexandros felt a momentary chill, feeling the intense scrutiny of the three sitting on the dais. He suppressed an urge to run his hand through his hair. *This is Pella! Remember that!* These were barbarians, true, but that did not mean they could not read the classics, or reason, or draw conclusions from the evidence of their own eyes.

"I make no heroic claims," he said. "What I have done, I have done. Your son speaks well of you, my lord, and through him I see the greatness of the Gutthilda."

"Haw!" Geofric barked in laughter. "You flatter us, Greek. You see our woolly-headedness, you mean."

"I do not flatter," Alexandros said in a flat voice, catching the reik's eye. "I am an impatient man and have never found time for anything but honesty. Ermanerich is young, true, but in him I see the strength and the weakness of your people."

"This may be so," Theodelinda said sweetly, cutting off her husband. Geofric looked pained but kept his peace. "But you have not said why you have come. Our dear nephew tells us that you come from the house of Gregorius

Auricus, our close friend and confidante. What do you bring us from him?"

Alexandros drew a folded packet from the pocket of his cloak. The letter was on a rich, creamy parchment, newly made, and tied with purple twine. He held it in his hands, still watching the face of the reik.

"Though I have been favored with the hospitality and grace of Senator Gregorius, I do not speak for him, nor do I come with his words on my tongue. To give my message legs, I wish to remind the reik of an offer made by the Gothic people to the Empire two years ago. At that time, with the Eastern Empire on the verge of collapse, the senator went before the Emperor and proposed no less than sixty thousand Gothic fighting men could be placed in the service of the Empire, should the Emperor but allow such a thing to happen."

"That offer," Geofric interjected, his tone verging on insult, "was rejected out of hand. It has been withdrawn. If the Western Emperor does not require anything of Gothic honor but policing the river, then that is all he will get!"

Alexandros ignored the outburst, turning the letter over in his hands. "Emperor Galen is a Roman. He believed Roman arms could succor the East and he was right. The lord Geofric may take exception to the Emperor's decision, but the honor of the Gutthilda has not been impugned. Many Goths fought in the army that broke the back of Persia. They gained great wealth and honor by those means. Their songs will be heard around many a campfire."

Alexandros raised the letter to the reik, holding it out to him. "My master is the Caesar and Prince, Maxian Atreus, coregent of the West."

This was technically true, though no one had seen the Prince in months. Still, Gaius Julius had proved a dab hand at forgery, and the scrawl on this letter could not be distinguished from the Prince's own. As the old Roman had said smugly, it was what the Prince would have wanted to say, if only he were around to write it down himself.

"He is a friend of the Gothic people. He knows the strength of the Gutthilda and their numbers. He knows these sixty thousand would be a royal gift. He knows the young men yearn to find glory of their own, glory which can only be won on the field of battle, in the company of their peers and under the eyes of their own chieftains."

Ermanerich, his eyes shining, nodded sharply to his father as Alexandros said this. The old reik watched and listened intently, gnarled old hands clasped in his lap.

"The Prince, in his wisdom, believes a great struggle is coming, one that will either see the Empire restored in full or cast down, at last, in utter ruin. In that final battle, the Prince would have the might and splendor of the Gutthilda at his side. This is why I have come to you, bearing this token."

Alexandros watched the subtle play of emotions on the faces of the old reik and Geofric. He had thought a long time about these words. Relations between the Eastern Empire and the Goths had always been strained, for they had been blood enemies before the coming of the Huns. The West, in comparison, had given them a new home. Like many of the tribes north of the Danuvius, the Goths were a moody and violent race, steeped in a long tradition of mutual slaughter and heroic death. Alexandros had listened carefully to the tales the Gothic boys told around the fire. Much like the Macedonian tribesmen of his youth, they longed for an epic final battle in which all would be decided and both the living and the dead, simply by taking the field of battle, would gain undying renown.

Rage—bright goddess, sing to me of Peleus' son Achilles . . . Old words, long dear to the Macedonian, came to his mind, and he knew the same yearning was in his own heart. *Murderous, doomed, he that cost the Achaeans so many men, hurling down to the House of the Dead countless souls* . . .

Only Theodelinda seemed unmoved, but Alexandros had already marked her as the one he must truly convince. She reminded him far too much of his own long-dead mother.

"The day will come," he continued, "and far too soon, I fear, when the Empire will call upon you for your full strength of arms. On that day, the Prince would have the Gothic people stand forth, showing their true mettle and might, unafraid of any enemy, well garbed and armored, staunch in the defense of their honorable vows."

"The Prince," Theodelinda said in a wry voice, "must be a miracle worker to conjure up this army of myrmidons. Honor and valor drive the heart to battle, but cold iron and steel do the dreadful work. Your dear Prince may dream of these sixty thousand, but can he feed the mouth of war from his purse?"

Alexandros smiled coldly at the woman and placed the packet in the reik's hand. Theodoric took the message, caressing the creamy surface of the parchment, and unbound the twine.

"My lord, these letters of credit, insured by Gregorius Auricus himself, will provide the funds to equip, train, garb and supply an army of forty thousand men. The funds may be drawn from accounts in Aquilea, Thessalonica and Salonae. There are also the names of men in those cities who can supply weapons, wagons, grain and livestock to support such an effort."

Alexandros did not mention that the noble senator did not, in fact, know the ultimate destination of the funds he—and the Imperial exchequer—were pouring into the private games now under way in Rome. Some Imperial estates, held in the name of Prince Maxian, were mortgaged to the hilt by Gaius Julius, acting as the Prince's agent. In time, these things would be discovered, but Alexandros did not care. It was on the old Roman's head to deal with such matters.

"This is a writ from the hand of Caesar Maxian himself." Alexandros drew a second letter from his cloak. Theodelina was watching with great amusement, while Geofric stared in sudden avarice at the letters in his brother's lap. To his credit, Theodoric was actually reading the papers, eyes flickering over the close-set lines of text. "It duly appoints the formation of a Gothic *auxillia* to assist the Legions in the defense of the public peace. An *equites comitatus* is appointed to command this formation, which of course will comprise these forty thousand men. While in the general course of campaign this *comes* will be under the authority of the Emperor, he may also undertake independent action, if warranted by circumstance."

"You've some papers then," Theodelinda said, leaning forward on the arm of her chair, "giving a thin veneer of respectability to raising a mercenary army within the Empire, one that would certainly be viewed with grave suspicion by the Emperor himself. Theodoric, this seems a short road to rebellion and the violation of your ancient oaths. We will all be a head shorter!"

Alexandros shook his head. "My lord, there is no rebellion here, no intrigue. The prince Maxian would *never* raise arms against his brother." The honesty in the Macedonian's voice was plainly apparent.

"What is this, then, if not a maneuver for the Purple?"

Alexandros kept his eyes on the reik, ignoring the baiting tone in the woman's voice. "This is what I have said, my lord. The Caesar Maxian has arranged to finance and field an *auxillia* for the defense of the Western Empire. A formation that will fight together, that will not be broken up, that will not be parceled out until no man knows his tentmates and no one sees his deeds."

Theodoric folded the letters of credit back together and took the writ from Alexandros' hand. He considered it for some time, reading the letter twice, and then he raised his bright old eyes up and squinted at Alexandros.

"Who," he asked, "will command this army?"

"I will," Alexandros said.

"What is this foolishness?" Geofric could not contain himself any longer. He gestured violently at his older brother. "So much talk of a Gothic army, but they send a foreign boy, a Greek, no less, to command us? This is an insult!"

Theodelinda placed a hand on her husband's arm and caught his eye. He glared at her for a moment, then subsided. Alexandros watched the exchange out of the corner of his eye. The reik was looking upon him with a musing expression.

"You have seen war, then, Alexandros." The reik made a bald statement, not a question, so the Macedonian remained quiet, hands clasped behind his back. "What do you want of the Goths? Why are you here, and not another?"

Alexandros felt his eyelid twitch despite an effort to show nothing to these vipers.

"This is what I know. I am not a man of peace. I do not dig in the earth or till the fields. I love the feel of a swift horse under my thighs, but I could not devote my life to them. I was sent to you because there is no other place that I could imagine being."

Theodoric laughed softly, tucking the letters away in the folds of his robe. The reik looked upon his two colleagues and his eyes grinned though his face did not.

"I know your mind, Geofric. Dear Theodelinda, what think you of this?"

The woman smiled coyly and inclined her head. Her fingers smoothed the line of her gown. Alexandros realized, watching her and the two men, she was not a Goth. The planes and angles of her face were subtly different from theirs, her hair a different shade and thickness.

"The young men trouble me, my lord. Something must be done to fill their hearts. If they remain at home they will only cause strife amongst the clans. They are idle and this breeds trouble. Those who wish to cut new farms from the forest or become tradesmen have already done so. You see them, restless, watching from the steps of their houses. If you do not choose a war for them, they will start one themselves. This, I know."

The woman's voice was heavy with hidden pain and hard-won knowledge. Alexandros felt for her. Once he had been a troublesome, bloodthirsty youth, desiring only strife to fill his cup of glory. Theodoric turned to Alexandros, a thin finger brushing his mustaches.

"You bring us no gift, young man. You are a heavy cost, with these pretty letters and bold words. How many young men will die if you lead them to war? Thousands?"

The reik seemed old then, exhausted by a long life. Alexandros knew the Goths had spilt oceans of blood—their own and their enemies'—to hold the frontier against the Huns and the Vandals and every other tribe which had come against them.

"My lord, send no man against his will. Let those that are restless, those that would cause trouble amongst the clans, let them choose their own way. If they seek war and glory, they will have it in plenty. But do not command men to follow me."

Alexandros watched Geofric and Theodelinda out of the corner of his eye. The man seemed puzzled by this turn, but the woman was laughing silently. Theodoric was no fool either; that was clear from the calculating expression on his face. Alexandros prayed silently for the old king's acquiescence. Things would be much more difficult if the King were directly involved in this. Let him keep his hands clean; leaving Alexandros' hands free.

"Perhaps." Theodoric made a gesture and Ermanerich rose, touching Alexandros' arm. The Gothic youth's face was stricken, but he obeyed his father's will. Theodelinda smiled as they walked away. Geofric watched with ill-disguised bile.

The bowyer was named Angantyr and he lived in a long, high-ceilinged building by the river. Two drying sheds and a laminating workshop formed a rough dirt square with his hall. After inquiring in the main building, which they found filled with craftsmen busy over their workbenches, the two men trooped down to the riverside. A long archery butt had been cleared along the bank, aimed at a great mound of dirt faced with logs.

"Master Angantyr!" Ermanerich called as they approached a man standing at the near end of the butt. The bowyer was whip thin. Unlike the usual run of Goths, he had narrow, dark features and quick black eyes. As they came up he was testing the pull on a heavily ornamented self-bow—a single curved stave of wood. Angantyr pressed it away from him, letting the corded horsehair string reach its full draw. Seemingly satisfied, he placed the stock against his shoe, bent the stave and unshipped the string. Without acknowledging them, he curled the string up and put it in a jeweled pouch strapped to his waist. The ornamentation on the purse matched that of the bow.

"A beautiful piece of work, master." Alexandros indicated the bow with his chin.

Angantyr looked up, his face tight with suspicion. "It is a passable device," he said, slipping the stave into a tubular leather case. Like the bow, the case was velvety leather with gold fixtures and an embroidered hunting scene. "The pull is sufficiently light."

"A gift, then, to a lady?"

Angantyr nodded, passing the case and purse to a servant standing behind him. The slave hurried away up the hill. Alexandros rested the foot of his own bow case on the ground. It stood nearly as tall as he did himself.

"Master Angantyr, this is Alexandros of Macedonia. He is a guest of my father."

The bowyer ignored Ermanerich and jutted his chin at the bow case. "You've something you need me to fix, then? Break a top ear?"

"No." Alexandros grinned. He had dealt with craftsmen

before, many times and in many places. "I've come about a consignment—you're well respected in these parts—but I'd like to know if you can fill a large order."

Angantyr laughed wheezily. "We're not some Roman *fabrica* to count success in job lots of a thousand, lad! I specialize in fine bows, in works of art!" His thin hand indicated the buildings and the jeweled bow just departed.

"My pardon, master. I need a copy of this bow and I was informed you could make one. However, if you no longer make *working* bows, then I will search elsewhere. Good day."

Alexandros turned, picking up the bow case, and began walking up the hill. Ermanerich, startled, hurried after. The bowyer's mouth dropped open and no sound came out.

"Wait, Alex! I thought you needed another bow for yourself!"

The Macedonian smiled, turning so Angantyr could hear him clearly. "I need more than one, and they are very difficult to make. I have heard, though, there is a man in Sirmium who might be able to help me."

"Wait." Angantyr's voice carried easily in the cool air. The afternoon sun was westering and the air was growing chill. "Let me see that bow."

The Macedonian turned. "Are you sure? I need a large number. Doubtless more than your shop can make."

Angantyr glowered. "Let me judge that."

"Very well." Alexandros stopped and laid the bow case on the grass. He wiped both hands on his woolen leggings. It would be an insult to get this weapon dirty. He knelt and opened the case. Inside was a bow covered in soft cloth, with another item bundled below it. Padding made from raw wool filled the case, keeping the objects from rattling. Alexandros stood, unwrapping the bow. As he did so, he watched Angantyr's face, which suffused first with delight and then, just as swiftly, fell back into anger.

"You're a fool," he barked as Alexandros held up the

bow for his inspection. "No one can make a bow like that, much less in quantity!"

The bow was a little over five feet long, with a sharp C-shaped curve. The stave itself was made of a wooden core with laminated sinew covering the inside of the C and the outside burnished with horn. In addition, the long, tapering ears ended in square knocks for the string, reinforced by two bone plaques, one on either side of the ear. Three bone plaques also reinforced the handle, where a man would place his hand. The top ear was very long and straight, while the bottom ear was short and curved. Alexandros unwound the horsehair string looped around the long top knock and reversed the bow so the knock rested on the tip of his boot. With a smooth motion, he laid the string along the back of the bow stave and drew it to the short knock. The end of the string threaded into a laminated bone hook on the square knock. As he strung the bow, the C shape reversed, straightening and curving back against the original orientation. The weapon gleamed in the sun, filled with subtle beauty.

"Master?" Alexandros reached down and drew a long flight arrow from the case. He presented the weapon to Angantyr, who was looking at the bow with a sick expression.

The craftsman shook his head and raised a hand. "No, there's no need for me to torture myself."

Alexandros turned to Ermanerich, who was looking back and forth between the two men in puzzlement. "Would you care to take a shot?"

The Gothic youth nodded and took the bow in his hands. With sure fingers he knocked the arrow to the bow and then tried to draw the string back towards him. It resisted him, stiff and solid as a log. Ermanerich grunted, muscles bunching in his shoulder, his fingers, cocked around the string, turning white.

"Lad . . . not like that. This is a Hunnic bow; you push the stave rather than drawing the string."

Alexandros took the bow back, slotted the arrow to the string and then laid the shaft along his left hand. With a simple pushing motion he pressed the stave away from him, drawing the head of the arrow to his finger. He turned, sighting across the river at a passing barge. It flew a blue flag ornamented with gods and sea serpents. The bargemen were lounging on the deck, watching the shore slide by as the current carried them down the river.

"Careful!" Angantyr barked, but Alexandros had already sighted, lifted the bow and loosed the arrow.

The arrow snapped away. It curved in a high arc, flashing out over the river, and then disappeared in the sky. Instants later, there was a cracking sound and the flagpole on the barge toppled over. The bargemen leapt up, staring about in alarm. Alexandros laughed.

"Gods! What a shot!" Ermanerich stared out at the river. The barge was at least four hundred feet away. "Can you teach me to shoot like that?"

"I can," Alexandros said, while Angantyr blurted out, "He can't!"

Alexandros caught the bowyer's eye. The man flushed.

"You mean," the Macedonian said, "you can't make a bow like this one, for the Prince to shoot. Or, should I say, you don't know *how* to make a bow like this."

Angantyr's lip curled up in a half-snarl, but he was at heart an honest man. After an obvious and almost comical struggle, he said: "This is the truth. I do not know how to make the Hun bow."

Alexandros smiled warmly at the man. Not many craftsmen would have been so honest.

"Why?" Ermanerich stared at the bow in his hands. "It looks like most any bow."

"True enough," Alexandros said, holding the weapon reverently. "In fact, I have in the case a written step-by-step description of how one builds such a weapon. From the selection of the proper woods and bone and horn, down to the mixture necessary to make the laminating glue. A

Roman *fabrica,* in fact, could churn out hundreds of these, all looking much alike. But they would not be *this* bow."

"It's the tuning," Angantyr muttered, staring at the ground and grinding his teeth. "A delicate matter. It takes months to make the bow shoot properly. And the glue . . ." He eyed Alexandros with suspicion. "How did you get the formula for the glue?"

Alexandros grinned and wrapped the bow back up.

"Rome is filled with all manner of people and foreigners. It's been that way for centuries. Master Angantyr, with what I have in this case, you can make these bows yourself—the same materials, the same design. But you are right, it will take months to tune each bow for optimum performance, for the longest flight, the straightest shot. That will take endless trial and error."

Angantyr shook his head violently. "It's impossible! How would I make a living, if all my time were spent fiddling with these damned Hun bows? What about my other commissions?" He paused, squinting at Alexandros. "What do you want these bows for, anyway?"

Alexandros smiled again and nodded to Ermanerich. "The Prince and his friends are going to use them, mounted, from horses."

"What?" Both Ermanerich and Angantyr exclaimed at the same time.

"Goths don't fight like slaves or brigands!" Ermanerich said.

"No one can draw a bow and fire with accuracy from a running horse!" Angantyr seemed outraged at the very thought.

"The Huns do," Alexandros said with equanimity.

"Nonsense!" Angantyr expressed himself violently. His eyes bulged with the force of his emotions. "The Huns are born and bred in the saddle! It's in their blood!"

"That *is* nonsense," Alexandros said quietly. He looked around and saw the sun was close to setting. A deep purple gloaming settled over the river. A huge flock of wading birds rose and flapped past overhead, black-and-white wings flashing with the last rays of sunlight. Night crept out of the east, covering the far hills and valleys. It was peaceful, listening to the soft murmur of the river. "Let's go in, it's getting dark."

The feasting in Theodoric's hall lasted late into the night, but the Macedonian watched considerable business being done at the reik's table. Of course, once the singing started, it was impossible to hear anything more than a foot away. Despite this, Alexandros observed the manner and custom of the men and women around him, taking note of their speech and deportment. After two hours he felt he roughly understood most of the politics in the kingdom. Or at least the portion which had been under way here, tonight, in the feasting hall.

A skald was summoned and instructed by Theodoric to recite one of the ancient lays. This was a sign, for the few remaining men and women at the lower tables now rose, paid their respects to the reik and departed. Theodoric motioned to Alexandros, indicating a seat now vacant at his side. There were four other men, each richly dressed, sitting beneath the high seat. Theodelinda and Geofric remained as well.

"Honored guest," Theodoric rumbled, "I have discussed this matter with my close advisers. We are blessed by the Caesar Maxian's friendship. We are flattered by his offer of assistance. The honor of the Goths is well known—how can we refuse such a request? Our strong arm has always been the bulwark of the Empire. We thrive under the Emperor's guidance."

Alexandros nodded, catching an undertone of bitter respect.

"I am sure," continued the reik, "many loyal Goths will be eager to join you. However, my advisers express concern over this business. We too have towns and cities to protect. Our own people cannot be left defenseless by this levy. Therefore I put upon you these strictures: no man may join you who holds land in our name; no man may join you who is married; no man may join you who owes a debt of blood or coin; and no man may join you who already serves as the *huscarl* of a lord. Within these strictures, you have my permission to undertake the Caesar's task."

Alexandros rose from the chair, feeling the weight of these men's eyes upon him. He felt a little giddy, for he could not have asked for a better outcome. He bowed to the reik.

"You are a generous king," he said, "and your renowned wisdom is shown in full. May I ask whom you will entrust with the execution of the letters I placed in your hand today?"

Theodoric smiled, eyes wrinkling in amusement. He was a king. Where coin lay, there was power.

"I am minded," Theodoric mused to himself, "that my youngest son, Ermanerich, should learn such business. It will do him good to grasp this thistle and hold it tight. He will see to the execution of these letters." The reik reached into his cloak and handed them to Alexandros. The Macedonian kept his composure, for two letters of credit were returned where three had been given.

As Gaius Julius had expected, Alexandros thought. The honesty of the Goths was like that of other men. A third of the planned funds would be diverted into the pockets of the reik. *No matter, no matter . . . I will take the rest from enemies of the Empire.*

"Go about this business, then, Alexandros of the Macedonians. Know that my eye is upon you and with you. My son, in this matter, will speak with my voice. I expect that you will do all honor to the Gutthilda and to Rome."

"I will, reik, you have my pledge on it."

Alexandros bowed deeply to the old king and then descended the steps to the lower tables. He needed to void the cold, leaden bread in his stomach, now bloated with wine, and he needed to write Gaius Julius a letter. Some matters had come clear and some remained obscure. Ermanerich was waiting, watching him with hopeful eyes. "Come, my friend, let's get poor Angantyr home to his workshop."

The Gothic prince nodded, glancing over his shoulder at his father. The old king was listening to the skald, seemingly asleep, a thin, blue-veined hand covering his face. Alexandros put a hand on the youth's shoulder, beckoning with his head.

"Leave them; your father has given us what we need. Let him rest. His time is passing swiftly enough."

Together, they went out of the hall and into the night.

[0]-[0]-[0]-[0]-[0]-[0]-[0]-[0]-[0]-[0]-[0]-[0]-[0]-[0]-[0]-[0]-[0]-[0]-[0]-[0]-[0]

THE PALATINE, ROMA MATER

)(

L ord and god, the Caesar Aurelian has arrived."
Galen, Emperor of the West, nodded to the servant, then returned his attention to the tablets and parchments covering his desk. Absently, he said, "Send him in and see that he gets something to eat and drink."

With summer full upon the city, Galen had moved his office into the cooler palace of Tiberius on the northern side of the Palatine Hill. The summer sun in Rome was strong enough, reflecting off acres of marble, to illuminate the rooms with a clear light. From here, too, the Emperor could look down upon the Forum Romanum. It also took him away from the Circus Maximus, all too visible from the windows of his winter office.

The circus should have been filled each day with boisterous, cheering crowds. Instead, the long racetrack lay quiet and abandoned, filled with drifts of dirty gray ash.

Galen chewed on the end of his quill pen, tapping it against his teeth while he considered the documents before him. One of his strongest supporters, the senator Gregorius Auricus, had laid before him a well-thought-out plan to resume the public round of tragic plays, chariot races, gladiatorial combats, wild-animal hunts, pantomimes, mocked-up naval battles and performances by tumblers, jugglers, fools and magicians that occupied the idle hours of the city's populace.

For no apparent reason, the Emperor could not bring himself to sign the papers and issue the appropriate edicts. These proposals meant nothing more than the resumption of Rome's daily routine. Yet, his mind was uneasy. Some nagging thought, half-formed, urged him to delay.

His forehead wrinkled in concern, but he set the proposal aside in a clearly labeled hinged wooden folder. Immediately, one of the scribes padded forward and took the book away. The walls were lined with alcoves and slots for storing manuscripts and books. The original contents— Tiberius' personal collection—had been moved to the huge, four-story Imperial library on the southern side of the hill. That left storage space for all of the paperwork generated by Galen's administration. The scribe filed the report away, then resumed his place behind a desk.

Galen, a literate citizen, drafted all of his own edicts and proclamations. However, they had to be duplicated en masse and that meant a veritable army of scribes to proof, copy and distribute his words. Six clerks usually worked in the room, heads bent over portable teak writing desks. The *skritch-skritch* of their pens, coupled with the susurration of slow-moving fans built into the ceiling, formed a relaxing background noise.

"Brother, how plays the day?"

The Emperor looked up and gave a wan smile to match the cheery expression on his brother's broad tan face. Aurelian, as usual, was kitted out in Legion cavalry half-armor and a maroon cloak. Coupled with his big red beard, it made him look like a friendly bear in gleaming armor. Heedless of Galen's orderly piles, Aurelian pushed aside the papers and sat down on the corner of the desk. The Emperor waved away two scribes creeping up to try and gather the scattered papers.

"Poorly, as it usually does, with giant lummoxes crashing about, disturbing the peace."

Aurelian grinned, teeth white in the thicket of his beard. "You spend too much time in here, mewed up with these ink-stained automatons."

"Huh. You held this chair while I was away in the East. I could retire to Tivoli and take my ease in the countryside, but then *you* would have to be here instead. Would you like that?"

"I would not!" Aurelian made a horrible face, miming disgust at the thought. "You deserve this, I'm sure. Better to be afield, on a fine horse, with sun and wind in my hair."

"Hmmm. Perhaps. You've just come from the south?"

"Yes," Aurelian said and, for a wonder, his expression remained cheerful. "Things are going well! The harbors at Puteoli and Misenum are cleared, so the fleet has a harborage closer than Syracuse, and the work at Stabiae and Neapolis is well under way. The air has freshened, too, so that the loss of life from poisonous vapors has all but disappeared."

One of the problems afflicting the men laboring in the dead cities were pockets of poisonous gas trapped in the rubble. Workers digging in the ash were often overcome. Many had died.

"And the graves?"

Aurelian's expression darkened. "All done, at last. So many of them . . . my clerks tally the total loss of life at just over forty thousand men, women and children. Countless animals also perished. We've burned all of them, lest they stench up the entire province, and the citizens have been either interred or cremated, when we could find a relative to tell us what to do. The towns of Herculaneum, Pompeii and Acerrae have been completely destroyed. Herculaneum and Pompeii, in fact, are completely gone, buried under cooling ash and lava. Acerrae still stands, but every last living thing in the *urb* was killed by poisonous vapors. On the other hand, the damage to the Via Appia and the Via Popila has been almost completely repaired. I spoke with Gregorius Auricus' man, Gaius Julius, who has charge of the project. He's done a fine job."

Galen put his chin in his hand and sighed, thinking of the plan to reopen the circus. Gregorius and this Gaius had put that together as well.

"Then matters are well in hand," he said.

"Yes," Aurelian said cheerfully. "There is even a chance of a harvest in the late fall if the weather remains mild. Some of the older farmers tell me that the lands under the ash will be even more fertile than they were before. Well, if there are reasonable rains . . ."

"Huh," Galen grunted. "Watered with the blood of the citizens! That is some good news. I am glad that you can be done with it, for I've another task at hand. This one will be outdoors, too, so you can rest easy about that."

"Really? What has happened?" Aurelian looked excited at the prospect of continuing his work in the field. Rarely had Galen met a man less suited for working in an office. The Emperor gestured to one of the servants standing by the door.

"Nilos, send in tribune Dagobert. He should be in the triclinium. Horse, have you had anything to eat today?"

Aurelian looked puzzled for a moment, then said, "By Hercules, no! I'm famished."

Galen made a face and then gestured to the servants again. "Bring something to eat for all three of us. We'll take it on the terrace."

When dour old Tiberius had built his residence on the Palatine, it had been a regular two-story Roman town house. Somewhat more richly appointed than most, but still traditional. Later, when Domitian the Cruel had torn down the patrician villas remaining on the hill to build his massive, integrated palace complex, a garden terrace had been added to the northern side of the Villa Triana.

The result, as far as Galen was concerned, was that he had a fine shady garden outside his office, where he could take a meal with his brother and the commander of the Rhine Legions in peace and quiet. Before he left the desk, he put it in order, then followed his brother out onto the terrace. The servants had already set up a brass table with a decorated cloth, plates and some wine.

"Something has happened," Galen said as he sat. Nilos appeared, leading Dagobert, who was looking around in appreciation at the garden and the view and the serving girls carrying out plates of cold meats, cheese, bread, candied figs, fresh-cut vegetables, sliced fruits and a honey-glazed duck. "Aurelian, you've met Dagobert, son of Lothair, before, yes?"

Aurelian nodded to the Frankish noble in greeting. The tribune was a very tall man with long fair hair. Like most of the northern barbarians, he was blue-eyed and sharp-featured. Dagobert bowed deeply to the Emperor and, at Galen's gesture, sat. With most men, the Frank would have been lordly, even remote, but seated in the company of his avowed lord he was diffident and humble. Like Aurelian, he was wearing the polished breastplate, greaves and leather *pteruges* of a Legion officer under a dark cloak.

"Ave, Lord and God," he said. "You are well?"

"I am," Galen said, picking at the food on his plate with an eating tine. "How stand things in Gaul?"

"They are good, Augustus," Dagobert replied. Aurelian, meanwhile, had piled an enormous amount of spiced lamb, bread and cheese on his plate. Apparently ravenous, the Caesar was digging into the food after anointing it liberally with fish sauce. "Recent actions in the south have restored order amongst the truculent Euskadae and the Bretons. The frontier along the Rhenus remains intact. In all, things are of a peaceful state, which I think will maintain for the rest of the year."

"Good," Galen said with heartfelt relief. "What of Britannia?"

Dagobert sighed and his good humor vanished. "Things are not so well. Last year it seemed reasonable to withdraw the Legion at Eboracum. Unfortunately, a great force of Scandians landed on the eastern shore in spring and the local chiefs, despite strenuous efforts, have failed to dislodge them. I have sent a mishmash of cohorts drawn from here and from there to aid Ammianus, who is governor of Britannia. It may not be enough."

Galen tapped his nose with a forefinger. He had other reports, sent by agents in Londinium, relating the same tale. Luckily, the Northmen had come ashore in the great fens and bogs near Branodunum, a poor and desolate part of the province. While the local governor could not get at the invaders, neither could they pillage the countryside.

"It will be enough for the moment," Galen said after considering the matter. "The Britons are doughty fighters. I will send Ammianus a rescript withholding taxation from the province and placing the sums so gathered in his own hands, to arm and outfit men to repel this attack. Between this aid and the reinforcements you have already sent, he should be able to punish these barbarians thoroughly."

"Perhaps," Dagobert said, unconvinced. "Ammianus is not a general. He may not be suitable for the task."

"Who commands the troops already sent?"

"My third-best legate, a Briton himself, named Uthar. He is a solid man, so he should be able to at least hold the Scandians at bay. Pepin, my second, I have left in command of the Rhenus Legions, in case the tribes beyond the river decide to try us while I am away."

Aurelian stopped stuffing his mouth with fried bread dipped in garlic butter for a moment.

"Not drive them off?" The Caesar seemed angry at the

prospect. "Not crush these barbarians and cast them back into the sea amid the ruin of their ships?"

"No," Dagobert said, shaking his head. A flinty look entered his eyes at the disbelief in Aurelian's face. "Things are changing in the north, beyond the frontier. The Scandian tribes grow very numerous, while our numbers of men under arms remain the same, or less, than they were before. In Germania and Gaul we are very lucky, for the Saxons and the Franks-beyond-the-River are our shield."

Dagobert took pains to distance himself as a chief of the Franks-within-the-Empire from those that remained outside of Roman jurisdiction. The near collapse of the Western Empire during the previous century allowed many tribes, including the Franks, to migrate into Gaul. When Imperial order had been restored, the various Emperors had adopted a policy of dissemination. Each household was allotted lands scattered throughout Gaul and the Narbonensis. In this way, by diluting the invaders amongst the mostly Romanized Gaulish population, it was hoped the outlanders would abandon their old ways and become Roman citizens.

Galen was not sure the policy was working, but it did provide a sorely needed reservoir of soldiery for the Western Legions. Dagobert was a good example. His forefathers had led the Frankish migration. Now he served in the Legion and had risen to a very respectable rank. In this way, the Empire directed the ambitions of those who might otherwise seek to carve a demesne from the corpse of the Imperial order.

"Britannia," the tribune continued, "does not have that luxury. Its long eastern coast is exposed to Scandian raids and invasion. Our northern fleet is in a parlous state as well, with most of the ships withdrawn to the Mare Internum. We are not able to contest these raids at sea . . . Lord and God, I know that you have won a great victory in the East, but we need to set our own house in order before too much more time has passed."

The Emperor curled his fingers into a fist. He knew all these things, but hard choices had to be made, and Dagobert lacked the latest news from the East. "Tribune, I take your words to heart, but let me relate what I have recently learned."

Aurelian, polishing off a cream custard glazed with Indian cinnamon, looked up with interest. Dagobert's long face grew longer.

"I have kept this news from common circulation," Galen began after taking a sip of wine. "Because I do not wish the people to be further troubled, still shaken as they are by the eruption of Vesuvius. However, this will be common currency in the Forum and the markets by the end of the week, for the ship that brought it to me will be only the first of many.

"In the recent war against the Persians, the Eastern Emperor used the Hellenic cities of the Decapolis and Syria as pawns to keep the main Persian army in play, while we struck out of the north. In the short term, this maneuver worked admirably and the Sassanid kings have been thrown down. Unfortunately, these same cities of the Decapolis and Nabatean Petra suffered heavily. In fact, the frontier city of Palmyra was utterly destroyed.

"To make matters plain, these diverse cities have risen up in revolt, aided by certain Arab tribes, against the Eastern Emperor. Further, they have won two great victories in Syria. First, they have smashed and scattered a great Eastern army under the command of Prince Theodore."

"Haw!" Aurelian smirked. "That pup didn't learn, did he? I remember what you've said of him, Gales. Got his soldier lopped off, did he? Waving it around in public, I warrant."

Galen stilled his brother with a stern glance and continued. "Prince Theodore then worsened the problem by abandoning the campaign and fleeing back to Constantinople, leaving the remains of his army under the command of an Armenian mercenary named Vardanes. Stripped of most of his troops, Vardanes fell back into Syria Magna. At the time that seemed prudent, since Damascus is the lynchpin of the Eastern frontier.

"However, the commanders of this rebellion are not short-sighted men. From the fragmentary accounts that I have received, it seems they split their army into at least three elements. One, I suspect the largest, has moved north to besiege Damascus. The second made its way in haste to the coast and stormed the great port of Caesarea Maritima. The third has moved south to threaten Egypt."

Aurelian and Dagobert's eyes widened. It was not enough that the entire Eastern frontier should collapse, but now the critical corn supply from Egypt—the source of nearly a quarter of the corn consumed in Rome and *all* of the supply for Constantinople—was threatened. These were daring rebels indeed.

"This is not all," Galen continued in a bleak voice. "I am assured the lamentable Prince Theodore also left these rebels a generous gift. At Caesarea, in harbor, awaiting his further command, was nearly half of the Eastern fleet, warships and transports alike. A very great portion of that fleet is now in the hands of the rebels."

"Bugger all," Aurelian hissed. He was no clerk, but he knew the value of a fleet in the Mare Internum. "There's not been a hostile, non-Roman fleet in the Inner Sea for centuries!"

"True enough, Horse, but no longer the case."

"The corn supply," Dagobert said slowly. "Unless this fleet is destroyed, they will threaten Egypt from both land and sea. The Eastern Empire will be crippled."

"And we will suffer as well." Galen gestured towards the south. "The loss of the Campanian farmlands in this eruption will require us to import an additional five million tons of wheat, rye and millet from the delta in the next two years. Normally, this would not be an issue, since the Egyptian harvests have been high for the past decade, but if Egypt is lost?"

"Famine," Aurelian muttered, looking out over the red roofs and white temples of the city. "Riots and insurrection, rationing . . . Can the African provinces make up the lack?"

"I have sent letters to the governors of Mauretania and Numidia, urging them to see more land placed under cultivation and all harvests are well accounted for. Some portion of their production is exported to the black kingdoms beyond the Gates of Hercules, but not enough to make up the difference."

Dagobert leaned back in his wicker chair, thick-fingered hand stroking his clean-shaven chin.

"What will we do?" Aurelian was pensive. "Egypt is our responsibility now, since you brokered that deal with Heraclius two years ago. We have, what? A half-legion of miscellaneous troops there? Not much of a garrison."

"True," Galen said, sitting forward, hands clasped. "They will need to be reinforced. I have given considerable thought to this matter in the past week. This is my intent: Aurelian, you will take command of the Western fleet and the three legions currently recuperating and retraining here in Rome. You will sail to Egypt as soon as possible and secure the province. Those three legions, comprising the First Minerva, Second Triana and Third Augusta, are our best troops. With them, you should be able to repel any attack."

"I'll say!" Aurelian got a gleam in his eye. "Do you suppose, if I take Judea and Syria back, we can keep them?"

Galen glared at his brother and Aurelian put up his hands in surrender.

"Dagobert, I've a task for you, too. As you know we are stretched very thin on all fronts. It is a necessity for us to put more troops into the field, particularly if the situation in Britannia grows worse. To that end, there are six fresh legions being mustered at Mediolanum. I want you to go there and take over the completion of their training.

It will be a task, since we are desperately short of experienced soldiers. But you will have to make it work."

"Six fresh legions?" Dagobert was aghast. It seemed impossible. "Where did you find sixty thousand men?"

Galen smiled grimly. It was a bitter pill to swallow, to come to grips with the fact that such a number seemed impossible to one of the highest-ranking military officers in the Western Empire. Galen knew the taste well, for it was constantly in his mouth, bitter as ash.

"They are not the best men," he said. "Most are freed slaves, others are barbarians, many are prisoners released from the mines and farms. A leavening of patrician youth has been thrown into the mix, but not enough. You must make it work, Dagobert. I am sure that the Eastern Empire will recover from Theodore's folly; we just need to hold things together for the rest of the year."

"Gales . . . I know you mean well, but I can't take all of our experienced troops to Egypt and leave the tribune with that lot! Let me leave him the Third Augusta and take two of these raw legions with me. Then he'll have a reliable core, and experienced officers, to get the rest in shape."

The Emperor frowned, pinching his nose. His instincts said Egypt was critical and urged him to protect it with his best men. Still, he could split the force, reducing the burden on Dagobert, while Aurelian and his experienced officers took the fresh legions to task.

"You want to dare this defense of Egypt with inexperienced troops?"

"Yes," Aurelian said firmly, sharing a quick glance with Dagobert, who looked vastly relieved. "You know that terrain as well as I—if they come at us by land, they have to cross the desert between Gazzah in southern Judea and Pelusium on the edge of the Nile delta. The avenue of approach is narrow and we can fortify it—these new men will be good for digging, if nothing else. Look, Gales, what if something else happens? You'll have no reserve at all if you send me everything."

Galen snarled, wishing that his brother would be a dumb cow and accept what he was given. Unfortunately, the Horse was right.

"I can call up the Goths," he said, half-heartedly. "I've been informed, more than once, that they can put another fifty to sixty thousand men into the field if I need them."

Both Dagobert and Aurelian paled at the proposal. Galen knew why—the Goths were a slowly festering sore on the flank of the Empire. They were vigorous and powerful, with a rapidly expanding population and a reckless eagerness for war. Despite the fact that they ably held a long section of the frontier, there were strict Imperial edicts in place limiting the number of men they could have under arms. The policies of dissemination also applied to the Legions, where men were enrolled as individuals, not as clans. The influx of such a great number of Goths all at once would break down that carefully controlled policy, leaving the West with a Gothic legion rather than a Roman one.

"That," Dagobert said slowly, "would not be wise."

The tribune looked like he had bitten into a sour olive. The Franks had been pushed into the Empire by the Goths after a series of humiliating defeats. The memory of those losses still haunted Dagobert and his kinsmen. Part of the balance of the northern frontier was held upright by the tension between the two nations. Galen, like his predecessors, managed to keep it from swinging too much in either direction.

"I know," Galen said, feeling the weight of his responsibilities crush down again. "Very well, the assignments will be reapportioned. Two veteran legions—the First and Second—and two novae—Fourth Scythica and Fifth Macedonica—will go with Aurelian to Egypt. Dagobert, you shall have the Third Augusta and the four remaining novae—Seventh Gemina, Eighth Gallica, Ninth Hispania and Tenth Fretensis at Mediolanum. My aides will provide you with all of the details."

Galen looked out over the city, thinking upon the effort it took to maintain peace and tranquillity here, at the center of the world. It was an old Empire that he ruled, weary and nearly done in by the long race against time and the tide of history. Perhaps . . . no, this was *Rome,* and while he breathed, it would survive.

In that moment, sitting in the sunshine, feeling the cooling breeze in his hair, listening to the watery sound of aspens swaying in the wind, he felt his spirits lift.

The Empire will endure, came a voice reminiscent of his father's. *The Empire is eternal. Our Roman duty is to the Senate and to the people, and while Rome stands, so stands the world.*

"Nilos! Come here, there is work to be done."

Aurelian clapped Dagobert on the back and raised his cup cheerfully. "No long face, lad. You're out of that dreary German forest for a bit, at least!"

"Yes," the Frank said. He did seem heartened by the prospect. "At least, my lords, we don't have to worry about the Persians anymore!"

THE DISTRICT OF THE CISTERNS, CONSTANTINOPLE

A woman stood on a stone platform, an elegant white hand resting on a burnished walnut table. The platform rose from a dark lake, shrouded in heavy mist. Four parchment sheets lay before her, arranged in a row. Her fingers, tipped with blue-black nails shimmering in the lantern light, were rolling a small glass vial back and forth across the glossy dark wood. Bracelets clinked softly together as the hand moved to and fro. The motion stopped and the woman turned, her pale, white eyes widening slightly in amusement at the sight of her visitors.

Two boys knelt as they stepped onto the carpet, dark eyes glittering in a pervasive golden light. The young woman in the dark cloak remained motionless, though she allowed the little black cat to spring down out of her arms onto the carpet. The little cat darted across the plush floor and then came to a halt beside the tall woman.

Her skin was rich cream. A long cloud of deep red hair spilled down her back and over her shoulders. Tiny jeweled pins sparkled and gleamed in its firmament, catching and reflecting the light of the lanterns. Laughing softly, she knelt down and ran her hand, long and thin, over the soft short fur of the little cat's stomach. It curled around her hand, biting gently at the webbing between her fingers.

"Wicked little creature," she said, her voice rich with amusement, "what have you brought me? A gift? A toy?"

The woman rose, the velvety black silk of her gown sliding effortlessly over a pert bosom and flat stomach. The cut of her clothing was archaic, filled with folds and drapes, but it suited her lithe frame. A twisted belt of golden cord circled her waist and the fall of the cloth almost covered her feet. They were bare, long toes tapering to almond-shaped nails. Around her shoulders draped a supple pectoral of ivory scales. The edges of the plate were serpents worked in gold, with tiny ruby eyes. At her throat, as a brooch holding the gown in place, was a tiny medusa mask with a projecting tongue.

"Anatol," said the Queen in Darkness, "who is this pretty young thing?"

The boy cowered on the floor, forehead pressed to the carpets. He was trembling so hard he could not speak. The Queen cocked her head to one side and sighed softly.

"Go, children. Go and play."

The two Walach boys crawled backwards until they reached the wooden walkway and their lanterns, then snatched up the hot copper handles and bolted off into the mist. The sound of their feet rattling on the planks echoed for some time. Then mist swallowed the sound. The Queen looked upon the girl in the cloak, frowning slightly, and passed a hand before her face.

There was no reaction.

Intrigued, the Queen folded back the hood, exposing the girl's head and shoulders. She was a little thin, with a strong face and well-formed lips. Her hair was a dark russet, curly and shoulder length. Her eyes were green and without expression. The Queen gently ran her hand over the girl's cheekbone, her ear, the side of her neck.

"Kitten," the Queen said, looking down at the floor with a disapproving expression. "This girl has no spirit at all. She is an empty vessel. Do I have some use for her?"

The little cat looked up and yawned, showing tiny sharp white teeth and a pink mouth.

"You are a troublesome creature." The Queen slit the leather cord holding the cloak together with the edge of her thumbnail. The woolen garment fell away, leaving the girl standing naked on the carpet. Her body was whole and without imperfection or flaw. Frowning again, this time in concentration, the Queen circled her.

"Child, this mute form is trying to tell me something. Do you know what it is?"

The little cat meowed and stretched, digging its claws into the carpet, tail lashing in the air. The Queen made a shooing motion at it with her hand, then stopped, standing behind the naked girl.

"Very fit," the Queen mused, slightly tilted eyes narrowing. "No bordello girl, no farm girl, no . . ." She took the girl's hand in her own, gently squeezing the fingers, blue-black nails tracing the patterns of callus and muscle in the fingers and palms. "Ah, how interesting. Where did you find her, daughter?"

The little black cat rolled on the carpets, yellow eyes gleaming. Then it sat up and meowed again. The Dark Queen let the girl's hand fall back and turned, face clouded with approaching anger, pale rose lips pursed.

"You followed that insufferable prince? He made this girl and then you stole her from him?"

The little cat affected not to notice the Queen. It continued to clean its fur. The woman smoothed back the dark wave of her hair.

"You are a bold creature. Do you know what she is— or was—before she was slain and then raised again? An ephebe of the Hidden Temple. One of the sacred ones . . . was she set to watch the Prince? I wonder . . ."

The little cat bumped its head against the woman's foot, then bit at her toes.

"Dreadful little creature!" The Queen laughed and moved her foot away. The little cat pounced, but the woman was far swifter. For a moment they danced on the thick piles of carpet, the pale white feet of the Queen flashing, the little cat leaping and bounding. The naked girl remained standing, staring straight ahead, while they moved counterclockwise around her. Then the woman stopped, her face showing astonishment for a brief instant.

"I will not," she said severely, flicking her gown back behind her. "You grow *too* bold."

The little cat rubbed itself against the girl's ankles. The Queen shook her head.

"I see your desire. No, I will send the girl back to where she belongs. The sisters will see her to final rest, as befits one of the ephebe fallen in battle. It will be a simple matter, and will give some relief from this . . . tomb of a place."

The Queen looked around, scowling. The platform held richly damasked couches, burlwood chests and a standing wardrobe, all things that she had collected over her long life. There were many things of beauty here, but the chill darkness weighed on her. She had not hunted in the night for some time. Things were very unsettled in the city above, the knighted streets filled with wandering bands of armed men. Her spies whispered to her of a struggle between the dying, cursed Emperor and his brother. Other powers moved too; she could feel their hidden presence in the air. Her own people were restless, bringing her odd rumors and fanciful tales. In such an atmosphere, it was impossible to remain inactive.

"Make yourself a useful creature!" The Queen picked up the little cat by the scruff of her neck and matched gazes with her, blue-white for yellow. "Go find the lax children who serve me and have them prepare my ship. We will go faring forth on the sea-green wave, as I did in the old time."

Then she let the little cat down and it darted off, swift, into the darkness and mist.

The Queen's humor did not improve. She returned to the table and stared down at the glass vial and its dark red liquid. She touched the glass vial with the tip of her finger. The liquid seemed to glow with its own light. Then she snarled, snatching the glass up and hurling it away into the clammy mist. The papers she tucked away in a pocket of her gown.

"Cursed boy," she hissed, nostrils flaring. "I will not be your servant, even in gratitude for your open-handedness! Laertes' whelp could learn from you and your crooked mind!"

The Queen brooded, sitting on one of the couches, staring into the darkness. "Mindless child," she suddenly snapped at the girl, who was still standing in a puddle of dark gray wool by the walkway. "Lie down and rest."

Dutifully, the girl lay down on the carpet, drew the cloak over herself and fell asleep.

)(

Gaius Julius entered the Colosseum near noon, head bent in thought. It was a hot day, the sun burning down out of a clear, azure sky. The old Roman found the heat pleasant, warming his cold bones and reminding him of summer days in his youth. He had been working for many days without going outside. By the simple means of entertaining one set of visitors and business acquaintances during the day at the baths, and yet another set at night in his rooms, he disguised his sleepless nature.

As Alexandros had said, once he forced his body and mind from their accustomed paths, it was easy to forgo sleep and food and drink. The body didn't care, sustained as it was by the Prince's will. Of course, it was necessary to partake of common meals, in moderation, lest his patrons and clients become suspicious.

What joy there is in life, he gloated to himself. *Such endless amusement in the struggle of men, in such cunning stratagems and plots! And to escape the tyranny of sleep, what victory!*

In life his critics had mocked him for writing letters and keeping his accounts while attending the theater. At the time it seemed insignificant, but later events had shown him—rather pointedly—his error. Every public moment in the life of a public man was a scene. In those days, he had believed himself quite charming enough to carry the role, regardless of his audience's desire.

No longer. Now he listened, with perfect attention, to anyone he dealt with. Each man, each woman, each delegation found his complete awareness upon them. Many found it flattering, as he intended. Some became alarmed and those he discarded, for they were weak. A few found his dedication and loyalty seductive and trusted him too much. Those were useful fools.

He passed through the shadow of a bronze four-horsed chariot as he entered the Colosseum itself. A hum of subdued activity met him and the old Roman weaved his way between scaffolds and ladders filling a huge barrel vault. Rickety wooden structures obscured stuccoed walls, ornamented with luxurious paintings and statuary. Slaves on their hands and knees, scrubbing with sponges and cloths, hid the vast, unbroken sweep of green marble floor. Women were carefully reapplying plaster and paint to the lower walls, covering up centuries of graffiti.

Gaius Julius passed through the apse, marveling at the effort invested in restoring the building. The hall narrowed to a doorway twenty feet high, surrounded by golden acanthus, holly and laurel. Heavy bronze statues of Hercules and Perseus flanked the entrance to the arena. They were draped in canvas to protect them from the painters working on the architrave above the door. Students in baggy tunics crouched on the scaffolding, faces intent as they touched up the bright colors on the faces of the gods with tiny horsehair brushes.

Gaius Julius stepped out into blazing sunlight again, shading his eyes against the glare. A particular heat beat against his face, radiating from a vast expanse of white and gray marble seating. The old Roman cast about, shading his eyes against the glare, looking for the man he had come to see.

The floor of the arena was surrounded by a flagstone walkway, separated from the main floor by wooden posts fifteen feet high. When the games were under way, the posts supported a fence keeping the wild beasts and criminals from reaching the actual wall of the amphitheater. That wall was twenty feet high, smooth faced with marble blocks, and pierced with doors at irregular intervals. Above its outward-leaning lip of burnished stone was the first rank of seats. These were reserved for the senators, the Vestals, and on the southern side of the arena, the Imperial box.

Two huge ranks of seats rose up behind the first tier. These rows were reserved for the tribes of the city, for the equestrians and the patricians. A pediment filled with statues of the gods followed, making a clear division between the upper classes in the lower seats, and the final two upper decks, one of marble and one of wood. The wooden seats on the topmost tier sat within a colonnaded portico circling the uppermost reaches of the arena. A series of wooden pillars, painted and plastered to look like marble, supported the portico roof. One hundred and fifty feet separated Gaius and the roof. Rising above the portico were tall masts. On a day when the *munera* or *venationes* would be celebrated, if it was not too windy or rainy, the masts held great canvas sails that swung out over the arena to shade the seats below.

Gaius Julius scowled in irritation. *Where was this Ovinius?* He paced to the right along the flagstone walkway. The cleaning activity was duplicated, on a vastly larger scale, inside the arena. Gangs of slaves, buckets and mops in hand, were cleaning the marble seating benches. Others labored on the ornamented stairways leading up out of the bowels of the building and into the tiers.

The old Roman passed a stairway whose carved panels had been completely removed from their concrete supports. A dozen workmen were easing a newly carved panel into place with the help of a crane and pulley. It showed a long-bodied dog tearing at the neck of an equally long-bodied deer. Gaius Julius frowned, seeing that the replacement panel did not match the quality, even worn with age, of the original.

A shame, he thought, *but this is not my project! There are still not enough hours for such small details.*

That was another lesson he had taken to heart. In his old life, he had tried to manage and order every last tiny detail of his affairs. This project was far too big, though it made him uneasy to entrust strangers with such responsibility.

No matter! he scolded himself. *These are professionals, let them execute their art, old man!*

The uppermost deck bustled with activity. Gaius could make out small figures in blue tunics climbing about on the wooden masts. Some of them were in the process of swinging in the boom-like extensions. The canvas awnings were nowhere to be seen. Gaius presumed they were being cleaned.

A booming shout rolled across the arena floor. "Master Gaius!" Gaius Julius turned and raised his hand in greeting, for here was the man he had come to see, striding across the expanse of wooden panels flooring the arena.

"Procurator Ovinius, I am glad to see you. I feared that you would be lost amongst all this commotion!"

Ovinius was a man of middling height, with a paunch pressing against his tunic and rapidly receding hair. He exuded an impression of bustling efficiency.

"Things are a little topsy-turvy here," guffawed the procurator. He looked around smugly. "It's been a good four centuries since the place got a really thorough cleaning. But, by the gods, she'll be in excellent shape when the games open."

"Good," Gaius Julius said. "I've a matter to discuss with you in private. Your office, perhaps?"

The procurator nodded, looking about with a trace of unease. "Of course, of course . . . is this a personal matter, or about the games?"

Gaius Julius did not smile but leaned close and said, "The games, good Ovinius."

The man relaxed visibly but avoided Gaius' eyes.

"Well, then, let's go below." Ovinius strode off across the arena floor. Gaius Julius followed at a more sedate pace, looking around with interest. This entire structure was new to him, built long after his death. The press of matters since his unlikely resurrection had kept him from attending the games. It was certainly Roman in scale. . . .

Ovinius paused and stamped his foot twice on the ground. Gaius Julius also stopped, watching with interest. The paneling under their feet suddenly shook amid a grinding sound. Gaius Julius swayed a little, but caught himself, as a twenty-by-twenty section of the arena floor began to descend. Chains rattled loudly through a pair of windlasses as they descended. Gaius flipped the edge of his toga over his shoulder, watching in amusement as they dropped below the arena floor at a steady, even pace.

Huge dark brown blocks of tufa formed the walls of the shaft. Channels had been cut in the stone to allow the chains to pass. An iron grating slid past, revealing a dim corridor. The air was sharp with musk, redolent of angry beasts and fear and urine.

"Have you been below before?" Ovinius raised his voice as the windlasses clanked and rattled to a stop.

"No," Gaius Julius said, letting his eyes adjust to the dim light. "I've heard tales, of course."

The lift ground to a halt, the blue square of the sky three storeys above. Now they stood in a cage of iron bars with doors on either side. Ovinius strode through one, thumbs hitched into the broad leather belt at his waist.

"It's quite a commotion down here on game day," he said as they walked. "There are three thousand staff at work, plus hundreds of animals and men appearing on the floor. That's not counting the sailors, of course, but they're not below. They work above, as they like to say."

Ovinius laughed at his own wit.

"I'm surprised that you still struggle with those acres of canvas and miles of cordage. Surely one of the Imperial thaumaturges could contrive some reflecting dome or cover that holds itself up with nymphs or gryphons."

The procurator made a sour face and a sign against ill luck with his hand. "Master Gaius, remember who built this place! Old Vespasian was a tax farmer and an accountant, by Hermes! A more practical Emperor never lived. He commanded his builders to raise this whole magnificent structure without any *special* help, if you follow. He had no truck with sorcerers and that ilk. Now his son, Domitian, he added the crystal lamps for night fights. They are a bit of work! The crowds like it, I think, knowing that all the marvels and feats that they see are conjured up by men with men's hands. Not by spirits or wizards! That sort of thing just isn't Roman."

"Still, wouldn't they be better pleased to have shade during the day?"

Ovinius shrugged, saying, "No one complains. The sunny seats are cheaper."

Gaius Julius ran a hand lightly along the walls of the tunnel as they walked. A thick, sooty layer of grime turned the brown and red bricks black as night. A heavy, fetid smell filled the air and troubled breath. Ovinius seemed not to notice. A column of slaves passed them, going in the other direction, carrying a long bight of chain over their shoulders.

"We've almost a hundred lifts, ramps and doors that open in the big floor," he said. "They're all being repaired, regreased, the chains fixed, the doors varnished and replaced if need be. I hope to have every single thing in the whole of the Flavian—every door, every wall, every toilet—refurbished, repainted and replaced by the end of next month."

"Are you going to clean down here?" Gaius Julius ducked under a low lintel as the procurator turned and stepped down into a cramped room.

"No! That would take another four months to try and scrub all of this down. I mean, of course, everything the public sees will be brought up to snuff. Everything hidden that's important, like the cages, lifts and gates, will be all new."

Ovinius' office was small, crowded with wicker shelves and a wooden table covered with papyrus and parchment rolls. A large copper plate bolted to the wall held etched plans of a dozen floors. Smoke from an ill-trimmed lamp coiled in the groined ceiling. The procurator sat heavily, his chair creaking under him. Gaius Julius took the other seat, brushing walnut shells and bread crusts from cracked leather.

"So, what is this business of yours?" Ovinius was still nervous.

Gaius Julius settled in the chair, looked around the room, then finally spoke. "I sent you a small note telling you that we had a business acquaintance in common. You'll remember him, a large gentleman named Syphax. A man of many varied interests."

Ovinius nodded, clearly unhappy. "I know him too well," he mumbled. "What do you want? Are you collecting for him?"

"Not at all," Gaius said in a breezy tone. "I made his acquaintance while providing entertainment for the workers on the Via Appia project. He knows so many people . . . we were discussing the amphitheater and your name, somehow, came up. I understand that you might, in the past, have borrowed some *small* sums from the good Syphax."

Ovinius looked sick, but he nodded.

"Well, you shouldn't worry about these things. Syphax is a businessman and he expressed concern and sorrow for your situation. His words moved me, I must say, and—in the interests of showing my generosity—I have undertaken to pay the interest on these *loans* of yours."

Gaius Julius smiled, examining his fingernails. Since his rebirth they had failed to grow, which was still disconcerting. He worried, when he had time, about the remains of his hair. Would it all just fall out, leaving him as bald as an egg?

"What do you want, then?" The procurator's voice was filled with even greater fear than before. Syphax, at least, was a blunt man in his business dealings. A fellow knew what to expect!

"These funeral games—when the Emperor commands!—are my concern. I'm sure you understand my feelings. A great tragedy has afflicted the Empire, and the festival to placate the spirits of the dead must be exemplary. My thoughts are close to yours; you want the Flavian to look fresh, as glorious as when Domitian first threw open the doors. I am close, very close, to being named the *editore* of these games."

Ovinius raised an eyebrow. This was business talk and he recovered his composure. "A juicy plum, indeed. Have you the coin to bear such a weight? The cost will be enormous!"

Gaius Julius waved the thought away. "Nonsense. The Emperor and the treasury will cover it. I, however, will be placed in the unenviable situation of having to provide the most spectacular entertainments seen since the Thousand Year games. Everything must be new, exciting, novel. Romans are the most entertained people in the world—you know how they respond to the same old tired spectacle."

"I do!" Ovinius laughed. "Stones and rocks and burning pitch thrown into the arena. Gladiators torn apart or stoned to death, emperors and senators abused! The people love their circuses dearly . . . I thought there would be riots when the Lord and God announced the games would be closed."

"Indeed," Gaius Julius said in a smug tone. "You agree, then, it is of the first importance to make sure these games are memorable and like nothing ever seen before."

Ovinius nodded eagerly. The matter of his debts seemed to have fallen by the wayside.

"It strikes me," the old Roman said, "that part of the problem is that the gladiators, the most popular part of the show, are too well known. Oh, women swoon and shriek over them, throwing tokens and falling out of their gowns to gain the eye of their favorites. Everyone counts the number of victories, the kills, the reprieves . . . but everyone, and I do mean *everyone* has seen the retiarius fight the Thracian, the Gaul against the Samnite. Where is the novelty in that?"

"So true," Ovinius agreed. "But that is traditional! If you try and change things, the people will be angry!"

"Not necessarily. Consider the popularity of the races. Fifty thousand people cram themselves into the Flavian on a regular basis. Two hundred and fifty thousand attend the Circus Maximus. Everyone agrees that the races are better than the gladiators. Why?"

Ovinius frowned and tapped his fingers on the tabletop. "Well . . . you follow your faction, Blue, Green, Yellow or White. There are as many races as fights. . . . Huh. I don't really know. More men die in the amphitheater, unless there are some good crashes in the turns. Hey, you get to sit with your family all together, rather than the women being sent up to the top deck."

"True," Gaius Julius allowed, shaking his head. "But the core of the matter is that you can follow a team over many races. There are standings—drivers move up and down; there's an ultimate goal, to win the season. It's not an individual contest, a single man on a single man, but something bigger. A whole team of drivers, handlers, grooms, horses, chariots . . . the people identify with the teams. Now, true, the senators and other idlers like to track individual gladiators and their schools, but there isn't as much there as at the races. Even the betting is more complex!"

"And so . . ."

Gaius Julius grinned, finally showing some of his hidden delight. "So, these funeral games will last thirty days. My intent is to field teams of gladiators in a tournament of champions. The best against the best, school pitted against school, with each contest of a different style and setting. It will be a great deal of work, but you and your staff can pull it off, I'm sure. Not simple killing, mind you, but each struggle with a goal and a purpose. In the end, there will be an individual champion and a winning team. The victors will go free."

"Huh." Ovinius did not seem convinced. "That might work. . . ."

"Good. I will have a messenger bring you the initial plans tomorrow and you can begin drawing up a budget and setting your craftsmen to work on the sets."

Ovinius nodded, but he was still troubled. "Is that all?"

"No," Gaius Julius said, "there is one other matter. Even with this change in format, there needs to be a new element, something never before seen on the arena floor. Something to shake up the old rivalries between schools and trainers. Do you know what the people love?"

"Roasted duck, delivered hot right to their seats?"

Gaius Julius chuckled, waving a finger at the procurator.

"No, my dear Ovinius, they love the underdog. They love the fighter with no reputation, of ignoble birth and uncertain antecedents, who makes good by sheer will and determination. They love the man who exceeds the strictures of his birth, who triumphs over all obstacles and receives the crown of laurels no one, *no one* expected."

"Hah!" Ovinius laughed. "No one is unknown and unexpected in the games! Every school extols the virtues of its fighters. They spy on each other constantly. Who could survive in the arena without training? Where will this underdog come from and live more than one bout?"

Gaius Julius smiled coldly. "That, dear Ovinius, is where I need your help. I know of such a person, but this individual is not a gladiator. He's neither taken the oath nor enrolled in a school. This person is currently in Rome, but he is free. . . . How may this parlous state be rectified? How will this prize be brought onto the sandy floor?"

"Well . . ." Ovinius scrunched up his face in thought. "Is he a citizen?"

"No, a barbarian, visiting from the provinces."

"Easy, then." the procurator smirked. "We bribe an urban prefect to charge him with one of the crimes punishable by service in the arena. Some men seize the poor fellow from a street at night and he gets put below until it's time to rise into the sun. A simple matter, requiring only the judicious application of gold."

"Excellent." Gaius Julius smiled. "You'll see to it, then, won't you?"

Ovinius blanched and a nervous finger tugged at the collar of his tunic. "Me?"

"You," Gaius Julius said, standing up. "Syphax is content, for the moment, but only while he receives your interest regularly from my purse. Find this malleable prefect and gather men to bag our dear barbarian. When you are ready, I will provide the locale and time to strike."

Ovinius swallowed and stood as well. "How . . . how will I get word to you?"

Gaius Julius smiled broadly. "Don't worry. When you are ready I will know."

The old Roman departed then, bending his head under the lintel and disappearing into the passageway. Ovinius wiped his forehead, his stomach churning. He peered out the door, but his visitor was already out of sight in the warren of tunnels.

"He's never been below, has he? But he knows the way out . . ."

THE SEA, OFF OF THE ISLAND OF CYPRUS

A gleaming iron beak clove through the water. White foam boiled away, washing over eyes painted on the ship's prow. The sea was a summery blue green, rolling softly between the galley and the pale, dust-colored line of the shore. Three banks of oars dipped in unison, driving the ship forward. Its square sail, striped brown and cream, was furled. A flute called an easy rowing stroke, letting the sailors in the benches stretch their muscles without exhaustion.

It was a still, hot day with calm, easy water. The trireme plowed unhurriedly northwest along the Lycian coast. Another hundred warships followed in two columns. Most were two-decked dromonds, though a brace of swift, single-banked galleys flanked the main body of the fleet. On the rear deck of the lead ship, the *Jibril,* Mohammed sat in the shade of a draped awning, looking out upon the quiet sea. The captain of the trireme, a Yemenite merchant, sat nearby. Zoë stood at the landward railing, face shaded by a straw sun hat.

"A placid sea," the captain said, dark face accented by a beard of small, tight ringlets.

"Yes," Mohammed said. "Nothing like the rough waters between your homeland and India. How do you feel about the fleet?"

"Good," the captain said, voice sharp and filled with pride. "The men have taken to the oars well, and my sailors have mastered this crude yardage and sail. A Yemenite dhow could cut closer to the wind, but these ships will do. They are solidly built."

"The Romans," Mohammed said, "are not an idle people."

"Where will we find them?" Zoë turned at the rail, her face pale and pinched-looking. "Why this shore and not another?"

Mohammed looked at her, meeting her eyes. "When we left Cyprus," he said, "I prayed and the voice from the clear air bade me sail north, along the coast, until the water turned dark. There, it said, I should turn out to sea."

"That is all?" Zoë's voice held a petulant snap. "If we burned out these cities as we passed, they would come looking for us."

The captain made to answer, but Mohammed quieted him with a gesture. The Quraysh chieftain stood, stretching his arms, and walked to the railing. The sea hissed past, foaming along the flank of the ship. The water gleamed and flickered, breaking the white ball of the sun into thousands of fragments.

"Can't we go any faster?" Zoë glared down into the rowing gallery, where three staggered decks of benches were filled with brawny men laboring over the oars. "Can they row faster?"

"They can," Mohammed said softly. "But they are learning on this voyage to row as one, to follow the commands of the flautist and the captain. If we rush to battle, or find ourselves trapped against the shore, they will not have the strength to row us out again."

Zoë stared at him, dark eyes glowering. Her anger faded. Her temper was still volatile, but the corpse of her queen remained in Caesarea Maritima. In its absence, her brittleness had begun to fade. "Are you afraid of battle?"

Mohammed shook his head, turning his gaze out over the waters. Mountains marched along the distant shore, thick with dark blue-green trees. A fruitful and prosperous land, with little cities and towns along the coastal plain. Sometimes, if the wind turned, the Quraysh could smell lemon and orange. There were orchards under the flanks of the mountains and fields of grain.

"Zoë, the Merciful and Compassionate One will provide, for I have submitted myself to his will. His voice bids me sail north until the sea turns, so I shall."

The young woman cursed, clenching her hand into a fist. "You have this faith, Lord Mohammed. I do not! I cannot see or hear what you see or hear. I must take you at your word—what if you are deceived? What if you are mad? Then we all die, and my vengeance will be unfulfilled."

Mohammed touched her shoulder and she turned back to him. His face was gentle. "You have seen what I see.

Do you forget? With your skills, with your art, can't you tell that I speak the truth?"

Zoë flinched, not from Mohammed, but from burning memory. "I have seen . . . things. They did not fill me with your confidence."

"Then sit with me and pray, as I do." Mohammed held out his hand. Zoë stared as if the tanned, calloused palm and strong, tapering fingers were vipers. Her eyes met his and they were filled with fear and confusion.

"I am not you," she whispered hoarsely. "If I look upon that face, hear that voice, I will be destroyed. The power that speaks through you is beyond comparison, like the sun to a candle. I will not do it."

"That is fear talking." Mohammed put down his hand and turned to the railing. "But I will not press you. At nightfall, I will pray and see what may be."

With a star-filled sky, the fleet rode at anchor, masts illuminated by sea lanterns. A rocky, treeless island lay between the ships and the farther shore, shielding them from prying Roman eyes.

On the raised rear deck of the *Jibril,* Mohammed knelt on a rectangular mat. He faced the south, knowing that at a great distance, the Ka'ba stood at the center of a city at last at peace. Mohammed bent his forehead to the thick pile of the rug and emptied his mind of all thoughts.

In that inner quiet, he could hear the voice of the Maker of the World. In truth, it filled the sky and the water all around him, singing softly in the rigging. Yet, like all men, the confusion of the day, the shouting of sailors, the matters of eating and breathing and tilling the soil distanced him from that single, pure voice. He closed his eyes, letting a litany of simple prayer wash all these cares away. As he did so, he felt a sensation blossom in his chest, as if a pure, joyous sound pressed against his ribs. He felt the spirit that moved the wind and tide drawing near.

You are almost there, O man, the voice whispered, as

if from a great distance. *Your enemy is coming. He comes in wickedness and sin, filled with fear and anger. He will destroy himself in rage. He is—*

"Mohammed, what . . ."

The decking beneath Mohammed's fingertips trembled. He sat up, ears ringing. To his amazement, he saw a burning white light illuminating the sails, the rigging, the sailors . . . everything within sight was harshly etched. Zoë seemed frozen, one hand flung up to cover her eyes, one hand on the railing of the steps. Mohammed tried to speak but no words came forth. He stepped forward, then froze himself. The source of the light moved as he moved, shadows swinging wildly.

Zoë crumpled, falling back down the stairs. Mohammed leapt to catch her. The light went out abruptly. Suddenly blind, he staggered, trying to grab hold of the railing. His knuckles cracked on wood. At their touch, the lacquered pine crumbled fill into dust. Mohammed fell heavily on his knees. The deck under him quivered and the once-so-solid boards seemed frail.

"Zoë? Captain?"

A chorus of groans replied, and Mohammed felt his tunic softly flaking away, settling onto the deck like wood ash. Delicately, stepping as lightly as he could, Mohammed descended the steps. The wood felt spongy and feeble, and he wound up crawling to Zoë's side, where she lay sprawled on the main deck. Distraught, his fingers brushed her throat, seeking a pulse. His heart was hammering.

Have I done this? His thoughts whirled like cranes in an updraft. *Have I become dangerous?*

She was alive, her chest moving, soft breath issuing from her lips.

"Praise the Merciful One," Mohammed said, vastly relieved.

"Mohammed." A rich, cultured voice issued forth from the prostrate girl. Her lips did not move. "You are being deceived."

The Quraysh bolted backwards, slamming his head against the stairs. His vision clouded for a moment with floating white sparks and he grimaced in pain. His heart beat furiously, like a runaway horse. There was a roaring in his ears, and he shook his head, trying to clear the pain away. "This is impossible!"

The night was dark and silent. The wind had fallen off, leaving the air still. Even the sound of the waves lapping against the hull of the ship seemed faint. He crouched forward, staring in astonishment at the supine body on the deck.

Zoë moaned, twitching, caught in some terrible dream.

"Impossible." Mohammed could not believe it.

NEAR THE TOWN OF AQUINCUM, PANNONIA INFERIOR

)-(

Comes Alexandros! A messenger approaches."

The Macedonian turned in the saddle, squinting into a cold wind. Dark trees lining the farm track bent in the gusts. Like his men, Alexandros was wearing a woolen tunic beneath a thick felt shirt. Above that was a mail hauberk reinforced with banded iron plates. An iron helmet with decorative horsehair plumes and hinged cheek guards was hooked to his saddle. Despite the threat of a blow to the face, he preferred being able to see.

A rider cantered up the trail into the meadow, his horse shining with sweat. It was one of the scouts. Alexandros waved the man over, and the companions crowding around him in an iron hedge parted, horses dancing aside to let the man ride up to his side. Ermanerich moved his horse closer, leaning towards Alexandros with a delighted expression.

"It could be a raid across the river," the Gothic prince said. His blue eyes gleamed with anticipation. Like Alexandros, he was armored from head to toe, both in the Roman-style lorica and in mailed leggings ending in heavy, reinforced leather boots. Ermanerich had declared himself the first of the "Companions." Alexandros did not attempt to dissuade him, though the moment gave him pause until he remembered the youth had a copy of Arrian's *Anabasis Alexandrou* amongst his belongings. "If it is, there will be some action."

The other Goths, hearing a fragment of Ermanerich's words, grinned in delight.

Alexandros held up a hand, quieting the Prince while the messenger caught his breath.

The scout was dressed in boiled-leather cuirass, reinforced with metal studs. His horse was dark brown, as were his accoutrements and armor. He work a dark gray woolen cloak, broken by inset patches of green cloth. A cylindrical leather quiver rode at his left stirrup, and he was armed with one of the new bows, stored in a wooden case. Like all of the riders in the new army, his saddle was fitted with the Sarmatian stirrup.

"My lord," the man said, dark eyes glancing around in interest at the heavily armored Companions. The scouts spent their time at the fringes of the army, snooping and spying; he may not have seen the heavy horse in full gear before. "A great force of Gepids has crossed the river a mile or more ahead. I don't think they saw us, as we advanced in light order as you have directed. There were many clan banners among them."

"How many?"

The man squinted, counting from a mental image in his mind. Alexandros waited patiently, feeling the cold wind eddy around him. The Goths loved the weather, which had turned chilly. High summer on the Pannonian plain was not that of the balmy coast of Greece. This morning, with frost on the leaves, it had seemed an excellent day for a road march.

"Almost three thousand, I would say."

Alexandros snorted in surprise. "This is a raid, not an invasion?"

Ermanerich nodded. "Yes," he said. "The Gepids are a numerous people, though they are cowed servants now. . . . Were there any Draculis banners amongst them?"

The scout nodded, the edge taken off his excitement. He raised two fingers. "I saw two of the red dragons."

Alexandros grinned, looking around at the faces of his companions. They were still eager for the fight, but now a tiny sense of fear pricked them.

"Two lamia then, these ghost knights of theirs?"

"Yes," the scout said, blanching a little at the prospect. "At least. We saw none, keeping back and out of sight . . . but where the red dragon flies, the nightwalkers ride."

"Good. How lies the land between here and there?"

The scout turned, standing up in his stirrups, and pointed down the meadow. "The river is ahead, through scattered stands of pine and oak, to the left. The land drops away sharply, making a moraine between this track and the water. When we saw them, they had come up out of the flats and were gathering on some open land about a mile away. There are thicker trees between here and there, but also some meadows."

Alexandros nodded and considered the warriors under his command. As he had expected, many men had answered his call to form a Gothic legion. Theodoric's ministers had kept a careful watch, turning away men who already held a debt or obligation. In effect, this denied him nearly every experienced warrior in the Gothic *feodorate*. Ermanerich grumbled about this, but it didn't bother Alexandros. His recruits were exactly what he wanted; younger sons who didn't want to clear new land, men who made their living only from war, the restless, the dispossessed. There were even Gepids and Bulgars who had crossed into Gothica in search of a new warlord. His men were eager, if not overly experienced. It made his task easier.

In an attempt to dilute possible opposition in the King's court, Alexandros had asked the lady Theodelinda to take charge of the effort to house, arm and outfit his men. Nearly six thousand strapping young lads ate a great deal, drank even more and had to sleep under some kind of shelter, even in summer. After demurring for a week, apparently for the sake of appearances, the lady had accepted his offer and set about the task with great energy.

She already owned a number of textile mills, ironworks and *fabricae* both within the Empire and in Magna Gothica. Her contacts amongst the merchants throughout the region were substantial. Alexandros expected her to find the armaments, goods and drayage he needed as quickly as anyone. He hoped that her familial connection with the king and his brother would keep her from taking a debilitating cut of the coin being poured into the effort. The extent of his aunt's effort and the breadth of her ability had dumbfounded Ermanerich.

Alexandros was not surprised. His time in Rome had not been wasted in idleness. He had spoken to many men, read every book he could lay his hands on, and gained a reasonable knowledge of recent Imperial history. A number of evenings in the company of Gregorius Auricus had provided quite a bit of juicy gossip. Even before he had met her personally, Alexandros had drawn Theodelinda's measure. Thirty years before, during a time of particular crisis in the Empire, she had been queen of a short-lived Lombard kingdom in northern Italia. Her realm had been destroyed in a bitter struggle with Rome, but the Queen had survived and accepted a new life within the Empire.

At her suggestion, Alexandros' men were billeted in the frontier town of Aquincum. The town stood at the northern edge of Gothica, beside the swift-flowing Danuvius. Theodoric maintained a strong garrison there, now reinforced by Alexandros and his men. Beyond the dark river, there were only barbarians and wilderness. Theodelinda thought the new levies should earn their keep. Alexandros didn't mind. If a Roman magistrate came by, then their presence would be easy to explain.

"Krythos, return to the vanguard and see that I receive regular reports as the enemy moves. Tell your commander to show the Gepids someone to chase, then fall back to meet us. There's no need to try and slow the enemy down."

The scout nodded sharply, heeled his horse around and trotted off. Alexandros gestured for Ermanerich and the other Companions to close up around him. "You have told me that these Gepids will fight in a mass of infantry around a few heavily armored nobles. Spears, swords, throwing axes. A mad, headlong rush into the enemy line. Yes?"

The Goths nodded in agreement.

"Very well." Alexandros felt a particular calm settle over him, even as it had done in his breathing life. "Clear the Companions from the track. Let the hoplites advance past the horsemen and stand at arms in the first big clearing that we come to. Ermanerich, you will go with them and see that they are fully arrayed in five ranks, but with their spears grounded."

The Macedonian had divided his six thousand men into three main groups. For his own ease, and to accommodate Ermanerich's romantic fantasy, he had named them as his old army had been arranged. The Companions fought from horseback, as well armed and armored as funds and equipment allowed. Their main weapon was the Sarmatian *kontós*, a flexible lance. Coupled with the stability afforded by their stirrups, they could deliver a fierce, sudden blow. These men were also armed with cavalry swords and heavy spiked maces.

The second division was composed of his Peltasts, who also rode into battle, but would dismount to fight until they were able to use their primary weapon, the Hunnic bow, from horseback. A few of them, even in the short month of training, were able to do so. Most, however, had to stand to be accurate. Luckily, nearly every man was able to sight and shoot a bow. Getting them used to using a horse bow from the saddle would take a long time. Until then, Alexandros had no qualms about letting them fight on foot. Accuracy would come with practice, and in the meantime, they would rely on volume rather than precision.

The bulk of his forces, at least at present, were hoplites, who walked to battle and would fight on foot. When sufficient horses were acquired, they would ride as well, at least on the march. The Macedonian had fond hopes of fielding a completely mounted army. Forage would be a limiting factor, but it seemed likely that any immediate campaign would be within the Empire, where local magistrates and governors could provide supplies. The hoplites wielded the *sarissa*, an eighteen-foot pike. They also carried the Roman stabbing sword and round shields slung over their backs.

"Ermanerich, remember to keep the men from moving once they are in position. When the Gepids appear, as I'm sure they will, all they are to do is take up 'at guard' with their sarissa and then hold ranks. Do not attempt to move against the enemy or to maneuver!"

The Gothic prince nodded in agreement. Learning to move in unison, without fouling the long spears, was going to take a lot more work. The last two attempts to march in ordered ranks had ended with a huge jumble of *sarissa* and crushed bodies after the men had failed to keep their ranks and pikes straight. The *hystrix* formation started with the men lined up in a honeycomb, sarissa laid out on the ground in line. When the signal was given, each man had only to bring his pike up at an angle. It was very simple.

Alexandros hoped they could manage it today without becoming completely disordered. "The Peltasts will take the hoplite left wing, dismounted. When the Gepids charge, the Peltasts will loose two or three flights of arrows into the enemy, then hold the flank with sword and shield. Chlothar, you will lead the left wing."

Chlothar was an expatriate Alexandros had tapped to command. He was an enormous blond man. The others said he was a Frank, out of the western reaches of Germania. Though he was not a Goth, he was so unflappable and calm in battle that Alexandros had made him Ermanerich's second.

"The rest of you are with me," Alexandros shouted, harsh voice carrying in the cold air. "We will take the right flank and wait for the enemy to commit themselves. Then we will level kontos and charge on my command."

The Macedonian slapped his horse, a fiery bay stallion, and trotted off among the thin pines. With care, his horse could make reasonable time through the avenues of the forest, leaving the muddy track to the infantry. Behind him, the Companions sorted themselves out and filed forward, pale sunlight glinting from their helms and shields.

"Damn that boy!"

Alexandros gritted his teeth against two equally fierce emotions. The first was respect for the bravery of the Gepids. At least two thousand of the half-naked tribesmen charged across the meadow, filling the air with a wailing screech. Another thousand, wooden shields forward, bronze caps covering their heads, advanced in a huge, loose crowd around the tube-shaped banners of their chieftains.

Peltasts, afoot, with one man in five holding his mount, were drawing and loosing as fast as they could. Long, black-fletched arrows slapped across the meadow, shearing through the charging Gepids. Dozens of barbarians fell, pierced through by pile-headed arrows. The turf was already littered with bodies.

The second emotion was churning disgust. The ragged front edge of the Gepid charge was only a hundred feet from the hoplites and their sarissa were still on the ground. Alexandros twisted in the saddle, watching sickly as his Companions continued to filter out of the forest in ones and twos. The open, parklike woods had suddenly become a bramble thicket as the horsemen neared the meadow. Alexandros reached the open plain in time to see the Gepids begin their mad charge across the high green grass and hollyhocks.

"Don't fool about," he shouted helplessly at Ermanerich, who was far out of hearing. "These aren't Phillip's men!"

Some of the Gepid warriors, hair thickened with white clay, hurled axes as they sprinted forward. One flickered through the air and sank deep into the skull of one of the hoplites. The man died instantly, sprawling to the ground, and Alexandros could hear the *thunk* echo across the field. The other barbarians, still howling battle cries, were armed with a confusion of axes, swords, spears and javelins.

At last, with only thirty feet remaining between the armies, bucinas blatted and hoplites began to raise their sarissa. Alexandros forced himself to watch. Ermanerich acted as if this were Phillip of Macedon's phalanx, as skilled a group of men with the long pike as ever had lived. Those men, all dead these long centuries, could dance with the eighteen-foot weapons. For them, the hystrix was a child's game, where they could move from rest to full array in under a minute.

These Goths had not been born and bred to the phalanx. They had not fought and died, ever victorious, under the banner of Phillip for thirty years. The pikes rose up, at first in good order, then someone fouled the man next to him, knocking the ash-wood shaft into the next man's pike. The disaster washed across the face of the Gothic line with a resounding clash and clatter of jarring wood and iron. Rising pikes fell sideways, like falling trees, with each additional pike adding more weight to the cascade. The Gepids howled in delight and rushed on.

Alexandros clouted the herald at his side. His mailed fist

rang on the man's helmet. "Sound attack, boy, all units advance and attack!"

The Macedonian drew his *spatha* with a flourish, spurred his horse and charged out onto the field.

"Alexandros!" A great cry went up, sending a chill through him, and hooves thundered on the soft, loamy ground. Only half of the Companions had managed to fight their way out of the forest, but they stormed forward, unlimbering their lances on the run.

The bay flew across the field, white and yellow flowers blurring past under his hooves. He ran strongly, even burdened by Alexandros' armored weight. As he rushed closer to the battle, Alexandros saw the Gepid charge smash into the disordered ranks of the hoplites. Many of the Goths were still trapped on the ground, crushed under the weight of their pikes, but Ermanerich had reacted quickly. The rear ranks, pikes ready, moved up.

The Gepid rush broke apart as they leapt across the struggling Goths or halted to stab and hack at the men pinned to the ground. The pikes and men made an unhappy barrier, and their attack slowed for a moment. A hideous slaughter was under way along the front of the phalanx, but the fourth and fifth ranks managed to brace against the rest of the charge. Gepids screamed, pierced by the thicket of iron. Despite two short rushes, they could not come to grips with the hoplites behind their long spears.

Alexandros spared a glance to either side, relieved to see that he did not charge alone into the midst of the enemy. A hundred of the Companions were at his side, lances leveled. Ahead of him, the flanks of the Gepid charge were curling out, spilling around the edges of the hoplite line. Even the center of the Gothic position was being forced back by the weight of the enemy. Alexandros reined in, deftly sliding out of the front rank of the charge.

The Companions, hooves thundering, banners snapping in the cold air, crashed into the Gepid flank. Many of the barbarians failed to notice the horsemen until they were ridden down or run through. Most of the Gepids were armored only with wooden, hide-faced shields. Some had shirts of iron rings sewn to a leather backing. The Companions clove into them, sending a shuddering wave through the mass of infantry. Alexandros trotted back, watching his armored knights hew into the masses of Gepid spear- and sword-men. Some of the Companions continued to stab with their *kontos*, though most had cast the weapons aside, or lost them, fouled in the bodies of the slain. This was *spatha* work, and the long swords flashed in the sun.

A great commotion of metal on metal and rising dust and shouts erupted on the far side of the Gepids line. Alexandros assumed Chlothar had pitched in with his Peltasts to try and relieve pressure on the center.

We'll have to start over with the phalanx, he thought grimly, turning his horse and trotting back towards the woods. More of the Companions were filtering out of the thicket and he stood up in his stirrups, shouting at them. "Form on me, form on me!"

They began to converge on him, riding forward in small clumps. Out of the thousand Companions, perhaps only half had managed to reach the battlefield. Alexandros spun his horse again, satisfied that they had seen him. His herald had gotten swept up in the charge, so his bannerman was a hundred yards away, mired in a desperate hand-to-hand struggle. He shaded his eyes, squinting into the fray. The hoplites seemed to be holding their own at least. They had not broken and run.

"*Comes!* Comes Alexandros! Look out!"

Alexandros whipped around, curveting the horse, sword bare in his hand. The scout Krythos was shouting, riding hard across the field, pointing off to his right. Behind him, the Companions were also in full gallop. They were shouting too, and some of them had drawn their bows and were shooting across the saddle. Alexandros looked to his left.

The mounted warriors in the second body of the Gepid

army cantered towards him. There were two men in the lead, on glossy black stallions, with their armor gleaming in the sun. Unlike the rabble they commanded, they were clad in full mailed armor. Long, trailing horsetail plumes danced on their helms. More mounted men rode at their back, holding a forest of banners and standards. The main ensign was a coiled dragon in black on a red field.

The Draculis, Alexandros thought as he faced them. *The dreadful enemy the Goths fear so much.*

The Macedonian raised his sword in salute to the noblemen riding hard towards him. They saw him, and a command was passed to the band that followed behind. The rest of the Gepid riders charged ahead, interposing themselves between the oncoming Companions and Alexandros.

"You wish to try my sword arm, then?" Alexandros shouted at the two men as he rode forward. In this crisp air, his voice carried a great distance over the battlefield. "Come ahead, I will not stint you."

The lead man, a fellow with a long, thin face and a neat black beard, urged his horse forward. Alexandros saw he wore a helmet contrived to make a beast face when the cheek guards and visor were down. The man unlimbered a long spear, leaf-shaped point catching the sun like a mirror. Alexandros, for all the time he had spent drilling the army, had not taken to the lance himself. He preferred a long slashing sword. Mindful of his enemy, he tightened the straps holding a painted oval shield to his upper left arm, leaving his left hand free.

The Draculis lord waved his companion back, stallion high-stepping forward. Alexandros saw a beautiful, spirited creature with a glossy pelt and powerful legs. The Macedonian circled left, keeping his sword arm on the man's side.

"You are a brave man," the Draculis called out. "If you swear to me and take the blood, I will let you live! These

Goths are children, they have no use for a *man* amongst them!"

"These are *my* men," Alexandros shouted back, making sure his voice carried to the Companions riding up behind him. "You try my patience with your rabble. Come, barbarian, let us see who is the better."

Alexandros watched the man carefully, seeing him guide the black stallion with his knees, watching them move as one. Luckily, these northern barbarians loved single combat, particularly between heroes or captains. The other Draculis lord had fallen back amongst the Gepids. They were laughing. It was an odd moment. Across the meadow, the struggling mass of Gepid infantry was still locked in frenzied battle with the Goths. The Companions that had charged into their flank had bent the barbarian line back into a V shape, but the second mass of Gepids had run up, forcing the cavalry back.

The Macedonian hoped that Ermanerich and Chlothar could extricate themselves without his help. He was about to be distracted.

The Draculis lord and his horse suddenly bolted forward, long lance tip slashing through the air. Alexandros had seen the rear legs of the stallion tense and he was already moving. The bay was a game horse and responsive, but it didn't have the weight or power of the black. Alexandros rose up a little, letting the horse handle the ground, springing to the left. The lance shifted in line, speeding at his chest. Alexandros felt his blood burn and his vision sharpened.

The lance slowed in the air, the stallion's hooves churning across the ground. Clods of earth flew up slowly. Alexandros' sword arm slashed sideways, his entire body turning into the blow. The tip of the spatha dug into the ashwood behind the lance tip.

Time resumed with a snap, and the thunder of the stallion rushing past was loud in Alexandros' ears. His spatha whipped back, parallel with the bay, and wind keened in his helmet strap. He turned the horse, arm stunned by the shock of contact. The Draculis was turning as well, but his powerful arm flexed, flinging the kontos, bladed head shorn away, to the ground.

Alexandros tested his grip on the spatha. His arm was not broken. If it had been, he would have changed hands. The Draculis lord drew his own sword with a sharp *ting!* The man gave forth with a high piercing cry and the stallion stormed forward again.

The Draculis cut overhand, trying for Alexandros' exposed head, but the Macedonian's spatha caught the blow at an angle. The two blades sang like a bell as they slid apart. Alexandros cut at the man's saddle strap. The Draculis' stallion snapped at the bay's rump, spoiling the stroke.

The horses circled, the bay nervous and jumpy. The stallion lowered its head and pranced sideways. The Draculis lord let the horse lead, waiting for an opening. Alexandros took the bay's reins in his left hand, keeping it in the fight. Confident in his advantage, the Draculis darted in, the stallion nipping at the bay's face. Alexandros let his horse spring back, clods flying. The Draculis slammed his sword down, catching the Macedonian's block full on. Alexandros' whole body felt the blow, and sparks sprang from grinding metal. A sense of despair lapped around the Macedonian's thoughts. *A sorcerer of some kind? That's not good!*

Alexandros attacked furiously, blade flickering, and beat the man's guard down. The Draculis attempted to strike back, but Alexandros crowded the gelding, making the stallion buck backwards. After a few seconds of loud exchange, steel ringing on steel, Alexandros turned the bay back to face the stallion. The Draculis thrust underhand, the tip of his longsword spalling across armored plates circling Alexandros' waist. The Macedonian grunted at the blow.

In that instant, as the blade grated across the solid metal,

Alexandros' spatha nicked the saddle strap on the opposite side of the stallion, shearing through the thick leather band. Crying out in rage, the Draculis lord whipped his blade back, barely stopping Alexandros' stroke inches from his face. The stallion lunged forward at the same moment, and strong yellow teeth chomped down on the bay's haunch.

Alexandros let the bay bolt for twenty feet, then reined in fiercely. The bay was shivering from head to toe, back leg held up. The Macedonian vaulted out of the saddle, spatha reversed and pointing up behind his head.

"Krythos! Take this horse away and see to its wounds."

The scouts were arrayed in a loose line thirty feet behind Alexandros, bows drawn and arrows ready. At least half the Companion cavalry had joined them. Matching them, behind the Draculis lord, who had fallen heavily from his horse, were the remains of the Gepid nobles.

The truce of single combat maintained. Alexandros caught a glimpse of the two lines fighting on the other side of the meadow; they had broken apart. Bodies were being dragged from the wreck of the phalanx by the Goths, and the Gepids had fallen back to form into a ragged mob behind their chieftains. Many of the men were watching the single combat as well, though their sergeants were keeping an eye on the immediate enemy.

Alexandros walked forward, boots sinking a little into the springy loam. Bluebells and a scattering of tiny white flowers peeked up out of the green grass. The sun was high in the sky, burning away the morning's chill. The spatha felt good in his hand. He drew out a long dagger from a scabbard at his left side. The Draculis stallion was unhurt, and had run off when the lamia had fallen. Alexandros' heart leapt to see the horse safe. The Draculis scrambled to his feet as the Macedonian approached. The man's helmet had been knocked askew, but he righted it with a swift motion.

"You are a cunning dog," the Draculis rasped. "Do you think that we are evenly matched now?"

Alexandros grinned, raising his sword and the dagger in guard. "I think I still have the advantage of you," he said merrily. "Let us see how well you fight without that beautiful horse!"

The Draculis moved warily, both hands on the long, wire-wrapped hilt of his sword. Like many of the northern barbarians, he favored a long blade, giving him at least six inches of reach over Alexandros. The Macedonian crabbed sideways, leading with the dagger in his left hand. The ground was a little uneven, littered with tufted clumps of grass.

"Ha!" The Draculis attacked with a wickedly fast diagonal cut against Alexandros' head. The Macedonian blocked with the shield on his upper arm and gasped at the power behind the blow. The oval shield, a laminate of pine on pine, faced with stiffened leather, cracked lengthwise. Alexandros reeled back, engaging the man's longsword with the tip of his own.

The Draculis beat Alexandros' blade aside with two powerful lunges and then slashed upwards with the tip of his longsword. The Macedonian flung his head backwards, barely escaping losing his lower jaw. Without pausing, Alexandros spun and the edge of his dagger clanged against the side of the Draculis' blade. He pressed hard, trying to turn the man and drive the longsword into the ground.

Heedless, the Draculis wrenched back, his entire body behind the motion. Alexandros' left arm flew back, unable to withstand the man's raw strength. The tip of the longsword blurred past an inch from his nose. Alexandros scrambled back, fending off two more slashes at his head.

Cursing, the Macedonian flipped the dagger into the grass behind him and took his spatha in both hands. The ruined remains of the shield on his left arm were a distraction. He had never faced an opponent so quick and strong. The barbarian even had some idea of what to do with a sword.

"You're the first of these children to last against me,

daywalker." The Draculis breathed easily, moving gracefully on the uneven ground. Alexandros felt a chill wash over him. There was something inhuman about the man, some cast to his face, something in the way he moved. "You will die with honor."

Snarling, the Draculis bulled in, his longsword snapping through the air. Alexandros blocked the first blow, putting his strength into it, and was not knocked back.

You are the master of this body, his mind shouted. *It does not feel pain or exhaustion!*

For an instant, locked hilt to hilt, he matched his gaze against the Draculis and saw the man's eyes were yellow and bisected by vertical black pupils. At the same moment, there was a shock of some power against his mind, something that clawed at his thought, trying to make him gibber with fear and run. The Macedonian laughed, for such phantoms had no power over him.

"You," he grunted, putting his shoulder into a push, "are a pitiful creature."

The Draculis sprang back as Alexandros broke their lock and slashed at his legs. The Macedonian circled, letting his awareness of the other man grow. He dragged his left foot a little. Then, as the Draculis lunged at the opening, he sprang into the man's motion. The spatha whipped sideways in a flat arc. The Draculis lord reacted just as fast, blocking with the haft of his longsword. Alexandros let his blade "stick" to the other sword, driving it into the turf. Again, they struggled, strength against strength.

The Draculis rammed his head at Alexandros, catching him on the side of the skull with his beast-faced helmet. It was a heavy blow and Alexandros was thrown back. By sheer will, he managed to keep his sword, but blood clouded one eye. The cut bled profusely. Alexandros tried to roll away from a half-sensed blow. The Draculis' sword arrowed down, grinding against the mail backing the Macedonian's lorica. Metal, stressed beyond its ability to withstand, popped with a tinny sound. Alexandros felt cold steel slide into his flesh, piercing his stomach.

He blinked furiously, clearing his sight. The Draculis, narrow face split by a tremendous grin of triumph, loomed over him. The man was trying to twist the longsword in the wound, but the flat iron plates held the blade straight.

"Well fought, child!"

Alexandros grimaced, willing his body to respond, and his right arm whipped the spatha across the front of his body, cleaving the Draculis' head from his neck with a meaty *thwack*. The skull, eyes wide in surprise, spun off across the green grass, bouncing to a halt amid a spray of daffodils. Alexandros raised his other arm just in time to catch the corpse as it fell heavily onto him. Blood flooded from the severed neck, drenching him in a thick bluish fluid. Spitting, Alexandros pushed it off. It was heavy, with all that armor and inert weight.

There was a great commotion all around him, howls of despair and hooves hammering on the ground. The Companions flooded past Alexandros as he staggered to his feet, charging into the mass of Gepid knights. Arrows whistled past overhead as the scouts loosed themselves onto the mass of spearmen beyond. Across the meadow, the Peltasts were shooting, their bowstrings humming like a lyre as they sent volley after volley into the barbarian ranks.

Krythos ran up to Alexandros, his face white with fear. Alexandros stumbled as he tried to walk forward, then looked down. The Draculis longsword was jutting out of his stomach, dark blood spilling off of it in a thin stream.

"Curse it," Alexandros gasped. "Give me your shoulder, lad."

Krythos seized his right arm, holding him up. Alexandros grimaced, took hold of the sword hilt and wrenched it from his body. The blade scraped and sparked on the edge of the armored plates on his midriff, but then slid free from his body with a greasy sensation and a *pop*. The scout swayed, almost fainting, but Alexandros caught him and held him upright.

"Don't worry, I've taken worse. It only caught my side." Alexandros laughed, staring down at the decapitated body of his enemy. "Did someone take that magnificent stallion in rein?"

Krythos nodded weakly, falling to his knees. His face was a bilious color.

"Good. I want that horse for my own."

Alexandros felt better, now that the wound had time to close. Though he couldn't see the gash beneath the heavy armor and felted shirt, he knew from careful experimentation that it was closing, leaving only a crust of dried blood around the scar. He flexed, turning, and the muscles in his side seemed to have already knitted back together. While the Prince willed that he live, the Macedonian did not fear death.

The sun seemed particularly warm, the air crisp with the smell of pines and flowers. "Ah, Krythos, a fine day to be alive! Look, the barbarians are running!"

The scout vomited noisily, his hands sinking into the bloody mud.

⊡〇-〔0〕-〔0〕-〔0〕-〔0〕-〔0〕-〔0〕-〔0〕-〔0〕-〔0〕-〔0〕-〔0〕-〔0〕-〔0〕⊡

AN INN, THE NAUMACHA DISTRICT, ROMA MATER

)●(

Vitellix was singing, his voice booming through the low-ceilinged room. It was a clear, beautiful voice, particularly with its edges smoothed by a great quantity of good beer. The clamor of the crowd in the *caupona* did not dissuade him. Both citizens and travelers were packed into the underground room, drinking and singing themselves. The smoky air was filled with many cheerful voices.

The Gaul's voice faded away, and he raised a cup high. "Let the Many-Handed hear our prayer and look upon our sacrifice with joy," he said, draining the cup.

Dummonus, Otho and Franco raised their own flagons and drank. Diana, squeezed in between Ila and the aerialist, sipped at hers. The wheaten beer was heavy and dark. She liked it very much, finding it soothed the throat and added to a pleasant sense of well-being.

Vitellix ended their day early, calling a halt to their unceasing practice. Diana hadn't paid attention to the gossip, but she gathered that the urban prefects had allowed artists and performers to use the theaters of Pompey and Marcellus to prepare for the upcoming *munera*. No date had been set for the funeral games, races and performances to begin, but an electric tension was palpable in the air. The diverse troupes that had been loitering in the countryside, observing the word of the Emperor's edict that "lest they debauch women and stir up tumults, disturbing the unquiet dead, they are banished from the city of Rome until such time as given leave to return," had entered the city in a flood.

Diana snorted in her beer, thinking of the previous "secret" traffic of the *lanistae* and their performers into and out of the city. No one had paid the Emperor great heed. She was pleased to work on a proper wire at last. The Pompeian Theater was equipped with a suspended harness and ring system that lowered from a crane atop the backdrop. With it, she could soar out high over the empty white seats, flipping and rolling at the end of the wire. Dummonus had begun teaching her how to use her muscles and strength to perform amazing feats. The weakness in her limbs was being driven out by hard work. Her leg and arm had healed up straight, too.

She leaned back into the wall, closing her eyes, one arm

tucked around little Ila, pleasantly aware of the warmth of Dummonus' thigh next to her own.

"Let's play a game," Otho was saying to his brother. Vitellix groaned in despair. "It goes like this," the acrobat continued, ignoring his father. "One man asks questions, while the others must answer without saying the words *yes, no, black,* or *white.* Simple, yes?"

Franco laughed, saying, "I think not. Are you going to begin?"

"This cup, what color is it?" Otho was holding up a Crotonese-style ceramic wine cup, white with a blue band around the lip.

"I'd say it had a light color." Franco grinned.

"Ha! You've lost! You said it was white!"

"Never. It is *light.*"

"I'm sure you're saying *white.*"

"You'll have a *light* eye if you keep this up."

"Will I? You'll have a black eye to match mine. Hey, is that Numismatix?"

Franco looked over his shoulder. A gang of burly gladiators were pouring down the steps into the inn, bodies gleaming with fresh oil. Most of them were wearing only cotton loincloths and banded leather belts. The noise level in the inn rose appreciably. The men waved to the proprietor for wine and began pushing people out of their seats near the middle of the room. The innkeeper bobbed nervously at them, then began hastily filling wine cups from wide-mouthed amphorae built into his counter.

"No, that's not . . . Curse you! You're a fine brother!"

Otho laughed like a donkey braying and Diana closed her eyes and put her fingers in her ears to try and block out the sound. Ila turned into her shoulder, covering her head with her hands. Franco, infected by his brother's good humor, started to laugh as well. Luckily, the room was so loud that you couldn't hear him. Vitellix grinned, trying to catch Diana's eye.

She had gone quite still. With her eyes closed, she felt

something, some sensation in the room. There was a cold feeling on her neck and arms. With all of the raucous merriment and the distractions afforded by sight, it was almost disguised.

Someone is watching us. The thought was unbidden, but once it had broached the water of memory, it was unmistakable. Diana swung Ila into her lap and then switched places with her.

"Hide under the table, little mouse," she whispered in the girl's ear. Ila looked up quickly, her face screwed into a mask of concern. Dummonus was also looking at Diana, his placid face questioning.

One of the gladiators pushed over a man sitting in a chair. The man jumped up, shouting. He was a drover, thick bodied with rugged features and arms stout as axles. The gladiators sneered at him and his friends, turning their backs on the rage percolating through the wagonmen. Diana stepped away from the table against the wall, motioning to Vitellix. The troupe master half rose, his face concerned, while Diana's eyes flicked across the crowd in the room. There were too many people in too small a space now. She felt hemmed in, trapped. It would be difficult even to reach the stairs going up to the street.

"Oh," came a voice, sharply clear in the angry murmur of the room. "Are you girls bleeding today?"

The gladiators gave out a great angry cry and spun on the wagoners. Diana watched, detached from the violent movement in the room, as the lead gladiator snatched up a wicker chair and swung it, hard, at the nearest drover. The burly man was already swinging his fist, which punched through the bottom of the chair and slammed into the gladiator's chin. The oiled man's head snapped backwards at the blow, sweat flying away from his nose, and he fell heavily to the grimy floor.

Diana was in motion a grain ahead of everyone else. A heavy pottery mug whipped through the air and her hand rose, fingertips flipping it away to shatter against the wall.

Men surged against her, some rushing the doorway to escape the riot, others striking out at anything around them. Three men scrambled up from their table. A body flew into them and they all hit the ground hard in a tangle of arms and legs. Diana turned sideways and let them fall past.

A hot eager fire wicked up in her breast as she ducked a flying wooden platter. With each motion, as she spun and danced, evading blows, limbs, bodies, thrown chairs and splintering amphorae, the fire mounted, hissing in her veins and making her head throb. This was not the usual gray pain. This felt *good*!

She glanced sideways and felt a stab of relief. Vitellix and the others had turned their table over and crouched behind it while wine bottles smashed on the wall and men punched and kicked, gouging at one another's eyes on the ground. The old Gaul caught her eye and pointed desperately at the door. With Dummonus holding up the rear legs of the table, they were edging along the wall, using it as a shield. Perhaps they could make the stairs that way. Diana leapt across the space between them.

Something swift slammed into her shoulder, cracking against the bone. She spun. Two men rushed forward out of the mob. One of them spun a heavy hand-sized bag from the end of a leather thong. Diana knew instantly what it was, and what they were.

Slavers! Man catchers, with a sap and a net.

That was enough. The black-bearded man flung a net with a practiced hand. It whispered out, the edges dragged wide by lead weights. The smaller, pox-faced man ducked left, avoiding the flight of the net. He whirled his sap high, waiting for her to be tangled. Diana was moving too, hitting the floor with her hands flat, taking the weight of her body on her biceps. The net whispered overhead. Diana spun hard, her legs arrowing out.

The bearded man was still moving forward, trying to crash into her and bear her down. The side of her spinning foot cracked into his kneecap. Sadly, she was not wearing heavy boots, only sandals. He staggered, clutching at his knee. Diana rolled up, legs coming under her.

Pockmark swung at her right-handed, face contorted by rage. The sap breezed by her head as she leaned to the side, coming up off the floor. Silence swallowed the room, the noise of the riot and the mob drowned out by a rushing hiss. She caught Pockmark's wrist, then wrenched down and away, in line with the movement of his body. It seemed right and natural that his elbow would bend back against the joint, that his mouth should open in a cry of agonized pain, that her left elbow should swing around, hard and pointed, to drive into his shoulder.

Sound resumed with a roar and a crash of splintering wood as a table flew across the bar and into wicker shelving. The proprietor ducked behind the countertop. Pockmark screamed, his voice high and thready, as Diana's motion snapped his elbow and then popped his arm from the shoulder joint. The rest of his motion threw him headfirst into the plaster wall where Ila had once been sitting. There was a wet sound as his face jammed into the bricks.

Diana spun back, left arm up in guard across her face, in time to see Blackbeard lunge with a knife. He was limping, his body turned to favor his injured knee. Diana drifted to his empty hand, her motion becoming languid. Everyone in the room clawed through tar, though she felt exhilaratingly light. She caught Blackbeard's thumb and bent it back with her left hand. The knife flew away, skittering across the floor, and she twisted her upper body into the blow, smashing the man's hand into his nose.

Blood gouted and she punched him in the throat with her right hand, fingers stiff and pointed. Cartilage and muscle cracked under her fist and Blackbeard's eyes widened in horror. Blood bubbled out of a crushed nose and he fought for breath. Diana pushed him away, turning, her face a mask of calm. A chair flew at her and she caught it by one of the legs.

The gladiators had cleared a space at the middle of the room, leaving the floor littered with moaning bodies. Those few drovers who remained standing were fighting with the press at the stairs, trying to escape. The floor was littered with broken pottery and wood and unconscious men and women. The leader of the oiled men turned towards Diana, eyes slitted. He was a tall, bronze skinned African, with high cheekbones and slick black hair.

"This must be her," he said, jerking his head. Two of his fellows turned as well, their faces lighting with interest. "A delightful morsel for our supper."

The other gladiators were dragging the innkeeper out of his poor shelter.

There was a loud crash as the door gave way and the crowd poured out into the street. Most of them were screaming, nearly crushed by their fellows. Diana could not spare a glance to see if Vitellix and the others had escaped. The three gladiators fanned out, moving across the low-ceilinged room towards her. The leader tossed a glass bottle over the bar.

Diana hefted the chair, vision narrowing to encompass the three men. The leader had stopped, drawing on a pair of boxer's spiked gloves. He was smiling at her as he tied the leather straps. The other two men glided across the floor, stepping easily over bodies and debris. The one to her right was wearing a scaled corselet at his shoulder, bound across his powerful body with leather straps. His head was a polished dark mahogany. The one to her left was pale, with thinning blond hair and arms like tree trunks. His skin, too, gleamed with oil, and his forearms with covered with sleeves of iron fish-scale mesh.

Wrestlers, she thought idly, watching them come. *Professionals.*

Voices whispered in her mind, sounding almost as if they spoke from the air around her.

When you cannot maneuver, you must kill. That was a lilting voice. *On difficult ground, press on; on encircled ground, devise stratagems; on desperate ground . . . kill.*

Diana breathed, centering herself, letting breath fill her, concentrating on a point just below her diaphragm. Her eyes lost focus and she shifted her feet, letting the sensation of the floor flow up through the thin soles of her sandals. She tossed the chair to one side. She seemed to have forgotten the two gladiators. The blond man laughed and strode up to her on the left, scarred knuckles clenching into a fist. Behind him, the leader looked up from the last of his laces and suddenly frowned. "Attalus, don't—"

Diana exploded into motion, even as the man's fist whipped short-handed towards her stomach. She didn't try to stop his blow; the scaled mail protected his arm and elbow. Instead, she spun outside his strike, which drove past with crippling power, and smashed an elbow into the side of his head. The blow rocked Attalus, throwing him back, blood smearing his ear, into the path of the black gladiator. They collided and Diana shouted, a deep, coughing sound, left leg lashing out in a high kick as she finished her turn. The black gladiator threw Attalus to the side just as Diana's heel intersected with his throat. There was a pulpy sound and then Attalus fell, choking.

The black man drove in, fists blurring in the air. Diana caught one blow on the muscle of her shoulder as she turned. The shock staggered her. Her left hand slapped down, catching the second punch on the inside of the man's wrist, deflecting it. He threw his forehead at her, and she had to wrench back, leaning backwards nearly double. The stench of garlic on his breath made her eyes smart. He jumped back, and Diana sprang backwards onto her hands, her toes brushing the roof as she contorted into a half-twist, and then was standing again, in guard, facing him.

"Well struck!" the boxer cried, shaking out his arms and watching with interest. "Watch her legs, Mithridates, she's a powerful length of thigh there!"

Mithridates circled to the right, his fists up, leading with his left foot. Diana circled as well, though she remained unfocused, waiting for the boxer to join the fray. He did not. The Numidian was watching her, waiting for her guard to drop. He seemed tentative, so Diana waited until she was again facing both men. The blood fire was running hot in her too, and she began to feel a furious anger welling up. These men had tried to hurt her, hurt her friends. Without knowing it, her face contorted in a ferocious snarl. Mithridates' eyes widened, then he danced in, feinting with his right.

He was very fast, much faster than Attalus, who was choking to death on the floor. Diana jerked away from the feint, then had to spring back violently as he followed with his left. His knuckles grazed her side, then she had to block hard with her forearm as his right fist plowed in, trying to knock her out. Diana screamed *kiiii* at the top of her lungs, then jumped up, snapping her left foot out. The gladiator dodged, but she clipped his chin and he rocked back. Furious, she plowed into him, slamming her right forearm into his face. The man blocked with his fist, but the force of her blow drove his hand into his chest.

She punched him in the diaphragm with her left fist, but he grunted, turning and catching the blow on muscle. He kicked hard at her knee and Diana jumped again, his hobnailed boot slashing under her. She came down, pivoted and snap-kicked the back of his other knee. Bone splintered and he howled in pain. A wild, glad look on her face, she grabbed the back of the leather strap running along his waist. He twisted, grimacing at the horrible pain in his knee, trying to get away. Diana kicked him in the cheek. There was a brittle cracking sound and his eye socket splintered, white bone jutting from his flesh. He howled.

Grunting with effort, she grasped both his shoulder and his belt strap and then threw him over her thigh. Mithridates hit the floor hard, winded.

Diana swayed, then stepped back, catching her balance. Her arms and legs were throbbing with effort and bruises were already wrinkling purple on her forearms. The room seemed blurry. She blinked, trying to clear her vision.

"You are *very* good," the boxer said, sidling towards her, spiked fists raised. "Like one of the heroes of old, standing on the bright sand, victorious." He grinned, though she could barely see him. The blood fire ebbed in her veins and she began to shake. Half sensing his approach, Diana scuttled sideways, then her foot clattered into the chair lying on the floor. Flinching, she jumped back, turning towards the unseen assailant.

The boxer stood up and back, motioning with his hand. One of his confederates, lurking by the stairs, flipped him a length of rope, which swung with a leaded bag. Nonchalantly, he let the rope swing easily around his head.

"Dear lady," he said in a loud voice, "you've me to deal with next."

Diana snarled, turning towards him. Her left arm rose across her face, right fist pointing to the floor. The sap flicked through the air, driven by the boxer's powerful wrist, and caught her on the temple with a soft *crack*. She toppled over.

The boxer flipped the sap back into his hand, smiling. He raised the bloody bag to his lips. "Faithful, faithful, faithful. Better than any woman. Pick her up, we'll go out the back way."

The boxer surveyed the ruins of the *caupona*, whistling idly to himself. One of his companions rolled Diana in a gray blanket and then hoisted her onto his shoulders. The other ran forward and held open the curtain to the kitchens. As he stepped over the body of the proprietor, the boxer struck an Apollo on the wall, and then tossed the burning spark into a pool of black fluid spreading behind the counter.

Flames leapt up, burning fierce and green, and licked along the smashed amphorae and the wicker shelving. The boxer closed the curtain between the kitchen and the main room of the inn, then walked quickly out the back door.

The crackle and spit of the fire was already loud behind him, spreading across the ceiling of the room. He whistled a merry tune.

Amid the ruined furniture, Mithridates struggled to rise, reddish light gleaming wetly on his skin. His ruined leg failed him and he cried out in despair. Smoke was already biting at his throat.

"Hamilcar!" His scream of rage was drowned by the roar of the fire.

THE ISLAND OF THIRA, SOMEWHERE IN THE AEGEAN

Waves slapped against the hull of the *Helios,* foaming across eyes and a sunburst painted above the ship's bronze beak. The *Helios* was a two-decked galley. The Queen waited patiently, her pale, white eyes shaded by a hood. The sea was quiet, limpid and azure.

"Ah, here they are at last."

A single-decked galley with flanks of silver gray sped across the water towards the *Helios.* The Queen watched as the *Herakles* drew alongside. A flute trilled and oars-women backed oar and the swift galley shuddered to a halt. On its simple deck—no more than a plank walkway down the middle of a rowing gallery—stood a woman in gray and shining white.

"Greetings, sister!" The Queen's voice carried easily over the water. "Good day."

There was no reply. The gray ship drifted closer. The Queen could see that the woman was very old, with fine white hair and a wrinkled yet regal face. Amused, the Queen drew back her hood. She saw the white figure stiffen, but there was still no reply.

"You have forgotten how to welcome a guest," the Queen said. "No matter. I've something of yours. Send over a boat, and we'll load it aboard."

"We want," came the thin voice of the woman, "nothing from you, Queen of Cats. Take yourself and your malice away from our shores."

"You want nothing from me? Then why come forth out of your sanctuary? Ah, but I know—curiosity. You wondered if the old tales were true, if the warnings and admonitions need carry any weight. Well, are your questions answered?"

"We have no questions for you, nor seek any answers. Your welcome was exhausted long ago. Begone!"

With that, the woman in white turned away. Two of her attendants stepped to her side, leading her back to a chair affixed to the deck. The Queen sighed. Now that she was here, seeing the arrogance of the Matron, she wondered why she had come at all. Was there some sentiment left in her after all these centuries? She realized, standing on the deck, feeling the sea wind ruffle her long hair, that she was tired of hiding in the dark. Her kingdom, once so prized, had dwindled to only a handful of outcasts and refugees. Even they were under a pain that she could not lift.

Her hand rose to her mouth, then clenched into a fist. *Enough!*

"Matron," she called out sharply, "you may ignore a guest, but I will fulfill my ancient duty. You may call me a traitor and the first of the fallen, but I know the duty of one sister to another. Nothing binds me to this act, yet I will satisfy honor."

On the deck of the *Herakles,* the Matron of the Island looked up. The Queen could see a look of grim surprise on the old woman's face.

"One of my servants discovered the body of a sister. I have brought her here to find that peace in death that eluded her in life. Will you take your lost daughter? Then I will go and leave you in peace."

The two ships rode on the swell in silence for a time, then the Matron roused herself from her chair and motioned that a boat be prepared. The attendants, and the captain of the galley, argued with her in low tones, and the Queen smiled, hearing all that they said. At last, the Matron stepped down into a shallow boat and was rowed across to the *Helios*.

The Cat-Eyed Queen reached down and helped her into the ship. The Matron felt tiny and birdlike in her hands. The old woman's eyes were quick, flitting across well-worn planks and rowing benches.

"Where is this lost daughter of mine?"

The Queen pointed to the funeral bier and the still, pale figure lying there.

"Here she is. She is not very lively, I fear."

The Matron stalked down the deck, staff tapping in counterpoint to her footsteps. She reached the bier and there was a sharp hiss of indrawn breath. Then the old woman reached out a trembling hand and gently touched the pale, pink cheek of the girl.

"She breathes," the Matron sighed.

"But she does not live," the Queen said in melancholy tones. "This is how she was brought to me."

"How did this happen?" The Matron turned abruptly.

"A man killed her," said the Queen, her voice soft. "A man she loved, who loved her in turn."

"She is not dead," the Matron snapped. "She is in perfect health. Where is her spirit?"

"Gone across the dark river," the Queen answered patiently. *Yet,* she thought, *perhaps the skills of the Order have decayed over the long years. What I see, this old, tired woman may not.* "Like all the shades of the dead. This man restored her body, hoping to rectify his mistake. Now the shell walks and breathes but is bereft of the guttering spark which makes us *live*."

"Who is this man?" The Matron was angry now, staring down at the girl. "I will not suffer to see one of us made a plaything or a toy."

"I do not think," the Queen interrupted sharply, "that he intended that she be a *toy*. I have met him, seen them together. He is wracked with guilt. He loved her very much. You should take this body and send it to the sky, as is proper."

The Matron leaned towards the Queen, old eyes bright with interest. "Who is this loving murderer? Tell me, for I wish to pay him back in kind."

"I think," the Queen said, "you should keep to your island. If you seek this boy out, you will find him beyond your power to punish. I have had some traffic with him, to my loss. His is a twisty mind, filled with traps baited by love and friendship."

The Matron angrily ground the ferrule of her staff into the deck. "No *man* harms a sister! The Goddess's arrows will find him, put madness in his eyes and tear out his heart! Tell me his name."

"No," the Queen said. "Would you set dear Artemis against Apollo? Was not the slaughter of Troy enough for you? This is a matter where the gods play! Stay inside, by the hearth, content in the strength of your doors!"

"A *god* did this?"

"Enough like one, I think. Have a care, Matron! The might of the Order has waned since the Drowning. You believe yourself a power, directing servants from this hidden place, but the world is changing, and the strength of your island fastness may soon be tested."

The Matron looked back at the towering walls of Thira. They seemed indomitable.

"You think it a strong place," the Queen said urgently. "But its strength is in being unseen. If you strike against this man, your hiding place will be revealed."

"This is not like you, to show such concern. What is your price?"

The Queen laughed, brilliant dark hair shifting like a cloud around her long neck and pale, white shoulders. She put a hand to her lips, almond-shaped nails glittering in the fading light. "You have books filled with lists of my crimes, Matron. Do you believe them all? There is no *price* for this girl! She is an innocent. I once swore the same oaths that you did: to help my sisters, to deliver them from danger, to work in all ways to serve the Goddess and protect the helpless."

"You? Help the helpless? Prey upon them seems more like it! Your name is black in our annals, bending your head to that *man* and doing his will."

The Queen stepped back, face washed with furious anger. She knew her own history well enough, she did not need reminding by some child! Her hand rose; the air distorted like a broken mirror as power flooded from the sea. The Matron blanched, then squared her shoulders, putting her staff forward.

"Go ahead, outcast. Strike me down. I have lived a long, full, *natural* life. I see no need to exceed my allotted span."

The Queen considered, then she laughed and waved the power away. Wind skipped across the waters at her motion, making the rigging creak and the light shape of the *Herakles* dance on the sea swell. "No. Come, take your sister. I have spent enough time in your pleasant company."

The Matron nodded, then called to the rowers in the boat. "Attend me, there is a body to be moved."

The Cat-Eyed Queen laughed again, this time in merriment.

"Matron, Matron . . . haven't you listened? There is no need of this burden. Watch."

Turning to the girl on the bier, the Queen leaned close and whispered softly. The girl moved, sitting up, and swung her legs off the funeral bed. With the same motion, she gathered up a robe and stood. The Matron stifled a gasp.

"Child," the Queen said, "go with this woman."

"Enter the boat," the old woman said. The girl walked to the ladder at the side of the ship, then climbed swiftly down, her movements graceful. The two rowers helped her sit, though they were loath to touch her pale skin.

"You see? She is quite biddable."

The Matron did not answer, hurrying to enter the rowboat herself.

The sun set, leaving the sky brilliant with stars and the sea gleaming with silver light. The Queen watched and waited, standing at the railing, until she was sure the sisters had returned safely to the hidden lagoon and the sea caves housing their ships. While she lingered, the Walach boys padded out onto the deck and took their places at the rowing benches.

"Take us away," the Queen said at last, "I will tell you when to stop."

Oars ran out, hissing into the water.

"Half a beat," she called out, pulling up her hood. "There will be watchers on the cliffs; let them see our wake bright on the dark sea."

The oars bit into the water and the *Helios* moved, slowly at first, but picking up speed. The Queen did not look back, but watched the sea ahead with glittering eyes. It had been a long time since she had plied these waters. Care was called for, among the peaks of the drowned mountains.

THE HIDDEN WAY, AELIA CAPITOLINA

Torches hissed, throwing smoke and a fitful light. Nicholas climbed down a wooden ladder into a dark pit. At the top of the shaft, Vladimir looked down, face dubious, holding out a torch. The ladder descended twenty feet and ended in the ceiling of a domed room. Nicholas jumped down, landing on a queasily soft surface. The two engineers, Sextus and Frontius, were waiting for him, standing on a lip of brick protruding from the wall of the room. Their miner's lamps threw giant shadows on the plastered wall behind them.

"What is this?" Nicholas moved carefully, feeling his boots sink into the spongy floor.

"A few centuries of garbage, centurion." Sextus' face was filled with shadows. "Just walk easy—there are soft spots."

"Delightful." Nicholas reached the wall and stepped onto the brick terrace with relief. "Where to now?"

"This way," Frontius said, squinting furiously in the bad light. "There's a second passage . . ."

The entrance shaft led down from the heating room of an old Roman bath house just off the *decumanus,* right in the middle of the city. Now the northerner bent down to pass under a crumbling arch. Some scratch-built steps followed and he found himself standing on the floor of a long, arched tunnel, easily twelve feet high. He breathed easier, looking around. "A hidden road?"

Sextus nodded, grinning like a fool. The engineer pointed off to the left. "It runs two hundred feet west, almost to the tetrapylon at the middle of town. Just like this, broad as a street."

"It *was* a street," Frontius muttered.

"Maybe," Sextus allowed, turning in the other direction. "This is the way we want to go. Another hundred feet to the wall, then we turn."

Nicholas followed them, walking quickly. The floor was covered with dirt, but he could see big round stones fitted together to make the roadway. Despite the vaulted roof, the workmanship did not look Roman. Greek? They walked on, passing under many arches, then the tunnel ended abruptly in a wall of cyclopean blocks.

Frontius stopped, running a hand over the smooth stone. "Each of these blocks, centurion, is twenty feet long, twelve high and who knows how deep. Massive, truly massive."

Nicholas looked up. The blocks ran up past the roof of the tunnel. "What are they above?"

"This is the platform holding up the Temple of Jupiter and the Perforated Stone. Not small, are they? That whole platform is artificial, built on this foundation over a hill and valleys on either side. The damned thing must be a mile long and a half-mile wide. Excellent work. We don't know how deep the foundation runs, either."

Nicholas nodded, duly impressed. If he didn't, the engineers would keep bending his ear until he admitted it was spectacular. They were like that.

"Sadly," Sextus continued, rubbing his nose, "there's no more time for poking about. Let's go this way." He turned right, entering a narrow corridor that ran along the base of the massive foundation. Smooth-cut blocks formed the left wall, while the right was dirt or brick or mixed round stones. The floor became uneven and descended sharply. After a bit, Nicholas had to bend down, for the passage roof became too low.

"We've excavated this," Sextus said, his voice muffled by his body. "It's a bit narrow. There seems to have been a passage here before, but construction in the city above caused it to be filled in."

They descended another seventy or eighty feet, then the narrow passage broke out into the side of a large room. Nicholas stood up, groaning with relief. Crawling about in these tunnels was a chore if you were in full armor.

"Fine-looking, isn't it?" Sextus was smiling.

Nicholas looked around, taking in smooth, plastered walls slanting inward at the floor. The room was large, easily seventy feet long and thirty wide. The floor was covered with the same loose dark soil filling the tunnels, but the walls were a creamy white, covered with irregular brown stains. To his left, just next to the exit of the tunnel, was the foundation of the temple platform, but here it was plastered as well. "What is it?"

"Another cistern," Frontius said, climbing out of the tunnel. "Once it was open to the sky, like one of those pools by the north market. Look up."

Nicholas followed the surveyor's pointing finger. Brick ribs vaulted the ceiling and slabs of stone had been laid down to make a roof.

"Someone decided that they could build something on top of the cistern, so they covered it over. Which is the very luck for us, centurion, because they could have just filled the whole thing in. Then where would we be?"

"I would be in bed, sleeping," Nicholas snapped. Despite repeated admonitions, the engineers had pressed ahead with their survey of the city waterworks and underground places. He couldn't fault them; the work on the walls and gates continued unabated.

"Please, sir, just give us a moment. Do you see this wall? See the curving brick?"

"Yes." Nicholas leaned close, for the wall—to the left of the tunnel as one entered—seemed a little strange. Its plaster had flaked away, leaving the arched courses of thin bricks exposed. "It's not like the other walls."

"Just so," Frontius said, shifting excitedly from foot to foot. "Once, when the cistern was open to the sky, this was a drain opening into the side of the pool. I figured a stream ran beneath the city from a spring north of the temple platform, parallel to the foundations, past here. Once, the stream filled this cistern. However, when they covered over the cistern they had to divert the water or the cistern would overflow."

"It's under our feet now?" Nicholas looked dubiously at the floor.

Sextus nodded, pacing his way across the cistern. "Yes, sir. We noticed the drain, then Frontius decided they ran a channel under the floor, then out again on this side. See this?" He pointed at his feet. Nicholas stepped closer, peering in the dim light. There was a large inset rectangular block in the floor, marked by two square holes, each about a hand's-breadth wide.

"I see it. Tell me what it is." Nicholas was getting snappish.

"It's a drain cover. Vlad, bring me those pry bars."

The Walach had been following along, quiet in his bare feet, but now he grinned in the darkness and hefted two long iron bars. Sextus took one, slid it into the square hole, then waited for Frontius to do the same with the other. Together they leaned on the pry bars and the stone, groaning and rasping, tilted up and away from the floor. Nicholas looked down into darkness, feeling cold, wet vapor rising up.

"How appetizing," he said, feeling clammy. "So?"

Frontius and Sextus shared a look, then shook their heads in despair. *Officers!*

"We sent one of our lads, one of the Roman lads, mind you, down into the tunnel. It's the stream right enough, and it runs down a brick-lined channel under the southern wall. Now, before you give me that look, centurion, the channel leads into the top of a shaft bored through the rock of the hill, spilling down in a waterfall. That shaft plunges down forty feet or so and into a tunnel. *That* tunnel, which is outside the southern wall, goes downhill quite a ways to a hidden spring that sits at the junction of the Hinom and Kidron valleys, almost a mile from the southernmost point of the outer wall."

Nicholas pursed his lips, considering the possibilities. His grim look faded slightly.

"Well, now," he said, scuffing his boot against the edge of the manhole. "These Arabs seem to have left the southern valleys alone. I'd say they didn't have the men to throw a cordon around the whole city. Can a body of men make their way through this whole mess of tunnels and shafts?"

Sextus nodded slowly, watching the centurion carefully. "You've not told the locals about this, have you?"

Frontius and Sextus shook their heads.

"All *Legion* business down here," the surveyor said. "We've put about that we're looking for hidden treasure. Only our men are allowed down into the bath house and we've not found any side tunnels that led to anything."

The centurion frowned but let it pass. If the locals wanted to dig around in their cellars, let them. Hopefully they wouldn't stumble across the excavation. "You say there's a spring at the other end? Can we get out?"

Sextus grinned merrily, rubbing his hands together. "We can, indeed. The tunnel comes out in a basin, just above the spring room, inside a ruined building. It's almost impossible to find the tunnel entrance. We've posted a watch, to make sure that the bandits don't find it without us knowing."

"How long does it take to get out?"

"About an hour and a half." Frontius raised a finger in admonition. "The only problem is this, centurion. If it rains, the tunnel floods."

"Rain? Here? There's little likelihood of that."

Nicholas turned to Vladimir, who was squatting at the edge of the pit, sniffing the cold air. "What do you think?"

"Me?" Vlad looked up, his dark eyes shining in the lamplight. He grinned, showing fine white teeth. "I like living better than dying or being a slave. When do we leave?"

"Not now," Nicholas mused, motioning for the engineers to close the stone lid. "We have to get ready. It would be best if we waited until the Arabs launched an assault, then they'd not notice us leaving. That will take a bit of planning."

The centurion turned away, thinking. The two engineers turned to each other and solemnly shook hands, then broke out in quiet grins.

·   ·   ·

A wasteland of stars filled the sky, clear and distinct in the cold desert air. Straight overhead they didn't even sparkle or shimmer. Dwyrin lay on the roof of the praetorium, head cupped in his palms, the bricks warm with the day's heat against his back. A guard leaned against the outer wall of the tower, watching the ramp and the roadway below, ignoring the Hibernian.

He had been coming here for days, spending hours lying under the glorious velvet sky. The nights were growing warmer, making it far more comfortable to lie out here than sweat in the stifling rooms below. It was quiet, too, without the racket of snoring and coughing in the barracks.

Dwyrin turned his attention from the sky and its burning, infinite depths. There was some work to be done before he let sleep take him. He was still troubled by exhaustion and a fading sense of solidity. He had difficulty paying attention to the centurion. Sometimes, if he didn't pay close attention, Nicholas became a transparent, shifting cloud of light, buzzing and whispering. The masters of his old school had warned against this. He needed to ground himself, to keep a steady anchor in physicality. Despite his growing power, he still needed to eat and sleep and shit, like other men.

It was difficult to remember, sometimes.

He brought forth the Entrance of Hermes in his mind. There was a brief sloughing sensation and then he was fully aware of the hidden world shimmering and flickering around him. Dwyrin frowned. The passage had become too easy, too swift. He needed a sharp division, requiring concerted effort to pass. How else would he know which world he walked in? With an effort, he retreated from the ghost realm, focusing on the solid feeling of the stones, the brush of night air on his hair, the darkness enfolding him.

Solidity returned, grudgingly, in fits and starts. It was difficult to make his mind see the mundane. He cursed, letting liquid sound flow out of his throat and across his lips. It seemed remote, unreal. Disgusted, he cracked his elbow against the bricks. Pain flashed bright and he was suddenly all too aware of his body.

"Too slow," he muttered to himself. "I need a discrete anchor."

He considered a peculiar vision that had come to him, soon after they had arrived in the city. He had woken from sleep, aware of the sky filled with pure white radiance. Dogs were barking. The watch had turned out to investigate. A half-familiar man had been sitting in Dwyrin's tent, watching him in the darkness. That memory had faded like a dream, but it had left behind a burning sign in his mind. It was always close to him now, drawing his thought like a lodestone.

The old man said it was "the sign of fire." Dwyrin let it assume a place in his mind, flowering from a bright point, unfolding an infinite array of bright geometric surfaces. The sign constantly transformed itself, wavering like a flame. Dwyrin could call fire from it with tremendous ease. The pattern let him smash the siege towers of the bandits, crush their feeble wards, rip the sky with bolts of flame. It felt good and right, as if he stared into a warm mirror.

"Are you my anchor?" he whispered at the night, letting the warm radiance of the sign drive the chill from his skin. "Should I look outside myself for solidity?"

It seemed to quiver, constantly unfolding in bright shape after bright shape.

"Are you what I need?"

The guard by the wall stirred, walking along the parapet. The night was getting colder, but Dwyrin was warm, even hot, in the effect of the sign. He smiled at the dark sky.

THE FORUM BOARIUM, ROMA MATER

❭❮

Night crept into Rome, making the alleys and narrow streets dim and gray. Gaius Julius walked quickly through the massive central hall of the Big Market. Despite the hour, the market was still bustling and alive, lit by many hanging lamps. The old Roman hurried; the merchants were preparing to close their shops to common trade and begin their nightly dealings. Wagons and wains were forbidden in the city by day, so at sunset the streets filled with great-wheeled vehicles, hauling all of the goods of the countryside into the markets. In this hour between the setting of the sun and full darkness, Gaius knew that he could cross the city swiftly, while other men were sitting at their suppers.

The day had passed in fruitful pursuits amongst the owners of the four great gladiatorial schools south of the Flavian. He had received news from one of his agents that his "package" had been acquired. Gaius had been torn, wanting to look in on his captive, but convinced himself to stay away. There were three cut-outs between himself and the kidnapping. His position was still a little too raw to risk any impropriety.

He turned left when he reached the colonnades and temples of the Forum, and passed under dark arches and down a tunnel. Beneath the remains of the ancient inner wall of the city, he turned right, following a long, narrow alleyway along the base of the crumbling ramparts. He remembered it from his lost youth, and was obscurely pleased that it was still here, even though six and a half centuries had passed. He would be home in a few grains.

He bent his head, quick mind considering the plans and plots he had in motion like a jewel raised to the light. There was much to consider, and too many hours passed in each day—even without sleep!—in negotiation and conference with his allies, servants or superiors.

Gaius Julius slid an L-shaped key into the door to his rooms. It clicked in the heavy internal lock and he went inside, being careful to close and relock the panel behind him. He had taken up residence in a private *insula* on the Quirinal Hill, not too far from Gregorious' mansion. Most important, the apartment was located at the rear of the building, with easy access from the alley. Gaius entertained many visitors at night and he did not want to disturb the well-to-do families occupying the other flats.

He turned, frowning. Warm lamplight spilled from his study. Quietly, he stepped to the arched doorway. His books and correspondence were in their usual sprawl across an oaken table and two desks.

"You've been busy, I see." The voice came from his right, and he turned, hand on the haft of a knife he wore on the leather belt under his toga. The circumstances of his untimely death were a constant irritant. Then his hand dropped and he made a half-bow.

"My lord Maxian, you cannot believe how surprised and happy I am to see you."

"I wonder," the Prince said in a harsh voice. Maxian reclined on one of the couches placed in the corner of the room, close by an iron brazier filled with coals. Gaius Julius did not notice any chill in the air, but he supposed that such things might slip his mind in his current condition. "I have been looking over your papers while I waited for you to return."

Gaius paced to his seat, a heavy curule field chair he had bartered from a cashiered Legion officer. It was comfortable and reminded him of old times. He missed being with his men. Rebellious Gauls were much easier to deal with than Roman building contractors. Gaius sat, sighing with relief to be home. "Do my efforts displease you?"

Maxian scowled and raised a cup to his lips. Gaius Julius tsked to himself. The remains of a rare amphora of Neapolitan wine sat by the couch. Such vintages were hard to come by, now that the vineyards were buried in ash or burning stone. He would have to hide the rest, he supposed.

"I confess," the Prince said, putting down the cup and sitting up, "I cannot fault your energy or activities. You seem to have set yourself to assist and aid the state in all ways. Given what you have told me before, however, I am puzzled. Where are your grand plans to overthrow the Emperor and set me in that place? Where is the cunning and guile that you offered to use for my promotion?"

Gaius Julius looked up, surprised at the bitter anger in Maxian's voice. "My lord! When we last parted, you told me rather forcefully that you were returning to your brother to seek his forgiveness, to attempt some reconciliation! With that in mind, I have bent my every effort to improving your patrimony and his. Have things changed? Have I misread your intent?"

"No." Maxian waved a hand negligently, swaying slightly with the motion. "I thought worse of you. I am very pleased with your work—particularly this effort to restore the highways in the lands around the . . . in the south.

"Gaius, when you left me, I intended to go straightaway to Rome, to make a clean breast of it with my brother. As perhaps you have guessed, this did not occur. I was . . . I tarried on the mountain. There was sanctuary there from the constant assault of the Oath. I waited too long—murderers came. I was attacked in the crater at night. They were very strong and well prepared. I barely escaped."

Gaius Julius leaned closer, straining to hear the Prince's soft voice. The red light from the coals shone on Maxian's face, making him seem old and tired.

"Really, they killed me, there at the end. Krista . . . Krista shot me with her spring gun, right here . . ." The Prince's fingers rubbed a space above his left ear. It seemed unmarked and undamaged to Gaius, but he said nothing. "I died, just for a moment. But the mountain was waiting. I took what it offered—then the structure of the Oath began to break down."

The old Roman felt a chill steal over him, remembering fragments of long discussions between the Prince and the Persian wizard Abdmachus.

"Gaius, the mountain should have erupted ages ago! But the Oath held it back, like a cork in a bottle. There was so much power built up behind the barrier. It was enough to restore me, and destroy them all. I escaped. The Engine took me away, far from the explosions and the fire. I was in the high air when . . . everything happened."

Gaius Julius stared at the Prince in horror. He had never considered such an outcome. "You . . . you were responsible for this disaster?"

"Yes." The Prince drained his cup with a convulsive swallow, then placed it delicately on the low table. "From your papers, I find that I murdered forty thousand people."

The old Roman flinched but then composed himself. "My lord, you were attacked. You defended yourself. When a man struggles for life, he may not be aware of the ramifications of his efforts. Who sent these men against you?"

Maxian's face collapsed, filled with anguish. He covered his eyes. "My brother."

Gaius Julius nodded, his long face grave. This was serious. All of his efforts might come to naught. "He accounts you a threat to the state, then."

"Yes. That woman will have put him to it, I'm sure."

The old Roman cocked his head to one side, thinking. His nets caught many fish, large and small alike. Some involved "that woman," presumably the Duchess de'Orelio, the Emperor's old spymaster. His quick mind arranged rumor and innuendo, added the Prince's news and came to a conclusion. "Lord Maxian, I have heard some things ... some news ... perhaps your brother did not countenance this plot."

"What?" The Prince looked up in surprise. "What do you mean?"

Gaius Julius stood and rummaged through the papers on his desk. He had recently established good relations with the clerks and ministers in the records office. His first goal had been to identify those properties directly owned by the Prince, so that he could borrow against them in the Prince's name. The project in Magna Gothica was consuming enormous sums. In the course of such efforts, he had found—*oh, here it is.* Gaius drew a parchment out of the stack. It had once been tied with colored twine and sealed with wax. A servant on the Palatine had neglected to burn the paper. A lamentable oversight. The old Roman smiled in delight.

"Here, my lord. This is only part of a larger document, but it tells enough of the tale, I think."

Gaius cleared his throat, holding up the paper and putting one hand behind his back, as if he were addressing the Curia. "It begins 'Galen Atreus, Augustus and God, Emperor of the West. From his servant and loyal subject, Anastasia de'Orelio, Duchess of Parma. Lord, I have committed terrible crimes ...' "

When the old Roman was done, the Prince was staring at him in shock, his face filled with conflicting emotions and a bare glimmer of hope.

"You see?" Gaius Julius put the charred paper away. "Your brother had nothing to do with this. He knew after the fact, surely even as you were being attacked at the villa. The Duchess is a cunning woman; she knew he would never allow your death. She had to move herself, then bear the burden of success or failure herself. By this admission of guilt, she hoped to shield the Emperor from the stain of murdering his own brother."

"By the gods, what a twisted path!" Maxian stood, unsteady from so much wine. "Is she dead, then? Executed?"

"Worse," Gaius Julius grinned, for his spies had been watching the Duchess. "She is a broken woman. She is thrice destroyed; first, that she did not kill you. Second, that her agents failed and died themselves. Third, that the mountain erupted and so many citizens perished. Like you, she has a conscience—a trait not to be admired in an intriguer!—and she blames *herself* for the devastation of Vesuvius. She still lives, for your brother pardoned her, but there is no spirit left in her. She is a husk, a shell of the power she once was."

"Good!" Maxian snarled, the raw pain of her betrayal fresh in his mind. Once he had thought her a good and trusted friend, but now? Even in defeat, she remained an enemy. Worse, one that knew him too well. "How fare Galen and Aurelian? Have you seen them?"

"No, no!" Gaius Julius sat again, warding off such a possibility with his hands. "I have toiled in blessed obscurity, my lord. I have no desire to traffic with these kings and emperors. You are quite enough of that for me." He shook his head in wonder. In his breathing life, he would have accounted a day wasted if he was not seen among the people, in the theater, in the circus, in the forum, entertaining and being entertained. Now, with his frantic dreams lying quiet, he took great pleasure in staying behind the scenes, unmarked and unrecognized. "But I have heard, from your dear friend Gregorious, that they are well, though greatly shaken by these events."

Maxian nodded, his chin on his hand, staring moodily at the wall. "The city seems lifeless. This damnable ash is everywhere a . . . I entered the city as a traveling player, hoping to avoid notice, but the soldiers at the Ostia gate held me up for an hour, questioning me! The theaters are closed?"

"Your brother suspended all public entertainments until funeral games could be arranged for the dead. This is a

singularly dull city, I would like to say, when there is
nothing going on but *work*."

Maxian summoned a gloomy half-smile at the jest. "This
is very unfortunate. Tell me, in your efforts, have you
made any friends in the Flavian?"

Gaius Julius' eyebrow slid upwards, but he restrained
himself from darting a shocked look at the table. Nothing
in this apartment should contain any reference to his intrigues in the amphitheater or among the circus factions.
One never knew when the Emperor's guardsmen or the
aediles might come knocking. "Perhaps . . . I might know
a man who works there. Why?"

Maxian turned to him, face intent, fingers intertwined.
"Gaius, I appreciate all that you have done to help restore
the state. By some miracle, you have divined my new purpose. I have been thinking, long and hard, about my rash
acts. I have been thinking, in fact, about that dog Abdmachus!" Fresh anger crept into the Prince's voice. "Do you
know what he did?" Maxian's jaw clenched.

Gaius Julius began to smile, thinking of Alexandros'
theories. "Mayhap I do. Tell me, Lord Prince, have you
found that he influenced your thoughts?"

"I have! The wretched creature inveigled a pattern into
my mind, bending me, all unknowing, to his will! He
guided me, pressed me to assail the Oath, to try and destroy it and Rome as well!"

Gaius clapped his hands in sly delight. His estimation
of the Persian wizard rose to new heights. The Prince's
face was a perfect cameo of the betrayed man, realizing
that he had been guided down a rosy path to certain destruction. "I hope, Lord Prince, that you have taken steps
against this *influence*?"

"Yes. It has been cast out, expunged from my mind. I
find that my thoughts are much clearer now. They are furious, but they are clearer."

The old Roman nodded, pinching his long nose to keep
from laughing out loud. "Then what will you do now?"

Maxian sighed, jutting out his chin, and scratched the back of his head. "I must make amends. I fear to face my brothers, to try and explain to them . . . Gods, I hear the dead of Baiae and Herculaneum shrieking when I close my eyes! There is such a black stain on me. I do not know if I can ever atone for these crimes."

"Lord," Gaius Julius said earnestly, "you are not responsible for these things! Your mind was guided, influenced, by the dark masters of Persia itself. You thought that you were doing the right thing. The Duchess, curse her, was trying to do the right thing too! Even your brother was only struggling to sustain the Empire against what seemed, what *was,* a dreadful threat! These things are not your fault. You were a pawn in Abdmachus' game."

Gaius settled back in his chair, watching the Prince very carefully. The old Roman, who had spent many years arguing in the Curia and the Forum, knew that his words were not wholly true. Every man made his own path, but the Prince should not be paralyzed by guilt, not when a clean break could be made from the past.

"Perhaps." The Prince stood abruptly and paced nervously around the room. Gaius Julius watched him with interest. "I have thought of something I might do, something that would help restore some of the damage the Empire has sustained."

The old Roman cocked his head to one side, waiting for the Prince to continue.

"Have you noticed that the odd pressure in the air is much less?"

"I have. I assumed that once I was no longer directly in your service, that once I strove to aid and assist the state, that the Oath had turned its mindless attention from me. You will note, however, that I have not discarded your amulet!"

Maxian wagged a finger, smiling. "That may be, but the eruption plays a part as well. Consider: at some time in the past, the mountain should have erupted, but the Oath viewed this as a threat to the Senate and the people. It undertook to prevent the explosion. Thus our cork. Now, if a pressure is not relieved, it builds. Centuries passed, I think, with the power in the mountain growing, and the Oath being forced to exert more and more counterpressure to hold it back. All this time, the other structures and lattices within the Oath are being strangled, leached of energy. More and more of the Oath itself was focused on holding back Vesuvius."

The Prince paused, arranging his thoughts. "Then there is violent and cataclysmic release. The mountain rages free, spewing fire, molten rock and deadly smoke. The eruption is far, far worse that it would have been before. The greatest damage is not to the land or to the people, but to the Oath itself. See it as a builder might see it; the dam breaks, causing devastation to the low-lying fields, but the worst effect is upon the arch of the dam itself. I believe, from what I can perceive, that the whole Oath has suffered a terrible disruption. Much of it is shaken or even destroyed."

Maxian stopped his pacing, looking at Gaius with a pensive expression. "I have given the Persians exactly what they wanted. The Western Empire is shaken, even crippled, by the devastation. Worse is the loss in the hidden world. Centuries of protections, of wards, have been torn down. If an enemy comes against the Empire now, all of those old sureties will be gone."

"Oh," Gaius said, remembering another tidbit of news, this from the East. "Oh dear. Such a thing may have already happened."

"It will get worse." The Prince was grim. "You will think me mad after all that I have said and done, but I am sure that I must restore the matrices of the Oath."

Gaius Julius made a face as if he had bitten into a rotten lemon. "Must you? It seems far more pleasant, not having to worry about being annihilated if I think wrongly."

Maxian grinned, though there was little humor in his

face. "I have an idea about that. But . . . where is our other conspirator? I would have expected Alexandros to be with you."

Gaius Julius shrugged, looking a little despondent. "He left. He fell in with some Goths and took off on holiday. To Siscia, of all places, which was dull, damp and dreary, as I remember. I don't imagine it has improved."

"Will he be returning?"

"If we send for him, he will come back. Rome wore on him, I think. Too civilized. Shall I draft a letter?"

"No." Maxian half closed his eyes, then sat for a little while, deep in thought. Gaius Julius, after watching for a moment, rose and began tidying up the papers on his desk. They had really gotten out of control in the past week. *Perhaps I should get a secretary . . . but who could I trust? There are so many secrets to keep.*

"He is well, though rather battered, I think." Maxian opened his eyes, looking at the old Roman with a slightly unfocused expression. "I see his intent, and yours, wily old goat! Vacation indeed!"

"Excuse me?" Gaius Julius felt a distinct and unpleasant chill steal over him. He struggled to hide growing horror. "You can . . . see him? Where he is?"

"I could look out of his eyes," the Prince said in a nonchalant tone, "if the need took me. I made him, as I did you, from dust. My will sustains him. If I desire it, I can see his mind."

"Oh. I am glad he is well."

The general good humor that had been with Gaius Julius for these last days vanished, leaving him with a sick, churning feeling in his stomach. He gripped the desk for support to keep his knees, unaccountably weak, from buckling under him.

"Have we done ill?" he asked tentatively.

"It doesn't matter. If it keeps our Macedonian busy and out of trouble, let him raise his army. I can see sitting around here with you, plotting and intriguing, would bore him. Besides, he would distract you from important work."

Gaius Julius made a face. The Prince was laughing at him. "Then, what now?"

Maxian rubbed his hands together. The effect of the wine seemed to have dropped from him like a discarded cloak, leaving him filled with energy. "I see you've been busy, planning the funeral games. That is excellent, truly excellent. Tell me, can this friend of yours get me a pass to enter the Flavian at any time, day or night?"

"I suppose . . ." Gaius looked suspiciously at the Prince. "What for?"

"You'll see." The Prince grinned. "Or rather, you won't see, but I will and that is all that matters."

What joy, thought Gaius Julius to himself, *I get to try to keep track of his machinations as well, while hoping that he ignores mine and keeps his naughty, prying fingers out of my thoughts!*

THE PALACE OF THE STAG, CONSTANTINOPLE

Master Tarsus?" The priest woke, blinking, and saw night had fallen. Someone was bending over him in the vestibule, gently shaking his shoulder.

"Excuse me! I did not mean to fall asleep." Tarsus sat up, grimacing at a twinge in his back. It did him no good to sleep on these cold stones. He was not a youngster anymore! The little room was dim, lit only by a single lamp. Then he recognized the man leaning over him.

"Master Hipponax!" Tarsus' bearded face lighted with joy. "I had not thought to find you in the city—they told me at the chapter house you had left."

Hipponax sat down, his round face smiling in a tired

way. He was a little man, with only a fringe of hair left on his head. Like Tarsus, he was dressed in the pale blue overcloak of the Order of Asclepius.

"Oh no," Hipponax said in a wry voice. "There's too much to do in the city. The high priest and all of his . . . friends . . . went off to his estates on Crete until this business with the Emperor's mood improves."

"Ah," Tarsus said, remembering the temple here was devoted to politics and currying favor in the Imperial court rather than actual healing. The simple-looking Hipponax was one of the few actually treating the ill. "You've been ministering, then."

Hipponax made a wry face. "I have! There are nearly a million people in the city, old friend. They have an endless litany of complaints. Far more than one simple priest not overly blessed with the gift can handle. But I try."

"What are you doing here? Have you come to see Prince Theodore?"

Hipponax shook his head, the faintest hint of anger showing in his eyes. "No, I've no desire to see men of war. I was invited by the Caesar, so that he might bend my ear for an hour or so. And a dolorous hour it was!"

Tarsus gritted his teeth. If he had stayed awake, he might have gained entrance to the Prince's chambers in Hipponax' company.

"What's wrong?" Hipponax took Tarsus' hand in concern. "Ay! You're waiting to see the Prince! I'm sorry, I didn't see you until I was coming out."

"No matter!" Tarsus said stiffly. "Do you think that he would see me now?"

Hipponax shook his head sadly, his voice low but cutting in tone. "A gaggle of patricians came in as I was leaving, and they were sitting to dinner. I doubt he'll find time for you tonight! If my interview is any judge, he will be a long time filling their ears with venom and bile directed at the Empress. His idea of plotting is remarkably blunt. Tell me, have you eaten? There is a fine inn not too far away—we could break bread, sip some wine!"

Tarsus felt his stomach grumble awake at the thought of a lamb shank and fresh bread. "I shouldn't," he said, looking out the door of the waiting room. The guards continued to ignore them. "But I fear this is fruitless. Let us find this inn of yours!"

Hipponax beamed, for he was very fond of good food and wine. Tarsus picked up his straw traveling hat and slung a stained woolen cloak over his shoulders. At least he was getting fit again with all this tramping about.

"How curious!" Hipponax cut a slice of garlicked sea bass, garnished with scallions and pepper paste, and skewered it neatly on an eating tine. The glistening, perfectly cooked fish disappeared into his mouth. He smiled beatifically, savoring the taste. "Your student claimed to have revivified the dead and imbued them with thought and spirit?"

Tarsus nodded glumly, picking at the spiced lamb on his trencher. As Hipponax had promised, the innkeeper provided an exceptional table. The bread could not be flakier, with a firm yet pliant crust. The lamb was divine, with a succulent aroma and swimming in rich gravy. But, as their conversation turned to Tarsus' mission, his appetite vanished. A sense of impending disaster gripped him, filling his thoughts with wild visions and phantasms. He saw the city burning, choked with the dead and prowled by abominations.

"Yes, he was certain, mad as it sounds. And his subjects! Gods above and below, I cannot think of a more dangerous pair to set loose upon the Empire. Can you imagine the trouble they could cause?"

Hipponax nodded, cleaning off his plate with a hunk of bread. "They are both notorious. . . . I wonder . . . could that be why he was able to summon them up as living men?"

Grimacing, Tarsus shook his head. "The passage of the *ka* into the underworld is no mystery. We debated that when *we* were students, The only way that a spirit returns—the only passage that the gods allow—is by rebirth in a new body, cleansed of all memory. Then the soul grows and learns again. Only the ancient heroes ever brought back the dead whole to the land of the living, and then, *then* by descending into Hades itself to lead them forth."

Hipponax dabbed at his lips with a cloth. "We've argued that point too. It's allegorical the heroes *led* the dead back from Hades. Obviously their physical bodies were cremated or rotted in the tomb. Some means must have existed to let their spirits return and inhabit a new body. Perhaps your student found this mechanism."

"No," Tarsus said in despair. "He related the incantation he used—it was one of the forbidden rites. He restored the body of his lover the same way. She became a husk, just as the old books warn. I fear this: malign spirits were nearby when the boy conducted the rites—they inhabited the freshly vivified bodies and are pretending to be these ancient despots."

"You," the little priest said, sitting back with his hands on his round belly, "are of a morbid turn of thought this evening."

"Do you see another possibility?" Tarsus' voice rose irritably.

"No." Hipponax shook his head, eyeing pastries laid on a platter next to their table. "I'll just have one of these." He took a square of thin dough, glazed with crushed nuts and honey. "Well, all philosophy aside, why tell Prince Theodore?"

"This is worse than just raising the dead, Hipponax. The boy has consumed the spirits of the dying as well, denying them their rightful passage into the underworld."

The little round-faced priest choked on his pastry. "What did you say?"

Tarsus nodded, angrily cutting at his lamb. The knife stabbed into tender flesh and red juice oozed out. "I could feel them around him. They made a soft noise wherever he went, moaning and lamenting. He said . . . you've heard of the great eruption of Mount Vesuvius in Italia?"

Hipponax nodded, his face growing paler.

"Well, the boy was there. He claimed he was responsible. I'm not sure that he realized it, but when all those poor people died, he swallowed up their spirits as they flew free. Gods, Hipponax, you can feel him from a mile away, a churning black cloud of malignity! He distorts the hidden world where he walks, warping patterns and crumbling bright matrices like a thunderhead. Just being in the same room with him is dangerous."

"Oh my." Hipponax put his fingers to his lips. "How . . . how many did he consume?"

Tarsus shook his head, his face bleak. The arching ceiling of the inn, built in an old underground water cistern, seemed to press down on him. "Thousands. Tens of thousands. A multitude. Their voices were like the wind on a field of grass, countless."

"I see why you wished to see the Prince, then."

"Yes, the high priest sent me to warn the Imperial government. To make them take action against the boy. He must be stopped, killed, somehow, before he consumes more innocents."

Hipponax sighed, all humor gone from his face. He seemed much older and careworn. The anger that had briefly surfaced before returned. "Prince Theodore is useless. Have you heard of the dispute between him and his niece?"

"Some rumors, some outright fabrications, I imagine."

The little priest leaned close, his face tight. "Here is how things stand in this troubled city: thanks to the pernicious nature of our dear high priest in the temple here, the Emperor Heraclius lies gripped by dropsy, a foul and debilitating ailment. Some months ago, we were summoned by Prince Theodore to treat his brother, but the high priest— the *fool*!—angered the Emperor with his rash words and we were sent away before I could examine the Emperor."

"Gods, why? What dispute lies between Emperor and temple?"

Hipponax shook his head sadly, round face sour as a lemon. "Here is the truth of the matter—I am surprised that you have not heard of it! Some years ago, the Emperor's wife, Eudocia, died and, after a period of mourning, he married his sister's daughter, the lady Martina. Now, I have met the new empress and she is a bookish and introverted sort of girl, but quite pleasant and respectable. I believe—worse yet—that she and the Emperor truly love each another. However! All of the temples, ours included, condemn this too-close match as an affront to the gods. So, when the high priest entered the Emperor's chamber, he demanded that Heraclius divorce his niece before he could be cured."

Tarsus grunted in dismay. Amongst his order, there was a strict rule that their powers, given by the gods for the benefit of all men, should not be used for political advantage or gain. He knew that the priests in the capital were not above leveraging their position for the betterment of their own purses. Now a man lay sick, perhaps dying, in violation of every sacred oath, for political advantage. Tarsus—who had not been involved in such matters before—felt ill himself.

"The Emperor was not pleased and, even in the extremity of death, banned the high priest, his fellows and all members of our order from his presence." Hipponax chewed on his thumb. "Now he continues to linger, half between death and life. His heirs are too young to take the throne and no regent has been appointed. The Empress and the Prince detest each other. Nothing can be done, no one will take action, while they strive for control of the ministries and the army.

"The Imperial government is paralyzed," Hipponax concluded. "I fear there is no one to help you."

"If that is so," Tarsus said, jutting out his chin, "then I will go to Rome."

Hipponax nodded slowly, playing with the wine cup on the table between them. "That would seem the best thing. Though, I wonder . . ."

"Wonder what?" One of Tarsus' eyebrows arched like the curve of a bow. His affable old friend, who had labored for so long in humble obscurity, sounded almost sly. The intrigues of the capital, he thought, must be infectious. Too, Hipponax seemed angry. Tarsus guessed that the corruption of the temple priests had gone too far.

"I can't imagine that Empress Martina, loving her husband as she does, is glad to see his body bloat with foul humors. Perhaps if we approached *her*—in secret—she could allow us to cure her husband. If the Emperor were well, then many transgressions might be forgiven. This breach of faith between temple and Empire might be healed. You would get the Imperial aid you need to deal with this dangerous student."

"And if Heraclius dies while we are attempting to heal him?" Tarsus fingered his neck, filled with mounting apprehension. "We'll both find ourselves in it. Not very enticing . . ."

"Nonsense," Hipponax said, smiling confidently. "We are both masters of the art. We can cure him."

Now it was Tarsus' turn to look sour. "Really? And who will cure us if things go badly?"

THE PITS BENEATH THE FLAVIAN, ROMA MATER

Iron bolts rattled back in their sockets. Diana became woozily aware of stone flagstones rushing up towards her. A spark of bright pain followed as her forehead rasped across the paving. She fell heavily on the floor. Freezing water sluiced across her face. The bolts rasped again and locked in place with a dull *clang*. Diana stared up at the ceiling, domed and arched with ribs of exposed sooty brick. Numbness clung to her like a heavy blanket, making the world—the grimy stones, the black roof, the chill, foul air—seem distant.

Get up, a muffled voice shouted. *Get up now!*

"Nikos?"

Diana rolled over, forearms tingling as if they had fallen asleep. The rest of the room swam into view. It was a rough rectangle, twenty feet long and fifteen feet wide. Behind her was a short flight of steps and a wooden door studded with iron bolts. Lamplight spilled down from recessed openings in the roof. She was dressed only in a grimy loincloth and a twisted breast band of patched wool. Her nostrils flared, taking in a truly horrible stench.

The room was dim, but she could see movement. Figures resolved out of the poor light and the smell grew worse. Her nose registered urine and feces and the bitter, metallic taste of fear. She crouched, shifting her feet. She felt slow . . . her arms and legs were so far away!

"It's a woman!" One of the figures creeping forward straightened up into the light. It was a scar-faced man with a patchy beard. There were five or six others behind him. Diana did not like their looks. Her face drew tight in a snarl. "They've given us a woman!"

"Given?" Her voice rasped like a wire brush on rusty iron. "Perhaps."

The men fanned out. Diana's nostrils flared, seeing skin pockmarked with open lesions. At least two were missing little fingers and one kept only the stump of his right hand. None of them had bathed for a long time. Feeling light-headed, she drifted to the left, putting the wall within arm's reach. Her left hand curled at her waist, palm up. Her right hand faced away from her body at chest height. Without considering the motion, which seemed to be the most seamless and natural thing in the world, her left leg slid forward slightly and her right went back, pointing to the floor.

The men paused, shifting from side to side. Diana could see them eyeing one another, wondering who would strike first. The tension in the air grew. She grimaced, becoming entirely still. When she did so, the largest of the men looked left and right, baring his teeth. Diana turned her direct attention away.

Let the pack determine precedence, she thought. *Ignore me for just a moment longer.*

Her whole body began to wake up, blood and muscle stirring with blood fire. She shuddered. A giddy sensation of delight and anticipation filled her. The numbness fell away. Each worn stone and pitted brick grew very clear and distinct.

The largest man strode towards her, shoulders swinging. But he was watching the other men out of the corners of his eyes. One of them jerked forward, his face raw with lust. The large man stepped sideways, cuffing the smaller man with his fist. There was a muffled curse.

Diana moved as soon as the pack leader turned away, her right foot knifing up, her upper body spinning away and down. The heel of her foot smashed into the back of the leader's skull, right above the spine, with the force of her full movement. There was a splintering *crack* and a gelid, wet sound. Blood sprayed away, dotting the faces of the prisoners with tiny scarlet marks. The big man toppled forward, eyes bulging out of their sockets.

Rage flowered in Diana, wiping away all thoughts of simply cowing the remaining criminals. Her right foot dropped to the floor and she spun through the motion, left fist flashing out. The first of the remaining men had turned towards her—mouth open in a bestial shout—when she smashed his nose into pulp. A great cry of rage rose up as the other men realized that she had killed two of their number. The man with the crushed nose fell backwards.

Three men plowed into Diana, knocking her back against the wall. The impact drove the breath from her body, but she squirmed away. She smashed her forehead into one face, feeling giddy delight at the resulting scream. Fingers clawed at her arms and she shoved hard in response. The man staggered back, surprised at her strength. All those hours working on the wire with Dummonus were paying off. A little man, his face like a terrier's, clung screaming to her right arm. With a jerk she bent his fingers back, hearing them crack and splinter, then she smashed his face. Like the others, he staggered away.

The remaining man picked her up and threw her against the wall. She twisted, hitting with her shoulder, then kicked off from the stone. The point of her shoulder plowed into his midriff, but he just grunted and wrapped his arms around her. He squeezed, trying to crush the breath from her. Diana let him turn her upside down, then brought her thighs together hard around his neck.

He bit at the flat, hard muscle on the inside of her thigh, but she'd already smashed a fist into his groin and while he was gasping in pain, she flexed her legs sideways, snapping his neck. He fell, voiding himself. Diana scuttled away from the twitching body. The two remaining men drew back in horror.

Diana ran forward, her feet light on the slick floor. A high-pitched scream rang back from the walls of the cell. The terrier-faced man was holding his broken hand, crying, when she ran past. Stiff-fingered, her hand chopped out, catching him in the neck. He fell, choking. The motion flowed into a spinning kick that drove her left heel into the groin of the last man. His eyes bulged, tongue protruding between blackened lips.

The last was scrawny, the weakest and smallest, cowering against mold-covered bricks, blood covering his face from a broken nose.

"Please! Please don't hurt me! Please, I wasn't—"

Diana dragged him back by his hair. "Was I *given* to you?"

Her fist lashed down, then again and again. He stopped screaming after a moment, then she shuddered to a halt, her arm red to the elbow with blood. Memory flooded her thoughts, bright and fresh. She let the body of the scrawny man fall to the floor, then turned, her face supremely grim. The terrier-faced man was still alive, vomiting on the floor. She twisted his head sharply, thumbs digging into his ears, until his neck popped. Then she was done.

Blood fire ebbed, leaving her shaking, but she did not fall to her knees. Instead, she braced her feet, hands over her face. Tears cut silver trails through the translucent red serum coating her face.

Oh, oh my dear friends! I miss you. I miss you. I miss you. Oh, Nikos!

She cried in silence, her shoulders shaking.

A pair of hands clapped softly overhead, signaling polite applause. "Magnificent. The people of the city will sing your praises, lady, for those men were all rapists and murderers of women."

Thyatis looked up, her head rising like a feral cat's. Another head was silhouetted by a warm glow in one of the ceiling recesses. She could not make out any features, but the voice was cultured and patrician, supremely self-confident.

"You are Diana? Late of the troupe of Vitellix the Gaul?"

"Yes. What is this place? Who are you?"

Soft laughter echoed from the ceiling. A hand rose against the light. "I am not important, and you will not be here long. Men will enter the cell. They mean you no harm, but if you attack them, you will be killed. They will tend to your wounds."

"I have no wounds," Thyatis bit out, turning towards the heavy door. There was a rattling as the bars withdrew. "I am a citizen; you will suffer if you do not let me go. My *familia* is powerful and they do not take kidnapping lightly."

"Ah," the cultured voice said, "but you are accused of a crime, and have been sentenced to execution. All quite laboriously legal, I assure you. Your family, if you truly have one, cannot go against the Emperor's will."

"What crime?" Thyatis' voice was steady and even, like the grinding wheel of a mill.

The voice laughed but did not answer. The cell door opened and two heavily armored men, dressed from head to toe in iron mail, entered. At the same time, Thyatis was aware that other men were watching from the small windows. Metal sang with the particular sound of a spring being pulled taut. The guards were not half-starved criminals thrown in a hole but professionals. She stood quietly and let them bind her hands.

A bath would be pleasant, Thyatis thought, walking out of the cell. Her feet made a sticky *pit-pat* on the floor. *Then escape.*

Gaius Julius stepped down from the wooden bench, twitching his toga straight. It amused him that so few people looked good in traditional costume. He did, which gave him a subtle advantage when dealing with the overweight senators clogging the Forum. He smiled genially at Ovinius. The prefect was sweating.

"You see? She's really a danger to leave loose on the streets."

The prefect had a haunted look. Gaius Julius put a comforting hand on the man's shoulder.

"Ovinius, you worry too much. Take care of her tonight and she'll be off your hands tomorrow. Later, if fortune allows, you will see her again."

"You mean," Ovinius whispered, "if she isn't put down like a rabid dog."

"This is possible," Gaius said, guiding the prefect back towards his office. "But the *lanistae* of Rome are well skilled in handling barbarian slaves, wild animals and other ferocious beasts. You've done your part well. Fully half of your debt to that ogre Syphax will be retired tomorrow. I will send a man with a bank draft in the morning."

Ovinius tugged at the neck of his tunic, though he didn't breath any easier. They passed a number of muscular young men loitering in the corridor. Gaius flashed their leader, a tall, darkly handsome African, a quick grin. The gladiator did not smile back, watching the prefect with cold eyes, while flipping a gold coin from hand to hand.

"This is quite illegal," Ovinius said in a low voice. "Sentencing criminals directly to the games without a public trial has been outlawed for centuries!"

"Pish," Gaius Julius said with an airy wave. "Watch and see. Diana *wants* to be in the Arena. There's nothing immoral about giving people what they want."

"How is he? Has he woken?"

Vitellix ducked under the lintel of the wagon door. He was very tired, having jogged back from the Aventine after a long night of drinking in the inns by the Flavian. Despite an itchy graininess in his eyes, he bent over the massive shape of the black man sprawled on the bed.

"No. But he'll mend." Ila looked at him wearily. She had a blanket pulled around her thin shoulders, and she managed a tired smile in greeting. "He shouldn't have tried to hurt Diana. She has a temper."

"I know!" Vitellix nodded his head ruefully. A half-smile played on his lips. "He's lucky you heard him shouting in that fire. Would have burned to death otherwise . . . a heavy brute." The Gaul massaged his shoulder. The African weighed two or three times his own weight. "I found her, Mouse."

"Where?" Ila's voice quavered, all possible fears clear in her eyes. "Can we buy her back?"

Vitellix sighed, running a wrinkled hand over his bald head. "I don't think so. She's been taken to the Flavian and put away below. I'm sure that lanista Gaius is behind this. But she's not a slave, she's been accused of some crime and sentenced to death by combat in the amphitheater."

"Well." Ila screwed up her face, thinking, brown eyes squinting ferociously. "Then we'll have to rescue her, like in the old tales. That'll teach those Romans to mess with us Gauls!"

Vitellix smiled and took the girl's hand. Ila despaired, seeing the bleak look on her father's face. "We won't, will we? We'll just leave and forget about her."

"Mouse, she's not one of us, not really. She just traveled with us for a while."

Ila turned away, sniffling, but she refused to cry.

The Gaul laid the back of his hand on the Numidian's forehead. The fever was dying down and his breathing had eased. Vitellix snorted; he'd never expected to do so much doctoring with a troupe of acrobats and aerialists! "Mouse, go to bed. I'll watch him until morning."

Ila refused to respond, staring at him with accusing eyes from the cocoon of her blanket. She scrunched up even smaller, curling into her chair. Vitellix nodded in resignation, then stepped out of the wagon, feeling exhausted himself. The night was cool. Wind moved in the branches of the holly trees, brushing their limbs across the curved roofs of the wagons. Vitellix looked up at the sky, seeing the Hunter rising in the east, a string of bright jewels at his belt.

What to do? We need a powerful patron, but we haven't got one . . . His thoughts began to whirl around, chasing one another.

"Oh, go to bed yourself," he muttered and stomped off.

THE GULF OF FINIKE, OFF THE COAST OF LYCIA

>❮<

Daughter, you must wake up. You've lessons today.
Zoë's eyes flickered open and she saw the
beamed roof of a ship's cabin. Wavering sunlight, reflecting through a porthole, danced on the ceiling. Tentatively, she flexed her fingers and then sat up. For a wonder, she felt fine and well rested. Something about the room seemed out of place, and after a moment she realized that this was not her cabin on the *Jibril*. The memory of a soft, familiar voice speaking to her faded, and she shook her head, swinging out of bed.

Her clothing was laid out on a cot and she slipped on her customary pantaloons and tunic. As she did so, she realized her skin was incredibly smooth, even glossy.

"How odd . . ." It was strange to feel so clean. She laughed at herself, realizing that it had been months since she had really been clean—hair, skin, even her nails. She had been so focused for so long—since learning Palmyra had been destroyed—being clean seemed unnatural.

"Well," she said aloud, binding up her hair with a black ribbon, "where are we?"

Stepping out onto the deck of the ship, she squinted in brilliant sunlight. A crisp wind caught her hair, flicking curls around her face. She felt a charge in the air—tension, anticipation, fear—and her head came up. Fully awake, she took the steps to the rear deck of the galley two at a time. The air was tainted with ozone, as if a storm were building in the clear air.

Mohammed stood at the rail, one hand on the curving stern post of the ship. Zoë looked around, trying to find her bearings. The fleet spread out to either side in a long line, white sails filled with a strong following wind. The iron beaks of the galleys surged through the water, throwing up a white spray. Every deck was filled with men.

"Lady Zoë," the desert chieftain said, distracted, "it is a good day to wake."

She turned, following his gaze. Another fleet bore down upon them at an angle, surging through choppy waves. A bleak shore, studded with barren hills, framed the enemy ships. Their red and orange sails were startlingly bright against a dim blue sky and washed-out mountains. "The Romans?"

"Yes, they have found us at last."

Mohammed turned, smiling, focusing on her for the first time. "How do you feel?"

"Alive!" She laughed, flipping the raven's tail of her hair over her shoulder. "I feel . . . well. Awake!"

"Good." The corners of his eyes crinkled up and she felt the warmth of his affection like a physical heat on her face. "I cannot offer you a quiet day of cruising amongst the islands. There will be a struggle. Do you feel the air?"

"Yes." She turned away, afraid she would blush. It felt strange to be greeted with such open warmth and relief. Zoë wondered how long she had lain unconscious.

Who washed me? she suddenly thought, feeling embarrassed. *Was it him?* She wrenched her thoughts back to the matter at hand. "Their thaumaturges are working against us?"

"I don't know." Mohammed laughed, running fingers through his beard. "I cannot see into their world, not as you can."

"They are trying to work something up." Zoë frowned, concentrating. She began to bring the patterns and symbols of the Entrance to her mind, but then stopped. Memory flooded back like water through a sluice gate and she felt suddenly ill. Afterimages of a brilliant white light echoed in her vision. She clutched convulsively at the railing. "Lord Mohammed?"

"Yes?" He turned back to her, startled by the alarm in her voice.

"You've not . . . prayed, have you?"

"Ah." He frowned, bushy white eyebrows drawing close like twin caterpillars. "The voice from the clear air is close, but it has not spoken. Not yet. Are you afraid?"

"Yes," she said, feeling sick. "I don't want to venture into the unseen world if that . . . power . . . will suddenly come upon us. I remember what happened."

Mohammed raised his chin a little, acknowledging her concern. "Our numbers seem even," he said, indicating the oncoming Roman fleet. "There may be no need to call upon the voice and its power. Can you block their sorcery?"

"By myself?" Zoë was alarmed at the prospect. "I'm not that strong! These ships are fragile creatures—if they send fire against us, or even stir up waves or winds, it will go very badly! If Odenathus were here, we might be able to interfere enough with their sendings . . ."

Mohammed squinted into the sun, gauging the hour and the wind. He had never commanded at sea before but it seemed the wind would not be an ally today. Nearly all of the ships on either side were dromonds, the heavy war galleys of the Imperial Navy, which relied on a triple bank of oars to maneuver. Indeed, the stiff white sails would be a liability once the fleets closed to arrow and scorpion range. They were flammable. With these steeds of wood, tar, cordage and canvas, fire was a deadly enemy.

"Can you keep fire from our ships?" he asked, catching her hands in his. They were thin and wiry, strong—Zoë didn't carry a cavalry blade for show. At the moment they were very warm. "As you did at Caesarea?"

"Perhaps. The sea will help." She retrieved her hands. Her fingers were tingling. "But that will leave them free for other deviltries."

The Yemenite captain hurried up, a legionary's helmet rattling, too large, on his head. Like his men, he was clad in thick cork armor. With his stubby tanned arms and round face, he looked like a seagoing pig with a mustache. "Lord Mohammed, we will be within range in a few grains. Do you have any orders?"

Mohammed laughed, a cheerful sound which carried easily over the heads of the men standing to in the rowing gallery. The sails were taut with wind, the ship making good speed. The rowers held their oars inboard, waiting to close to battle. In only moments they would have to bend their backs . . . but not yet. The Quraysh chieftain smoothed his mustaches and looked out over his fleet plowing through the dark green water.

"Signal our fellows this—that God is great and his will is victory!"

The Yemenite nodded sharply, then shouted orders to his signalmen on the foredeck. Colored flags were raised, fluttering in the breeze, waving and dipping as the men passed the message on. In the rowing gallery, the Sahaba looked up, seeing the great green banner of their Lord rise up to the top of the mast. It snapped smartly, trailing stiff in the wind.

"Allau Ak-*bar!*" The sound was a great roar, amplified by the curving shape of the hull. It carried across the water, borne by the wind. "Allau Ak-*bar!*"

Zoë marshaled her thoughts and tried to calm her queasy stomach.

You need not fear, daughter. You have looked upon the furnace and lived. This will be a little matter.

The Palmyrene girl's head snapped around in alarm, looking for the speaker. There was no one standing on the deck. She felt a touch, a caress on her forehead.

There is nothing to fear.

Zoë swallowed—her throat was unaccountably dry. These hallucinations were a distraction, but they could be ignored. She slipped down the steps and latched the door to her own room behind her. The oaken walls of the ship would give her a little protection, far better than trying to concentrate on the open deck. Seating herself on the bed, she closed her eyes. An dodecahedron flowered before her, constantly in motion.

Mohammed swung from the top of a ladder into the elevated fighting platform on the rear deck of the *Khuwaylid,* feeling the ship pitch and roll under his feet. It wasn't quite a spirited horse, but the motion reminded him of riding into battle. The Yemenite captain and a pair of Sahaban marines were waiting, crouched behind wicker shields lining the platform. From this vantage, the full length of the deck was visible. Sailors were hauling the mainsail down and furling the canvas into a long box-shaped bin running along the spine of the ship. In the rowing gallery, the oarsmen had run their oars out and the leaf-shaped blades waited above the water.

The Quraysh captain smiled grimly to himself. It had been centuries since someone tried to fight a land war on the waters of the Mare Internum. The sailors in the opposing fleet were professionals, well trained and experienced. His Sahaba were reckless, wild fellows used to fighting on land, from a horse. Even with a leavening of Yemenite sailors, there was no way they could win a naval battle against the Imperials. But in hand-to-hand, on the crowded decks of a pair of ships, he would put his men against the best of the Romans.

They just had to get to grips, denying the Imperials room to manuever.

Flutes trilled on the deck below and oars plunged into the water. Three banks of oars on either side bit, then pulled, and the *Khuwaylid,* which had been slowing without sails up, surged ahead again. Behind the flagship, the following galleys picked up speed. On the fighting platform, the Yemenite captain eyed the fleet with a worried expression.

"Only a few grains now, only a few grains." He was

muttering under his breath. Mohammed noticed he was sweating. The Quraysh shaded his eyes with a hand, watching the Roman fleet begin to move. The enemy lines were splitting, fanning out on either flank. Their ships moved with a delicate grace, striding over the water on long, flashing limbs.

"Prepare to fire scorpion for range!" The captain's bellow carried easily to the foredeck. The crew of the weapon swarmed into action, manhandling a smoothed stone into the throwing cradle. Other men cranked furiously on spoked wheels, drawing the curving wooden bar of the "sting" back.

Mohammed took a firm grip on the railing of the platform, then closed his eyes. *O Lord of the World, we place ourselves in your hands, knowing your mercy. Here is our enemy, and our hearts are pure and filled with devotion. Grant us victory this day!*

The sea burned with blue fire to the limit of Zoë's perception. Each ship spidered across translucent foam, the resistance of the water to the cleaving prow a burning white lattice. The matrices of the water surface cracked as the bronze rams cut through, sending out rippling shock waves not only in the liquid itself but through the pattern in the hidden world. The Roman ships were even brighter, outlined with intent and fear and hope and anger. Two of the Roman dromonds, hanging back from the main line of battle, glittered within gold domes. Brassy glyphs and signs drifted across the spheres like shadows thrown on a wall.

Zoë was surprised; it felt like there were only two enemy thaumaturges.

But they might have learned caution, she thought to herself. Until a mage attempted to impose her will upon the fabric of air and water and wood around her, she might evade detection. As yet, Zoë had not raised a ward of defense. It was Legion doctrine to do so, but if she distorted reality around her, a wary eye might find her in the chaos of the battle. With a shiver, she suppressed instinct, letting her self open itself to the hurrying lights and blazing, cold fires of the unseen.

See, Zoë? The sand lizard's coloration, whispered a soft voice, *lets it hide among the rocks.*

Zoë shook her head again, trying to drive the sound away. Ahead of her, a building pyramid of potential suddenly fractured and a shining sphere flew away from the fighting platform, falling with a cracked, glassy burst into the sea a dozen yards from the leading Roman ship.

Now, she thought, *the fight begins.*

Zoë's patience was rewarded as the first two lines of galleys crossed. The even lines of ships almost immediately dissolved into a swirling melee, but the two big Imperial galleys forged straight ahead, protected by a wedge of smaller, single-banked ships. The shape and pattern of the air around the two dromonds began to flex and a distinct gradient formed, coiling and writhing. Thaumaturges on the enemy ships were drawing power from the air and the sea, preparing to unleash it upon the Arab fleet.

Time to get to work. Zoë grimaced, narrowing her concentration to a pinpoint. The enemy galleys rode through a writhing storm of energy, reflecting off the glowing wards, refracting up from the surface of the water. The division of air and sea rolled endlessly, as sharp in the hidden world as it was in the physical. Zoë sent her perception winging out, then plunging like a cormorant into the sea. There was a moment of resistance, a tugging, and then she was below the waves in a completely different realm of shifting subtle patterns and deep abysses. Sharks flew past, drawn to the spreading red stain in the waters above. The hulls of the ships plowed overhead, leaving a swirl of countless tiny vortices in the hidden world. It was difficult to guide her sight at first, but she managed.

The hulls of the two great galleys loomed up. Even here, under the water, the glittering shields of the wards shone in the dimness. In truth, there was no less light than above, but it was obscured, scattered, fouled by sparkling motes of plankton and microbes. Everything in the sea, even the density of the water, distorted raw perception. Zoë struggled with the roving Eye. It got harder to control the farther it flew from her.

She sped closer to the wards and saw, as she closed in, that they were weak and diffracted by the constant motion of the water and the ship. They swelled up before her, glittering and splitting her vision of the black-tarred hull above her into a dozen distorted images. For a moment she hung just out of the pattern of the ward, waiting.

A crosscurrent surged past, thrown out by the churning oars of another ship. As it washed across the ward, the pattern fractured and Zoë leapt into the breach. There was a burning sensation and then the curving hull was directly before her. In her sight, ghostly fingers stretched out, giving shape to her intent. Fingertips caressed the black tar Imperial shipwrights used to seal the planks. A dozen coats had been applied during the last careening. Only a few barnacles had managed to attach themselves.

Zoë bent her will to the incredibly complicated pattern of the tar. It was smooth and composed of uncountable flat ribbons sliding across one another, intertwining like a coil of snakes. The structure formed a watertight barrier, but it was filled with hidden fire. Zoë brushed invisible fingers across the ribbons, calling on a fragment of the sign of fire that Dwyrin had shown her.

A white-hot spark lit in the surface of the ship's hull.

Zoë released her Eye, snapping violently back into her own locus of perception.

The *Khuwaylid* cut in across the wake of a Roman galley, ram breaking free of the blue-green waters, then plunging down again. Mohammed clung to the railing, feeling the whole ship flex as it plowed down into the trough. On the deck, sailors slid amongst sea spray and blood fouling the channels along the rowing gallery. They were busy stripping the bodies of the dead. Naked corpses were thrown over the side. The Imperial galley had turned away, but the *Khuwaylid* had not given up the chase. Another Roman galley was busily stroking forward, directly across the Arab ships' line of sail. The Yemenite captain shouted for a double-stroke and the flautists shrilled wildly.

Mohammed felt the air tremble and looked up.

A mile away, through a drifting forest of ships' masts, he saw a massive, four-banked Imperial galley shudder violently. The huge ship, main deck easily fifteen feet higher than his own, advanced at a stately pace through the battle. The air around the galley was hazed with mist. Red banners flew from the foredeck and painted eyes snarled at every enemy in its path.

Then the sea heaved around her flanks, and a blinding flare of red-orange fire bloomed out of the water. Mohammed's jaw dropped open and he raised a forearm to shield his eyes. A tremendous *boom* snapped across the water as the Imperial galley convulsed, rising up in the air, spilling men and oars into the sea. Fire rippled up the hull, burning white-hot, and steam billowed from every oar port. Blazing fragments of mast spiraled into the sky, trailing curlicues of smoke.

The debris slammed back down in a concussive roar, disappearing into the boiling sea. Waves leapt up, hissing and steaming, swamping the nearest single-bank galley, which was turning away. Even across the distance, Mohammed's blood ran cold as he heard the shrieks and screams of agony from the doomed ship. Boiling water smashed into the smaller ship, turning the galley sideways, then swamping her. The men within perished in the scalding water, swallowed up in the dark sea.

"Ramming speed!" the Yemenite captain screamed, completely focused on the enemy ship dead ahead. Oars dug deep into the water and the *Khuwaylid* leapt forward. Mohammed bowed his head in prayer, wishing the souls of the dead a swift journey into Paradise.

The *Khuwaylid* ground into the flank of the Roman ship, bronze beak shearing through oaken planks and hide-wrapped shields. An enormous screeching followed as the ram crushed through the planking. Water poured into the wound, drowning men trapped in the wreckage of their oars. Sailors clawed out of the rowing gallery, dragging their fellows down in panic. The Imperial galley shuddered, then began to list to one side.

"Back oars!" the Yemenite captain howled. Obediently, the rear half of the *Khuwaylid's* oarsmen began rowing in reverse. The fore half had shipped oars back into the body of the ship to avoid having them fouled or shattered in the collision. The bronze ram scraped and squealed out of the stricken galley. The sea poured into the gaping hole, causing the Imperial ship to wallow deeper into the waves. Sailors plunged into the water. Grayish-black shapes were already busy in the wreckage, rolling and diving, fins cutting above the water.

Mohammed heard another *crack* and caught a glimpse of a scorpion stone, wreathed in green fire, whirling through the air towards him. With a warning shout, he leapt from the fighting platform. He hit the deck hard, but managed to get his legs under him and rolled away. The stone shattered the platform with a *boom,* then rolled out of the wreckage and bounced across the rear deck. Fire spattered from the missile, leaving burning trails on the deck. Splinters scythed through the air. Mohammed flinched, wiping blood from his cheek. One of the Yemenite captain's legs was lying on the deck. The rest of the round little man was nowhere to be seen.

Mohammed picked up a helmet and tied the strap tight under his chin. The battle was growing fiercer. He stood scanning the horizon. The first two lines of Arab ships were fully engaged with the Imperial fleet. Driven by the wind, the entire battle was drifting towards shore. Mohammed's reserves were hanging back, though the right wing of the Imperial fleet was trying to swing upwind.

The shattered Imperial four-banked galley burned furiously, sending up a thunderhead-shaped pillar of smoke. Steam boiled from the sea around the wreck. Mohammed's lips drew back in a snarl. The sinking ship was still burning underwater, lighting up the dark sea with a shimmering blue-white light.

Wizardry! He did not like this kind of war. He felt very tired for a moment, but roused himself. *There is work to be done.* He stepped away from the burning deck. A pair of Arab sailors ran up onto the rear deck with buckets of sand. There was nothing to be done about the captain or the archers. They were just gone.

"Signal the reserves," he shouted to the remaining signalman. "Go after the Roman wing with all speed."

The sailor, face half covered with blood, nodded weakly and began running up banners on the rear signal mast. Mohammed turned back to more immediate concerns. A pair of Roman galleys were cutting in from the *Khuwaylid's* port beam. Unlike the Arab ship, neither vessel boasted a ram at its prow. Its decks were thick with men.

They'll want to board us, Mohammed thought, fingers drifting to the hilt of his sword. *Well, now; that we can accommodate!*

Eager to keep the Roman thaumaturges distracted, Zoë bent her will upon the sea itself, trying to rouse the choppy waters to new heights. In moments, she realized she had made a serious mistake. The sea had its own mind about such things. Affecting the waves required a long reach and greater power. The gelid patterns in the water slid away from her intent, leaving her drained and the sea undisturbed. Worse, the effort flared bright, drawing the attention of the enemy.

Violet fire licked across her pattern, hissing and snapping in the matrices forming her battle-ward. Zoë sweated, still kneeling on the quilts. At least two more thaumaturges had been lying low amongst the Roman ships and now they attacked. By great good luck, neither had taken the time to raise his efforts into the realm of the physical. They strove against her solely in the hidden world.

Zoë invoked a quicksilver lattice, a shining gradient drawing away the stabbing power, dissipating it into the body of the sea. Even that response was too weak and too slow. While she deflected one attack, the other struck. Heat flashed through her and she gritted her teeth, retreating behind a hasty blue sphere. The poorly formed shield buckled and cracked within half a grain, crushed by licking black flame.

I need help! she wailed. If Odenathus, or even Dwyrin were here, he could have easily overmatched these children! There were vast reservoirs of strength in the long-familiar matrix of her cousin's mind.

Here, here, my child! See the brightness? See the strength it offers you?

The whispering voice returned. Distracted, Zoë rocked back, flung against the wall of the cabin by a hammer blow from the Romans. Desperate, she collapsed the remains of her other shields and curled back into a spiky violet tetrahedron. Brightness swam close at hand, a singing glow waxing and waning with the beat of her heart. More black fire raged around her, the tetrahedron cracking under the attack. Zoë wept, seeing annihilation sweep in upon her.

You've stood in the furnace, the voice snapped, now quite clear and familiar. *You're just afraid! You'll die if you don't act!*

Zoë gurgled, blood seeping from her mouth. The Romans, sensing victory, redoubled their attack; the woolen quilts began to smoke. The Roman mages drew swiftly closer, their efforts strengthening. It was becoming difficult to breathe.

The Roman attack suddenly slackened and Zoë caught a glimpse of arrows zipping through the windows of a cabin much like hers. A young man with flowing blond hair was throwing himself to the floor, shouting in alarm.

She snarled, white teeth bared in defiance. There was no more time for quibbling. She reached out to the close white radiance as she had done so many times with Odenathus and Dwyrin. Zoë's pattern mingled with encompassing warmth and the shining power folded around her. Raw strength poured in, rushing like a wadi in a spring flood. For an instant, her concentration frayed, overwhelmed, but the voice was there, hectoring her, and she composed herself. Her control would be crude but far better than nothing! *Mohammed does not have the skill for this,* she realized, *though this splendor flows through him.*

Her attention turned, hawk swift, to the enemy and saw they were very close.

Zoë felt light, insubstantial. A giddy sensation plagued her focus, but she concentrated, bringing to mind old, familiar sequences of the basic signs and transformations. As she progressed through the sixteen symbologies, her mind calmed and familiar patterns reasserted themselves. The flush of power faded, but she did not relinquish control. There was still need of the blazing flower and its strength.

She cast about for the remaining *quinquereme* and found the ship pulling away under all oars. The golden lattice of wards and glyphs had doubled and trebled since her first glimpse of the enemy. Smiling grimly, she perceived the interlocking maze of signs reaching under the ship as well as above.

They've not liked the taste of us. She laughed to herself. *We bite!*

Then she put forth her will, drawing power both from the shining radiance and from the sea. The defenses shrouding the great ship were angled to block any blow she might strike in the hidden realm. There were other ways . . . she could tap power that rivaled the ancients'!

The sea groaned, whitecaps flattening, and then a single swell rose up, sliding past the rear ranks of the Roman fleet. It picked up speed, aiming for the quinquereme.

Zoë laughed, feeling the will of the Roman thaumaturges suddenly shift in alarm. The golden dome flickered and then dimmed. The wave rushed closer, rising and rising. An Imperial *liburna* rode up on the face of the swell, crew clinging to every stay and mast in horror. Then the wave passed and the single-banked galley slid down the following slope, oars askew, rolling wildly.

There was a flash of power and the front of the rising wave lit up like the sun. Zoë laughed again, a gay, glad sound, for the thaumaturges on the Imperial ship had tried to shatter the interstices of the form driving the wave. But there was none. It was only simple water, relentlessly following an ancient pattern. Zoë had set it in motion miles away. Light stabbed in the deep, glowing blue-green through the wave. The wave towered over the ship, which had been frantically crabbing, starboard oars pulling hard while the port rowers reversed with all their strength.

The Roman quinquereme had managed to turn only a quarter of the way to face the wave when the swell crashed down on the deck. Zoë blinked, momentarily blinded by a flare erupting as the golden dome crumpled under thousands of tons of water. A hollow *bang* echoed across the waves from the impact of the wave front on the deck. A grinding sound followed and then the wave was sluicing from the starboard tholes and running in rivers from the deck. For a moment, the quinquereme wallowed, spinning back onto its original heading. The four banks of oars were hopelessly tangled, splintered and shattered. The upper decks were empty.

Too, the hold flooded and now the ship listed hard, rolling to port. Zoë wondered if anyone inside could free himself from the tangled wreckage of oars and dying men. *Probably not,* she thought with satisfaction. Memories of the plaza of bones and skulls greeting her homecoming came to mind. *Here is my justice!* echoed in her thoughts.

The quinquereme settled in the frothy wake of the swell. One side dipped under the waves, seawater pouring through the oar ports. The galley slid beneath the waves.

"One by fire, one by water." Zoë clenched her fist, feeling wonderfully alive. She grinned in delight, eyes hungry for the next ship she could touch with her power.

THE CROWN OF THIRA

)I(

Kettledrums boomed in predawn darkness, setting the pace for a line of mourners climbing the mountainside. A thousand steps were hewn from the stone, from the lagoon below to the peak above. Each step gleamed pale white in the starlight. Along the sacred path, statues of winged maidens faced the sea, and bas-reliefs of deer and wild animals emerged from black basalt. Among the carvings, three-faced, six-armed goddesses peered out. The women walked slowly, heads bent, each bearing a lighted torch.

Carried at the head of the procession was a chair of ivory and horn, wrapped with garlands of white lilies. In the chair rode the living body of the girl Krista. Above her floated a canopy held aloft on long poles by unsworn maidens. Torchlight gleamed and flickered on the cloth of gold as if it were a sheet of living flame. The spiritless girl's hands were folded on her lap, holding fresh-cut peonies. A flowing samnite gown draped her limbs; her rich, dark curls were bound up with ribbons of gold and pearl. She stared straight ahead, gaze unwavering.

The steps ended and all around, the horizon bent away into darkness. Six muscular attendants walked to the center of the platform. Gracefully, they knelt and set the ornamented chair on the ground. The rest of the mourners entered the circle, pacing to either side until they filled the edges of the peak. The torches wavered in a slight wind, casting moving shadows on the stones.

The drums ceased, the drummers laying hide kettles on the smooth flags. Flautists and women with bells and triangles halted their gentle noise and knelt. A ripple passed through the maidens standing near the head of the stairs and they parted, like the white sea before the prow of a black-hulled ship. The Matron entered, her face hidden by a wax mask, her fine white hair loose around her shoulders. Two others accompanied her, a younger version of herself and a slim woman of indeterminate age with pale golden skin. They too wore masks, all the same visage of a stern woman with curling hair.

The bearers brought forth urns of oil and pitch, then waited while the Matron entered the middle of the circle and stood before the seated girl. The Matron bore a pomegranate, a quarter cut away, revealing red seeds. Her voice was firm and strong from behind the mask:

> "Here is a pyre a hundred feet in length and
>   breadth.
> Borne aloft, the corpse is laid with aching, heavy
>   hearts.
> Droves of fat sheep and shambling crook-horned
>   cattle
> Are led before the pyre, skinned and dressed.
> Here, the great-hearted goddess flenses fat from all,
> Wrapping the corpse with folds, from head to foot.
> Then she heaps the flayed carcasses round the
>   corpse.
> Here are set two-handled jars of honey and oil
>   beside her,
> Leaned against the bier."

The night wind softened as the Matron sang, and then died as she finished. Her two companions joined her, each facing out, standing back to back. The Matron raised her hand and the bearers approached the body of the girl. Singing softly, they anointed her with oil from the urns and poured pitch around her feet. Shallow channels in the stone captured the dark liquid, which spilled into a triangle.

"Here is our sister, fallen in battle, heroic and glorious. She died honorably, striving to cast down our foes. Let all praise her and remember her name! She is Krista, daughter of Anna, child of thrice-blessed Achaia."

The assembled women gave a great, deep shout and held their torches aloft. In the still air, the brands sputtered, sending up aromatic white smoke. The Matron turned so that she faced the north. The golden-skinned woman faced the chair and the girl. Now the bearers wrapped the spiritless body in lengths of waxed cloth with gentle fingers.

"But the pyre does not burn," Mikele sang, lilting voice rising like a flight of birds. In her hands she held a chalice of beaten gold, worked with hawks and falcons around the rim.

> *The swift runner thinks, what to do?*
> *From the pyre she prays to the two winds,*
> *Zephyr and Boreas, West and North—promising*
>   *splendid victims*
> *Pouring generous, brimming cups from a golden*
>   *goblet,*
> *Begging them to come, so that the wood might burst*
>   *in flame*
> *And the dead burn down to ash with all good*
>   *speed.*
> *Iris, messenger, hears her prayers, rushes the*
>   *message on*
> *To the winds that gather now in stormy Zephyr's*
>   *halls*
> *To share his brawling banquet."*

The Chin woman poured thick wine into the channel at her feet. It mixed, swirling ruby and black, with the pitch.

The bearers finished with their task, leaving the girl wrapped in gentle cloth, covering her limbs and body, all save her face, which was calm and still, staring out upon the mourners.

The three women turned again, and now the Matron's disciple faced the girl. In her hands there was a slim candle of beeswax, unlit. She, too, sang, her eyes closed.

"No time for sitting, cries the swift-winged
*   messenger to the assembled hall.*
I must return to the Ocean's running stream, the
*   Aetheopians' land.*
They are making a splendid sacrifice to the gods,
I must not miss my share of the sacred feast.
But hear me, I bring the prayers of the daughter of
*   Artemis!*
She begs you come at once, Boreas, blustering
*   Zephyr,*
She promises you splendid victims—come with a
*   strong blast*
And light the pyre where a brave warrior lies in
*   state*
And all the Argive women mourn around her!"

The young disciple touched the lit candle to the dried flowers. Around the circle of the platform, the mourners raised their voices in song, all in harmony, ringing like a great bell. Fire flared and sparked in the petals, leaping up in orange and green. The disciple stepped back, as did the Matron and Mikele, and cast the candle into the pitch.

Flame roared up, licking along the circumference of the seated girl. The wax cloth dripped and then caught, burning a clear blue. Within an instant the center of the platform was a writhing column of fire and smoke, leaping towards the sky. The faces of the assembled women gleamed with firelight.

"At that hour, the morning star comes rising up," sang the massed voice of the sisterhood,

> To herald a new day on earth, and riding in its
>   wake,
> The Dawn flings out her golden robe across the
>   sea,
> The funeral fires will sink low, the flames dying.
> And the wings will swing round, heading home
>   again,
> Over the Thracian Sea, and the heaving swells will
>   moan.
> Then at last Artemis, turning away from the corpse
>   fire,
> Will sink down, exhausted. Sweet sleep will
>   overwhelm her,
> Giving her ease, sending these dreadful thoughts
>   away."

The Matron turned her face away from the pyre. She walked slowly, stiffly, to the head of the long stair. Her old bones would feel every step as she descended to the city hidden below. One by one, each of the women on the mountain peak approached the raging fire and bowed, throwing her torch into the conflagration. In the end, as the rising sun filled the east with pink and gold, only Mikele remained, watching the dawn.

The funeral ash rose up in a gray cloud, thick and heavy, then scattered to the west, across the jagged cliffs and steep slopes of the island, lost amongst tumbled boulders and black sand. Within a few grains, the platform was swept clean and the Chin woman turned her face from the rising sun, cold, swift wind nipping at her gown. Then she, too, descended.

THE WALLS OF AELIA CAPITOLINA

)I(

Dwyrin stalked along the city wall, a cloak pulled tight around his thin shoulders. A fierce wind blasted out of the east, flinging grit and sand in a brown haze over the surrounding hills. On the battlements, it was growing colder as the day faded. As the Hibernian paced, his head bent low, he chanted to himself. A dull red glow followed him like the wake of a ship, spreading across the parapet's limestone slabs. The sentries along the wall stayed well away, either sitting on the roofs of nearby buildings or standing around in the darkening street below. After he had passed, they tentatively returned to their positions.

Dwyrin paid their fear no heed, concentrating on laying his fire ward. Nicholas had been fretting for days. The enemy attacks had ceased. The bandits were lying low, barely stirring from their camps. The centurion was sure it meant a trick in the offing. Without sufficient troops to guard the entire wall, he pressed Dwyrin to find a sorcerous answer to the riddle. Dwyrin couldn't give him an answer—he had no idea what the enemy was up to. He had never learned the mnemonics to invoke the Eye of Mercury or raise some spirit to spy on the enemy. That, he reflected sourly, had been Zoë's job. *Not mine! Not the too-young recruit, too late and too slow to learn those things.*

He smiled mischievously. The next time the Arabs attacked, they would get a surprise. He might lack many skills, but he was becoming fire's master. They would burn hot, if they tried to scale these walls. The pale, white limestone was the perfect matrix; the stone would burn by it-self, if sparked to the proper temperature. He could feel that yearning tugging against his feet as he walked. The sign of fire burning in his own heart inspired other flames to life.

Vladimir had banned him from the kitchen of the prae-torium. It was too dangerous!

No dishes for me to wash! The memory of school brought a pang of remorse. He wondered how his teachers were doing, Ahmet and the others. He hoped that they were safe and sound, lazing on the banks of the Nile, herd-ing the gaggle of junior boys through whitewashed halls. He shouldn't be here, locked in a death struggle with an old friend.

Dwyrin looked out over the dun fields and the scraggly line of Arab tents, his heart heavy. Twilight was on the land now, making everything hazy and indistinct. Odena-thus was out there, somewhere. The Hibernian had tried to touch his friend's mind through the vestige of their battle-meld, but he had found only a blank sensation. Odenathus had more than enough skill to block him out. Too bad. Maybe if they could have talked, they could have ended this. . . . *Probably not.* He sighed. *I've killed too many of his friends.*

He reached stairs leading up into a tower flanking the Damascus gate. The red glow dripped from his cloak and seeped into the flagstones. Below him, under the light of many torches and lanterns, the gate tunnel echoed with hammering as the Roman engineers levered blocks of stone and brick into place. Today, Sextus and his stone-masons hoped to complete work on sealing this gate. The gate tunnel near the praetorium was already closed and work had started on the Dung gate at the southwestern corner of the city.

The stairs led up into a large room with arrow slits on the outer wall and murder holes cut through the floor. Now, of course, the openings to shoot down at attackers in the gate tunnel showed only dirt and bricks. Dwyrin ignored the citizens clustered in the room. They were men of the city, clad in heavy leather jerkins reinforced by metal plates. It wasn't nearly as good as the Legion armor, but it could be turned out by the tannery and the black-smith's shops within the city. Their arms were no better, mostly old swords dug out of attics or cellars and new-forged spears. The few militia officers were Legion veterans settled here decades ago. They were a grizzled lot, but the backbone of the defense. They ignored Dwyrin in turn, keeping the other men occupied while he worked.

Placing a hand over the middle arch of the gate tunnel, Dwyrin bent his will upon the keystone, etching a sign and pattern to tie together the fire-ward he had scattered along the rampart. A fierce glow radiated from the stone, lighting the room and silhouetting his hands as they bore down on the floor. Then he let go, feeling pressure release and a *pop* as the pattern locked into place. Now, while the key-stone remained intact, the walls would make any assault costly.

The fire-barrier wasn't anything Odenathus couldn't overcome, but then, the Palmyrene couldn't be everywhere at once, could he?

Dwyrin wiped his forehead. It was damp with sweat. This was hot work, even on a chill evening like this. The desert weather and its moods never failed to amaze him. It was coming on full summer, yet the nights were still bitterly cold and a stiff wind could make you reach for your cloak. The day's work done, he clattered down the stairs to the street, thinking with anticipation of a stein of corn beer in the praetorium mess hall. Maybe there would be something other than the usual mutton to eat, too. Rations weren't short in the city, but there was little variety.

" 'Ware! 'Ware!" The dissonant clanging of an alarm bar suddenly cut the hazy air as he reached the street. Cursing, he turned and leapt back up the flight of stone steps. "They're coming!"

Dwyrin frowned, hearing panic in the lookout's voice, but when he reached the top of the tower and looked out upon the darkening plain, he knew why.

The enemy had not been planning some trick, they had been waiting for reinforcements.

A vast number of lights covered the rocky fields before the walls, flickering orange and red. They advanced swiftly in winding columns of torches. A low rumble of boots and sandals thudding on the rocky ground reached the ears of the men on the tower. Where before the Arabs had come against them in thousands, now there were tens of thousands.

"Signal the praetorium!" Dwyrin's voice cracked like a whip and the men leapt to obey. A shuttered lantern, backed by a silvered mirror, was uncovered and it flashed towards the southwest. The soldiers on the wall were shouting too, calling down to their mates in the street behind the rampart. Men rushed forward, weapons in hand, struggling to pull on their helmets or armor. "Keep everyone back from the face of the wall when they put the ladders up!"

The columns of men on the plain jogged closer, their helmets and spears glinting in the torchlight. On the road there was a great racket as two siege towers rumbled towards the wall. The shouts of sergeants and captains rose up to the defenders. With a rattling of armor and weapons, the attackers began to fan out as they came within arrow range of the walls.

"Wait for it!" Dwyrin hoisted himself up on the walkway behind the tower parapet. Two of the citizens followed him, each carrying large rectangular Legion shields. While he peered out into the gathering darkness, they covered him on either side from enemy arrows. "Hold your shot until I've a chance to work."

The Hibernian closed his eyes, a soft chant on his lips. He felt the sign of fire calling, its voice irresistible. He struggled to contain the swiftly growing power. An indiscriminate release would kill thousands and set the city ablaze. Clenching his jaw, Dwyrin bore down, trying to master the sign. He felt shaky, trembling with effort. It was growing stronger.

Arrows cracked against the wall and whistled past overhead. Dwyrin turned his attention outwards, seeing the plain swarming with men. His mage-sight let him see through the darkness and make out battalions of spearmen, masses of archers and ranks of cavalry waiting on the road behind the siege towers. The towers themselves flickered with a corpse light, showing the faint tracery of fresh wards and shields. Dwyrin grimaced, half sensing the pattern of *aqua* and *terra* striving against his *ignis* and *ventus*.

He had prepared for this day, too. A word formed on his lips and he stabbed out his fist, letting a tiny portion of the sign raging within him billow forth.

Fire ripped across the plain, shattering the ranks of the first wave of Arabs. Huge jagged waves of flame consumed the men. Most of them simply disappeared in the actinic white glare. A halo of red light wavered in the air around Dwyrin, though he no longer had time to notice such things. The two shield men screamed and fell back, their faces burned. Steam hissed from their clothing and armor. Arrows filled the air, flaring bright against the fireward as they sought out Dwyrin's life.

On the plain, now lit by shuddering red light from pyres burning amid the scattered rocks, the massed ranks of the Arabs raised a great cry like the ringing of enormous trumpets: *Allau Akbar!*

Then they surged onwards, the siege towers rumbling forward in their midst.

Nicholas squinted to the north, pale violet eyes straining against the gloom, one hand leaning on the parapet of the praetorium tower. Lurid orange and red stabbed on the horizon. A series of thunderous *booms* rolled over the roofs of the town, shaking dust from the rafters and startling the dogs awake. There were fires in the city, too, but luckily most of the buildings were brick. Something was throwing up a huge column of smoke, though, which glowed from below with a baleful red light. Amid the fumes the centurion could make out the flicker of a signal lantern.

"Tens of thousands," he muttered to himself, reading the slow pulse. "Shit."

Vladimir padded up, lanky frame jingling with a coat of heavy mailed armor. The Walach bartered a sheep for the old-style hauberk of overlapping leaf-shaped plates. He wore the mail cinched with a broad leather belt and a linen surcoat. One of the townswomen had stitched a snarling cat in black and white on the chest. It was poorly made, but Nicholas kept his peace, seeing the pride filling his friend. The Roman guessed the sign was the clan-totem of his people. A long-bladed ax was slung over the barbarian's shoulder. "Runners just came in, Nicholas, there are armed men on the western ramp."

Nicholas bit his lip, then came to a swift decision. The last day had come. "Vlad, round up the engineers, as quick as you can. We're going out. I'll get the boy and meet you in the tunnel. Go!"

Raising a thick black eyebrow in surprise, Vlad nodded sharply and then bolted down the stairs, taking the narrow steps three and four at a time. Nicholas would have tripped, broken his ankle and then stove in his fool head trying such a thing. The Walach was sure on his feet, though, and never seemed to step wrong. The centurion listened, cocking an ear to the darkness. Sure enough, he could hear the clink of metal on metal and the sound of men running in boots below the western wall. He did not risk looking over the edge. The enemy counted many fine archers among their number.

Sighing, he looked out over the domed roofs of the city, taking it all in. The thunder at the northern gate was still rising in pitch, with the entire line of the wall lit up by a violent red glare. The boy was making quite a noise, but if the enemy had enough men to test the whole length of the rampart, there was no way they could hold the city.

Another command wrecked, he thought, caught by a tinge of remorse. *Another lee shore in a bad wind.*

He pushed away thoughts of the Dannmark and the memory of men shouting in fear in the darkness. The fog-shrouded coast of Scandia was far away and those men had been dead and rotting in the cold ground for years. Shouts from below the wall roused him to action. In a moment, ladders and grappling hooks would crash against the parapet. He needed to move swiftly. Despite his haste, he took the stairs only two at a time, one hand brushing the wall to steady himself.

Nicholas struggled through the plaza behind the Damascus gate, pushing through fleeing citizens. Despite their solid construction, the houses along the street were burning furiously with transparent blue-white flames. The northerner crouched low, scuttling along the ground. Women and children were running in the other direction, wailing in thin, high-pitched voices. Some of them were on fire. Things seemed to have gotten out of hand atop the gate tower. He paused, trying to draw breath in the superheated air, sheltering behind a tall column standing in the middle of the plaza. The carvings of marching soldiers and triumphant emperors were hot to the touch.

In his hand, Brunhilde was keening with fear. The blade's watery surface reflected a hundred leaping flames. Another titanic *boom* rocked the city and clods of dirt and stone rained down into the street. Nicholas could feel power surging in the air, bitter with the smell of discharged lightning. He mustered his courage, peering around the column.

The main tower seemed intact, though a whirling orb of red light wrapped the upper third. Flashes and sparks danced against the northern face of the sphere. Nicholas gripped Brunhilde tight then thrust her forward and sprinted for the base of the stairs. She shrieked in outrage, but the blade cut through the wavering red light, leaving a whirling tunnel of breathable air. He took the stairs as fast as he could, bending his shoulder forward. There was a burning hot resistance and each step was a struggle. Brunhilde began to smoke and glow but he reached the roof of the tower alive. The rectangular space was littered with corpses, most of them charred beyond recognition.

Nicholas felt sick. These were Romans from the look of the puddled, melting armor. The stones cracked underfoot, broken by the intense heat. He skipped across them, hoping that his boots would hold out. Bending nearly double, he peered between the merlons out onto the plain before the city.

The plain burned and smoked, pitted by huge craters. Columns of Arabs continued to rush forward into the conflagration, their helms glowing orange in the flare of the sphere of fire. Pillars of smoke boiled up, clouding the sky, and fiery stones plunged from the heavens among the running men. The remains of two siege towers smoldered on the road before the gate, shattered, logs and mantlets scattered in all directions. The war cries of the attackers were faint, almost drowned out by the burning hiss of stones bursting amongst them.

Nicholas flinched back from the carnage, seeing the ground carpeted with . . . He stopped, then looked again. Then he did curse, violently and at length, but it was too late to do anything but what he had already done.

"Dwyrin!" His scream was lost in the ripping sound of a bolt of fire leaping from the boy's fingertips to lash down amongst a charging battalion of armored horsemen. The ground erupted at the blow, spewing dirt and rock and limp bodies into the air. Nicholas lunged to the boy's side, feeling the feeble protection afforded by his sword fail. Heat beat at him like the mouth of a furnace. He grabbed Dwyrin's arm, then stifled a cry, feeling his hand burn.

"Come on, lad! It's fake, it's all fake! We've got to run!"

The boy turned, head swiveling like that of a hunting cat, and Nicholas felt his heart go cold at the sight of Dwyrin's eyes. They were slits of brilliance, blazing with incandescent light. Nick slapped him hard across the face, wincing at the pop and bubble of his flesh as he touched forge-hot skin.

Dwyrin's head rocked back at the blow and the burning light flickered in his eyes.

"Look! Look at the ground! Where are the bodies?" Nicholas pointed, his hand smoking. Dwyrin turned, staring out over the battlement. Hordes of Arabs, their armor bright, continued to pour across the blasted landscape, their banners and spears held high. They ran across empty ground. Amid the chaos of rubble and smoking craters, there were no bodies. Not even one.

An arrow flicked out of the night and burst into flame against the sphere. A droplet of molten iron struck the breastplate of Nicholas's lorica and clung there, hissing. He grabbed the boy by the shoulder and dragged him away from the parapet. The sphere flared up for a moment and then suddenly went dark with an audible *pop*.

Nicholas stumbled on the stairs, blind in the sudden darkness, but then hauled the boy over his shoulders and staggered down. The light of the burning buildings would do to light his way. Flagstones cracked under his boots, turning to dust as he ran. Behind him, the limestone face of the tower was burning too, with a hot green fire as the rock sublimated into the air in a glowing cloud.

Allau Akbar! rang across the dark sky, roiling with columns and drifts of smoke.

By the time Nicholas found the others, they were crowding into the white cistern. He squeezed out of the narrow tunnel and gasped in relief to come out into the vaulting room. He had pushed Dwyrin, now half awake, in front of him the last fifty feet.

"Hoy, it's the centurion! Optio!"

Nicholas nodded to the nearest legionaries, who stood back from the opening, swords bare in their hands. It was hot and close in the chamber, but it was still better than being in the dark passage. He looked around and found Sextus coming towards him, a glad look on the engineer's face.

"Sir, we were about to give up on you and the boy!"

Nicholas scowled, but was glad to hand off the red-haired Hibernian to the nearest soldiers. "See he gets some water and a lie-down, lads. He's a bit used up, I think. Sextus, I heard on the way down that the south gate has fallen."

The surveyor nodded, his grin wiped away. "Vlad and Frontius went down the tunnel first. They sent a runner back to say the enemy put his main strength against the southern wall. I'd guess that all the storm and thunder in the north was a ruse?"

Nicholas nodded sharply, thinking hard. "Yes," he said absently. "They took the boy right in—some kind of phantom army, filled with noise and motion. He surely drew everyone's attention with his response! Listen, Sextus, we need to start sending the men through the tunnel. Someone upstairs is *sure* to notice that we've disappeared. You know the temper of the men left in the city—those Armenians, for one, will change sides immediately. The rest will be out for our blood."

"I know, sir." The surveyor's humor returned. "I left a little something to delay them, though. A Phyrgian gift, as it were, which I hope will be as good as any Dionysus ever gave."

"What?" Nicholas was scowling again. He was supposed to know what was going on, by the gods!

Sextus fingered a heavy chain around his neck, turning it to the light of one of the lamps his men were carrying. It glinted ruddy red gold in the light. "A whole wagonload of treasure—coin, specie, jewels, chain like this, statues, everything to incite greed and lust in a man's heart—is scattered across the great ramp leading up from the *decumanus* to the temple platform. More than any single man could carry—when these bandits reach it, I think there will be some time wasted."

Nicholas shook his head, wondering if that were true. These weren't bandits. "Perhaps," he said. "How long will it take to get everyone out of the tunnel? Who has the robes?"

"About two hours to get everyone out," Sextus said, rubbing his nose. "Each man is carrying his kit and clothing on his back. We started as soon as Frontius' runner came back."

"Not great, but it'll have to do. Send two men back down the narrow passage. Make sure our tracks in that hidden road are wiped out and any litter picked up. Then start knocking down this tunnel, try and fill it in behind us."

Sextus stared at the centurion for a moment. Nicholas could see the man's thoughts—the narrow passage and the hidden road were their only way out if the enemy found the springhouse entrance to the tunnel. The engineer didn't want to be trapped in the stifling dark with no way back. For his part, Nicholas didn't either, but it seemed more likely that pursuit would come from inside the city.

"Do it," Nicholas growled and the centurion nodded sharply before turning to his men. The northerner went to the side of the cistern where Dwyrin was laid on a cloak. The boy looked bad, his face sheened with sweat. He looked pale and empty, like a vessel that had been poured out on the ground.

"Hey, lad." Nicholas knelt by the boy's side and put the back of his blistered and swollen hand against Dwyrin's forehead. "How do you feel?"

Dwyrin didn't speak, but the anguish in his eyes said the Hibernian knew the enemy had played him for a fool.

"Rest now, we'll be moving soon." Nicholas turned the

corner of the cloak over Dwyrin's chest, then sat down, his back against the wall. Dwyrin closed his eyes, squeezing them tightly shut. Nicholas was determined to be the last out of the cistern. It would be a long wait, here in the close darkness, watching as his men dropped, one by one, down into the tunnel. The pain in his hand was almost blinding, but he pushed it away. There just wasn't time for that now.

Odenathus rode through the gates in a weary daze. The huge statues paid him no heed, for he was part of a flood of Sahaba trooping up the long ramp. Men and women of the city were mixed in amongst the soldiers, all a pressing, noisy mass spilling out of the gateway into the gardens surrounding the towering shape of the Temple of Jupiter. Every inch of the Palmyrene's body cried out in agony, for he had sustained his illusions and phantasms for nearly two hours before he felt the bright ravening flame of Dwyrin go out like a snuffed candle. It had been enough. Much of the city was still burning, lighting the night sky and throwing a reddish light down from the clouds. The white pillars of the temple seemed stained with blood.

The Palmyrene let his horse find a patch of grass and stop. Then he crawled down out of the saddle and fell asleep on the ground. The horse, which was accounted wise among its kind, moved to stand over the exhausted sorcerer and continued to graze with its rubbery lips on the leaves of the tree. These humans were quite foolish, needing a calm head to watch out for them.

Not far away, within the towering halls of the temple, a lone man crossed a broad floor of hexagonal marble tiles. His lean face, long ago burned dark by the desert, was filled with fear and wonder in equal parts. His dark robes, made from the finest cloth, were tattered and worn, scarred by war and long travel. His boots, which had been worth two mares to acquire from a Persian merchant, made a soft sound on the tiles. Uri Ben-Sarid, the chief of his people, came to the sanctuary of the temple and looked upon the seated figure of Jupiter Maximus, god of the Romans. The marble sculpture was twenty feet high and painted in the likeness of a brawny man with riotous dark hair. A fierce look of disgust passed over Uri's face, but then he put such things aside.

"Cursed shall be the idolators," he whispered to himself. In this thing, he and Mohammed understood each other perfectly. The Ben-Sarid did not believe, in his heart, that his old friend heard the voice of the nameless god speaking from the clear air. There could be no prophets in this debased and corrupt time. But he did know Mohammed was a wise man, a cunning leader and a man filled with hate for Rome. Even as the Ben-Sarid hated. Slowly, his eyes intent on the floor, he circled the statue. Behind the platform, screened by the bulk of the figure, there was an opening and a stairway that descended below the floor of the temple.

"Oh, my good and gracious Lord . . ." Uri felt faint, seeing that it was possible to descend below the elevated platform. It might, he thought in rising panic, be possible to step below and stand . . . stand upon the rock of the hill itself. There might be a stone, in the darkness below, a stone that had once crowned this low mountain. A slab of pitted gray basalt where . . .

"No." Uri backed away, frightened by his impious thoughts. He bit his thumb, trying to keep from crying out. Despite all that he had learned at his father's knee, he felt compelled to walk down into the darkness. His people, at last, had returned to the holy place, to the temple of their fathers, and he could not descend, he was not allowed to look upon the most sacred place of all the tribes.

He was not a Kahane; he was not of the sacred line. The priesthood had been slaughtered long ago, the survivors scattered to the four corners of the earth, if any had lived through Ben-Yair's apocalypse. His blood was weak, diluted, perhaps even contaminated by the blood of lesser peoples. This, his heart's desire, the prize the lives and blood of the Ben-Sarid had paid for on the walls of the city, was beyond his reach.

Uri leaned against the flank of the Roman statue, cold stone burning against his arm. His other hand covered his face, trying to stifle the desire tormenting him. Tears seeped between his fingers and fell, one by one, sparkling to the marble floor.

Outside, the Sahaba reveled in their victory, raising their swords and spears to the burning red sky, raising thunderous cheer after thunderous cheer. Jalal strode among them, a giant among men, his face split by a tremendous grin. Mohammed would be pleased!

Allau Akbar! Allau Akbar!

Shuddering at the noise, Uri turned away from the stairway. He had to find the Arab general and make sure that no one went down those steps. No one.

───────────────────────────────

THE PALATINE HILL, ROMA MATER

The Emperor sat in the rooftop garden amid a drift of white parchments covering a camp table fitted with golden legs. Two well-muscled Africans stood nearby, ready to adjust the canopy of white Indian cotton protecting Galen from the midday sun. The palace staff ignored the long years Galen Atreus had spent in the field with his Legions, exposed to the rough elements.

Gregorius Auricus entered the garden, toga snow white and thinning ivory hair oiled back. In place of his usual jeweled rings was a single golden band on his left hand. Likewise his tunic, though of exceptionally fine linen, was plain and unadorned. Gaius Julius followed the senator at a respectful distance, weighed down by a thick sheaf of parchments. The plans and schedules for the games grew heavier by the day. Like his patron, Gaius Julius was dressed very simply, though he had taken care not to rival the quality of his benefactor's garb. Instead, he had selected a cut of cloth which said *middle-rank bureaucrat* to the discerning eye.

Of course, with the monies he was accumulating, he could afford much better. Impatience in such matters was his enemy, he reminded himself, particularly today. It was much wiser to hide himself in anonymity. So, with his eyes downcast, he entered the garden of the Lord and God of the Empire as the very picture of humility.

"Gregorius! Welcome, old friend. Sit, sit." The Emperor sounded cheerful.

Galen took the older man's hand and led him to one of the swan-back chairs beside the camp table. Gregorius met him in kind, embracing the younger man. Gaius could hear the warmth in the Emperor's voice as pleasantries were exchanged. He could see the elderly senator was equally pleased.

"Galen," Gregorius said. "Have you met my secretary? This is Gaius Julius, of notable name, and with a great and welcome passion for hard work." Gaius smiled at his patron's kind words and bowed to the Emperor.

"I have not had the pleasure," the Emperor said, seating himself. He nodded to Gaius, dark eyes examining him carefully. Gaius felt a chill, seeing Maxian's likeness refined in his elder brother and feeling the strength of his intellect and personality. "You are well recommended to us, Gaius, and *not* for your name. I have had reports of you, from the military commanders in Campania."

The Emperor paused and Gaius leaned forward slightly, a concerned look on his face. "Nothing untoward has happened?" he said, expressing businesslike concern. "The bridge at Beneventum hasn't collapsed again?"

"No." The Emperor laughed. "I understand it was a bit of trouble to rebuild. No, all I have heard of you is good. We are grateful for your assistance in this troubled time."

Gaius nodded in acceptance of the praise, forcing himself to blush slightly. He had found, to his amusement, that such things had to be considered in this new . . . body. "It is my duty, Lord and God."

"I understand," Galen said, leaning back in his chair. While they had been talking, the maids had quietly delivered wine, fresh fruit, steaming fresh bread and sliced meats glazed with honey to the table. Galen ignored the repast, turning his attention to Gregorius, who was smiling contentedly, his hands on his stomach. "Old friend, you've been badgering me for months, so I think I know why you're here."

Gregorius nodded, a half-smile on his face. "Is this a good time to discuss it? I have heard there is trouble in the East."

"There is trouble everywhere," Galen said in a peevish tone. "The matter of Egypt is only the most pressing. My whole business is finding trouble and putting it out. It is not a good time, but various and diverse persons have informed me that I *must* do something." The Emperor and the senator laughed at a secret, shared jest. Gaius did not see what it was, but kept his face bland and interested. He did not laugh with them.

"She is bored, then?" Gregorius' voice had a gentle needling quality.

"She is," the Emperor dryly answered. "And I know that I have been remiss in my sacred duty. Each day, you know, the Pontifex Maximus and the priests of the temples are in here, moaning and crying about the insult to the gods and the plague of ghosts in the countryside."

The Emperor suddenly turned to Gaius. "Did you see any ghosts, any manes, any lamiae when you were touring the road works in the south? Any foul, undead creatures?"

"No, Emperor," Gaius said with a straight face. "I did

not. But I know that every citizen in the whole of Campania is beside himself with fear of them."

The Emperor made a *harrumph* sound and put his chin in his hand. Gaius fought hard to keep from laughing aloud. The money he had spent encouraging the temple priests had been an excellent investment. Without his prodding, the priests would have continued to loll about in their town houses and temples, idle and unthinking of their duty.

"There shall be games," the Emperor muttered, smoothing back lank, dark hair.

"Did you say something?" Gregorius, still possessed of a smug humor, leaned closer to the Emperor, his eyebrows raised.

"I did," Galen allowed, glaring at his old friend. "Do you want me to shout it from the rooftops?"

"The people," Gregorius said quietly, "would rejoice to hear it."

Galen sighed, accepting the rebuke, then sat up straight. He shuffled some of the papers around on the table and finally drew out one, a creamy-white sheet of parchment, carefully scribed in dark ink. Gaius Julius guessed, from the depth of the color, that it was the fruit of the Sabean octopus. One of the guilds maintained special farms in the shallows near Misenum to raise and harvest the gelatinous creatures. The Emperor, looking relieved, handed the paper to Gregorius, who settled back into his chair to read.

While he did so, Gaius found himself subjected to the Emperor's scrutiny.

"You have a familiar face," Galen said after a moment. "Yours is a cadet branch of the ancient Julians?"

"Yes," Gaius said, trying not to fidget. He made his hands lie still, gripping the leather carry case. "Not the . . . famous line, of course."

"It would be difficult," Galen said, watching him closely, "for they are all long dead. Still, you have done well since coming to the city. I applaud you—too few men these days have your energy or stamina."

Gaius raised an eyebrow and inclined his head again. "Fulsome praise from you, Lord and God. You are well known for your long hours and dedication to the state."

"Perhaps," Galen said, smiling a little. He indicated the paper. "I wager if Gregorius accepts the duty represented by that paper, he will task you with its contents."

"I will," the senator said, looking up, the white storm cloud of his brows drawn down over keen eyes. He handed the paper to Gaius, who took it gratefully. This Emperor was too perceptive—the old Roman had not missed the comment about stamina. He would have to be more circumspect with his working hours in the future!

"I accept your trust, Lord and God. I vow we will not dishonor or embarrass you in its execution. Gaius is a hard-working man and honest, a boon to Rome. Between us, we should be able to provide what the Senate, the people, the gods and the Emperor desire."

"If," Galen laughed, "you can satisfy all those powers, then you will be gods yourselves!"

Gaius Julius put the paper back on the table. He allowed himself a tiny smile. As he had hoped, the Emperor had bestowed a great honor on his old, dear family friend. Traditionally, the Emperor kept the right to produce games and plays of all kinds to himself. This had been an Imperial prerogative since the time of that whelp Octavian Augustus. However, that boy had also occasionally allowed his favorites, particularly the noble general Agrippa, to stage *munera* and *venationes* in the Emperor's name. Galen, no mean student of history himself, had borrowed some of Octavian's words for his own proclamation. Gaius Julius read it over again, frowning inside. *Why can't anyone write plainly? This reads like one of that fop Cicero's tracts!*

The "elegant" Latin the Emperor favored recalled the opprobrium heaped on Gaius' own literary efforts by his political adversaries. Cicero had been an enemy for a long time. The old Roman looked up, his face filled with what he hoped was dedicated concern and responsibility. He could not afford to scowl! "Lord and God, has a date been set for the first of the games?"

Galen shook his head, saying, "No. I entrust this matter to your hands, Gregorious. The Treasury has set aside considerable funds to pay for the games, but I will not force a day and a time upon you. It is up to you to set the day. But even I feel the discontent in the city—so let it be soon! I will not trouble you with directives about what kind of shows or events or celebrations, but remind you of the great sacred games that the Divine Augustus endowed upon the city, after his victory at Actium. We honor the helpless dead of our sister cities, much as he honored the people for supporting him in the civil wars."

Gregorius nodded in agreement and Gaius Julius mentally discarded at least a quarter of his planning—all thrown aside for that damned brat Octavian's memory! Still, the idea had merit. Gaius had been envisioning something along the lines of the millennial games Emperor Phillip Arabicus had staged almost four hundred years before. The Divine Augustus' games, however, had been much simpler, more refined. If anything, they would be easier to emulate than Phillip's grandiose phantasmagoria.

"Of course," Gregorius answered, while Gaius was fuming, "we have made some few plans and preparations already—they can be easily adjusted to provide what you desire. Would you like to review the high points? Gaius has them here."

Galen laughed, a sharp bark of sound, and raised his hands in surrender. "Am I little more than a puppet? Is my every move watched? That case, I presume, has these small, even insignificant plans and schedules of yours? It seems weighty . . . I can guess the name of the spy. She *is* impatient!"

The Emperor shook his head *no* at Gaius when the old Roman moved to open the case.

"I know you're not wizards—so my desire to emulate the Divine Augustus will send your efforts awry. Take a few days to consider, to plan and to revise. Then come and see me again and show me what you'll present in my name. Go ahead, put those papers away!"

Galen turned to Gregorius and took the senator's wrinkled old hands in his own. "Old friend, you have always stood by me, offering unstinting aid and counsel. You are a true Roman, a pillar of the state. We have had some disputes, but I pray that they are in the past. A great test is upon the Empire. We will all have to strive, together, to mend the ills that afflict the state. Tell me, is there any enmity between us? Any hurt unrevealed? Is this task I set you too much?"

Gregorius shook his head, then raised one veined hand to his face, covering his eyes. "Lord and God, I am an old man and I have always striven to do right by the Senate and the people of Rome. But my days grow short. I can feel the weakness of my limbs and heart. It is enough, for me, to give what aid I can to the family, to the man, who has rescued our people from disaster."

Galen blushed, looking down. "Then things are well between us?"

"Yes," Gregorius said, and it seemed to Gaius the senator looked upon the past, unaware of the two men and the sunlit garden. The old man seemed very frail. "Perhaps this will be my last task before the Boatman comes for me."

"Do not say that!" Gaius Julius was half out of his chair before he could stop himself. Both he and the Emperor sat back down, sharing a sideways glance. They had echoed each other's words.

"Your heart is still young," Galen said, standing up and beckoning for his servants. "Come, this is enough for the day. I know that you walked from your house, as a patrician should, but I will send you back in a closed litter. You're noble enough to bear that burden too, I think."

Gregorius laughed and accepted Gaius' arm as they walked back into the palace. Galen accompanied them to the great serpentine stairwell at the heart of Tiberius' villa, where they were met by a phalanx of guardsmen, link boys, litter bearers and two bull-throated men who would clear a passage for them through the crowded streets of the city.

The Emperor watched the litter leave from an upper window in the library. "Are you quite pleased with yourself?"

"Perhaps. Maybe. I shall have to think about it." Helena was sitting on a curving window seat. The louvers were angled out, letting afternoon sun fall into the room. There was an untidy pile of scrolls around her. A wax tablet lay on the windowsill, along with an ivory stylus. "Why were you so hesitant? The circuses and the gladiators are part of the daily routine of the city. It's not like you to fly in the face of tradition."

Galen paced across Persian carpets that had come out of the sack of Ctesiphon. "I have never loved the games! They *are* traditional, they are part of the business of being Emperor, they are part of Rome—but that does not mean that I enjoy them. But the people love them, you love them. I see their place in showing the power and the generosity of the state. I just . . ."

He paused, searching for the right words. Helena looked up at him, dark hair lying smooth and sleek on her shoulders. She waited, smiling, letting him grope and fumble in his heart.

At last he said, "I think the games are wasteful. They burn gold and lives and even animals in enormous numbers—I have reports, love, on my desk from the praetors of Africa and Numidia; they report that the ibex and the gazelle and the elephant and the tiger are gone, hunted out, impossible to find. For what? I sum the ledgers showing the vast sums invested in these entertainments, and I see granaries and bridges and dredged harbors and aqueducts and baths. I see the lives of the people made better, rather than titillated by the antics of the pantomimes and the deadly heroics of the gladiators."

Helena shook her head and rose, the silk train of her dress sliding from the window seat like snakeskin. She looked up at her husband and took his head in her hands. She was frowning, giving him a look which said she was perplexed and amused at the same time.

"Dear husband, you are a fine emperor, but you do not understand the people at all. All the classes of the city, the patricians, the workers, the craftsmen—they don't care about these bridges and aqueducts. They are dull! Oh, surely they must have them, they must exist—grain must move, trade be conducted, rivers flow within their banks— but the man who mills the bread or hauls a bale of goods, he is concerned with three things. Three things only."

Galen raised an eyebrow, then took her hands in his. "What three things?" He was wary of her sharp tongue.

"These three things." Helena smiled gently. "First, that he and his family have bread to eat."

"Surely," the Emperor said, "which weighs heavy on my mind! This Egyptian business—"

"Shush!" Helena put a slim finger to his lips. "Listen. Second, that his family is safe, that he may live in peace and undertake his trade undisturbed. And yes, you have done this. But third, oh, third! You must *not* forget the third thing—there was a poor, lonely emperor who once lost a great deal for his miserliness!—the People *must know* that their emperor loves them and is one of them. That he is not a god. Here, husband, is your failing."

Galen tried to turn away, his face sour, but Helena held him close, looking up at him with extremely serious gray eyes. "Will you be Tiberius, dying alone and friendless on some corrupt island?"

"No!" Galen shook his hands free. "I will not be Prince Caligula or Commodus either and live within the confines of the circus!"

"No one asks you to!" Helena's voice was sharp. "But

if you become distant from the people, if you deny them the due that has been theirs for many centuries, their hearts will turn away. They must *see* you and know that you *love* them. They must take bounty from *your* hand and not from another. Even a great man like Gregorius will not suffice. If you do not partake in this, it will make your troubles worse, not better."

"Fine," Galen snapped, eyes narrowing. "Let the people have their circuses. Bread is the true test of their loyalty. I will not stint them."

Then he stalked out of the library, shoulders set in anger. Behind him, Helena threw up her hands and let out a breath in a long, slow hiss. She was angry too, but someone needed to tell the pig-headed, self-centered, ignorant clerk of a man the truth. "Hah! We are such enlightened sorts ourselves."

Helena laughed to herself, then bent to pick up the stylus and the tablet. She was collecting ancient gossip from the early chapters of Suetonius' *De Vita Caesarum.* One of her correspondents, Artemesia, had begun tweaking her about ancient follies. Helena did not intend to take the worst of such an exchange. She tucked the stylus behind one ear and wondered if the long-dead historian's invective against Tiberius and Caligula and Nero was affecting her judgment. "Men! Live or dead, they trouble me."

NEAR TYRE ON THE COAST OF PHOENICIA

A cold night wind blew from the sea, causing Khalid to wrap a heavy silk-lined cloak close around his broad shoulders. He was sitting in the ruins of a Hellenic temple, astride a broken marble bench. The young general had kindled a small, smokeless fire among the tumbled stones, just enough to warm his feet and give him a little light. The camp, thronging with Sahaban light horse, sprawled across the slopes of the hill below, overlooking the sweeping harbor of Tyre.

Khalid spat into the darkness, frowning out at the battlements of the island city. His small army had made a swift advance up the Phoenician coast, seizing many towns. In some places he had been welcomed as a liberator, in others merely not resisted. This place was different. The ancient city was built on an island, connected to the mainland by a massive mole faced with granite blocks. Below the hill, a warehouse district spread along the shoreline, fronting two harbors formed by the mole itself and barrier islands offshore. A stout wall protected the warehouses, but a swift assault had carried its gates. It was the island itself that defied him. The last sixty feet of the mole had been built as a bridge, which the Roman defenders had collapsed when the Arabs reached the harbor. Khalid lacked a fleet and the docks had been carefully emptied of shipping.

Khalid smiled, thin features half lit by firelight. "Well, Patik, what do you think? Should we leave these wolf cubs mewed up in their stone den?"

The stolid Persian did not answer, remaining a quiet, comforting shape in the darkness beyond the glow of the coals. The mercenary was sitting with his back to the fire, horse bow on his knees, watching the night. The young Arab tossed another twig into the embers.

"A troop of horsemen could be left, I suppose . . . they could watch the island-city and keep the Romans penned within. Hmm." He tapped his narrow chin with another twig. "But if Mohammed and the beautiful Zoë cannot hunt down and destroy their fleet, then each of these ports will be a spear point against our belly."

The Arab wished the "great leader" had allowed him to move the infantry and siege equipment north from Caesarea. However, Mohammed had been strict about the operations allowed in his absence. Jalal, Uri and Odenathus were away in the south, securing the road to Egypt. Shadin held the great port itself and was responsible for mustering even more men from the towns and villages newly fallen to the Arabs. All Khalid had been allowed was a moderate force of swift-moving lancers and bowmen. Enough to scout for any Roman armies loose in the north, but not enough to assay the capture of a strong fortress like Tyre. "Perhaps, if we built some rafts, we could slip up to the seawall under cover of—"

"Someone is coming." The Persian's voice rumbled like stone sliding downhill.

Patik moved in the darkness and Khalid sensed a bowstring being drawn back. The Arab stood gracefully, right hand sliding under his cloak and around the hilt of a straight-bladed cavalry sword. Looking away from the fire, Khalid listened. After a moment, he heard stones rattle on the slope and then branches in the laurel trees rustling. Only a single man seemed to be approaching. Khalid turned, his boot brushing a tied bundle of grass into the embers. They sparked, sending up little yellow jets of flame, then burst alight.

A figure was standing at the edge of the firelight. It was tall and broad-shouldered, clad in a long dark cloak with a deep hood. Red glimmered on its chest, reflecting back from close-fitting scaled armor. Its boots crunched on the broken *tesserae* covering the floor of the temple. Khalid could not see the face. He felt the air grow chill and he tensed to draw his blade.

"Salaam," it whispered in a faint cold voice. "You are Khalid al'Walid."

Khalid steeled himself, disturbed to glimpse Patik lowering his bow.

"I am," he answered, shrugging the cloak from his right shoulder. "Who are you?"

"A messenger."

"What is your message?" Khalid moved to put the dying fire between himself and the figure. "Who sent you?"

A sound came from the shape, something like laughter, but from a throat unused to such sounds. A dry hiss rattling amongst the bones of the dead.

"You know my master," it said, remaining at the edge of the temple. "He knows you."

Khalid felt the cold in the air steal over him. It became hard to breathe. Patik remained motionless at his side. The young man remembered a day under a burning white sky.

Towers of brick and carved stone rose from a barren plain. The wreckage of two of the towers lay scattered about. Something had smashed them down, pulverizing the rock and marble statuary that had adorned them. Khalid crawled amongst the stones, shaking with fear. Smoke and fumes rose from the blasted soil, which hissed and steamed in agony. Only moments before the sky had rippled and fractured like bad glass drawn from the forge. He alone, of all the men in the army cowering in the hills, had dared to come down onto the dusty plain before the city.

Trails of white smoke curled up from a ravine cracked open in the parched earth. Something dark had fallen there. Khalid had seen it. Now he crept to the edge of the crevice and looked within. There was something there in the shape of a man, curled up, skin blackened by titanic forces. Once it had worn a robe; now that was burned away. Once bracelets of gold and platinum had adorned thin wrists; now they were puddled droplets on the sandy ground. A reek rose up from the ravine like the smell of a charnel house. Khalid wrapped the end of his kaffiyeh around his face, then slid down into the crevice.

More cloths over leather gloves protected his hands, which was wise, for the ebon skin of the shape burned like fire. Khalid rolled the figure over, then felt his mind go cold as he looked upon the face of the sorcerer. Slitted yellow eyes burned into his, making the world grow dim and faint.

"I remember," Khalid grated, his voice distant. "What is your message?"

"This," hissed the thing wearing the shape of a man: "the army of the Great King has seized Antioch in the north. Soon, he will come south. He comes in friendship and with open arms for all those who defy Rome. It would not be wise to resist him, for he is your friend."

Khalid felt a shock like a blow to the face. He steadied himself, thinking of Patik's strong arm at his side. Even this thing might find it hard to overcome both of them. Still, he hesitated, remembering the power of the sorcerer. It was not wise to defy such powers. Not for a young man without any clan or tribe save that of a madman. Perhaps not even then. "How has this happened? Antioch is a strong city."

The shape laughed again, the same rattle of dry bones. "Many strong places have fallen to the King of Kings. That city is only the least. You would do well to greet the Great King in honor, bowing before him, for he is lord of the world."

Khalid mustered his thoughts, though they spun and whirled like leaves in the khamsin. "When will he be here, this King of Kings? Does he come to make war upon Rome?"

The figure turned, heavy boots scraping on the ground. At the very edge of the dying firelight, it looked over its shoulder and Khalid thought he saw two points of pale fire burning in the shadows under the hood.

"The Great King is already at war with Rome," it hissed. "This lord Mohammed has done him great service and he will not forget."

Khalid sneered, but the thing was already gone. The Arab groped amongst the stones, casting more kindling onto the fire. Soon, an aromatic smoke rose up from bright flames.

"What was that?" Khalid looked up at Patik. The Persian remained standing, his bow half drawn, looking out into the darkness. At last, he turned, his grim face still. Though Khalid felt chilled and uneasy, it seemed that the mercenary was unmoved by their night visitor.

"It is gone."

"What *was* that?" The Arab's voice rose a little.

"A messenger."

Despite Khalid's insistence, the Persian said no more while the night lingered.

The next day was blustery but not cold. Full summer was upon the coast of Phoenicia, and the sun was hot in the olive groves and the vineyards. Khalid remained in the temple on the hilltop, watching white-sailed boats coming and going from the island fortress. They seemed insolent, mocking his siege with their flitting about on the pure blue water. His companions accounted him a devious man, but he could see no good way into the city.

"Many strong places have fallen to treachery," he mused, liquid brown eyes roaming over the outline of towers and gates and steep walls of limestone slabs. "I wonder if there are ulcers I might stir to life?"

Horns sounded on the plain behind the hill. Khalid did not turn to look, comfortable in the wariness of his scouts and pickets scattered through the olive groves and farmsteads radiating out into the coastal plain around the city. The Romans built well, with hard-surfaced roads and fine bridges all through this country. It was rich here on the gently sloping plain edging the sea. He wondered if all of Rome was so flush with fields and orchards and flocks of fat-tailed sheep and longhaired goats. There were even cows here, thick with heavy, fat meat. And there were so many of them! Even the nominal population of the warehouse district along the harbors far exceeded the citizens of Mekkah in the far south.

The young man frowned, knowing from his brief travels in Persian lands that Tyre did not even approach the size of such cities as Damascus or Antioch, much less a metropolis like Constantinople or Ctesiphon.

What does our brave leader intend? He has seen these lands, too. He must know that Rome is beyond our power to throw down. Why this mad plunge into the heart of the enemy?

Mohammed claimed he was guided by the voice from the clear air. Refusing to believe this had become part of Khalid's view of the world. Even the miracles he had seen performed did not sway his belief. Mohammed was a man who had found power within himself to do these things. There was no *god* that spoke to him. The gods were long dead.

A dim murmur rose up from the camp at the bottom of the hill. Khalid turned and walked to the edge of the temple. A troop of brightly caparisoned riders entered the camp down among the hedgerows and rosebushes. Even from this height he could make out the embroidered saddle cloths on the horses and the red and gold shields of the riders. Fifty or sixty armored men rode in from the countryside, escorted by Arab scouts. Their bows and lances were stowed on their horses and a trail of pack mules followed, heavily laden with rolls of armor and barding. *A scouting party, then.*

The young general sat in the shade of the laurel trees and waited, thinking while the Persian commander labored up the hill. Khalid's agile mind worried at the problems inherent in this struggle against the Empire. *How does Mohammed hope to win?* he wondered. *Does he intend to win?* A thought occurred to him and he turned suddenly, looking for Patik. The Persian was standing nearby, his bronze single-piece helmet resting at his scale-armor-covered hip. Khalid took in the man's rugged features, the classic Persian nose, the thick arms. He wondered, then, what the mercenary thought of all this. "Patik, why did you join me?"

The Persian looked down, flinty eyes expressionless. "You were going the way I was going."

Khalid raised an eyebrow. The mercenary's presence was comforting but unexplained. "Did you have to flee Persia? Are you an outlaw?"

"Does it matter?" Patik's thin lips quirked into something like a smile, but the expression was as forbidding as a scowl. "Would you send me away if I was?"

Khalid laughed, surprised to get so many words from the stoic mercenary. He rarely spoke. When he did, a cultured baritone was revealed. "No," he said, "but I wonder—if we must fight the Persians, whose side will you choose?"

"We will not fight them. You will see."

The surety in the man's voice took Khalid aback. Voices from the trail down to the camp distracted him before he could respond. The head of a man appeared among the bushes and then a stout fellow of medium height stomped into the circle of broken pillars. Like the riders Khalid had seen entering the camp, he was clad in lamellar armor of small metal lozenges, covering him from shoulder to mid-thigh. The armored man stopped within the circle and bent, pulling off his heavy helmet. "Salaam, Khalid, son of Walid, chief of the Makzhum."

The young Arab stepped back in surprise. He knew this man, though he had never expected to see him again. "Salaam, Lord Khadames! By the prophet, General, I did not think to see you here!"

Khadames grinned, his round face beaming behind a neatly trimmed gray beard. Khalid was surprised to see the Persian had grown markedly older in the last two years. His noble face was lined with wrinkles and he seemed to carry a heavy burden. His hair was streaked with white and gray. Despite this, he smiled genially, nodding absently to Patik, and sat down on one of the broken columns. "You've come up in the world, lad. That's a hardy troop of men you've down below—and I hear you and your friends have tasted sweet victory over Rome."

"We have," Khalid said cautiously, sitting himself. Patik had disappeared into the brush, leaving the two of them alone. "An . . . ominous . . . messenger came last night, bringing word that you were coming. That one said the Great King rides to war on Rome again. Is this true?"

The shadow in Khadames' face returned, but the old general turned his face to the noonday sun and sighed, visibly drawing strength from the gentle warmth. "It is true. The Great King's army captured Antioch. Our . . . allies have seized the Cilician Gates from the Roman garrison, opening the passes. The Great King stands poised to strike into Anatolia once more."

"A stunning victory." Khalid's eyes narrowed and he watched the Persian closely.

"We have your master to thank for that," Khadames said, managing a smile. "Did you know that the Great Prince Theodore stripped the entire Eastern frontier to muster the army you defeated at Yarmuk? The garrisons in Mesopotamia, at Antioch, in Armenia, were all drawn down to fuel his campaign against the desert cities." Khadames shook his head in amusement, scuffing at the broken *tesserae* with the tip of his boot.

"That army was destroyed," Khalid muttered, feeling ill used. Both Persia and Rome traditionally set the desert tribes against each other, using the Arabs as pawns in their ancient war. "They could not stand against the power of the Lord of the Wasteland."

"Or against your arms," Khadames said quietly. Khalid looked up, his face still.

"Yes," the Persian said. "We have many reports of the battle from captive Roman soldiers. Your army fought with great valor. You might have won even without the storm out of the desert."

"Perhaps," Khalid snapped, seeing hidden malice in the open face of the Persian general. "You would do well to mark that power, for if you desire to test yourself against it, you will lose."

Khadames raised a hand and waved away the hot words. "Khalid, you were only a scout when last I saw you, but no man in that cursed army was accounted braver than you. Twice you did Persia great service and showed yourself a man of honor. I will not bother to try and deceive you with pretty words. There is respect between us, I think, and the Great King hopes that from respect, friendship may grow."

"Friendship?" Khalid was incredulous. "Friendship with that . . . monster? You must be mad!"

Khadames cocked his head to one side, smiling slightly. He drew a cloth out of his belt and wiped his forehead, then laid it on the column next to him. "I would not call the Great King a monster," Khadames said at last, filled with secret amusement.

"I would!" Khalid said hotly. "You've seen the atrocities that come from his hand! Didn't you hear the shrieks of the Palmyrenes as their city was consumed? Didn't you feel the horror in the air?"

"Ah," Khadames said, affecting surprise. "You speak of the lord Dahak and his . . . *appetites*."

"I do," Khalid snapped. "Who do you speak of?"

"I speak of the Great King, Shahr-Baraz, King of Kings, lord of the Persians and the Medes. A commander whom you, I believe, once respected as the greatest general in the world."

Khalid stopped, his face screwed up in a scowl. For a moment, he could not speak. "What?"

Khadames half turned where he sat and slipped a wooden shield from his back. It was small and round, barely enough to cover his bicep, three layers of laminated cross-bound oak faced with an iron boss. It was painted, too, with the likeness of a snarling boar, white fangs streaked with red. The Persian held it up to the young Arab.

"Six months ago, as they reckon it in Ctesiphon, the Great Lord Shahr-Baraz, the Royal Boar, adopted the twin daughters of the late emperor Chrosoes in great glory and splendor. He is the protector of the Twin Radiances, Azarmidukht and Purandokht, the glories of the East. From their loins will spring a new dynasty, joining the house of Sassan to his own ancient lineage. It is he, the best of us, who sits upon the Peacock Throne."

"What?" Khalid was stunned, his quick mind hurrying to reshape its view of the world.

"You said that before, I believe." Khadames was grinning fit to burst as he put the shield away. "Know this, lad, that the Great King remembers you and he remembers the lord Mohammed as well—did they not spar, lance to lance, on the field of Emesa and in the early days of that lamentable siege? Know too, the creature Dahak is his servant and his loathsome ways are bridled by the Great King's hand and will."

Khalid raised a hand for silence and thought for a moment. Looking up, he squinted at Khadames, sitting so easily on the ruined stones. "What do you want with us?"

CHERSONESOS, A PORT ON THE SEA OF DARKNESS

)•(

This is poor news," Dahvos said, toying with the gnawed remains of a lamb shank. "It seems we've come too late."

Master Nomes nodded, spreading thin, gnarled hands wide to show that such things were the will of the gods. A Greek from Trebizond, the old merchant controlled the business interests of the House of de' Orelio, here on the northern shore of the Sea of Darkness. Lank, stringy hair fell to his shoulders and he was lean to the point of cadaverousness. When he spoke, it was in a hurried, accented Greek punctuated with wet-sounding coughs. Jusuf had to listen closely to make out what he was saying.

"Young man," the merchant wheezed, "you're too late to hire any sizable number of hulls. The governor has already sent off all those ships that are rigged to carry horses or cohorts of men. This new trouble in the Syrian provinces is ruining commerce as usual." Nomes paused, hacking, and dabbed at his mouth with a handkerchief. "At best, there are some coasters, each able to carry ten to fifteen fully grown horses, plus an equivalent number of men."

"That's not enough," Dahvos said in a remote tone. Jusuf saw the authority of a prince had come stealing over his brother like a graven mask. The carefree youth pranking and laughing on the road from Itil was gone, replaced by a stern young man, a leader. "We would need substantially more ships than a *few* coasters. The grain fleet will not return?"

Nomes shook his head sadly. Jusuf was sure the man saw considerable profits disappearing in the wake of the Crimean grain haulers, so recently recalled to the capital. The pinched look on the merchant's face indicated he felt the missed opportunity keenly. "Not until the summer harvest is in, my young friend. A ship could be dispatched, I—*cough!*—suppose, to carry word to the capital. But when the Imperial authorities might respond, I do not know. It could be months."

Dahvos mulled this over, sipping from a copper goblet filled with steaming spiced wine. Jusuf watched his brother with interest. This expedition might be his idea, but its execution was in the hands of the young kagan.

"Master Nomes," Jusuf ventured, while Dahvos was thinking. "Have you any news from Italia or Syria? The last message that reached me told of Theodore's defeat in southern Phoenicia."

The old merchant shook his head sadly. "No," he said. "Not so much as a scrap. All the news I've heard of late is bad, and out of the capital. There is a bitter struggle in the Imperial household, though none of it, I warrant, is in the streets yet. The factions are waiting for Heraclius to die."

Jusuf settled back in his wicker chair, disheartened. "Nothing new from Italia?"

Again, Nomes shook his head.

"Well," Dahvos said suddenly, "we will have to go around, then, if we cannot take ship directly to Constantinople. It will take some time, I'm sure, but the distance is not much greater than what we have already covered, if memory serves."

"Around? That's a long road through lands we've just crossed, and over two sizable mountain ranges to boot."

Dahvos wagged a finger at his brother. "Not east, dear Jusuf, west. Through southern Sarmatia, across the Danuvius and then down the coast into Roman Thrace."

Nomes guffawed. "To the west? Young sir, all that land is fine riding, but also the domain of the Avar khanate! They are ancient enemies of both Khazaria and Rome— you will have to fight your way through such a passage, and that will delay you for a long time indeed."

"I wonder," Dahvos said, with an unprincely twinkle in his eye. "The Avar khan was soundly beaten during the siege of Constantinople last year. His dependent chiefs will be restless, his own status debased. We are a strong force and we can move swiftly, with your help."

"My help?" Nomes squinted suspiciously at the young man. "How can I help you with this business of armies? I'm a simple merchant!"

"Yes," Dahvos smiled, "a merchant with numerous shallow-draft coasters and extensive contacts all along the coast of the Sea of Darkness. I think it would not tax your abilities too much to provide us with a following fleet."

"A what?" Nomes' lip curled up, gnarled hands wrapped around his walking cane.

"A fleet," Jusuf interjected in a dry voice, giving his little brother an arch look. "A fleet that will sail along the coast while our army rides on land—a fleet that can bring us fodder, food, supplies, news. A fleet to ferry us across the mouths of the Danuvius and other rivers barring our passage along the coast."

"Hmph." Nomes settled in his chair, wrinkled face filled with distrust. "And who will pay for this excursion? You?"

Jusuf looked to Dahvos, who raised an eyebrow, then withdrew a folded, sealed packet of parchment from his tunic. He placed the papers on the table between himself and the merchant.

"I am an agent of the house of de' Orelio," he said softly, so that the servants loitering in the alcoves around the dining room could not hear. "As are you. This is a draft upon the Duchess's account in Constantinople. I think you will find it covers your expenses in this matter."

Nomes raised an eyebrow, then poked at the edge of the parchment with a knobby finger. "Did the Queen of Day set you about this business, then?"

Jusuf wondered at the strange title, but nodded. "We have discussed it, she and I."

Nomes coughed again, suddenly seeming tired and very old. "Then I'd best help you, I suppose. But not tonight. I am tired."

Jusuf rose and bowed to the old man. Nomes ignored him and, helped by his servants, shuffled out of the hall. Dahvos also stood, pocketing some early apples from a tray on the table.

"A good idea."

Dahvos nodded amiably, saying, "I thought so. Your fault, really."

"How so?" Jusuf slung his cape around his shoulders. Rooms had been provided for them in the upper story of the merchant's house, but the Khazar was planning on spending the night in the stables with the horses. It promised to be cleaner, quieter and less infested with biting insects.

"All that hideous Greek you made me read when I was a stripling lad and didn't know any better."

Jusuf frowned at his brother. "What are you talking about?"

Dahvos sighed, shaking his head, then scooped the remainder of the lamb roast into a fold of his own cloak. Jusuf shuddered, thinking of the pungent smell the grease would leave after turning rancid on the inside of the heavy wool. Dogs would follow them for miles!

"Herodotus," the kagan chided. "Don't tell me that you didn't read it yourself?"

Shrugging, Jusuf strode out of the dining hall. "I wasn't the prince in waiting, *you* were! So what did this Herodotus say?"

Dahvos scowled and followed after, grumbling. "A fine brother you are! Can you even *read* Greek?"

"I can make do." Jusuf paused outside the doorway to the courtyard. The air was a little nippy, but quite pleasant. A breeze was coming down off the hills above the port. Above the flat roofs of the town, the stars were out and burning with a fierce brilliance. Jusuf felt a delicious anticipation—he had never ridden in the Sarmatian steppe or seen the snowcapped wall of the Dacian Alps rising on the horizon. The birds of the Danuvius marshes were said to be extraordinary in their diversity. "Was this Herodotus a general?"

"No," Dahvos said, still disgusted. "He was a historian. A Persian, Xerxes the Great, invaded Greece long before Rome or even Alexander. He built a great fleet in Syria and used it to supply an enormous army. A force far larger than the land would allow, if they had to forage."

"Did he win?" Jusuf turned, interested.

"No," Dahvos allowed, breathing deep of the clean night air. "But we will."

)⊢(

"Everything is ruined," Martina wailed, her voice and image distorted in the fiery disk of the *telecast*. "The fleet is destroyed and old Andrades is dead! Everyone blames me for this, I can tell! I can see them, scheming and talking about me!"

Helena frowned in distaste, watching the girl's face grow streaked with tears. She had been in her solarium, detailing the latest scandal among the Vestals, when a runner had come from the "viewing room" upstairs. Generally, the telecast lay unused during the day, as experience had shown the device more reliable by night. The Emperor was out of the city, viewing the dredging work under way in the great hexagonal harbor of Portus at the mouth of the Tiber. The thaumaturge on duty, a large overdressed German named Gart, had dithered about for an hour before sending for her. Helena glanced sideways at him, viewing the side of his head—all sweaty under his red beard—with mild nausea.

"Dear, you must calm yourself." Helena stifled a sigh and pinched her nose. "Weeping and blubbering will gain you nothing in this business. Look, you've already ruined your eye powders. Martina!" She raised her voice and the Eastern Empress looked up, wiping her button nose. "One of the rules of being empress," Helena said sternly, "is that you do not cry, whimper or generally act like a spoilt child denied a sweet. Certainly not in public! That includes the young man there, who does such good and loyal service."

The image in the burning disk was poor and streaked with shuddering lines of blue and white, but Helena could see the Eastern Empress turn, staring at the portly young priest who was maintaining—with considerable effort—the operation of the mechanism. Some of the Western thaumaturges thought the influence of the sun was in opposition to the motive elements inherent in the disk. Martina turned back, obviously trying to muster herself.

"But things are impossible now! I've been placed under close watch by the Faithful; even Rufio is distant and cold. No one will listen to me at all—everyone knows I sent the fleet out to stop these bandits! It's not *my* fault they defeated that smelly old man!"

"Martina! You will stop whining." Helena's voice cut into the girl's tirade. "Tell me this; has any of the fleet returned?"

"Yes," Martina sniffled, blotting her nose again. "Some. Everyone says that most of the ships were destroyed or captured by the bandits."

Helena nodded. "I do not think," she said in an acerbic tone, "that these people are *bandits* anymore. I think they are a *nation*. But, be that as it may, tell me—where is the Imperial army?"

"I don't know!" Martina managed to stop crying. It was a small improvement, but it made Helena feel much better. Dealing with her colicky son and his noise was enough for her without some spoilt princess as well. "No one talks to me about those things. Rufio, he might know . . . but I can't even see him anymore."

"Can you send him a message? Do you know any of the generals personally?"

"No," Martina muttered, looking at the floor. "I didn't like them. I just saw them at court or when we had a party or something."

Helena restrained her tongue, though she longed to verbally disembowel this child-queen. Memory held her back, for she had felt the same when she became empress. Luckily, the egotistical lady from the provinces had found a mentor in the city. Anastasia had been waiting for the new empress on her first day, even before Galen had received the Purple and the acclamation of the Senate. The Duchess, impeccably dressed as ever, had taken her aside and begun to teach her about being an empress. This child had not learned those lessons yet. Helena was disappointed—only a few weeks before, Martina had been maturing to meet the challenge. Now, given this reverse, she had lost confidence in herself.

"Do you," Helena bit out, "know their wives?"

Martina hung her head low and then shook it *no*.

Helena sighed in disappointment. "They've not sought you out? Looking for favors or your husband's ear?"

"Oh yes." Martina brightened. "They are always about, snooping for crumbs. But I don't *know* any of them. They're not . . . friends or anything."

"Crumbs are good enough," Helena said, considering what to do with this girl. Emperor Heraclius was bedridden, an invalid, his brother, Theodore, disgraced, the Empress isolated by her unwise marriage, the Faithful distrusted by the Legion commanders . . . who did that leave? "Martina, are there *any* of the ministers or high priests who will speak to you?"

"No," Martina moaned, looking like she was going to cry again. "The temples have turned their backs on us. Only the priests of the Asclepiun wanted to help my husband, but he sent them away. The ministers—they're afraid of me—or . . . wait. There are two that would talk to me, I think. But only one of them could help . . . maybe."

"Who are they?"

Martina shuddered slightly, clasping her arms over her chest. The movement pushed her breasts up in the low-cut palla. The image in the telecast suddenly flickered and went out, leaving a vision of swirling green fire. Helena sighed, then sat back in the cane chair positioned before the ancient bronze mechanism. The boy-priest Alexos was very easily distracted. Even through the poor image of the telecast, it was clear the priest was helping the Empress due to a bad case of puppy love. His masters, in fact, would probably be very angry if they knew the boy was allowing the Empress to spy on them.

"Gart, who made this device?" Helena pointed at the slowly rotating sphere. It had reverted to an image of the world as seen from on high. White clouds covered most of the Western Empire. If one watched long enough, one could see them move. "Is it Egyptian?"

The big sorcerer shook his head.

"No, Empress. It was found in Hispania, though the signs and symbols incised in the bronze are reminiscent of Egyptian glyphs. There has been some discussion, amongst our order, as to its antecedents. Most of us believe it is an artifact from before the Drowning."

"Really?" Helena sat up, straightening her back. Sitting in this chair for hours gave her aches and pains. She would have to visit the baths afterwards and have one of the masseurs restore the proper humors. "Can anyone read the signs?"

"No." Gart sighed, an oddly feminine sound to come from such a large man. "It is beyond our art. We can ken the basic use of the device, we can make it perform some feats, but understand it? Read the lines of symbols? I cannot. Perhaps they cannot be read at all."

Helena coughed politely. The thaumaturge sounded just like the old men in the *ludi historiae* who bickered about the ruins along the Nile or the strange, unnamed tombs in the hills of Etruria. When one of the historians said, "It cannot be known," it meant "I haven't a clue." All scholars were loath to admit ignorance. The Empress found it amusing. Her correspondence showed nothing clearer than men barely knew what was going on in their own homes, much less the world at large. "Gart, we have one of these useful devices here. The Eastern Emperor owns one. Are there more?"

The German nodded, his red beard bouncing on his fat

chest. "When the device is woken from sleep there is a moment when I feel it reaching out, attempting to find its brothers. All these devices were made by one hand at one time. They were forged from the same metal, drawn from the same ore. This is an old technique—the same craftsman incised the runes and smoothed the edges of the metal with the same motions. In this way, they are very close to being the *same* device in the hidden world. They yearn for each other."

Helena raised an eyebrow at the fat German's poetic interpretation. However, she was not a thaumaturge, so perhaps his description was accurate. "How many are there?"

Gart raised a finger, saying, "This cannot be known with surety, but I believe besides this one and its brother in Constantinople, there are five more. If you press me, I could not say why, but I believe it is so."

"Interesting," Helena mused, but she turned back to the spinning world. A rising hum was beginning to emanate from the telecast. "They are trying again?"

"Yes," Gart hissed, attention focused on the burning sphere. "Here!"

Martina, her hair half in front of her face, wavered into view. Again, Helena could see the dim chamber in the distant city and the sweating, pale face of Alexos off to one side. His cheek was bright red, showing the outline of a small, furious hand.

"Empress!" Helena barked and Martina's eyes widened at the tone. "Do *not* strike the man who aids you! If you do so again, I will neither speak to you nor help you. Do you understand me?"

"Yes," Martina said, blushing. "I'm sorry."

"Don't say it to me," Helena growled. "Say it to him." She jabbed a carefully manicured finger at Alexos. "And stop distracting him with those flimsy tight gowns. Wear something elegant and refined, suitable for an empress, not a Persian harem girl."

Martina scowled, jutting her round chin out. "I can wear what I want," she said defiantly. "At least people look at me when I dress this way. I hate being ignored! Some of the men like it—is that so bad?"

"It is," Helena said, taking control of her temper. "An empress does not care if she is loved by her people, only if they fear her. Would you want your uncle Theodore to look at you with desire?"

Martina flinched. A moment of violent emotion passed in her eyes, though her face itself remained frozen. Helena's carefully plucked eyebrows narrowed in concern. Raw hatred leaked out of the Eastern Empress for a moment, but then it was gone.

"No," Martina said, her voice cold. "I understand what you mean."

"Good," Helena said gently. "Tell me—each thematic governor must send regular dispatches to the capital, yes? Who receives those reports? Is there anyone who acts upon them?"

Martina nodded, pressing the heels of her palms to her eyes. She seemed very tired.

"There are reports—they are delivered to the *logothete* of the *notitia*, who collates them and produces a summary for the Emperor and his council. With my husband in seclusion, these summaries and the letters were being left in the office, where I could read them and respond. Unfortunately, since the ministers have found me out, I do not know who reads them now. Certainly none of these fumblekins has the wit to act on his own."

Helena tapped the back of one almond-shaped nail against her lips. "The destruction of the fleet leaves your enemy with many options. He can now strike all along the Asian coast or even against Greece. No city or province is safe until the enemy is driven from the sea. Listen, Martina, you said that there are two ministers or officials who will listen to you. Who are they?"

"One is Nidus, the logothete of the tombs." Martina's

voice revealed a clammy terror at the thought of the man. "The other is really no one, just the master of the kitchens. He's a funny little gray man, but he doesn't seem to care that I married my uncle."

"Martina—you need any kind of ally now, so do not dismiss even the cooks. This Nidus, now, you've told me before that the other ministers fear him. Will they listen to him if he orders them to do something?"

"I don't know." Martina frowned, which did not improve her looks. Helena suspected the girl had been spending far too much time mewed up in the damp, underground room housing the telecast. Her complexion was suffering. "I don't believe that he's *ever* ordered anyone to do anything! But they will listen to him."

"That is enough." Helena glanced sideways and saw that Gart was tiring. It was taxing work to hold the two devices in communication. "Quickly now—you must change your dress. Look as Imperial as possible at all times! Seek out Nidus and press him to call regular meetings of the ministers. Have the dispatches from the provinces read aloud to everyone. If no one can *order* the others to act, perhaps they will do so on their own. You must find more allies amongst the priests and the nobles—stop ignoring them! Listen attentively to them, no matter how boring. Someone will want to help you, if only for his own advancement."

"I will!" Martina stood, raising a hand in parting. The sphere shimmered and collapsed, whirling down into a flurry of green and white and blue sparks and then, with a rattle, to a set of flat, interlocking bronze disks.

Helena tapped her teeth with her thumb again, nodded to Gart and hurried out.

Twilight was falling as Helena stepped down from her *sella* onto the street in front of the Villa of Swans. She waved irritably at the troop of husky men, then waited, face covered by the edge of her stole, until they had trooped off down the hill with the covered litter on their shoulders. There was moderate traffic on the street—slaves on their masters' business—but no one approached the gate of this house. A drift of leaves had blown up in the recess of the doorway. The Empress' nose twitched at the mess, but she tapped on the door regardless.

There was no answer for a long time, and the sun was close to the western horizon before Helena heard movement in the yard behind the high gate. She redoubled her efforts, using the heel of a small knife she carried to trim pen quills and cut twine. It made a tinny sound on the travertine panel.

At last the gate opened a crack and a pair of smudged blue eyes stared up at her, surmounted by a cap of blond hair.

"Go away," the little girl said. "Her ladyship is not accepting visitors today."

"Or ever, I warrant," Helena said in an acerbic tone. "Let me in, Betia, or I'll have the Praetorians up here and they'll knock the door down."

For a moment the maid considered this, then pushed the heavy door open enough for Helena to turn sideways and step inside. The inner yard, which was little more than a court for people to dismount from their litters at parties, was strewn with dead orange and red leaves. Willows hung over the walls on either side, planted in the garden circling the house. Betia padded away, ghostly in a plain white tunic and gray shawl. The Empress followed, slowly taking in the disrepair and ruin that had overtaken the villa. She was outraged by its poor state. Once, this had been the most gracious and elegant home in the city. Her own summerhouse in Catania followed the same floor plan.

Now the house was dark and silent. Even the great sea hall with its mighty Poseidon seemed dingy and filled with gloom. Following Betia, Helena passed through many dark rooms until, at last, they climbed a flight of stairs and reached the roof. The sun had set, though the western sky was a riot of color. The white domes of the villa glowed copper in the last vestige of the day. A wooden pavilion stood on the roof at the end of one wing of the house. It commanded a sweeping view of the seven hills. In the purple gloaming, the city was beginning to blaze with light. Lanterns and torches glowed in windows; bonfires lit the docks along the river; sacred fires gleamed in the temples. It would be a clear night, allowing the glory of the stars to shine down on Rome.

Helena stepped into the pavilion and saw Betia kneeling next to a wooden chair facing the south. A figure sat in the chair, swathed in dark cloth. Helena stepped to the edge of the pavilion and turned, one hand on the painted wooden half-wall marking its edge. "Anastasia."

The woman in the chair leaned on one arm, chin resting on the back of her hand. In the poor light, her face was a pale oval marked by the dark smudges of her eyes. She did not appear to notice the Empress.

Helena jerked her chin at the slave girl. "Betia, fetch some lamps and wine and something hot to eat."

The figure in the chair moved slightly, rustling, but then subsided at Helena's glare. Betia slipped off into the twilight, quiet as a dove.

"There is trouble in the east," Helena said in a matter-of-fact voice. "I need your help to sort it out." The Empress moved about until she found, painfully, a chair with her shin. She drew it over to where Anastasia was sitting, then sat herself, folding her shawl over her hands. It would grow cold as night deepened. The Duchess said nothing, but Helena thought she could sense a weary interest.

"The Emperor Heraclius remains sick, an invalid. His policies in the Decapolis have yielded insurrection and the rebels—aided by Arabian mercenaries—have seized half the Eastern fleet from the great port at Caesarea. To compound these troubles, I learned today the *drungaros* Andrades has been defeated off the Lycian coast, losing the *other* half of the Eastern fleet. Empress Martina and her uncle, Prince Theodore, are locked in a stupid but inevitable struggle to control the Imperial bureaucracy in Constantinople, playing at draughts while the Empire burns."

There was a breathy laugh from the Duchess's cowl and a white hand emerged from the heavy robe. Helena took the cold fingers in her own, controlling a flinch.

"Succinct," Anastasia said, her voice weary. "Why do you trouble me with this?"

"I don't care if you are stricken with grief," Helena said in a fierce voice. "I know your adopted daughters were killed in the eruption, that you sent men to murder my brother-in-law, that they may have failed. You account yourself responsible for *all* the dead. This means nothing to me. These events are in the past. This trouble is in the present and my husband will have to deal with it. You will help me, or I will have you given to the Praetorians for their supper."

This elicited a second, slightly fuller laugh.

"Dear," Anastasia whispered, "I'm past the day when I could entertain a whole cohort. You'll do just as well by setting a gaggle of schoolboys upon me. I know you are beside yourself with worry, but I am of no more use to anyone. My policies have led only to ruin."

Helena closed her eyes briefly, overcome by her own weariness, then opened them again as warm light flowed into the pavilion. Betia returned with a lamp and a covered plate. Helena held her tongue until the blond maid hung the light on a hook and laid the plate on a table between them. A linen cover was removed, allowing steam and the aroma of fresh bread to rise up. There were strips of cut meat, steamed vegetables and a round of cheese. The smell reminded the Empress she had forgotten to eat during the day. She accepted an eating tine gladly.

"I don't care about your policies," Helena said, chewing on a rare slab of lamb covered with pressed peppercorns. "You know things that no one else does. You will answer my questions."

Anastasia looked up, violet eyes glittering for a moment

over the lip of her wine cup. The vintage had been heated with iron plugs and spiced with cinnamon and nutmeg. Steam curled around the older woman's high brow and the oily curls of her hair.

"Will I?" There was a trace of amusement hiding in the tired voice.

"You will," Helena said, her voice cold. "You may have been replaced by my husband, but I do not trust your successor and I *know* that he does not have the grasp of the whole empire as you do. Tell me this, do you still receive reports from your various agents and factors throughout both empires?"

"I do," Anastasia allowed, staring at the steamed vegetables. Betia had settled in beside her mistress and was watching like a hunting falcon, ready to respond to any command. The Duchess picked out a single carrot from the plate and nibbled on it. "They are downstairs, in the study, if you wish to see them."

"Do you still read them?"

"No," the Duchess said, chewing thoughtfully. "But Betia insists on interrupting my naps by reciting them aloud." The woman turned slightly and made a face at the maid. "She is a very irritating girl."

"Have you heard of these matters before I spoke of them?"

"Some," Anastasia said, poking about on the plate with an eating tine. "This business of the fleet is new."

"Yes," Helena said, biting at her thumb. "I heard of it just today. The news is fresh in Constantinople."

"Is it?" Anastasia found a carrot and carefully broke it in two, then ate the smaller of the pieces. "They must be in quite a panic."

"Empress Martina is at her wits' end," Helena said in a dry tone. "Is there a man you can trust in the Eastern capital? Someone I could send word to? Someone who can *do* something there?"

Anastasia sighed and put her eating tine away. She

slumped back in her chair, letting the cowl of the robe fall over her face. "I will give you the lists of names and cities, if you so desire. Then you can play at this business yourself, without wearying me. There is a man there, a tribune in charge of the Office of Barbarians. He's supposed to be Heraclius' agent, of course, but we've had an understanding for years."

"Good. Could he see about killing a man?"

The Duchess made a sound like a snort and a laugh mixed together. She raised herself up in the chair and motioned for another glass of wine. Betia pressed it into her hands. She drank deep, then put it aside. "You've taken to this business, haven't you? Do you really think that you can change anything with plots and murders? I thought so once . . . it's addictive, you know, but then I don't suppose that you care, either. It's too much like a story in one of your letters."

Helena put down her own cup, wondering bitterly if she would have to summon guardsmen to threaten the Duchess. It seemed they had come a very long way from that first day, when Helena had been the nervous young woman out of her depth and Anastasia the wise councillor. Their respective ages could not be that far apart—perhaps only a decade. Were they enemies now? "Will you answer my questions? I will tend to the details."

"Will you?" Anastasia said, her voice sounding almost normal. "Would you trade the citizens of two large cities and countless towns to destroy a single man? Ha! I see the look on your face—you wouldn't, would you? You think these things can be finessed, avoided, fate circumvented because you are *smarter* than everyone else!"

The Duchess's voice rose to almost a shout. The cowl fell away, revealing a face lined with tiny fine wrinkles and the burden of age. The artful powders and unguents that normally composed a perfect visage had not touched her face in weeks. Coupled with her anger, she suddenly seemed terribly real to Helena and the Empress drew back in confusion.

"Do not play at these games, child," the Duchess said in a sneering voice. "Go back to your letters and your gossip and your dream worlds. You could not stomach the smell of blood."

Helena clenched her jaw, biting back a furious retort. At least Anastasia seemed to be taking an interest in the world around her. "And you, O arbiter of what is real and what is not—will you come forth from your grave? Put aside your funeral cloth and rejoin the living? You are hiding in your own dream, a luxury that I cannot afford." The Empress's eyes narrowed and she scowled at the Duchess. "I will not abide the living dead in my husband's realm. You must either be alive or I will see that you find the grave with my own hands!"

Anastasia laughed aloud, a full, belly laugh that spilled out of her like water from a shattered dam. Once she started, the Duchess was unable to stop. Helena sat back in her chair, feeling the hard grain of the wood under her fingers. Betia was alarmed, then went for a towel and dabbed tears from her mistress's eyes. Finally, exhausted and aching, Anastasia was able to take the cloth from the blond slave and clean her face.

"You have been reading those melodramas of Petronius' again," she gasped at last. "The living dead? What fine dialogue you write for yourself!"

Helena shot her a look, then folded her arms over her chest. "You're no better," she said in a surly voice. "Languishing about in sackcloth and ashes. Sitting in your abandoned, empty house with servants hidden away in the cellars. Artful drifts of leaves and dirt scattered about. The next time you try this flummery, make the gardeners use the right kind of leaves! The oak make a pretty red display, I agree, but not in high summer!"

Anastasia harrumphed, then clapped her hands for more wine. She moved like an invalid. The Duchess took another cup from Betia, who remained in her shadow. "Leave me alone. I do not want to go through all of this again, Helena dear. I feel it in my gut now, like a Spartan fox. All those men and women . . . I must go away. Far away."

"There's not going to be anyplace far enough," Helena snapped, "to get away from me. My husband may be a big fool, spurning you because you did what he feared to do, but I am not. Please, Anastasia, help me! Help us."

The Duchess turned her head away, putting the back of her hand to her mouth. Helena sat quietly, watching. Betia remained motionless, right by the older woman's side. Night deepened outside of the circle of warm light thrown by the oil lantern. Bats fluttered over the roof of the pavilion, darting around the edge of the garden. The night promised to be warm.

At last, Anastasia turned back to the Empress, her eyes in shadow. "You are a poor friend, Helena. You barge in and demand food, drink, conversation—then want help for no particular reward. In some circles, you would be a boor!"

"I cannot be a bad guest." Helena smirked. "I'm an empress."

"I had noticed," Anastasia answered in a dry tone. "Very well. I do not think there will be any rest for me, here or anywhere."

"You would hate rest." Helena smiled knowingly. "How would you know you were alive?"

"I am not like that," the Duchess said, a distant look in her eyes. "Intrigue is no longer my elixir. I am afflicted by worse than lotus blossom—conscience bears on me."

"Then give in," the Empress said, leaning forward and tapping on the table. "This mess in Constantinople needs to be cleaned up—if you have a man in place, let us dispatch a message to him."

"To what end?" Now the Duchess's voice was sharp and she seemed fully awake. "Whose death will 'clean up this mess'?"

"Prince Theodore, of course! While he is stirring the pot in the Eastern capital, Martina cannot direct the Imperial government as Heraclius' regent. With him gone—"

"There will be civil war," the Duchess interjected, shaking her head. "Your correspondence with the girl has turned your head. She is entirely unsuitable to manage that snake pit and even less able to command a defense of the capital."

"A defense? What are you talking about?"

Anastasia let out a long, slow sigh, then motioned for Betia. "Dear, bring us a map. You know the one."

The slave hurried off, white legs flashing in the darkness that lay upon the villa.

"The matter of her marriage has compromised her role in Constantinople," Anastasia said. "Her regency would be constantly under attack. Consider: young Constantius, the son of Heraclius by his first wife, Eudocia, is the heir. Martina would have to put him ahead of her own son. How likely is this? No, she would intrigue against her stepson and try and put the infant Heracleonas in his place. The great nobles would revile her and the state will be paralyzed—again.

"Theodore is an equally bad choice. These rebels have bested him twice and he is of poor character. No, a third option is required. Of course, the optimum outcome would be to restore Heraclius to good health, then all of these problems would fall by the wayside."

"Martina," Helena ventured, "believes that he is near death. The captain of the Faithful Guard is attempting to treat the Emperor in secret with some herbal remedy, but it does not seem to work. The priests of Asclepius are at loggerheads over the marriage issue, so they will not help."

Anastasia nodded, thinking. Then she smiled slightly as Betia returned with a rolled leather map. "Ah, let us examine the other problem." Betia unrolled the map and laid it out on the table.

"These rebels out of the Decapolis have a canny leader,"

Anastasia said. "He knows victory in this war depends on control of the sea, thus his efforts to obtain a fleet and to drive the Eastern ships away from the Phoenician coast. This done, he has one of two objectives—Constantinople or Egypt."

Helena nodded, examining the carefully painted depiction of the eastern end of the Mare Internum. "Galen believes Egypt is the target, for it is the richest province in the Empire and without its grain, Constantinople will starve."

"This is possible." Anastasia paused. "But our enemy has moved swiftly and with an obvious plan. Look, he could have seized Egypt by land if he so desired, marching swiftly down the coast and crossing the desert at Pelusium. He did not. His first blow was to capture the great port and the fleet at Caesarea Maritima. I think his aim is here instead."

Her thumb laid alongside the tiny figure of Pallas Athena marking Constantinople at the junction of the Sea of Darkness and the Mare Aegeum. "The Imperial Army has been shattered. Theodore is disgraced. Heraclius is bedridden. There is no fleet to defend the approaches to the city by sea. A daring man might sail into the Propontis and land an army, besieging the Eastern capital by both land and water."

"Impossible! The walls of Constantinople are impregnable! It would be a disaster."

"Perhaps. Perhaps this rebel thinks he can force a peace settlement if he blockades the city. How long could Rome stand if the flow of African grain were cut off? Constantinople is even bigger, with even more mouths to feed."

"Oh." Helena stopped and considered. "That could be . . . the rebel king would gain time and land to mount a proper defense, or further attack."

"Exactly. He moves very swiftly, this one, because he knows that keeping the Empire off balance is his only hope for victory. A negotiated settlement will give him legitimacy amongst the Eastern cities. Persia is in disarray, so there is a sliver of time for him to build a new state between the old empires."

"Then we must move swiftly, too."

"Yes, dear. Is Galen in the city?"

"No." Helena shook her head. "He's gone off to Portus for a few days to oversee the dredging operations—they're clearing the channels in the harbor of Trajan with some contrivance of Aurelian's."

Anastasia raised an eyebrow approvingly. "A boring but worthy project. Your husband is sometimes wise, I see."

"I suppose, but I am reminded of Nero and his lyre."

Anastasia laughed, but nodded in agreement. Then she said, "There are several new legions being mustered at Mediolanum, I believe."

Helena shrugged. She had no idea.

"Here is a solution to this business in the Eastern capital, my dear. Listen closely, for you must make your dear, dull husband believe this is *his* idea. Some time ago an arrangement was made between the emperors of East and West regarding the command of military detachments operating in the other's territory. Do you know of it?"

"No," Helena said, a little taken aback by the Duchess's effortless command of the situation.

"It was agreed that each emperor, or his designate, would serve as the *Dux Militaris* for the other, if a combined operation were undertaken. Thus, during the recent war in Persia, Galen was Heraclius' dux. If a war were fought here in the West, Heraclius would be Galen's second. In this case, if a Western army were to arrive at Constantinople under the command of a Western caesar, then that leader could take command of *all* the Roman forces in the area."

Helena nodded, committing the proposition to memory.

"This will allow someone competent," Anastasia continued, "to deal with this invasion. It is unlikely the entire Eastern fleet was destroyed in this latest disaster—the Western fleet will have to gather up the survivors and then hunt down these rebellious ships."

THE PRACTICE YARD, THE LUDUS MAGNUS

)H(

Narses crossed the sand with a slight limp, leaning on his walking cane. In youth his body had been powerful and strong, but years in the Legion and the arena had taken their toll. The stump of his left arm was bound across his chest with a leather strap. Today, with the sun high and heat sizzling from the sand, he was stripped down to a loincloth and sandals. His muscular body was etched with scars and old, puckered wounds. Short gray hair frizzed the top of his head. Sand crunched under his sandals and squeaked under the tip of his cane.

The Amazon, Diana, was waiting for him at the center of the practice yard. The school mirrored the oval shape of the Flavian, in a quarter-scale replica. Seats under painted canvas shades and behind a tall wooden wall surrounded an oblong of white sand. The practice yard lacked the Flavian's various elevated platforms and hidden doors, but it served. Narses had canceled morning practice so he could consider his new prize.

She waited quietly as he approached. Archers stood ready atop the barrier wall, bows taut. Narses did not think he was in danger, but there was no sense in taking chances. Hamilcar followed him, lean and sun-bronzed, carrying a pair of wooden practice swords.

"My name is Narses," he said, coming to a halt. He approached her from the south, with the sun at his shoulder. Her eyes were gray slits, but she made no motion toward him. The *lanista* pursed his lips, looking her over. After a moment of observation he circled her, keeping two strides away, looking her up and down with a careful eye. Her only garments were a soiled breast band and loincloth. Narses returned to his original position.

"What is your name?"

The woman regarded him, then a half-smile passed over her lips. "Diana."

"Fitting. Is it your real name?"

"It is now."

Narses nodded, squinting a little with his left eye. "May I see your hands?"

"You need to ask my permission?" Thyatis' voice was filled with brittle humor.

"I am asking your permission," Narses responded, leaning on the cane. "Out of professional courtesy."

"I'm not a gladiator," Thyatis snapped.

"No." Narses smiled himself. "You are a soldier. I was a soldier once. May I?"

Thyatis held out her hands, palms up. Narses stepped to her, aware of Hamilcar stiffening with tension, poising to leap to his defense. Too, the archers on the wall sighted and drew their bows, ready to loose them. The woman did not move. The lanista ran his right hand over her palms, thumbs, wrists, feeling the calluses and tracing the pattern of scars on her arms. When he was done he stepped back. Narses seemed sad, even regretful.

"You shouldn't be here," he said. "You're a soldier, not one of these toys."

"Toys?" The woman almost laughed aloud but she restrained herself, clasping her hands behind her back. "I don't think your friend likes being called a *toy*."

Narses could feel Hamilcar's anger too, but he just chuckled. "Did you know that, with one famous exception, gladiators set against legionaries lose? The man who is trained to fight in the arena lives in a world of careful constraints. He is like an actor on the stage, with a role and a script to follow. He is not a soldier, who does not care for effect or spectacle but only to live and to kill his enemies so that he might survive. A soldier thrives in chaos, a gladiator in order. When chaos and order meet, the soldier is the master."

Thyatis raised an eyebrow. "You are an odd gladiator."

Narses smiled ruefully, shaking his stump at her. "Not much of one now. I should have been an innkeeper, then I'd have two good arms. Hamilcar, toss us those blades!"

The African underhanded a practice sword first to Narses, who caught it deftly from the air, and then to Thyatis, who let it fall to the sand.

"Pick it up," Narses said, tossing his heavy wooden blade into the air and then catching it for a better grip. "I would like to see you with a sword in your hand."

Thyatis looked down at the weapon, then knelt and picked it up. It was long-hafted, with room to wield it hand-and-hand. Wood wrapped in canvas made for a heavy blade, easily twice the weight of the equivalent iron. She took it in both hands, her right wrapped around the hilt near the crossbar, her left against the pommel. Her body relaxed, left leg sliding forward, bent, while her right slid into balance behind. The tip of the wooden blade pointed down and to the right, in line with her body. Narses' eyebrows rose in surprise, seeing the woman's balance and poise. He raised his own weapon, turning it over so that his palm faced the sand.

They stood, facing each other. A grain passed, then another.

Narses shifted his position, turning his body into line with hers, knees settling. Thyatis responded, swinging the sword up in a smooth motion, weight shifting slightly forward. Her balance remained, as did his.

Again a grain passed, then Narses brought his sword hilt to his forehead, the blade pointing at the sky, and said, "Well done. Hamilcar, take these tools away." He bowed, then tossed the wooden sword to the frowning African. The gladiator caught the sword deftly, then tucked it under his arm. Thyatis waited a beat, then bowed herself, grounding her weapon,. then flipped it to Hamilcar.

Narses bent and picked up his cane, shaking his head.

"You have a powerful enemy," he said, looking up at Thyatis. "Do you have a patron? Someone who can pay for your freedom?"

"No," Thyatis said, voice acid with bitterness. "I do not want freedom."

Narses stepped back, surprised by the hatred and anger in the woman's voice.

"I don't understand. You want to fight and die in the arena?"

"Yes." A distant look entered Thyatis' face, showing an echo of terrible loss. "That is fitting."

The lanista shook his head in puzzlement. He had seen many men enter the arena and most leave in death, dragged to the Black Gate by dark-robed attendants. There was nothing worthwhile on the bloody sand.

"You are still young," he said, "and you've all your limbs! Your anger will grow less with time, then fade. Turn away from this slaughter! It is foolish. Wasteful."

Thyatis shook her head. "You don't understand. I want to fight."

"You will not have to wait long. The funeral games for the dead of Vesuvius begin soon."

A strange light came into her eyes. "The Emperor honors those slain in the eruption? The *munera* have been approved?"

"Yes," Narses said. "You didn't hear?"

"No," she said, smiling. "But I am glad. Find me suitable opponents, Master Narses! The shades of the dead will be hungry after this long wait. I would send my friends into the underworld with full bellies!"

Narses backed away, on edge. He saw the woman was

suddenly glad, even cheerful. Hamilcar joined the lanista and they hurried toward the gate in the wall.

Thyatis knelt on the hot sand, ignoring the guardsmen moving toward her. In a moment, they would try and herd her back to the cell with long, barbed spears. She would go without trouble, but at this moment, she clasped her hands, putting her fists to her forehead.

O Huntress, she prayed, *let my friends find their way to golden fields, rich with grain. I have failed them, failed my mother, failed you, goddess. My heart is broken, but I will do them honor! I will send brave men down to the black river to hold their cups, to serve them, to bring them choice cuts of meat, thick with fat. I swear it will be so!*

Then she stood up and allowed the guards to take her back into the holding cells lining the practice yard. The faces of the dead still haunted her, but she thought now they might smile, where before there had been only torment.

"A strange sort of test," Hamilcar ventured as he and Narses walked through the tunnel into the main building. "Not even a blow struck?"

Narses grunted, his cane tapping on the tile floor. "No need. I saw enough."

"Of what? Her sleek breasts and thighs?" Hamilcar laughed, his bronzed face glowing in the light of the high windows. "She is pretty and vicious all at once!"

Narses stopped and turned, looking up at the African, his chin jutting out. "Do you think that her victory over the criminals was a fluke?"

Hamilcar nodded, looking down at the old man. "Of course," he said, brushing back rich, dark hair. "They were drugged or poisoned. No woman has *ever* been triumphant in the arena."

Narses grimaced, curling his fists over the head of the cane. "Hmm, in your memory, perhaps. I remember differently, though it was a long time ago. Listen, when you walk onto the hot sand, do you care if you live or die?"

"Yes," Hamilcar said in a curious tone, "who does not?"

"Her." Narses turned away again, thinking. The patrician Gaius had put a proposal to him. Now, seeing the woman up close, marking the pattern of her muscles, the skill inherent in her motions, the odd scars and welts on her, Narses was intrigued. "This woman is good, young lad. She does not fear death. I would not want to face her over bare steel."

"I could kill her," the African mused, turning his noble head in profile as they passed a polished metal mirror. "I am the best fighter in the city."

"Are you?" Narses laughed as he climbed the stairs to his office. "Perhaps the best *male* fighter in the city. But, you could be right. Many strange things have come to pass. I am too old to be surprised anymore."

The old lanista settled behind his desk, looking pensively out the window. Across the rooftops, the arches and arcades of the Colosseum rose up against the sky. From this vantage, the amphitheater was a marble and concrete cliff, towering over the city. Narses felt a little sad, thinking of all the men he had sent to die on the sand. Gaius' proposal troubled him, though he could see the benefits for himself and for the school. The Ludus Magnus was the foremost gladiatorial school in the Empire, revered and respected. Narses had been the master for sixteen years and had seen emperors come and go. He had a reputation to uphold. These funeral games needed to be special. Galen's delays had raised the anticipation of the people to a fever pitch. The usual fights and spectacles would not suffice. "Hamilcar, listen closely."

The African, who had been checking the fit and polish of the leather straps girding his loins and chest, turned. He was an attentive lad, even if he was quite amoral.

"Go to the slave market, the prisons, the whorehouses. Find me every fierce girl that you can, every barbarian, every madwoman. Bring them here and put them in the cells on the third level. But quietly! Don't purchase them all at once. We have one real Amazon, but she should not stand alone on the bright sand."

〖回-〔0〕-〔0〕-〔0〕-〔0〕-〔0〕-〔0〕-〔0〕-〔0〕-〔0〕-〔0〕-〔0〕-〔0〕-〔0〕-〔0〕-〔0〕-〔0〕-〔0〕-〔0〕-〔0〕-回〗

CAESAREA MARITIMA

〗《

The wooden flank of the *Khuwaylid* slid past a limestone quay and came to rest, guided by gentle oars and ropes flung from the ship. Sailors swarmed from the ship, tying up and running out a gangway. The planks flexed under Mohammed's boots as he strode ashore. He found the heat of the day pleasant, though anyone else would find it oppressive. The white buildings and wharfs flung the sun into his eyes, but he squinted with the ease of long practice. Behind him, the rest of the Arab fleet was entering the huge harbor. Mohammed was delighted to see a large number of merchantmen tied up at the docks, busily loading and unloading bales and crates of goods.

Commerce endures. The thought was very comforting.

"My lord, welcome!" Khalid was waiting, handsome face wreathed with a smile. The young man bowed before Mohammed, bending his knee and putting fingertips to his forehead. The Quraysh tapped him on the shoulder and motioned for him to rise.

"Greetings, young Eagle. Well met, Odenathus! If you are here, then the road to Egypt must be open in the south!"

"It is." The Palmyrene smiled, bowing. "Though there was some difficulty. Cousin! Oomph!"

Odenathus and Zoë embraced, her dark hair flipping around her neck. Mohammed smiled, seeing the young woman was allowing a little happiness to show. He left the two of them to make their greeting, turning back to Khalid. "Is Shadin here? Good. Let's find somewhere to sit and have a cool drink."

Khalid gestured toward the graceful three-story building that served as the port offices. "My lord Mohammed, I've made this building our headquarters. Your staff is billeted there, and . . . we have a guest. A royal guest. You will be surprised to meet him, I think."

Mohammed raised an eyebrow at the stress the young man laid on the word *royal*. "Do we?"

Zoë shaded her eyes with a hand, staring at the merchantmen riding at anchor in the harbor. "Is that the *Tigranes*? It surely looks like her . . ."

"It is," Odenathus said, walking at her side along the quay. "I found the Palmyrene factor still in business here when we returned from Aelia Capitolina. He was surprised to see me, and very glad. I bade him send out messages to all the ships owned by the city—they are gathering here; a few arrive each week."

Zoë smiled, teeth brilliantly white in a very dark face. The time at sea had burned her dark brown. She tucked a stray tendril of hair behind her ear. "That is marvelous! The city is not dead, then."

"No." Odenathus nodded in agreement. "We still own warehouses and ships throughout the whole of the Mare Internum and down into the Sinus Arabicus. Many citizens who were abroad are gathering here, as they hear that the Queen lives. They are heartened by your presence, Zoë, and they are very angry with Rome."

"Good," Zoë said, dark eyes shining in delight. "We need more ships to carry men and supplies. Did our courier galley reach you?"

"Yes. It arrived yesterday!"

Zoë frowned, shaking her head. "How strange! We sent it away days and days before we turned back from the Roman shore. . . . No matter. What matters is that the way is open to Constantinople. The Imperial fleet is scattered and many ships were destroyed or captured."

"That is good news," Odenathus said, but something in his voice made Zoë stop.

"What is it?"

Odenathus shook his head, raising a hand. "Nothing, I suppose. I just . . . Dwyrin was at Aelia Capitolina when we were besieging the city."

Zoë's eyes widened. "He was?"

"Yes. He was aiding the defense, you know. They must have posted him there, after we left him at Antioch. Oh, Zoë, he's so strong! I never would have guessed it . . . not the way he was when we were together."

Zoë looked ill and sat down on one of the stone mooring pillars that lined the quay. She stared at Odenathus with a sick expression. "You didn't . . ."

"No. I think he lives. At least, he did not fall by my hand. Some of the Romans in the city escaped through a hidden tunnel. Very clever, really! The whole city is honeycombed with secret passages and adits. Jalal was beside himself!" Odenathus sat as well and Zoë took his hand.

"Did he hurt you?"

"No." Odenathus shook his head ruefully, squeezing her hand. "But it was close! His fire-calling power is incredibly strong. Luckily, he doesn't seem to be able to do much else—but don't get in front of him. You'll be a cinder!"

"It must have been strange to match power with him for real. I mean, not in training."

"It was very difficult. You know, I found something . . . after the first time. You see, the first time we fought, I couldn't bring myself to strike at him, not really. I couldn't . . . I didn't *mean* it, if you know what I mean."

Zoë made a face, shaking her head. "No, I don't understand."

Odenathus laughed, scratching the back of his head. "I didn't either. Jalal almost ran me through for cowardice in the face of the enemy. No . . . there was a *geas* upon me, a pattern. A working that turned my mind from fighting Rome with my full strength."

The Palmyrene rolled up the sleeve of his tunic, showing the scar of a mark on his upper arm. "See this? The Legion brand they put on me when we enlisted to fight the Persians. Do you remember?"

"Yes," Zoë said, running slim fingers over the waxy flesh. "I didn't have to swear, not like you or Eric, because I was a woman . . . did it mean something?"

"It did." Odenathus pulled his sleeve down. "When we swore the oath, we accepted a binding—not to raise arms against the Empire. When Dwyrin came at me, I couldn't really fight him. I was lucky to escape alive. The geas is very weak."

"Clever," Zoë allowed begrudgingly. "A good idea to keep rebels from really fighting!"

"Just so." Odenathus wagged his finger at the town. "Everywhere we go, I watch the citizens. Many join us, hating Rome, but never the old soldiers. They swore this oath, too, and they fight us. It's difficult through this whole province—any settlement of retired legionaries has to be watched. They raid our supply caravans if we don't."

Zoë sighed, rubbing her face with both hands. "It doesn't matter. Mohammed intends to pack up the entire army and strike against the Imperial capital in one massive blow."

"Oh," said Odenathus, taking the concept in. Zoë seemed suddenly tired. "He won't have to worry about garrisons, then."

"No," she said, rising and wiping her hands on her pantaloons. "Let's go inside."

Mohammed stopped sharply just inside the room. It was a large, dim chamber with a high-beamed ceiling. A long table of burnished oak stood in the middle. The Quraysh felt a chill, seeing who was rising from a seat at the head of the table. Khalid stopped behind him, waiting.

"Lord Mohammed," the youth said in a clear voice. "This is the King of Kings, Shahr-Baraz, Shahanshah of the Persians and the Medes, lord of many lands. Your . . . guest."

Mohammed took two steps into the room, hand light on the hilt of his ebon sword. The towering man behind the table inclined his head in greeting. Another man was standing against the wall behind him, a thickset gray-beard wearing a close-linked shirt of mail. The big man smiled, showing fine white teeth behind a vigorous thicket of beard and mustache.

"Good day," the Emperor of the Persians said. "I apologize for my early arrival, Lord Mohammed, but I was in haste."

The Quraysh waited until Khalid had entered the room. Shadin followed, his heavy frame and ready sword easing Mohammed's mind.

"You are unexpected," the Quraysh said, voice cold. "And not welcome, I must say."

Mohammed turned to Khalid, his face a mask. "Have you broken bread with this man?"

"Yes, lord." Khalid gulped, seeing the strict displeasure on Mohammed's face. "He arrived two days ago on a spent horse, with only the lord Khadames and an escort of lancers in tow. He spoke of peace, so I let them stay."

Mohammed's eyes glinted in anger, but he mastered himself and walked to the head of the table. Shahr-Baraz topped him by a full head or more. Mohammed looked up at his old enemy, lips compressed in a thin line. "Do you think that you can fight your way out of this place?"

"No," Shahr-Baraz said, shaking his massive head. "My life is in your hands. You are king here, not I."

"I am not a king," Mohammed said. He placed the sword, still sheathed, on the table. "Men follow me by their own choice. I rule only myself."

"More than most can say," Shahr-Baraz rumbled and he too placed his sword on the table. "I have a proposal for you, but if you do not wish to hear it, I will leave."

"There is little that you can say to me," Mohammed snapped, letting some of his anger show. "Persia, and you in particular, have little honor in my eyes."

The Boar raised a bushy eyebrow in surprise, but then he nodded, remembering. "Ah . . . you were at Palmyra. I had forgotten. Yes, you would think that I acted faithlessly there. But I did not—let us not dispute the past, but the present. Much has changed since those black days."

"Has it?" Mohammed paced to the far end of the table, his head bent. "Khalid, bring us something to eat and drink. Find Zoë and Odenathus and bring them here."

The young man stared at Mohammed, his face one of plain entreaty. The Quraysh stared at him, scowling, until Khalid turned and left, his boots rapping sharply on the tiled floor. "You say things have changed. Your mad emperor is dead, I understand, and you now rule in the name of his daughters."

"Yes," the Boar said, seating himself. He spread his huge hands wide. "More has occurred since last we tested wills across the sand and battlements of fair Palmyra. Rome has destroyed both our capitals. Chrosoes is dead, his dismembered body buried in a common grave. I have taken his daughters under my protection. Some measure of order has returned to Persia. You have broken the back of Rome in the East."

A flinty smile passed over Mohammed's face, but he remained silent, listening.

"I am tired of war." Shahr-Baraz leaned forward, face serious and intent. "I have fought my whole life—first against the T'u-chüeh on the Oxus, then against the Usurper, then against Rome. I have won battles and lost them. Now, I am king and I want one thing—peace."

"When a Persian speaks of 'peace,'" Mohammed quoted, "he wants a piece of your land. Tell me, O King, what have you heard of me? Have you heard that the voice from the clear air, the voice of the Maker of the World, has spoken to me? He tells me that a struggle is coming, one between light and darkness. I have seen that evil—it stood at your side, it was your *champion* when you tested the honor of Zenobia."

The Quraysh paused, seeing Zoë and Odenathus entering the room. Both of them looked perplexed, then Zoë saw the man sitting at the table and her face turned white with rage.

"Abominations! A Persian?" The Palmyrene girl's mouth twisted into a snarl. "Strike him down, Mohammed, or I will!" Her fingers curled, sketching a sign in the air. A chair rattled behind Mohammed, but he stepped forward, interposing himself between Zoë's anger and their visitor.

"Do nothing," Mohammed barked, catching Zoë's hand in motion. A cold fire burned among her fingers, but at the Quraysh's touch the flames flickered out. "He is our guest, for the moment."

Mohammed saw Odenathus was equally outraged, but he caught their eyes with his own and shook his head. "Control yourself. Patience." Mohammed's voice was a sharp whisper.

He released Zoë's hand and turned back to the Persian. Shahr-Baraz was sitting again, though the general Khadames had come forward and was standing just behind him.

"You serve a monster," Mohammed said. "I had intended to strike against Rome, against Heraclius, but if you have restored Persia, then you had best ride swiftly, for my anger will be hard on your trail. The Romans are in disarray. I can leave them be for now."

Shahr-Baraz opened his hands, palms out. "Lord Mohammed, I know what you believe. I know what you are thinking. The late Chrosoes trafficked with dark powers. He entertained demons. Servants crawling from the pit of Ahriman's domain flocked to him.

"But I am *not* Chrosoes! I am not his wife, Maria, who first threw wide those doors, whose desire for revenge upon her father's murderers led down this evil path. I am the Boar! Shahr-Baraz! I do not serve evil. I am my own master."

Mohammed snorted, sounding very much like a camel. "Prove it."

"I will," Shahr-Baraz said, motioning to Khadames. The general bent down and, with a grunt, hoisted a barrel onto the tabletop. It was old and grimy, stained almost black with age. It sloshed as the general set it down. The Boar, making a face at the smell oozing from the barrel, snapped the clasp of a chain holding the lid closed with his bare hands.

The smell worsened and Mohammed felt the hairs on his arms rise up. An aura of indefinable evil washed over him as the lid of the barrel came away in the Boar's hands. The lord Khadames turned away, his face pale. A gelid sound of something slopping back and forth filled the air. Steeling himself, Shahr-Baraz reached into the barrel and dragged forth a head.

Mohammed stepped back, heart thudding with remembered terror. Behind him, there was a hiss of indrawn breath from Zoë, Odenathus and Khalid. Only Shadin, in his stoic way, did not react. The Boar raised the face of a demon from the barrel. It dripped with viscous slime and it was dark, blacker than pitch, dark as coal. Despite the advanced state of decay, some recognizable features remained.

"That is the one," Mohammed rasped, mind filled with violent memories. "That is the creature that strove against Ahmet on the Plain of Towers, that threw down the gates of the city."

"This is the head of the demon Azi Tohak," Shahr-Baraz rumbled. "I hewed it from his body myself. He was a servant of uttermost darkness, of Ahriman, of the chaos that boils and bubbles at the center of the universe."

Surprisingly, a sad look passed over Shahr-Baraz's face. "He was once the younger brother of my friend, dead Chrosoes. Their father banished Rustam when he was very young and he fell into evil ways. After Chrosoes reclaimed his throne from the usurper Bahram Choban, his brother returned to the court. But Rustam had a new name and a new face. No one knew the truth, not until Empress Maria was seduced and destroyed and the King's face ruined."

Mohammed stepped closer, though every instinct screamed he should flee. Up close, the thing's face was even fouler. In some ways it approximated the human, but in every plane and feature it revealed an alien, inhuman nature. Overlapping black scales formed the skin, smoothing to delicate fluted plates around dead eyes. Sharp, pointed teeth jutted from the rotting jaw, and the ears folded back into an elongated skull. At the neck there was a jagged tear revealing nacreous-green bones. The Quraysh felt ill simply looking upon the remains.

"It is a token to reclaim my honor," the Boar said, leaning close. "I had already left Palmyra when the city was destroyed. I will rue that decision for the rest of my days. I did not mean it to happen—it was this thing, this Dahak, that shattered the city of Silk."

"Will that bring back the people of my city?" Zoë's voice rose like an arrow. She strode forward, her face cold and still. "Will it bring back my aunt? Will it restore the dead to life?"

"No," Shahr-Baraz said, sadly shaking his head. "It will not."

"And you expect to leave this place alive?" Zoë made to raise her hand, but Mohammed took it in his own.

"Lady Zoë, only the great and merciful god can restore the dead to life. No power on this earth can give you back your aunt, or your city, as it was in life. All things pass, whether we desire it or not."

"You accept his apology then?" Zoë snarled and snatched her hand away from the Quraysh. "Is Persia your *friend?*"

"No." Mohammed's voice was firm. "We will not bow to either empire. Lord Baraz, if you desire peace between us, you will go and leave us to our own devices. If what you say is true, if you have turned your back upon evil and walk the straight and righteous path, then the Lord that moves the sun and the tides will reward you. But if you lie, if this is a trick, then you will surely burn in torment, tortured for all eternity."

Shahr-Baraz nodded, shoving the head back down into the barrel. His face was screwed up against the stink. "I do not lie," said the Boar. "But I would say something to you, as a king to a king."

"Go on." Mohammed's voice was very cold.

"There will be no peace for your realm, or mine, while Heraclius is shah of the Romans. We have both seen the depth of his treachery. He is a murderer, faithless, without conscience or honor. *He* will not rest while either of us lives."

Mohammed nodded in agreement, but his face was stiff and remote.

"This is why you press him so hard," Shahr-Baraz continued. "You smash his armies, wreck his fleets, you drive him before you with whips. He cowers in his city of stone, unable to resist you. Victory, Lord Mohammed, is very close at hand."

The Boar paced to a window overlooking the port. He tugged at the long silver tips of his mustaches. "You have done what Persia has never done, broken the Roman control of the sea. You can strike directly at Constantinople, blockade the city, cut off all supply. You know, I think, what an advantage you have gained. Oh, there were many days when I stood on the shore of Chalcedon and begged great Ormazd for a fleet . . ."

Shahr-Baraz turned away from the window, almost snarling at the memory. He put his hands on his hips and stared at Mohammed, a blunt expression on his face.

"Together, Lord Mohammed—"

"No!" Zoë shouted, throwing off Odenathus' arm and striding to Mohammed's side. "We will not have an alliance with this dog! He is tomorrow's enemy. We should kill him now, while we can. Then Persia will be thrown into chaos again, and we will have time to deal with Rome."

The corner of Mohammed's mouth twitched up. He settled back against the table. "Lord Baraz, your . . . offer will be discussed. Good day."

The Persian king nodded, then strode out of the room. The gray-beard followed him, nodding amiably to Khalid and Odenathus. Zoë watched the two men go with ill-disguised hatred. When they were gone, she turned to Mohammed, smoldering. He raised an eyebrow, then sighed. "Khalid, where is that food?"

Shahr-Baraz walked along the seawall of the port, his attention idle on the waves rolling against the sloping wall of rubble. Khadames paced along beside him, head sunk in thought. The Boar stopped, looking out upon the broad waters of the Mare Internum. He had seen it before, many times, as his armies marched along the Roman shore. "I have always wondered, old friend, if Egypt is as grand as travelers say."

Khadames snorted, hooking his thumbs into his belt. "I don't think we'll see, my lord. Not without some blood spilt."

The Boar laughed, a big, booming sound that drowned out the waves for a moment. "We've spilled so much, you and I. Why not a little more?"

The general frowned, pursing his lips. His eyes seemed very old. "Not so long ago, you said that you wanted a realm at peace. You vowed it, in fact. Have you changed your mind?"

Shahr-Baraz tugged at his mustaches. "I have not. But, do you see another way? I cannot."

Khadames shook his head, feeling very weary. "We do not have to fight. We can go home—aren't Antioch and the lands around it enough? Our nation is still splintered, racked by chaos. Let us set things right there, in the land between the two rivers!"

Shahr-Baraz looked out to sea, watching the late-afternoon light glitter on the water.

"My lord," Khadames continued, his voice low and urgent. "You are Shahanshah now! King of Kings—you have all the choice in the world. Let us go home."

The Boar's chin rose a little as he looked to the west. "Rome is weak now, stunned by these two defeats. If that dog of a Hun is right, the road lies open from Antioch all the way to Chalcedon."

"We have been on the shore of the Propontis before!" Khadames' voice was almost shrill. "It gained us nothing. Constantinople is invincible. We would waste another ten thousand lives trying to break her walls. Yes, even with this fleet of Mohammed's! The Western Empire will come to Heraclius' aid and we will have to fight two empires on their own ground."

"If Mohammed accepts my help," Shahr-Baraz said, grinning, "then there will be two empires to match against these Romans. You know the power I can command now. It would be enough to break even Constantinople!"

The old general cursed then, violently and for a long time. His face turned beet red under the thick, graying beard.

"You are a fool," Khadames said at last, when he had mastered himself enough to speak intelligibly. "I have seen this power you dote on. You do *not* control him. That is a charade! This strength will control you, if you use it. You have not seen the pits under Damawand, or the forges and furnaces that labor there, unceasing."

"I *am* King of Kings," the Boar snorted, standing up from the wall. "I rule Persia now. You forget yourself, Khadames. Even the power of Damawand bows to me."

"Does it?" Khadames coughed, feeling a little faint. "You forget that I have seen the true master there, though it almost destroyed my mind. The will of a king is insignificant."

"Old woman." Shahr-Baraz snorted, sounding like his namesake, rooting in the forest. "Well, then, since you are overwrought, I will say this—if the Arabs accept my offer, we will make war on Rome. If they do not, we will go home and I will see just what occurs in this mountain valley of yours."

Khadames nodded weakly, heart thudding violently in his chest and vision blurring.

"Zoë, listen to me." Mohammed maintained his composure, even when the Palmyrene woman's tirade reached particularly violent levels. She stopped, breathing heavily, and brushed her hair out of her eyes. "Do you just want revenge? Nothing more, just to destroy your enemy?"

Odenathus, Shadin and Khalid had been watching in interest as the Quraysh and the Queen went back and forth. An hour or more had passed. Neither side had budged. Mohammed wanted to discuss the Persian offer, Zoë did not.

"If that is all that you want, then we will reject this offer. Indeed, we should try and capture Shahr-Baraz and his men and hold them for ransom, at least. But if you want anything more than to destroy the nations who brought down Palmyra, then we will have to consider this."

"He," Zoë jabbed a finger at the window, "set that monster upon the city. This *noble* Boar of yours fed my family, my people, my home into the furnace. It does not matter that he left—if he had not been there, this creature would have been elsewhere too. You urged me to strike against Rome first, and I agreed, for we thought Persia would be mired in civil war for a decade or more. We were wrong! Well, now chance comes around again, driven by the Fates. Let us seize this moment and strike a double blow!"

"Do you only want revenge?" Mohammed, at last, raised his voice a little. "Does your city mean nothing to you?"

"It means everything!" Zoë glowered at the Quraysh. "But it is dead and buried in the sand."

Mohammed shook his head, pointing at the harbor with his chin. "I saw the ships come in, just as you did. Palmyra was a mighty trading empire, not just a single city in the desert. Thousands of her citizens are still alive, scattered and disheartened. *They* are not dead. The city is not dead. It can rise again, built by Palmyrene hands, repaired by Palmyrene wealth. But it can only do that if there is peace."

Zoë was silent, her fists on the tabletop. She looked over her shoulder at Odenathus. "Cousin, what do you think?"

"I think," he said, his long, tanned face grave, "the city can live again, but it will be a mighty undertaking. We are rich, true, and many of our people still live, but our city was a fragile thing, balanced at the edge of the desert. It had been carefully cultivated over hundreds of years, built up stone by stone. All of that has been destroyed. Perhaps it cannot be regained. Perhaps we should abandon that dream of a new home."

"Is revenge enough?" Mohammed's voice was soft, making Zoë turn back to him. "Would you rather have victory? A victory where Palmyra is once again the queen of cities, mighty and cultured? If that is what you want, then revenge will not suffice."

"I want," Zoë said, grinding her fist into the table, "my aunt back, my mother back, all the dead haunting me back. But I will not get that, will I? No, there is only this war and this struggle. What do you intend, Lord Mohammed? Shall we make peace with this Persian? Shall we ally ourselves with him to defeat Rome? What then? What happens after Rome is cast down?"

Mohammed nodded, rubbing his nose. "That is the crux, Lady Zoë. What happens after victory?" He sighed and picked up a cup of water from the table. It was cool on his throat.

"Lord Mohammed?" Khalid ventured to break the silence. "I have not asked before, since there seemed to be no point . . . but can we, ourselves, take the Imperial capital?"

"No," Mohammed said, smoothing his beard with a scarred hand. "It is far too strong for us to take, even with this fleet and the army we have gathered."

Odenathus looked around, surprised, then coughed.

"Yes?" Mohammed was smiling.

"Then what did you intend?" Odenathus was nonplussed.

"I hoped," Mohammed replied, "to draw Heraclius into a field battle outside the city. With a fleet to blockade the ports, he would have to come out to drive us off so food could come into the city. I knew we could not possibly field and ship an army large enough to *capture* the Imperial capital, but we could lure the Emperor out to crush us."

Khalid laughed and slapped his thigh in delight. "Like baiting a leopard out of its den!"

"Yes, just so. Then, in open battle, I could kill this faithless emperor and have done."

Zoë raised an eyebrow, summoning a ghost of a smile on her weary face. "That was enough for you, then, just the death of one man? This smacks of revenge, Lord Mohammed."

"It does." Mohammed smiled back. "It does. It is romantic, too, one man against one man. The kind of thing that would appeal to any warrior of the tribes. Great honor could be had that way, for the daring."

Zoë stepped to Mohammed's side and put her hand on his weathered old face.

"You didn't think anyone would follow such a reckless romantic, did you? You've been surprised all along that an army came to you, and a fleet, and victory after victory."

"Yes, I was surprised." He took her hand and held it in his, searching her face. "But I should not have been, for the voice from the clear air guides me and it has the power to overcome all obstacles."

Zoë blushed at the softness of his voice and drew back her hand.

"What will you do now?" Odenathus pulled a chair out from the table and sat. "What comes after victory?"

"Peace, I hope." Mohammed stepped away from Zoë, smiling gently. "I think we must take this Persian offer, if for only one thing." The Quraysh glanced at Khalid, who nodded in agreement.

"For time," Zoë growled, pacing across the room to the window. "We cannot fight both Persia and Rome. Did you see his face when he spoke of standing on the shore of Chalcedon?"

Mohammed nodded. "I did. It galls him like a cancer. For all his valor and cunning, he could not defeat those walls. It is a lure for him, too. You saw the expression on his companion's face, I imagine." The Quraysh laughed softly. "The Boar could not live in peace. He is a man of war, of violent action; it is a drug to him. This Khadames sees the truth, but I wonder if the Boar kens his own nature."

Mohammed looked around the room and saw, in the faces of his companions, decision. "Very well. Khalid, send a runner to the lord Shahr-Baraz. We shall sit and eat and strike a bargain with this fellow, something suitable to both parties."

"Suitable?" Zoë snorted in laughter. "You've a merchant's tongue!"

Mohammed did not smile. A distant look passed over his face, reflecting loss. "I suppose," he said, "but a wise man once told me that there is no finer path in life than to weigh fairly and in full measure in all your dealings, no matter how small or how great. So does the merciful and beneficent Lord weigh the lives of men."

A sharp wind gusted out of the southeast, snapping the banners of the Sahaba on the masts of the harbor towers. Mohammed stood on the docks, a troop of men in full armor behind him. A Palmyrene coaster was loading from the main quay. Persian soldiers filed aboard while their horses, eyes covered, were being hoisted into the hold of the ship. Luckily, the Romans had equipped the port with big, double-winch cranes. The Quraysh watched the commotion with an experienced eye, finding a simple joy in the practiced motions of the harbor crew. The Persians were very nervous, going aboard ship with their horses. Mohammed supposed that it was quite new to them. Persia was not renowned as a maritime power.

"Lord Mohammed?" Shahr-Baraz approached, accompanied by a pair of horses and grooms. "My thanks for lending me the ship. It will cut days off our journey to the port at Seleucia Peria and then Antioch."

"You seemed a man in haste," Mohammed replied evenly. "Allies should help each other. It is my pleasure to speed you on your way."

The Boar laughed at the gibe, wiping a tear from his eye. "Well said. You are a rare man, Mohammed, a king without a crown or throne. We shall see each other again, I expect, before the city of the enemy."

"Yes." Mohammed nodded at the other quays and wharfs, where thousands of men were in motion, beginning the long process of loading the army of the Sahaba onto the Imperial fleet and the merchantmen the Palmyrenes had summoned. It was a huge effort, for the soldiers had stripped the warehouses and Legion armories of everything they might need. Long lines of wagons and mules crowded the roads into the city as well, hauling food and other supplies and fodder in from the countryside. Detachments of Arab troops placed in garrison throughout the highlands were marching in, too. Mohammed had resolved to sortie forth with every man he could put under arms. "You will have to march swiftly to join us in time. It is a long and weary road from Antioch to Constantinople. If the good god smiles upon us, we will hold the crossing for you."

Shahr-Baraz grinned, running a thick-mailed hand

across the heavy breastplate on his chest. "That will be a sight! It has been a long time since a Persian army crossed the Propontis. I have dreamed of such a day."

"I know," Mohammed said in a wry voice. "Do not tarry."

"We will not!" The Boar nodded fiercely. "Here, brother king, I've a gift for you."

Shahr-Baraz motioned and the grooms led two horses to the King's side. Each was alike as to be a twin: glossy black with long fetlocks and wild manes. There were no markings on them save the whites of their eyes. Even the hooves were coal dark.

"These fellows are from the stable of the Shahanshah, bred to the wind and foaled from the storm. They are my gift to you, to seal our bargain. There are suits of armor, too, for I would not lose my new friend to an errant blow, and blades—Indian steel—finer than any seen in Roman lands! Please, take them; they are yours."

Mohammed raised an eyebrow, hand smoothing his beard. He walked around the horses but he did not touch them. They were powerful creatures, very tall, and they watched him with liquid, intelligent eyes. They looked strong, strong enough to run a day and a night. Strong enough to carry a man in full armor and not tire.

"They are Bactrians," Mohammed said, smiling in delight. "They are very fine."

He ducked down, then stood again. "Ungelded yet. A rich gift, Lord Baraz."

"Will you take them?" The Persian king rubbed his hand across the shoulder of one of the chargers. The horse blew at him and nosed his armored shoulder, looking for an apple or a biscuit.

"No." Mohammed shook his head sadly. "They are a king's gift and I am not a king. Your generosity, sir, does you proud. But I will not take them and I do not mean offense by this. I have a horse, a sword, armor, a helm. I carry them in the name of my city, and I will not dishonor my home by bearing another's gear."

Shahr-Baraz nodded, but Mohammed could see the man was disappointed. The merchant in the Quraysh yearned to take the horses and send them south to stud the horse herds of Mekkah. Such fine animals were very rare. At the same time, he was certain that he should accept no gift, however small, from the Boar.

"Well," said Shahr-Baraz, "I will see you again, not-king, and our enemies will know despair!"

With that, the Boar turned and strode up the gangway into the ship, his men hurrying after. Mohammed watched him go. Then, when the ship had cast off its mooring lines and the longboats were towing it out to sea, he turned away and walked back to the praetorium. Unaccountably, his heart was heavy and he wondered if he had done the right thing.

The wind died at sundown, leaving a limpid, warm night. Mohammed was walking on the terrace of the praetorium, letting darkness wash over him, smelling the sweet scent of hyacinths and whiteflower vine. A trellis covered most of the veranda, supporting a riot of flowers. It was peaceful there, far from the eating hall and the barracks. He stopped, looking out at the nighted city, seeing the pale yellow glow of lamps shining from many windows.

"Lord Mohammed?"

The Quraysh turned, surprised to find anyone on the terrace. A slim figure was seated on a bench, well in shadow. "I am sorry, Zoë, I did not mean to intrude."

"It's nothing," she said. "I'm just hiding."

Mohammed sat down. "Why are you hiding? Do you want to keep hiding by yourself, or can I join you?"

Zoë laughed and the sound was blessedly free of her habitual brittleness. Mohammed wondered, sitting in the warm darkness, if she even visited her aunt's catafalque anymore. Since they had returned from the sea, the girl seemed almost herself. Mohammed did not assume the vit-riolic, insanely angry woman he had first met was the true Zoë. "Do you know why I am Queen?"

Mohammed shook his head *no*.

"I will tell you." Zoë smoothed back her bangs, which had grown overlong and were constantly getting in her face. "My aunt Zenobia was the eldest child of the old king, Hairan. He doted upon her and, when time came to declare an heir, he chose her over his younger son, Vor-odes. My mother, Antonia, was the middle child. Time passed, as it does, and Zenobia became queen of the city. Despite tremendous pressure, she did not marry. Always, she would say to the city fathers that she would marry soon, or next year."

Zoë sighed, and Mohammed heard an echo of despair. "Mama Antonia bore me and tended me, but Auntie Z was always there. When I raced in the city games, she was waiting at the finish line, a crown of laurels in her hands, just for me. When the witch finders said I had this talent, she brought me the finest tutors and teachers. When the call came from the Empire to fight against Persia, Auntie clasped the winged eye on my cloak. She said I was her daughter, even if Antonia had done the hard work."

There was a rustling sound and Zoë unfolded her hands, revealing a golden brooch. In the soft darkness, the metal gleamed with a pale inner light. Mohammed touched the ornament gently, tracing a rimmed eye, double wings and a clasp pin.

"When we set out, she sent an escort of archers with us and bade me hurry home. Later, Mama Antonia sent me a letter—Auntie had issued a will, saying that I was her heir. Vorodes signed too, for he had no desire to be king. He liked hunting and playing too much."

Mohammed folded the girl's hands over the brooch again, shutting out the gleam of light.

"And now?" His voice was soft, befitting her gentle, quiet tone.

"Now I am Queen." Zoë put her hands over her face. "Odenathus is such a . . . man sometimes. He has been busy, writing letters, sending messengers, buying drinks for strangers. He is gathering all of our people, slowly, in fits and starts, but steadily in his Odenathuslike way. There must be thousands of us in the city now. They all want me to be Queen . . . I mean, to rule them. To judge their disputes, to issue writs and edicts . . . I don't know how to do those things."

"I know what you mean." Mohammed's voice was filled with laughter. "Khalid and Odenathus spend too much time together, I think. They are always plotting. Did you know Khalid has a man who writes down everything I say? He says it will be important someday. I wonder . . ."

Zoë nodded, leaning back against the carved wall. Marching soldiers flanked her, passing mutely in the stone. "You are a king, despite what you told that Persian braggart. You rule armies and cities, even nations. You see how Prince Zamanes is—he should be a king himself, yet he defers to you in all things. Ha!" She laughed, a liquid sound. "*You* are a king of kings."

Mohammed snorted, folding his arms over his chest. "Foolishness. Hubris."

Zoë turned, bringing her legs up before her and wrapping arms around her knees. She looked at him in the darkness, barely able to pick out the noble nose or the short, neatly trimmed beard. "You might think him foolish, but this is real. You are a king and make a king's decisions. Do you know why Khalid has that man writing down what you say?"

"So his own place in the histories will be assured, I warrant!" Mohammed sounded vexed.

"No," Zoë said, poking him in the side with a finger. "He calls it the Shari'a—the law—and the lives of your men, of all the tribes and cities who follow you, are guided thereby. Like the Romans, he believes every man should know. the law, so it might direct his life."

"My words? The law? Oh, that is a sure course for confusion!"

"Is it?" Zoë sounded pensive. "Would the Lord of the World, who speaks from the clear air, guide you astray? Shouldn't men, exposed to the revealed desire of the Creator, follow his precepts?"

Hot words on Mohammed's lips were quenched and he put a hand to his chin, thinking. "If they are the words of the Great and the Beneficent One, then yes, man should abide by those strictures, keeping to a straight path. But what if the words this scribe takes down are only *my* words? Then I may speak from my human heart and mind, which may be confusing or misleading. I may be wrong in what I say."

"Are you?" Zoë's hand slipped over his. "I think this power has changed you. I can hear the echo of a mighty voice, even when Mohammed the man is speaking."

Mohammed shook his head, his hand curling into hers. "No. I am not an infallible deity. I am little more than a mirror to reflect the glory of god."

"Hmm." Zoë's nose twitched. "Perhaps."

Then they sat in the quiet darkness for a long time, undisturbed.

The wind shifted again, coming out of the south, hot with the smell of the desert. Almost a month of backbreaking labor had been completed and the army of the Sahaba was, at last, boarding the fleet. Zoë stood on one of the smaller quays in the merchant harbor of Caesarea. A fat-bellied merchantman was tied up, allowing the dockhands to run out a double-wide loading ramp. The Palmyrene ship was painted a sea green with yellow eyes. Zoë had chosen the coaster for its capacious hold. Even as she watched from the shade of a papyrus parasol, fifty men were carefully rolling the catafalque of Zenobia onto the deck of the ship.

The funeral car had sat for weeks in a Palmyrene warehouse, watched over by the Sahaba. Craftsmen labored

over every detail with care, expanding the simple ornamentation added while they had waited in Petra. Plates of
gold and silver covered the sides and the canopy was colored with paints made from crushed jewels. Even the cof-
fin within had been replaced with a thin-walled alabaster
sarcophagus. Zoë had added her own touches, making the
wheels run light and smooth. Khalid donated a pair of
glossy black stallions to draw the catafalque.

It was beautiful and precious and Zoë bit hard on her
thumb, watching the dockhands grunt and strain to roll the
heavy wagon, inch by inch, up the ramp. As the catafalque
moved, slaves walking alongside slid bracing logs behind
the wheels so that it could not break free of the ropes and
crash back to the dock. On the deck, men waited with
hooks that would let the cranes lift it up and lower it into
the hold. Creaking, the wheels topped the ramp and rolled
onto the deck. A dozen men slowed the wagon, bringing
it to rest.

"Oh, this is too much to watch!" Zoë turned away, trying to push thoughts of disaster out of her mind. She
walked along the quay, armor jingling, sword rustling at
her side. Despite a general improvement in her humor, she
had not set aside the silvered helm or the long knives slung
at her waist. The only touch of vanity she allowed herself
was freshly trimmed hair and regular baths. The air of the
port resounded with the creak and groan of wood and ropes
and men loading the last of the equipment and supplies.

She passed a sleek galley, newly flagged with the green
banner of the lord Mohammed. The newly repaired *Jibril*
was a wicked-looking thing, all smooth lines and curving
rails. A hooked prow surmounted its foredeck. A line of
Arabic script ran along the outboard above the oars: *There
is no god but Allah, and Mohammed is his prophet.*

Zoë smiled, for she knew this to be true.

Walking, her boot touched something and she heard it
skitter away, making a jingling sound. Puzzled, she
stopped and searched the ground. After a moment she

found a single earring caught in a crevice between two heavy flagstones. She squatted, one hand on her knee, and carefully worked it loose.

A single black Gerrhaenid pearl, set in gold, gleamed between her fingers. She rose and looked around. There was no one else in sight who might have dropped such a bauble. Pursing her lips in annoyance, Zoë turned it over in her hand, wondering what to do. The dark pearls of the Sinus Persicus were extremely valuable, and the setting and workmanship of this one were exceptional. Zoë had not gone unchanged by her time in the court of Zenobia; she had gained a fine awareness of valuable things.

A horn sounded in the distance, a mournful, wailing sound. It was the signal for the first ships to leave the harbor. She needed to be aboard. Shaking her head at the folly of some women, she put the earring in her right ear, just to keep it safe until she found it a good home. Then she hurried away, her boots jingling on the quay.

A little distance away, on the rear deck of the *Jibril*, Khalid al'Walid raised his sun hat with a thin finger and watched the Queen of Palmyra depart. He smiled, teeth white in the tanned darkness of his face.

"Well," he said to Patik, who was sitting next to him on the deck, carefully oiling a suit of lamellar armor with a rag and an unghent from a small clay bottle, "she has some appreciation of beauty."

The Persian looked up, his long face calm under his short, curly beard. When Khalid had first made his acquaintance, the mercenary had been clean-shaven, but now he was letting it grow out. It promised to be mighty. "You should not play this game. Leave this to the powerful."

As always, Khalid was impressed by the rich tones and cultured voice hiding behind that stoic, even mulish face. "Please, Patik, how will I grow great if I do not emulate those who are?"

The Persian did not respond, turning back to his careful work. Al'Walid wondered if he should have taken the Persian's gifts. *Too late now!* Setting aside these qualms, Khalid leaned back, letting the hat slide down over his face. The weather promised an easy journey to Constantinople and he intended to make the most of it. There would be little rest once they were at grips with the Romans.

◻▣◦(0)◦(0)◦(0)◦(0)◦(0)◦(0)◦(0)◦(0)◦(0)◦(0)◦(0)◦(0)◦(0)◦(0)◦(0)◦(0)▣◻

NEAR PELUSIUM, LOWER EGYPT

)¤(

His camel groaning, Nicholas topped the crest of a long, striated dune. The sand was soft here, driven by a steady wind off the sea, and the creature's splayed, three-toed feet dug into the loose slope.

"Heyup!" Nicholas slapped the camel with a thin cane, making the beast lope down the side of the dune. Weeks of practice kept him in the saddle, though the swaying motion made most of the legionaries ill. Years on the heaving pine deck of a Dansk *drakenship* had given the barbarian a great tolerance for such things. The motion was oddly comforting. Behind him, in an irregular line, the rest of his small command descended the long sweep of the dune. The ground was rockier below, though ahead he could see a line of palms and the spreading green of a canebrake and mud flats. They had come, at last, to the edge of the great delta.

Nicholas wheeled the camel, drawing another *gronk* of outrage, and waited for his companions to join him. Vladimir loped up a moment later. Despite some half-hearted attempts, the Walach had given up on getting the camels to carry him. They shied from his smell and tried to bite or kick. Instead, Vlad's gear rode on one of the pack animals and he jogged alongside the line of march, stripped down to a pair of dark green breeches. His heavy pelt would have been impossibly hot, save for Dwyrin's power.

The Hibernian rode up, cane rod snapping against the flanks of his camel. The young man looked rested and cheerful in his white kaffiyeh and desert robes.

"Pelusium should not be far away," the Hibernian called as he switched his camel's ear. The beast had been trying to bite Nicholas' leg. "Then the channels of the delta— we'd make better time on a ship."

Nicholas nodded. The lad was their Egypt expert. No one else had been there before. "What? Give up these fine friends and their smell and noise and ill-humor?"

Dwyrin smiled lazily, leaning forward on the saddle pommel. "At least these ones aren't attracting flies."

Vlad laughed, squatting on the ground and letting his legs rest. The Walach liked to run, but this heavy sand was hard going for him. He didn't have the advantage of four big splayed feet. "I don't miss the flies or the heat, Dwyrin. I think we'd have shriveled up without your help."

Nicholas knew that was true! Their flight from Aelia Capitolina had veered into rough water once they left the inhabited regions south of the city. A long stretch of barren wasteland separated the southernmost Judean towns from the coast at Gazzah. Beyond the crumbling, half-abandoned port was a worse passage across the top of the Sinai wilderness. There was no water to speak of, and the heat of summer baked the land. By great good luck, the boy recovered from his exertions in the siege before they had ventured out of Berosaba.

"Just doing my job," Dwyrin said, looking out at the cane fields and the blue line of the sea beyond. Flocks of birds were slowly rising and falling over the mud flats, feasting on dark clouds of insects hazing the air. "I'm glad I figured out how to do it. I hate the heat."

The rest of the engineers rode up, making a milling crowd of camels, mules and stubby-shouldered horses.

Sextus and Frontius cantered up to join Nicholas and his little command group.

"*Ave,* centurion!"

"Gentlemen, I think we've come to the end of our journey. If Dwyrin is right, Pelusium is not far ahead through these palms and cane. By rights, there should be a Legion outpost. Hopefully we'll be able to find someone in charge and report in."

The surveyor and the engineer nodded, though they looked a little disappointed.

"We'll be reassigned, then," lamented Sextus. "Parceled out to some other unit."

"Scattered to the winds," Frontius complained. "Like so much straw on the threshing floor."

They both sighed. Frontius jerked his head at Dwyrin. "Centurion, can we keep the lad on?"

"I think not," Nicholas growled. "We're sticking together. It's . . . ah . . ." He grinned. "It's cooler."

Sextus groaned and put his hands over his eyes. Frontius just shook his head.

"Centurion!" One of the surveyors was pointing towards the sea. Nicholas turned, shading his eyes. There were riders there, silhouetted against the sparkling blue waters. They seemed to be hurrying towards the palms. As they moved, there was a slow rippling across the mud flats and a great cloud of flamingos rose up, shifting and sparkling in the sun. The birds had been feasting amongst the shellfish in the muddy pools.

"Oh, that is fine." Nicholas raised his hand to signal the men. "We've been seen and the blind fools are sure to think we're bandits or the whole Arab army! Come on, let's go find the sentry pickets."

With another chorus of groans and bleats from the camels and some whickering from the horses, the column shook itself out and ambled across the sandy scrubland, heading for the road running beside the sea. They kept away from the coastal road during their long journey, fearing possible Arab patrols. Now they were forced to the coast by the mud and bogs and quicksand that sprawled out from the easternmost arm of the Nile.

Dwyrin took up his accustomed place at the middle of the group, lazing in the saddle, attention only partially focused on the camel. The rest of his effort, such as it was, spun slowly in the hidden world, a faint purple disk around the entire group. The hair-thin layer passed heat out and cooler air in. Too, above the column, it diffused the rays of the sun, providing a veneer of shade for the men riding below. The strength to reflect the sun came from the air itself as it calmed and grew cool. Flies and other insects were unable to penetrate the barrier, providing welcome relief from their biting and buzzing.

The Hibernian was heartened by the speed of his recovery from the effort of the siege. It seemed to him that his core self, that indefinable mote that spun and glowed at his heart, was growing stronger. He could shrug off the illusions and phantasms once tormenting him. A great sense of focus and solidity had come upon him as they crossed the desert. The emptiness let his mind find strength. His skill, though still raw, was growing. Over any kind of heat or flame, he wielded swift and encompassing power. Dwyrin thought of his friends and was glad that he had not killed Odenathus in their struggle.

The row of palms and waving green cane grew closer.

"Halt! *Quo vaditis?*"

Nicholas let his camel amble to a stop, a hand raised in greeting. The line of palms disguised a shallow, meandering channel filled with saltbush and waxy-leafed scrub. Beyond the stream, a high bank of black soil led under more date palms to a crumbling brick building. The road in front of the customhouse was half buried in sand. Nicholas hadn't expected there to be much here, so he wasn't disappointed by the dilapidated buildings.

The legionaries appearing out of the brush, swords

bared, were a different matter. It took Nicholas a moment to realize what was wrong, but by the time that two iron spear points were pressed against his chest, he raised both hands. The grim-faced men in plumed helmets and shining lorica were Western troops, not Eastern. It was disorienting, since Egypt was an Eastern province.

"Whoa, there, lads! I'm Nicholas of Roskilde, centurion of the Fourth Engineers cohort of the First Minerva . . . you can put the pointy sticks away."

Behind Nicholas, the rest of the column came to a halt, surrounded by more soldiers in the brush and among the palms. Despite the tension in the air, none of the men around the column seemed to have noticed the clouds of flies under the palms were suddenly gone, or the steady drop in air temperature. Dwyrin, Sextus and Frontius pushed their way up to the head of the line.

"The First Minerva?" The Western commander stomped up to Nicholas' camel, glaring suspiciously. The man was sweating heavily. "You're a little lost, I think."

Sextus doffed his straw hat and clambered down off the horse.

"We were loaned out to the Easterners," the surveyor said. "Barely got out of Judea alive."

The Western centurion glowered at the rest of the column, then tugged absently at his chin strap. "You're the first men down this road in weeks. Been mighty quiet."

"Yes," Nicholas said, leaning forward on his saddle pommel. "The Arab army is in Gazzah, I imagine. No one's going to come down the road except them now."

"Well," the centurion said, looking sour, "you lot look Roman enough. I've orders to take anyone who comes out of the desert to the legate, so you'd better hop along. I'll get my horse."

Nicholas sat back and exchanged a bemused glance with the others. The centurion did have a horse, a nag with a mottled face, but it got along well enough and didn't mind the camels. The rest of the Western troops in the scrubby trees disappeared again and the column, after some jostling about, managed to get moving.

For a mile or two past the customhouse the land was thick with stands of green cane and muddy pools. The road was still in disrepair, blown with sand and dangerous with loose paving stones. Slender trees grew thick on the banks of the channels, hiding mottled green logs sleeping in the hot sun. Gleaming white cranes stepped through the water, hunting for frogs. Then, after passing through a belt of tall, willowy trees, the column passed under an ancient archway flanked by huge sandstone statues of men with tapering beards. This was the first time Nicholas had seen the detritus of the ancients. Dwyrin ignored the pharaohs, chewing on a piece of flatbread, but the centurion craned his neck to look up at them as they passed. Even the stone was cracked and chipped, dilapidated, oozing hoary age.

Beyond the archway, everything changed.

Great plumes of dust rose from a land crawling with men. Suddenly, the road was clear and wide, lined with columns of workers trudging along under bundles of freshly cut stakes. Roman soldiers were everywhere, directing traffic and keeping a close eye on thousands of fellaheen digging under the blazing sun. The Western centurion urged his mount onwards and Nicholas had to swat his camel hard to get it to keep pace. Winding their way through crowds of laborers hauling dirt up out of a dry river channel, Nicholas and his men passed over a great wooden bridge.

The northerner looked down in awe at the river bottom. It was swarming with workers, digging furiously with mattocks and spades. A dark haze buzzed and drifted over the riverbed—flies and darting shapes of thousands of small brown birds preying upon them. Endless lines of brown men in white loincloths bent under the effort of hauling thick black dirt out of the excavation and up a series of ramps to the western side of the river. Even the bridge, obviously ancient, had been torn down to huge stone plugs on the riverbed. The ancient stone span had been replaced by a wooden road.

Upstream, past clouds of slowly rising yellow dust, the sloping face of a dam filled the channel.

"What is happening?"

The Western centurion looked back, grinning. "The legate likes to dig!"

They trotted down off the bridge, through another decaying triumphal arch and onto a crowded road. On this side of the dry river, dirt was rising into a sloping berm running in either direction as far as the eye could see. It too swarmed with brown men and soldiers. In some places, the top of the long wall was finished and Nicholas made out stonemasons and carpenters busily erecting a wall of fired mud-brick. Below the parapet, lines of fellaheen worked, pounding stakes into the outer face with mallets. The sky ahead was dark with smoke, rising from hundreds of brick pits.

An opening in the berm, shored up with massive stone blocks, let them through the barrier. Behind the sloping wall there was a half-mile-wide area stripped clear of brush and trees. The rear face of the berm was sharp and built up with a fighting platform and packed-earth ramps leading up to the walkway. Ahead of them, they saw the edge of a second river channel. Here there was less activity and another wooden bridge. As before, the roadway had been torn down to the pilings, though the water was high, rushing past in a brown flood. Western soldiers manned a pair of towers on the far side. A second wall of packed earth rose up at the water's edge.

Lines of camels and mules passed through the gates, carrying bundles of wicker, straw and cane. Nicholas and his escort waited for a dozen grains while the caravan passed by.

"This channel is wet," Nicholas remarked to the centurion. "Is the work finished here?"

"Not started yet," the Western officer grumbled. The man made a shooing motion in front of his face, though no flies had bothered him for over an hour. Nicholas assumed the motion had become automatic. At the edge of the invisible barrier riding around Dwyrin, little drifts of dead flies were piling up while Nicholas watched the camels and mules pass. Now the caravan was laden with fresh bricks wrapped in straw.

"The dam isn't done for this section yet." The centurion pointed off to the south.

Nicholas shaded his eyes, squinting, and made out—two or three miles away—a low ridge of earth and stone being built across the channel of the river. Like the river bottom they had passed, the levy swarmed with men, visible at this distance only as a rippling motion on the great mound of earth.

"They need to finish dredging the first channel," the Western officer continued. "Then they'll divert this channel into that one and close this dam. Then everyone will fall back here and finish this wall."

Nicholas looked north along the line of the berm and saw that it only ran a quarter-mile and then petered out. Obviously the bridge crossing needed to be defended first. "How long has all this taken?"

The Western officer grinned. "We've only been under way for six weeks. Not bad, eh? That's what you get from His Worship! Swift action. Come on."

The last of the mules passed and the column wound its way through the gate. A mile ahead, Nicholas could see the outskirts of a town and rising above it, squat and ugly as all sin, a whitewashed brick fortress hard on the sea. Banners and flags flapped in a desultory breeze, but they were obscured by the reek and fume of fires burning in the flat between the last bridge and the town. A huge camp sprawled in all directions. The ground on either side of the road fell away, gouged out for brick pits. Between the bowl-shaped excavations there were wilted fields of corn and onions. Legionaries and fellaheen passed in the opposite direction in a steady stream. Their progress slowed.

It was worse in the camp. Nicholas recognized the general outline of a traditional Legion encampment, but the tent city that housed the workers sprawled riotously in thickets of dirty tan tents. The brick-surfaced road was clogged with people coming and going. It was worse in the dust and mud off the highway. Nicholas schooled himself to patience, closing his nostrils against the humid stink of thousands of unwashed bodies, dung, flies, oil, smoke from green wood and the stench of bricks drying in the sun. Slowly, the walls of the fortress rose up, closer and closer.

Inside Pelusium, the crowds thinned, replaced by grim-faced couriers and legionaries on every corner. It seemed the city had been emptied of citizens, everyone turned out for billets and workshops. Still riding, Nicholas passed a long, low building. Through the open windows, he saw rows and rows of women squatting on the floor, splitting marsh cane for wicker and weaving it into mats.

"We use it to stabilize the face of the wall," the centurion commented. "Or to make brick forms. Need a lot of it."

At the center of the town was a plaza serving mainly to frame a giant gate into the fortress. The gate was flanked by huge round pillars and a flat, squared-off roof. Carved into the walls of the gate were figures of men and gods and tall ibis. Both doors were chocked open by column roundels and guarded by a full cohort of Western troops. The standards and battle emblems of four legions hung above the portal.

Nicholas whistled, seeing that two of the ensigns were brand-new, lacking the metal plaques depicting famous victories. It was strange to see the bronze eagles shining new and fresh in the sun, without the nicks and patina of age that marked their fellows. The other standards did show their age, though, and Sextus slapped his thigh in delight.

"Frontius, my friend, we've come home! I thought I saw Scortius directing the workers on the first bridge. Centurion . . ." Sextus pointed, drawing Nicholas' attention. "That's the standard of the First, by the gods, our own blessed Minerva, may she watch over us!"

Nicholas smiled at the good humor in the faces of the engineers. They would have quite a tale to tell to their comrades when they were reunited.

"Dismount and follow me, centurion." The Western officer swung off his nag and led them through a crowd of slaves waiting inside the fortress gate. Nicholas followed, making sure that Vladimir and Dwyrin were right at his side. He didn't want to lose track of them in this mob. Following the centurion, they crossed a yard of sun-baked brick and entered another monumental gate, this one guarded by twin sphinxes painted as lions. White plaster walls rose up behind them, etched with long rows of writing. Nicholas could not read the signs, but he didn't care. Sextus and Frontius, without an invitation, hurried to join them.

The centurion pushed open a door of polished cedar twice the height of a man and they entered a long, cool room. It was open on two sides, to the north and west, giving a fabulous view of the green fields of the delta and the sea. An arm of the ancient Nile lay alongside Pelusium and from the top of the fortress, broad brown water could be seen, rolling slowly north to the sea. High above the fetid stink of the town, the room was airy and comfortable. A breeze rustled through the windows. The rest of the chamber was cluttered with long tables, a mismatched collection of chairs and numerous staff officers, sitting and writing.

"Legate, *ave!*" The Western officer saluted a tall redheaded man standing over the largest table. Nicholas saluted as well, but said nothing. An immensely detailed map covered the big table. Even from his poor angle, Nicholas could make out the two channels they had crossed and the main river. He guessed, from the profusion of marks, that three lines of defense were being prepared.

"Centurion?" The redheaded man looked up, square face framed by a rich, curly beard. Like the officers hunched over the tables, he was wearing a segmented breastplate of hooked iron bands over a red tunic. A pleated kilt almost reached his knees, doing little to disguise powerful thighs and thick calves. "What news?"

"A cohort of the Fourth Engineers of the First has come in from the desert, sir. This is their commander, Nicholas of Roskilde. You wanted to see anyone from the East, quick as may be."

Nick stepped forward and made a half-bow to the man. The legate smiled, his whole face lighting up, and reached out a thick hand, clasping Nicholas' wrist. "Well met, then! You've come from Judea?"

"Yes, sir. I'm an Eastern officer, but my men are Western. This is Vladimir, my aide, and Dwyrin, our thaumaturge, and these fellows are—"

"Sextus and Frontius," finished the legate, grinning like a fool. The two engineers saluted sharply, sunburned faces wreathed with unexpected smiles. "I know them from when I commanded the First myself. Good to see you, lads. I'm glad you're not dead!"

"Not a chance, Your Worship!" Sextus jabbed at Nicholas with his thumb. "Centurion wouldn't hear of it! Bit of a close shave, though."

"True," Frontius interjected, rubbing his chin. "Nary a whisker left!"

The redheaded man shook a thick finger at Sextus. "None of that 'Your Worship' business, Sextus. You know I hate it."

"Your 'Worship'?" Nicholas said, feeling peeved at being left out of the joke. The man turned back to him, nodding.

"Sorry, centurion. I am Aurelian Atreus, Caesar of the Western Empire and commanding legate of the expeditionary forces in Egypt. Come, sit and tell me what you've seen and done. Someone will bring us something to eat, I think."

Aurelian did not lie, and a large and highly spiced lunch was laid out for them. Nicholas found the Western prince forthright and blunt. It took a long time to relate everything that had happened since he had set foot on Judean soil, but when Nicholas was done, Aurelian was nodding to himself as if much once hidden had been revealed.

"These Arabs are well equipped with siege equipment, then?"

Nicholas, Sextus and Frontius all nodded in agreement. Dwyrin and Vladimir had fallen asleep in the cool room, stuffed full, but the three officers remained alert and focused. Being interviewed by a prince of the Empire had an invigorating effect. Two scribes joined them, quietly writing down everything they said.

"Would you say that they've fielded a real army, then?" The Prince was curious, watching Nicholas with interest. "Regular camps, siege works, infantry and cavalry—thaumaturges to support their efforts?"

"Yes, sir. It's very clear they are not some raiding band, or even rebellious militia. They have clever commanders who adjust to circumstance and attack weakness with strength."

Aurelian nodded, rubbing a fist against his chin. His eyes narrowed. "You're thinking of the way they caught out the boy, sending phantoms against him."

"Yes," Nicholas answered. "Whoever is in command of the army that rooted us out of Capitolina is a canny fellow—he knew he couldn't get in the front door, so he made sure we were busy watching it while he unlocked the back."

"Good." Aurelian smiled, rubbing his hands together.

"You've seen our little earthworks effort, then?"

"I have." Nicholas sounded impressed because he was. The massive effort to fortify the approaches to Pelusium beggared anything he had ever seen the Eastern army attempt. There was a great deal of professional rivalry between the two armies, though from everything Nicholas had seen since taking service with the Eastern Empire, the Western Legions were far superior in logistics, planning and discipline. Very few of the Eastern officers had the technical skill to direct such a project. None of their troops would have been willing to dig, either, but that had always been a foundation of the Western army, even in the days of the Republic. "I doubt they will be able to get through."

"I know." Aurelian sprang up, seemingly filled with limitless energy. "I don't expect them to, really. I just want them to go around for that back door, but the way I want. Plus, it gets my men in shape. Too many of them are recruits, so we alternate days of drill, marching and digging."

Nicholas swallowed a laugh, but the Prince caught his expression and grinned back.

"No, centurion, I'm not a popular commander right now. They hate me, I'd guess, but they have to get used to it. Our desertion rate is high, but most come back after a week or so. Men don't really like to leave, once they've been in the Legion awhile. The citizens outside"—he pointed out the window at the town and the fields beyond the river—"don't understand us so well."

"Lord Aurelian? What happens to us?" Sextus got up and took a parade rest, feet wide, hands clasped behind his back. The Prince nodded at him, acknowledging the question.

"Well, I'm keeping you and your cohort here, Sextus. I have a project in the south, down by the Reed Sea, that will be to your liking. I've been putting it off because my other surveyors and engineers were busy up here with the diversion channels and the dams. You'll have a few days to rest up the men and get your gear sorted out—I'd guess you had to abandon your wagons and tools in Aelia?"

"True, sir!" Sextus and Frontius both groaned, shaking their heads in dismay.

"Better your heads stay on your necks," Aurelian growled. "Those can't be replaced."

"And us, sir?" Nicholas straightened too, though he had never been drilled in the various forms used by the Western troops. "Do you have a place for us?"

"I do." Aurelian sighed, looking over the three of them. "But you're Eastern property, according to the agreement between the two emperors. I'll have to put you on the next courier boat for Constantinople, though I'd rather keep you. You seem a man with a good head, Nicholas, and I have few enough of them under my command. Your young friend would be a boon, too, but he is strictly off limits."

"Sir?"

Aurelian grimaced, but spread his hands wide. "Heraclius and my brother struck a deal last year, where Egypt would be placed under Western administration so that Eastern troops, clerks and staff could be moved east into Persia to form the core of a new administration in the captured provinces. Under the terms, the taxes are split half and half, but all military personnel of Eastern origin are remanded to the offices in Constantinople. Most everyone left last fall, but you're here now and you're Eastern. A pity."

Nicholas nodded in understanding, though he was disappointed. Dwyrin had been telling him about the vast monuments and temples of the land along the river. Nicholas had already seen more of Constantinople than he had ever wanted to see. The prospect of spending some time amongst the tombs and dead cities of this ancient land had intrigued him.

"Thank you, sir. I appreciate your candor and your hospitality. The pickled eels were particularly good."

"Aren't they? My brother always complains about my taste, but everything's better with garlic, I say."

Nicholas smiled, delighted to find the Prince a man after his own heart.

◻-[0]-[0]-[0]-[0]-[0]-[0]-[0]-[0]-[0]-[0]-[0]-[0]-[0]-[0]-[0]-[0]-[0]-[0]-◻

THE FLAVIAN, ROMA MATER

)◻(

C hunk-chunk-chunk-chunk.

Wheels rattled and the roof above Thyatis' head split open, flooding the stone shaft with sunlight. The platform beneath her feet shuddered and creaked as it rose up, iron pulleys squeaking. Sound flooded the shaft as she ascended, a booming, rolling roar that made the air shudder. Thyatis flexed her arms and legs, seeing them shine with oil, rolling back and forth on the balls of her feet. She knew what made the sound and it filled her with an unexpected thrill. She checked the twine tying back her hair, the snugness of her loincloth and breast band.

Sunlight touched the crown of her head and then she rose through the floor of the arena at the heart of the Flavian. The wooden doors covering the elevator fell back onto the sand. Her sudden appearance in the center of the great oval was greeted with a low roar of applause. Thyatis blinked in the sunlight. It was early and only half of the marble seats were filled. Still, tens of thousands clapped hands to shoulders as the platform rattled to a halt. She raised her hand, greeting the crowd.

Jeers and shouts met her gesture. Thyatis turned, surveying the arena. All around her other trapdoors were swinging open. She stepped away from the platform.

The nearest elevator clanked to a halt and a woman in rags stood up, staring around in horror. Thyatis raised an eyebrow, seeing that the next platform had also stopped. This one deposited a very large, angry-looking lion. It was a magnificent beast, tall as a woman at the shoulder, with a heavy dark mane and tawny pelt. The lion was blinking in the sun, puzzled by the noise. *Lions again,* she thought, becoming very still. *But no high grass!*

At a glance, she guessed there were sixteen women and sixteen beasts; more lions; a handful of bears; some scrawny leopards and a pack of wild dogs. She assumed, watching the animals stare around, growling and yipping, they had been starved, perhaps baited with human blood. Diana grinned in relief, seeing an elevator to her left had delivered a spear. Moving softly to avoid drawing the attention of the angry black bear just beyond, she stepped to the weapon and picked it up. It felt good in her hands, a smooth ashwood shaft tipped with eight inches of polished iron.

A great shout echoed from the walls of the Flavian, distracting Maxian for a moment. He was pacing along a wooden roof circling the top of the arena. The roof was forty feet wide and served as a preparation area for the big canvas sails that shaded the seats below. The Prince stepped to the edge, one booted foot on the lip, and looked down onto an oval of sand a hundred and forty-eight feet below. Black dots ran on the sand, chased by other black dots. The crowd was howling with laughter. To Maxian, his hair blown sideways by the breeze, it sounded like the surf on a rocky shore.

All of the people in the seats seemed very small and insignificant, like ants. Maxian turned away and resumed his measured pacing. The sailors handling the canvas awning ignored him. Some of Gaius Julius' men followed him at a distance, keeping watch. The old Roman had begun to accumulate retired soldiers and barbarian mercenaries. Such men were easy to find in Rome. Maxian did not think he needed bodyguards, but Gaius ignored his protests.

The Prince began a soft chant, a little mnemonic to keep pace as he measured the distance around the oval. As he walked, he dropped tiny copper beads onto the planks, grinding them under his heel to fix them in place.

Maxian ignored the heat and the noise of the crowd. The fragile pattern around the people in the stands was far more important. It was almost drowned by the shuddering power bound into the stone, sand and wood of the building. Bound by centuries of blood sacrifice.

The black-maned lion crashed to earth, throwing down one of the running women. Her scream choked off as powerful jaws bit through her neck, splintering bone. Blood spattered across the white sand and the lion roared in anger, shaking the suddenly limp body. It didn't understand why the creature that smelled so good tasted so bad. The corpse flew away and the lion turned, blazing yellow eyes blinking.

Thyatis sprinted in, shouting. Blood streaked her side, oozing from four long parallel cuts left by a leopard's claw. The spear, slick with blood, was in her hands. Snarling, the lion reared, batting at her with giant paws. The spear punched into its chest, ashwood flexing with the blow, and Thyatis gritted her teeth, feeling the point grind across bone and then slip wetly between ribs. The lion screamed, a long wail of pain, and staggered aside. The spear was wrenched from her hands as the beast toppled over.

The lion thrashed on the ground, blood gouting from the wound. As it rolled over, the spear broke, drawing another howl of anguish. The lion staggered up, then fell over on one side, panting heavily. Thyatis wiped sweat from her bow, continuing to chant. With each kill, she urged the spirits of the dead on, to placate the gods and grant her friends swift passage into the golden fields beyond the dark river.

"Help me!" A cry drew her attention. Thyatis turned,

seeing the pack of wild dogs circling closer, driving a woman in a brief tunic towards her. The woman's skin was dark as fine ebony and she had snatched up a sword. She held it in both hands, keeping it between herself and the nearest dog. The pack was crouching low, slinking over the sand, ready to dart in and catch her ankle or knee in sharp teeth. Thyatis looked around, ignoring the woman.

"Please, help me!"

Three of the female lions were still alive and had found one another. Now they were hunting in a pack, confused by the thick smells and the massive sound that reverberated from the amphitheater walls. In the stands, the matinee crowd was in a cheerful mood. They had waited a long time to see the games again, and the usual sad spectacle of slaves or criminals driven before the beasts was proving unexpectedly amusing. The bears and leopards were dead, along with most of the women. Only Thyatis and the Nubian were left.

"Give me the sword," Thyatis shouted, rushing the nearest dog. The Nubian looked wildly over her shoulder, then tossed the blade—a Legion-issue gladius—to the redheaded woman. Thyatis caught it out of the air in a deft motion, then leapt sideways. The first dog bolted back from her movement, but the pack itself turned, yelping. The gladius slashed down, shearing through the muzzle of the nearest dog. It yelped, then staggered away, pawing at its ruined nose. The others bolted, but Thyatis was quick, catching the slowest dog and hamstringing it. Crying mournfully, the dog tried to drag itself away, but the gladius punched down, severing its spine.

The Nubian woman backed up, finding a spear on the ground. Thyatis darted towards her. The pack circled again, yipping in high-pitched anger.

"Spear," Thyatis barked and the Nubian woman threw her the weapon. It was lighter than the one she had lost in the lion, but it would do. The gladius slipped into the side of her loincloth, pressing tight against oil-slick skin.

Just after dawn, the guards had hustled Diana out of her cell and into the baths at the northern end of the Flavian. Two slaves had scrubbed her down, even washing her hair with an eye-stinging soap. Thyatis hadn't minded the rough treatment—it had been weeks since she had been clean. When they oiled her, she was alarmed. The oil did not have the usual sweet, lemony scent dispensed in the baths and gymnasiums of the city. It was rank and musky, like a cat in heat.

"Keep behind me." Thyatis advanced on the dogs, keeping the three lionesses in her field of vision. They were tearing at a dead body sixty feet away, growling and snapping at the air. The dogs were a greater concern in this frozen instant of time. "Pick up any weapon you can."

The Nubian nodded, gulping, but controlling her fear.

Another roar of delight rose up from below as Maxian completed his circuit. He knelt, hands gentle on either side of the copper bead. Each metal orb had been drawn from the same ingot, spun in heated air and formed into equal weights. That had not really been a sorcerer's job, but being able to manipulate temperature made it very easy. The Prince touched a finger to the bead and felt the chiming echo of its siblings. Maxian let the shape and pattern of the Flavian take shape in his thought.

The amphitheater loomed over the city, instantly recognizable. For the tens of thousands of barbarians and foreigners passing through the Imperial capital each year, it was a symbol of the Empire. More, it stood at the middle of the city, square between four of the seven hills. Once, in an earlier age, the focal point of Nero's Golden House had rested here. Now it was the heart of urban Rome.

Maxian, feeling the play of power in the building, knew it for the heart of the Empire as well. His brother Galen might be the symbol of the state, the living divine emperor, but this place was the keystone of the pattern sustaining the Empire itself.

In every town and city throughout the Empire, there were replicas of this arena. The ceremonies that acclaimed the Empire, the Senate, the people, the city, were conducted here and there, like and like. In all those places the power and majesty of Rome were made flesh, manifest and unavoidable. Here, on the white sand, the lifeblood of criminals and traitors was spilled. There, in the provinces, the amphitheater was Rome. Only citizens could sit in the marble seats, enjoying the games, watching barbarian slaves and wild animals driven to their destruction. In each death, the glory of the state was reinforced and the triumph of civilization over barbarism reaffirmed.

The Prince breathed out slowly, letting his mind settle. This was something he had never attempted before, an act of such a delicate nature that he put aside the humming power flowing within him, part and parcel of his sinew and bone, since Vesuvius. The constant muttering and whispering were shut away. Bit by bit, carefully, he began to disassemble the matrices and forms protecting his living body from the onslaught of the Oath.

There were only four dogs left and they slunk away, growling.

"Ready with another spear," Thyatis called over her shoulder.

"Ready!" The Nubian woman had a good arm. It made everything much easier.

Thyatis sprinted at the dogs, shrieking. The sound echoed back at her from the marble wall circling the arena floor. The dogs had had enough and they bolted, yelping in fear. She turned her body, still running, and threw in a single, graceful motion. The spear plunged into the body of the largest dog with a gelid *slap*. Howling in pain, the dog crashed to the ground. It tried to rise, whining and licking at the blood welling up from matted fur.

Turning, Thyatis caught the second spear from the air. She grinned at the Nubian woman, getting a pale grimace in return. Then Thyatis froze, the spear half raised. The lionesses were padding up behind the Nubian, heads low, tongues tasting the air. The black woman froze as well, seeing Thyatis pause.

"Lie down, slowly." Thyatis found her footing, spear at her shoulder.

The first lioness bolted forward in complete silence, haunches and paws blurring over the sand. Thyatis felt her nostrils flare. Muscles burning with effort, she ran forward, the spear firmly held at her waist.

The Nubian woman pressed herself to the sand, hands curled over her neck.

Pale shades of blue faded from the air with the last of Maxian's shield. He sat, legs crossed, at the southern edge of the amphitheater, high above the Imperial box. Far below, his brother was attending the games, sitting in regal splendor under a crimson canopy, his wife, Helena, doubtless at his side. Maxian calmed his thoughts and let physical sensation flow away. It was very difficult to remain still, to hold an image of a quiet pool foremost in his mind. He strove to banish all intent from himself.

The power of the Oath curdled around him, shimmering darkly in the wooden planks, in the marble statues of the gods, in grains of sand far below. A tendril, rich with destruction, flowed across him. The Prince struggled to keep the pool calm and serene. Flight or resistance would mean destruction in the instant it would take to raise his wards and barriers. He lay open to the power of the Oath, here in the very crucible. It lapped up against him, flowed over him.

It was like ice, freezing and cold, a perfect lattice of forms admitting no deviation.

Maxian exhaled, slowly and evenly, and let death enter him with a drawing breath.

Krista, in her desperate attempt to destroy him, had shown him a glimpse of the way. Though she had strug-

gled against the Oath in his company, though she had been
an enemy of the mindless power, she had escaped destruction. She had seen a road to survival where he had not.
Fleeing from him in his exile at Ottaviano, she had embraced the dark power, vowing Maxian's destruction. A
cancer it sought to drive from the body of the Empire.
Maxian had laughed, realizing his earliest diagnosis had
been correct in all but one critical element.

The Oath was not an infection upon the body of the
state and the people. He was.

Sand scattered away as Thyatis crashed to the ground. She
cried out, pain jolting through her side. The lioness bit
down, claws raking the sand for traction. Gasping, Thyatis
managed to wedge the haft of the spear into the beast's
mouth. Five-inch fangs sheared past, inches from her face,
grinding at the wood. She tried to roll, but the lion had
her thigh pinned. Frantic, knowing the huntress would rake
with a hind leg at any moment, Thyatis stabbed at the
beast's eye with her right hand. It turned away, yowling,
and she managed to roll free. The lioness spat out the
spear, snarling, tail lashing furiously. Thyatis scuttled back
and her foot ran into the Nubian girl's prostrate form.

"Weapon!" Thyatis hissed, scrabbling behind her. The
girl pushed something hilted into her hand. The lioness
shook her head, then padded to the right. The other two
lions were circling outside her arc of motion. Sweating
now, heart racing in her chest, Thyatis turned as well, digging her feet in, trying to find purchase in the sand. The
lioness doubled back, yowling, and Thyatis checked the
heft of the blade in her hand. It was a large, single-bladed
knife.

Delightful.

The lioness put its head low, tail lashing, eyes burning
with rage. Thyatis went still, poised, waiting for the charge
or leap. In a corner of her mind, her sense of smell told
her the lioness thought she was a rival in heat, come to

steal her mate. A flicker of sadness passed through her; black-mane must have been the male of the pride. His life was spilling out on the white sand a hundred feet away.

The lioness leapt, a blur of motion, but Thyatis was ready. She twisted, taking the lion's charge on her moving arm. Her fist caught a ruff of fur at the neck and then she threw her own strength into the movement. The lion catapulted over, yowling in surprise, and slammed onto the sand with a *crunch*. Thyatis staggered, her arm burning with effort. Her teachers in the Open-Hand Way would be disgusted, her putting her own energy into the throw, but . . .

The smaller of the other two lions charged in, fangs bared, biting at her neck. Thyatis' right forearm ground into the animal's neck, blocking it away from her head. The knife in her left hand flashed and then blood spattered as it sank into the lioness's shoulder. Thyatis staggered back, pressed by the beast's weight, striking again and again. The lioness yowled and leapt up, rear legs lashing out. Thyatis screamed, feeling her right thigh split open under razor-sharp yellow talons. Furious rage boiled up in her and she grappled as they rolled on the ground. Steel turned crimson as the blade stabbed, again and again, into the lion's chest. Thyatis suddenly found herself on top of the lioness and ground the knife down with both hands on the hilt.

A huge, flat paw slammed into the side of her head, throwing her onto the ground. Blinking blood and sweat from her eyes, Thyatis rolled up, knife clenched in her hand. Blood covered her whole torso and flew from her hair. The young lioness was making a horrible bubbling sound, trying to yowl in fury, but her throat was torn out. Blood spilled onto the sand with each breath. Swaying, the lioness tried to move forward, but fell, the fire in the yellow eyes dimming like a fading lamp.

"Here." The Nubian girl pressed a spear into Thyatis' hand, her face a cold mask. "Finish her. They shouldn't suffer like this."

Thyatis took the spear and ran forward, lightly, her sandals slapping on the sand.

Above her, in the stands, the crowd cheered wildly, sun hats held aloft. This was the best show they'd seen all year.

Thyatis thrust the spear with all her strength, pinning the dying lioness to the ground. Iron grated on sand. A last spark of life guttered in the lambent eyes and then it was gone. Turning, blood and sweat streaming from her limbs, Diana felt a giddy rush of relief. The other lions slunk away. Attendants in black tunics advanced from iron-gated doorways set into the wall. They would kill or capture the remaining animals.

Sound washed over her as Thyatis raised the spear in salute to the Emperor and the crowd. They were clapping and cheering.

For you, my friends, find these gifts in the cold darkness, let this victory guide you, light your path in the dead world. O my friends, find the golden fields heavy with wheat. Drink deep of this life, sweet as wine.

Sweat purled from Maxian's forehead, pooling in the cavity of his throat and shoulders. His shirt was sticky, clinging to his wiry torso. Yet, he lived and breathed and found himself suspended in an ocean of darkness. His balance was a delicate thing, keeping his perception alive, retaining his ability to flex power and alter the world. He struggled to blend into the pattern. The Oath was all around him, in him, pervading all things.

I am not an enemy, he whispered into the darkness. *I am a friend. A friend.*

He had not been annihilated. Indeed, it seemed that he floated in darkness, carried along with so many other patterns and forms. The Prince breathed slower, finding a welcome sense of relief in the balance.

I am still alive.

He opened his eyes. The sun was sliding down into the west. He wiped sweat from his eyes and rose, almost stumbling. It was draining to do nothing in this way. One of the guardsmen approached.

"Bring me wine and something to eat." Maxian was startled by the raspy sound of his voice.

"Of course, lord." The man hurried off.

Maxian sat back down, his arms trembling. "Whooo . . ." He grinned, then smoothed back his hair. Salt stung his eyes, but he felt elevated, free.

In the Imperial box, under the shade of a large canopy, the Empress Helena looked up from her letter. Though the Emperor had to sit and observe the games, reacting with the crowd, indicating his pleasure or displeasure, the Empress was free to curl up in a large wicker chair. Some soft pillows were wedged behind her back and neck. Her attention had been drawn by a change in the sound of the audience. The bowl shape of the amphitheater funneled sound into the Imperial box, magnifying it as if it were the mouth of a horn.

Helena craned her white neck, looking out onto the sand. The first battle was done, some foolishness of wild beasts and slaves. One eyebrow, tinted with antimony and carefully shaped by the application of small golden tweezers, rose in surprise. The victors were a pair of women, one dark, one light. It seemed the animals had been defeated. This was unusual. Slaves and criminals rarely lasted long against the beasts. Against the professionals—the *venatores*—half-starved animals rarely triumphed. The two victors approached the Imperial box, herded forward by attendants in black robes and grotesque gray masks. The redheaded woman reluctantly yielded up a knife, a sword and a bloody spear, throwing them on the ground.

Galen rose, sighing, heavy robes rustling. He stepped to the edge of the Imperial box, taking his time, making sure that everyone in the huge building could see and hear him. As he did so the murmur of the crowd fell away into silence. The matter of the prize monies and the palm branches was of considerable interest to the crowd. Helena sat up as well.

"We have all waited for this day." The Emperor's words carried in the silence. The design of the amphitheater made his voice audible even in the highest seats. "I know many of you have been impatient for these games, fearing the spirits of the dead would take their displeasure out upon those who still live."

A low rumble came back in response. Everyone in the city had expressed their opinion, at one time or another, of the Emperor's delay, usually in unflattering terms. Now that the games had begun, ushered in by a fabulous parade and three days of feasting on the Imperial ticket, the mood of the people had mellowed.

"It is my belief," Galen continued, raising his voice slightly, "that something should be done well if it is to be done. Excellence in such things takes time. The people of Rome deserve the best games that can be provided. Are the citizens of this great city not the finest in the world, deserving of the best in all things?"

A cheer rose, echoing from the statues on the highest level, reverberating from the encircling wall and the huge canvas sails now run out to shade the northern side of the amphitheater. More and more people had entered the Flavian as the day progressed and now it was near capacity. Everyone liked to hear how important they were and how much the Emperor cared to put on a spectacular show.

"The portents are good," Galen declaimed, "and the first fights auspicious! Let these two brave Amazons come forward for their reward!"

The Charon-masked attendants motioned for the red-headed woman and the Nubian girl to approach the Imperial box. They did so, but seeemed paralyzed by fear. Helena frowned, seeing the Gaulish woman was staring down at the sand under her feet, unable to look up.

"You are victorious," Galen cried, looking out at the crowd rather than down at the two convicts below him. "As Rome is victorious over the world! Your reward is not just life, though that is precious, but the acclaim of these citizens!"

Again there was a tumult of cheering. Most of the people in the crowd weren't paying attention yet, this was just one of the warm-ups, but those that were had gotten good value for their money. Helena shook her head and rolled her eyes at the thought. Admission was free, though the allotment of seats was carefully controlled and the seats awarded only to the patricians and certain classes of the city. She turned back to her letter, ignoring the two convict women as they were presented with palm leaves and, in a Greek touch, crowns of holly.

Dear Artemisia, she wrote, quill nib squeaking slightly on the parchment. *I hope that you are well, or as well as can be, married to a flatulent ox. . . .*

Thyatis stared at the crown of holly in her hand. It didn't seem right to put it on.

"Go ahead!" The Nubian girl hissed out of the corner of her mouth. "It's expected."

Keeping her head low, Thyatis put on the crown. One of the black-robed attendants jabbed at her with a spear and she turned, glaring at the man. It would take only one swift motion to snatch the spear away from him . . . but she did not. She put on the crown and raised her arms again. Scattered cheers came back. Then she and the Nubian girl were herded away into one of the tunnels that led out of the arena at ground level.

"What is your name?" The Nubian girl was giggling. Thyatis understood perfectly—they had escaped death. It felt good, being alive. There was a delicious lassitude in her limbs, a fine afterglow. Far better than the gray dullness which had held her captive for so long.

"Diana," she answered, clasping forearms with the slave. "And yours?"

"Candace." The girl grinned, showing fine white teeth. "I guess we *are* Amazons!"

THE DISTRICT OF THE CISTERNS, CONSTANTINOPLE

)H(

"Carefully, children, carefully!" The voice out of the darkness was fierce. Four of the Walach cowered on the walkway, clustered around a heavy pine crate. They had been trying to move the crate down a narrow path of stone and rotting wood. Oily, dark water of unknown depth lay under the walkway. Mist pooled in the air, making vision and breath difficult. "Those things are precious."

The Dark Queen appeared out of the fog, a black shape against gray mist. Lanterns hung from poles beside the walkway, throwing a shifting, fitful light across the mossy planks. Her face was a pale oval, white eyes gleaming in the darkness. The Walach crawled before her, pressing their faces to the wood.

"Two of you ahead," she hissed, looming over them, "and two behind."

The Walach boys took hold of the crate, musk glands oozing fear into the close, humid air. The Queen brooded, watching as they hauled the crate onto their shoulders. The walkway creaked alarmingly but did not give way. With careful steps, they inched down the path. The carved jade-ite vases in the crate were absurdly heavy. Shaking her head in disgust, the Queen stalked up onto the platform. It galled her to have to move like this, in a hurry, rushed.

Her platform was empty, stripped down to ancient beech planks. The Chin vases, covered with coiling dragons, birds and mountains wrapped in delicate cloud, were the last to leave. Snarling to herself, the Queen drew a vial out of her cloak and wrenched off the cap. A hiss escaped and she quickly turned her face away. Preserving her beauty had cost too much already; she hated the thought of losing what little remained. A flick of her thin hand scattered silver dust across the platform.

She stepped back, the hem of the cloak over her face, and paced quickly away down the walkway. Behind her the platform began to smoke, sending up dark, curling wisps. Even in the heavy, warm air, she could feel the heat of the fire build. Within the hour, nothing would be left but the gorgon's heads, caked with soot. At the entrance, she leapt up the stairs, driven by anger.

These Fates will rue the day they trifled with the Queen of Night!

Her fury had not abated by the time she reached the highest point in the old acropolis. Zeus Pankrator had not visited his temple in millennia, but it remained a glorious structure, perched on a high hill overlooking the watery junction of the Golden Horn and the Propontis. From this vantage, the Queen looked out to the east. Below, in the harbor, her ships were putting out to sea, driven by long oars and the tireless backs of her children. There were six of them in all, fast merchantmen, and then the swift *Helios* pacing them as a guard. Huddled in their holds were the last of the *surâpa* remaining in the city.

She had always expected this day would come. Her people had dwelt in the city for over a thousand years, living and hunting amongst the daywalker herds. Now they were few and driven into hiding. The Queen scowled, her fine-boned face transforming into a mask of hate. Pale fingernails, long and sleek, dug into the marble railing around the tower. She bent her head, concentrating, and felt power shift in the earth. She no longer had the strength of youth, but wind and air were still hers to command. Fog boiled up off the cold waters of the Propontis, spreading like a stain of ink in clear water. Within a few grains it covered the seven ships plowing south, then enveloped their masts and began to mount the massive granite seawalls. Beneath that shroud, her children fled.

She hoped that they would find safety in the west. Long ago she had made arrangements for their sanctuary, but who knew if such ancient trust would hold? The Queen turned away, drawing power back to her, letting the wind and the air and the sea resume their wonted course. She pulled the hood of her cloak over her head and began to descend the steps.

At the far edge of the water, where fog and mist crept towards the Asian shore, the tide of white suddenly stalled, boiling and seething. The Queen's head jerked up and she stopped, hand pressed against the crumbling wall. Something touched the fringe of her artifice. Even with her power withdrawn, she could feel an echo. Swiftly, almost without her thought, the air around her flickered and shaded to an impossible hue. She leapt back up the stairs, lighting on the railing, her feet bare on cold white stone.

In the east, at the edge of vision, lightning flickered in sullen clouds. At the edge of the water, power was working in the night. Her fog had disturbed some hidden pattern. A wind rose, and she could feel zephyrs rush across the cold waters, driving back the mist. For a moment, she considered putting forth her power to deny this. Then a strange sensation came over her, a flickering touch, riding on the wind. She knew it, recognized it, feeling memory stir. It was an old thing, something she had thought destroyed or banished. For the first time, the Queen knew the source of her dread and the strange feeling of doom filling the day-walker city.

The destroyer, she thought, feeling truly old. *The lord of the ten serpents.*

Thunder rumbled in the east, echoing the dim flash of light in the clouds.

The Queen snarled, in defiance now and not simple rage. She was glad, lighthearted, even, knowing why she had waited. She would not flee to the west. She would wait and prepare. It would be interesting. Even the faint pain lingering in her blood seemed insignificant. *How will you get over the water, I wonder?*

━━━━━━━━━━━━━━━━━━━━━━━━━━━━━━━━━━━

OFF SESTUS, THE EUROPEAN SHORE OF THE PROPONTIS

)╫(

There are the signal flags." Odenathus shaded his eyes, looking out at the sun-hazed shore. "It is Khalid. His men are within the walls of the town."

"Good," two voices echoed as one. Odenathus turned, raising a sharp eyebrow. Both Mohammed and Zoë stared at each other, then laughed. The Palmyrene sorcerer stepped under the canvas shade covering the rear deck of the *Jibril.* The galley moved softly under him, rolling on the swell. Sunlight glittered on the water on all sides, broken only by the sleek, low shapes of war galleys and the round bulk of merchantmen. It was hot on the water, without even the morning's breeze. Odenathus hooked his thumbs into his belt and looked questioningly from his cousin to the lord of the Sahaba. "Well? Do we go ashore here?"

"No, not yet," spoke Zoë, Mohammed nodding in agreement. "The Romans still have a fleet—so we will keep full crews on the galleys. The troop ships will unload under our sheltering wing."

"I am troubled," Mohammed said, smoothly following on her statement. "We saw many Roman ships flee our previous battle and I cannot hope storms destroyed them. Too, there are other ships in their hand. We have seen nothing of them, so I would guess the Emperor hoards them, waiting for us to present ourselves in a favorable vantage."

Zoë rubbed her right ear, thinking, then nodded as well. "We must assume our fleet will be destroyed if they bring us to battle."

"Yes." Despite the prospect, Mohammed seemed quite calm. "If all goes well, it will take another three days to unload the army. We must then move overland to Constantinople with all good speed. Shadin will command, with Khalid and his scouts in the van. We have not landed too close to the city—we will have time to forage and spy out the lay of the land. A week, perhaps, until we look upon the walls of Constantinople."

"Yes, and from good, solid land too!" Odenathus laughed. It would take a day or so for the men and the horses to find their land legs again. "And this one-well town? Do we leave a garrison?"

Mohammed's eyes glinted, catching a reflection of the mirror-bright sea. "No. A watch with a fast ship will do. They can bring us news if the enemy comes this way. Our army is not large enough to fight more than one battle at a time. There are ports closer to Constantinople to serve our needs. Perinthus has a good, deep harbor."

Odenathus nodded, turning back to stare at the shore. The hidden world was quiet. The enemy had not put forth his strength yet. The Palmyrene wondered what would happen when he did. Zoë had told him a little bit about her experiences with the power that flowed through the lord Mohammed. It seemed very dangerous.

The whinny of unhappy horses carried very clearly across the still water. Zoë opened her eyes and sat up, clutching a thin blanket to her chest. A series of rattles and clanks and groans followed. The Palmyrene closed her eyes and counted to ten. It did little good. The wind had dropped at sunset, leaving the Propontis very quiet. The army, despite the late hour, continued to unload onto the docks of Sestus, making an unholy racket while she was trying to sleep. Zoë pressed her palms to her eyes, then gave up. Sleep eluded her. A faint muttering sound filled the air, making her irritable and nervous. She let the blanket drop to the bed, then carefully eased up, her movements soft and quiet.

It only took a moment to pull on her pantaloons and a heavy woolen tunic she had found in the market at Caesarea. Bare feet would be best on the deck of the ship. A raven-haired ghost, she slipped out of the big cabin and padded up onto the main deck.

She breathed in, settling her mind, and let the true world open before her. In the darkness, the blue glow of the sea was bright, filled with the patterns of sleeping fish and the dark green surge of currents far below the surface of the water. Keeping her eyes away from the abyss of the sky, Zoë let her mundane perception come to the fore. A hundred yards away, the bulk of the Palmyrene lug *Archelaos* filled the night. Zoë smiled to herself, letting the rise and fall of her breathing and the beat of her heart center her.

Then, with a single light step to the railing, she leapt up. Cool night air rushed in her hair, flowing under her hands, and she lit, breathless and grinning, on the deck of the cargo ship. Lights twinkled on the water, reflecting ceaseless activity on the docks. The crew were sleeping. She heard nothing but snoring, loud and soft alike, aboard. The entrance to the hold drew her, a dark magnet. Zoë padded down the steps from the foredeck and then climbed down a short ladder.

Invisible in the darkness, the presence of the catafalque filled the hold. Zoë stepped close, letting her fingers find the ornamented scrollwork on the four corner posts. She shivered, feeling a deep chill in the air.

The muttering grew louder and she shook her head. A sick feeling grew in her stomach. Memories of death crowded her thoughts—the dead of her city, the acres of bones, the tumbled ruins, the shattered, smoke-blackened buildings—clutching at her with dry, twiglike fingers. Gasping, Zoë fell against the side of the catafalque, tears streaming down her cheeks. All of the pain that had filled her before the night journey with Mohammed came welling up, crushing her with its vast weight.

Daughter, listen to me.

Zoë's head jerked up, all her focus and concentration gone. It was very dark in the hold. A creaking sound echoed from the floor, coupled with the lapping sound of water against the side of the ship. The air grew cold. Zoë shuddered, afraid to move, afraid to touch anything that might be squirming close to her in the darkness.

Listen. Listen to me. Please, Zoë, hear me. The words were faint, almost drowned out by a near-audible muttering and hissing.

The Palmyrene woman pushed herself up from the floor, sliding away from the sarcophagus lying on the wooden platform, garlanded with flowers and rare spices. It was hard to move, an effort even to raise her head. Something dragged at her, trying to crush her down to the planks. Zoë started to choke, feeling nausea well up in her, biting at her throat. She clenched her teeth, biting back on vomit. There was something hot on the right-hand side of her head. Trembling, she raised her hand, touching her hair.

Something was at her ear, a spidery web of metal whiskers and wet, chitinous surfaces. Her fingers dug at it, tangling in sharp wires and rustling, clacking mandibles. Zoë snarled, a guttural animal sound, and ripped at it. Horribly bright pain blossomed and there was a tearing sound, coupled with a gelid, wet *slurp.*

"Aaaah!" Zoë tore at the thing, screaming in rage. "Aaaah!"

The thing writhed, cutting her fingers. Blood welled, spilling down her neck. A bright spark guttered alight in the darkness as Zoë called in desperation upon her power. In the flickering light, she saw a staccato image of something like a huge black spider, covered with waving ebon fronds, squirming in her hand. It was wet with blood and some shining fluid. A whiplike tail lashed in the air, darting at her eyes, a triple-pronged mouth flashing at the tip.

"No!" Her scream ripped the air and was followed by a brilliant white flare of light. She hurled the thing away from her, clacking and chittering. It struck the side of the catafalque and bounced away. Flames leapt up from the dry wood, burning brightly among the dead flowers and drifts of incense and cardamom. A billow of stinging white smoke rose from the platform. Zoë crawled away, hands on the floor, heading for the ladder to the main deck. A swift, rustling sound followed her and she jumped aside, catching sight of the spider-thing leaping at her out of the darkness. This time she was ready.

Fire roared out from her hand, filling the air. The thing was caught in the blast, silhouetted for an instant before it was set alight. It shrieked, flung back against the far wall of the hold. There was a sickening crunch and then Zoë chopped her hand down, face contorted with disgust. A jagged arc of lightning lit from her clenched fist and smashed into the creature, blowing it to fragments. The wall leapt with flame and the catafalque was burning fiercely. A hissing scream rose from the platform and there was a dry, rattling sound. Zoë backed away, her shield raised, flame roaring against the wavering blue surface. The side of her head was cold and wet. She pressed a hand against her ruined ear, trying to stop the flow of blood.

The ship groaned and the shattered side of the hold suddenly buckled, letting a flood of water into the burning room. Steam hissed up, filling the chamber and billowing out of the hatchway. Zoë, surrounded by licking flames, leapt up, springing out of the hold and onto the deck of the ship. A grinding sound followed her and the decking shuddered under her feet. Water continued to pour into the hold, drowning the flames. Hand bloody, her head throbbing with pain, Zoë staggered to the railing, ignoring the panicked cries of the crew. The *Jibril* floated peacefully, now lit by many lanterns. There was shouting. She choked back nausea. Waves of pain washed over her. The moment of fierce energy she had summoned up was fading, leaving her weak.

Legs trembling, she climbed onto the rail. The ship listed as the hold flooded, making balance difficult. Planks and beams ground violently, snapping as the hull cracked under the pressure. Focus came, but only slowly, like a drunk weaving down a street. The entrance to the hidden world eluded her, coming and going in fits and starts. The sky flowered open into an abyss of burning lights, then grew dark again. Steeling herself to the effort, Zoë tried to shut out the pain and the weakness. Suddenly, the matrices of perception coalesced and she could see the pattern of the sea and the air.

Desperately she leapt, soaring into the sky, the rush of her passage blowing back her hair.

Something metallic wiggled in her bloody ear and she screamed in fear, smashing her palm against the side of her head. The dark surface of the water rushed up with dizzying speed.

THE OFFICE OF THE EMPEROR, THE BUCOLEON,
CONSTANTINOPLE

A soft, insistent tapping sound filtered through the air. Martina blinked woozily, realizing she had fallen asleep at her desk. She raised her head, tasting something foul on her tongue. Across the room, beside little Heracleonas' bassinet, Arsinoë rose, gathering a gown around her dark shoulders. The maid padded to the door, then leaned against the close-grained panel, listening. "Who is there?"

There was a soft answer and the maid turned to Martina, her black eyes wide. "Mistress? It is Rufio, with two priests of Asclepius."

"Oh, what now?" The Empress rose, trying to clear the taste from her mouth. "Can't they let me sleep?" She tugged her tunic straight, then draped a woolen stole around her shoulders. A heavy *krater* of wine on the desk made a poor mirror, and she made a face when she saw the heavy smudges under her eyes. "Let them in."

Rufio entered quietly, sliding through the door as it opened. Two men, one large and heavyset, the other small and old, followed him. Arsinoë, looking very worried, closed the panel behind them. Martina flicked her head, pointing the maid to the bassinet. The African girl scurried to the baby.

"Well, what do you want?" Martina failed to keep scorn from her voice. The two men with Rufio were clothed in the archaic himation and chiton of their order. The taller man, his face dignified by a thick dark beard, bowed politely.

"Dear lady, Empress, we must apologize for the abuse you have suffered at the hands of some members of our order. Please know that neither myself—and I am Tarsus— nor my colleague, Hipponax, agree with or condone the insults offered you and your husband."

Both priests bowed again and Martina found her expression softening in response. Years had passed since any priest she had met in the city greeted her with such civility. "I see! You are well-spoken priests, at least. My apologies. How can I help you?"

The two men shared a glance, and then the smaller one bobbed his round head and smiled gamely. "Lady, we hoped that we would be allowed to tend to your husband. Both of us are blessed with the healing art and we were thinking . . ."

Tarsus followed smoothly, ". . . that we might do some good, for everyone."

Martina sat down in her chair, overcome by a surge of emotion. She fought back tears, motioning weakly to Rufio. "The captain of the Guard can tell you what has happened before."

"We know," Tarsus said, stepping around the desk. He knelt in front of the Empress, his light brown eyes kind and his voice gentle. "The captain told us of the previous attempts and of their failure. Please, mistress, let us try. We are loyal citizens. You must know the Emperor's sickness is like a poison in the body of the state."

"It will do no good." Martina pressed a hand over her mouth, closing her eyes. Tears seeped from between the lids, stained black and leaving a gray trail down her cheeks. "The gods have cursed him."

Tarsus stood and looked at Hipponax, a grim look on his face. "Have the other priests said this? Or do you fear such a thing?"

"The other priests," Rufio rumbled from the shadows, "have said many things. That does not mean they are true."

"My lady," Hipponax urged, "may we see him?"

"What harm can it do?" Martina waved at Rufio, her eyes still pressed tight. "Take them through the passage."

Rufio nodded, his eyes glinting in the light of the candles. "This way."

Tarsus dithered for a moment, then turned away from the Empress, Hipponax' hand on his arm. Together, they followed Rufio, who had pressed a concealed latch and opened a panel in one of the walls. The shadows swallowed all three men.

Once they were gone, Arsinoë crept up to her mistress, who was clutching the side of the chair, shaking violently. The maid laid a quilt over the small, brown-haired woman, then pressed a cup into her hand. Martina drank swiftly, spilling a thin trail of dark red wine down her chin. The stain on her tunic spread slowly, creeping down across her breast.

Each time Rufio entered the Emperor's presence, the foul smell struck him as if for the first time. The guard captain wondered if there had been any change, really, since they had begun feeding the Emperor Sviod's remedy. The glassy, distended skin, the puffy limbs, the hoarse, croaking breath—they all seemed the same.

Tarsus and Hipponax knelt on either side of the Emperor, knees sinking into the plush quilts covering the Imperial bed. Both men discarded their bulky himation, rendering Rufio a grim, armored clothesrack. As soon as the two priests entered the chamber, a change fell over both of them: their timidity and nervousness were gone, replaced by a swift, professional manner.

"Dropsy." Tarsus met Hipponax' eyes and the smaller man nodded in agreement. "Fluids are gathering in the limbs; the lungs are being crushed by the weight of clear humors in his chest." Tarsus gently laid back the silk sheets covering the Emperor's grotesque body. Neither man flinched at the fish-pale flesh or the bulging navel standing up like a tiny phallus. Hipponax ran his hands down the swollen legs, his fingertips close to but not touching the gray flesh.

"The motive threads in his legs may be damaged." Hipponax pulled the sheets from the Emperor's feet. "His toes are beginning to turn dark. Blood is pooling in them, perhaps stultifying. His circulation of bile and blood must be very poor."

Tarsus laid a hand on Heraclius' forehead, eyes closed. There was a soft humming sound and the Emperor suddenly lost some of the stiffness in his body. Rufio moved slightly, hand moving towards a knife at his waist. Hipponax looked up, then shook his head. "Do not be alarmed, Captain. Tarsus has only made him sleep without dreams."

The little round priest sat up, tapping a thumbnail

against his teeth. "Tarsus, if this were simple dropsy, any priests who treated him before would have been able to set the balance in his body aright."

"Yes." Tarsus leaned close, smelling the gargling breath issuing from the Emperor's slack mouth. "Captain, is he drinking an infusion of juniper berries?"

Rufio started, then said, "Yes. Compounded with some other herbs."

"Parsley seeds. How much have you been giving him at a time? For how long?"

"Only a little, but over the last several months." Rufio shrugged. "He refuses to drink when he is awake, he fears any liquid, and at night it must be done in secret. There are too many hostile eyes in the palace."

Tarsus looked at Hipponax, disturbed. "Such a course of treatment should have greatly reduced these symptoms."

The little priest bobbed his round head in agreement, the fringe of hair around his ears catching the faint light of a single candle. "Not a normal disease, then, something else."

Tarsus settled back, closing his eyes. Hipponax did the same. After a moment, Rufio jerked his head around, thinking he heard a sound in the hidden passage. When he looked back, the two priests had placed their hands on the torso of the Emperor. A soft white glow was seeping from under their fingers, trickling across the swollen flesh.

Rufio's face contorted, filled with undisguised horror and loathing. His nerveless fingers dropped the two cloaks to the ground in an untidy pile. Then he looked away, his fist clenched around the knife at his waist. His knuckles whitened with a crushing grip. Silently, his face gyrated between anguish and rage. Then—with an effort visible in his shoulders and neck, where the veins bulged—he mastered himself. When he turned around, the soft white light washed over a stoic face, unmarked by tears or any kind of emotion in his black eyes.

·   ·   ·

"You failed." Martina's voice was dead and cold.

"Yes." Hipponax seemed drained, reduced, his face graven with weariness. "But there is the tiniest seed of hope, Empress."

Martina raised an eyebrow, her powders and colors a ruin. Neither of the priests looked any better in this dim orange light. "Tell me."

"The Emperor has made himself sick." Tarsus leaned forward, haggard face intent. He met Martina's eyes with a candid look. "We used our arts simply to divine the cause of his ailment. I—*we*—believe he ate too much dry salted meat while on campaign. This caused his body to begin retaining fluids. A common enough occurrence in the desert, particularly when a man's humors are out of balance. But—*but*—when the swollen feet and distended limbs struck him, he believed the gods cursed him. Now, the mind torments the body."

Hipponax nodded in agreement. "My lady, your husband cannot be treated by our arts because he will not let himself be cured. He is consumed by fear. I would guess, from what I have heard, he believes his marriage to you has brought the wrath of the gods upon him."

Martina jerked up, face white with rage. Her wine cup flew across the room and shattered, making a shockingly loud sound in the quiet room. "I am *sick* of hearing this is my fault! Get out, both of you. Rufio, take them away. You are no better than these other priests—at least they had the bravery to say this from the first."

Tarsus stood, shocked and dismayed. "My lady! You've no fault in this I can see! The Emperor's mind is set against his body, to the detriment of both. If he can be convinced to live, to set aside this self-loathing, then he can be cured. Please—you can help him—your *son* can help him. From your love, he can find the strength to become well."

"What pap!" Martina groped on the desk for something heavy and sharp. "My son is weak, his blood corrupt. He

will follow his father across the dark river soon enough."
Her hand found a marble blotting pin. It felt good in her
hand. Rufio stepped in front of the priests.

"I will take them away," the captain said, muscular hand
pinning hers to the desk. "They mean you no disrespect,
Empress."

"Get out." Martina's voice was reduced to a hiss. "What
is he doing? Get away from him!"

Hipponax, his brows drawn together in dismay, had
stepped to the bassinet. The priest laid a gentle hand
against the sleeping baby's head, ignoring the scuffle behind him. Warm light reflected in the little priest's eyes,
then he smiled.

"Empress, your son will be healthy." Hipponax turned,
then raised an eyebrow at the sight of the captain of the
Faithful Guards forcibly restraining the Empress, one hand
over her mouth. A trickle of blood seeped from fine white
teeth biting into his palm. Rufio did not seem to notice.
"You should have someone see to that, Captain. Bites sup-
purate quickly.

"Empress." Hipponax walked to the struggling woman,
his voice gentle. "We are not your enemies, though I know
you have been poorly treated by our order. Your son is
suffering from too much bile. He needs more sun and the
comfort of your arms. Do you feed him yourself?"

The priest gently moved Rufio's fingers away, letting
Martina take a breath. She glared at both men with undisguised fury. "No. There is a wet-nurse. It is painful for me
to nurse him."

Hipponax nodded, then placed Rufio's hand back over
the Empress's mouth. The guard captain seemed amused
by this, then his face darkened with anger as the little priest
cupped each of the Empress's breasts, his head cocked to
one side as if listening. Martina surged violently in Rufio's
arms, but he lifted her up and her legs kicked violently in
the air. Hipponax removed his hands, bowed and stepped
back. "Your pardon, my lady. I am sure my head will be

easily loosed from my shoulders, if that is your wish. Listen. You should not nurse yourself, and you should find another wet-nurse for your son. There is a subtle balance in the humors of a nursing mother's body. Yours, I fear, is unsuitable for your son. I venture his current wet-nurse is also unsuitable."

Rufio set Martina down. He took his hands from her body, then stepped quickly back. The Empress spun, her face white with rage, lips smeared with blood. "You. You . . ."

Her head snapped around and a finger jabbed out at Hipponax. "I do not want to see you *ever again*, little man. If I do, I will have you torn to pieces by wild dogs or hacked into sections with cleavers."

Both priests bowed deeply and then, with Rufio behind them, slipped out the door. Martina stood in the middle of the room, shaking with anger. Then her face slowly cleared and she steadied herself with a hand on the table. She took a breath, then another, then shuddered. Her face wrinkled, then her tongue darted over her lips, tasting something like iron and salt.

"Oh, how foul! Arsinoë! Where did that wretched girl get to?"

She spat blood on the floor, then wiped her mouth clean.

THE FLAVIAN, ROMA MATER

I am sure it is her, my lady," Betia shouted, pushing through the crowd. The arcade surrounding the amphitheater was stifling. Tens of thousands of citizens pressed forward in a huge snarled mass. There were marked walkways, delineated by stone plugs and ropes, but today the city was gripped by a tremendous sense of festivity. Everyone was eager to get to the games. The hawkers in the park north of the Colosseum were doing a frantic business in seat tokens. "Everyone says the leader of the Amazons is a tall, redheaded woman with incredible skill. She slew a dozen wild beasts by herself!"

Anastasia snorted, holding a gray veil before her face. She hated crowds in the city and today was worse: hot, sunny, without so much as a breath of air to alleviate the heat. Some people, crushed in the crowd, had already fainted. Men jostled her on either side, trying to push ahead in the line. The queue inched ahead slowly, disappearing into the black maw of the northern gate of the Flavian.

"I don't believe it," Anastasia sniffed, nearly stumbling when a pack of stonemasons surged up behind her, pressing her into Betia's thin little back. The blond girl braced her mistress with both arms, then wiggled forward between a group of bakers. Most of the seats in the Flavian were allocated to guilds, the ancient clans or patrician families. Anastasia had her seats by virtue of her late husband's position as Duke of Parma. She had never been to the games before. If this hot, sweaty crowd were the norm, she didn't intend to go again. "The possibility of her survival is insignificant."

Betia turned, watery blue eyes flashing. "I think we should watch and see for ourselves!"

The Duchess sighed, knowing what pitiful, tiny hope drove the blond girl. She had tortured herself with the same dreams. It was useless; all of the men and women whom she had sent to murder the Prince were dead, annihilated in the mammoth explosion of Vesuvius. Despite the dead feeling in her heart, she continued on, sweating and suffering in her dark gown and shawl. The garb of mourning was not designed for a blisteringly hot day down in the center of the city.

.   .   .

The sand burned white, throwing long shadows down the tunnels on the north side of the amphitheater floor. Thyatis squatted in a nameless grimy passage. A great clamor was under way out on the arena floor. Chariots were parading past, decked with white and silver, holding bronzed men in armor. Gladiators raised their arms, glinting with metal, to the adulation of the crowd. Robes of purple and gold were draped over brawny shoulders. The horses, bedecked in tassels and flowers, stepped past, fetlocks rising and falling in careful unison. Thyatis was sure it all made a fine show from the marble seats. A drumming sound could be felt through the wall at her back, the pounding of tens of thousands of feet against the seats.

A sandaled foot kicked her thigh gently. "Don't be so foul."

Thyatis looked up, eyes slitted with anger. The Nubian girl, Candace, was standing next to her. Like Thyatis, she was dressed in a short kilt of pleated linen edged with badly sewn gold patches. A half-*strophium* covered one breast, leaving the other bare. A crown of cheap copper flashed with gold paint held back her hair.

"This is ludicrous," Thyatis growled, picking at her breast band. "I don't want to flop around while I'm fighting."

"Well," Candace cocked her head to one side, grinning, "it is a little droopy, but very traditional . . . oomph!"

Thyatis was standing, her fists clenched. Candace looked up with disbelief from the floor, rubbing her stomach. "That was uncalled for, Roman!"

Thyatis's voice was sharp. "I've no time for levity." She looked down the corridor. A dozen women were huddled against the walls, sunk in their own hopelessness. They were dressed in the same ridiculous costumes. "Do you know when we go on?"

"My apologies." Candace stood, dusting herself off. The poor-quality linen kilt was already smudged and torn. "You hear what they call us—we're supposed to be Amazons. This is our *traditional* costume. So we get to prance around half naked."

Thyatis raised an eyebrow at the Nubian girl's perky breast. "Really. I'm thinking that I'd prefer a mail shirt, greaves and a shield instead. Have you talked to any of our fellow victims?"

"No." Candace shook her head, surveying them as well. "More like us—flotsam from the prisons or the market or the bordellos. Poor chicks."

"Give me your strophium."

Candace raised both eyebrows in surprise. "Excuse me?"

"Hand it over." Thyatis gestured impatiently with her right hand. "The Queen of the Amazons gets to cover both breasts."

"Oh. Of course, *Your Majesty.*" Candace gave her an arch look but unwound the cloth. Thyatis wrapped it across her own chest, crosswise, and sighed in relief to draw it snug across her left breast. "Won't you have a hard time shooting a bow now?"

"I doubt," Thyatis said, pacing to the iron grillwork closing off the end of the passage, "they will give us bows today. The *editores* are not stupid. One dead senator would quash their pensions." She put her hands on the iron bars, pressing against them, letting her body flex in line with her extended right leg. It felt good. Sitting in the stone pits under the arena for a week had not improved her temper. Worse, it had been hard to exercise and keep herself limber.

"You lot," Thyatis barked at the other women. "Stand up. Candace, help anyone that can't stand by herself."

The other women stared back in confusion. Two of them stood tentatively. Thyatis jerked her head at them while she reached down and pulled up the nearest slave.

"Listen to me. We're going to be set against some opponent—probably male criminals—as the opening act today. A bloody warm-up for the crowd, not just the clowns thrashing about. There will be weapons set out on the floor of the arena. I'd guess, since we're in a tunnel, that the men are in a tunnel too, on the south side of the arena. We'll have to run and grab what we need."

Thyatis stopped, frowning. Except for Candace and the two older women that were standing, no one seemed to be following her. "Do any of you speak Latin?"

Another round of blank looks.

"Capital. Just capital."

Maxian stopped climbing, thighs burning with effort. He pressed himself to the side of the stairwell, letting the crowd continue past. There was a little niche at each turning of the stair as it snaked its way up through the warren of the Flavian. Usually a statue of one of the gods resided in the alcove, but this one was empty. The pungent smell of onions, garlic and fish sauce choked the air. The upper deck of the amphitheater was reserved for the poor, for women and for barbarians in from the provinces to see the show. Maxian let them surge past.

A family passed him, led by a round-faced merchant, sweating furiously in his games-day toga. His wife followed, drawing Maxian's eye. She was cool and collected, possessed of a magnificent mane of curly dark hair under a gauzy veil. She had a baby in her arms.

She reminded Maxian, suddenly, of the Duchess Anastasia. He wondered what she would say to him now if they met. Their last meeting had been over an interrupted dinner. He had ignored her in main part and she had, politely, left. Soon after, Krista had left his side, then tried to murder him. Melancholy filled the Prince and he leaned against the wall, fist to his chin. There had been a brief time when it seemed they were friends. More than friends.

I wonder, Maxian thought suddenly, *if our assignation meant anything to her? Did she play me, even then?* It hurt, thinking that she might have just used him for her own pleasure, or worse, for some scheme. *No matter.* He shook his head, then slipped into the flow of men and women climbing the stairs. He could have banished the pain from his legs, but he was intent on a delicate process today. It might put a monkey in the henhouse to throw power recklessly about within the Flavian.

Only another hundred and six steps remained before he reached the broad pine decking under the awning poles.

A phalanx of tubas *blatted*, signaling the beginning of the games for the day. Helena waited until the cacophony died down, then removed her hands from her ears. Galen was laughing at her, his eyes wrinkling up.

"Stop that," she chided him. "I hate all this noise."

"You mean it distracts you from your writing."

"Perhaps." She frowned at him, giving him a good, solid glare. "It's my turn to complain about the games, not yours."

"You should be pleased today," Galen said, leaning close to her, his hand sliding on her knee. "The Amazons are the opening act. There should be plenty of dead men if this notable Diana proves her mettle."

"Stop that. You'll scandalize the Vestals," Helena hissed, narrowing gold-dusted eyes at him. "Here, give me our son."

Galen, distracted from her thigh, nodded to the slave behind him. Little Theodosius had shaken off his colic. Now he was a healthy, squalling baby. Today, matching his mother, he was wrapped in pale violet silk. Galen took the boy in his arms, his face lighting up with a smile as the baby grabbed at his nose. The Emperor turned, facing the crowd. Today the arena was filled to bursting, with buttocks in every seat, as Cicero might have said. A riot of color, a mutable sea of faces filled the great bowl. Galen settled the baby on his hip, mindful of his golden crown of laurel, and raised his other hand.

"Let the games begin!"

.   .   .

The iron grill rattled up. There was a deafening roar of sound, the unleashed joy of forty-five thousand human throats. Thyatis sprinted out, legs blurring over the white sand. Behind her, she hoped, Candace and the other women were running out as well, keeping close together. The sky was very blue and the heat from the sand beat up at her like an open flame.

Five hundred feet away, on the southern, shady side of the arena, another gate was rising. Men spilled out onto the brick walkway circling the arena floor, confused, looking about in fear. The city magistrates sentenced useless criminals to the arena. Those worth sending to the mines or city farms were not wasted on the amphitheater. These would be murderers, rapists, cripples. Anyone whom the state could spare.

Thyatis ran, letting her muscles find their own rhythm. The walls of the Flavian rose up on all sides, half in shadow, half in sun, vibrant with color. The initial cheering died, replaced by a hushed anticipation. The audience had seen this play before, many times. Two gangs of criminals would be urged out onto the sand with whips and smoking-hot brands. The attendants, dark in their archaic masks and robes, would kill those who did not fight.

No one ran to battle, certainly not with such speed.

The elevators rattled to a halt, leaving spears, maces, swords, axes exposed on the floor of the arena. Thyatis glimpsed that they were arranged in two rows, one near each tunnel mouth. Some of the men looked up, staring at her rushing towards them with all the speed she could manage.

The men's line of weapons was only a hundred feet away now. Two of the criminals suddenly darted forward, shouting, realizing that the women behind Thyatis had already reached their own line of weapons and were snatching them up. Thyatis redoubled her efforts, head down, sprinting recklessly.

•   •   •

"These are our seats, noble sirs." Betia smiled prettily at the two men squeezed into a block of seats reserved for Imperial governors and tribunes posted to the frontier. They looked up and Anastasia was pleasantly surprised to see the pair were her guardsmen. The larger of the two nodded sharply, then squeezed over on the marble bench. There was an outraged cry from beyond him, but the guardsman turned and glowered at a portly official until the man gulped and went silent.

"Thank you." Betia sat, wedging a basket of snacks between her pale legs, and helped Anastasia sit down. The Duchess had been nearly overcome by the heat and was feeling rather sick. Betia pressed an alabaster flute of lemon water into her hands. "Drink this, mistress. The heat is dreadful today."

The Duchess nodded, lifting her veil and drinking deeply from the cool jar. The tart water was a blessing on her throat. A great roar of sound rose up from the stands and she looked around speculatively, violet eyes drinking in the scene. The crowd was in a festive mood today. The Emperor had promised spectacular games and so far they had not been disappointed. The parades had been grand, the fights bloody and without mercy. The wild animals had even put on a good show. Anastasia felt a pent-up energy in the crowd. Months had passed without any games at all. Now that they had started again, everything was fresh and unexpected.

Betia was standing on her seat, on tiptoes, staring down at the floor of the arena. There was another burst of cheering and clapping. Anastasia tugged at Betia's skirt. "What is going on?"

"It's her!" Betia looked down at the Duchess, her face glowing. "It *is* her!"

Sighing, Anastasia stood, though her whole body seemed sore. Her depression had taken a physical toll. Cursing at the forest of heads and arms that prevented her from seeing the arena floor, she climbed up on her seat.

This was very rude, but any kind of social politeness seemed to have gone straight out the window today.

She could see the sand at last, and she staggered in surprise. Betia, concerned, caught her elbow. Down on the white oval, engaged in furious, whirling combat with a brace of men, leaping and striking, a spear grasped firmly in both hands, golden-red hair startlingly short, was a woman who looked very much like Thyatis. Her adopted daughter, presumed dead, seemed quite alive.

"Oh. Oh, dear." The Duchess found it very hard to breathe.

Thyatis blocked fiercely, slapping aside a wild overhand cut. The sword bit into the haft of her spear, then bounced away. She gave ground, pressed by three tattered men. Her first rush into the body of the criminals had laid two of them low, their bright blood smeared on the walkway. The rest had scattered in all directions, some hobbling on stumpy legs. Two of them, grimy creatures with broken faces, she had hunted down and slain. They had begged for life, crawling on the bricks, but she did not have time for mercy. The rest had run for the weapons on the elevator platforms, then had turned to hunt her.

The other women, with Candace at their center, had taken up all the spears and swords they could find and now parked themselves near one of the walls. The attendants, venturing out from the tunnel beneath the Imperial box, were cursing them, trying to get them to take part in the battle.

One group of the condemned men had turned on Thyatis immediately. She had killed one in their first rush, tearing his throat out. His body, limbs askew, was sprawled a dozen yards away. The three facing her began to circle, trying to flank her. She paced sideways, keeping the wall of the arena at her back. It struck her as funny, suddenly, that the men were alike as peas—ragged dark hair, filth-stained bodies, emaciated frames. Prison reduced all men to constituent parts, it seemed.

She shouted, lunging at the nearest one. He scrambled back, crying out in fear. She rushed into the gap, whirling the spear. The butt end, a stocky length of oak, cracked into the side of the man's head. He went down, nerveless, sword spilling from lax fingers. The other two attacked, slashing wildly. Thyatis flicked the spear to the right, batting aside an oncoming sword blade, then driving the corroded iron head into the man's mouth. He jerked to a halt, gargling blood and filmy bubbles. Thyatis let out a hoarse *kiii* shout, then whipped the spear butt around to her left and forward. The third man crashed into the butt, breath shocked from his body. He staggered. Thyatis wrenched the point free of the man choking on his own blood.

Before she could kill the last of the three, a frenzied shouting drew her attention.

The phalanx of women was under attack from both the remaining criminals and the attendants. It broke, women fleeing in all directions. One of the men waded in, hacking around him with an ax, splitting the skull of one of the older women. She died instantly. The man, his red beard flowing down almost to his waist, screamed in victory.

Thyatis knew the sound; the barbarian had lost himself in the frenzy of battle. She spun, kicking the stunned man in the side of the head with the heel of her foot, then sprinted towards the slaughter. The crowd was howling with laughter and cheers, but she let the thunder of sound wash over her, unheard.

Each copper bead was still in place along the circumference of the arena. Maxian rose from the last one, satisfied that no one had tampered with them or dislodged them by accident. There was a strange feeling in the air, a fragile sensation, and the Prince swallowed nervously. He had never attempted anything this delicate before. At least, not without Abdmachus at his side. The old Nabatean wizard had a lifetime of experience in such matters, the Prince barely three years. Maxian shook his head and shoulders, trying to dispel his tension.

I don't have to do this today, he thought, still trying to calm himself. *I can wait. I am in balance with the Oath.*

His previous effort had proved illuminating. The constant struggle he endured had lessened and then disappeared. No longer did he maintain the Shield of Athena at all times, even when sleeping. It was still ready, the pattern well used and close to hand in his thought, should he need it. He did not think that he would. With the change in his own intentions, as he directed himself to go with the flow of the enormous pattern, he found that it did not abrade against him.

A smooth stone, slick with moss, lying in a running, rushing stream. That was how he thought of himself. There was a great sense of peace within him now, too. It held the kind of serenity that he had found on Vesuvius, before its destruction, when he had dwelt in a point of balance between the fury in the mountain and the power of the Oath itself. It would be very easy to do nothing, to let things stand as they did. To let the stream continue to flow, rushing down to the sea as it had done for millennia.

That, Maxian thought, *would be the safe course.*

He looked down into the arena, seeing the small figures of men rushing to and fro on the white sand. Across from him, perched amongst the lowest stands of the arena, was the Imperial box. It was gay with color and thronged with people. His brother would be there. Maxian was overcome with a sense of loss. His brother, doubtless, thought him dead. At the very least a monster or a madman.

You could go see him, tell him what has happened, what you've done. He will embrace you, take you in. He loves you, your brother. Go to him.

Maxian blinked and looked around. There was no one nearby. The sailors who raised and lowered the giant awnings were clustered in the shade beneath the masts, eating a hearty lunch. He could hear them chattering amongst themselves like monkeys in the trees. Had he really heard something?

"Odd," he said aloud. It was lunchtime. He should eat. Galen would have a veritable feast laid out in the box. Everyone would be there. Maxian turned away from the copper bead and strode to the head of the stairway leading down into the courses of the amphitheater.

Even the attendants scattered before the barbarian, picking up their long gray robes and sprinting out of the way. The redheaded man had hewn down two women and one criminal before running out of immediate victims. He turned, mouth white with spittle. Thyatis skidded to a halt, taking in the frenzied look on his face and his massive chest and mighty thews. Here was a man who would never accept the yoke or the collar. He was too dangerous to put in the mines or on a farm. The overseers would find his hands, thick as tree roots, around their necks in the darkness.

Thyatis shouted, drawing his attention. The berserker spun, seeing her, then charged forward, screaming a high-pitched war cry. The ax, spilling blood, rose high above his head. Thyatis let him come, then hurled the spear with all her might. It flickered across the gap between them and plunged into the man's chest with a meaty *thunk*. He staggered, but the madness in his face did not change and his steps did not falter. Thyatis leapt aside, but he plowed into her, smashing her to the ground. She rolled, frantic, and his free hand grasped her ankle.

Bellowing like a wild aurochs in heat, he dragged her toward him, blood welling around the spear. She kicked at his face. A meaty fist came down, smashing into her stomach. Thyatis gasped, feeling her breath flee. The spear haft ground against her side. His fist crashed down again and this time she cried out in pain, feeling ribs grind against one another. Pinned, she tried to roll, but he fell on her, sweat and blood dripping from his wounds. Slick red fluid smeared across her. Thyatis gouged at his eyes, but he seemed impervious to pain. He was still screaming unintelligible words in her ear, smashing his fist against her shoulder again and again.

A wave of darkness shuddered across her vision, followed by trailing sparks. It was difficult to breathe, his massive weight pressed down on her diaphragm. Thyatis cracked her head forward, catching the barbarian's nose. It broke, splintering, but he bit at her head, catching her hair. His fist ground against the sand. His entire upper body shook like a dog, wrenching her back and forth. Incredible pain blossomed. She nearly passed out.

The haft of the spear scraped across the ground into her right hand. Gasping in pain, Thyatis shoved on it hard, away from her body. The wooden shaft twisted in the man's torso, and blood and entrails flooded onto her stomach. Now, for the first time, the barbarian screamed in pain and she levered him away, spilling vitals and urine and blood from the gaping wound. Now his eyes were free of the madness and he was howling, a hoarse, endless sound.

Thyatis stood, dripping blood and serum, grinding the spear into the man's guts. He flopped like a gaffed fish, then she tore the spear point free. He was done. She turned, seeing that the other criminals had cut down three more of the women. Only two were left, gamely trying to fend off the attackers. Candace was bleeding from a cut on her breast. Thyatis swallowed, relieved to breathe freely again.

Betia hurried, sprinting up the stairs two and three steps at a time, white legs flashing under the short skirt. The din of the crowd, howling for blood and getting it, roared in her ears. The stones of the Flavian were shuddering with the noise and the hammering of feet on the seats. The blond slave had only seen bits and pieces of the fighting on the sand, but it was enough to convince her that the redheaded woman down there was her mistress' *sicaria,* returned from the dead.

Oh, she thought, almost weeping with joy. *If only this means Nikos is alive, too!*

Behind each section of seats, ascending from the patricians close to the floor to the plebes high up under the wooden roof, there was a circling tunnel cut with arches that looked out upon the city. These passages were filled with people coming and going and the few lucky merchants allowed to sell their wares within the amphitheater itself. The Duchess needed more water—the poor woman was suffering terribly in the heat and sun—and Betia knew there was a stand not far away. She hoped the queue wasn't too long.

Hurrying around a corner at the end of the ramp, she dodged between a pair of men arguing about the next day's races, then found herself in a crowd of people wanting to buy candied figs and sweetmeats.

"Oh! Bother." Everyone in this city was much taller than she was. Fuming at the delay, she pushed through the citizens, then found herself in a bit of an aisle between the people at the sweetmeats stand and those wanting to buy water. She looked left, trying to find the end of the line. There was a man there, just passing by as she looked, one hand on the outer wall, his face filled with worry, pensive.

She knew him. Betia's heart seemed to stop, frozen with fear.

A tall man, with long rich hair that hung below his shoulders. He came to the Villa of Swans very late, pounding on the door. She had let him in, annoyed by being woken at such an hour. The mistress wanted to see him. Betia had led him upstairs. He followed her like a dark cloud, distracted by his own concerns. He left when the cock crowed and morning light crept across the villa walls.

The girl knew who he was but could not move. Prince Maxian walked on, deep in thought. When he had passed out of her sight, she shuddered and then shook herself. Taking a deep breath, she followed him. The water was forgotten for the moment.

The crowd continued to mill about, taking their ease out of the sun. The eddy of sound from the amphitheater echoed here like waves crashing upon the shore, rising and falling in pitch. The Prince continued down the passage, then turned into one of the sloping rampways that led down to the ground floor. Betia padded after him, heart in her mouth, trying to keep him just in view.

Suddenly, halfway down the ramp, he stopped, his head rising. Betia froze, pressing herself against the plastered wall. It was painted with scenes of the fights and games, long processions of victors and victims in turn. Every five feet or so there was a roundel painted with a man's torso and face. Below each portrait was a listing of their victories and exploits.

"Fool! You've been taken again, in just the same way!"

Betia stared, eyes wide, as the Prince turned abruptly about, a rueful grin on his face. Without even looking at her, he stormed back up the ramp, laughing. In a moment, he was gone, though she could still hear him berating himself. She put a hand over her mouth, giddy with relief, then ran down the ramp as fast as she could. The Duchess needed to know that the enemy was here, in the Flavian, with her, right now.

Thyatis hefted the ax, gauging the balance. The weapon had a long haft, with a single-bladed head and a sharp tine. She jogged across the sand, feeling the soles of her feet slip and slide in the goo inside her sandals. Candace and an older woman were still alive, though backed against one of the temporary nets that separated the contestants from the wall of the arena itself. Four men were hedging them in, jabbing with a spear and swords.

Rushing forward, Thyatis swung the ax up to her left shoulder, settling her grip.

"Look out!" shouted someone from the crowd, whistling and clapping only a dozen yards away. The nearest of the criminals looked around wildly. He saw Thyatis rushing at him and shouted in alarm. The men scattered, abandoning their attack on Candace, who slumped with relief against the netting. Thyatis skipped back, watching them spread out.

"Help me with these dogs!" Thyatis' voice was harsh. She was getting tired. The berserker had almost done her in. "To me!"

Candace pushed away from the net and grabbed the other woman. Together, brandishing their swords clumsily, they hurried to Thyatis. The Roman woman turned toward the men, swinging the ax easily from side to side. One of the criminals lunged in, his gladius nosing towards her. She ignored him, watching the other men, her vision unfocused.

One of them had a spear. He was the most dangerous right now.

"What—*gasp*—now, Your Majesty?"

"Keep behind me." Thyatis grunted. "Watch my back."

Thyatis crabbed forward. The men edged warily away. The spearman circled to her left. He had not raised it up to throw. *Maybe,* she thought, *he doesn't know how . . .* It was a possibility. Recklessly, she darted to the right, exposing her back. She whirled the ax, forcing the swordsmen back. The other men scuttled back, too, staying out of range.

Candace yelped, trying to cry out a warning, then parried furiously as one of the men rushed her. Thyatis ducked and whirled to her left. The ax blurred out of her hand, whirling towards the spearman. He was already recovering from an overhand cast. The spear whispered over her head. Thyatis tumbled and rolled up. The thrown ax hit with a *thunk*. The spearman stood shock still, staring down at the sharp tine buried in his chest.

The swordsmen attacked. One cut high, the other low. Thyatis sprang up, left leg striking sideways, her body flattening as she brought her head down. A sword flashed past beneath her. The kick caught one man in the arm, cracking bone. She hit the ground, rolled and sprang up, face-to-face with the other swordsman.

She shouted violently, and the heel of her right hand smashed into his nose. Blood and mucus spurted. Her left leg rose, then snapped forward, twice, from the knee. The blows drove into the soft flesh of his stomach, then his chin as he jerked forward. Her left foot touched the ground; she shifted, and plowed her right hand, clenched, into his face. He was thrown back sprawling on the sand.

The man with the injured arm cut at her with a knife in his other hand. Thyatis slipped the blow. She hooked his arm with her left hand, snapping it back to her chest, trapping the blade behind her. Her right fist, still smeared with blood, cracked across his face, snapping his head to the side. Her right elbow followed, smashing his nose. His neck made a grisly, cracking sound.

Thyatis, shuddering with blood fire, threw the body on the ground. She spun, everything slowing, as if the world were winding down. Candace and the older woman hacked at the body of the remaining swordsman, their faces contorted in fury.

Breathing was very difficult, but Thyatis gasped, drawing in huge gulps of air.

The crowd was chanting, screaming at the top of their lungs: *"Habet, hoc habet!"* The sound rose and rose, rattling the statues ringing the arena.

"I am not a stone in the stream," Maxian said to himself, once more on the deck high above the arena floor. "I would be a dam, a channel, a culvert."

He settled himself by the first bead. The wood around the copper had begun to rot and fade, turning papery white. Another day and the copper pellet would work free of the decking and fall to the sandy floor hundreds of feet below. Maxian frowned, running his hands over the boards. In the hidden world, he could feel the tiny frisson of resistance generated by the bead. The copper was warm to the touch. He sighed, settling himself. This would be very delicate work.

He closed his eyes, shutting out the riot of color ringing the amphitheater. He chanted, settling his mind. He eased delicately into the hidden world, insinuating himself into folded matrices and angled patterns. He took his time, denying himself the soft, peaceful comfort the Oath offered. He would be its master, not its slave.

It seemed very likely to him, on reflection, that he would have been beset and killed if he had approached the Imperial box. The Duchess, at least, would be watching for him. Maxian's head bent to his breast, his breathing slowing until it seemed that he did not breathe at all.

In his mind, a glorious panoply of forms unfolded and unfolded and unfolded. . . .

Betia squeezed in beside the Duchess, breathless and sweating. The crowd was even more closely packed than before. A bald man with stiff white mustaches was crammed in tight behind their seats, shouting himself hoarse.

"Mistress!" Betia shouted in Anastasia's ear, though the older woman seemed to be crying, her hands covering her eyes. "Please, you must listen!"

Anastasia turned, her glorious violet eyes tinged with red. She snuffled, wiping her nose with the hem of her gown. "What is it?"

"What is wrong?" Betia suddenly registered the poor state of her mistress. "What happened?"

"Oh." Anastasia dabbed at her eye. "Nothing. Nothing. That wretched daughter of mine," the Duchess jabbed a finger at the arena, "nearly got herself killed two or three times! Dear, I think we should go home, this can't be good for my heart or my complexion." Anastasia flapped the edge of her veil, trying to cool herself.

"An excellent idea," Betia growled, grabbing one of the

guardsmen. The two men were shouting lustily, waving their hats in the air. Everyone in the arena was doing the same. "It's too dangerous to stay here. *He* is here, on the upper course."

"He? Who do you mean?" Anastasia put her hand on the blond slave's shoulder.

"I mean," Betia looked around slowly, scanning the faces in the crowd, "the prince Maxian. I saw him, I'm sure of it, on the upper promenade."

Anastasia felt a chill, and then she stood up, fingers digging into Betia's shoulder for support. She drew the veil across her face, her eyes cold. Men and women were in motion all around her, crying and cheering, waving their hats or boards painted with racing slogans. The Duchess saw nothing of the Prince. "Come," she said, stepping down. "We must find the Empress immediately."

Thyatis staggered, pushed by one of the gray attendants. A carved wooden mask in the shape of a tusked demon hid his face. Its black eyes stared at her, huge and round.

"Move!" The mouth was a funnel, magnifying and distorting his voice.

She stumbled forward, utterly drained. The *strophium* at her chest oozed a thin red fluid when she moved. Candace held one arm, the nameless older woman the other. All three wore crowns of golden holly, studded with small gems. Waves of applause rolled over them, then slackened as they entered a tunnel. Slaves in black tunics were waiting with buckets of water. Thyatis collapsed against the wall as soon as she could, gasping for breath. The slaves doused her with water. Bloody froth swirled away on the floor around her feet.

"You did well." A smirking voice penetrated the drumming in her ears. Thyatis looked up and saw the boxer from the inn leaning against the wall, grinning. He was sleek and clean, clad in a red kilt and leather armbands. His skin gleamed with oil and his hair was a glossy black crown. Silver fish-scale armor covered his arm and shoulder. "You impress me. I admit I thought Narses mad when he bought you."

"Did you?" Thyatis turned away, taking a towel from one of the slaves. The fluid on her skin was oily and slick, untouched by the water. She began rubbing it from her arms and chest. "Does it matter?"

"No." Hamilcar shook his head sadly. "They posted the last of the matches today—we will not meet on holy ground. They've decided that you should not die until the last day and not by my hand."

With that, laughing, he strode away down the tunnel, gathering up his fellows as he passed. Thyatis ignored him, crouching down next to Candace and the older woman. They were both shivering with reaction. One of the slaves had bound up the Nubian girl's wound. Thyatis clasped both of their hands in hers.

"What is your name?" Her voice rasped like an awl on strong wood.

The older woman blinked and whispered: "Agrippina."

"Good. A strong name." Thyatis stood before her knees locked up. "Now we are three."

"What do you mean," Anastasia bit out angrily, "I may not speak with the Empress Helena?"

"I mean just that, madam." The Praetorian centurion's eyes glittered back, half hidden by the visor of his helmet. "The Imperial family is enjoying the games—they are not interested in seeing scarecrows or beggars today. The fifth day is set aside for such petitions; go see her on the Palatine with the rest!"

"I am not a beggar," Anastasia snarled, raising her hand and her voice. Betia fumbled at her arm, trying to restrain her. "I am an Imperial officer and a close friend of the Empress. She *will* see me."

The Praetorian shook his head, scarred face impassive. "You've not been given leave to see her. Now, if you don't go away quietly, my men will throw you out, Imperial officer or no."

Anastasia hissed in disgust, but she saw the man was determined. In these mourning clothes, all gray and black, without any makeup and half dead from the heat, she couldn't awe a street urchin. Helena had no idea she was here, and Anastasia wanted a private meeting, not a scene. "Very well. Good day."

The Duchess spun on her heel and stalked away through the crowd loitering in the passage behind the Imperial box. Various ambassadors and bureaucrats watched her with interest as she swept past. Her guardsmen peeled away from the walls to follow her and Betia hurried ahead, trying to remember where they'd left the litter bearers.

"Mistress?" Anastasia's head turned, her face filled with incipient fury. There was a solid-looking man, bald as a hen's egg, with a nervous expression on his face. "I don't mean to be a bother . . . but, I was sitting behind you in the crowd, and I heard . . . I heard your girl say you knew the redheaded woman fighting today?"

"Yes." Anastasia was suspicious. This fellow looked like a barbarian, a Gaul, in fact. There was something about him, though, something familiar. Could it be the long, tusklike mustaches? "Do I know you?"

"Oh, surely not," laughed the man, making a sketchy bow. He was very well built, almost like a wrestler, save with flatter muscles, rather than bulging round sinews. "I am a visitor to the city. My name is Vitellix. I am a very, very minor *lanista*."

Anastasia raised an eyebrow, though its usual daunting effect was lost on the self-effacing man. "You have met Thyatis before? In Persia, perhaps?" She made a sign to her guardsmen, who closed in around the man, their bodies sliding between her and this stranger.

"Oh, no," Vitellix said, starting to sweat again, though the passage was shady and cool. "I know nothing of any Persian business! She was with my troupe, for a little while, while her wounds mended! Please, my lady, I mean no disrespect or harm—it cuts at me to see her thrown to the dogs like this!"

"She is proving a wolf." Anastasia smiled grimly. "More than these curs can stomach. You will come with us, I think."

The Gaul blanched but did not resist when the guardsmen took hold of his elbows. Anastasia marched out of the tunnel, her mind, at last, waking to the chase.

THE OLD CAMP OF THE XTH LEGION, AQUINCUM, MAGNA GOTHICA

Bucephalas tossed his big square head, flipping his glossy black mane at Alexandros' face. The Macedonian moved his head to the side with the ease of long experience. The horse stared at him mournfully with one large brown eye. Alexandros ignored the entreaty, continuing to brush the flanks and back in even, strong movements. He had a curry brush of wood and ivory strapped to one hand. He was taking his time, letting his thoughts wander far away from his daily effort of routine and discipline and instruction.

"Vittam croceam ea circum crinem flavum gestavit
In vere cum nove Maia gestavit."

Sound from five hundred throats, a little breathless from running, filled the late-afternoon air. Oak and pine crowded the fringes of the field of Mars. Out on the uneven ground, *syntagmas* of men were drilling. Two trembling rectangles of motion, each two hundred and fifty-six men, sixteen rows of sixteen, jogged across the field. Their long spears were held straight up over their heads like a thicket of newly planted saplings. They jogged at half-time, up and down the field, file leaders growling and barking like hunting dogs. The men ignored the threats and curses, concentrating on their marching cadence and step.

Alexandros smiled. Weeks had passed since anyone had fouled a *sarissa* in simple marching practice. There was progress, but it was very slow. They were far better at singing, which pleased the Macedonian, for he loved the sound of men's voices raised in rough harmony. Only this glorious Draculis horse and the prospect of power pleased him more.

"Et si rogasses pro quo gereres
dixisset pro milite suis gestare
quo absit procul et longe
procul et longe
procul et longe.
Gestavit pro milite suis quo absit procul et longe!"

Bucephalas whinnied and bumped Alexandros' shoulder heavily.

"No," said Alexandros, his voice light. "No apples or biscuit for you yet. I have to get these burrs out."

In the darkness before the sun, Alexandros had rousted out his Companion cavalry and made them dash five Legion miles to the outpost at Castra and then back again, all without warning. The run woke him up, set his blood in motion, though he was sure the Goths were sound asleep, sprawled on the floor of their long house. He continued to brush, taking his time.

"Cunam infantis ea circum insulam in urbe tulit
In vere cum nove Maia tulit.
Et si rogasses pro quo tulisset
dixisset pro milite suis impellere

> *quo absit procul et longe*
> *procul et longe*
> *procul et longe.*
> *Tulit pro milite suis absit procul et longe!"*

One of the syntagmas shifted step and the cadence rose, now sounding very hoarse. The men in this group had been marching for almost three hours. When the drill was done, Alexandros expected many of them to collapse on the ground, exhausted, arms and legs burning. The rectangle stopped with a faint rattle of sarissa on sarissa, then grounded the butts of their sixteen-foot weapons. A centurion, the syntagmatarch, shouted more commands and, as one, the men angled their long spears forward. Alexandros stopped brushing for a moment, tangling his hand in the stallion's mane so it couldn't eat his shirt. If the men kept individual distance, when they angled their sarissa, they should make a solid front of iron and ash, impervious to cavalry.

> *"Floras pulchras ea circum sepulcrum posuit.*
> *In vere cum nove Maia posuit.*
> *Et si rogasses pro quo possuisset*
> *dixisset pro milite suis ponere"*

The spear points lowered en masse. At the right edge of the formation, some of the sarissa tangled, knocking against one another. Men struggled to keep formation and clear their fouled weapons. There was some success. Alexandros spilled wine and grain on the altar of Skyfather Zeus each day, thankful the Gothic race was endowed with great strength and endurance. Handling the sarissa took raw strength. The pale-faced Romans, short of stature and weak-limbed, would never have managed.

> *"quo absit procul et longe*
> *procul et longe*

procul et longe.
Posuit pro milite suis quo absit procul et longe!"

The Macedonian thought the city-dwelling Latins had been very clever, fielding an army which relied on maneuvers, precision and skill to fight rather than raw strength. These Romans were sometimes wise, knowing where they excelled and where they lacked. Alexandros sighed, turning away. The centurions were kicking and shouting at the men who failed to keep formation.

"Wretch!" Bucephalas had snaked his huge soft nose into Alexandros' shirt, snaring an apple. The horse grinned, whuffling a cloud of moist, horsey breath into the Macedonian's face. "Ah! That is foul. . . ." Alexandros buried his head in the stallion's mane, drinking in the clean smell, letting himself dream—just for an instant—of home. Not the home of his youth, not violent, fratricidal Pella, but his ever-victorious army. There was safety there, a chance to rest. *My brothers walk in golden fields,* he thought mournfully, *and I am all alone.*

"Comes Alexandros?" A pained look passed over the Macedonian's face, but when he turned, his face was open and welcoming. Krythos, subcaptain of the scouts, jogged up. "Lord Ermanerich says a messenger has come from the reik in Siscia."

Alexandros raised an eyebrow. Perhaps his impatience was driven by the Fates. "Good," he said, "are Chlothar and the others in the longhouse?"

Krythos nodded sharply. The man had been very close mouthed since the battle with the Draculis raiders, which had earned him Alexandros' approval and a promotion. The scout seemed to be a canny man, well traveled and skilled in the woods. Such men, used to spending long periods of time alone, perhaps in enemy country, were naturally circumspect. Alexandros was pleased.

"Feel like running?" The scout nodded and together they

ran swiftly back across the green field towards the praetorium and the regularly spaced buildings of the camp.

A messenger had come, a tired-looking Goth already snoring on one of the sleeping benches by the time Alexandros and Krythos reached the praetorium. As always, a crowd loitered around, hungry for news. Soldiers were worse than horses. Ermanerich and Chlothar were waiting, too. The big Frank was stuffing his face, digging spoonfuls of grain mash and honey out of a bowl. The Gothic prince was almost beside himself with fidgeting. Alexandros grinned at them, then picked up the message tube from the praetor's desk. He unscrewed one end, then unrolled the parchments inside.

There were letters inside, one open, one sealed. The sealed letter was from Gaius Julius in Rome. The other, a missive from the Gothic reik, Theodoric. When he was done, Alexandros rolled them up again, thinking, and put them back in the tube. Then, dragging the moment out, he called for a jug of wine. The slaves, who had been keeping out of the way, dashed forward, deposited the red clay amphora and then scuttled away again. Alexandros looked around at the faces of his men, measuring them with his eyes. He poured unmixed wine into a shallow cup. Putting the cup to his lips, he drank. The wine was bitter, a poor local vintage.

"Word has come," he said at last, "from the Emperor of the West, Galen. He calls upon the Gothic people to come forth to aid Rome in war. He has sent an edict to Theodoric, stating the feodorate may put a wholly Gothic army into the field."

A sigh of relief passed through the room. Goth would fight beside Goth in the line of battle, and everyone would see their deeds. Their glory would not be lost, forgotten amongst the Romans.

"There is more. Various disasters have occurred in the East, where rebellious men threaten the Eastern Emperor.

The Augustus Galen, invincible and wise, has resolved to support his brother emperor. Four Western legions are sailing to Constantinople to join the Eastern army in repelling these invaders. We, the Gothic Legion, are to meet them there, traveling overland."

Ermanerich was grinning, fit to burst, and even the usually morose Chlothar began to smile. The other subcaptains were pleased in a grim way. Alexandros raised a hand before they could begin congratulating themselves. "This is not all."

He paused, tapping the end of the message tube with his fingertip. "Theodoric, your reik has the settlement of who and how many will go. He directs me thus in this letter:"

Alexandros cleared his throat, summoning up the words from memory.

"It has come to the ear of the King," he quoted, "that many Gothic men, even those barred from service under the Comes Alexandros, have joined the band gathered at Aquincum. Too, many barbarians and outlanders, even Franks and Gepids, have sworn themselves to the banner of the *comes*. In this way, the band has grown large, larger than the reik intended. This both pleases and displeases the reik. In the matter of the Emperor's will, the reik directs only those men who are not of noble Gothic blood to follow the *comes* to battle in the East."

Alexandros looked around again, the hint of a smile on his lips. There was stunned silence. "Those men," he continued, "who do not go into the East will return to Siscia to serve the reik himself, as his own *thegns*."

Ermanerich, beside himself, growled in outrage. "Curse him! What is this? We cannot go to war? We cannot fight?"

"Some of us," Alexandros gestured to Chlothar and the other outlander captains, "will go to war. The reik will keep his own men close to hand. You most of all, I think."

"But . . ." The Goth was speechless.

"It means more than half of the Companions will not go," Chlothar rumbled, heavy face composed in thought. "But the rest of the army, it may march. There are few princelings among the Peltasts or scouts. He is clever, this King of the Goths."

"How? He insults us, he insults me, his own son!" Ermanerich was turning a dark red color. "Are we children? Babies? Do we need shelter, hiding behind our mothers' skirts?"

Alexandros put a hand on the youth's shoulder, his face grim and set. "You are a soldier, Prince Ermanerich. You will obey the orders of your reik as if they were orders from me. If the reik wishes the noblemen in this army to stand by his side, they will." The Macedonian raised his voice so that everyone in the hall could hear him. "I will abide by the orders of Theodoric, reik of the Goths, as will any man—*any* man—who serves under me."

Alexandros held their gaze, his eyes glittering, until each man nodded in agreement. Ermanerich was the last and the angriest, but in the end, he too bent his head. "Very well. Bring the roster. We must adapt to this circumstance."

Krythos already had the mustering book opened on the table. Alexandros hooked a chair with his foot, then sat. After a pause, his captains did so as well. The Macedonian was in an unexpectedly good humor. He could feel fate, turning like a fulcrum, in the air around him.

THE SUB-URBS OF CONSTANTINOPLE

Mohammed leaned close, bristly white beard brushing against Zoë's shoulder. "How do you feel?" The Palmyrene girl smiled weakly, her face pale and wrapped with bandages. She raised her hand, gently touch-

ing the side of his face. The Quraysh smiled, taking her
fingers in his own. He was sitting on a stool on the rear
deck of the *Jibril,* beneath the big canvas shade. Early
morning light fell in long slats across the wooden ship.

"I am well. I feel . . . drained and sore, like I've ridden
a long way on a lame camel."

Mohammed nodded, fingertips brushing across the right
side of her head. "Do you remember what happened?"

Zoë shook her head, swallowing. She licked her lips.
They were very dry and a little crusty. "Is there something
to drink?"

Mohammed tipped a clay jar to her lips and she drank
slowly, letting the cool water moisten her face. Then she
lay back, still pale, but in the morning light he thought she
was regaining some color. Zoë looked around and saw
Odenathus leaning on one of the poles supporting the canvas. His lean dark face was filled with worry.

"Cousin." Zoë tried to smile at him but thought it came
out as a grimace. "You look poorly."

"He has not slept," Mohammed said, voice lifted by
quiet laughter. "He and I and Khalid have taken turns
watching by your side. You look better, I think, than we
do!"

Odenathus nodded in agreement, then came to her side
and squatted on the deck. Zoë frowned at him, seeing
worry lines and wrinkles around his eyes. He seemed much
older than she remembered. "How long have I been sleeping?"

"Not long," Mohammed said, voice a gentle rumble.
"Three or four days. We were only worried at the beginning—you had water in your lungs. Luckily, one of the
Palmyrene sea captains knows a trick for getting it out
again. Your ear will heal, too, though I fear there will be
a scar."

"My ear?" Zoë raised her hand, surprised at the effort
it took, and touched the side of her head. Thick linen band-

ages were tight against her flesh. "What happened to my ear?"

"You don't remember?" Mohammed frowned, sharing a glance with Odenathus. "It was ruined, torn up, bleeding fiercely. There was some kind of metal sting in it, and small red wounds on your neck. Do you remember what happened on the *Archelaos*?"

"No." Zoë's eyes widened and she tried to sit up. The effort was too much and she fell back on the pallet. "Did something happen to the Queen? Is she safe?"

Mohammed sighed to himself and a shadow passed over his face. "The merchant ship sank, holed, and the Queen's funeral car went down with it. Khalid has some divers working in the wreck, I believe. They may recover it."

"Khalid thinks it will be soon." Odenathus leaned close, laying the back of his hand on Zoë's pale, sweaty forehead. "The catafalque may be destroyed by the fire and water, but the Queen will be lying safe in her sarcophagus. They have a barge with a crane. She will see the sun again soon."

Zoë nodded, relieved, and her eyes closed. Within a grain, she was sleeping deeply, her breathing regular and her face slowly resuming a normal color. Mohammed stood, pensive with worry, and motioned for Odenathus to follow him. The Quraysh stepped to the rail, ignoring the shoreline, crowded with houses and temples. They were very close to the city itself.

"There was something on her, some device." It was a statement, not a question. Odenathus nodded in agreement. He did not possess any of the healing art, but there had been remnants of some odd power in the wound. The Palmyrene sorcerer had driven the pattern out. The working had tried to dig deep, perhaps attacking her mind.

"There was an earring she was wearing, a black Gerrhaenid pearl, very rare. She never said where she got it. It was in that ear. Did she bring such a thing from Palmyra?"

"No." Odenathus remembered the jewel as well. The pearls of the Sinus Persicus were renowned the world over, but the black ones, they were a treasure. "It was a Queen's ornament, surely, but I did not see her take such a bauble from the ruins. I thought she found it in the market at Caesarea."

"Perhaps." Mohammed's face grew long, thick hand smoothing his beard. "Or perhaps it was a gift. Gerrhae has long been in the domain of the Persians. The lord Shahr-Baraz might easily possess such a thing."

Odenathus made a face at the thought. "She would not take such a thing from him!"

"No, but another might give her a gift, not saying who had sent it."

"Who?" Odenathus looked around in suspicion. Mohammed was being circuitous and the young man's mind turned to treachery. "You think there are Persian agents among us?"

"I am sure of it!" Mohammed laughed, but it was not a merry, joyful sound. "The Boar is not a fool. I am sure there are many agents among our men. Persia is well known for having an extensive network of informers in the Roman East, where the majority of our troops have come from. One of them, however, has made the acquaintance of the lady Zoë. She came close to death from this. We will have to be careful."

"And watchful!" Odenathus felt a heavy weight settle upon him. Soon the struggle would begin in dire earnest and this only added to his burden. "I will keep an eye on her."

"Good." Mohammed looked away, out across the waters, at the rich countryside. This land was thickly settled, with gyres and barns and vineyards in endless array. Streams spilled down out of the fields into the waters of the strait. Even from here, he could hear cattle lowing on the shore. He was sad, but he kept the feeling to himself. The desert was so much cleaner, more open, the sky and the horizon visible. There was no thickness to the air, no clinging heat and dampness. In this place, a hawk might spiral in the sky, invisible, the sight of one's eye muddied by the heavy air. "Our cause is too poor to afford treachery."

Near dark, the clouds parted. A violent golden sunset covered the land, sending down shining beams through the remaining clouds. On the deck of the *Jibril,* Mohammed was heartened, seeing the rose and violet wash the sky. It had not rained much on the ships, the scudding clouds keeping to the land as sheep to the flock.

"It is very beautiful." Zoë's voice was weak, but she could walk unaided.

"Yes, almost like home." Mohammed pulled over a wicker chair, one draped with his cloak. "Sit. There is news."

"I could feel it," Zoë said, dark eyes smiling up at him. "This ship is too small for secrets. Everyone started to act busy and 'on important business.' What happened?"

Mohammed pointed at the shore with his chin. The Arab fleet was pacing the advance of the Sahaban army on land. Now they were anchored in shallow water off the harbor of Perinthus, the second largest city on the Propontis. It was a strongly defended city on a peninsula, flanked by steep-sided banks above a narrow beach. A tall wall cut off the base of the headland, protecting the city.

"The city fathers will not surrender, and we are pressed for time. We need this harborage. Khalid and Jalal have been arguing over assaulting the port. Odenathus has gone ashore to see if he can do anything."

Zoë raised a sharp black eyebrow. "Such a place will have old, old wards and patterns. They will be difficult to break."

"I know. A sticky point. We cannot get mired in a siege, not when a greater one lies just ahead. Jalal also sends word his scouts have reached the belt of open ground around Constantinople itself."

"Has there been fighting?"

Mohammed nodded. "Some. Our patrols have clashed with theirs for the past several days, but they have not come out in force. They are certain we cannot get into their city if they keep the gates closed. They can be patient."

"What about the Persians?"

Mohammed tilted his head in the other direction, to the southeast. "I have had some correspondence with the King of King's messengers. A swift-riding force of horsemen has taken possession of the southern shore—I believe they are Hunnic mercenaries, if you can believe that—and are waiting for Shahr-Baraz and his main army to arrive."

"Well!" Zoë smoothed back her hair, which had been washed while she slept. Still weak, she had not bothered to don her armor, content to hobble about in a thick white shirt and baggy pants. "Everyone is gathering for a party . . . but when does it start?"

"Soon." Mohammed curled his fingers over the hilt of his black sword. "A courier galley arrived only an hour ago—that was the trouble you heard—Roman ships, in numbers, have been sighted in the Hellespont."

"Riding up on us," Zoë growled, looking over her shoulder at the dying sun in the west. "Are we trapped?"

"Yes." Mohammed seemed pleased by this. "We cannot go back, not without fighting our way out of the narrow strait. The enemy, however, will not be able to get *in* unless I withdraw the fleet from Sestus. Or, if we give battle and they defeat us."

"What are we going to do?" The Palmyrene woman's attitude shifted subtly, and Mohammed knew that he was speaking to a fellow ruler now, not a dear friend. "I do not think the Roman emperor is going to come out and fight you, hand to hand, on the field of honor."

Sighing, Mohammed unclenched his hand from the

sword hilt. "I fear you are right. If the Persian army can be shipped across the strait, we can attack the city with a great army. Perhaps it will be enough to break the gates. But, more to the point, we don't have enough shipping to ferry the Persians about *and* blockade the city *and* hold the Hellespont closed. I have already sent a ship back with orders for the galleys at Sestus to join us. We will let the enemy in behind us."

Zoë smiled, thinking of flexing her power in the hidden world. Ships seemed particularly vulnerable to sorcery. "Two dogs in a pit, with no easy way out."

"Exactly." Mohammed's face was very grim, forbidding. "Only one of us will leave alive."

THE VILLA OF NARSES, OUTSIDE ROMA MATER

This is a villa?" Betia did not bother to hide her disgust. Anastasia did not respond, climbing down from her litter and being careful not to step in anything. The Duchess was dressed very simply—her humor had not improved enough to indulge in her usual extravagant dress—and she was on a business visit, so it seemed proper to dress like a revered matron. "It's so . . . *small*."

Anastasia waved the litter bearers away and they trotted off down the lane, all husky backs and stout legs. Raising a carefully plucked eyebrow at her servant, she ducked under a trellised archway and into the garden. A high wall of mud-red bricks surrounded the lot, faced with a simple wooden gate on the country road. A house—well, more of an ambitious shed—sat at the back of the property.

The owner was squatting on the ground behind rows of feeble-looking grapevines. Anastasia stepped carefully along the path and stopped. "Hello, Narses."

The master of the Ludus Magnus, the greatest gladiatorial school in the city of Rome, indeed, in the Empire, looked up from under a sun hat of badly woven straw.

"Why," he said, squinting into the afternoon sun, "you must be the Duchess of Parma."

"You know who I am." Anastasia was determined to be blunt and open. In her peripheral experience with the man, nothing else seemed to work. They had never met face-to-face before. "I've come to make you an offer. I want to purchase one of your fighters."

"Hmm." Narses looked to his vines. "I'm busy right now. Come back later, or better, see me at the school."

He looked back up, a length of twine in his mouth. "You're young to be buying playthings."

Anastasia gave a short, cool laugh. "I don't want to buy a man."

"That one, eh? She's not for sale, not for any price."

"No?" Anastasia shifted so the sun fell in Narses' eyes. He blinked, then started to squint. "How much?"

Narses shook his head. "Even in this foul old city, there are some things that are not for sale. She is one of them. Fate put her in my hands, fate can take her away. But I won't sell her."

Anastasia looked around, seeing patchy walls and a sagging roof on the shed. The plot was in a section of the Tiber Valley leased out to the middle classes for bits of garden. It was no patrician's villa, for sure. "She must make you a great deal of money."

The *lanista* made a *harrumph*ing sound. "It's forbidden for the schools to bet on the fighters."

Anastasia made a half-smile, watching the stocky cripple stand up. It was difficult with only one arm, making him do a little half-step dance. Betting on the fights, the races and the games was illegal, but that just meant enormous sums of coin changed hands without being taxed by the Imperial government.

"Narses, I am not looking for a toy. I want the woman out of the arena."

"Sorry." Narses rubbed his nose. "She's in on a criminal charge. I'm just representing her, picking up the tab for food, water, boys, things like that. She's not mine to sell. Go ask the Emperor to let her out!" The lanista chuckled at the concept.

"No," Anastasia growled, "I won't. Please, you'd let one of the younger men out if their . . . mother paid you. I know these things happen."

"Diana is not a child." There was a bite in his voice. "Are you her mother?"

The Duchess gave him a steely look. His smirking attitude made her angry—she wouldn't give this *peasant* anything. "No. Just a friend."

"Duchess, I cannot help you. The woman is in the arena on a prison charge. Only the Emperor can release her."

Anastasia hissed in disgust, then turned away and strode out of the garden. The man was a dumb stone. Betia hurried after her after carefully putting down some flowers that she had picked while waiting. Narses shook his head in disgust. *Rich people. Always wanting to buy something shiny they saw in the market.* He walked to the gate, closed it, then knelt and picked up the flowers. They were red peonies and very pretty. He tucked one behind his ear.

He waited by the gate, listening. Men ran up and the two women got into a litter, then jogged off down the road. Narses sighed, blowing his lips out, and frowned. He had hoped to finish the last row of trellises today. Instead, he put everything away, then tied up the gate with a bit of rope to keep the goats out. Narses jogged off at a regular, easy pace. There were shortcuts along the river. He could easily beat the litter back to the city.

Rapping hammers echoed in the big open bowl of the Flavian. Dozens of men were working around the fringes of the arena floor, repairing damage sustained in the last series of fights. More men were high up on the marble walls, suspended by ropes, washing the statuary and travertine walls. Gaius Julius paced along the first deck of seats. It was a pleasant morning. The arena custodians were making the best of an off day. The old Roman tipped his hat, squinting up at the higher rows.

A dark figure crouched there, on hands and knees, above one of the vomitoria capping the internal stairways. Gaius sighed in exasperation, then climbed up two flights of narrow steps to reach his master. The old Roman had not expected to find Maxian here today, but since he was, there was a question that had been bothering him.

"My lord? What are you doing?" The old Roman tried to keep weary resignation from his voice but failed. *Who knew the business of sorcerers? Who wanted to know?*

Maxian looked up, dark brown eyes hooded. He grunted, then turned back to the slab of marble under his feet. Numbers were cut into the surface, a V on one side and a VI on the other. Both were almost illegible due to wear. Maxian ignored Gaius and ran his thin hands over the stone, slowly, an inch at a time. He chanted softly, letting the words form of their own accord.

Gaius shook his head in dismay, but remained sitting quietly until the Prince was done. The memory of black lightning lingered with him, and men howling in agony, trapped in the jagged light.

"Well?" Maxian stood at last, stretching his back and grunting a little. He brushed white dust from his tunic. "You didn't climb all the way up here to keep me company."

"No . . ." Gaius Julius smoothed down the fringe of hair around his head. "Aren't you worried that someone will recognize you, skulking around like this in broad daylight?"

Maxian smiled and raised a finger. The air around him shuddered, bending this way and that, wavering like an open flame. Then the Prince was gone, leaving a nondescript worker in baggy clothing and an annoyed expression. "Do you feel better?" The apparition spoke with the Prince's voice.

"I suppose." Gaius Julius' voice had a strangled sound and he sat down on one of the benches. "I should have guessed. What are you doing with the section markers?"

The Prince wavered again and resumed his own shape. He scuffed a toe across the marble slab. "I am trying something delicate—even with you hulking brutes hanging over my shoulder. I do not want to be disturbed. So I have been laying my own pattern, some signs and symbols to watch and listen and warn."

"Down here?" Gaius Julius looked around. These were the middle seats, which would be swarming with lower-caste patricians and their drinking companions on game day. "I thought you were working up there." The old Roman pointed at the roof high overhead.

"Oh, I've already seen to that. But I found some interesting things in the pattern of the building while I was finishing up. I've been . . . patching and mending. Making sure these signs have the power of their first making. These section markers ring the whole arena, each imbued with its own mild purpose."

Gaius Julius lifted his sandal, peering at the slab. "There is a spell on them?"

"Oh yes. Old Vespasian was no fool. He built this place with a purpose beyond just entertaining the citizens. I think the Oath spoke to him in his dreams, guiding him."

Gaius Julius laughed, thinking of some of the histories he had read. "Dreamed? Vespasian?"

"Yes, Gaius, he dreamed of gold and its orderly collection. He dreamed of an empire at peace."

"An empire of citizens who had no excuse to avoid paying their taxes, you mean!"

Maxian laughed, but nodded. "At the same time he began construction of the Flavian, each regional governor began his own amphitheater—hundreds of them, one in each town and city. All of them match the plan of the Flavian in some degree; all of them are dedicated to the gods of Rome and to the state."

Gaius Julius raised his hands. "All praise the Capitoline Triad and the Divine Emperor! I see your point. The provincial amphitheaters are the warp and weft of the Oath."

"Even so. Like so much of it, the signs and patterns here have been damaged over time. I'm just making sure they are restored."

"Why?" Gaius Julius tried to keep overwhelming curiosity out of his voice.

Maxian did not answer. The Prince began to pace away, measuring his footsteps, counting under his breath.

I'll ask him later, Gaius grumbled to himself.

Anastasia's gloom had not lifted by the time she reached the Villa of Swans. She was displeased by her handling of the *lanista;* she should have known everything about the man, about his operation, about Thyatis' captivity before she revealed her interest. She was out of shape, like a gear fouled with rust. It would take time—time she might not have—to restore her network of informers and chatty friends. She entered the gardens at the rear of the house, ignoring the wild display of summer flowers. Even the chuckling of the fountains and streams flowing down from a hidden reservoir at the top of the house failed to cheer her up.

Betia followed along, equally depressed. The Duchess's mood infected her own. There was no sign anyone other than Thyatis had escaped from the destruction of Vesuvius.

"Find the Gaul and his friends, bring them to me."

Betia's head snapped up, her face blank, and then she hurried off.

Anastasia looked around wearily. She was in the hall of the Poseidon. The god loomed over her, regal face staring down the hallway of sea-green marble, his limbs straining against the sea breaking around him in stone waves. He

failed to lift her spirits, though this had once been a favorite room. Like much of her house, the Poseidon was
cast in shadow, echoing the gloom in her own heart. The
villa seemed very empty.

"Oh, you gods, you torment me, showing me happiness,
then snatching it away."

Anastasia dabbed at her eyes. Tears were welling up,
making sparkling tracks in the antimony on her cheeks.
Precious months had passed while she wallowed in despair. Jusuf was gone, sent away like Tros; Thyatis thought
dead; Nikos and Krista surely killed. Shirin's babies, who
had brought such lively chaos into her life for such a short
time, had been in Baiae, right in the path of the eruption.
Their tiny corpses had never been recovered. So much
death. So little life.

But now, with her mind awake, she was no longer
gripped by despair. She was angry. Very angry. Everything
had happened because of one man—this prince, this child,
this boy—who was destruction for her dreams. Even the
bittersweet memory of their closeness was a goad to her.

"Betia!" Anastasia's voice rose, ringing from the vaulted
ceiling. "Attend me!"

The blond girl appeared, her hair disordered from running, with the Gaul, Vitellix, in tow. Both of them seemed
wary, but Anastasia did not care.

"Gaul. You and your troupe found a man, a Numidian,
in the burning inn. Is he here?"

"Yes, my lady. A priest of Asclepius has tended to
him—his cheek and knee were broken—but he will be
well soon, I hope."

Anastasia considered glaring at the man until he burst
into flames, but there was no time for such petty fancies.
The Gaul matched her gaze, a little nervous but resolute.
"I would talk to him."

"This way." Betia bowed nervously. "He is in the west
wing."

The Duchess swept past, the train of her gown picked

up in one jeweled hand. "Good. I want to know everything about the Ludus Magnus. Betia—have a scribe join us, immediately."

For a moment, she considered sending a messenger to Helena to ask her for an appointment and for advice. Just as quickly, she discarded the thought. If she was to pick up her old life, she would do so entirely. She would speak with the Emperor and the Empress when she knew exactly what she wanted to say, and to propose.

Heavy age-stained wood groaned on stone and the cell door swung open. Thyatis rose stiffly, her hands in plain sight. The guards were simple men; if she did not stand quietly in the middle of the grimy room, hands out to her sides, there would be no food. She had been squatting, mind empty, in the exact middle of the cell, waiting. At least two days had passed since she and Candace and Agrippina had survived the battle against the criminals. She was pleased with this room, it was much larger than the last. Exercise was possible, though she couldn't really work up a sweat.

"Hello." It was the crippled man, Narses, standing in the doorway. He leaned heavily on his walking stick. Thyatis guessed the cane was an affectation, playing to the missing arm. "Would you like better quarters? A bath? Edible food?"

Thyatis did not answer, waiting for the other boot to drop. Narses chuckled a little to himself, then stepped down into the room. He banged on the door with his stick and it swung closed behind him. Thyatis raised an eyebrow, but the old gladiator just leaned against the wall, tapping his scarred chin with the hawk-headed cane.

"I am serious, Diana. I would like to put you and your two fellow 'Amazons' in better quarters—with beds, for one thing, and a private practice yard. Ah . . . now I have your attention."

"Why?" Thyatis put her hands behind her back, fingers

clasped. She stood straighter. "What do you want from me?"

"Now? Well, previously I wanted to make my money back. But you've done that already . . . I think I'll protect my investment."

Thyatis laughed, cracking her knuckles and staring up at the groined ceiling. "An investment. Like a stud horse or a milk cow."

Narses nodded, but there was a merry glint in his eye that took some of the sting away. "If you like. Your skill makes you valuable. Let me reward you."

"In exchange for what?" Thyatis leaned forward, a smirk on her face. "For not killing any slave, attendant, guard, wayward tourist that I come across in your house? For not trying to escape?"

Narses nodded, chin jutting out. "A fair bargain, I think."

Thyatis laughed, a harsh bark. "How many days until I—we—go on the sand again?"

Narses held up three stubby fingers. "Your next opponents are prisoners of war, taken in Persia and the East."

"A big show. Just the sand, or with some kind of set?"

The lanista clapped his hand to his chest. "You've been to the games before! Yes, twenty Amazons against twenty Persian prisoners of war—they're building a replica of a city called Tauris. It's supposed to ape some siege, a river crossing . . . What is it?"

Narses paused, humor draining from his face. Thyatis' expression had not changed, but her eyes lit with furious anger. "Diana?"

"A rich jest." The woman bit out the words. "I will not attempt to escape. You will give us training weapons, just wood, of normal weight so that these women you are sending to their deaths can have some faint hope. You will let me speak with these other women and show them some rudiments of defense. We will play out your scene. You will not be disappointed."

Narses nodded, then rapped on the door again. The

woman turned away, leaning against the wall, both hands pressed against the bricks. She remained that way while he stumped out. In the hallway, he shook his head in amusement. He had seen so much in the arena, far more than he would have thought the first day he stepped into this bloody house.

"You lads! Take these three women out of their cells, put them in the first sword's quarters!"

Narses stomped off, whistling to himself. Hamilcar had been getting used to such plush accommodations! The boy needed to remember who was the master here, and who the oath- and contract-bound slave. Of course, Hamilcar might be a little angry about losing his privileges, his better food, his private bath. But that didn't matter to Narses. The lanista smiled to himself, supremely happy, and made sure that the peony behind his ear was still there. Behind him, the slaves and guards stared after him in surprise. Then they shook their heads and went to unlock the cells. Stranger things had happened, though no one could say when.

When he got to his office, a thought occurred to him. He banged on the wall until one of the clerks in the outer room came in.

"Jordanes, send a boy over to Gaius Julius' office with a note to come by when he can."

"Yes, master!"

THE PROPONTIS, NORTH OF THE GOLDEN HORN

A rrows fell like rain, some burning, streaking across the night. Men struggling on the shore screamed, dying under the iron hail. Shahr-Baraz, King of Kings, lord of the Persians and the Medes, spurred his horse forward, hooves rumbling on the plank road. Around him, Persian spearmen surged forward, every third man carrying a torch. The night was a wild confusion of burning lights and darkness. Bonfires roared on the shore, throwing a ruddy, red light on the faces of the soldiers. The Boar cantered down off the bridge, his sword raised, catching the firelight. "Forward! Clear the road!"

A deep-throated roar answered him and spearmen and *diquans* in full armor poured down onto the beach. Roman soldiers fled before him, throwing down bundles of pitch-soaked brush and lanterns. The King reined in his horse, laughing—a huge booming sound that rolled and echoed across the battlefield—to see the Romans running like hares. More arrows fell amongst the fleeing men. Dark shapes ran between them, gore-streaked swords flashing. More men died. Shahr-Baraz sheathed his sword with a *ting* and raised the silver visor of his helmet. The metal plate was worked into the face of a man, with a nose and eyes, and inlaid with gold. Wearing a full suit made for hot work, but gave excellent protection.

"My lord?"

The shahanshah looked down, tugging at his mustaches. "Yes, Lord Piruz?"

The Eastern diquan made a sharp bow, then pointed up the road. "The Romans are falling back along the road, too; should we pursue?"

"No." Shahr-Baraz' voice was firm. A troop of men with long axes and maces clattered past down the wooden ramp from the last of the ships. "Push down the road until you can only just make out the bonfires. Round up the guards and beat the bushes for more Romans and our own men. We'll begin sending the army across at first light. You had better have secured the area by then."

Piruz made another bow and then clanked off into the night. A score of men in full mail and swords followed him. Shahr-Baraz sighed. The Easterner had a black scarf knotted where his breastplate and shoulder armor joined. One of Purandokht's tokens. Some days, the King wondered which of his adopted daughters had more followers. *No matter!* he thought. *They are here, these hotheaded youths, and they fight for me. We can deal with the suitors later, after the war has culled them!*

Shahr-Baraz nudged his horse and trotted back up the ramp. The surface swayed under the charger's heavy tread, but the Boar was not concerned. His engineers had built well on the foundation provided by the Arab fleet. Lines of men marched in the other direction as he let the horse trot along. The Boar knew them, passing in the night, by their standards and ornamented shields, by the make of their helms and the fletching of their arrows. Khorasanians, Medes, Daylami archers, Gaur mountaineers, lowlanders from Mespotamia, the hill chiefs of Tabaristan. All the panoply and glory of Imperial Persia. He passed lanterns too, suspended on the stern posts of the ships making up his bridge.

Khadames had not believed such a thing could be built, even when Shahr-Baraz showed him the passage in one of the old books. A hero of ancient times had done this, crossing over the Hellespont. He had been fighting Greeks, too. Most of the Arab fleet did yeoman duty, lashed together with ropes, making a wooden bridge from one side of the Propontis to the other. A wide swath of buildings across Chalcedon had been looted for the timber to make a roadbed on the back of the fleet. Shields flanked the sides of the wooden road, giving men on the precarious bridge shelter from Roman attacks.

Shahr-Baraz grinned in the darkness, torchlight catching on his strong white teeth. An enormous weight was taken from him, knowing the Arab fleet prowled out in the darkness, watching the approaches to the city, keeping Roman boats from attacking this fragile lifeline between Europe and Asia. He raised a gauntleted hand in salute—the folly of Heraclius and the noble honor of Palmyra and Arabia made this possible. *Bless you, Emperor!*

"King of Kings." The voice was flat, emotionless, without a hint of human warmth.

Shahr-Baraz gentled his horse, which was not used to the odd smell, and halted. He was on the third ship from the Asian shore, now confronted with two dark figures, cloaked and hooded, showing only the barest glint of iron scale at their hands. "You have news?"

"Yes. Our brothers say the Romans are all dead."

"Good." The Shanzdah had been set to watch and wait, while the guard at the western end of the bridge slept. A wise decision. Shahr-Baraz did not bother to ask how these figures knew what transpired a mile away, where their fellows hunted in the darkness. "Is there more?"

"Yes. You are wanted beyond the hill."

"Ah. Tell your master I will be there in a little while."

The King of Kings did not bother to wait for a response. He had not managed to get to the scene of the abortive raid in time to even swing a blade, but the dash across the water had roused his appetite. He would eat before he went down into the valley behind the hills. The black wagon could wait, having nowhere to go, save where he directed.

The sun had risen, wallowing up out of an eastern sky thick with clouds and haze, by the time Shahr-Baraz rode down into the dell hiding the wagon. Cold mist clung to the ground, coiling among dark-skinned trees and tombs. Slabs of cracked stone rose out of the ground, covered with thorns and vines. The path narrowed, passing between a pair of standing stones. The Boar was sure the locals had chosen this marshy hollow for their graveyard because no one wanted to live there anyway. Surely no land worth planting with wheat, grape, olive, flax or rye had been lost! Even at midday the damp ground under the trees seemed dark and close. A chill hung in the air. The charger snorted, shaking its head, but the King urged it on. Horse and man passed through an opening in a paling of iron poles driven into the ground.

Shahr-Baraz felt the cold eyes of hidden guardians watching him but showed no sign of fear. Tomb houses loomed up out of the dim light, their doors cracked and splintered. Moss hung from carved lintels and oozed across dirty floors. It was very still, without the sound of bird or man. Only the *clop-clop* of the charger's iron hooves on the tilted stone road disturbed the heavy silence. He reached a particular tree and stopped, swinging down off the horse. The charger stared at him with wild eyes, but the Boar ignored its entreaty, tying it securely to a low-hanging branch.

"I'll feed you when I get back." His voice sounded hollow in the air.

Beyond the tree, he walked to the left, then right, then ahead, following a path marked by small lead cones placed on the ground. The wards were etched with tiny, spiky symbols. Shahr-Baraz felt their presence as a growing resistance in the air, tugging at his beard, the passage of cold, ghostly fingers over his face and hands. At last he climbed a flight of ancient, crumbling steps and into the ruins of a temple. Only the snag-teeth of columns remained, marking out a double rectangle among tumbled blocks of stone and carvings. The black wagon sat at the center of the platform, heavy and forbidding. Broken mossy slabs floored the temple. Lines and patterns were scratched into the stone. A figure squatted, hands on knees, before the wagon, facing Shahr-Baraz. The King paced forward, stepping carefully, and the resistance in the air suddenly lessened.

Darkness folded around the Boar and he stopped, planting his feet, thumbs hooked into his belt. Though he stood under an open sky, here there was only twilight. High overhead, the sun was reduced to a dim bloated red disk. Walls of slowly moving gray smoke bounded the temple, shutting out the sight of the leprous trees and oddly pale undergrowth among the tombs.

The figure moved, raising its head. There was a rasp of metal on metal. Black-painted ears rose, smooth, muscular limbs flexed and the thing stood. It had the body of a man, olive skinned, belted with leather and a black kilt. The head was that of a great dog, a jackal, shining with red-painted eyes and a glistening iron finish.

What has happened? A voice echoed from the iron mask, splintered and broken by the shape of the mouth. *My Eyes tell me that the Romans came against the bridge.*

"They did. The Shanzdah were waiting and slew many. My soldiers drove off the rest. The bridge is safe and the army will begin moving across today, if the weather holds and the waters in the strait are quiet."

Excellent. Has the Axumite brought you the box?

"Yes." Shahr-Baraz nodded, curious. He reached into the tunic lying over his armor and pulled forth a small obsidian box covered with glyphs and figures. Some of the pictures were disturbing, showing coiling worms and an odd-looking city like the domain of enormous termites. "I have it safe with me at all times. Do you want it?"

No! This thing must stay closed and with you. Its contents are precious. G'harne does not give up her secrets easily . . . when the time is right, I will take it from you.

Shahr-Baraz smirked, pocketing the box. "You're afraid of this little box? It's barely big enough for a hen's egg."

Even so. Even so. There was a chuckling sound. *Now, where is the Arab, this Mohammed?*

Shahr-Baraz laughed, a rich, booming sound. "You cannot see him with your dead eyes?"

No! If I could see him, in the waking world or the hidden, he might perceive me as well. Tell me, is he still across the water?

"Yes," Shahr-Baraz nodded, "safe on the European shore. His army screens the city, watching for us while we labor on the bridge. It has been slow work—he failed to capture the town of Perinthus, so he lacks a good harbor for his ships—but we have finished. Soon we will be able to assail the city itself."

Do not hurry. There are friends coming to join us, from the North.

"Ah. The Avars have agreed to fight at our side, then?"

Yes. The khagan Bayan is coming with a great host of men. With them at our side, we will field more than a hundred thousand fighters.

"Can you send a message to your Eyes with Bayan?" The Boar tugged at his mustaches, thinking.

Yes. It is difficult, hidden as I am, but possible. What would you have him learn? The voice seemed puzzled, which brought a brief flicker of amusement to the Boar.

"Our situation here is precarious—though I'm sure you don't think so. Our army is far from home, living from forage and looting amongst the Roman villas. The Arab army is in equal straits. I have learned from a friend amongst the Arabs the Roman fleet blockades the southern mouth of the Hellespont, trapping our allies in the Propontis. The Roman fleet may have brought more troops—a new army, perhaps a Western army—which will attempt to relieve the city. At the moment, we have the strength to besiege and surround Constantinople, but not to take it by main strength."

We have discussed this. All you need to do is force a battle. I will take care of the rest.

"So you say, but I do not trust your plan. It is too complicated. The Fates are fickle and unkind, always waiting to trip up unwary men. Now—the Romans have spies everywhere, watching us. It is impossible for us to root them all out, to hide ourselves from their eyes, not in their own country. Bayan and his Avars, therefore, must move into the vicinity of the city quietly and carefully and out of sight. There will be no communication between us, save by your powers. The Romans will not come out of their city unless they think victory over us is assured."

Ah, we must appear threatening, but weak enough to

defeat in open battle. An injured rabbit, thrashing in the underbrush. Very well, I will influence the khagan.

"Good. We will see if we can defeat the Romans by *human* skill and arms. If I fail, then you will have your chance." Shahr-Baraz smirked, wondering if the jackal-headed man could understand what passed between the sorcerer and the King. "When will you cross over?"

Not soon! This is not a simple matter. I will continue to sleep, watching and waiting.

The Boar snorted. "Missing your head, are you? Afraid of this Arab?"

Do not mock me! The power that moves in the Quraysh is like the sun, indescribable, unsurpassed. If he knew—if that power knew—that I was your ally, he would turn against you. That would be a deadly struggle.

"You could not defeat it, then?" Shahr-Baraz pressed, stepping a foot closer to the black wagon and its inhabitant. Inside, encased in gold and lead, bounded around with spells and wards, lay the corpse of a prince. Despite its missing head, the body remained alive in some horrific way. "Could you fight it to a draw?"

I am not afraid of this Arab or the power that has woken in him. The voice was petulant. *But such a struggle would wreck all these lands, perhaps shatter the world. Even I, who know the secrets of death and life alike, prefer to walk and speak and live in a green world.*

"Ah. Then we must avoid discovery, eh? Well, you seem snug in your box. I have heard from our 'friend' the lord Mohammed carries your head in his ship, safe and sound. Of course, if the ship should sink . . ."

Do not say such things!

"Hah! Don't worry—it is quite safe, I'm sure. A bold ploy of yours—I'm not sure that I would be so free with my head." Shahr-Baraz swallowed the rest of his laughter. The chill in the air deepened and an almost palpable anger began to radiate from the wagon. "Peace! Peace. I will not mock you . . . much. Tell me this, if you can; when the time comes to move you, will a ship suffice, or will we need the bridge?"

A dry hiss echoed in the air, but the chill withdrew and the air lightened. *The bridge would be best . . . if the wooden road were covered with earth, or the boats lined with saplings, that would be very effective.*

"Saplings?" Shahr-Baraz shook his head. "I'll keep a fast galley on hand, waiting below these cliffs, on the shore. Once the army is across, we dare not keep the bridge up—it's too easy a target for the Roman fleet and impossible to protect. I want those ships free."

There was no answer, only a brooding silence. After a few moments, the King retraced his steps, careful to leave the tiny lead cones untouched, and returned to his horse. The jackal-headed man remained, squatting once again, waiting patiently. The dim red sun continued to ride high in the sky, casting a baleful light on the dead tombs.

▣Ю-[0]-[0]-[0]-[0]-[0]-[0]-[0]-[0]-[0]-[0]-[0]-[0]-[0]-[0]-[0]-[0]-[0]-[0]Ю▣

THE LUDUS MAGNUS, IN THE DISTRICT SOUTH
OF THE FLAVIAN

)(

A t Narses' nod, one of his guardsmen lifted the bar locking the first swords' quarters. The lanista stepped inside, his cane's distinctive *tap-tap* loud in the night. A lamp, burning low, illuminated a table littered with the corpse of dinner. Diana lay, her head sprawled on the tabletop, snoring softly, one hand still curled around a wine cup. Narses stumped up to her side, then rolled back an eyelid with his thumb.

"Sleeping." He grunted. "Check the others."

His men entered the room and found Candace and Agrippina asleep on their couches. Carts with padded wheels were waiting outside, each long enough for a tall man, which left plenty of room for the two shorter women. Narses watched with a paternal air while the slaves loaded the women onto the carts, swathed in blankets.

"Go on," he chided the men. "Use the tunnel and be quick about it."

Narses closed the door himself, once the others were gone, then picked up the bar and put it in place with his hand. He smiled at his fist. It was still strong. An Ethiopian merchant had once sold him a black springy ball, advising him of its many medicinal powers. The lanista found it relaxing to squeeze the ball in his fist seven or eight hundred times a day. Even one arm could still serve, if the will behind it was resolute.

He picked up the cane and walked back to his office, tapping it on the floor at regular intervals, whistling softly. Everyone else in the sprawling complex of buildings was sound asleep. Within the hour, a messenger would come back through the long underground tunnel connecting the Ludus Magnus to the Flavian, bringing word that Diana was safe in the heavily guarded pits under the amphitheater. They would not languish in mean cells, either, but in certain quarters reserved for special prisoners. His Amazons would not want for creature comforts!

"Well?" Gaius Julius was waiting in the office, a dark gray cloak thrown around his shoulders. The man's pate gleamed in the light of a brace of candles. "Are they safely put away?"

"They are. They ate heartily and sleep deeply." Narses sat in his old leather chair, feeling it creak comfortably under him. "Everything is very quiet. Perhaps nothing will happen tonight."

"Perhaps." Gaius Julius shook his head ambivalently. "The Duchess is a canny woman—if her agents enter the Ludus Magnus and find that their quarry has fled, there will be no violent demonstration. Such things are poor technique; her men will retire quietly, seeking advantage on another day."

"Humph! Not very sporting. My lads are very restless—they want a good brawl. Of course, Hamilcar really wants to test his skill against Diana."

"You mean the kohl-eyed African?" Gaius Julius sneered. "He wants to put his *sword* in her, all right! He's like a boy in love for the first time—it would be useless to pit them against each other. Keep her unique, separate from the usual dreary business of *retariius* and *murmillo*."

"There would be some heavy betting," Narses said in a sly voice, "if Diana and Hamilcar were to be put to the test. My lads already waste hours of practice in fevered argument, comparing the two, measuring their strengths and weaknesses. Wouldn't you like to see it youself? You love the games, the fights. I know, I've seen your face!"

Gaius Julius shook his head, raising a hand, palm out. "I will tell you a secret of the showman's art, my friend. You should know this! When a man and a woman are at odds, there is no finer show in the world. Sparks, lightning, storms—all pale beside a feuding pair. But if they grapple in the test and one wins? Or they reach compromise? Well, everything is lost. There's no show there—only marriage! Who wants to watch that?"

Narses nodded in agreement, but raised a finger. "Friend, I have already been informed bets in the excess of five and six million *aureii* would exist, if such a thing were to happen. She has captured the imagination of the whole city!"

The old Roman whistled silently. That was an emperor's sum. A cunning man in control of events could make a suitable profit from such a frenzy. Greed was not unknown in the dead man's heart, and good red gold was the fuel for all his ambitions. His finances were already stretched to the absolute limit, not just by the massive and continuing series of games, but by Alexandros and his army. That project consumed all the coin Gaius could shovel into the trough, with no end in sight. Someday, perhaps, the investment would reap a rich reward, but until then? Only endless loss . . .

"If you want to set them against each other," a contemplative tone crept into Gaius Julius' voice and he smiled, leathery skin creaking up around his eyes, "then do so in a way no gladiators have ever dueled before. . . ."

A huge figure moved against the night. The man tensed, setting his legs, then reached down and cupped his hands. His companion crouched at the corner of the Ludus Magnus. Heaps of rubbish clogged the alley.

"Hup!" The man straightened, powerful legs and arms moving in swift unison. The girl flew up, then deftly flipped and landed on the top of the wall. Crouching, she peered around, looking across the canted tile roof of the school. Ila's nose itched and she rubbed it with the back of her hand. This section of the outer wall was relatively free of metal spikes or crushed glass, so she took a moment to take a wooden bobbin from the pouch at her belt and toss it down into the alley. Below, Mithridates caught it from the air, feeling the twine uncoil. He crouched down, holding the wooden spool gently in his huge black hands. On the rooftop, Ila picked her way swiftly across the tiles, moving in silence. Her bare feet trod lightly on the rooftop. Twine unspooled behind her.

The gladiator had patiently described the compound, scratching maps in the sand, telling her how to move quietly and unseen. Pairs of guardsmen patrolled after dark. Gladiators would be locked away in their rooms or cells, but many entertained "friends" in the evening. Gladiators were richly rewarded, if they lived. Suitable company was only one compensation. Because of this, the night watch was not quite as strict as it should be.

Ila did not intend to set foot on the ground floor. She was light and nimble enough to make her way by roof and arch. Clambering over the roof ridge, she found herself below the rear wall of the main building. Softly, she crept to the wall, then eased along it, feeling with her hand for a . . . drainpipe.

Despite the darkness, Ila was sure of her touch. Fired-clay piping was bolted to the side of the building, letting the rainwater that fell on the roof find the cisterns below the school. The beneficence of the gods was not to be wasted.

Her nimble feet on either side of the pipe, Ila took a firm grip with her hands, then swarmed up the drain, her toes splayed against the rough brickwork. At the edge of the upper roof there was an overhanging lip. Clinging with her knees, the girl reached up and felt around for a good hold. A thirty-foot drop dangled below her, but she paid it no mind. Even without a net, she was sure of herself. Her fingers found a solid hold and she grabbed on, pushing away from the wall below with her feet. She bounced, then rolled up, swinging over the lip. Rough tile scratched her leg, but no blood was drawn, so she pressed on.

"Bah!" Narses snorted. "That is the stupidest idea I've ever heard!"

"Is it?" Gaius Julius waved his goblet at the other man. The remains of two bottles of Campanian wine lay between them. "Or just *unheard* of? I've never seen such a thing."

"Ay, that's because no one would agree to it—the Greens and the Blues would have a fit! They've their own traditions, you know, and it would anger the gods to flaunt them."

"Oh, please!" Gaius' voice was slurred. The wine was very good and the discussion thirsty. "What gods? Have you seen them? When did storm-crowned Jupiter last grace Rome with his presence? Never! Not even in the old tales. He's always frolicking around with the Greeks, but not with old, dull Rome."

Narses made a sign with his goblet, seeking to fend off

evil. Wine splashed on the floor and the lanista cursed. "Look at the waste! Bacchus will be enraged. No, gods or not, my friend, the racing factions would *not* agree to such a thing. If it didn't work, they'd be a laughingstock!"

"Really? Even with so much money to be made?" Gaius Julius grinned over the edge of his cup. "I'll bet . . . I'll bet I could convince the Emperor to allow it. That would shut them up."

"How?" Narses' eyebrows crept up on his forehead like a pair of caterpillars. "You know the Emperor?"

"He and I," Gaius Julius said in a dignified voice, "have broken bread together." Then he hiccupped. "Damn this wine, it's betrayed me!"

Narses laughed, but a contemplative look came over him.

Ila crouched at the edge of the roof, looking down into the center of the main building. Just below there was a balcony, lined with sleeping benches and partially covered with an awning. Slaves sprawled on the deck, snoring and snuffling. Like many Romans in this mild summer weather, they had moved out of their close, cramped dormitories to sleep under the bare sky. Ila frowned, looking for a way down.

Gulping, she eased to the edge of the roof, swung her thin legs over the side, then dropped down between two large sleeping men. She landed softly, drew a quavering breath and found her balance. After waiting a moment, she slipped between the sleeping bodies to the outer railing. A balcony lined with stout pillars faced the lower floor. She hoped it would be free of snoring layabouts. Ila hopped up on the railing, then prepared to swing down.

"Did you hear something?" The voice was startlingly clear and not far away.

Ila immediately swung over the railing. Her heart was pounding, but she became very still, barely breathing.

Footsteps clomped on the balcony, making it shiver slightly.

"I see a lot of lazy slaves," said a different voice.

"Oh, they work hard enough during the day, when we're sitting in the shade! Let them sleep—no, there was something. I saw it out of the corner of my eye, maybe a child."

"Haw!" the other voice said, turning away. "If there was a child here, it would be squealing."

Rough laughter receded and Ila peered out. The guards were gone. Crabbing sideways to the top of a pillar, she monkeyed down, clinging to either side of the fluted column. This floor was deserted, save for rows of orderly worktables and looms. Ila hopped down, crouching below the level of the tables, and then scampered off, towards the north, where Mithridates thought the women would be held.

"Narses, do you believe in the gods?" Gaius Julius was maudlin now, deep in his cups. The lanista nodded blearily. "I used to, I think, but now? Where are they? Why don't our prayers move them?"

"Maybe they do." Narses managed to untangle his tongue. "The gods are the gods! They can pick and choose just like men. No one ever said that the gods would do what we wanted. If they exist, we are their playthings, no more than insects."

Gaius Julius scowled. "I hate the thought! A Roman lives and breathes freedom. Are we only tokens, moved on some board? Did the gods make us, put spirit in our bodies? Do they make us live?"

Narses poured the last dregs into Gaius' cup. "It sounds like you hate them. I would praise them, for if they made me, then I live and breathe and take joy in the world! Is there a greater gift than life?"

Gaius Julius closed his eyes. "Am I a living man? I think, I feel, I hope . . . but what if these feelings are just

the dreams of the gods? What if I am only their memory
. . . then I am nothing. I hate this!"

"Then drink more wine." Narses hiccupped, then started
to dig under the table for another amphora. "And it will
all become much more bearable."

"No." Gaius Julius stood, now showing no effects of the
alcohol, and gathered up his cloak. "I am tired of this. I
am going home."

Dawn stole over the rooftops, throwing a fine gown of pink
light over the city. Mithridates stirred, still crouched at the
base of the wall. There was no sign of Ila.

Mithridates listened and waited. His brown eyes
searched the rooftops. No alarm had sounded. The tiny bell
attached to the length of twine lay silent. Mithridates
picked his way out of the alley, careful to disturb nothing.
The ground was littered with smashed glass and pottery.
It would be easy to leave a trail.

A block away, to the east, an *insula* of flats crowded
under the vast shape of an aqueduct. Ranks of plastered
arches rose over the houses, carrying three tiers of water
pipe from outside the walls into the center of Rome. Mithridates climbed the back stairs, finally reaching the top
floor and knocking on a peeling wooden door. A husky
man in armor under his cloak opened it. The African
slipped inside, finding the room close and crowded.

Mithridates said, "She did not return, though there was
no alarm or confusion. I think she is still hiding inside the
school. Doubtless circumstances changed and she could
not leave."

Anastasia snapped her fan closed. "Rumor tells me that
some slaves were moved from the Ludus Magnus to the
Flavian overnight, by a secret way."

"Yes," Mithridates answered, "there is a tunnel that con-
nects the cellar of the school to the lower levels of the
amphitheater. It is used to transport criminals or particu-

larly popular fighters or just when the streets are crowded on game day."

"Thyatis may be in the pits, then. Can we get her out?"

"No." Mithridates met the Duchess's furious gaze with equanimity. His life was already forfeited, his oath and contract to the Ludus Magnus broken—there was little this woman could do to him. "Not by force of arms. The Flavian is well defended and under Imperial protection. A favor, a pardon, gold—those things might fetch her out."

Anastasia turned away, the back of her hand to her mouth. She had wanted to deal with this herself, in private, but the effort had been both too rushed and too slow. There was another possibility, however. "I will speak with a person of my acquaintance. A favor might be arranged."

"What about the girl?" Mithridates remained, solid as a column, watching her.

"Keep a watch," Anastasia growled, glaring at the African and at Vitellix, who was leaning against the wall, chewing on his nails, worried. "She is a deft creature, she will find her way out."

The Duchess left, followed by a cloud of her servants.

Mithridates looked at Vitellix and smiled, showing fine white teeth in his ebony face. "Why don't we pay the school a visit? You can return me, seeing as how you found me all lost and injured. Perhaps Hamilcar will be there and I can break his neck."

"A fine plan." Vitellix looked ill with worry. "Let us watch for a day, and see."

In the alley behind the school, the tiny copper bell at the end of the length of twine shifted on the breeze, making a small ringing sound. Then it fell still, then swung again. A stray cat, nosing among the piles of refuse for fish heads, heard it and slunk close. Tawny eyes gleamed and it batted at the bell with a dirty paw. The bell rattled and rang, and the cat bit at it with sharp yellow teeth. Twine frayed and then tore loose. Amused, the cat chased the bell down the alley.

"Oh, now, what fresh torment is this?" Nicholas hung out over the railing of the galley, staring ahead in disgust. Roman galleys and merchantmen crowded the harbor, making a forest of masts and rigging. Clouds of dust rose into hot sky over the town. Full summer had decided to weigh in on the Thracian hills and a white haze cloaked wooded ridges above the port. "Another delay!"

The northerner swung down from the rail, bare chest gleaming in the midday sun. The heat had driven all of them to strip down, even Vladimir, though both he and the Hibernian wound white cloths around their heads in Judean style. Nicholas didn't like having his head covered, but they claimed that it was cooler this way. He was happy to sweat.

"You're in a rush to fight, then?" Dwyrin lounged in the shade of a sail section, feet up on a coil of tarred rope. Nicholas sat down next to him, sighing with relief to enter the invisible field of cool air around the boy. "We can't get into the city, so we'll have to wait while the army unravels the mess."

"We're—I'm—supposed to report to the tribune . . ." Nicholas groused, chin on his knees, staring moodily out at the acres of ships trying to enter Perinthus. In addition to swarms of war galleys, there were a multitude of fishing boats, merchantmen, coastal lugs and, worst of all, huge Egyptian grain haulers, pressed into service to move the Western army. ". . . as soon as possible. I don't like being late or disobeying orders."

"Well," Vladimir drawled, his accent thicker than usual,

"you are trying hard to get there! We've even the Caesar's writ to smooth our passage."

Nicholas flicked a barnacle at the Walach, who ducked, laughing. Neither he nor the boy viewed the current delay as anything but extra vacation from work. Nicholas, unfortunately, could not shake the feeling that they should *already* be in Constantinople, not mired here, waiting for a berth at the docks of this backwater. He stood again, nervous, and went to the railing.

Two of the huge grain ships, each three or four stories tall, lumbered into the docks, guided by dozens of longboats filled with sweaty men bending hard on their sweeps. The railings of the grain ships were thronged with soldiers, waving and shouting encouragement at the rowers below. Beyond, the docks themselves were crowded with wagons, shouting centurions, confused soldiers and a few harried townspeople trying to buy fish for their dinner. Nicholas kicked at the deck in disgust—they had been sitting offshore for three days now, waiting.

"Wine! Pomegranates! Wine!" A young voice called across the water. Nicholas looked up and saw a brown-skinned boy, maybe eight years old, poling a skiff towards them. The front of the boat was filled with baskets of fruit and amphorae of wine in wicker and straw holders. "Honeycomb!"

"Boy! Over here!" Nicholas waved his hand. The youth, spying him, turned the skiff with ease and darted across the water towards the galley. "You slugs, get our gear, right away!"

Dwyrin and Vladimir each opened one eye, glared at Nicholas, then shut them again. The Hibernian had the cheek to start snoring. Nicholas jumped back from the rail and gave each of them a good kick in the feet. "Ow!"

"Get up, we're leaving." Nicholas leaned back over the railing, smiling at the youth. "Lad, how much to take three of us to shore?"

"Five sesterces!" The water bandit raised a tar-stained

hand, fingers outstretched. "Luggage is extra!"

"How much extra? We've got legionaries' kits." Nicholas was fingering a solidus in his belt pouch. The Caesar Aurelian had sent them off stuffed with good food, clutching a travel pass with his name on it, and some coin to ease their passage. The northerner had been very impressed by the Western prince, who seemed a man after his own heart.

"An extra sesterces per man! But not too heavy," the youth rocked the skiff from side to side with his bare feet, "or you'll swim!"

"We'll take it." Nicholas swung easily over the rail, surprised to see Dwyrin get up and scrounge their gear out of the hold. The northerner dropped down into the skiff, landing easily and immediately finding his balance. Feeling the galley pull against the sea on their passage up from Egypt had felt good, but this little boat was better, since it was taking them somewhere! "Hand me the packs."

Dwyrin leaned over the rail and passed down the first bundle of equipment and carrying poles. Nicholas caught and stowed the gear in one smooth motion. Vladimir handed down the next and within ten grains they were crowded into the skiff, sliding across the water towards the port.

Galleys and *quinqueremes* rose up around them on all sides, draped with flags and colored awnings. Bored soldiers stared down at them from the railings. Equally bored sailors watched idly from the rigging. The boy was quick and sure with his oar, sending them gliding under hawsers and the sterns of massive ships. The air was filled with the caw of gulls and terns, the rattle of tackle and rope, the ever-present bellowing of centurions trying to get their fumble-kneed charges safely on land.

"How long has this been going on?" Nicholas looked up, watching with concern as a crane swung a military *reda* overhead at the end of a pair of cables. A shadow passed over the boat as the wagon occluded the sun, swaying from side to side. Despite the creaking of the ropes and a great deal of shouting, the reda reached the eager hands of its owning maniple safely.

"Almost a week," the boy chattered, smooth brown arms twisting the oar to guide them around an anchor rope. "The big boats just keep coming and coming. Plenty of business for me!"

The skiff darted out of the shadow of a grain hauler and up to a stone staircase plunging into the water at the dockside. "You pay now!" The boy stuck out a hand black with tar.

Nicholas gave the boy two solidii, slightly more than the eight sesterces he demanded. Then he hopped ashore, hobnailed boots scraping on wet stone. The bottom step was eroded by the sea and slick with moss, making the footing tricky. Despite that, and a small crowd of buskers and children gathered at the top of the stairway, they managed to get ashore only half drenched and with all of their gear. Dwyrin settled a straw sun hat on his head and, sighing, let the sphere of cool air around them fade away.

Vladimir groaned, but Nicholas just shook his head. "We don't want someone noticing us. It'll be trouble enough to just get through this mess in town without being commandeered into Western service. Get used to the heat again."

Dwyrin patted Vlad on the shoulder. "Sorry."

"Why did I agree to come back here?" Vlad looked morose, already sweating. "I daren't go into the city, you know. The Queen will be waiting."

"I know." Nicholas began to push through the crowd of children and beggars. "We'll figure it out later—after we report in!"

Vladimir glared at the beggars touching his arms, then bared his teeth. They backed off, eyes white with fear. "You always say that . . ." He was growling.

Thick dust clouded the side of the road, painting Dwyrin's face a tannish yellow. Cloth covered his mouth and nose, but he still blinked furiously. A troop of armored horsemen had just clattered past and this particular road was not the traditional Legion road, with a hard surface and drainage ditches on either side. It was more a shallow trench filled with very fine, well-churned dust. The three friends were slogging up out of the broad low valley holding Perinthus at its mouth. Cohort after cohort of legionaries passed them. Each time, they scrambled out of the way and took advantage of whatever shade was offered. This part of Thrace was very rich and lush, which made it easy to pass the time under peach or apple trees.

A rolling series of hills lay around them, stretching into the blue haze of the north. None of them had ever come this way before, but Constantinople could not be far off.

"Gahhh! It's getting under my fur." Vladimir banged his hat against his arm, trying to shake off the dust. "This is *so* much better than sitting on that ship, sleeping or stuffing ourselves with grilled fish."

Nicholas ignored the Walach and his whining, peering ahead, one brown hand shading his eyes. They had come out of a belt of trees and were at the edge of fields sloping down into some kind of valley. "Look at this . . ."

Dwyrin looked up, waving a hand in front of his face to clear the dust.

A hundred yards away was a farmhouse surrounded by a cluster of Legion standards and tents. Cavalrymen were milling around under a stand of olive trees. Many of the trees were only stumps and the house itself was blackened ruins. Beyond that, bands of men were sitting and standing under more trees. Thin trails of white smoke rose from their cookfires. The road turned left at the farmhouse, then ran down into the valley beyond. Dwyrin guessed that they had found the main part of the army.

Across the valley, which was very shallow, a city rose up into the haze, vast and gray, with walls stretching out in either direction, both to the north and to the south. Dwyrin swallowed a whistle, seeing rampart after rampart rising up into the sky. He knew the place, though he had only been there briefly. Constantinople, the greatest city in the world, capital of the Eastern Empire.

"What's the matter? We'll be in the city this afternoon." Vladimir cheered up, then sneezed. "That can't be more than five miles as the crow flies. Come on!"

Nicholas shook his head and pushed his hat back. For a moment he chewed his lip, then spat on the ground. Dwyrin and Vladimir looked at him curiously, then at each other.

"What is it?" Dwyrin scratched the back of his neck. A long line of infantry, once-shining armor caked with dust, sandals squeaking in the dirt, swung past, water flasks banging at each hip. A brace of javelins and a carrying pole were over each shoulder. More dust puffed up. They were not singing, as the Legion usually did on a march. Even their standards, proudly carried before the lead men, hung limp in the still air. Dwyrin sympathized. He had done his share of marching. "Nicholas?"

"Look, there, down in the valley. Do you see a dark line?"

Dwyrin turned, raising his hands in front of his face, thumb to thumb and forefinger to forefinger. The air between his fingers shimmered and shifted, then suddenly sprang clear and distinct, showing him a magnified image of the valley floor. The dark line was a rampart of earth, faced with sharpened stakes and surmounted by a palisade of cut logs. Men in cloth headdresses labored along it, digging and hauling earth in woven baskets. Officers moved among them, exhorting them to greater efforts. Men in armor stood guard, watching the hills with arrows laid across their bows. In front of the rampart was a steep-sided ditch, and the ground before it was cleared of brush and trees.

"It's the Arab army!" Dwyrin was dumbfounded. They

seemed to have come so far from Aelia Capitolina, escaping the rebels, and here they were again. "They've built a wall along the valley."

Nicholas nodded, then picked up his bag and pole, slinging them onto his shoulder. "They have. My eyesight isn't as good as your trick there, but I'd venture to say that it stretches all the way around the city, one wall facing out and one in."

Vladimir hurried to catch up and Dwyrin stumbled after, dispersing the pattern he had formed from the air. "Why would they want to do that?"

"It's an old Roman trick. One wall keeps the people in the city penned up, the other keeps their friends on the outside from getting in to help them. The first Caesar did the same thing once, at a Gaulish town called Alesia."

"We can't get into the city, then?" Dwyrin looked down into the valley again. His power might be able to make them an entrance. Logs could burn, and even stone and earth could crack in the heat, if the fire was hot enough. "Are we going to try?"

"Perhaps." Nicholas looked over his shoulder. "First I'm going to see if I can find someone who can tell us what's going on."

"You men! You're Eastern troops, aren't you?"

Nicholas looked behind him, then back to the Western centurion walking quickly towards him. The three friends had been angling towards the cookfires set up by the farmhouse. Nick figured the cooks would know all the latest news. "Me, sir?"

"You." The centurion was scowling already, but Nicholas waited with a placid expression on his face. "You're not one of our troopers—and that boy is wearing the caduceus and lightning flash. What's your name and rank?"

"Nicholas of Roskilde, sir, centurion of the Eastern army. These are Vladimir and Dwyrin." Nicholas turned towards them, motioning with his hand. "But we're on assignment already. Official business, if you know what I mean."

"Too bad," the centurion growled, brown eyes narrowing. "The legate wants to know where in Hades the Eastern army is and what's going on!"

"Sir." Nicholas kept his voice even, but he matched the Western officer's glare. "We just got here, we don't know what is going on. I can't help you right now."

"Really?" The officer sneered. "Let me see your transit papers."

Nicholas sighed but made a *shush*ing motion at Dwyrin, who was starting to get a mischievous look in his eye. The boy's confidence had improved a thousandfold since they escaped Aelia Capitolina. His color was better, he was cheerful, even the small exercises of his power seemed ably done. Best, he no longer drifted into the dream state afflicting him during the siege. However, he was becoming fond of using his skill to make trouble. Nicholas drew out the pass Caesar Aurelian had provided, though he was loath to do so. Unfortunately, he had no other papers to hand. "Here. Read it carefully, centurion."

The Western officer unfolded the parchment. His face, which could not be called pretty in the best of times, grew forbidding as he read. When he was done, he nodded, then jerked his thumb towards the command tent. "You're free to go, centurion, but I'd appreciate it if you took a minute with the legate."

"Fine." Nicholas nodded at Dwyrin and Vladimir. "Can my friends get a bite to eat while they wait?"

The Western centurion nodded sharply, then turned on his heel and walked back up the hill towards the farmhouse. Nicholas let out a slow hiss of breath, shaking his head. "Vlad, Dwyrin—don't talk to anyone, understand? And hide that damned badge."

Dwyrin nodded guiltily and unclasped the bronze snakes-and-lightning from his tunic, slipping it into his bag.

"I'll be back soon."

True to form, Nicholas was left to sit, sweating in the afternoon sun. The Western centurion stormed off, on "important business," and did not return. Messengers came and went; officers wandered by, deep in conversation with one another. Servants hurried into the tent with food and drink but didn't offer Nicholas any. The northerner fumed and tried to find some shade. Two hours passed and the sun began to set. At last, as he was about to give up and leave, the centurion suddenly reappeared.

"Legate Dagobert has time for you now." Nicholas considered punching the man. His tone implied Nicholas had been making a nuisance of himself. "Inside."

Like most command tents, the pavilion was large and crowded at the same time. Clerks sat on the floor, writing desks on their laps. Couriers loitered against the walls, trying to be helpfully unobtrusive. Two staff officers eyed Nicholas as he walked in, then ignored him. A portable field desk dominated the northern wall of the shelter, occupied by a tall man with long hair. Nicholas raised an eyebrow at this, seeing that the commander of the Western army was a Frankish barbarian, and probably a noble to boot.

"Nicholas of Roskilde, centurion, assigned to the Eastern Office of the Barbarians." Nicholas followed his terse delivery with a sharp salute, arm raised to his shoulder. "Reporting as ordered, legate."

The man turned, pale gold eyebrows raised, and nodded to the centurion. The soldier sidled off. "You've come from Aurelian, in Egypt?"

Nicholas nodded soberly, taking his measure of the man. The barbarian was stoutly built, with fine-boned features. His armor was serviceable and lacking the usual silver wash and filigree sometimes afflicting Eastern officers. His eyes were mournful. Nicholas didn't know if this was the man's usual countenance, or if he had suffered some recent calamity.

"You've a thaumaturge in your care?" Nicholas nodded again. "Aurelian directs you be given all aid in reaching Constantinople so you can rejoin your unit. In particular, I see he is being a stickler about this sorcerer of yours— they are supposed to be under direct Eastern command. You wouldn't happen to know where the Eastern army is, do you?"

"Ah . . . no, legate, we've just arrived in these parts." Nicholas was nonplussed. *What kind of question is that?*

The legate nodded, though more to himself than to Nicholas. "Things in the capital seem to be . . . confused. I expected to sail into Constantinople itself, but I find an enemy fleet blockading the approaches. We advance on land and find our way contested by the enemy, again. He has matched his seaborne efforts with the same on land. Have you seen their circumvallation?"

Nicholas nodded again, mustering the courage to ask, "Does it go all the way round, sir?"

The legate nodded, long face looking even more mournful than before. "My scouts tell me it does, though the northern end is still under construction—but there they found the Persian army, in all its numbers."

"The . . . Persians, sir?" Nicholas felt the news like a blow to his stomach. Through the three years the city had been besieged before, the Persians had never been able to get across the Propontis. *Of course*, he cursed silently, *they hadn't had a real fleet in the strait, either.* "How many Persians?"

The legate shook his head. "We've no idea, centurion. There has been some fighting between our scouting parties and their light horse. Now, this business of your travel pass—I'm not going to ignore the Caesar Aurelian's directive, of course, but I can't help you go any farther. Indeed, it would be unwise of me to let you try yourself, as this precious thaumaturge might be killed."

Nicholas kept his face still, though he had the usual feeling of nausea that accompanied meddling from on high. The legate shuffled some papers on his desk, then drew one out, looked it over and put it back.

"By my order, you and this sorcerer are temporarily attached to the third cohort of the Ars Magica, attached to the Tenth Legion. You'll report to their mess and get acquainted. When we have cleared our way to the city, of course, you're free to report to your own commander." The legate laughed, in an irritating sort of way. "This thaumaturge can help us across that ditch and wall. It must be fate."

THE FIELD OF BLACK BIRDS, MOESIA SUPERIOR

)•(

The Goths were singing as they marched in the rain, voices rising in rough harmony above close-packed pine and fir.

"Dux grandis vetusque Eboraci,
decem milia habuit!
quos ad summum collis
et rursus ad imum duxit!"

Alexandros turned Bucephalas off the road. The stallion was glad to get off the metaled surface—Legion roads were not built for horses, but for men in hobnailed boots. Traditionally, a horse path would have paralleled the main roadway. Here in this rough country, that had proved impossible; on the road was laid through high-sided cuts faced with local stone. The horse cantered up a steep grassy hill standing over the road. The Macedonian was wrapped in a heavy woolen cloak with a hood, though he didn't mind the rain and wind. Not as much as his men, anyway. Alexandros heeled the stallion around and swung down, boots crunching on the rocky soil.

"Cum eis ad summum, superpositi,
cum eis ad imum, depositi,
Sed cum eis in semicollem,
Nec ad summum nec ad imum fuerunt!"

Rumpled hills covered with thick dark forest stretched away in all directions. Isolated tors of barren slate rose out of the woodland, harboring eagles and great-winged hawks. Coupled with the heavy, low clouds, the forest was claustrophobic. The Macedonian felt his heart lift each day the army pressed south, winding down narrow roads and tracks, following the Imperial highway towards Greece and the sea. These highlands reminded him of home, with their lightly settled wilderness and staunch, proud people. He counted the centuries since he had seen green Macedonia. In his first life, he had reached India and the Hydaspes but had never returned to Pella and Macedon. Alexandros laughed, turning his face to the gray sky. Rain spiraled down, spattering on his face.

It felt good to be alive. So good. He held up his hand, catching the rain.

"General?" Alexandros wiped his face with the corner of his cloak and turned. Chlothar climbed the hill, armor rattling and jangling. Mud caked the man's boots and legs, and his stringy blond hair was plastered back against his head. His face was grim, high forehead creased with worry. "We've come to a bridge—it's too weak for the wagons. The stream is high, too, and running fast."

Alexandros grinned in good humor, thumping the man on his broad shoulder. "There's no way around, I suppose. No other bridge, no ford?"

Chlothar shook his head, a morose expression on his face. "No, Lord Alexandros. There are heavy woods on all sides and the span is ancient and high, two courses of stone—I went out on it myself—well cut, but old, too old. Some of it has fallen away on one side, taking away the retaining wall."

"Good." Alexandros breathed deep, smelling wet pines and stone, hearing ravens quarreling in the trees crowning the hill. "There are some engineers with us in the siege cohort. Send them forward to examine the bridge. I will speak with them after they have had a chance to see it themselves. The men are to break out by syntagma and make camp—the file leaders must choose the ground well; we will be here for a time."

Chlothar grimaced, wiping water from his eyes. "What do you intend, lord?"

"We'll rebuild the bridge, like new, or better if we can."

Water roared over black rocks, swirling white between the foundations of the bridge. Broken branches, mud, grass, leaves, pine needles and bits of bracken swept past. Chlothar had not lied; it was a mighty span, nearly a hundred feet high at the center of the stream. Four massive pilings rose up from the swollen flood below, forming a series of heavy brick arches. The roadbed ran on a second, lighter series of arches faced with fieldstone and slabs of granite. Alexandros stepped over a dark brown log, shining with rain, and looked down upon the side of the bridge. His engineers clustered behind him, taking shelter among the pines. The sky was even darker now, with heavy gray clouds rolling out of the north.

"Two of the upper supports, my lord, have cracked." The lead engineer pointed. Alexandros nodded; he could see the fifth and sixth upper pilings had lost their facing, revealing a core of thin red brick. Weather and rain and wind had gouged away nearly a third of the roadbed. The other pilings looked bad, too, with sections of facing missing. "Water seeps in through the breaks, then freezes in the winter, splitting the bricks."

Alexandros nodded again, looking up and down the

stream. The water plunged through a steep-sided ravine, cutting across the base of the valley. He already knew, just from the fold of the hills and the thickness of the trees on the far side, that there was no other way through. The old Romans were fond of building in straight lines, but this highway wound back and forth like a snake. Here, in this rough country, they had followed the path of least resistance. This would be the only place suitable to put a road across. "We will have to tear down the last two pilings, hopefully only to the foundation pier, and rebuild them."

"Aye, that is probably so." The engineers muttered among themselves, but Alexandros knew the sound—they saw a great deal of hard, dangerous work ahead of them. "If we're lucky."

"Can you do it?" Alexandros faced them, eyes hard, chin out, challenging. "Do you have the skill?"

The lead engineer stepped back at the sharp words, face screwed up in disgust. "Sir! We're Romans, my lord, not these Goths and Germans you've got in the ranks. Our kin built this bridge and we can make it good as new."

"Good." Alexandros grinned, still challenging them. "How long, to build in stone?"

"Four weeks," the lead engineer snapped, brown eyes flashing.

"And wood, just for the two broken pilings and the roadbed?"

"Two—maybe less."

"I want stone," Alexandros' voice was cold, cold as the rain falling in a steady sheet around them. "In three weeks. Tear out the damaged piling; throw the debris in the river. You'll want a wooden roof over the whole road, too—a pitched one, so it won't collapse under winter snow. Each syntagma will be tasked for stone or lumber or road work. Chlothar, you and I will decide who does what. Dismissed."

The Macedonian leaned against one of the pines, digging his fingers into the mossy bark. A rich, woody smell, redolent of mushrooms and rotting vegetation, filled his nostrils. It made him feel clean, invigorated. There was a cough from behind him. He turned and found Chlothar, looking morose again. "Chlothar, you're a fine officer, but you don't have to look like you've had to sacrifice your last white bull all the time. What is it?"

The Frank handed over a message packet, then ducked under the eaves of the pine. Next to the trunk, the body of the foliage blocked the rain. Alexandros held up the parchment, swiftly scanning the chicken scratching. "Huh. You read this?"

Chlothar nodded, brawny arms folded over his chest. "Yes. They want us to hurry."

"We won't." Alexandros folded the parchment up and put it back in the oiled leather packet. "We will get to the Eastern capital as fast as we do—no more, no less. There will be other delays like this bridge. At a guess, I'd say we will reach the Hellespont in six weeks."

"They sound desperate." Chlothar had learned some caution. He kept his voice neutral.

"It doesn't matter." Alexandros rubbed the side of his jaw, thinking. "These men are not ready for a campaign yet—not a hard one. They are just starting to be soldiers— not that they lack courage, but they must learn to move and fight and think as one. The bridge will help. Is there a goldsmith among the servants?"

Chlothar nodded, puzzled again.

"Good. Send him to me. We have need of three crowns—one gold, one silver and one bronze. Each week, the three syntagmae that complete their tasks swiftest shall win a crown."

Alexandros turned away from the swollen river and the rain-slicked trees. Bucephalas needed currying and his feed. The stallion's wounds had already healed, but the Macedonian was keeping a very close eye on the animal. Already, as he and Chlothar descended the hill, the sound of adzes and axes was echoing through the dark wood. Above, the sky was a slate gray, pregnant with more rain.

THE PITS BENEATH THE FLAVIAN

)•(

An iron grate rattled open, and Hamilcar, first sword of the Ludus Magnus, entered a high-ceilinged room. Thyatis looked up, her face still and grim. Two slaves were lacing her into a suit of Legion armor. She had her arms up over her head. Agrippina and Candace were just finished getting into their armor. The slaves whispered that today was the last day in the Flavian, the massive culmination of month-long celebrations. The Amazons had been moved up to the second to last act, past a battle between *bestiarii* and a poisonous snake of unusual size. The best of the gladiators would follow, putting on a bloody finale.

"I've brought you a mouse," Hamilcar chuckled, pushing a slim little figure in front of him. "I caught it in my pantry. She wanted to meet the 'famous Diana,' so here she is."

Thyatis stood and clasped Ila, who was shuddering, her face bruised, to her breastplate. "Did you strike her?"

Hamilcar laughed, teeth flashing. "She struggled while we were digging her out of her hole. Someone may have been rough, but even mice can give a nasty bite."

The African was freshly bathed and oiled, his armor and leathers gleaming. His usual languid grace was even more apparent—a sign to Thyatis that he was mentally prepared for the arena. He seemed more like a hunting cat than ever, as his well-muscled hand smoothed back his dark hair. She showed her teeth in a humorless grin. "I understand that we will not meet on the sand. You must be very disappointed."

Hamilcar shrugged, drawing a tendril of fine black hair in front of his face. "I have seen the posted schedule, but you know? I do not believe it. I think that the gods mean for us to test each other, pretty girl. I am looking forward to matching skill with you."

"Good." Thyatis put Ila behind her, pressing the little girl into Agrippina's waiting hands. She stepped close to the African, meeting him eye to eye. Hamilcar was not used to facing men his own height, much less a woman. He grew still but did not back away. "I would be happy," she said, "to see that day."

"Good fortune to you, then. Do not die too soon!" Hamilcar stepped back into the frame of the door. He gave an oily smile. "Perhaps the mouse can carry your shield today." Then he was gone and the door swung closed.

"What does he mean?" Thyatis knelt, taking Ila's face in her hands. "How did you get caught?"

Ila sniffled, putting the back of her hand to her nose. "Sorry. I was being very quiet."

"Where did they find you?" Thyatis' fingers gently probed the bruises. Ila stood very still, trying not to wince. Thankfully, the girl's cheekbone was not broken, and the skin was intact. "Were you in the school?"

"Yes." Ila hung her head, whispering. "I was supposed to find where you were being held. Vitellix and Mithridates were going to come and get you with some other men."

"What other men? Who is Mithridates?"

Ila looked around and saw that Candace and Agrippina had moved away, herding the other "Amazons" to the far end of the room. "That mean lady's men—they are fierce killers, professionals! Vitellix says that they are *sicarii*. Mithridates is the black man you fought in the inn—you broke his knee, remember?"

"I remember. This 'mean lady,' what color are her eyes?"

Ila screwed up her button nose, thinking, then said, "A funny purple, like the petals of a flower."

Thyatis felt a chill as violent memory intruded into her thoughts. Sighing, she sat down, holding Ila's hand. "She knows I am here?"

"Oh yes," Ila said, sitting as well. "Vitellix saw you fight in the arena. So did she. It's not hard to tell you're you, Diana! Everyone in Rome thinks you're the most beautiful woman alive!"

"Thank you, Mouse." Thyatis hugged the girl to her. "I don't want to see that woman again, though. I'm done with her, I think, and her sicarii."

"Vitellix doesn't like her either," Ila said in a conspiratorial tone. "She's arrogant and mean, and she always talks to him like he was a servant."

"She thinks everyone is her servant, sometimes." Thyatis remembered a brief moment of humanity between them, of caring, perhaps even love. "But she is a human being, too. It's too late for a rescue, though. We fight within the hour."

Ila gulped, her eyes getting big and round. "I have to fight?" she squeaked.

"No." Thyatis' eyes narrowed and she stood, motioning with her head. "Not you. Candace, Agrippina, a word."

The two women clanked over, eyes smudged with tension. No one had slept well for the last three days. The aftereffects of the drugged food and wine had been slow to wear off, making everyone irritable. Thyatis had been pressing them hard, too, trying to show them how to fight with a sword and a spear. Thyatis knew that most of the latest victims—more slaves, prostitutes, women from the city prison—would die. At least this was the last day, the last fight. If they could just live through this, they would be fine. Some of them might even be freed. She had tried not to tempt them with false hope.

"Will they count us," Thyatis said softly, "when we march out?"

"Maybe." Candace looked at Ila, who was scrunching

herself into the smallest possible space at Thyatis' feet. "What did that sleek pig say?"

"Nothing," Thyatis growled, her hands on Ila's shoulders. "Mouse won't last a grain out there; we need to leave her behind or hide her somehow."

"If we can," Agrippina rumbled, "we will. But these poor dears . . . they won't last long either."

"No. Just try and keep them together. I'll do all the killing, if I can."

Candace shook her head, tight ringlets bouncing on teak-colored shoulders. "You can't expect to win by yourself, Diana. These Persians will be veteran soldiers. Not half-dead slaves or convicts blind with hunger."

"I know." Thyatis hooked the shoulder pieces onto her breastplate. "They've given us armor this time, though, and we'll get real weapons. Is everyone suited up?"

Agrippina nodded, looking over her shoulder. "As best we can manage. Most of this stuff doesn't fit."

Thyatis made a crooked smile, feeling her breasts compress under the armor. *Thank Artemis it wasn't her time of the month!* Agrippina, who was well endowed, had foregone the full suit. This was old Legion equipment, purchased at a reduced rate in the market. The armor had never been designed for a woman. "Just keep them shoulder to shoulder and pointed at the enemy. Don't try and kill anyone yourselves, just hold them off."

The Butcher shook her head in dismay. "The attendants will be at us again with the whips and hot irons. They want a good show!"

"Hold them off too." Thyatis' eyes narrowed. "I'm not ready to die yet."

"Yeah," Ila whispered, scowling fiercely. "That oily man needs a good whipping."

"Empress."

Helena turned in surprise, surrounded by a cloud of her maids and attendants, dark brown eyes widening at the sight of an old friend. The tunnel behind the Imperial box was floored with agate and decorated like a palace in its own right. At intervals, there were side chambers where notables could take their ease between acts. The box itself was open on three sides, though covered by an awning, and dusty if the wind got into the arena. This room was usually used for the musicians—flautists, lyre players, tambourine shakers—who provided background for the esteemed conversations of the Emperor and his favorites. The Empress halted, though her maids, eager to see the colorful scene in the arena itself, passed on, chattering and laughing. "Anastasia?"

"May I have a moment of your time?" The Duchess was no longer draped in mourning cloth, though she had not resumed her usual flamboyant dress. Today she was dressed in traditionally cut dark gray edged with black, her classic oval face barely painted, save for some smoothing powder around her eyes. A veil covered her hair. She seemed, not shrunken, exactly, but leaner and stripped of anything extraneous. Anastasia stood aside, letting Helena enter the empty room.

"What has happened?" Helena turned, concerned, as Anastasia let the curtain fall over the door. "Are you well?"

"I am awake." Anastasia did not smile, though she raised one white hand slightly. "I would like to ask you a favor."

Something in the woman's voice made Helena pause, though her first instinct was to say *yes, of course.* The Empress had a mother-of-pearl and silk fan in her hands. Helena bought a moment to compose herself by unfolding it. "What is it?"

Anastasia paused, seeing the subtle change in the younger woman, and she realized her retreat from the world had cost her more than she had realized. The Duchess sighed, feeling very old, and sat down on one of the padded benches that lined the walls in the little room. "I am sorry, Helena, I have no right to ask you for anything.

I know you are disappointed in me, and I have already betrayed the Emperor's trust."

"Oh dear." Helena sat as well, her light linen gown folding under her. Even with today's games being an evening program, the Empress knew it would be dreadfully hot in the Imperial box. The marble seats and walls soaked up the heat of the day, then yielded it slowly as night came on. To compensate, she had adopted a confection of silk and linen designed by her seamstresses to be as cool as possible. Helena was sure that the Emperor would find it pleasing, too, since it exposed far more cleavage and bare shoulder than she wanted. The seamstresses wanted to get her pregnant again. Helena wrenched her thoughts around to her old friend. "Anastasia, you have my trust. This must be dire, then, to have you moping about in such a funk."

The Duchess nodded, keeping her hands clasped in her lap. "It is. My failures compound like bad debts, Empress. You have seen the young woman they call Diana, the fighter?"

"I have indeed!" Helena could not help but smile. "Along with the entire city, of course. Isn't she magnificent! Do you . . . wait. You know her?"

Anastasia nodded, and it seemed to Helena that the weight on her old friend grew even greater. "I do. She is . . . she is my daughter, my adopted daughter. One of the ones . . ."

". . . you thought had been killed in the eruption." Helena pursed her lips. "One of your agents."

"Yes."

"Why is she fighting in the amphitheater? That seems odd, even for one of your stratagems."

"It is not my plan!" Anastasia's voice was almost brittle. "She has been charged with crimes and sentenced to the arena. I have not been able to discover the nature of the charges; the court records are sealed or missing. I did not know where she was until I saw her myself the other day."

The Empress nodded, idly fanning herself. "You want her pardoned."

"Yes." Anastasia stared at the floor. A year ago, she would not have needed to ask. Her position would have allowed her to forge release papers, grease the proper palms, lean on the right officials. In another six months, perhaps, she would be in such a position of strength again. But not today. "Please."

"You," Helena said slowly, arching an eyebrow and putting the fan to her nose, "will have to ask Galén for this yourself. The Empress, no matter how wise and beautiful, cannot pardon criminals, even ones that have been falsely accused."

Anastasia paled, her fine-boned white hand going to her throat. "He will not speak to me."

"He will." Helena's eyes narrowed, glinting. "That much, I can promise you."

A muted roar suddenly intruded, the tumult of fifty thousand people standing and cheering. The stone bench under the two women trembled at the sound.

"The games begin," Helena said briskly. "Come with me."

Anastasia stared at her friend for a moment, then stood, taking the Empress's hand.

"Come, now," Helena chided, "he rarely bites!"

The light was failing as Thyatis rolled out onto the sand, standing in the back of a silver chariot garlanded with bright flowers. Four pure-white horses led the high-wheeled vehicle, their manes twined with ribbons, tall plumes of feathers bobbing over their heads. Night was beginning to climb into the eastern sky, and the roar of the crowd, welcoming their new hero, rose up like thunder.

"Hail, Amazon!" they screamed, round faces lit by a fading golden glow. Long, slanting beams of light fell through the arches on the western side of the arena, shimmering in the dust raised by the day's fights. The people in the upper seats were standing, shouting, their arms raised. In the lower ranks of seats, where the patricians sat, the crowd was quieter, though there was still a drumming of feet on the stone benches.

"Hail, Amazon!"

Thyatis flicked the reins and the horses picked up to a trot. The chariot sped across the sand, wheels grinding across dark red stains and the rake marks left by the slaves who smoothed the floor between each bout. Raising her hand, Thyatis greeted the crowd. They met her with acclaim, their voices huge, like the gods roaring in the heavens. Coins and flowers and tokens filled the air, thrown by eager admirers. They pattered on the sand like rain. Behind Thyatis, four more chariots came, carrying her fellow Amazons. Candace smiled for the crowd, too, though Agrippina was more concerned with keeping her footing in the chariot.

"Hail! Hail! Hail!"

Thyatis raced the horses to the entry tunnel, feeling the hot, close air of the arena rush past. The horses were glad to run and she swerved to a stop, throwing a spray of dust and sand into the air. It hung, glowing gold in the late-afternoon light, and she sprang down. Her armor was cinched tight and close, clinging to her supple body like a skin. Blood fire hissed, filling her limbs with strength. She felt glorious, invincible. "Hail!" she cried.

The other chariots rolled to a stop, the slaves in the tunnel darting out to take the reins and lead the white horses away. Thyatis looked over her sisters, nodding to each one. She tightened a strap here, adjusted a helmet there. The women's eyes were filled with fear. Some of them could barely stand.

"We fight together," she barked. "We survive together. Do not try to run, or hide or beg for mercy. Together, we will triumph." She turned away, pacing across the sand towards the Imperial box. From the corner of her eye, she caught sight of Ila in the tunnel mouth behind an iron grating. Thankfully, Hamilcar had forgotten to tell the magistrate in charge of the amphitheater that a very small new Amazon had been added. She stopped, legs firmly planted, before the marble wall of the Imperial box. This time they had given her a helmet, an open-faced thing, chased with silver and gold, with copper wings sweeping back over her shoulders. For all its glamorous appearance it was heavy and unwieldy. Facing the Emperor, she tucked the helmet under her arm.

"Hail, Emperor of the West. We who are about to die, we salute you. Let our blood, spilt in these holy games, give rest to the uneasy dead. Hail!"

Twenty feet above, the figure of the Emperor looked out upon the expectant crowd, which had grown silent, hushed, and raised his hand. It was white against the darkness of the box. The sun was setting quickly. Crystalline spheres rose all along the rim of the amphitheater. Each burned bright and the whole bowl of the massive building was lit as if by day.

"Let the game begin!" The Emperor's voice rolled out, magnified by the shape of the Imperial box and the cupped bowl of the building. His words echoed back from the statues crowning the arena wall. No sooner had they died than a rising moan filled the air, a magnificent and unearthly sound. A dozen men worked the levers and stops of an enormous water organ, calling forth a sound like the gods speaking.

She turned, sliding the helmet onto her head. Already the arena was filled with the rattle and clank of the elevators. Figures were rising from the sandy floor amid wooden structures that aped walls and buildings and an arched bridge. The torchlight glinted from armor and helmets. Thyatis looked to Candace, seeing the Nubian woman drawing her sword. Agrippina held hers in both hands like an overlarge cleaver.

With a rasp, her gladius rippled from its sheath. Now there was nothing but the sight of her enemy, moving tentatively towards her over the sand. This would be her last moment of respite. She stopped, raising her sword to the sky, saluting her enemies.

"Avete, morituri estis, vos saluto!" she shouted, and the crowd, hearing her words, gave forth with a bellow of appreciation. The sky rang with the sound.

The skyline of Rome glowed with fading sunlight. On the uppermost deck, the great sails and their masts shimmered with red and gold. The sailors had drawn them in and were busily lashing them down against the night wind. Maxian, shrouded in gray and black, strode across the pine deck with Gaius Julius at his side. The Prince paced his usual circuit, ignoring the cheers and howls that rose up from below. The rising and falling sound of the mammoth water organ rumbled, making the decking tremble. Bending low at each copper bead, the Prince checked the wood around each sphere. This time, the pine was not discolored. The markers had achieved a balance with the Oath.

"Is there anything we can do to help?" Gaius Julius' voice held an interested but distant tone. The Prince shook his head, rising from the last bead.

"No," he said, distracted. "Watch over my body. See that I am not disturbed. If I fail . . . then I think it will be obvious!" Maxian shrugged the black cloak away. Now they were standing directly above the Imperial box, though it was at least a hundred and thirty feet below. "Are you going to be in the stands, watching?"

Gaius Julius shook his head. He was trying to avoid Imperial attention. "I've done my part for the celebration. This effort of yours concerns me more."

The Prince settled himself onto the deck, arranging his legs and arms just so. He faced outward, across the breadth of the arena, toward the statue of Jupiter the Best and Greatest. The marble figure glowed pearlescent in the failing light, looming large amongst the statues that ringed the interval between the forth and fifth sections of seats. Maxian breathed out slowly, then drew a deep breath. Despite the roars of the crowd and the thundering of feet on the seats, he let his mind empty.

"What happens if you fail?"

The Prince opened one eye, glaring at Gaius Julius, but then both opened. The old Roman had a pensive look on his face and seemed, of all things, to be worried. "What is troubling you?"

"Nothing." Gaius turned away, waving a wrinkled hand in dismissal. "It's nothing."

"Tell me." The Prince sketched a sign in the air with his finger. It gleamed blue for a moment, then faded. The symbolism broke apart the forms he had begun to draw around him in the hidden world. Power beginning to flow to him dissipated, spilling across the wooden planks, dripping down into the air over the crowd. Some of the citizens packed into the seats below looked up, puzzled by some half-heard noise or flash of light. Maxian stood, facing Gaius. "You were going to ask me a question the other day, when I was working in the seats."

"Yes." Gaius Julius turned back, shading his eyes with a raised hand. The setting sun grew enormous, a vast, flattened red disk as it touched the western horizon.

"What is it?" Maxian's voice was tinged with anger. He did not want to be delayed. He had no time for idle chatter. The pressure of the Oath against his shields was very low, barely more than the rush of water over gravel in a stream, but he would have to raise himself into the full flood once more if he was to accomplish his task.

"Why am I alive?" Gaius Julius was nervous. "You could not make Krista live, or the little Persian. Not like Alexandros and I are alive. We think for ourselves, we feel pain, hunger and fear. How did this happen? Are you a god, guised in mortal flesh, that you can bring forth our *spirit* from dead clay?"

Maxian stepped back, surprised by the vehemence, the

sorrow, the pain in the old Roman's voice. "Don't be absurd! I am not a god."

"Then why do we live?" Gaius Julius' voice was sharp. "How did you do this?"

"I don't know!" Maxian let his own anger show. The thought had tormented him for a long time—why could he bring the two men to full life, complete with humor and mirth and joy, when Krista became only a dead thing, a corpse that walked, something to be controlled, guided by his will alone? "There is more *power* in you than dwelt in Krista or Abdmachus. Perhaps that gives you spirit—your legends are strong, eternal. Who knows the names of a pretty slave girl and an exiled necromancer? No one! But you—you and your Egyptian queen, your conquests, your books—they are known to everyone! And Alexandros!" Maxian's voice gained a brittle, furious edge. "Who does not know him?"

"Our legend?" Gaius Julius looked stricken, his face filling with comprehension. "O you cruel gods . . . That statue, it looked just like *him,* the other looked just like *me.* And I . . . I am old and bald, my face wrinkled . . . what fickle memory made him young!"

Maxian stared at the older man in incomprehension. Gaius laughed, seeing the puzzlement on the Prince's face. "You don't see? You just spoke the truth! You gave our *legends* flesh, not our mortal selves! I am . . . what they made me, the historians, and the gossipmongers, my enemies in the Senate. I am what the puppy Octavian enshrined!"

The Prince stepped back, disgusted and frightened as the unflappable old man suddenly began to weep. Then he realized it was laughter drawing tears from Gaius Julius, not grief. The words penetrated, at last, and Maxian's lips quirked into a smile. He understood. "Then praise your nephew, for his adulation has given you new life."

Gaius Julius just nodded, choked with bitter laughter.

"A mystery solved, if it is true." Maxian settled himself

again, turning his back on Gaius. Again, he raised his hands, marking a sign in the air. The Prince shut all thoughts of Gaius and his mysteries out of his mind.

"Now go away, he's busy."

Gaius Julius, who had started to turn away, stopped, surprised. The voice seemed to come from the Prince, but it had a distinct accent, far different from the Prince's provincial Narbonensis twang. The old Roman stared at Maxian, then looked all around. No one was anywhere near. Shrugging, he hurried away, smelling a familiar sharp odor building in the air.

Gaius Julius stopped at the top of the narrow flight of stairs leading down into the tunnels behind the seats. When he looked back, the air between him and the Prince was hazed with mist, distorted, and the blazing white spheres around the arena made the sky glow in a great reaching column.

On the floor of the arena, the false buildings cast shadows on the sand, making a patchwork of dark and light. Thyatis advanced, leading with the point of her gladius, the Amazons a solid wedge at her back. Agrippina and Candace anchored each end, armed with swords. The rest of the women, nervous, crying, bunched together, were armed with a confusion of weapons. Thyatis was sure that the servants bought them in lots from the Imperial army. Some of them, she had never seen before.

The false buildings had been arranged so that to get from one side of the arena to the other, an arching bridge would have to be crossed. It was a dozen paces wide, with a low railing on either side. Thyatis looked back. The attendants were issuing from a tunnel mouth, dark cloaks making them shadows against shadow. Only their silver and gray masks caught the light, shining like phantoms. Some of them wielded whips, the others smoking, red-hot rods. At intervals along the top of the retaining wall that circled the arena, archers were posted. Anyone who refused to fight would be whipped, scourged, shot if he or she did not comply.

"Victory or death, my friends," Thyatis shouted. Candace and Agrippina answered her, "Victory or death!" The other women wailed in despair, but as the three ran forward, they ran too, fearful of being left behind. Ahead, the bridge was empty, though Thyatis was sure the enemy was close at hand.

Her boots rang on the planks as she leapt up the ramp. Something glittered in the air, and she ducked aside, slashing sideways with the gladius. A spear whispered past, hurled with tremendous force from the shadows of the nearest building. It missed Thyatis, but there was a slapping sound from behind her and a gurgling cry. She ran forward. Men appeared from the shadows, shouting, voices hoarse and foreign. The words were unknown to her, though she had picked up a little Persian during her time in the East.

A massive figure lunged out of the darkness, spear point glinting, and Thyatis' hand blurred, driving the sword in a block that sent the spear ringing away. A huge man, standing a good head taller than her, wielded the weapon. He was clad in scraps of armor, ring-shaped mail with flaring shoulder protectors. His beard was dark and curly, hanging almost to his stomach. His spear whipped around, cutting at her legs. Thyatis sprang up, avoiding the stroke.

The Persian fell back a step, reversing the spear into a guard position. Thyatis adjusted the winged helmet, which had slipped a little. The leather strap didn't fit properly. They circled while she considered throwing the helm away. More Persians—if they were really Persians—moved out of the shadows, torchlight glinting on their scaled armor.

"Hold the bridge!" Thyatis shouted, shifting her balance. The spearman dodged suddenly to the left, slashing at her head with the broad leaf-shaped blade. She ducked again, then lunged left, cutting at his head. He parried deftly with the tang of the spear, catching her blade on the metal. Thyatis' concentration focused, narrowing down to just the man, the spear and her footing on the bridge.

Behind her, there was a clash of arms and screams. Persians pressed past their champion, while he dallied over bright steel.

Thyatis danced back as the spear licked at her again. She cut hard at the shaft, but the man was very quick and jerked it back in time. Out of options, she charged in, throwing a blizzard of cuts and slashes at him. He blocked one stroke hard, then reversed the spear haft in a blur and caught her on the ribs. Metal squeaked at the blow and she staggered, her thigh striking the edge of the bridge. She blocked, the point of the gladius pointing down, and drove the spear point into the wood on her left. Her right leg lashed out, a snap kick, and caught the Persian on the elbow with the iron-shod heel of her boot. He shouted, his eyes wide with pain, and jumped back.

Thyatis caught the spear with her right hand, spinning into it, and twisted. The Persian gasped, feeling his broken elbow take the strain. The spear haft slipped in his hand. Thyatis rammed it back into his gut. He choked, losing breath. She rotated sharply, the tip of the gladius shearing through his cheek and into the back of his mouth. Bone cracked and then metal ground against metal. The sword whipped back into guard, slick with blood. The Persian fell sideways.

Picking up the spear, Thyatis cradled it under one arm while she sheathed the gladius in a seamless, smooth motion. Her arms were trembling, glistening with sweat. The crowd, seeing that she had struck down her first opponent, gave a cheer, followed by a chanted shout.

"One! One! One!"

"What? You must be mad?" Galen, Emperor of the West, turned sideways in his golden chair, staring at his wife and at Anastasia with equal disbelief. The Emperor's usually lanky hair was carefully combed back and slicked with oil. A crown of golden laurels wreathed his head—an ancient diadem from the time of the Principate, commissioned by Augustus himself—and he was draped in a toga of pure white silk. For a wonder, it was not incredibly hot, though he was sweating slightly. The press of bodies in the amphitheater made it far warmer than the cooling night would have suggested. "This criminal is one of my soldiers?"

"Yes, Lord and God." Anastasia kept her voice low, half kneeling at the Emperor's side. She kept her face turned from the crowd. Part of the positioning of the Imperial box allowed the common people to see the Emperor and his family, to know they enjoyed the festivities too, that they shared the games and the smell and the heat with their subjects. Of course, this meant it was very difficult to have a private conversation in plain view of fifty thousand people. "I sent her with you to the East; Thyatis, a centurion. She did you good service at Tauris."

"I remember." Galen stared out at the arena floor, seeing the Persians and Amazons fighting and dying. Blood streaked the bridge and pooled on the sand. Despite their attempt to stand together, some of the women had been hewn down by the easterners.

"I sent her on, to Ctesiphon, and there it *seemed* she perished with her men in a fire."

The Emperor gave Anastasia a steely look, his face pinched. "Is she my soldier or yours?"

The Duchess struggled to keep her face calm, though now she was sweating. Thyatis' mission in the East had been to secure the princess Shirin, a Khazar noble-woman, for the Western Emperor, to use as a bargaining chip in the quiet, subtle struggle with the Eastern Empire. But Thyatis had stolen Shirin away, faking her death, and had brought her back to the West. Unfortunately, at this moment, the Princess had not been delivered into the Emperor's hands.

"I am your servant, Lord and God. So is she. Any fault is mine."

Galen scowled. Anastasia could see he did not want to have this discussion now, or ever. Their last official meeting had been emotional and dangerous. Telling the Emperor you had ordered his brother's death was not wise! Particularly when you forced his hand into agreeing it must be done for the good of the state. "How did she come to be in the arena? The truth, woman!"

The Duchess swallowed, her throat dry. Here she would be tested in the balance.

"Lord and God, she led the team I sent to Ottaviano, to deal with . . . what they needed to deal with." Anastasia heard Helena's sharp intake of breath at her side. The Emperor's eyebrow lifted slightly, his face going completely cold. "They failed, my lord. I thought they were all killed—*everyone*—but it was not the case. Thyatis lived, though she was terribly injured. Some travelers in the wasteland found her and nursed her back to health. I fear her memory was damaged, lost. I only found out she lived when she appeared here, in the arena."

"Someone lived?" Galen's voice was soft, even gentle. "Someone whose death you desired? This is the . . . failure you speak of."

"Yes, Lord and God."

"My brother?" he whispered, his lips barely moving. Though the roar of the crowd had grown to such proportions she couldn't hear his voice, she could see the shape of his lips.

"Yes, Lord and God." Anastasia bowed her head, pressing it against the cushions at his feet.

"How do you know this?"

"One of my servants, Lord and God, saw him with her own eyes."

"Where?" The Emperor's voice was a hiss of anger.

"Here, my lord, in the Flavian, on the occasion of the last games."

Galen sat back, his eyes hooded. He seemed to have sunk into himself. Irritably, he motioned for Anastasia to leave. She started to back away, but Helena stopped her, an elegant hand gripping the Duchess's shoulder.

"Husband? What about Thyatis?"

The Emperor had a glare for his wife, too, but she met his eyes with equanimity. After a moment, Galen looked away, watching the struggle on the sand. More of the Amazons had died. But the crowd was in a fine humor, chanting in a huge voice that echoed and rolled back from the walls. "Four! Four! Four!"

"What is her crime?" Helena looked at Anastasia, raising an eyebrow.

"I do not know, Lord and God. All of the papers are lost or missing. She was ambushed and captured by thugs, then remanded into the custody of the Flavian."

"A kidnapping, then. By who?"

Anastasia raised her head, pale face making her violet eyes seem very large. "That would be a scandal, my lord. It would touch the hem of the Imperial authority. Perhaps such things should be let to lie—if you pardon her today, nothing need be explained or revealed."

Galen laughed, sitting forward in his chair, looking down at her. The golden diadem slipped down a little over one ear. "Duchess, are you trying to protect me or someone else?"

"You, my lord. These games must be orderly and without blemish. Too many have died to have their honorable funeral spoiled by the connivance of a few."

"You do not seek revenge?" The Emperor sounded incredulous. "Your daughter, if I remember the papers of adoption correctly, is fighting for her life down there and you don't want to see the men who sent her onto the sand punished?"

Anastasia shook her head. "No, my lord. I believe they saw an opportunity to put on a show as has never been seen in Rome before."

A glint appeared in Galen's eye and Anastasia knew that he had divined the culprit from her answer. "I see. Yes, that is wise, at this juncture. Charges against such a personage would make things very complicated. . . . Very well, if she lives, she is pardoned."

The Duchess nodded, relieved, her hands trembling. Of course, the matter of the Prince would be raised again, in a more private meeting. Helena, however, frowned at her husband and leaned close, her voice fierce. "She may well die in this fight, husband, and then what?"

"Then," he snapped, irritated beyond measure, "the gods willed she die. Are you satisfied, wife?"

"Yes," Helena said, sitting back. His anger left a mark on her, sparking her own, like a shrouded coal burning behind parchment. Anastasia slipped away, while the two of them were furiously ignoring each other. There was a dry taste in her mouth. She needed to find Vitellix and Betia as soon as possible.

Sand spurted away from Thyatis' feet as she sprinted off the bridge. Two Persians whirled to face her, their weapons slick with blood. Bodies were scattered on the ground around them. Both men carried spears. The nearest one shouted, whirling his spear around. It was too late. Thyatis' rush slammed her own spear into his side, cracking through his armor, snapping the wire loops holding scale to scale. The iron tip ground on bone. She twisted the spear sideways, then felt it slide through flesh. Grunting with the effort, she threw the Persian, croaking with pain, aside.

In an instant of perfect balance, she took in the scene around her. The spearman to her front was sliding closer, the point of his weapon angled low, butt high behind his head. To her right, Agrippina was locked in a fierce grapple with another man, this one helmet-less, but built like an ox. They strained back and forth, each with a knife in hand. Other men were fighting the remaining group of Amazons, led by Candace, behind Agrippina. Two men with round shields and swords sprinted towards Thyatis.

The spearman attacked, stabbing at her thigh. Thyatis blocked with the ax, but it was heavy, clumsier than the sword. The Persian reversed his stroke with incredible speed, then lunged at her head. Thyatis threw her head back, turning away, throwing her whole body into the motion. The point of the spear smashed into the side of her helmet. Blinding pain jagged through her head and the helmet crumpled at the blow, crushing her ear. She hit the ground hard, half blinded. The ungainly thing slid against her nose. One eye was blinded. She rolled again, frantic, dropping the ax, tearing at the copper wings, trying to wrench the helm from her head.

A spear point slashed into the sand, barely an inch from her stomach. She kicked out, blindly, then turned the motion into a spin, the sand of the arena floor grinding under her back. Then she managed to break the strap and fling the helmet away. The Persian jumped back from her wheel kick, but now he dodged in low, leading with the spear. He was very fast. Thyatis twisted but could not avoid the thrust. The spear point rang on her armor and she felt ribs bend. The lorica held and the spear sprang back. Gasping in relief, Thyatis rolled, taking her weight on her forearm, then flipped up, landing on both feet. Immediately, she fell into an open-hand guard stance.

Now three men faced her, the two shield men flanking the spear. She gasped for breath. Fatigue was setting in. Blood from her ear covered her neck and the side of her face. Without waiting for his fellows, the spearman charged in, slashing at her in a cross pattern. This time she was ready for the quicksilver speed of his attack. A hoarse *kii* escaped as she slapped the iron blade away with her left hand, grasping for the haft of the spear. At the same time, she sprang up, her right leg arrowing out, her body turning into line with his in the air. Her heel smashed into his face as she seized hold of the spear shaft.

The Persian rocked back, stunned, and Thyatis hit the

ground, facing away from him. One hand on the metal tang behind the point of his spear, the other on the ashwood shaft, she spun, levering it against her body. It tore free from nerveless hands, whipping around. The spearman crumpled to the ground.

One of the sword and shield men lunged in at her, shield high, spatha arrowing at her heart. Her face a mask of rage, she slapped the blade away with the haft of the spear, then snapped it back, low, catching him behind the shield, in the stomach. Breath *oof*ed from him, and she jammed the butt of the spear into his eye socket. The wooden shaft fit perfectly into the eye hole in his helmet and there was a violent *thunk* as it slammed home. Bone cracked but did not break. Blood flooded out of the man's helmet. Thyatis spun, suddenly remembering the other swordsman.

He hacked overhand, sword biting deep into her shoulder plate. It *spanged* violently and she went down, driven to her knees by the force of the blow. Her left arm seemed to go numb, and she twisted away, trying to bring up the spear. He kicked her in the face, snapping her head back. She sprawled on the sand with a *thud*. Dust puffed up around her. He settled his grip on the sword, raising it for a second blow. Thyatis stared, frozen.

Agrippina stormed in from the side, shrieking, her sword in two hands like a cleaver. Heedless, she swung at the Persian with the full weight of her body. He leapt back, blocking with his shield, and was driven back five or six feet by the blow. Agrippina struggled, her biceps bulging with the effort. Thyatis scrambled up, snatching up the spear. The Persian smashed his sword hilt into Agrippina's face, rocking her back. Thyatis lunged, the spear fully extended. His sword clove sideways, biting into Agrippina's thick neck.

The spear tore into his armpit. Light mail parted and Thyatis' heave powered the point into his heart. Gasping, the Persian staggered back, blood foaming from his mouth. Thyatis wrenched the spear free, throwing the man to the ground, red spurting from his side. She turned, but Agrippina was already lying still on the ground. Her throat was torn open, big head lolling to one side.

Mouth tight, Thyatis stepped over the dead woman and stabbed the unconcious spearman in the neck, killing him with a sharp, violent blow.

"Nine! Nine! Nine!" The crowd was in a frenzy. Men tore their clothes, shrieking in delight, baying like a vast, uncountable pack of dogs. Women fainted or shuddered, slick with sweat. A great heat built in the amphitheater, the air flooded with sweat and blood and the hot breath of tens of thousands.

Thyatis staggered up, ear bleeding freely, torchlight gleaming on her face. Her arms and torso were red, her hair plastered with gore. "Victory!"

The crowd answered her shout with a howl. She limped forward, the spear held up, the point wavering before her face.

A realm of phantoms and shadows unfolded before the Prince, filled with glittering swift lights that flickered and pulsed, tracing the matrices of power defining the waking world. Visions passed before him—cities and emperors and battles—as pale and transparent ghosts. He looked out upon the skyline of Rome and saw it change as he watched, one building rising, another falling, fires sweeping across the tenement blocks, then roaring up in a haze of brick dust, scaffolding and smoke. A towering golden statue of a man was built and destroyed in the blink of an eye. Temples were raised, forming out of the mist, and then torn down. Palaces were flattened, then rebuilt. Time and history surged around him in a buffeting torrent.

Maxian's face aged, his hair turning white, then it grew young again. Wrinkles faded from his skin; age spots mottled, then receded. For an instant he was bewildered by the sensation, losing his concentration, and his face changed again, his hair vanishing. He was shorter, more powerfully built, his head brown and bald, a snarl on his lips. Then Maxian's training took hold and he centered, drawing upon the power that burned steadily in the very heart of his pattern. Here was solidity, a foundation, an anchor. The Prince let events unfold around him while he regained himself. The brown man vanished, clawing at the air, fighting and struggling.

Then the Prince was whole once more, a shining beacon of power. When he became aware of this, the glow faded. He wanted to be a phantom himself, invisible to the enormous strength in the Oath. Bit by bit, with great patience, he disassembled the wards and shields that guarded him. As he had done before, he let power flow over him. He offered no resistance, letting the inertia in the matrices seize him, whirling his spirit form away.

A shining palace stood on a hill—not the confused warren of rooms that crowned the Palatine in the real, waking world, but what Augustus had built at the dawn of the Empire. Classical, severe buildings gleaming white under a clear sky and a pure yellow sun.

You found a city of brick, whispered Maxian's ghost, *and left it a city of marble.*

Vaulted rooms passed him, filled with throngs of people. Africans, Germans, Numidians, Persians, Scythians—an infinite array of diverse colors, faces, garb, jewels—all come to the city at the center of the Empire. He drifted through chambers of gold and silver and pearl, coming at last to the audience hall at the heart of the Palatine. Here, crowned in living laurel, his toga a simple white edged with the maroon so dear to the Empire, sat the Emperor in state, dispensing justice, granting mercy, a living god.

Maxian felt himself fray, nearing the center of the vortex. He abandoned physicality. He would hold on to only one thing, even though the storm of power around him wore away everything else. Memory, emotion, his physical body—all would be sacrificed. The shining, interlocking spheres of self that hissed and spun and burned at his core would remain. This was the thing that let him exert his will upon the world, his spirit, and its great power above all else was to press, ever so infinitesimally, upon the hidden patterns of the world.

The Emperor turned, his bearded face grave, one hand raised, holding a sphere of brilliant gold in one hand. The other gripped an ivory rod capped with a ram's head in dark bronze. In the figure, Maxian saw order and law and the regular passage of the seasons. In the staff abided power over all the lands of the earth. The Prince stared, compelled to obey, to bow down, to follow the rule and the law of the ancient city. The pressure on his will increased, the dissolution of his self rushed forward. Beyond the shoulders of the seated King, Maxian saw barren, stony mountains, like nothing that had ever risen on the Roman horizon.

A great pressure beat upon him, threatening even the tiny mote of self. It whirled this way and that, unable to withstand the King's awesome majesty. Maxian cried out, but there was no one to hear but the dreadful ruler, looking upon him with reproach and dismay. The lamb at the Emperor's feet bleated, begging for the stern judge to show mercy.

Thyatis lurched across the sand. The crystal lights blazed with a pure, colorless radiance. The sky high above was fully dark, leaving the walls of the arena a shimmering sea of white faces. Blood oozed down her arm and she had to keep shifting her grip on the spatha. Ahead, four Persians surrounded Candace. The other women lay in heaps, throats cut, bellies slashed open. The Nubian woman dodged this way and that, desperately trying to avoid their blows.

A raw low growl escaped Thyatis. Blood clouded her vision, spilling from a long gash on the side of her head. Despite her wounds, she felt a burning fire driving her limbs to move, her heart to beat.

The crowd grew hushed, seeing her dragging one leg, each step bringing her closer to the foe. Flowers began to rain down, cast from above. Thousands of petals, flung out in silence. Thyatis did not look up, did not see the shining faces of women and girls and young men crowding close to the retaining wall, watching in silence as she staggered forward.

One of the Persians, a man with a forked black beard, shouted and rushed at Candace. The Nubian woman slashed wildly at him, making him jump back. He laughed, a giddy, mad sound, whirling a curved sword over his head. Candace stabbed at him again but missed. While her back was turned, another man, this one armed with a hooked pole-arm, slashed at the back of her thigh. Candace screamed and the hook tore open her flesh. Thyatis began to run, her head down.

Pain flared in her wounded leg, sharp bright flashes as her sandals hit the sand.

The Nubian woman tried to spin, hacking with her sword, but two of the men rushed in, chopping at her with axes. She was thrown down, one blow cracking her armor. Thyatis felt her legs grow light, blood fire roaring in her ears, speeding her across the sand. The man with the hooked pole scurried to one side, trying to get a clean blow at Candace, who rolled feverishly on the ground, trying to evade the blows raining down on her. Thyatis ran up beside him, face twisted into a mask of rage, and slashed the spatha across as she came even with him. He glanced sideways, suddenly, catching sight of something out of the corner of his eye. The sword bit into his neck and he choked, stumbling, and then Thyatis ripped it out through his spine. The head, spinning in the air, gave out a choking wheeze and bounced away across the sand.

A hushed sort of moan rose from the crowd, and a soft *thud-thud,* almost unheard, began to fill the air.

Candace cried out as an ax chopped into her stomach. Red fluid welled around the shining metal. Thyatis, still soundless, rushed in, the spatha blurring in a figure eight. The swordsman on the left, his face wrapped in a blue scarf, shrieked, his shoulder suddenly laid open. The man on the right threw himself away from the flashing weapon, sprawling on the ground. Thyatis swung around, feet planted on either side of Candace, who struggled for breath. Thyatis settled her grip on the spatha's hilt.

Fork-beard charged her, screaming, the curved sword a glittering whirl around his head. Thyatis let him come, seeing his wild white eyes grow huge, then flowed into the blow. A haze of blood drifted over her, but she was already moving, spinning away from a new attack.

The thudding became a drumming, though no voice broke the silence, only the massed beat of a hundred thousand feet on the stone.

The last axman leapt in, hewing wildly, his ax cleaving the air with manic energy. Thyatis skipped back, parrying and parrying again. The man was screaming, a high, wailing sound which flew up into the air and vanished, swallowed by the night. Blocking, Thyatis caught the haft of his ax on her sword guard, and they grappled, faces inches from each other. Thyatis let him come, throwing his full weight upon her. She twisted and he flew, slamming into the ground. She kicked the ax away, then knelt, reversing her own blade and driving a convulsive blow into his chest. Ribs cracked and splintered, red fluid bubbled up through the armor, then the light faded in his eyes.

She stood, unsteady, her limbs trembling like jelly. She turned and saw Candace's head rolled to one side. A thin trail of bile and mucus spilled from her mouth. A roaring filled her ears, but it seemed only she could hear it.

"Are there more?" Her cry echoed back from the marble walls. *Are there more?*

Maxian guttered, his spirit lashed by an invisible wind, but he did not surrender. The power that gazed down upon him contained order and the regulation of all things. The

Prince bent his will into the wind. Here, in this gleaming palace, in the perfect world that it contained and represented, there was one thing missing. Maxian bent his will upon the Emperor, upon the air around him, upon this hidden, invisible space. He grappled with the power, striving to bend it, ever so slightly, to his will.

It would take so little, for he had the book of Khamûn to guide him. Not so long ago, though it seemed an age had passed, he had summoned the ancient tome from the air, binding it from dust and hair and the flesh of the earth itself, all from a single page. That ancient sage, one of the masters of the art, had built this hidden world in a frenzied burst of genius, driven by fear for his own life.

Augustus had not suffered the Egyptian to live, but Khamûn's work had outlived his master. The pattern embraced Maxian: buildings and palaces, bakeries and forges, the tramp of soldiers in the ghost streets of this phantom city, the cut of women's clothing, the hairstyles of men. The lives of millions had been yielded up, a day at a time, to reinforce and extend that perfect vision. Each life painted the colors a little brighter, filled in some hidden corner, made everything richer. All it lacked was one . . . simple . . . thing.

Beside the Emperor, seated on his carven throne, the air distorted and flexed. Sparkling motes flowed to it, flying from the hair of the seated king, from the polished stone that gleamed underfoot, from the air, from gardens half seen through the arched windows. Maxian's spark burned low, crushed into the marble floor, ground under the invisible heel of the guardian of all that was and all that is. His sight failed, his mind fled, darkness lapped around him. He raged against the night, calling on all powers and deities to aid him.

There was no answer.

The shimmering form standing at the Emperor's right hand faded and then grew stronger, burning with colors, filled with wavering patterns. Something new was trying to force its way into the hidden world. It met resistance; the strictures of the form of the palace did not allow it to be born. Pressure grew against it, faster and faster, even as it took shape.

At the center of the chamber, surrounded on all four sides by signs and symbols, a tiny burning white mote compressed and compressed, until, at last, there was only a pinprick of light. And then, with a rippling in the stone and air, it went out.

Galen stood, his face a tight mask, and looked down upon the sand. His right hand was clenched tight, wrapped in Helena's fingers. Full silence filled the amphitheater, disturbed only by fifty thousand people breathing. Below the Imperial box, four of the masked attendants approached, bearing the bloody, torn body of a woman. They halted, silver masks staring up at the Emperor, firelight glinting on their tusks.

"Does this woman live?" Galen's voice rang out, clear and distinct. Every single person in the vast crowd could hear him, from the senators leaning raptly forward in the first tier, to the sailors hanging over the edge of the deck at the uppermost level. "Has she breath in her body?"

"Yes, Lord and God." The attendants spoke as one. They seemed to speak from the depths of the earth itself. "She lives and is victorious."

"Then I grant her, not only the crown of the victor," Galen raised a crown of holly in his hand, showing all the prize, "but also her freedom, for she has expiated any crime, any accusation, any calumny in noble combat, before these witnesses and before the gods."

Thyatis lay on a bier of spears. There was a noise, and she raised her head, seeing above her, suspended in darkness, the face of a man. He held high a crown and she knew it was hers. Struggling, she turned to one side and raised an arm, strong and muscular, still garbed in mail, links fouled and spattered with blood, and saluted him, the Emperor, Lord and God.

"Ave, Imperator!" Her voice was weak, but like his it carried in the silence. Then she fell back, exhausted and spent, and she knew nothing more.

High on the wall of the Flavian, Gaius Julius crept out from the stairwell. The trembling air around the Prince had suddenly stilled, then a wind had risen, fluttering the torches. The old Roman felt unaccountably weak, barely able to walk. He stumbled, then fell to the pine decking. His vision blurred; a hissing filled his ears. Gasping for breath, he crawled forward, his fingers barely touching the body of the Prince.

Gaius Julius collapsed, unable to move, his mind in a vise of pain. Just beyond him, the Prince lay, still and cold, without breath, one hand flung out. Wind rustled through his cloak.

THE WALL BEFORE CONSTANTINOPLE

)|(

A single lantern gleamed, hanging from the back of a wagon. Nicholas blinked sleepily, then crawled out of his tent and into the pale circle of light. Centurions moved in the darkness, passing from tent to tent, rapping sharply on the posts with switches. Men woke at the sound, yawning. The northerner rubbed his eyes and stood up. Morning was not far off, but the predawn was pitch black and cold. Even in summer, the wind from the Sea of Darkness was chill. "All right, time to get up."

Nicholas kicked Vladimir's large and hairy feet. The Walach growled menacingly but crawled out anyway. His hair was a wild mess, all tangled and greasy. Dwyrin followed, yawning cavernously. "Pack up," Nicholas whispered, beginning to gather up his own gear. "If the gods smile, we won't be back here."

"Good," Dwyrin mumbled, shrugging on his tunic. Both men pulled on their boots and laced up the straps. "A nice warm bed in the city—a feather bed!—would be better than this bramble patch."

Vladimir laughed—he liked sleeping out under the stars. "You don't sound like a barbarian to me. Always going on about baths and beds and cooked, hot food!"

"Who ever said Hibernians were *barbarians*?" Dwyrin said, an arch tone in his voice. "We're not mud people like the Britons!"

Nicholas ignored their banter, his mind dwelling on the day's battle. He pulled a heavy felt shirt, the *thoracomacus,* on over his undertunic. Getting kitted out—putting on layers of padding, then armor, then lacing up the armor and checking the straps—took almost thirty grains. Unlike the simple mail shirts of the Dann or the Germans, the Romans used a complicated, overlapping set of metal bands. When it was properly fitted, it could turn a spear or a sword. There would be plenty of use for it today.

Around the three friends, in the darkness, the Roman army roused itself, rustling and clanking, hushed voices filling the gloom. Some lanterns and torches were lit, but not too many. The legate hoped to catch the enemy unaware with a dawn attack. Nicholas snorted, thinking of the possibilities of success. An army in motion was *not* quiet!

Zoë rode in darkness, letting the mare find her way, following a rutted, muddy road winding between the outer and inner walls of the Arab circumvallation. Her heart was heavy, both to leave the warm bed in her tent, and from the summons she had received. Weeks ago she had furiously demanded immediate notification when the body of

her aunt was recovered from the wreck off Sestus. She
hadn't expected to be roused before dawn by an exhausted
courier. A ship had docked at the pitiful harbor the Arabs
had built on the Propontis, carrying the sarcophagus of the
Queen. Somehow, in this chill night, the matter didn't
seem urgent.

Shivering, Zoë pulled the cloak tighter around her shoulders. The heavy wool helped a little, though the slowly
healing wound on the side of her head was sensitive to
changes in temperature. *Why was it so cold in this damned
damp country? Why did Khalid have to be so insistent
about recovering the body? Why couldn't it have waited
until dawn! Why did I get out of bed? I must be mad.*

Ahead of her, the shape of a wooden tower appeared
out of the gloom, gray against black. The mare turned,
following the path, but Zoë's attention was drawn upwards. The men in the tower were stirring and she could
hear them whispering to one another. "What is it?" Her
voice carried well in the quiet darkness.

"There's a noise, upslope. The Romans are moving
around."

Zoë reined in the mare and turned to the west. Sighing
at the interruption, she settled her breathing and brought a
litany to mind, letting the words focus her will and sight.
Patterns unfolded in her mind, brilliant flowers with infinite petals. When she was done, she raised her head and
looked upon the nighted world with burning eyes. The
slope stood out in sharp relief, studded with burned-
out farmhouses, copses of trees, hedgerows and stone
walls.

In this early hour, it boiled with movement. Thousands of
flamelike apparitions filed down the slope, wending their
way through the hedges and yards, crowding on the roads.
Zoë felt a cold shock run through her, seeing the glittering
yet subtle array of patterns moving with the army, rolling
across the fields. Thaumaturges walked at the head of each
column, a shuttered lantern held up behind them, guiding

the legionaries. Others would be crouching in the darkness, on the ridgeline, bending their will upon the Arab soldiers sleeping behind the parapet and wall, soothing their minds with thoughts of sleep and home and safety.

"Rouse the camps!" she shouted. The side of the tower was close at hand and she leapt from the back of the startled mare, seizing the rough wooden poles. She swarmed up into the tower, a battle meditation hurrying through her mind. "Sound the alarm! The Romans are attacking!"

The men in the tower gaped at her, faces glowing in her witch-sight. The enemy pattern clung to them like a gossamer web, fouling their thoughts. Zoë cursed and sketched a sign in the air, drawing power from the mud and earth below, then made a ripping motion. Both men suddenly startled awake, alert. "Now, you fools!"

Turning, she drew her hands fiercely inward, bending her will onto the stone and rock and wood surrounding her. Below the tower, pools of water dried up, hissing into the soil, and the air trembled. An alarm bar began to ring, hammered by one of the watchmen. Zoë stabbed her hands out, unfolding her palms, and light blossomed in the dark.

There was a shockingly loud *boom* and the sky lit with a brilliant white flare. All across the slope, suddenly transfixed by the burst of light, thousands of Romans halted in shock, seeing every gyre and barn and tree silhouetted by the intense radiance.

"To arms!" Zoë shouted, her voice magnified, rolling like thunder. "To arms!"

Dwyrin did not pause at the flash. He had seen the sudden surge of power behind the enemy line, the spiking gradient indicating a sorcerer at work. He ran forward, his own witch-sight showing the rocks in the road, the twists and turns of the path. Vladimir was right behind him, relying on his own preternaturally keen vision. Nicholas huffed along at the rear, trying to keep both of them in sight. He flinched away from the blinding radiance.

"What in Hel's name was that?" He sounded surprised. The Hibernian was not.

"The enemy just figured out we're coming," Dwyrin shouted over his shoulder. "They've their own thaumaturges, you know."

An hour before, Dwyrin had presented himself at the thaumaturges' encampment. He had been met by an all-too-familiar set of dour faces. The Western sorcerers did not approve of having an Eastern neophyte foisted on them. It spoiled their charts of organization and hierarchy. Worse, the intruder was a mere boy and only a second-circle apprentice at that. After some vigorous discussion between Nicholas and the tribune in charge of the thaumaturges, it was grudgingly agreed that he would act as a "skirmisher" in front of the main body of the army.

Dwyrin stayed out of the conversation, telling Nicholas *sotto voice* that the Western Emperor Galen had used junior thaumaturges in such a way during the Persian campaign. The historical precedent did not appease the Western mages. They had a plan for the coming battle, and it depended on the skill of many working together. Dwyrin felt a chill in his stomach when the Western tribune deigned to explain it to him.

When he and Zoë and Odenathus and Eric had worked together, they could have done such a thing. Now, with their five scattered by fate and reduced by death, Dwyrin didn't have the training or the rapport with these Western sorcerers to attempt such a working. In the battle today, he would be a dangerous irritation.

Running in the darkness, letting his physical body work up a sweat, was an excellent distraction for his angry mind. Of course, most of the Western plan had just been thrown out the window, too, so that was fine. Now he could improvise! He skidded to a halt. The column of legionaries he was following poured past a farmhouse with a stone barn. He grabbed Vladimir and Nicholas, drawing them off the road. "There's a barn here. We can get on the roof. Come on."

"The roof?" Nicholas panted, his armor weighing heavy. Long sea voyages filled with a lot of eating and sleeping did nothing for his physical conditioning. "Why?"

"So I can see the enemy. Come on, you've got to keep my body safe."

"We do? Who would want to eat you?" Vladimir made a face, but Dwyrin was already scrambling up the side of the barn. "Ah, Nicholas, the barn is this way."

"Right. Climb a barn in the middle of battle." Nicholas found the wall with an outstretched hand. He hated being the blind one. "A fine plan. Sounds like one of yours!"

The attack is here, Zoë snapped, feeling Odenathus' surprise through the battle-meld. *Opposite the second military gate.* Around the base of the tower, the Sahaba swarmed up onto the wall, many carrying their helmets and armor. The last two days had been quiet, interrupted only by scattered clashes between Khalid's light horse and the Roman picket lines in the woods. Yesterday there had been a fight near the northern end of the circumvallation. Sahaban troops cutting firewood had been attacked by a Roman cohort, but Shadin's heavy horse had driven off the Western troops after a brief melee in the olive groves. Mohammed and Khalid had been sure the enemy would wait for more troops to come up from the port at Perinthus before they attacked.

Yes, tell Mohammed it's the whole bloody Roman army. I can see them from here. Zoë ignored her cousin's imprecations, turning her attention to the broad swath of barren ground before the wall. Arab archers crowded the parapet, stringing their bows, dragging up baskets of arrows to sit beside them. The sea voyage from Caesarea had given the Sahaba plenty of time to cut, trim and fletch. Men in heavier armor were waiting close by, ready to swarm up to the fighting platform when things came to hand strokes.

Zoë frowned, watching the enemy moving forward, swiftly, even in the darkness. Patterns began to emerge, cohorts and maniples forming up. They came on at a steady pace, ignoring the fading brilliance in the sky. The faint blue glow of a battle ward rolled forward with them. Now, as she watched, it strengthened and the muted noise of an army on the march swelled. *They are adapting,* she thought, her mouth dry. *Where are Mohammed and Odenathus?*

The Palmyrene queen decided to take matters into her own hands. Even on fast horses, the two men would take at least an hour to reach her position. "Blessed Dusarra, stand by me," she whispered, raising her arms to the sky. Silvery mail rippled, her cloak falling behind her. Power flowed in the air and the ground, some hidden deep, some riding on the surface. Her fingers dragged at the flow, summoning strength. "Smite our enemies," she shouted, stabbing out a fine-boned hand at the advancing ranks of the Romans.

The earth shook and there was a deep-throated *boom.* The barn trembled, spitting dust from cracks between the stones, but did not collapse. A half-mile away, on the sloping plain, a huge blossom of flame roared up. Even at this distance, Dwyrin could hear the screams of men and the panicked shouting of their fellows. The Shield of Athena that the Western thaumaturges had been extending over their soldiers rippled, fracturing. The Hibernian nodded to himself, fists clenching and unclenching.

"Gods!" breathed Vladimir. "They've a firecaster!"

"No." Dwyrin's voice was hollow. "*Here* is a firecaster."

In his heart, the sign of fire blossomed, and he knew that his time had come at last. His talents and fate had led him to this place and this day. Now, with a grim face, the boy from a distant island would show his power. He chopped a hand down, letting the sign fly free.

The hidden world shuddered, a brilliant trace of pure white light leaping from the barn roof to the distant wooden tower. The arc of lightning shrieked above the heads of men, driving many to the ground, cowering in fear, and struck the base of the tower like the hammer of the gods.

BOOM!

Zoë screamed, hurling herself into the air in a mad effort to flee. Her personal ward was suddenly slammed with an enormous, sky-encompassing blast of fire and light and shattered wood and vaporized, superheated mud. She tumbled in the air, flying over the camp of the Sahaba, and slammed to the ground against the other parapet wall. Behind her, the tower was gone, flung skyward in a thousand burning fragments. Men shrieked, burning, thrown down in drifts by the blast. The roar of flames and the rush of a huge column of smoke swallowed their cries. White clouds boiled up, painted violent red and orange by the lake of flame leaping and hissing where the tower had been.

The Palmyrene queen rolled over, groaning in pain. She hurt all over, but the ward had deflected the brunt of the explosion. She rose, dripping with mud, clods of earth clinging to her armor. Someone was there, out in the darkness, a familiar figure, a power that she had once tutored herself. Tantalizing familiarity reached out to her, a missing place in the battle-meld.

O Great and Merciful One! Dwyrin?

"I hear you, Zoë." The Hibernian was glowing, a shining orange sphere rotating around him. Even Nicholas could see it in the darkness, a mottled, translucent surface brilliant with signs and arcane symbols. The northerner cowered on the roof of the barn, hoping that the straw did not burst into flame. Orange shadows danced around him, thrown by the glittering ward. "You should not be fighting me. You swore an oath, once, have you forgotten?"

Dwyrin's mouth continued to move, but Nicholas could no longer hear the words. A rushing sound filled the air, like the passage of a vast flock of birds. Wind sprang up out of the west. Through the shifting sphere, Nicholas could see the boy etch a sign in the air, then stab out his hand again.

The earth shook. Nicholas curled up into a ball, armored hands clasped behind his head. Another flare of azure light filled the sky with a shattering roar. A half-mile away, the Arab wall erupted skyward. Burning logs catapulted through the night, trailing smoke and sparks. More fires were burning on the plain where flaming debris had landed. A vast billow of smoke was mounting into the sky, lit by flames from below.

"You should not have betrayed me." Dwyrin's voice was rising, catching a strange edge. His fist curled and drew to his heart. Nicholas grabbed Vladimir and together they rolled off the roof, landing heavily in the yard. The pair scrambled to the wall, pressing themselves against the cold fieldstone. The earth heaved, rippling with the echo of a titanic blast, and a hot wind rushed over them. The straw roof finally caught fire.

Zoë staggered away from the burning ruin of the wall, her face streaked with blood. Everything behind her was aflame, wrapped in smoke and jets of steam hissing out of the earth. The air was filled with drifting embers and sparks. Some touched her cloak and clung, burning. Hundreds of men fled past her. Some of them were wreathed in flame, yet they still ran. Her shields flickered into sight, then faded again. Desperately, she turned, crouching on the ground. The second wall had been smashed down as well. She had crawled in the mud, struggling out of the ditch that faced the city.

Odenathus! Her cry was faint, but he was there instantly. She caught a fleeting glimpse of a horse's neck and rushing wind. *Dwyrin's here! He's stronger than I am! Help me!*

We're coming was his reply, breathless and hurried, and there was wind rushing past. *Fall back to the north, if you can.*

Another explosion ripped the night, throwing another watchtower into the air. Zoë pressed herself to the cold earth. Burning logs smashed down around her, bouncing across the ground, spewing sparks and smoke. A man a dozen feet away leapt up, screaming, and tried to run. A log toppled out of the night and crushed him, grinding him into the earth. Vast pyres burned in the wreckage of the wall. Every tent seemed to be alight.

Zoë limped away, to the north, throwing aside her charred cloak. Transient blue patterns gleamed in the air around her, though in the face of the power that was walking upon the earth to her west, she knew they were little defense.

Light stabbed in the north, and there was a ringing like a great bell being struck. Odenathus was putting forth his own power.

Is Mohammed there? Zoë tried to run and found that her left leg was weak. She stopped, running her hand along the muscle. Something was sticking out of her leg. A splinter had arrowed through the center of one of the links in the mail. Gritting her teeth, she knelt and yanked it out. Fresh pain flooded her leg and she gasped. *Odenathus! Answer me!*

The sky lit up, furious bolts of azure and crimson arcing out of the west. Three sharp explosions followed and the battle-meld with her cousin vanished. Zoë grimaced, fighting back tears, and fumbled at her leg. She needed a bandage.

"Sahaba! Sahaba, to me!" Zoë's voice was hoarse. Smoke bit at her throat. Men ran in the darkness, fleeing past her. None of them stopped. She ripped the sleeve from her shirt, wrapping it around the wounded leg. "In Allau's name, to me!"

The bandage clenched on her thigh and the pain ebbed,

but she was weak, very weak. Smoke drifted over her, glowing orange and vermilion in the light of the burning walls and towers. She crawled towards the north, mud squelching under her fingers. Behind her, in the huge gap torn in the Arab circumvallation, Roman soldiers appeared, scrambling across the ruins. As they advanced, the fires died, guttering out, swallowed by the earth.

Something came, a spectral orange glow that crept across the ground. A figure was at the center of the radiance, drifting across ditches choked with charred bodies. Lines of armored men hurried forward on both sides, their faces in shadow.

Mohammed turned from the south, face black with anger. The horizon was a sea of flame. Great clouds of smoke covered the land, lit from within by infernal lights. The Quraysh's face was half lit by the terrible radiance. "Is this your help, King of Kings? My men are dying, but you will do nothing?"

Shahr-Baraz shook his head. His visage was grim, mustaches gleaming in the firelight. "Lord Mohammed, I do not believe my men could do any better in the inferno than yours, even with the hearts of lions. Come, order your army to fall back upon our camp. Let my priests join their power with yours and the prince Odenathus. Perhaps together we can defeat this *daeva* the Romans have brought against us."

Mohammed's eyes glinted dangerously, but he restrained his anger. Staring into the darkness, he saw the fires were beginning to die down. No messengers had come, which must mean disaster. He mounted his horse, the same old flea-bitten mare he had ridden since the Sahaba ventured forth from Mekkah. Looking down at the King of Kings, standing in the gate of the Persian camp, he nodded his head. "Very well. If the Romans have broken the wall, then we will fall back and take up positions here. Be ready."

The King of Kings, resplendent in golden armor, returned the nod with a raised hand. At his side, Khadames scratched his nose, then turned away and began to bellow orders. The Persians had leapt to arms, scrambling out of their tents, at the sound of the first explosion in the south. Now they would have to take up positions along the ramparts raised at the end of the bridge. The general would also have to prepare for thirty thousand Arabs to pour into the camp, baggage and all.

Mohammed rode off into the darkness, accompanied by a troop of heavy cavalry. Their banners fluttered in the darkness. Shahr-Baraz watched them go, tugging softly at his mustaches. He was not smiling, though on another day he might have, to see his ally humbled. He had exchanged words before with the lord Mohammed about the vast effort the Arab army had invested in the long fortification. Now their fleet would have to anchor directly off his camp, rather than on the far side of the city. It would make the blockade more interesting. . . .

"Now, this is a puzzling turn." He frowned at the south, watching lines of flame advance across the fields. "What is this power that the Romans have woken—an Egyptian, a druid? They have never been blessed with something this strong before." The Boar turned his head, raising his chin in summons. One of the Shanzdah stepped out of the darkness, the eye slit of his helmet showing only darkness. "Go south and see what walks in the fire. Tell your master, and tell me."

The silent figure bowed its head, then turned silently and loped off into the darkness. Shahr-Baraz felt a chill on his neck, seeing the creature go. This trafficking with dark powers made him uneasy—but now, with the Romans coming against him in strength, he would not gainsay their help! He looked east, his lip curling in a snarl. A line of lights marked the ramparts and towers of Constantinople. He hated the city and its invincible defenses. Of all the battles and campaigns he had ever undertaken, only this place had defied him.

"Not this time," he hissed. "Not this time!"

◼〇◼〇◼〇◼〇◼〇◼〇◼〇◼〇◼〇◼〇◼〇◼〇◼〇◼〇◼〇◼〇◼

THE VILLA CASTIMONIA, OUTSIDE ROMA

)+(

Pipes and flutes wailed, carried by wild drumming. A ring of gladiators, their oiled bodies gleaming in the lamplight, danced, a young woman on each arm, their faces bright with laughter. An entire wall of musicians produced a swirling, hypnotic sound, much to the delight of hundreds of revelers packed into the main hall of the villa. Anastasia, her face swathed by a gray veil, pushed her way through the crowd on the staircase. Helena, even more heavily gowned, with two veils and a positively prudish hood, followed close behind. Vitellix, his face smiling and open, led them, his shirt a virulent mustard yellow. He was wearing red-and-white-checked tights, his head freshly shaved. The Duchess kept close behind him, letting his wide shoulders clear them a path.

The creamy-white marble steps of the grand staircase were already stained with spilled wine, crushed candied figs and drifts of young men and women in all states of undress. The *lanista* descended the stairs into thick crowds of people who were packed around the dancers. Eeling his way through, he reached the wall, Anastasia's hand clinging to his belt. It took nearly five grains to reach a doorway only a dozen feet away.

Anastasia felt faint and ill. The air was close and hot, filled with spices and incense and the battling pomade and perfume of a great number of sweaty people. Even in her own parties—which had, in their time, been noted for their decadence—she had never seen such indulgence. Every gladiator in the city had been invited to Narses' victory party, and they hauled with them the wild patrician youth, the prostitutes and acrobats and actors and pantomimes and hustlers who thronged the Aventine and made the Subura so dangerous by night. Vitellix shouldered aside a drunken youth, his toga slipped to the floor, a crown of holly tangled in his hair, who was feverishly copulating with a young girl pressed against the door. Faces flushed, the girl crying out, they barely noticed being pushed aside.

The Duchess squeezed past, turning her head. She had seen such things before, even done them, but since the eruption of Vesuvius she had lost her taste for senseless abandon. The frenzy in the air grated on her. She saw despair hiding behind the glad smiles and the violent dancing. *Is everyone desperate to feel alive?* They entered the chamber beyond, Helena treading close on Anastasia's heels.

This room was dimmer, filled with thick, bitter incense. The Duchess blinked, catching sight of Vitellix stepping carefully across the floor. Deep-pile rugs, fabulously expensive, covered the room. There were many more people, most of them naked or nearly so, writhing in their own lost dreams. Some of them had the glazed eyes of lotus eaters, others were making use of the couches and cushions. The Duchess swallowed, feeling the air bite at her throat. She hurried forward, oiled limbs brushing against her ankles. A doorway flanked by porphyry naiads led into a arched hallway. Vitellix was waiting, his head cocked, listening.

"Narses has done well by the school," Helena commented in a dry tone, looking around at the walls faced with dark green marble striated with gold. "I had no idea the salary of a lanista was so generous."

Vitellix blushed, then pointed with his chin. "This villa

is owned by a patron of the school. I was here once before; these rooms are reserved for the master's guests. If Diana is in such favor, she will have one or more of them for her own."

"Privacy?" The Empress raised an eyebrow. "Luxurious?" Even in the palace, her own bedchamber was rarely private, plagued as it was by servants, maids, guardsmen and her husband. "Perhaps I should be a famous gladiatrix."

Anastasia pushed past Vitellix, pacing along the hallway. Each door was painted with scenes of forests, beaches, mountains. They were cunningly done, affording the illusion of opening into some fantastic world. At the third one, she heard a hoarse voice laughing. It sounded familiar. She paused, swallowing, nerving herself, and then pushed it open.

Despite her haste, Anastasia's effort to snatch Thyatis away from the clutches of the arena staff had failed. She had found Vitellix among the crowd of spectators and touts in the domed rooms behind the entrance tunnel. The Gaul had been beside himself with worry, but only the dead had been carried out through the Portia Libitina. There was no Thyatis. One of the slaves, pressed with gold, had shown them a second tunnel that led from the Portia into the lower tunnels. Guardsmen had blocked their way. Despite threats and bribes, they had not been able to enter the catacombs under the amphitheater.

Anastasia was sure Narses had expected something, secreting his prize fighter away. Inquiries in the Flavian the next day revealed the master of the Ludus Magnus had posted a contract between the school and Thyatis. She would be one of his free gladiators now, who had a special relationship with the Ludus Magnus. The Duchess's opinion of the crippled man sank to a new low. With a horde of scrawny-necked lawyers involved, she was tempted to start having people killed.

The room was opulent and garish, decorated with an astounding amount of brocaded red, green and yellow drapery. A huge bed, crowned by four carved posts, filled at least half the chamber. Gauze drapes covered the posts and hung down on three sides of the plush expanse. A man's feet were sticking out from under the gauze. Bits of clothing, armor and discarded bottles of liquor covered the floor. Like the lotus room, the floor was piled deep with carpets and rugs. Anastasia's sandals sank into them. There was another laugh, a hoarse, smoky voice.

"Lower, slave, lower! Yes, that's it . . . aaaah!"

At least two masculine voices answered with the sounds of laughter and oiled flesh on flesh. The Duchess grasped the embroidered gauze and flung it aside, face still and cold, revealing a tangle of bare limbs and sweat-dampened hair. Thyatis was lying back on a huge mountain of pillows, one leg hooked over the shoulder of a brawny young man. He and his companion were attending to her.

"Oooo! Dears, we've a guest. No—I haven't given you permission to stop!" Thyatis pushed the man's head back down, tangling her scarred hand in his thick, curly hair. "Hello, Anastasia. What do you want?"

The Duchess took hold of the nearest post, her fingers wrapping around the thigh of a carved sylph. Her fingernails turned white with the pressure of her grip. "Hello, Thyatis. I've come to fetch you out of this place."

"Have . . . oooo! . . . you?" Thyatis' face flushed and her lip curled. She met Anastasia's eyes with a glittering anger, but the Duchess refused to look away. After a moment, a petulant look entered the woman's face. Grimacing, she pushed the two boys away, a hand caressing the smooth cheeks of each. "Sorry, sweets, but I've got to deal with this rude person. Go find someone else to play with."

The boys scuttled away, gathering up their clothing— skimpy silk confections that showed off their fine thighs and muscular, smooth chests. Helena watched them go

with interest, winking at one. The boy simpered back, his
kohl-rimmed eyes a luminous green. The Empress closed
the door after them, then stood against it, a handkerchief
pressed against her nose. An overbearing cloud of incense
drifted in the room. Vitellix was still outside, in the hallway.

"I am done with you." Thyatis' voice was bitter and
filled with venom. "You have no hold on me, Duchess.
You should go unless you would like a pair of boys yourself?"

"No. I am done with that life. Please, Thyatis, I need
your help. Come with us, I have a litter waiting outside.
Vitellix is in the hallway—in this throng they won't even
notice that we've left."

Thyatis stepped off the bed, her naked body gleaming
with oil and wine. A strange expression was on her face,
compounded fury and grief. She loomed over the Duchess
by nearly a head.

"You need my help? For what? To murder someone, to
make them disappear, to clean up the Emperor's dirty laun-
dry? To die for you?"

Anastasia stepped back from the raw hatred in the
woman's voice, a hand coming up to her breast. "I need
you at my side, Thyatis. The prince Maxian is still alive!
We have to do something."

"The Prince? Alive? How shocking!" Thyatis' voice
grated like a knife on stone. Her face paled, becoming
almost arsenic white. "He threatens the very Empire, I suppose! Do you think that I don't know he survived? I saw
him escape in his iron servant!"

The Duchess was forced back again, her face turned
away from Thyatis' shouting. "I did not know if you knew.
Who knows what happened on that mountain, save you
and he?"

"I know." Thyatis stopped shouting. Her voice was low,
almost choked. "I know everything that happened. Listen,
Anastasia, I will *not* fight for you again. I will not take the

lives of the innocent. These games, they are my penance. I hope—no, I pray—that the spirits of the dead will find comfort in my acts, that they will fill their cold bellies with the blood I spill in the arena. Oh gods, let them fly to the golden fields! Let them be waiting for me with glad smiles!"

Thyatis fell to her knees, her face an anguished mask, but no tears fell. Anastasia knelt at her side and tore her veil away, bending her head close. "Thyatis, daughter, listen to me. Please come home. Until I saw you were alive, I thought I had lost everything. But you live and I have found some hope."

"Hope?" Thyatis drew back, her eyes dark, disgust plain on her face. "Hope of what? Of sending me out to kill for you, to die, in the end, like the others? Like Nikos, incinerated? Like Krista, burned to a crisp, then her poor dead body dragged away?"

"We have to fight!" The Duchess was still kneeling, and her voice was plaintive. "The Prince is a monster! He still lives, Betia has seen him lurking in the Flavian. You know what he is capable of! We failed, *we* together, but we must try again. That child must be stopped."

A ghastly look came over Thyatis' face and Helena, still standing by the door, silent, unobserved, thought it was like the very pit of torment had opened in the young woman's face. The lamplight caught in those sea-gray eyes and burned with a leaping flame.

"I know failure. You know nothing of it." Thyatis spit, catching Anastasia on the side of her face. The Duchess flinched, but could not rise, transfixed by the horror in Thyatis' eyes. "Failure is only a grain—a single grain— from victory! I had him, Anastasia, I had the Prince in my hand. His body was broken, pierced with arrows, his heart transfixed with my sword. My fist was in his hair, drawing back his neck for the final blow!" Thyatis' hands clenched into rigid claws and she stared into some abyss only she could perceive.

"One cut! One blow! One swift chop and his head was my trophy! But I turned away." Tears came, choked out like her voice. "There was a commotion—that thing, the *homunculus* was among the men, slaying. I ran to help. *I thought that the Prince was dead!* Who knew his power? Who could grasp that while any spark of life remained in him, he could rise up, his shattered body made whole?

"Do you know what is worse than failure? Worse than seeing your friends die, smashed down by an impossible power? Worse than seeing Nikos try and fail to make good *my* mistake? Worse than watching Kahrmi and Efraim lunge into certain death at the monstrous hands of this boy? Do you?"

Anastasia, speechless, shook her head.

"This is worse. Knowing, *knowing* that you could have ended this, *knowing* that forty thousand innocent people— mothers, husbands, children, cripples, slaves—all died, choking on poisonous gases, burned alive, crushed beneath a rain of stones, drowned by a violet sea, because *you* turned aside for just . . . just a *grain*! It was only a moment! Just the tiniest moment!"

Rage boiled up in the woman, her tendons standing out stark against her flesh. Thyatis loosed a guttural howl, ripping the bedpost free, tearing the gauze. Her muscles twisted under the gleaming skin and she grasped Anastasia by the shoulder of her gown. Thyatis raised the length of wood, screaming. "This is worse! Knowing that four little children, innocent, who went to the seashore because they wanted to see a *sea serpent*, who wanted to run in the surf and catch octopuses and be sea monkeys, are dead because of *one moment*! I loved them, Anastasia, and they are dead because of *my failure*. Baiae is destroyed. Not one house stands. Everything is ash and ruin. . . ."

Her voice trailing down, Thyatis suddenly let go. The Duchess slumped to the floor, her makeup in ruins, streaked with tears.

"Get out." Thyatis turned away, her back stiff.

Anastasia rose from the floor, unable to look at her adopted daughter. She moved to the door but was barely able to walk. Helena caught her hand, taking her weight, then turned the latch for her. Vitellix was right outside, his face pale. The door was only thin wood and veneer—he had heard everything. The Empress shoved the Duchess into his arms, then closed the door again. Her face was still and calm, like a statue. She unfolded her fan, letting the *click* of it draw the gladiatrix's attention.

"I know what you have lost," Helena said to Thyatis' back. "You have my sympathy and prayers. My name is Helena Julia Atreus. If you ever need my help, come to the Palatine and ask for me. It will cost you nothing, for the debt that Rome owes you is greater than I can repay."

Thyatis turned, her eyes hollow. "You mock me, lady."

"No. Never." Helena replaced her veil, which had come loose from its tiny silver pins. "Remember this, in the days to come, that the Emperor has freed you. You have left one kind of servitude; do not rush to take up another. Narses is an honorable man, in his own way, but your grief will not find an answer on the floor of the arena."

The Empress put her fan away, then stepped close to Thyatis and raised her head. Gently, for the redheaded woman was trembling, Helena pressed her lips to one cheek, then the other. Tears brushed her lips and then she turned away. Again, Vitellix was waiting outside the door, holding Anastasia, who had drawn the edge of her cloak over her face.

"We are leaving," Helena said. "Now."

The lanista nodded, though his eyes went to the door.

"Not now," Helena said softly, putting a hand on his arm. "It would do no good."

"What about my daughter, Ila?" Vitellix' voice was charged with emotion. "We have to find her, too."

"I think," Helena said, glancing at the door, "she is well protected."

)(

A desultory wind gusted out of the west, carrying the smell of burning tar and wood. Dark clouds of smoke hung over the roofs of the city, masking the massive walls from view. In the distance, indistinct, a dull gleam of fire lit the sky. Parts of the Arab fortifications were still burning. She could smell the corpses, dry and dusty with a sharp aftertaste of broken stone and thorn. The Dark Queen paced along the roofline of the temple of Hecate, her humor foul, a heavy dark gray cloak wrapped around her thin shoulders. Smoky zephyrs tugged at her hair. The sun was shrouded, passing down into a heavy bank of cloud filling the western horizon. Though the day was not yet done, the gloom of twilight covered the city. Down below her, fires tended by nervous priests burned on the altars of all the young gods.

The Queen snarled to herself, wrapping a white hand around a painted statue lining the edge of the roof. She stared to the west, bending her will to penetrate the murk and smoke rising before the city. She knew from the frightened whispers of the daywalker children that a great army had come, breaking the siege, clearing the highway leading down the Thracian coast to Perinthus and on to ancient Macedon.

The army of the West has come, they said, confused, *but the Emperor will not let them enter the city.*

More than just an army had come out of the west. Two brilliant stars burned subtly in the firmament of the hidden world. She could feel them at a distance, one away in the north beyond the Horn, one in the south, across the Thracian hills. Powers were gathering for battle. Amusingly, many black-hulled ships were drawn up on the beaches across the Horn on the Galatan shore. The sight brought back ancient memories.

Snorting at the thought, the Queen folded herself up between two of the lithe statues—maidens bearing bowls of wheat and olive and grape—the hood falling forward over her face. Dark red lips quirked up in a smile, watching the priests below her vantage raising their voices to the sky in entreaty. *There is no one to hear you, fools. All your gods are dead or sleeping.*

A chill came upon her with the thought. *All but one, and he is a god of darkness.*

She had not felt the power in the east for days. But it was still there, subtly disturbing the patterns and flows in the hidden world. That, she could feel in her bones. The dark power was hiding, covering itself with signs and wards, but it pressed at the fabric of the world like a heavy stone on a canvas sail. Against these dark thoughts she held one faint hope: her children were all safely away in their fat-bellied ships. Months would pass before she would hear from them. She wagered against herself that this battle would be done by then. The heaviness in the air promised doom and slaughter.

THE CIRCUS MAXIMUS, ROMA MATER

Blinking in the noon sun, Thyatis trudged across a vast expanse of clean hot raked sand. The monumental shape of the circus rose up around her, empty and desolate. A hundred yards away, a line of slaves in green tunics were working their way around the sweeping turn at the end of the raceway. The slaves were smoothing the sand with iron-tined rakes. Distantly, Thyatis could hear the bang of hammers as laborers worked in the stands, setting up festival banners and religious icons. Today the circus was empty. There were no races scheduled, no battles of *venationes* against wild beasts, no triumphal processions, no vast crowd of citizens baying for blood and victory.

Thyatis' head throbbed viciously. She pressed a hand over her eyes, trying to block out the glare from the sand. It was hard to walk and harder to think. Her body felt like it had been beaten with oaken staves, then rolled down a rocky hill. The throbbing in her skull held a constant, repeating, echo of the roaring crowd in the Flavian. She felt sick.

"You shouldn't have had so much wine or been with those boys. They're very athletic," Ila ventured, walking alongside her. The mousy girl was trying to be very quiet and unobtrusive. Thyatis had not woken in a good humor. Being summoned to the stables of the Blue racing faction at such a dreadfully early hour did not contribute to her well-being. "You look like Otho and Franco the time they got run over by a wagon."

"The best mice are quiet mice." Thyatis had a hard time speaking. Her throat seemed swollen. "Please, your feet on the sand are loud enough."

Ila made a face but started tiptoeing. She was vexed but didn't want to get Thyatis mad.

They were cutting across the eastern end of the circus. The messenger had told them to meet Narses in the racing-day stables of the Blue faction. The fastest way from the Ludus Magnus was through the monumental triumphal arch of Titus, then down the long straightaway. A marble reef, or spina, ran down the middle of the raceway, crowned with temples and statues and a huge red granite Egyptian obelisk spearing into the sky opposite the Imperial box, or pulvinar, which jutted into the circus stands from the side of the Palatine Hill. The ends of the spina were decorated with three huge bronze cones, the turning posts for the race. Just behind the metae, at the eastern end, was a temple building with seven huge golden eggs on the roof. Ila eyed them with distaste—they turned over to mark each lap—but she thought they were too garish. At the far end of the spina was a matching building crowned by seven golden dolphins.

They passed men in white smocks busily painting over a long red smear on the wall separating the sand from the first deck of seats. Four of the workers were fitting a fresh marble panel into an area that had been damaged by a crash. Ila wrinkled up her nose. *Sloppy driving!* she thought. *Popped his wheel right into the wall.*

Thyatis had her head down, eyes still shaded, but a cheerful whistling made her look up. A young woman walked past, carrying a bucket of paint on her shoulder. Her thick black hair was tied up into a bun and her slave tunic left her olive shoulders bare. The Roman woman blinked in surprise, then stopped, a strange look on her face.

"Diana?" Ila stopped too, staring after the slave. "What is it? Do you know her?"

Thyatis swallowed, blinking tears away. "No. Not her."

A dark-haired woman with a perfect oval face and glorious dark brown eyes smiled at her. Sunlight dappled the water behind her. They were sitting on a beach, under a cloth awning, looking out over the green sea. Thyatis was happy. Her life had purpose, a destination, everything was so certain. . . .

Ila took her hand and squeezed. "Did she die?"

"What?" Thyatis shook her head, retreating from memory. "No. No, she is safe, far from here. But I will never see her again." Ila thought Thyatis might cry, but she did not.

"Why not?" Ila held on to her hand and they continued to walk, now passing the temple of Victoria, sitting on the southern side of the stadium, opposite the Imperial box.

Drudges were sweeping and washing the walls with horsetail brooms. "Don't you care for her?"

"I do." Thyatis' voice was dull and lifeless. "But, mouse, she had four children and they were supposed to be cared for in Rome! I said they would be safe. They were killed. She is far away on an island, but—oh gods!—her children are dead because of me. I can never face her again."

"Oh." A sad expression passed over Ila's face. "She would blame you."

"I blame myself. She will be heartbroken, crushed. They were her precious babies." Thyatis stopped, unable to continue.

The little mouse girl was depressed too. Together, they continued to trudge across the sand, though it was getting hot and burned their feet. All Thyatis could see were the faces of the dead, looking upon her with mournful eyes.

Anastasia bit her quill idly, staring out the window of her study. Afternoon sun spilled through the tall arched casement, illuminating a worktable strewn with papers and oddments. Despite the shock of Thyatis' words at the party, she had revived enough to wear something that was not wholly black and gray. Instead, she had ventured into cream and light green, which was certainly cooler on such a hot day. She sighed, then put down the quill. Tiny indentations marked its length.

"All the time that she was with you," the Duchess asked, "she did not remember who she was?"

"No." Vitellix was sitting in a chair across the room, out of the sun. Dark circles shadowed his eyes. Anastasia knew the Gaul had not been sleeping well. He worried a great deal, particularly with his daughter missing. "She seemed distant from the world. Sometimes, she described a gray numbness between her and the past. If what I heard through that door was true . . ."

"It was." Anastasia bit out the words, feeling hopeless anger rise in her again.

". . . then I can see why. Can't you let her go? The past is nothing but horror for her!"

"No!" The Duchess surprised herself with the vehemence in the single word. "I will not admit defeat in this or in anything." Her lips thinned into a tight straight line. "We all bleed and suffer loss in this life. It is the way of the world. I am concerned with larger issues."

"Like your own grief?" Vitellix raised an eyebrow and sat back, slumping in the chair. "You still struggle to leave your own villa! I saw your face the other night, at Narses' party and afterwards. You are not the same woman you were. So many of your servants and family are dead—you cannot have escaped unchanged."

Anastasia glared at him, violet eyes narrowing. She lifted her chin, giving him a cold look. "That is my business, not yours, Gaul. You are here because I feel some compassion for you, for your stray daughter. Do not think to tell me how *I* feel."

Something like anger glittered in Vitellix' eyes, but then it passed, submerged in a wry look. "Oh, your pardon, noble lady. I thought I was here because I know the business of the games and I know Narses and his school. I *thought* we wanted to get our daughters back."

Anastasia's forehead creased, and she looked sideways at the man. He seemed familiar again, but she could not place him at all. The mordant sarcasm in his voice was impossible to miss. She raised her hands in mock surrender. "Enough. I am tired of bickering with you. How much do you know of the prince Maxian?"

Vitellix sat up again, his face intent. The Duchess offered an olive branch. He had to get Ila back *somehow*. Losing his wife had been bad enough; he did not want to lose the little mouse too. "Only what I have overheard between you and Helena Julia. He is Emperor Galen's younger brother?"

"Yes." Anastasia took a deep breath, smoothing her gown over her thighs, thinking. "Ah, but where to start? I suppose it began at a party here, in the Villa of Swans. . . ."

Thyatis stepped through the arch of the number-twelve starting gate, delighted to be out of the sun and into cool shade. Ila was still holding her hand and pressed close to her side. It took a moment for her eyes to adjust to the dim light, but the redolent smell of horses, hay, oats, oiled leather, waxed canvas, burnished metal and wood was all around them.

"Diana! Welcome!" Narses limped forward, leaning on his cane. The stout man's smile was wide and genuine. He laughed, seeing Ila hiding behind the redheaded woman. "Come in, little mouse, no one will hurt you here, not even this sleek cat."

Hamilcar was leaning against the side of a two-wheeled chariot, squinting and looking bilious. He was not smiling. Much like Thyatis, he was pale and green in the face. In a marked contrast to his usual physique-displaying raiment, today he was wearing a heavy blue woolen shirt that hung down to his thighs. Checked linen pantaloons covered the rest of his legs. Ila hid a smile, thinking that even the thought of the sun or loud noise would probably make him double over, heaving.

"Well, both of you seem to have drunk from the same well." Narses was cheerful, his round face wreathed in a smile. Thyatis blinked at him, thinking him the most evil creature she had ever seen. How could he be so *sunny* this morning? She had slept for a day and a night, barely able to move, much less speak before she could rouse herself out of the big plush bed in his villa. Ila had helped her to the baths, then scrubbed her down. "I trust that neither of you have gone blind or lost the use of your limbs?"

"No," Hamilcar and Thyatis growled in unison. Then they glared at each other.

"Good." Narses looked around, taking a deep breath,

smelling the pungent air. "A business proposition has been put to me." Narses voice was suddenly quite businesslike, cool and composed.

Hamilcar opened one eye, showing it red and throbbing. "You didn't bring us here to talk about advertising, did you? Do we have to appear at some taverna and play at swords?"

"No, not at all." The lanista tapped his cane against one foot, smirking. "If you have not heard, the final celebrations of these funeral games are scheduled for three days hence. The Emperor, of course, will be in attendance, as will a great proportion of Rome. Over three hundred thousand people are expected to attend! There will be a great beast hunt in the circus and then chariot races. Unfortunately, of course, the gladiatorial games are all done with. Sad, really . . ."

"What," Thyatis bit out, "do you want with us?"

"Oh, sorry. A patron of the art—you needn't know his name, it's entirely unimportant—has been begging me to arrange a match between the two of you. But of course, the fights are over and tradition is tradition!"

Hamilcar stood up, swallowing bile, and put his hands, gently, on the lanista's shoulder. "What are you talking about?" The African swayed a little, then caught himself, blinking.

"Well . . . the school has been offered a great deal of money—the two of *you* have been offered a great deal of money—to arrange a match between Diana the Amazon and Hamilcar the Glorious! Oh, what a draw!"

"With swords?" Thyatis began to look speculatively at Hamilcar. "In the Flavian?" She smiled, a tight grin that showed the tips of her teeth.

"No, no, no!" Narses shook his head, stepping between the two of them and looking out the starting-gate arch. "The gladiatorial contests are finished—closed out with that stunner of yours, Diana, and Hamilcar's fine victory. Only the last day is available on the schedule." He turned, his head silhouetted against the vast sweep of the stadium. Thyatis could see the obelisk rising up over one of the lanista's broad shoulders. Bright pennons and banners lined the roof of the stands, silhouetted sharply against the blue sky. "You'll race here, of course, four-horse chariot against four-horse chariot, seven laps in all."

"A race?" Hamilcar's face lit up.

"With chariots?" Thyatis scowled, staring at the high-sided vehicle behind the African.

"Exactly." Narses smiled genially. He tapped the chariot with the tip of his cane. "In three days Hamilcar will race for the Greens and you, Diana, will race for the Blues."

"I've never raced a chariot." Thyatis was outraged. "It won't be much of a contest!"

Ila tugged at her sleeve, making Thyatis lean down. "Yes, it will," whispered the mouse girl, her eyes narrowed to slits, glaring at the African. "I'll show you some more tricks. We're gonna get that smirking cat." She stuck out her tongue at Hamilcar.

The African laughed, his confidence suddenly very high. The news shook off his hangover and he ran a hand along the curved surface of the chariot. "Three days! It seems so long—"

"You seem so short," Thyatis said dryly. "You may wish it were long, when you cross swords with me."

Hamilcar grinned, his teeth brilliant and white in the gloom. "Well, then, we'll finally have a chance to see who masters the other."

Thyatis grinned again. "A good choice of words. You already have a collar, don't you?"

Hamilcar's face went cold. Like most of the gladiators, he was a slave. Thyatis laughed.

"I suppose," Anastasia said softly, depressed, "the Prince must have fought there on the mountaintop, and his power—exercised so violently—woke the volcano to life. Disaster followed disaster."

Vitellix stood by the window, staring out at the garden. "Diana says she saw all the other men die at his hand, yet he had been wounded to the point of death himself. Is he truly so strong?"

"He must be!" Anastasia raised her head, glaring at the Gaul. "He *does* live, if we are to believe Betia. He was sent away to the school at Pergamum, you know, when he was young. The whole family was so proud—a healer with the true art is born to perhaps one family in a million— and they seemed blessed. Who knew things would turn out in such an evil way?"

"Do you think," Vitellix knelt by Anastasia's chair, his face pinched and intent, "Diana was right when she said she *could* have killed him by striking off his head?"

"I don't know." The Duchess looked away, closed fist bumping her lips. "We know so little about his powers. Krista . . ." Anastasia stopped, her face bleak, then made an effort to gather herself and resumed. "Krista told me the Prince could raise the dead as creatures without will, though they could speak and act if he directed them. He healed her hurts more than once, wounds which should have killed her. I gathered, from what little she said, he could draw upon the strength of those like Gaius Julius and Alexandros. She said their legends made them powerful."

Vitellix made a sound like a snort and a laugh at the same time. Anastasia stared at him, her eyes dry but desolate. "I have seen them both, I think, the golden youth and the gray old politician. At the house of Gregorious Auricus. In fact, I believe the esteemed senator is Gaius Julius' patron."

"What? His patron?" The Duchess pursed her lips, considering this news.

"Yes . . . Gaius Julius—if the man that I am thinking of is he—is responsible for the funeral games. He is the actual *editore,* though Gregorius—for obvious reasons—is the magistrate in charge. Gaius met Diana—pardon, Thyatis—at a party hosted by the senator. He conceived a desire for her, I think, but she rebuffed him."

Anastasia sighed. "Being in such a position would make it easy to have her captured and put into the Flavian as a criminal."

Vitellix nodded, still thinking. "I do not know what happened to the youth, though he suffered some kind of fit at the party. They took him away to a private room."

Nodding, Anastasia rose from the chair, absently smoothing her gown. Nervous, she took a corner of the sleek fabric between her fingers and began to fold it over and over, making a sharp edge that she rubbed against her thumb. "The histories say Alexander was sometimes afflicted with seizures. The physicians call it *morbus comitialis,* I believe. So—the two legends are here in the city. The Prince is here in the city. I do not believe, from the Emperor's reaction when he and I spoke, that Maxian has approached his brother."

"Does Maxian know?"

"That his brother acceded to my act?" Anastasia shrugged, lifting her white shoulders. "I do not know. If he does, then he will be very angry. The Emperor's life would be in grave danger . . . or would it?" The Duchess suddenly stopped. "There is—I do not know how to put it—there is apparently a magical guardian, if you will, watching over the Emperor and the Empire. It is very powerful. Part of the Prince's madness is his desire to overthrow this guardian. He believes the guardian exerts a baleful influence upon the people, sapping their vitality. However, it may be strong enough to keep Maxian from taking revenge upon his brother."

"Would he?" Vitellix clasped his hands behind his back. "Would he kill his own brother?"

"Galen would have him killed." Anastasia's voice dropped and she looked down. "Once a man is Emperor, then his actions are guided by the welfare of the state, not by his heart."

"Like yours?" Vitellix raised an eyebrow, but there was no censure in his voice. "I praise the Many-Handed each day I do not have to carry your burden. It would be too heavy for me."

Anastasia met his eyes and he felt enormous compassion for her, for there was such desolation and loss in them. Despite this, he knew she would never surrender her purpose, even if the weight of it crushed the life from her body.

"I will set my men to watch the house of Gregorious Auricus," Anastasia said. "We will find this dead man and the Prince. Please, if you will, see if you can speak with Thyatis and Ila. Narses may extend you that courtesy. He certainly will have nothing to do with me! If necessary, I will have them kidnapped so we can discover what Thyatis knows of the Prince. Also, I will speak with the Emperor and the Empress about this. Strenuous steps must be taken if the Prince is to be captured."

Vitellix nodded, his round face sad. He had hoped to leave this life behind long ago.

◻◦⊙◦⊙◦⊙◦⊙◦⊙◦⊙◦⊙◦⊙◦⊙◦⊙◦⊙◦⊙◦⊙◦⊙◦⊙◦◻

CONSTANTINOPLE

)‖(

The tramp and clatter of hobnailed boots rang through the Great Gate. The ancient towers were blackened, scarred and scorched by the impact of stones and bolts. Constantinople had endured far too much in the last five years. Nicholas marched through shadow, Dwyrin right behind him, Vladimir bringing up the rear. They marched in the legionary cohort assigned to guard the Western legate, Dagobert, as he entered the city.

A crowd was waiting inside the gate, held back by the

leveled spears of Eastern troops. The people stared at the foreigners with dead eyes and wan faces. No one seemed happy to see them. Noting the grim Eastern troops standing in the gatehouse, Nicholas wondered what had happened. These men looked defeated. Odd, considering the Arab army had been driven off into the fortifications held by the Persians north of the Golden Horn.

The Western legions held the Perinthus road, as well as most of the Arab works. The enemy, in fact, no longer directly threatened the city. The long, watery tongue of the Golden Horn thrust between the opposing armies. A stream fed into the Horn from the west, making a border between the Roman pickets and the Arab and Persian scouts. The mass of Constantinople lay south of the Horn on its own peninsula. Nicholas expected that once the Western and Eastern commanders put their heads together, a massed attack on the Persian camp would be launched, supported by a concerted effort by the Western and Eastern fleets to smash or drive off the Arab squadrons blockading the city.

In the aftermath of the dawn attack, Nicholas found himself and his two friends welcome guests of the legate himself, who seemed both appalled and overjoyed to have such a powerful weapon at hand. Nicholas watched the Western officers fawning over Dwyrin with growing disgust. The hatred and envy in the faces of the thaumaturges was worse. His gut told him to get the boy into the city as quickly as possible. Nicholas had pressed the legate to abide by the treaty. Dagobert wanted to demur, but he was not bold enough to imprison them. Thus, they entered the city under his protection, though they did not feel particularly safe.

"The dux Dagobert, son of Lothair, tribune of the West, commander of the Legions!" A bull-voiced guardsman crashed the butt of a heavy double-bitted ax on the floor. Dagobert entered, Nicholas, Vladimir and Dwyrin at his back. Two of his staff officers followed.

A man turned, face flushed with anger, from the table

at the center of the room. Nicholas raised an eyebrow, seeing Dagobert stiffen. The easterner was tall and broad shouldered, with a neatly trimmed red-gold beard. He was wearing full cavalry armor and boots with a red stripe along the seam. *Ah,* Nicholas thought, taking the measure of the man, *this is the prince Theodore, of whom so much was expected and so little delivered.* Five or six Imperial officers, their silver-washed armor gleaming and burnished, their cloaks made of fine wool and silk, stood around the table. Each man pretended to ignore the interruption.

"Pardon me, my lord," Dagobert said stiffly. "I have come to speak with the emperor Heraclius about driving these Persians from his land."

"Have you? Well, then, long-hair, you will speak with me! I am Theodore, Caesar of the Eastern Empire and commander of the Imperial army. When I have time, I will discuss the disposition of your forces."

"Is Emperor Heraclius dead?" Dagobert's voice rose a little, putting a sharp emphasis on the word *Emperor*. "Are you his heir?"

Theodore's lip curled a little and he finally faced the Frank squarely. "Dead? No, he is not dead! He is ill, but I command the Legions in the city and am his royal brother. Listen, tribune, you are most welcome, but I do not have time for you right now. Return to your camp and I will speak with you in the morning!"

Nicholas could see that the tribune's temper was fraying. The plain dismissal in the Eastern Prince's voice was an iron goad. Nicholas motioned with his head and Vladimir and Dwyrin, both wide-eyed, began to inch back out of the room. The Western staff officers moved up, smirking.

"Lord Theodore, Emperor Galen has declared me *magister militatis* of the Western Empire." Dagobert drew out a short ivory rod capped with gold. He held it up, light from the high, narrow windows catching on the bright metal. "By treaty, within the confines of the Eastern

Empire, while I am here, I outrank all other officers in the Legion save the Eastern Emperor. This includes you. Now, where is Emperor Heraclius? I need to speak with him immediately!"

"The Emperor," Theodore snapped, face growing red, "is not here!"

Nicholas reached the door just as the Prince started to shout and eased it open. The two burly red-beards on either side looked down at him with interest, but he smiled and made a little wave with his fingers before slipping out.

"Nicholas! That was interesting! Why leave?" Dwyrin pressed his ear against the door, a sly look on his face. "Wait—I can still hear them. They're shouting."

"We can all hear them," Vladimir said dryly, cleaning out one ear with his finger. "I think everyone in the palace can hear them."

Nicholas rolled his eyes. "Come on. Let's find my tribune and report—then he can hide us somewhere! Bickering generals are nothing but trouble."

The northerner turned to go, but found himself face-to-face with a very angry young woman. She was short, richly dressed and blessed with a tousled head of brown hair. At the moment, she seemed ready to chew iron pigs and spit nails. A brace of very large men in armor were behind her. More of the Faithful Guard, though they were wearing closed helmets and their hands were tight on their weapons. "Out of my way, centurion!"

"Of course, milady!" Nicholas backed up, running into Dwyrin and Vladimir, who were trying to see what was going on. "Martina?" Dwyrin sounded surprised and embarrassed at the same time. He hurriedly tried to smooth his hair back and tug his tunic straight.

The woman paused, hand on the door, squinting at the Hibernian. "Oh, you're the boy from the stream. Hello! I'm sorry, I haven't a moment." Then she slammed the door open and stalked in, already spoiling for a fight. "Dear Prince Theodore! Why, I'm surprised to see you out and about. Weren't you under house arrest?"

Nicholas closed the door gently, grimacing, and then the three of them hurried away down the corridor. Luckily, Nicholas knew the palace fairly well and they were able to escape before something else happened.

The fires on the plain died down at last, letting the air clear. Nicholas and Dwyrin walked along the upper battlements at the far-northwestern end of the city. From their vantage, they could see across the Golden Horn, into the Galata suburbs and the Persian camp. Evening was close, drawing a dark gray blanket across the land. The only lights to be seen were the cookfires of the Persians and the Arabs. Sometimes, lanterns winked on the galleys patrolling the waters of the Horn. Nicholas drew a breath, taking joy in the clean, cold air. Their barracks were in one of the old palaces down in the lower city. They were cramped and crowded and filled with vermin and lice. Vladimir refused to go out after dark, leaving Nicholas to squire Dwyrin around. The lad had taken an active, even ghoulish interest in the campaign.

Such as it was. Despite the passage of a full day and a night, the Western troops remained outside of the city, still in their encampments on the Perinthus road and in the wreckage of the Arab *limes*. Rumor in the barracks and the markets said Dagobert and his staff had left the city empty-handed, without so much as a glimpse of Heraclius. What *was* clear was Prince Theodore's open disobedience. Despite his presumed arrest, he was widely seen in the city, speaking earnestly with the various Legion commanders and the cohort tribunes. Nothing came out of the Bucoleon but silence.

Nicholas leaned on the wall, one shoulder resting against a smooth granite merlon. An arrow slit opened out beside him, giving him a good view of the last touch of the sun on the Propontis. A haze had come up with sunset, covering the water and the land. A few lights flickered, but even the stars in the east seemed dim. Dwyrin put up a booted foot on the embrasure, staring fixedly out at the Galatan shore.

"What do you see?" Nicholas was curious. The boy wanted to walk the walls all day, but they only just managed to get out of the barracks a glass or two ago. Now the Hibernian had a look about him.

"There is a great army moving in the darkness.". Dwyrin's voice was distant. "The fire-priests are trying to hide them. Fools, I am inside their pattern! Look, do you see the starlight on their spears?"

Nicholas peered out into the gloom, but he could see nothing. "You've the witch-sight, lad, not I."

"Here." Dwyrin put his hands over Nicholas' eyes, then bent his head. A low muttering followed, while Nicholas blinked in the darkness. At his side, Brunhilde trembled, woken by some current in the hidden world. Nicholas laid his hand across her hilt and she quieted. "Now. See?"

Nicholas opened his eyes and gasped in surprise. The shroud of night parted, leaving the rising hills of Galata illuminated by a directionless clear light. Every tree, every wall, the houses, the barns and temples seemed perfectly distinct. Nicholas tried to blink but he could not. There *was* movement, there among the rolling hills. Endless lines of lancers were winding their way down out of the northeast, the white fetlocks of their horses splashing through the stream that fed the Horn. Nicholas squinted, then staggered. Dwyrin caught him, firm hands on his shoulders. When he narrowed his vision, the scene leapt dramatically closer. Now he could see the men—flat Asiatic faces, like those of Huns or Turks, with long mustaches and pointed metal helms fringed with mail. Horsetail banners flapped at the head of each column and their long *kontos* glittered like a forest of steel reeds. Many of the riders were wearing long red and black coats with bow cases slung at their hips. Huge mobs of brown- and blond-haired men crowded the sides of the road, marching in loose order, with spears and painted oval shields slung across their backs.

"The Avars," Nicholas hissed. He had spent months fighting them during the last siege. "The khagan Bayan has returned . . . ten or fifteen thousand of them, it looks like." He blinked suddenly, his eyes watering furiously. "Ahh! That hurts!"

"Sorry!" Dwyrin dabbed at Nicholas' eyes with the edge of his tunic. "I don't know how it feels for someone else."

"Tyr!" Nicholas sat down, squeezing his eyes shut. They were burning like someone had ground a red-hot ember into each socket. "Ahh!"

Dwyrin left, then returned with a wooden cup. Gently, he laved Nicholas' eyes with the cool water and the pain receded. Nicholas' eyesight sparkled with drifting white motes for a time but then cleared. It was full dark, though the mist had cleared away, leaving a brilliant wash of stars in the heavens. The Hibernian was squatting opposite him, a chagrined look on his face.

"Sorry! I wasn't thinking . . . we used to practice that sort of thing in my old five. But you've no training for the witch-sight."

"No matter, lad. I can see at least. Come on, we've got to make a report. Those idiots in command will need to know this right away." Nicholas stood up, finding his balance returned.

"Do you think we'll attack them?" Dwyrin sounded positively eager.

"Hey, now, don't rush ahead, lad. You proved yourself in the wall attack, but those Persians will have more than one wizard on their side. The next time we go up against them, they'll be ready for you."

"Maybe." The boy sounded smug. "But I'll be ready for them."

Nicholas raised an eyebrow, but the confidence of young men was eternal and boundless, like the tide and the sun rising. "That's a good trick, with the far-seeing. We make a good team, you know, the three of us."

"Thanks." Dwyrin sounded like he was blushing, but Nicholas said nothing.

Mohammed ducked through the tent door, his face filled with disgust. Outside, it was raining, and he flipped back the hood of his cloak. He sat down heavily in one of the camp chairs, then put his head in both hands.

"What was all the commotion?" Zoë put down her brush, a delicate ivory-backed antique she had recovered from the palace in Palmyra. Her thick hair was down and loose, falling around her tan shoulders in a dark cloud. "It sounded like an army banging around out there."

"It was." Mohammed remained deep in thought.

"Mohammed?" Zoë rose, gathering her shirt, and knelt by his side. A bandage covered her wounded ear; the battle in the dark had added bruises on her arm and thigh. "What happened?"

"An army is arriving, under cover of darkness. They are the Avars, from north of the Roman frontier. I believe the Persian priests are trying to hide the sound of their movement from the Romans, much as they attempted to deceive you. That is what Shahr-Baraz has told me, anyway."

"Ah." Zoë took his weathered old head in her hands, smoothing his wrinkled brow with her thumbs. She pursed her lips, considering his words. "No one told you they were coming to join us? I certainly did not hear of it."

"No. I have spent the better part of a week in constant argument with the King of Kings, urging him to join us in driving the Western army from the Perinthus road. Each day he has said *wait*. Now I know why, and I am very uneasy about his reticence."

Zoë nodded, then turned and sat against his knees, handing him the brush. "Tell me, but you have to brush my hair."

Making a snorting sound that passed for laughter, Mohammed took the brush, holding it up for a moment. The silver back was smooth and reflected his face, inverted.

Even upside down, he seemed old and tired, with deep shadows around his eyes. *Where is the young man who rode to Damascus with a pack train of fine plates and goblets?*

"Don't sigh. Tell me what you are thinking." Zoë glowered up at him.

"Ah, I don't know where to begin." Mohammed gathered the young woman's hair, exposing the sleek line of her neck, then began to work the brush through the violent curls with a slow, even motion. Long ago, when he first married Khadijah, he had done the same for her. Little rituals like this were easy to fall into. They occupied the hands while the mind was disturbed. "I do not like these Persians. Shahr-Baraz and Heraclius are far too alike in my mind for him to win my trust. He and Khalid are close, too. I have seen them talking."

Zoë grunted. "Did you know," she said, "Khalid served in the Persian army as a youngster, before he joined you? He was a scout. He was at Palmyra."

"Yes, I remember." Mohammed began working through a tangle, keeping the hair slack so that the brush did not pull. "He seems quite devoted to our cause, but I wonder . . . Your cousin and he are thick as thieves. They are constantly larking about."

Sniffing, Zoë raised a hand, critically examining her nails. "Odenathus is a lout sometimes. Some days it seems he has grown up, then he'll be an . . . an ox again! He plagues me! Khalid is a bad influence on everyone. What will you do about him?"

"Do? I'm not sure that I need to do anything. Not yet. Shahr-Baraz, the kagan Bayan and I will have words again tomorrow. The Boar says that he has a plan for taking the city, which I am interested in hearing. If it seems likely to work, we should make the effort. Otherwise, we must put our heads together and think of something else."

"I will come." Zoë made her pronouncement, complete with a regal snap of authority. "I am Queen of Palmyra and command half our forces. I will have my say in this. You men will make a mess of it, I'm sure."

Mohammed ran the brush through the last of her hair, smoothing it out across his thigh. "As you command, O Queen." His voice was very dry. "You and Shahr-Baraz at odds will be amusing, at least."

"Amusing?" Zoë stood, drawing her shirt close and narrowing her eyes. "Do you think that I am *amusing*?"

"No." Mohammed stood as well, his expression gentle. "Thank you. I will be glad of your company."

Zoë frowned, then relented, letting her brief anger flow away like a desert storm. She met his eyes, drinking in his calm, ineffable strength. "The end of this is close at hand, my friend. Our long road leads to this gate of stone and this ancient city. Can you feel it in the air?"

"Yes." Mohammed was suddenly calm, his expression distant. "The voice from the clear air is quiet. I think that means that we have come, at last, to the hinge of fate."

"Nicholas." The door to the barracks room swung open and two men entered. Nicholas stood, arm stiff in salute. Vladimir rolled out of bed, grabbing up a shirt to cover his pelt. Dwyrin, poring over a book he had found in the market, looked up, puzzled. The third watch had just passed and the three friends were preparing to bed down. The rest of the maniple quartered in the high-ceilinged, drafty, rat-infested room was out on watch duty, pacing the miles of wall protecting the city. "Well met."

"Tribune Sergius! I hadn't thought you were still in the city." Nicholas clasped the heavyset officer's forearm in greeting. "I am glad to see you!"

Sergius smiled, short-cropped white hair gleaming in the lantern light. "I'm glad you weren't killed in the desert. There is little time—I've read your report of the movements in the Galata hills. I've brought someone that wants to talk to you."

The man behind Sergius stepped forward, coming into

the circle of light. He was thick-set, with short, oily black hair and a craggy, grim-looking face. Everything about him, from his thick wrists and knuckles to the small scars on his neck said *soldier* to Nicholas. A very experienced professional. The northerner straightened, seeing a killer's look in the man's eyes.

"This is Rufio," Sergius continued, "the commander of the Faithful Guard."

"Oh." Nicholas raised an eyebrow. "Well met, sir, but why are you here?"

"I'm here for the boy." The man's voice was cold and direct, like ice grinding through the flanks of a ship caught in the floes off Grönland. "I'm here to take you under my wing. Sergius and I, given the political situation, have come to common cause. We need each other, I think. Get your kit, we're moving you to the Bucoleon itself, close to the Emperor."

"The Emperor?" Dwyrin squeaked, but hurried to gather up his gear.

"Yes. The situation is rushing to a violent conclusion." An edge of great weariness leaked into Rufio's voice, but Nicholas saw that the man was in complete command of himself. An aura of effortless competence surrounded the officer. Nicholas liked to think that he was a professional, but this man was an exemplar. "I need you where you can do some good."

Nicholas shoved the last of his equipment into its carry sack, then checked to make sure that Vladimir and Dwyrin had left nothing behind. Sergius had moved to the door and was watching the corridor. "We're ready."

Rufio didn't waste any words but moved swiftly down the hall. A pair of the Faithful were lurking at the junction of the main hall and a cross corridor. The two Scandians fell in behind them. Nicholas guessed that they were pure-blood Svenska, from north of the Gray Sea. Old and implacable enemies of the Dann lords, though he didn't suppose that mattered here, in the south. There was plenty of everything to go around, not like in the icy wastes.

"What is the political situation?" Nicholas picked up his pace, matching Rufio's.

The captain of the Faithful gave him a sideways glance, then said, "You know the Emperor is ill?"

"I heard. There are some wild rumors about."

Rufio nodded absently. They passed into a kitchen, filled with steam and the smell of baking bread. Behind the ranks of cone-shaped ovens was a staircase leading down. Rufio took the steps two and three at a time.

"The Emperor is slowly recovering," Rufio said in a low voice. "But Theodore and Martina have been at each other's throats for months. They hate each other and Theodore has scored two coups in recent days—first, the Emperor's first son, Constantius, has taken refuge in his uncle's residence. That gives the Prince an heir to control. Second, the commanders of the Legions in the city have agreed to let Theodore command them in battle. Martina cannot even appeal to the people or the circus factions for help—her marriage has turned the priests against her."

Nicholas stopped, eyes narrowing. "Where do you stand, Captain?"

"I am with the Empress." Rufio turned in the narrow space. The stairwell continued to plunge downwards. Nicholas was sure they had passed below street level and were entering the catacombs and tunnels honeycombing the city. "The Emperor's desire is known to me and he would not want his brother in command. Unfortunately, his illness has progressed to such a point that he is delirious most of the time. I have been forced to take extraordinary steps."

"Won't Theodore win?" Nicholas held up a hand, causing Vladimir and the others to stop. "You say he has the support of the army and the priests and the people. What does the Empress have, then?"

"She has me." Rufio turned away and continued down the stairs. "She has Sergius and the Office of the Barbarians. Even one of the *logothetes* supports her."

"Will that be enough?" Nicholas called down the stairs, voice filled with dismay.

"Perhaps," Rufio's voice echoed up from below, out of the darkness.

囗〇-〇囗

THE TEMPLE OF VESTA, ROMA MATER

)I(

Draped in white wool, her face and head covered by a folded wimple, Thyatis climbed a short flight of pale marble steps. Her head was bent low, unable to bear the glare of the sun. She stopped inside the doorway, clinging to a fluted pillar. Within the central room, a fired burned. The garden surrounding the temple was filled with the quiet noise of bees and crickets. Thyatis swallowed in fear. This place was forbidden. Only the priestesses of Vesta were allowed in this inner sanctum.

The gate to the larger Atrium Vestae had stood open at her approach. The lectors with their bundled rods and axes were absent. A brazier had burned in their empty watch house. Thyatis had called, hearing her voice die among pillared halls. Searching for one of the priestesses, she had ventured into cool, dim chambers, then to this garden tucked behind the building. *This is forbidden! I will be buried alive!*

She stepped into the inner room, feeling the heat of the fire beat on her face. Nestled in a deep marble bowl, the flame of Rome burned bright, licking up from the coals. Thyatis knelt, her forehead pressed against the marble lip of the bowl. Her fist ground into the stone, drawing blood. Tears dripping on the tessellated floor made a soft sound.

Meteors plunged out of a sky burning with orange and

vermilion light. Vast roiling clouds surged across the heavens, shedding sparks and a black rain of ash. The sea surged, crashing against a shore filled with low-lying buildings. Temples and villas were inundated, their tile roofs cracking under the shattering wave. Foam boiled up, sweeping through the streets. Thousands died, drowned or crushed, their corpses lifted high on the black waters. Beyond the harbor mouth, the wreck of a ship broke apart on the long mole protecting the wharves and docks. A spar tossed in the boiling sea. A figure clung to it, trapped in the rigging, dead, blind face staring up at the burning sky. Beneath the water, a red light gleamed and flickered on the woman's chest. Her dark hair spread in the water like a fan, her face shrouded by steam.

"No! Oh no. Oh no." Thyatis levered herself up from the edge of the bowl. Every horror she had suffered paled, becoming faint and indistinct. This was raw, a jagged wound torn open inside her. Sea-gray eyes wide, she stumbled back, away from the fire hissing in the center of the temple. She fell against a wall, her shoulder cracking one of the wooden panels. "Oh, not her too, not her! Oh, my love!"

Little sister, you must not believe these visions.

Thyatis stiffened, feeling a cold breath on her shoulder. The broken panel revealed a hidden chamber. She turned, rising, left hand groping for a sword. Her fingers found only folds of heavy cloth and a braided girdle. In the opening, a pair of gray eyes blazed, shining in the darkness. A figure of a woman stood in shadow, hidden, wrapped in deftly woven robes, a spear leaning against her shoulder.

"What are you?" Thyatis could barely speak.

Your guardian, sister, your patron, a guide in these dark places. Listen, as the Crooked One once listened to me. Closely, for my words are wisdom, winged from the heavens. You must keep hope, child, and tend it in your heart. While you have that hope, you will win. Victory will come, though the seas break and storms swallow the world. You, of all women, must keep hope you will come home again, through torment and illusion and betrayal. Ignore these qualms in your heart.

There is no truth in fear.

"Wait!" The figure grew dim, the brilliant eyes fading. "Does she live? Does Shirin live?"

The figure smiled, though it was more felt than seen. Thyatis turned away, her mind racing. What if Shirin had fled the island, come to Rome? What if she had taken ship, some coaster or merchant lug from Athens? It would beat up the coast, fat sails filled with wind, coming under the shadow of the mountain. Many ships that made for Rome harbored in Misenum overnight . . . such a ship, Shirin aboard, might have laid to in the wide bay at Neapolis on a warm summer evening. In the night, the mountain would wake, raising tumult in the sea, flinging meteors, a rain of burning ash.

"O you cursed gods, you have taken everything from me! Everything!"

Thyatis fell to the floor, nails digging into the tile, weeping uncontrollably. She had driven her body to its limits the past days, training while light remained in the sky, pressing herself and Ila harder than they had ever been pressed. She had lamed horses, smashed chariots, feverish to master the skills she would need to beat the smirking African on the raceway. At night, when visions tormented her, she drank until her pain was dulled and she could find some rest in the arms of gentle Morpheus. Now that failed too, and she shuddered uncontrollably.

Not everything is taken from you, the gray-eyed voice whispered, faint, as if from a great distance. *Not everything. Open your eyes.*

Thyatis woke, hot sun beating down upon her back. Puzzled, she rose, arms heavy with armor. She looked around, her face lighting with awe. The heavy gown and robes were gone. She wore high-strapped boots, a tunic of linen clasped at one shoulder, iron bracelets. Her other shoulder and bicep were covered with fitted bronze. A helmet rode on her head, heavy and tight. A sword lay on the ground at her feet and she knelt to pick it up. A hilt of bone ran into a half-moon guard, set with an eight-rayed star. The blade swelled towards the tip, making it point-heavy, but the edge was keen and a thick tang ran down the center line. Her hand fit perfectly.

A temple rose around her, glowing in brilliant hot sunlight. Huge round columns rose up in a stone forest on all sides. Thyatis stood at the intersection of two colonnades. Before her, the columns opened out into a half-circle. Enormous stone lions rose up, flanking a monumental doorway. The great beasts stared down at her, dead eyes rimmed with flaking paint. Long beards curled from their chins. Every surface on that rising doorway was covered with carvings. Plaster clung to the sandstone, holding the remains of bright colors on a white background.

Thyatis gulped, then gripped the sword tightly and advanced. A thin, dry wind blew past her, whirling sand across her path. Everything seemed ancient and abandoned. Distantly, at the edge of the temple complex, she knew an army was waiting. The darkness within the doorway loomed, growing deeper as she approached. All light seemed to fail at the boundary. Broad, flat steps led up, and she ascended with a sinking heart. She stopped in the portal, one foot touching the darkness, her body in the light.

Within, she could see nothing. Great dread seized her. There was something waiting just inside, waiting to tear into her, shedding her life. Her foot moved back into the light. The wind moaned among the pillars, making a ghostly sound.

Thyatis jumped, startled, and then settled her nerves.

She would enter the darkness. The sword raised in her hand, she slid into the gloom like a snake's tongue. For a moment it glowed, passing from light to dark, and she saw a vast statue within, rising up fifty or sixty feet above her head. Empty stone eyes stared down at her from the seated king. Thyatis entered, feeling the heat of the sun fade from her back. It was very dark.

Enter, my son. The voice was enormous, ringing back from the sky like a striking gong.

"Aah!" She started awake at a light touch. Thyatis stared around a poorly lit room. Someone was seated at the side of her bed, tiny hands pressing her down. "Oh. Ila, what is it?"

"You cried out." The mouse girl shifted and lamplight showed her face pinched with worry. "You sounded afraid. I thought you were having nightmares again."

"I was . . ." Thyatis groped for the memory. Titanic voices had been ringing around her, telling her things, important things. Her heart was hammering and a chill sweat dripped from her as if she were a cold jug on a hot day. "I was wearing armor. There was a helm of snakes. . . . Oh, it's all gone now." Thyatis glared at the mouse girl, who sidled away, shamefaced.

"Bad mouse. No cheese for you." Then Thyatis laughed and Ila climbed back onto the bed, grinning. "How do you feel, Ila?"

"Tired!" The girl raised an eyebrow. "Aren't you?"

"No." Thyatis sat up, brushing back her hair. Something poked her in the eye. Frowning, she opened her hand. A lock of gleaming dark hair lay in it, folded over like a keepsake. Thyatis held it up to the light in wonder. "I'm not tired."

)((

Sweating, Nicholas stepped back, raising his blade in salute to the Scandian. "Well struck, Olaf!" The axe man nodded his big head, wild beard jutting from his chin like the prow of a ship. Nicholas turned away, picking up a towel from the bench at the edge of the fighting square. All around him was a constant murmur of gruff voices. Many of the Faithful spent their free time in the hall, sparring and drinking. The sounds and smells made him feel at home. These Scandians were all from the eastern lands, but their dialect was still close to that of the Dann: a comfortable sound, coupled with the familiar smell of oiled metal and mead and roasted meat. The Faithful Guard were well kept by the Emperor, with plenty to eat and drink.

"Centurion." Nicholas pulled a tunic over his head, then turned. Rufio approached, nodding to some of the men, clasping forearms with another. "I understand you speak Scandian?"

"Yes, sir." Nicholas did not know what proper rank the captain of the Faithful Guard held, but the black-haired Greek seemed to deserve immediate respect. "The Dann dialect, but it's close enough . . ."

"Good." Something like a smile crossed Rufio's thin lips. "Traditionally, the Faithful are commanded by Greek officers, but I think you'll fit in, even if you're a Latin."

Nicholas was surprised. Very few people ever realized he was a Latin Roman, and not the northern barbarian indicated by his dress and accent. "Not many people notice, sir. It doesn't matter to me if it doesn't matter to you."

"No." Rufio handed him a golden clasp worked in the shape of a dragon biting its own tail. "Here's your flash. I've put you on the list just below me. When things come to blows, you'll have the Hibernian, your pet Walach and half the men. I will command the left, you the right."

Nicholas donned his cloak, replacing an iron clasp he had picked up in Aelia Capitolina with the golden one. Then he strapped his baldric on, making sure Brunhilde was snug in her sheath.

"A fine blade," Rufio nodded at the hand-and-a-half sword. "Scandian make?"

"Yes."

Rufio smiled, turning a little so that he was between the nearest of the Faithful and Nicholas. His voice was soft, barely carrying past Nicholas' ear. "You should keep it sheathed until the men are comfortable with you. Olaf is as dense as a stone, but one of the others might mark what you've got there. Then they might be minded to ask where a Roman was getting a runesword."

"She was a gift." Nicholas felt very uncomfortable talking about this. Brunhilde began to tremble at his waist and he clamped his hand down on her hilts. Rufio raised a thick black eyebrow at the motion.

"I'll not try and take it from you, lad. If you won it in fair battle, it's yours."

"I was *given* her," Nicholas said, voice rising a little. Rufio met his look with perfect calm in his black eyes. Nicholas flushed. "I understand, sir. I'll spar with another weapon."

"Good. Now listen, events are beginning to move. Now you're my staff officer, you get to come with me and watch the powers that be bicker like old hens in the farmyard."

"What happened?"

Rufio gave a half-smile, jerking his head. "A new player has entered the game."

The Bucoleon, Nicholas found, was actually composed of many palaces and buildings, all intertwined in a confusing maze of levels, halls and chambers. Rufio walked swiftly, though he was slightly shorter than Nicholas. They passed quickly through rooms filled with intricate mosaic designs on the floor and stunning paintings—now peeling or sagging with age—on the walls.

"The Western legate entered the city again, with some new friends." Rufio was using his briefing voice, which amused Nicholas, since it was clipped and quick and leaned heavily on some kind of regional Greek accent. Luckily, Nicholas had a good ear for dialects. "I have heard, from the commander of the number-six gate, that Western scouts have been watching the Persians and their allies. Another five or six thousand Avars have filtered in from the north. Of course, I wouldn't even know this much save Sergius is working overtime, visiting old friends."

Nicholas nodded, wondering how much the captain of the Faithful knew about Sergius and the Office of the Barbarians. With the current struggle in the city, it seemed unlikely that Prince Theodore knew who Sergius *really* worked for—otherwise the white-haired tribune would have lost his head. Nicholas was a Latin, sent by the Western Office to help Sergius with his messier problems. The Western Office had taken great pains, over the last twelve years, to secure control of the Eastern office. It was an old game, made more interesting at the moment by the Prince's play for power.

"We—a term I use loosely—are guessing the Persians and Arabs field nearly eighty thousand men. With another twenty thousand Avars and Slavs, they are well over our own strength. You think Dagobert brought four legions?"

"Yes, I saw their standards and flags myself." Nicholas nodded. "One veteran, three fresh, all full strength—so perhaps forty thousand or a little more."

"After Theodore's little debacle in Syria, there are perhaps thirty thousand Eastern troops mustered here."

"Not good odds, seventy to a hundred."

"No." Rufio shook his head. "But this has changed. A report came in last night from a man selling wine to the Western troops in the forts. He says a great host of barbarians—not Turks but some other horse-people—arrived out of the north and have joined Dagobert."

"Who?" Nicholas stared at the Greek in surprise. The Avars controlled everything north of the mountains dividing Thrace from Moesia Inferior. But there were scattered bands of Sarmatians, Slavs and Walachs in the vast Rus forest. "Another Western army?"

"No." Rufio was smirking. "The wine merchant did not know the banners, but I recognized them from his description. They are Khazars, from the lands far to the east around the Mare Caspium. Their khan Ziebil aided Heraclius and Galen in their war against the Persians."

"How did they get here?" Nicholas was nonplussed.

"I don't know, but we might find out. Their commander is coming into the city with Dagobert, to try and meet with Theodore."

"Not the Emperor?"

Rufio shook his head and Nicholas saw the weariness in the man again. It was easy to miss behind his confident expression. There was something else, too.

"How long have you served Heraclius?"

"All his life, the brat." Rufio's face brightened, weariness falling away like a dropped cloth. "His father hired me, when young Heraclius came of age, to be his bodyguard. We were in Africa then, at Carthage. The old man—he was governor—decided to take a hand in Imperial politics. Everything was in chaos then. A right bastard named Phocas was wearing the Purple. We did him in, though. A long time, I suppose."

Nicholas nodded. *That tells me where Rufio's placed his coin!*

"Why did you want us in the Guard?"

A brief smug flicker crossed Rufio's face. "I don't know

if you've seen it, but the boys' effort to break the Arab wall woke up every priest, wizard and hedge-witch in the city. I gather, from their whispers and complaints, no one has ever cut loose with that kind of display before, at least not in their memory, which is liable to be short." The captain snorted dismissively. "When Sergius said that you'd reported in, I convinced him that you needed to be near the Emperor, to protect him."

"Is that true?"

"Not at all! I've been around a bit, Nicholas. I know exactly what kind of disaster a young man with incredible power can be. My job, my *only* job, is to protect the life of the Emperor and his family. Having you and the boy under my eye means one less thing to worry about."

Frowning, Nicholas said, "You think the boy is a threat to the Emperor?"

Rufio shrugged his shoulders. "I think he is a threat to every person in the city and the immediate surroundings. He's young, Nicholas, very young. I've seen his face, how he is with you and Vladimir; he has no conception of what the exercise of his strength might do, what it might cost him."

Nicholas whistled, remembering the siege in the desert. "I see your point."

"Good. Now, we're going to be observers at this meeting, so just keep your trap shut."

"Yes, sir!"

Prince Theodore had taken over a building at the margin of the Bucoleon complex, near the old Acropolis of the city. Rufio and Nicholas entered through a passage from the main palace and were immediately stopped by armed legionaries. Six cavalrymen watched the entrance. Rufio smiled pleasantly, then turned over his gladius and a knife from his belt.

"The prince feeling well today?" The soldiers did not

rise to the bait, keeping their faces neutral. "Nicholas, you should give them your sword."

The northerner felt physically ill at the thought, but he pressed Brunhilde's plain leather sheath into the man's hand. "Take good care of that," he said in a tight voice. "It was my father's."

Shrugging, the legionary put the long sword against the wall behind the guardpost. Nicholas marked the place, glared at the other men on watch and then hurried after Rufio. The captain of the Faithful seemed quite content to go unarmed into the lair of the enemy. When Nicholas caught up with him, the captain clapped him on the shoulder.

"Don't worry," he said softly. "Thirty of the Faithful are within call of us, even in here. Try to stop sweating so much. Eventually, even the prince will notice."

Nicholas hadn't managed to calm down by the time they entered the main hall of the building. Wooden panels lined the walls and there was a long table in the center of the room. Prince Theodore, flanked by some of his staff, stood near the head of the table. The Eastern officers had their heads close in conversation. Rufio stopped within polite distance and folded his arms, observing the scene. Theodore glanced up, frowned to see the captain, then resumed his conversation. Nicholas tried to be invisible, hiding behind Rufio.

A grain or two passed, then the guardsman at the end of the hall cleared his throat. "The Western legate, Dagobert, the King of the Khazars, Dahvos, and his staff."

The newcomers entered, dressed in field armor, though they were weaponless. The same two Goths accompanied Dagobert. The Khazars were a pair of tall men with curly hair and short, neat beards. Nicholas looked them over, seeing muscular, lean horsemen. They were clad in scale mail and weather-worn, patched cloaks. Their boots, though recently cleaned, were scuffed and mended. Both of them were very tan and Nicholas sensed they had been on the move for a long time.

"Greetings!" Theodore turned to them, flashing an instant smile. "Please, sit. Would you like wine or refreshment?"

"No, thank you, Prince Theodore." Dagobert did not sit and the others in his party followed his lead, standing at the third point of a triangle made by the Eastern officers, Rufio and the Westerners. "I have brought the khagan Dahvos to join us, as his army has joined ours, to discuss driving the Persians and their allies away and lifting the siege."

"An excellent plan." Theodore seemed intent on being as friendly as possible. Nicholas felt the hair on the back of his neck stand up. There was an odd feeling in the air, but more than the tension between the various parties, it felt like someone was watching him. He tried not to fidget.

"I received your dispatch this morning," the Prince continued, showing his teeth. "Our numbers now exceed those of the enemy. I am currently adjusting the disposition of my forces in the city, but when that is done, we shall advance together and destroy them."

Nicholas, listening, translated the prince's words into *When I've managed to get all of the cohort commanders to follow me, or replaced those that won't, I'll dare to poke my nose out of the city.*

Dagobert raised a skeptical eyebrow. "You agree to lead the Eastern troops under my command, then?"

"Well . . ." Theodore shrugged. "I think we can all work together, Legate. There's no need to force change upon our lieutenants at this time."

The Frank stepped forward, eyes glinting. "Our emperors have already agreed to a working arrangement, and proved its efficacy, Prince Theodore. I will command the combined army. You and your officers will follow my directives. The three of us, and our staff, will devise a plan of attack together, but we will execute it under my authority."

"That is not necessary," Theodore snapped, temper fraying. "If we agree to a plan, the Eastern Empire will stick to it."

Dagobert's face darkened and he smoothed his mustaches down with a sharp movement. "Without a single guiding will, we will not be able to use our army effectively. Three commanders are worse than none."

"This could be," Theodore said in an offhand way, "but you are not used to the capabilities of our troops, our way of fighting. There are differences between our Legions. By the way, do you speak Greek?"

"No," the Frank grated out, anger beginning to rise in his sad-looking eyes. "I do not."

"Then how will you direct my troops?" Theodore's voice gained a patronizing edge. "Some of my officers may remember some schoolboy Latin, but not all. You will have to rely on me and my staff, I fear. So there is no reason to make the arrangement top heavy."

Dagobert bit back a curse, his eyes thinning to slits. "Sufficient courier riders who speak both Latin and Greek, Lord Prince, can be found to carry messages from me to the cohorts. I do not think there will be a problem."

"That is unacceptable." Theodore turned away with the air of a man who has been patient with an impossible situation. "There is far too much room for error in such translations. We will be in battle against a canny and powerful foe! We cannot afford a misunderstood order."

"Very well." Dagobert seemed to have made up his mind during the Prince's speech. "The Western army and the Khazars will deal with the Persians. We would appreciate it if you would remain inside the city with your army, Prince Theodore, so that no orders are misunderstood."

Nicholas swallowed a whistle, feeling the cold tension in Rufio. Nervous, the northerner looked around, counting the number of Eastern guardsmen along the walls. As he did so, a glint of light from one of the wall panels behind him caught his eye. An elaborate hunting scene had been carved into it, leaving deep, shadowy recesses between the figures of horses and dogs and rearing stags. Something had been there for an instant. But it was gone now. The sensation of being watched remained.

"Do you think you can defeat the Persians without me?" Theodore's voice dripped with sarcasm. "With your raw troops and these ragged barbarians?"

"Any army," Dagobert replied, face stiff, "fighting as one can defeat an enemy fighting as three. Do I have your word your forces will remain inside the city?"

"You do not!" Theodore barked angrily. "You presume a great deal to order *me*, barbarian!"

"When your emperor is well," Dagobert snapped, "ask him what he would have you do. I do not think that you will like the answer."

Theodore stepped forward, his motion violent, but brought himself up short before he struck the Frank. The two men exchanged a long and pregnant glare, then Dagobert smiled icily, bowed and turned away. "Good day, Lord Prince. Please extend my best wishes to the Emperor, when you see him next."

Rufio touched Nicholas' shoulder and they retired, quietly, through the door they had come in through. Theodore was already raging, his voice low and vehement, behind them as they slipped out. "Both of those men are fools," Rufio said quietly as they hurried down the hallway. "Things are worse than I expected. Turn here, we can catch up with them before they leave."

Nicholas followed as Rufio ducked through a series of interconnected rooms, mostly filled with boxes and hampers of indefinable baggage. They came out into a high domed hallway filled with a pleasant green light slanting down from above. Windows of close-set colored glass studded the domes, providing a soft and diffuse illumination. Statues of ancient emperors and heroes lined the walls. The Western and Khazar officers were hurrying past, their boots making a loud rattle on the tiled floor.

"Legate, Kagan. May I have a moment of your time?" Rufio pitched his voice to carry, but not far. Dagobert paused, frowning, but then caught sight of Nicholas standing behind the captain's shoulder.

"Ah, the missing agent! And you are?"

"Rufio, captain of the Faithful Guard, my lords." Rufio bowed, both to the Frank and to the Khazar. "I believe we can speak in this room undisturbed for a moment."

Dagobert glanced over his shoulder. "Very well."

Rufio led them into a small alcove set with benches on all sides and ornate stone carving on the three facing walls. The stone was painted to resemble vines and roses. A circular glass window filled the ceiling, shedding a faint greenish light onto the five men. Nicholas took up a position by the door, keeping an eye on the hall outside.

"Do you speak for the Emperor?" Dagobert seemed aggrieved and distracted. The two Khazars were watching the byplay intently. Nicholas guessed that they were brothers.

"I fear, my lord, no one can truly speak for the Emperor at this time." Rufio sounded both sad and professional. "He is in the grip of a serious illness. Despite all our efforts, he refuses to become well. You cannot count on his aid or assistance in these matters. I do, however, speak for the Empress Martina. She supports the Western Emperor's plan, though her power in the city is, currently, severely circumscribed."

"Theodore controls the army, then? I understood he was under house arrest."

Rufio shrugged. Some things could not be helped. "Theodore has gained the support of nearly all of the Legion commanders and his house arrest was never enforceable. Are you going to attack the Persians?"

Dagobert shared a glance with Prince Dahvos. The Khazar, at last, spoke in a pleasant, barely accented voice.

"Even with the addition of our horsemen, master Rufio, we do not outnumber the enemy. It would be madness to attack them in their camp. They have a strong position behind the stream and the hills."

"Then there is a stalemate, unless Theodore brings his army out of the city."

"Yes." Dagobert's face became morose again. "Unless the Persians are lured out of their encampments . . ." The Frank tugged at his long nose, thinking. "Their supplies must come across the strait, on the Arab fleet?"

Rufio nodded, his arms crossed. "If our combined fleet defeats theirs, they will be trapped. Soon they would run short of food. They would have to come out of their encampments to search for supplies, and the Khazar horse could harry their foraging parties. That would force a battle. Also, we can wait."

"For what?" Dahvos seemed interested, handsome face lighting with speculation.

"While the Perinthus road is open," Rufio said, "food can enter the city. They have no chance of reducing us by blockade and starvation. To take the city, they would have to close the road again. That will bring them out."

"And if they come?" Dagobert said in a sour tone. "Then we are outnumbered! Dare we give battle against the Boar?"

Rufio snickered, rubbing his pox-scarred jaw. "Even the West fears him! Listen, if there is battle in the offing, Theodore cannot remain in the city. He will lose face among his supporters. These Arabs have already beaten him once; he must be itching for a rematch. If he knows that you are going to give battle, he must join you."

"But he refuses to be under my command!" Dagobert frowned. "That would be a disaster."

"Is there another option? Without the Eastern troops, you may well be defeated and driven back. With them, there is a chance for victory."

The Frank mulled this over, slowly stroking his mus-

taches. While he did so, Rufio turned to the Khazar prince.
"Khagan Dahvos, my condolences for the death of Sahul.
He was a wise king and a mighty warrior."

"Thank you." Dahvos smiled, clasping forearms with
Rufio. "You were with Heraclius in the campaign at Kerenos, weren't you?"

Rufio nodded sharply. "Yes, lord. Though we never
spoke at the time. I am greatly relieved to see you and
your men here, though I am surprised—I had not heard
someone had sent a messenger to Khazaria requesting your
aid. Surely Theodore didn't?"

"No." Dahvos' expression changed subtly, becoming
guarded. "We heard that there was trouble and guessed that
our aid would be welcome. A long journey, master Rufio,
if you don't come by sea!"

"Ah." Rufio glanced sideways at the Western legate,
who looked like he had bitten into a sour melon. "It does
not matter how you came. I will not flaunt the goodwill
of the gods! Legate? We do not have much more time—
Theodore's guardsmen will come looking for you soon."

"We can press the Persians, try to get them to come out
of their hole." Dagobert's words were abrupt. "But I won't
do that unless you can guarantee the Eastern army will
sortie from the city to support us." A thought seemed to
occur suddenly to the Frank. "With the boy!"

Rufio bit his lip, looking back and forth between the
Romans and the Khazars. "I cannot guarantee the entire
Eastern army will come forth—it would not be wise, in
fact, to leave the city unguarded—but I think most will.
And, of course, the boy will come."

"The boy?" Dahvos looked amused. "Which boy?"

"The firecaster." Dagobert was visibly relieved. "He got
us through the wall, perhaps he can overmatch the Persian
magi."

"Don't rely on him!" Rufio stepped close to the Frank,
a grim, fixed look in his eyes. "Putting your trust in a
wizard is like trusting the gods! They are not reliable. Cold

steel and the courage of men, those can be relied on, not these fickle powers."

Dagobert did not step away. Instead an avaricious gleam entered his eyes. "But you will bring him forth?"

"Yes," Rufio growled, the tone of his voice sending a chill down Nicholas' back. "He will come forth."

The Frank nodded and left the room, gathering up his officers. The two Khazars stayed behind for a moment, the black-haired one joining Nicholas at the arched doorway. Dahvos was reaching into his belt for something.

"I am Jusuf," he said, extending a hand. Nicholas clasped it, then saluted.

"I am Nicholas of Roskilde, centurion of the Faithful Guard. Well met."

The Khazar cocked his head, staring at the northerner. "Your eyes . . . they are an odd color, if I may say so without giving offense. Are you from Rome?"

"No!" Nicholas laughed, blushing a little. "Well, I don't know that. I may be, but I was orphaned and don't remember my birthplace. I was raised among the Dann, in Scandia."

Jusuf nodded, distracted by his own thoughts. "Of course."

Dahvos and Rufio finished their conversation and the blond Khazar strode up, his eyes sparkling with delight. The kagan nodded to Nicholas. "Jusuf, we'd better hurry or the legate will think we're plotting against him. Gentlemen, we will see you on the field of battle."

Nicholas kept silent while Rufio stepped back into the room and went to one of the corners where the benches left a cleared space. "Follow me." The captain pressed on a section of carved thorns and the corner folded back, making a sudden opening. There was an outraged squeak from the darkness, then Rufio entered. "Don't wait for the sun to set" floated back out of the darkness.

Ducking his head down to enter the low tunnel, Nicholas followed. A heavy smell of dust and mouse droppings and hyacinth perfume met him, but he took a breath and then hurried after the receding tread of the captain. He was suddenly very worried. *How the Hel am I going to get Brunhilde back?*

⊡()-⊡

THE CIRCUS MAXIMUS, ROMA MATER

)(

Leaning over the side of her chariot, Thyatis gave Ila a fierce hug. Around them, dozens of slaves and attendants swarmed among the horses and chariots, oiling axles, testing tack and harness, fitting tall feather plumes into the bronze headdresses of the animals. "You must hide, little mouse," Thyatis whispered into the girl's ear. "There will be a great deal of confusion today; you might be able to get away."

Ila nodded, her eyes wide. The girl was both worried and disgusted. "Why did they have to choose a four-horse, single-driver race? Why can't I drive in your place?"

Thyatis managed a half-smile, though the despair in Ila's face struck at her heart. "Narses arranged this, Mouse. The people want to see me and Hamilcar race. I'm sorry."

"Oh, I'll never get to race! No one wants to see me! Only you."

"Ila!" The mousy girl blinked back tears, but she held Thyatis' hand tightly in both of hers. "If I win today, or even survive the race, it will be because you taught me how to drive one of these things. If I win, you win, for you trained me."

"Maybe." Ila pressed her forehead to Thyatis' hand, then let go, a sad look on her face. "Watch the turns! It's a rare race that doesn't see a driver killed or crippled. Do you hear the crowd?"

Thyatis nodded. From the starting gates she could see part of the long sweep of the circus. The seats were a sea of people in a festive mood, wearing their holiday best. Everyone who could cram into the stadium was here today, making a brilliant display of gold and purple and white and cream and blue. Only an hour ago, the Emperor had ascended to the temple of Victoria and watched while the priests sacrificed nine sheep and nine goats to the Fates. The animals were then burned in the Greek style. Curls of smoke rose from the white pillars of the temple. The crowd noise sounded like an enormous flock of angry birds.

"I do," Thyatis said, wrapping the reins around her left hand. "They are eager for sport."

"For blood, you mean." Ila looked around, her eyes narrowed in suspicion. "The slaves whisper—they say everyone expects either you or the fat cat to die today."

"I know." Thyatis fitted a bronze helmet onto her head. "It would be a proper sacrifice if it were me, but I would not want to give that oiled panderer the satisfaction."

"Don't you dare die!" Ila scowled up at her, one little hand on the curving rail of the chariot. "You have to see me race *my* horses."

"Very well." Thyatis grinned down. A simple tunic of blue cloth covered her body from shoulder to thigh. Despite the weight it added, she managed to work herself into a corselet of close-fitting iron rings. The horses wouldn't be happy, but she *was* going into battle. Leather straps covered her arms from wrist to elbow, and high boots ran up to her knees. The helmet sported a pair of stylish back-swept wings, but she had broken the copper off with her bare hands. She wondered why Amazons were supposed to have huge, unwieldy wings on their helmets. Was it traditional? *No wonder they nearly became extinct!*

Cornets and bucinas winded, a brave, glad ringing sound. The slaves and grooms in the starting gates flooded away, carrying their bags and boxes and ladders with them. Ila padded off, waving good-bye. The Roman woman turned, snugging her helmet strap tight. She tested her balance on the chariot, rolling from side to side. It was very light, made of wicker and pine, with scenes of the ancient gods painted on the sides. The horses looked over their shoulders at her, rolling their eyes and blowing. They were a matched set of dark brown Parthian mares. Two grooms remained with each chariot, holding the leads for the teams. The horses were eager to run, tossing their heads. The long ostrich feathers danced in the air.

Thyatis tightened the reins around her hand, staring straight ahead at the brilliant white sand. The blood fire was beginning to hiss in her veins, making the world slow down and become preternaturally distinct. A hush fell over the drivers and teams in the starting gate.

Galen, Emperor of the West, stepped down from his golden seat, arm raised in salute to the people in the stands and the drivers arrayed below him. As he descended the steps, a slave on either side maneuvered a canopy of purple silk to keep him in the shade. The sun was bright today. The Emperor took a deep breath and lowered his arm. Another slave placed a dark red handkerchief in his hand. Dropping this was the signal for the race to start. He stretched out his arm, the cloth in his fist.

"Citizens of Rome," Galen's voice rang out, strong and clear, echoed around the sweeping length of the stadium by heralds repeating his words, so that all might hear. "I call upon the gods to protect and increase the power of the Roman people, to bless their empire and their armies with victory and good fortune, to be gracious and favorable to the plebes, the patricians, the College of the Priests, to me, to my family and my great household."

At the words, a deep-throated cheer rose up, for Galen had loosened his purse enough to see every man, woman and child in the city feasted for two days and two nights in preparation for the last day of the games. Well lubricated with food and wine and sweet pastries, the people were in a mellow and forgiving mood. Whispers of the Emperor's penuriousness had fallen quiet.

"The oracles," he continued, "have instructed spotless white bulls be led to the altar of Jupiter by day, not by night, for the heavenly gods love sacrifice under the light of the sun. To please the honored dead and the gods who watch over us and make Rome strong, performances have been given in the theaters, all have rejoiced and I have laid cakes upon the altar of Eilithyia."

Again, there was a murmur of general approval. The strange weather afflicting the land had passed, leaving blue skies and clean-falling rain. It seemed, with these proper sacrifices and the veneration of the dead, the displeasure of the gods had been turned aside.

"One hundred and ten matrons have prayed on bended knee, asking Divine Juno Regina for her blessing and forgiveness. I have knelt myself beside the Tiber and given up a pregnant sow to the goddess Tellus, so she might make the fields thick with wheat and the harvest rich. All these things I have done to restore the health of the people and the state."

The crowd responded in kind to the words, raising their voices in praise for the Emperor and for the gods. Galen gestured to one of his Praetorians, then raised both hands to the heavens. As he did so, soldiers began to descend from the heights of the stadium in pairs, heavy baskets in hand. They began to scatter tokens of copper, stamped with letters and numbers, into the crowd. The people surged to their feet, raising a glad cry. The poorer citizens were traditionally forced to sit in the highest seats in the stadium and now this largess—for everyone knew that the tokens could be redeemed at the Imperial storehouses for cloth, salt, grain, meat, tools, lumber, iron ingots, fired pottery, lambs, kine, all matter of goods and wealth—was being distributed to them first.

"Already," the Emperor called to the people, "Already Faith and Peace and Honor and ancient Modesty and neglected Virtue are venturing to return, and blessed Plenty with her cornucopia appears. Our voices ask for aid and we feel the presence of divine spirits. We beg for these soft showers from heaven, pleasing the gods by the prayers that we have learned, trusting them to turn away disease, drive out fearful dangers, gain peace and a season fertile with fruits. Our song of piety winds grace from the gods above, our song from those below."

On either side of the pulvinar, massed ranks of maidens and young men began to sing. The hymn was powerful and ancient, first raised to the sky in the time of fabled Romulus and Remus, primordial kings of Rome. Many in the assembled multitude joined in, filling the stadium with the booming roar of their massed voices. The Praetorians continued to descend the steps, their hands sowing a sparkling cascade of copper.

Galen waited, sweating in his heavy toga and cloak, until the gift givers reached the walkway separating the patricians and senators from the lower classes. Then he raised the red handkerchief again, drawing the attention of a rank of trumpeters arrayed on the *spina* across from him. At the motion, the grooms loosed the bridles of the chariot horses and ran out of the way. The drivers took up their reins, waiting tensely for the signal.

"For the glory of our ancient gods, let this race begin!" Galen's voice rang out into the hushed silence left by the end of the hymn. He dropped the handkerchief. As it drifted to the ground, the massed trumpets sounded in a sharp bleat of noise. Motion exploded along the line of chariots, the drivers whipping their horses to the race. Hooves thundered on the sand and the chariots leapt forward, wheels spinning furiously.

Behind the Imperial box, a tunnel ran through the bulk of the stadium and into the Palatine Hill itself, allowing the Emperor and his family easy, secure access to the circus. With the race under way, the usual crowd of servants, courtiers, clerks and Praetorians departed. An old man, his back bent with weariness, shuffled along the hall, one gnarled hand pressed against the wall for support. Near the small complex of rooms at the back of the viewing platform, the ancient stopped to catch his breath.

A servant, looking out for him, hastened up to his side. "Master Gaius? The senator has kept you a seat, close by the balcony."

"Give me a moment, lad." Gaius Julius' voice was little more than a croak, strained and hoarse. His fingers curled around the man's arm, though the servant barely noticed the weight. "I am not well. Tell me, has anyone been asking for me?"

The man nodded, then motioned off to the side, where an alcove was half hidden by a wooden screen. "He did not give a name, master, but he was generous."

"Good." Gaius Julius gathered his strength and then hobbled to the alcove. His limbs, which had once seemed so tireless and strong, had been reduced to this pitiful state. Even his mind seemed clouded and slow, though he was certain that his mental faculties remained unimpaired. He had taken to checking and then double-checking everything he did. It made for slow work, but it was necessary. A wrinkled hand thrust aside the screen. The man waiting in the alcove was nondescript, perfectly ordinary in appearance. Even his toga and tunic were an indefinable color. Gaius Julius expected that the courier was well remunerated for this particular skill. "You've my chits?"

The man nodded and pressed a leather case into Gaius' hand. The old Roman felt the weight of the bronze betting tokens and smiled. Even in his reduced state, the thrill of a dangerous gamble fired his blood and set his mind in motion. "Excellent. Here."

The nondescript man took the bag of coin, bowed and then slipped out. Gaius Julius leaned against the wall, weary beyond measure. *Damn the prince! He toys with our lives too, not just his own!*

Luckily, the old Roman had foreseen that the prince might come to grief, and his men whisked both of them away to a safe house on the Ianiculum Hill. A priest of Asclepius had been summoned as planned but could do nothing. Nearly three days had passed before Gaius Julius could open his eyes. The worst part of the whole experience had been being aware but unable to motivate his body to action. The prince remained comatose, barely breathing, his skin waxy and cold. Gaius Julius wondered with growing fear if he would be trapped in this half-life forever. What if the prince did not die? Would he remain this ancient, withered figure, barely able to walk without assistance? It was maddening!

By a stroke of luck, all of the preparations for the final day of the games had been completed. Gregorious Auricus, in fact, had been able to resolve all of the last-minute problems and controversies without a hitch. Gaius Julius sneered at the wall, thinking that the senator would reap all of the glory and public acclaim for this, when the old Roman had done all the work. *Well, nearly all the reward* ... He tucked the pouch of betting tokens away in his robe, taking considerable satisfaction from the weight that pressed against his side.

Thanks to some spurious rumor that the races would be fair, a great deal of wagering revolved around whether the Amazon Diana would win the race. Nearly every serious connoisseur of the races thought it impossible. The woman might be a very demon with the sword, but she had never raced before. Gaius Julius heard she had been training nonstop for the past days, trying to learn the tricks of maneuvering the four-horse chariot, but he knew that three days could not match a lifetime of experience. Hamilcar, however, was a more likely prospect.

The gladiator had never raced in the circus either, and the odds against his victory were long. In fact, the current leader in the yearly standings—Robertus of the Greens—was the odds-on favorite. Gaius Julius, however, paid close attention to all kinds of obscure information. Once, when they were in their cups, the *lanista* Narses mentioned the African Hamilcar was skilled with a chariot.

Gaius Julius had taken a risk, betting nearly all of the capital that he had accumulated in Prince Maxian's name on the young gladiator. He had also taken some small steps to ensure the wagers he had laid *against* Diana would pay off as well.

Croaking with laughter, Gaius Julius hobbled out into the passage and then into the back of the pulvinar, his dark toga and cloak flapping around his scrawny legs like a raven's tail.

Wind rushed past, whistling through Thyatis' helmet. She leaned into the turn as her chariot thundered around the *metae*. The entire chariot shuddered and flexed under her feet as it swung. The wheels skidded sideways across the sand as the horses, heads down, manes flowing, roared around the corner. Four other chariots, two White, one Red and one Green, were neck and neck with her. Their drivers were screaming imprecations at the horses, whipping them with the reins. Above the thunder of the wheels on the sand, the roar of the crowd was very distant and faint.

Thyatis tugged the reins to the right and the horses leapt the same direction. Cursing, she tried to guide them back towards the inner track. The *spina* was raised in three steps; first a small ledge, then a wall seven or eight feet high, then the platform that held the statues and obelisks. Her left wheel had been veering towards the ledge. Ila's voice was loud in her memory; *don't let the wheel hit the ledge; it'll splinter!*

The White driver on her right, trying to swing past her on the turn, had his horses running flat out, sweat streaming off their flanks, when her chariot jumped out. The horses were keyed up and overresponsive and she overcorrected in the turn. Her right wheel slammed into the side of the White chariot, throwing the driver against his front rail. The man shouted in rage. The crowd erupted in cheers, sensing a wreck in the offing.

A Red chariot suddenly surged past on her left and Thyatis cursed herself, wrenching her attention back to the race. The Red driver hunched low in his car, whipping the horses furiously. They sped past, blowing sand and dust across Thyatis. Choking, she swung in behind him. At the turns, the inner track was critical; a driver could gain one or two lengths in each circuit.

A hundred yards ahead, the three leaders went into the turn in front of the starting gates. Hamilcar was hanging a little back from the Blue and Green, running without an opponent on either side. Thyatis was seized by a fierce desire to beat the sly young man. She flicked the reins to the right and her Browns surged into the gap between the Red and the White chariots. Hooves blurred across the sand and she caught a glimpse of the White's wheels seemingly spinning backwards.

They came into the turn, Red on the inner track, then Thyatis' Blue, and the White, screaming insults at her. She felt the tension in the rattling, bouncing car change as they slewed into the turn and she let the rear of the chariot kick out. The back of her chariot swept across the front of the White's horses and they veered away. The White driver lashed at them, losing sight of the ruts torn in the sand by the passage of the first four chariots. The wheels hit a wedge of sand and suddenly bounced skyward. Screaming, the driver tried to cling to the reins, but the horses turned, trying to catch Thyatis' mares. The driver was flung out of the car, which toppled over. The man hit the ground with a crunch and then rolled, shrieking, as he was dragged, his leg tangled in a strap. The chariot car bounced twice, shedding a wheel, then slammed down on the driver and broke apart.

Thyatis lost sight of the man, concentrating on swinging back in behind the Red chariot, which had opened a length or more in front of her. They were in the straight again, stinging dust and sand striking her face. She ignored the pain and let the horses take their head. The browns opened up, their stride lengthening, and she roared forward, rapidly closing in on the Red chariot.

"I'm sorry," said the armored guard at the entrance by the starting gates, "but the stables are closed until after the race. You can come back then, if you want. The drivers like to meet their fans." He smiled down at Betia, broad brown chin crossed by the strap of his helmet. The little blond girl smiled up at him, swinging her shoulders from side to side.

"Are you sure?" she wheedled. "You couldn't just show me the inside? I love the Blues! They're the best, you know, particularly that Amazon Diana! She's amazing!" Betia put her right hand on the man's forearm.

"I'm sorry, Miss, but that's against the rules. Now, if you want to wait, I can maybe see you go in later?" He smiled back at her, showing heavy yellow teeth.

"But I want to go in now!" Betia sounded petulant. Her left hand remained behind her back. She thrust her chest out, letting the thin fabric of her tunic stretch. "Please?"

"No, no." The guard looked away for a moment, to see if his mate had come back from the latrines. "I can't . . . urk." He looked down.

Betia slipped her knife out of his stomach. The thin space between his shirt of linked mail and his belt was oozing blood. She pressed a hand over his mouth, ignoring his stunned look, then the knife slid across his throat. Blood welled against her hand, dripping down her arm, but she levered him to the ground, letting the stable door carry most of the weight.

Four men appeared and picked up the guard. Another man, dressed in much the same armor and clothing, took his place. Betia wrapped her bloody arm in the dead man's cloak, then pushed the heavy wooden door open with her shoulder. Her blue eyes were bleak, but she kept moving, concentrating on the task at hand. The door swung open and the four ducked in with the body. Four more nondescript figures slipped in behind them and then the door closed.

"Quickly, quickly." Anastasia threw her hood back. Her face was pale but perfectly arranged. The grim light in her eyes matched her cold perfection. "Find the rest of them. No sound. No alarms!"

At her side, Vitellix looked down sadly at the dead guard, his throat seeping dark blood from the razor-thin gash. With the toe of his sandal, he flipped the edge of the man's cloak over his face. The four men split up, moving quickly through the high-ceilinged rooms of the stable. Two of the men had swords, two bows. Mithridates touched Vitellix on the shoulder and then the two of them hurried off, their own weapons bared.

"Ila? Ila!" Vitellix' voice was soft as he passed down the line of horse stalls. "It's Vitellix!"

Anastasia sighed, watching the lanista disappear into the gloom. Her gown under the robe was a deep cerulean, low cut across the chest, showing the curve of her smooth white breasts. Without urgency, she reversed the cloak, revealing a sky-blue silk lining, and draped it low on her bare shoulders. "Betia, are you done?"

"Yes, mistress." The blond girl had shed her soiled tunic and dragged the body on its cloak into the nearest stall, covering its feet with straw. Then the girl pulled on a new tunic that matched the Duchess's colors. "All done."

"Good." The Duchess smoothed her round forearms with a dusting of lead powder, turning them a seamless, perfect white. She checked her earrings and the fall of her hair. Gold and sapphire bangles tinkled at her wrists. "Let us see if they are done."

Betia went ahead, her knife bare in her hand, lamplight glittering on the blade. Anastasia followed at a stately pace, her liquid violet eyes taking in the signs of a scuffle as they entered the main area of the stables. At the end of the race, the Blue chariots and their drivers would return here. Once the horses had been unhitched, the drivers—victorious or not—would mingle with their adoring fans and then go off to some banquet held in their honor. The Duchess smiled, wondering what the little cripple Narses would think when he found that his prize Amazon had been snatched out from under his very nose.

That will show him not to trifle with me.

Horns blew and the fourth dolphin turned nose down, golden tail swinging towards the sky. Thyatis hung on for dear life, letting the chariot slide around the turn, axles and wheels squealing. Despite Ila's warnings, she had let the horses take their head, running flat out. Now she was only five lengths and one other chariot behind Hamilcar, who had continued to run swiftly and alone in third place. The lead Blue and Green drivers were dueling for first, an intense game of inches and tight margins at the turns.

Thyatis didn't care about them and she urged her four browns on as they burst out of the turn and into the straight in front of the temple of Victoria. The remaining Red chariot was ahead of her, driver lashing the horses to keep his lead. Thyatis hurtled towards him, running up hard behind his car, trying to get her horses between him and the wall. He caught sight of her out of the corner of his eye and swerved inwards, trying to force the browns into the wall. They ripped past the Victoria, the crowd raising a lusty cheer to see them duel.

Seeing the Red driver swing in, Thyatis jerked hard on the reins and let the browns bolt, away from the wall. She lost a half length but swiftly made up the distance, letting the mares storm ahead. She swept up behind the Red's car, angling for his right wheel with the crossbrace on the front of her chariot. He caught sight of her again and turned his head, snarling in rage.

Thyatis made a rude gesture. The man lashed out at her with the whip in his right hand. The steel tip flashed through the air at her, but this was something she could deal with. She switched reins and snatched the whip out of the air with her left hand. Her right flicked the reins and the browns swung left. The crossbar on the front of the chariot speared into the spinning wheel of the Red chariot.

The driver struggled to reclaim his whip, but Thyatis looped it around her forearm with a blur of motion. Then his wheel blew apart with a shriek, shredded by the iron ferrule on the crossbar. The Red chariot dipped and Thyatis added to the man's motion with a swift heave of her left arm. Screaming, the driver spilled out of the car, cracking his head against the sand, then Thyatis gasped in pain as she let the whip slither off the leather bracings on her forearm, a trail of black smoke hissing from the heavy leather. The Red chariot was splintering across the track, its horses scattering in all directions.

Thyatis shouted gleefully, lashing the horses with her reins. They thundered on, rushing towards the turn. Hamilcar was dead ahead, his horses running easily, barely exerting themselves. The African was braced against the inner wall of the car, left hand on the reins, right raised to the crowd. He swung the chariot around the turn with ease, shifting his weight just so. A storm of girlish screams and squeals echoed off the high arched roof of the triumphal arch of Titus, which was packed with his younger supporters. Even through the haze of dust and grit, Thyatis could see the man smiling like Apollo.

Her own chariot wallowed around the turn, spewing sand and making an ominous rattling sound. The left panel of the car suddenly splintered away, the wicker worked loose by the collision with the Red chariot. Thyatis kicked it free, sending it spinning back behind her on the track. She crouched low, letting the browns hurl her forward. They closed, heads racing the wind, a length and then another.

Hamilcar looked back and smiled, paying attention at last. He waved.

Thyatis' whip licked out and snapped over the heads of the browns. They sprinted forward again, gaining another length. Now they were very close.

The end of the *spina* loomed up, the *metae* sparkling in the sun, a crowd of slaves in red tunics hanging out over the track, screaming encouragement. The two leading chariots made the turn, but Hamilcar goosed his horses and was right behind them, taking the turn at very high speed, one wheel off the ground. The African, one foot hooked under the rail, leaned way out to canter-balance the suspended wheel. Thyatis cursed. She was taking it too close herself. The browns drifted out, clearing the turn, but she lost a length. The African's fingertips brushed across the face of the outer metae.

The crowds in the stands around the turn were on their feet, clamoring, their applause for Hamilcar's feat ringing to the sky.

"Little mouse? Where are you?" Vitellix moved into the room with caution, leading with the point of his long knife. Anastasia's men were supposed to have killed or subdued all of the Blue grooms, slaves and hangers-on who had been waiting in the stables. That didn't keep one of them from escaping and waiting in a closet with a hay fork.

The main room was large enough for three chariots and their teams at once, a huge vaulted hallway with a dirt floor to spare the horses' hooves. Opening off it were the stables themselves, with stalls for the horses and storage for the chariots. A waiting chamber also opened from the main room, with storage behind it. Vitellix was searching the storage rooms. "Mouse!"

"Perhaps she's not here." Mithridates had been following him quietly, a heavy spear in his hands. "Perhaps," rumbled the African, "she has gone out to watch the race."

"No . . ." Vitellix sighed. "That would be too painful for her, I fear."

The black man shrugged, his eyes flitting across the tumbled boxes and broken chairs crowding the storage space. A glassy scar surrounded one eye, making it seem half shut at all times. "Wouldn't she know the sound of your voice?"

"Yes!" the Gaul snapped, rattling the wooden crates around. "She would."

"Then," Mithridates rumbled, "she must be somewhere else."

"Fine." Vitellix turned on his heel and strode out into the main part of the stable. The four men whom Anastasia had brought were opening the doors to the starting gates, their armor covered by blue tunics. The Duchess was standing nearby, her blond shadow almost invisible behind her. "My lady!" Vitellix called out as he approached, "have you seen any sign of my daughter?"

"The little one with mousy-brown hair?" Anastasia suppressed a smile, checking the drape of her veil with almond-shaped fingernails. "I have seen her, I think."

"Where?" The Gaul looked around, his head moving in swift, jerking motions.

"There." The Duchess tried to keep amusement from her voice, but she sounded very droll. Vitellix stepped to a door and stared out into the starting gates. Ila had climbed up the nearest one and was clinging to the ironwork at the top of the arch with her hands and feet like a monkey. She could see out over the track. Vitellix ran up underneath her, his heart thudding in his chest.

Ila was screaming her lungs out as four chariots swept around the turn.

"Diana! Inside, inside! Diana! Go, go, go!"

"Mouse." Vitellix sounded aggrieved. "Come down from there."

Ila looked down, surprised. "Poppa! What are you doing here? Did you see Diana?"

Vitellix held up his arms and Ila sighed, letting go of the ironwork. He caught her deftly and set her down. He looked very sad for a moment, then clutched her to him, squeezing the breath from his little mouse.

"Poppa! You'll break a rib!"

"Sorry, Mouse." The Gaul squatted down so they were at eye level. "Someone hit you in the face." His fingers traced the outline of the bruise and his expression darkened.

"Yes, it was that African Hamilcar and his friends. They caught me in the Ludus Magnus before I could find Diana. They'll pay for that, I bet." Cunning and anger glinted in the little girl's eye. "I'll fix them if Diana doesn't."

"Did anything else happen? Anything bad?"

"No." Ila sighed in exasperation. "Nothing. Very dull, really. They were all afraid of Diana, once she killed all those people." Then her expression brightened and she turned to the gate. "Perhaps she'll break Hamilcar's neck while they're racing. She's very good at that . . . but, Poppa, she's not a good driver! Her horses are already winded."

"It doesn't matter," a cold voice said. Ila and Vitellix looked up to see Anastasia standing over them, flanked by her men. "She just has to finish and get back to the stables."

"She doesn't want to work for you anymore!" Ila glared at the Duchess. "Leave her alone!"

Anastasia stared down at the little girl, a mixture of grief and anger in her face. "Your father didn't abandon you, Ila. He came looking for you, worried half to death. I don't want to make Thyatis *work* for me, I just want my daughter back."

Hot words died on Ila's lips. The Duchess's eyes were so sad and desolate. Ila took her hand and led her to the corner of the gate. The little mouse pointed out at the track.

"This is the best place to watch from. See? The finish line is at the temple of Victoria."

The sixth dolphin dove for a sea of stone and the massive crowd was on their feet, cheering themselves hoarse. Thyatis was still clinging on, a length behind Hamilcar. The African had tried to run her into the wall of the *spina* on the fifth lap, but had failed, losing a length. Now they thundered forward, horses lathered, their chariots shuddering with every hoofbeat, almost neck and neck. The African's blacks were still running strong, tireless, their hooves speeding over the sand like the winged feet of Hermes. Thyatis felt her browns tiring, though they were giving a game effort. Her poor skill was costing them too much strength.

Barely two lengths ahead, the Blue and Green leaders were still neck and neck, jockeying into the inner turn on the last straightaway. At the moment the Blue driver had managed to swing ahead and capture the path along the wall. Thyatis risked a look and saw the *metae* of the last turn looming ahead, shining through the cloud of dust. Gritting her teeth, she slid the horsewhip out of its holder on the right side of the chariot car. Shouting, she lashed the browns with the reins and they jolted forward.

Beside her, Hamilcar stared across in surprise, his hands light on the reins. His glance flicked forward, seeing the backs of the Green and Blue leaders barely half a length in front of his horses' noses. He cursed. Thyatis again lashed out with the whip, letting it extend to its maximum length. The Blue driver suddenly jerked, a red welt across his shoulder. The man wrenched his team sideways, shouting insults at the Green driver. Their wheels locked for half a grain, sparks fountaining up from the metal bosses on their hubs. Both chariots swerved away from the wall, slowing infinitesimally.

Thyatis's browns lunged into the gap and she pressed their flank sideways against Hamilcar's blacks at the same moment. He reined in, slowing his team to keep his left wheel from grinding against the granite flank of the spina.

Thyatis bolted ahead, suddenly in front of him. The African glanced swiftly to his right and saw the Green leader now abreast. The other two drivers had freed their wheels and now rushed forward, in line with Hamilcar. Thyatis turned, looking back over her shoulder, a wild smile on her face.

All three men lashed their horses as one, their teams redoubling their efforts. Thyatis snapped the whip again, just over the heads of the browns. They were laboring mightily, but they were straining and she could feel them beginning to fail.

A whip snapped beside her head, a sound like the crack of ballista firing. She ducked aside. The browns moved with her and her left horse was suddenly running only inches from the wall. A horrible screeching sound assaulted her ears and hot sparks flared up through the broken side of the chariot car. Her left wheel ground against the spina. Without looking, she lashed backwards over her shoulder with the whip.

Somewhere, a man screamed in pain. Though she could not see it, the sudden hoarse roar of the crowd told her something had happened. There was a sickening *crack* and then double screams and a metal hub boss whipped past her, caroming off the red granite obelisk as she passed. A violent, crashing sound followed and the screams of wounded horses filled the air. Her heart turned cold, but she kept her head down, urging her browns on into the last lap.

For an instant, there was only the sound of her chariot wheels hissing across the sand and the thunder of her horses' hooves. The crowd was silent, holding its breath. Even the musicians on the spina had stopped playing, their tubas and trumpets falling quiet. Thyatis glanced to her right.

Hamilcar was there, his face an intent mask, his helmet gone, his long glistening black hair streaming out behind him like a horsetail. His blacks were running hot, foam streaking their sides, their powerful muscles surging and rolling as they darted past. Now he was pressing his horses, forcing the last gasp of strength from them. He looked across and met her eyes as they roared into the final turn. There was an instant of communion, two proud souls that could not admit defeat or loss, locked in the grip of combat.

A *crack* rocked Thyatis' chariot as it swerved into the beginning of the turn. She looked down in time to see the abused axle disintegrate into a mass of whirling splinters. Without thinking, she leapt up onto the crossbar that rode behind the horses, still gripping the reins. The chariot car exploded, torn apart in an instant by the stress of the turn and the incredible speed of the horses. Chunks of wood and lengths of wicker spewed across the sand. A wheel spun away, bouncing towards the starting gates. The horses, suddenly bereft of the car's weight, leapt ahead. Thyatis clung to the reins, her body quivering in balance on the crossbar.

Hamilcar shouted in rage, rising up, his arm scything back with the whip.

"Kill him!" Anastasia shouted, her white arm stabbing out at the man hurtling by. At her side, one of the men in blue had drawn an arrow to his bow. Now he drew it to his cheek and sighted, his movement smooth and assured. Vitellix jerked around, seeing the last two drivers swing out of the turn, right into line with where he stood.

Hamilcar's whip lashed out, lighting across Thyatis' shoulder. It sprang back from the armor under her tunic, but her balance was lost. She fell, her arm still tangled in the reins, and gasped in pain as her right foot hit the speeding ground. The leather sole of her boot shredded away, then she heaved herself back up. Her body flexed, vaulting, and she twisted, swinging up onto the back of the third brown mare. Her left leg was still tangled in the harness. She tore at it with her hand, freeing herself.

A dozen feet away, Hamilcar lashed his blacks and they sprinted ahead, pulling out of the turn. He looked back, a smug smile on his face, but then it was wiped away by the sight of Thyatis rising up onto the back of the mare. He cursed and his whip snaked out again.

"Kill him!" Anastasia's knuckles turned white, gripping the iron bars of the gate. The archer loosed, his breath sighing out, and the arrow flicked away, arcing high into the air.

Thyatis dragged at the reins of the brown, forcing it right. Hamilcar's whip snapped in the air, only inches to her left. The brown team, following her motion, surged to the right, cutting behind the African's chariot. Thyatis swung one leg back, scrabbling to find footing on the horse's hind-quarters, her left hand digging into its mane. *One leap,* she thought wildly, *and I'll be in his chariot! Then we'll—*

The arrow smashed into her back. Her mouth opened, crying out. Her foot slipped and she tumbled from the mare, cracking her head against the crossbar that ran across the horses' chests. Spinning, her body hit the ground, bounced and then rolled over, limbs splayed out. Thyatis caught a glimpse of the sky cartwheeling above her, then the marble rim of the stadium, and then the sand plowed into her face and there was darkness.

"No!" Anastasia staggered as if she had been shot herself. Her hand rose to her mouth, trembling. Betia was already clutching her elbow, straining to keep her from falling. Vitellix and Mithridates were shouting and the starting gate opened with an explosive *bang* as Ila threw the locking bar. The mouse girl was already running, her legs and arms pumping.

"Diana!" Tears streamed down her round face and she was running, all alone, on the hot sand.

In the Imperial box, Gaius Julius let himself breathe, a long hissing gasp of relief. On the far side of the spina, Hamilcar had just swept across the finish line to a peal of trumpets and the clash of huge gongs that stood in the portico of the temple of Victoria. A lone Red chariot followed. "Oh yes," he breathed to himself. "Oh yes." He closed his gray eyelids, letting himself feel the shudder of relief in his body, even with its aches and pains and terrible weakness. "Oh yes."

Narses sprang up and, to the alarm of the Green merchants staring out at the finish line in glad surprise, swung over the lip of the balcony. The lanista could see the still, skewed form of the woman Diana lying alone on the sand. He could see the black fletching of an arrow on the ground too, and his quick eye had caught it in flight. Grunting, he landed on the seats below the box, then leapt down them, three and four at a time. No one seeing him move, flitting across the crowded seats, never setting a foot wrong, would have called him a cripple.

The lanista's face was incredibly grim and he tore the holly from his shoulder and discarded it as he ran. When he reached the retaining wall, an ugly murmur was already rising from the huge, stunned crowd. "Diana is dead," they were shouting.

He vaulted over the marble lip of the wall, then folded up as he hit the ground below. He rolled up on the sand, letting his tumble break the energy of his fall. He ran forward, towards the still, crumpled body on the sand.

Above and around him, a vast beast with three hundred thousand throats suddenly gave vent to a howl like Cerberus itself. "The Greens killed Diana! *Kill the Greens!* KILL THE GREENS!"

Just beyond the victory line, Hamilcar swung his team around, brown face beaming at the crowd above him.

There was a huge tumult of noise and he raised his hands in answer to their acclaim. Attendants were running out from the tunnels to take his horses in hand. Despite his expectation, the air was not filled with thrown garlands, coins, hats—all of the things that usually met the victor in such a race. He squinted at the crowd, suddenly realizing that they were angry. Thousands of people were staring back down the track. Then he heard the shouts.

"No. No!" He turned himself and saw the ruins of Diana's chariot scattered across the track, her prone body, the figures of people running towards it. "That's impossible! I beat her! *I beat her!*"

A rotten fig flew out of the crowd and spattered against the side of his chariot. Hamilcar looked down, stunned, then up again. Hundreds of people were swarming down out of the stands, shouting in rage. The sound of the crowd had turned ugly. The African vaulted nimbly out of the chariot car, then cut one of the blacks out of the team with his boot knife. The arch of Titus was two hundred yards away, over the glimmering sand. Perhaps he could find safety there.

〔◎〕()-()〔◎〕

THE BUCOLEON, CONSTANTINOPLE

〕〈

W hat do you think you're doing?"

Martina, Empress of the Eastern Empire, strode into the vault with her head high and a glint in her eye. Arsinoë followed, hurrying to keep up, with little Heracleonas on her hip. The Empress was not disheveled as usual, having let her maids have their way with her. She had been bathed, scrubbed, oiled, scraped, her hair piled on top of her head in an artful way. Tiny golden pins held the curled mass in place. Subtle paints and powders accented her round face. A stiff, brocaded dress was fixed around her body with a sleek train of silk.

Rufio, captain of the Faithful Guard, turned, black eyes taking in the scene. The vault was buried in one of the oldest sections of the palace, only reachable from the main floors by a hidden flight of stairs. Four of his men were busy lifting a huge golden blazon down from the wall of the room. "Empress. I'm surprised to see you down here in the dark."

Martina stopped, her lips drawn into a thin line. "You are not allowed to touch that, not without my husband's permission."

Rufio nodded, his grim expression unwavering. "I know."

The guardsmen lowered the icon to the ground, their movements slow and controlled.

"Put it back." Martina strode to the captain's side, her face filled with growing horror. "This is treason, to take the Emperor's standard! Have you gone mad?" Her white hand clutched his forearm.

Rufio looked down, then gently took her hand in his own. "Touching the body of the Empress," he said softly, "is also treason."

"So it is!" Martina jerked her hand back, scowling. "What are you going to do with the icon?"

Rufio motioned for the guardsmen to take the standard away. They did, two men on each pole, gripping it by the carrying handles welded onto the iron. When they were gone, Rufio looked back, then frowned at Arsinoë. "Girl, you should take the boy back to the nursery."

"You will not!" Martina threw a glance over her shoulder and the African girl paled, clutching Heracleonas to her chest. "Stay right there. Captain, you *will* tell me what you are doing."

"There will be fighting soon," Rufio said, though it was not clear whether he was answering her question. "Your uncle, the prince Theodore, has decided to place Legion cohorts that are loyal to him around the palace—to 'secure the safety of the Emperor.' Your husband is too sick to move, so I am removing these things"—he gestured at the bare wall and a number of high wardrobes whose doors stood open—"to a place where Theodore cannot lay hands upon them."

Martina stepped back, stunned. "You are going to leave?"

"No." Rufio said, his voice level and quiet. "I will be back. I am leaving half of the Guard with you, under that Latin officer, Nicholas. We will fall back, quietly, into the suite of rooms around Heraclius' bedchamber and barricade them. Even if Theodore attempts to force his way in, they can be held for a day or more."

"Held! For a day? What are you talking about?" Martina's fists clenched and unclenched convulsively.

Rufio nodded, black eyes flickering to Arsinoë's terrified face and then back to Martina. "Your uncle is preparing to seize the palace and declare himself regent for his nephew Constantius. He will need to possess Heraclius' body for this, either alive to sign a will, or dead to show that the Purple must be passed on. Our hourglass is down to the last grain."

"Impossible!" Martina shook her head violently. "I would know if this had transpired! He just spends all of his time bickering with the cohort commanders and trying on his brother's clothes. . . ." The Empress paused, eyes widening at the expression on Rufio's face.

"How do you know that?" The guard captain cocked his head, taking a half step towards her. "How did you know that we were moving the regalia? Were you hiding in the walls again?"

"No." Martina quailed away from the fierce expression on his face. "I wasn't! You have no right to question me!" She rallied, jutting out her chin and matching his growing fury with her own. "I am the Empress! You are a guard captain! You must obey me!"

"Must I?" Rufio's voice was still very calm and level, but she could feel his anger building like storm clouds over the Propontis. "Do you have a spy in his camp? A woman? One of the slaves?"

"No." Martina gave him a disgusted look. Then she smiled. "I have my ways."

"Do your *ways* tell you what is happening in the Persian camp?"

"No. Why would I watch them?" Martina flipped her hand in dismissal. "They're boring and safely on the other side of the walls, digging and rooting about in the mud."

A look of contemplation crossed Rufio's face, then he stepped back, making a sketchy bow. "Empress, my apologies. I spoke out of turn. What are your orders?"

"Well." Martina straightened her stole and the pleats of her gown. "That's better. You think Theodore will try and capture these things?"

"Yes, Empress. They are being moved to a safe place." Rufio's expression cleared, becoming its usual stoic mask.

"He will try and seize my husband?" Martina's brown eyes were thoughtful.

"I believe so."

"Your treason is forgiven, Captain. But I require your assistance today."

"Of course, Empress. How may I serve?"

Martina gave him a look, daring him to mock her. Rufio clasped his hands behind his back and met her eyes. She almost sneered, but then gave it up. "I am going to take Heracleonas to see his father. You must order the guards to let me into the bedchamber."

One of Rufio's eyebrows rose. "Is that wise? He has banned you from his presence. If he is angry, I would have to imprison or exile you."

"I know." Martina sighed. "But if those two foul priests were right, then his fear is killing him. I will show him his son—his healthy son—before he goes into that darkness. Now, take us there."

Rufio nodded, though he was torn. He needed to catch up with the men carrying the regalia and the standard. They might encounter difficulties in the tunnels. He had no margin in his plan for a delay like this. Martina was still staring at him, her chin raised. Inwardly, he sighed, and then strode through the door. "This way, Empress."

Martina swept after him, Arsinoë hurrying to catch up. The baby was almost asleep, drooling on her shoulder.

"Husband?" The Empress pushed open a heavy door. Although it was midday, the room was dark, the high windows covered with black drapes. A single dim candle burned on a table near the door. "Heraclius?"

Martina wrinkled up her nose, trying not to breathe. The fetor in the room was heavy as oil. She pinched her nose and advanced into the darkness. The bed loomed out of the gloom, thick with quilts and tangled sheets. Her outstretched hand touched a bedpost. "Husband, where are you?"

Arsinoë and Rufio stood guard in the doorway. The captain had sent the guards away to join their fellows in the outer ring of rooms. Martina looked to Rufio, who shrugged in puzzlement. The Empress circled the bed and found the blankets thrown aside in a tangled mass. Hiking up her dress she crept onto the bed. Her small white hand searched among the covers, finding them cold with sweat. Martina shuddered and rubbed her palm hurriedly on the quilts. The Emperor was gone.

The smell clung even when Martina wiped her hand repeatedly on the blanket. Shuddering, she stepped away. Her heart was beating faster and a sense of disaster was growing on her. Had Theodore already struck, stealing her husband's body? Was he dead? The Empress stepped to the nearest window, feeling for the casement in the darkness. She found the heavy fall of a drape and yanked the cloth aside. Dust puffed out, filling the air. A thin slat of pale sunlight appeared, striking through the darkness, making the dust sparkle and shine. Martina blinked. In this gloom the pale gleam seemed very bright.

A muffled thumping came from behind her. She spun, trembling. Something was there in the darkness. "Rufio!" Her voice quavered. "There's something there!"

The guard captain was across the room in a blur, bare metal gleaming in his hand. He crouched, sidling towards the corner. Martina stepped out of the beam of sunlight and saw, as her eyes adjusted, a huge armoire standing against the wall, faced with two doors each the height of a man. The corner itself was empty. Rufio shifted his body, his sword arm pressing Martina back behind him. The Empress clung to his hard, muscular shoulder with relief, pressing against the solidity of his back. Blood thudded in her ears and she felt faint. The captain eased the wardrobe open, revealing a mass of robes and tunics. A foot twitched in the light, greasy and gray and covered with sores.

"Husband?" Martina gasped, palm pressed over her mouth. The foot twitched as if the light burned the flesh, then drew back under the shadow of the robes. "Heraclius? Please, it's Martina, please come out."

Gathering herself, the Empress motioned for Arsinoë to join her. The maid scuttled forward, the baby pressed to her chest. "Give him to me."

Martina took Heracleonas in her arms. Then she knelt down in front of the wardrobe. The little boy made a burping sound and immediately squirmed out of her arms. Despite her simmering hatred of all priests, and those of Asclepius in particular, Martina was forced to admit changing her child's wet nurse had made a big difference.

"Go away . . ." A bubbling wheeze issued from the robes. Martina steeled herself, composing her features, then reached in and pushed the clothes aside. "Ahhh!"

Heraclius cowered away from the dim light, arms raised, body contorted to fit into the tiny space. For a moment, all she could see was a pasty-white thigh covered with sores and dead gray skin. Then she made out his head, long red-blond hair clinging wetly to his scalp.

"Husband! Oh, my love . . ." Martina squeezed herself into the wardrobe, ignoring the mess made of her delicately pinned hair and the gown. Her hands touched his face, finding it wet with tears. "Come out of this place," she whispered, sliding her arm under his. "See your son? Yes, this is Heracleonas, strong and healthy. Look at him!"

"No." The word was slurred, almost unintelligible. Weakly, the Emperor tried to pull away from Martina. She caught his hand and put it against her cheek. "My son . . . is . . . corrupt. Cursed!"

"Look at him!" Martina's voice caught a tone of command and she turned his head. Heracleonas stood at the edge of the wardrobe, fat little fingers clutching the tunics. He was smiling. "See his bright face? He is a terror, always getting into trouble."

Heraclius stared at his son, face puffy and gray, but he could still see and he blinked. Tears seeped out of the corners of his eyes. "He can stand." Now Martina could make out the words. "He's standing."

"Come, love." Martina squeezed out of the wardrobe, then bent and took her husband under the arms and lifted. She grunted, bracing her right foot against the lip of the wardrobe. "Arsinoë, get Heracleonas. I don't . . . *grunt* . . . want to trample him."

The maid ducked in, face averted from the naked, swollen body of the Emperor, and snatched Heracleonas away. Rufio disappeared out the door. Martina managed to help Heraclius up, carrying most of his weight with her shoulder. He had lost weight while he was bedridden, even though his legs and abdomen were swollen. His skin squeaked as he moved, and bubbles of clear fluid moved under the surface.

"Can you stand?" Martina panted with effort.

"No." Heraclius wept. "It hurts, it hurts!"

A disgusted look flickered across the Empress's face and she staggered towards the bed. At the edge of the mountain of quilts, her left hand seized the bedpost. "You can stand," she gasped, "your body is *not* corrupt. We are *not* cursed for our marriage."

Martina stepped back, suddenly leaving Heraclius on his own. He cried out in fear, staggered forward a step, then caught himself weakly on the edge of the bed. "You see," she said, brushing the wild fall of hair out of his face. "It's not so bad."

"My feet, my legs . . . are useless." Tears were streaming down Heraclius' face. "I'm a cripple. Unfit to be Emperor."

"You have two legs, two arms, a nose, both eyes!" Martina took Heracleonas from the maid, then stepped close to the Emperor. "Like your son. Look at his face. Look at *my* face."

Heraclius, Emperor of the East, looked up, his blue eyes bloodshot and red. Martina met them with her own and smiled, putting the child in his arms. "I love you. Don't fear me."

The Emperor clutched the boy to his chest, staring down at the round smiling face. His swollen fingers gently brushed back the child's thin blond hair.

"Da-da!" Chortled Heracleonas and grabbed his father's nose in his tiny fingers. "Poopy!"

Heraclius coughed, then sat down on the edge of the bed, holding his son. Martina and Arsinoë were immediately at his side, keeping him upright. "Yes . . . son . . . I am."

Rufio paused at the door, Sviod and Nicholas at his side. Both men were carrying ceramic jars of the juniper tea. The captain of the guard took in the tableau before him, then motioned for the other two men to step back.

"Do you feel the air?" Rufio looked at Nicholas, who nodded. There was a tension, a bitter smell, something half heard, only felt. "Battle is coming. There's no time for a slow cure. Nicholas, there are two priests of Asklepius at their temple, named Tarsus and Hipponax. They can't have gotten out of the city. Get them here immediately. He's ready to be helped."

Nicholas nodded sharply and took off at a run. Sviod looked down at his jug, then he raised it solemnly to the north.

"Vell," the Scandian youth said, "I guess Grandma vas right about those juniper berries!"

Rufio did not answer immediately, black eyes bare slits. Martina stood over her husband, a shaft of sunlight falling on her, sparkling in the tumble of brown hair cascading down around her shoulders. She seemed very beautiful. She was smiling at her husband and her son.

"Your grandmother was a wise woman, Sviod. A wise woman."

THE PLAIN OF MARS, BEFORE CONSTANTINOPLE

)⚬(

W*ake! You are at the balance of fate.*

Mohammed's eyes opened, at first seeing nothing but darkness. Then a glimmer of firelight appeared, illuminating the roof of his tent with orange and gold. He lay still, feeling the warmth of his bed, the heaviness of the horse blanket lying over him. The world outside was cold and dark. Men passed by outside with torches. He felt the motion of the earth and knew the time to rise had come. Throwing back the blanket, Mohammed stood, his head bent to the south.

O Lord of the World, you have guided me to this day in all ways. I have believed and I have been delivered. Give me the strength to throw down your enemies, to free

*the world, and I will yield up blood, bone and heart in
your service.*

"There is no god but Allah," he said aloud to the darkness. He was awake and alert. Stepping to the door of the tent, he looked out. Torches and lanterns dimly lighted the tents of the Sahaba, but the men were rising, breath puffing white in the cold air. The two guards in front of his tent were awake and looking up at him.

"Bring something hot to drink," he said. One of the men rose, armor clinking softly, and went off in the direction of the cook tents. Mohammed went back inside. His hand found an oil lamp on the folding table by the head of his bed. A moment's effort with flint and steel had the wick lit and a soft yellow glow filling the tent.

"Zoë, it is time." Mohammed put the back of his hand against the Palmyrene woman's cheek. Her wounds had healed well, leaving only tiny, glassy scars around her ear and the side of her throat. In this soft light, they were almost invisible. Her hair lay across the folded quilt like a glossy black fan. She woke silently, eyes flickering open, then turned towards him. A warm hand emerged from the blankets and covered his, pressing it against her cheek.

"Hello." Her voice was very soft and filled with sleep. "It's cold."

"I've sent for something hot to drink." Mohammed smiled, kneeling on the heavy carpets covering the floor of the tent. "You have to get up. Today is the day."

"Oh." Zoë slid deeper under the blankets, leaving only her dark brown eyes visible. "Is everyone else up?"

"No." Mohammed tried to keep from laughing but failed. "You have to get up now."

"It's cold." Zoë's forehead creased in a frown.

"Yes, it is."

"But I have to get up, even though I can see your breath in the air?"

"Yes."

"Oh, very well." Zoë made a face but sat up, pulling the

blankets around her shoulders. Her bare feet poked out from under the covers, then slid hastily back. "It's very cold."

Mohammed was saved from having to answer by a soft whistle at the door. The guard handed the Quraysh two copper flagons. Steam rose from the surface of the liquid they held. Mohammed sniffed it, then wrinkled his nose. "Hot mare's milk with honey."

Zoë took her cup with a wary look. "Who drinks milk? It'll spoil."

"Not in this cold," said Mohammed, draining his flagon. "The Avars make it, I think. Not bad."

Ignoring Zoë's foul look, Mohammed stripped off his sleeping robe. His body was firm and muscular, the benefit of years in the saddle and unstinting physical labor both in war and peace. He had put on some muscle since escaping from Palmyra. The Sahaba ate far better than they had during the siege! Rummaging in one of the soft bags at the foot of his bed, he drew out a pair of woolen pantaloons and tugged them on. A thick tunic followed, then a stained felt vest. By this time, Zoë had managed to finish her drink. She helped him pull a shirt of heavy iron links over his head, his beard tucked out of the way. Her hands clasped a leather belt around his trim waist and drew it snug. The weight of the iron felt good on his shoulders, comfortable and familiar. Thick pads were sewn into the inside of the shirt, protecting his neck and upper chest. He sat on the blankets and began to wrap lengths of fleece around his feet.

Zoë retrieved his boots from near the door and helped him tug them on. They were heavy, with three layers of leather stitched together. Vertical iron slats were fitted between the layers, reinforcing the sides of the boots and protecting the tops of his feet and his shins. Standing again, he wiggled his feet around until they seemed to fit. A dark green surcoat went over the mail shirt. Zoë straightened it in the back, then held up his djellabah. Arms extended behind him, Mohammed stepped into the desert robe. Another belt secured it and he untangled the hood before laying it flat on his shoulders and back.

"Good." Zoë smoothed back his white-shot hair, standing on tiptoe. "You'll frighten the enemy for sure." Mohammed smiled, catching her hands as they withdrew. A helmet and reinforced leather gloves lay beside the bed.

"Thank you," he said, bending towards her. Her eyes met his and she smiled faintly. "Things are much easier with you at my side."

"Hmm." She gave him an arch look. "That's almost a compliment."

"It is." Mohammed turned away, untangling his beard with his thick fingers and arranging it on his chest.

Behind him, Zoë rolled her eyes, then slipped out of her sleeping robe. Beneath it, she was wearing only a thin breast-band crossed behind her neck and a loincloth. Like him, she drew on long woolen Persian-style trousers and a light tunic. Her felt vest was heavier, clean and didn't smell like a camel.

"It's safe to turn around." Zoë sat cross-legged on the bed, hands busy behind her head plaiting the riot of dark hair into a long, snakelike braid. She curled the braid around and tucked in the end to make a cap. Besides making a moderate cushion for her helmet, it would stay out of her eyes. "Help me, please."

With Mohammed's assistance, Zoë wriggled into a very light shirt of mail covering her body and arms down to her wrists. Unlike his heavy disks of flattened iron, hers was a supple gleaming snakeskin of tiny, perfectly fitted rings on a lambskin backing. The shirt had been originally made for her aunt as a girl, and came to Zoë as an heirloom. Even on her, it was getting tight around the shoulders. The Palmyrene breathed in and out, letting the mesh settle across her chest.

Mohammed lifted up a polished steel breastplate, his muscular arms easily taking the weight. The armorers of

Palmyra had done a fine job fitting the gleaming metal to her torso. The armor was made in three parts, one solid section running from throat to waist, then two hinged half-pieces in the back that met in a row of clasps and hooks along the spine. Zoë held her arms out in front of her and stepped into the armor. Mohammed folded the backplates in, letting them meet behind her, then hooked each clasp in turn. "Good?"

"Oh yes," she groused, "I feel like a statue now."

"But a safe one." Mohammed strapped curved steel vambraces to each of her forearms. Gloves made of the same fine mail slipped over her hands, padded inside with leather and backed with a solid metal plate. A pleated, Roman-style skirt of heavy leather tongues circled her waist and fell down to her knees. The Quraysh shook his head in dismay, running his hands down her legs. "You should wear something to protect your knees."

"If I do that," she said in a grumpy tone, "I won't be able to walk. Besides, I'm not supposed to be fighting on the front line, am I?"

"No." Mohammed gathered up her djellabah. "You and Odenathus are far more valuable defending us in the hidden world."

"True." A bleak expression suddenly overcame the woman's features. She was thinking of the strength of their enemy. "Will you help?"

Mohammed paused, staring at her. "If the Lord of the World decides to help us, then . . ."

Zoë sighed and held up her hand. "I understand. You cannot control the power that moves through you. We will suffice, if we must."

"Can you stop him?" Mohammed had not discussed the matter of the Roman firecaster with Zoë, but he could see it weighed upon her. Odenathus had not raised the subject either, keeping to himself or spending his time with Khalid.

"I don't know," Zoë said after a moment. "To win, we must."

A great number of torches illuminated the tunnel of the Great Gate. Hundreds of giant men packed into the broad space, helmets gleaming in the ruddy light. Clouds of smoke drifted up, pooling in the arches of the building. Nicholas was fully armored, a conical helm with a T-shaped eye slit tucked under one arm. The Latin officer was trying to keep from losing his temper. "Captain, Vladimir and I and the boy are a *team*. We've fought together before; we have a system. His body needs to be protected while he's working his power. An arrow or spear could kill him just as easily as you or me!"

Rufio nodded, his face thrown half in shadow by the torchlight. "Centurion, I understand, but I *have* to leave someone I can trust in the palace. That means either you or me. We have to go forth with both the Hibernian and the standard or we're dog meat. Now, if this works, then Theodore will follow and someone will have to deal with him. That means me. You have to stay in the city."

"I don't like this. . . ." Nicholas felt queasy, but he couldn't refuse an order. He looked sideways at Dwyrin, who was fairly vibrating with eagerness. "Will Vladimir be enough to protect your back?"

"Yes, sir." Dwyrin grinned at Nicholas, white teeth brilliant in the darkness. "We'll be fine. The Emperor is more important anyway."

Nicholas rubbed his face with an armored hand, shaking his head. "This doesn't feel right. Vlad?"

The Walach was draped in heavy iron armor and a huge black cloak. Never a small man, he looked positively enormous in this light, yellow-gold eyes glittering. Vladimir smiled, showing long incisors and strong sharp teeth. A long ax lay over his shoulder. "He'll be safe with me."

"Centurion, I can do this." Dwyrin rubbed his hands together, though he wasn't cold at all. An invisible sphere of warmth surrounded the boy. Nicholas assumed it must be a tiny exercise of the art, but it seemed wrong and out of place in this bitterly cold predawn. "Go back to the palace."

Nicholas looked back at Rufio with a grim expression on his face. "I hope this works."

"It will." The captain's confidence seemed unshakeable. Nicholas saluted, then nodded to Dwyrin and Vladimir. "All right, then. I'll see you tonight."

The Hibernian waved at the retreating back of the northerner. Dwyrin felt good, very good. His sleep had been deep and free of dreams. Rising early, when the first of the Faithful stirred, he had dressed quickly and run down to the massive gate. Vladimir, grumbling and complaining, had followed. Something about the city night did not sit well with the Walach, and he was constantly looking behind him. The Hibernian didn't care—today was the day of days! A subtle tension in the air heralded battle.

From the watchtowers on the Great Gate, Dwyrin could see across the long plain lying before the city. Just before the double ramparts, there was a dry ditch. Then a space of a hundred yards or so and the ragged shape of the Arab circumvallation describing a long arc. Beyond the wall was a long slope dotted with burned-out farmhouses and temples rising up into irregular hills. At some time in the past, there had been orchards, gardens, fields of wheat. All of those things were gone, leaving acres of stumps and tumbled-down walls. Shallow streams ran down from the hills, making spots of marshy ground.

Dwyrin reached the gate before anyone else, so he had a good view of the Faithful assembling, marching out of the darkness with their thick fur cloaks and round helms. Huge round shields hung over their backs, adorned with black figures of crows and ravens on red backgrounds. Each man carried a long single-bladed ax and a heavy straight sword on a baldric slung over one shoulder. Their deep voices carried up to him as he sat on the tower wall.

The captain, Rufio, had followed soon after, accompanying a regiment of men carrying something draped in black canvas.

"Well, lad, can you make something glow?" Captain Rufio turned to him, dark eyes glinting under a heavy iron helm.

"Yes, sir!" Dwyrin clenched his fists, concentrating. After a moment, soft white light spilled from between his fingers. "Will this do?"

"It will." A flicker of something—it couldn't be despair, could it?—crossed the captain's face. "But not yet, not yet. When we march out, then I will need your aid. But first, we must watch and wait."

Rufio motioned to a man leaning out of a door high on the side of the tunnel. The man nodded, then ducked into a room inside the wall. Almost immediately there was a deep, grinding sound. Before Dwyrin and Rufio, the outermost of the massive gates of the city began to open, swinging in on huge hinges. A dozen men guided each door, walking alongside. Night yawned before them. The sun was still an hour from peeking over the eastern horizon. A faint light was growing in the east, but in the torchlight spilling out onto the road everything seemed pitch black.

Mist and fog rose from the ground in wisps. A cold gray day was in the offing.

The Persian camp sprawled across the Galatan hills in an untidy mass, fitfully lit by torches and lanterns. The muffled sounds of thousands of men moving carried easily in the night air. Mohammed and Zoë watched with interest from a hill just north of the stream feeding into the Golden Horn. Nearly a half-mile of water separated their vantage from the ramparts of the Roman city. Constantinople was invisible behind a wall of fog curling up from the water. Mohammed finished a ripe fig. Zoë had refused to eat any breakfast.

"It will be cold," Mohammed said. Zoë nodded, face wrapped in the tan linen tail of her riding cloak. The Quraysh studied the sky, making out a film over the stars. "It may even rain."

The *clip-clop* of horses approaching drew Mohammed's attention and he tucked the remains of the fig into his cloak. He turned his flea-bitten mare, leaning forward on the saddle. Around him, arrayed on the hill, were his Sahaba, their camp torn down and packed. Each man was mounted and armored, lance gleaming softly in distant lantern light. The lean shape of Odenathus appeared out of the gloom, with Khalid following. Both men seemed tense, but then, everyone in the army was on edge. Mohammed raised a hand, beckoning the two young men to his side. Shadin moved up, out of the ranks of the *qatib* lined up on the crown of the hill.

"What news?" Mohammed spoke softly, though anyone with eyes to see from the walls of the city knew that the enemy was on the move. "Are there any changes?"

"No, Lord Mohammed." Khalid's eyes were alight with amusement. Odenathus turned his horse to stand by Zoë and the two cousins exchanged a brief hand clasp. "The Boar is already enraged with the slowness of his men breaking camp. Even the Avars are already crossing the stream." The young man pointed off in the darkness to the northwest.

"Very well. Is the road still clear?"

"Yes, lord." Shadin's voice was gruff but confident. "Our scouts secured the bridge over the stream last night. The Romans have not been seen on the far bank." The hulking swordsman pointed at a dim gleam of light tracing a path down the hill. Lanterns hung from trees or posts.

"Excellent." Mohammed raised his voice so that all of the men and women around him could hear clearly. "As agreed, we have the right flank of the army. We will follow the path laid out for us by the *muqadamma*. We will need to move swiftly to avoid clogging the road. Beyond the stream there are rising hills to the right. By dawn, if the great and merciful Lord blesses us, we should be in position on those hills, screening the Persian right flank."

Shadin and the others nodded. Mohammed and Zoë had taken them over the plan in detail the previous day. They, and the Persians and Avars, faced difficult ground on both the left and the right of the plain. To the left, there were both the remains of the Arab fortifications and then the ditch before the walls. After some argument, Shahr-Baraz convinced the Avar khagan Bayan the key to the whole battle lay there, under the gray battlements. The nomad chieftain wanted to command the right wing. Shahr-Baraz insisted the Avars take the left. Mohammed kept quiet during this bickering. He did not want his army exposed to bow shot from the city walls, or broken in two by the double ditch-and-wall of the circumvallation.

The Persians would array themselves across the center of the plain, where the ground was best for their heavy horse and masses of spearmen and archers. Mohammed didn't care about the presumed honor, but he was glad to have the right under his command. Low sloping hills covered with old walls and copses of trees broke up the ground, but most of his force was actually the heavy infantry of the Decapolis. They would do well there. He assumed that they would face the main body of the Western legions. His precious band of heavy cavalry, the *qalb* of mounted Arabs and Palmyrenes, would cover the join between his line and the Persians'.

"Zoë, Odenathus and I will go first," he continued, "with the qalb directly behind us. Then the *maisarah* and the *maimanah* will follow with all speed. The heavy horse and the muqadamma will protect the infantry until they are in position."

Everyone nodded, so Mohammed clucked to his horse and she ambled down the hill, following the trail of lanterns. Behind him, tens of thousands of men began to move, armor rattling and clinking in the gloom. A whispered chant filled the air, raising the hackles on the back of his neck.

"Praise be to God, Lord of the Universe,
the compassionate, the merciful,
sovereign of the day of judgment!
You alone we worship, and to you alone
we turn for help.
Guide us to the straight path,
the path of those whom you have favored,
not of those who have incurred your wrath,
nor of those who have gone astray."

Dawn was starting to break in the east, shedding a gray light. Dwyrin and Rufio stood in the shadow of the Great Gate, looking out across the plain. Drifts of mist and fog clung to the ground. The Hibernian could hear, though. The tramp of booted feet and the rattle of hooves on the stone road carried across the fields. Rufio laid a hand on his shoulder. "Can you see them? The legions marching?"

"Yes." Dwyrin blinked and the mist faded away from his sight. "They are coming down the road in long columns, shields shining in the light of their torches."

"Yes . . ." Rufio squinted into the gloom. Long lines of lights appeared, winding down out of the hills. Some branched off like rivers of fire flowing into the east. "All right, lad, time to make our standard burn like the sun."

Dwyrin smirked, cracking his knuckles. Directly behind him, filling the gate, was the tall icon of the Emperor. The black canvas had been removed and an especially sturdy troop of the Faithful were waiting for orders. Rufio called out, voice sharp in the cold air. "Raise the standard!"

The Faithful were quick to heft the platform to their shoulders. The visage of the Emperor rose up, rocked back and forth for a moment, then steadied. Dwyrin opened his hand, thoughts far away. The background of gold and pearl began to shine, glowing like the rising sun. The Emperor's portrait lit with carefully applied colors, the pigments as fresh as the day they were first applied.

Rufio smiled, then paced out onto the road. With a measured stomp, the Faithful advanced behind him, the Emperor riding high on their shoulders. Light spilled out from the icon, lighting up the road, the ditch half filled with debris, the broken teeth of the Arab wall. Dwyrin walked alongside, one hand on the platform. Vladimir paced him, keeping between the boy and the misty plain.

Where the light fell, gray mist fled and within a few grains, as the procession walked west, more and more of the plain was revealed. The golden radiance lit even the grim towers flanking the gate. In the city, bells began to ring, pealing in the cold air. All along the vast wall, men stirred themselves from sleep and stared out in wonder.

"The Emperor goes forth!" rang the massed voices of the Faithful. "The Emperor goes to battle!"

At the head of the procession, Rufio smiled grimly, hand ever on the hilt of his sword. Before him, the mist parted and was driven back by the golden light. Soon the helmets and spears of the Western troops hurrying down the road would appear.

White fog drifted between the trees, leaving them shining and dark with moisture. Jusuf urged his horse forward, letting it find its way across the stubbled field. High grass stood in clumps, the long stems bent down by heavy dew. On either side of the Khazar, columns of riders moved slowly forward, feeling their way through the mist. A line of trees rose up out of the gloom and Jusuf ducked under a branch.

"Hold up," he called to the men on either side. The ground descended. The trees made a windbreak at the top of the hill. A slope covered with low bushes fell away below his feet. He whistled, the fluting call of a marsh gant. "Dahvos?"

The brushy ground swallowed the noise of horse's

hooves, making the kagan and his escorts appear as suddenly as phantoms. Dahvos was fully armored, with a conical steel helm sporting a horsetail plume. His guardsmen wore solid-iron masks, worked with geometric designs, and heavy mail fell in a swath around their shoulders and necks. Much like the Roman knights, they wore vambraces and greaves of spliced metal strips. Just behind the Prince, a rider held the banner of the house of Asena socketed into his stirrup. The flag was barely visible in the poor light, hanging limp, but the green field and red horse were plain.

"Order both columns to halt on this ridge." The kagan's voice snapped with authority, carrying easily, even in the heavy air. "Send scouts forward and to the wings. Particularly the right—find the Roman Legion there; it should be the Tenth Fretensis. We must close up with them."

Couriers peeled off from the escort, cantering off through the mist. Dahvos turned to his brother, blue eyes intent. "What do you think?"

Jusuf shook his head, lips pursed. "We should slow up and make sure we're in line with the Roman advance. There must be a swale between these hills, probably marshy ground down there. Shall I take a party forward?"

"No." Dahvos had grown into his duties during their long ride around the fringe of the Sea of Darkness. Though he would often consult with Jusuf, the younger man knew his own mind. Jusuf was pleased by his half-brother's maturity—he would make a good kagan for the people. "The Western cohorts must travel farther, on foot, than we. We will wait and let this fog lift and make sure that our flanks are secure." The kagan turned in his saddle, gesturing for another courier to come up to him. One of the young men, not yet warriors, rode up, his face eager.

"Zachar, go along the crest of this ridge and make sure that everyone has come up and stopped. No one is to go down the valley without my command. Only the scouts are to advance." Dahvos turned back, peering forward into the murk. "Is this a foggy country? How long will this last?"

"Not long," Jusuf said, shifting the hilt of his sword forward in its scabbard. "This is some freak of the weather—it's high summer here! I think it will burn off soon, though the day may be cold."

"Good. When the air clears a little, I want you to take command of the far left. I am going to shift the heavy horse to the right, more towards the Romans, and I don't want any surprises behind me."

"I understand." Jusuf raised an eyebrow. "Remember—the ground in this swale will be soft; a charge might founder."

"I know." Dahvos grinned. "The Western troops are nearly all infantry, though. The Persians are sure to try and turn their flank with their own clibanarii. When that happens, I'd like to be able to strike as they turn."

Jusuf was about to answer, but a rider came spurring up the hill, his horse's mane flying. Both men turned, watching as the scout made the last length up to the crest. "My lords!" The man heeled his horse around, pointing out into the fog. "The valley is shallow and only a half-mile or so across. The hills on the other side are low, but there are many men there."

"Persians?" Dahvos' expression sharpened, becoming predatory. "Or Avars?"

"Neither, lord! These are men I've never seen before! Their skin is dark and they ride under a green and white banner—a sword and letters I cannot read."

Jusuf rubbed his chin, feeling the oily curls. "These must be the Arabs from the desert."

Dahvos nodded in agreement. "How are they armed? How is the ground?"

"All afoot," the scout said, "but they stand in close ranks, like the Romans, with bows, square shields and longish spears. Some horsemen chased us off—a few arrows, though they do not seem to be great shots. There is a shallow stream and the ground is soft and muddy."

"They do have some lancers," Jusuf interjected crisply.

"But they come from Roman cities, these rebels, so they will fight like the Legion. Triple lines of infantry in a shield wall, with archers and javelins in support."

"Where are the Avars, then?" Dahvos mused, tapping the helmet with the back of his hand. "Not in the center, certainly; they must hold the far right flank of the enemy line."

"Do we advance?" Jusuf's fingers were busy, testing straps and buckles, making sure nothing was loose or frayed. "Or wait?"

"We wait. No sense in charging across soft ground and then up a hill. Let these townsmen come down into the flat, then we'll see what they're made of."

Dahvos nodded to the scout and the man trotted away down the hill. Jusuf unhooked a wineskin from his belt and took a long drink. Even in this cold air, the armor encasing him was hot. If he was right, it would just get hotter as the day progressed.

"Here they come. At last!" Shahr-Baraz felt a great weight lift from his shoulders. The King of Kings stood at the center of the Persian line, a hundred yards behind a huge sprawling block of spearmen. He sat astride a high wooden seat, formed of precut timbers, draped with cloth of gold and silk cushions. His engineers assembled the watchtower in darkness, guided by torches and markings cut into the logs. There were no protective shields or hides, but it offered him a huge advantage—he could see clearly from the hills on the right to the walls of the city on the left. Armored gloves shaded his eyes, and he saw, across the plain, long lines of soldiers pouring out of the city. "He is coming out!"

Forward of the tower, a great mass of archers and slingers and javelineers stood at ease, some sitting on the dew-soaked ground, others counting their arrows or slingstones. A space of a dozen paces separated them from the backs of the spearmen, who waited silently in uneven rows, wicker shields facing front, in five deep ranks. Armored diquans paced between masses of lightly armored infantry, helmets glowing in the diffuse light. Groups of men in heavier armor, armed with maces and long, straight swords, were interspersed amongst the militia spearmen. The mass of the Persian infantry needed some stiffening to face the Roman legionary one-on-one.

Behind the tower, standing beside their horses, talking in low tones, were the Immortals, the pushtigbahn, Shahr-Baraz' reserve. Each of the noblemen were armored from head to toe in overlapping mail coats, and armed with heavy spiked maces, lances, long swords, and the heavy recurved horse bow they had inherited from their Parthian predecessors. Nearly six thousand of the finest fighting men in the world. Shahr-Baraz could name only three other nations that fielded so professional and skilled a force.

Of course, all three of those powers faced him across the field. The King of Kings was not concerned. He didn't need to win this battle, only fight to a bloody draw. That would be enough. The mere fact the Eastern Legions issued forth from their city made him giddy with relief. Everything depended on Heraclius coming out to give battle. Shahr-Baraz saw the battle emblem of the Eastern Emperor glowing and flickering like a star in the mist. The Eastern troops were having trouble negotiating the Arab fortifications.

"Bless you, Lord Mohammed. Your men built well!" Shahr-Baraz turned to the west, raising a hand in salute to the Arab forces arrayed on the hills. In any other battle, he would have been forced to deploy Khadames and his clibanarii to cover the right, greatly extending his frontage. Today, however, he was pleased to let the Arabs protect his flank. He had never before met a man, much less a *king,* who was as honest and honorable as this Mohammed. Shahr-Baraz was certain, from the top of his gilded helm to the iron spikes on the toes of his boots, that the Arab chieftain would stand firm at his right, through fire and storm and even defeat.

Shahr-Baraz sighed, leaning on his armored thighs. *If only I could make this man my friend. Then all would be well in the world. His honor is unimpeachable! Our alliance would doom Rome and leave Persia the master of the world.* But such a thing was impossible. The Boar felt a little guilty—he had not revealed the whole plan to seize Constantinople. If Mohammed knew what was to come, he would be an enemy rather than a friend. Thus the Arabs were safely tucked away on the right. Shahr-Baraz owed Mohammed this much, for destroying the Roman fleet.

But the Avar khagan, now, he will gladly pay my price! The Boar smiled, teeth glinting behind tusklike mustaches. Off to his left, the Avar Slav infantry were swarming forward in a great undisciplined horde. They spilled around the earthworks of the old Arab forts like oil, spears, axes and swords glinting, blue-painted bodies and bright-checked trousers merging into a great colorful mass. The barrier of the ditches had already broken the Avar force into two distinct groups—one group of nearly eight thousand on foot on the Persian side, then beyond the circumvallation another mass of infantry backed up by the kagan's mounted nobles. The horsetail banners and dragon flags of the Avars were snapping in the morning breeze.

The Avars would be attacking straight into the teeth of the Eastern Legions, but if they broke through to the Perinthus road, the bulk of the Roman army would be separated from the city itself, unable to fall back into the massive fortifications. That would be an excellent outcome. . . .

Horns winded across the plain, where the morning fog was blowing back in streaming tatters. In places, the pale white mist still clung to the ground, but the Boar could see his enemy advancing on a broad front, their ranks perfect, with good separation between each column. The old general's heart lifted to see such precision on the field of battle.

Ah! A thing of beauty! My spearmen should look so good after an hour's effort in the melee.

That was part of an old problem—the Persians could march as well as the Romans, engineer as well, fight a-horse far better, but the Romans could fight all day and not lose their damnable order and efficiency.

Four Western Legions advanced across the plain at a walk, lines undulating with the uneven ground. Shahr-Baraz watched them carefully, seeing that they were moving slowly, centurions walking backwards ahead of each cohort. A thin line of archers and skirmishers ran ahead, slings and bows at the ready. Behind the ranks of the legionaries were two blocks of reserves, but even with the height advantage of the tower it was impossible to see what kind of troops they were.

Mercenary horse, he thought, *or auxiliaries of some kind.*

"Signal flag!" The Boar's voice cut through the murmur of the *pushtigbahn* like a cleaver. "Prepare to advance!"

Down on the ground, four men hoisted colored flags in a prearranged pattern, letting them snap in the breeze. At the same time, trumpeters raised long bronze horns to their lips. The *blat* of sound carried well. Shahr-Baraz raised his head, watching the western hill. Flags responded. The Boar was pleased to see Mohammed had deployed his infantry in a stout line just below the crest, behind a screen of light horse. He could not see the opposing soldiers, hidden by the last scraps of mist clinging to the hills.

The Boar swung down from the tower, muscular arms easily taking the weight of his armor and gear. Two boys ran up with his horse, all covered in quilted armor sewn with metal plates, as he lighted on the ground. "Immortals! Mount up!"

Ten thousand Immortals scrambled onto their horses, raising a huge clatter and noise. Shahr-Baraz felt his blood quicken. Soon . . . victory would come closer with each Roman corpse. One of the boys placed a stool on the ground, easing his climb onto the horse. He felt gloriously alive, the mighty beast solid under his thighs, armor clinging to him like a second skin. A mailed hand swung down his face plate, clicking it into place.

"Hey-yup!" The Boar spurred his horse off to the left. He intended to throw his main effort against the Eastern troops around the gleaming icon of the Emperor. As the Arab wall split the Avar advance, so it divided the Eastern Legions. But under the eye of their Emperor, they would stand and fight. With a little luck, he could press them back into the broken ground and drive them from the road in disarray. The great weakness of the Roman formations was susceptibility to a sharp cavalry charge if they were disordered and their line ragged.

Dwyrin climbed up the blackened slope of the Arab rampart, sooty ground falling away under his boots. Vladimir and two of the Faithful followed close behind, fur cloaks flapping in the cold wind. At the top of the slope were jagged burned stumps and the remains of a fighting platform. The Hibernian stopped, looking out in delight upon the plain before him. Just to his left, thousands of Eastern legionaries were marching at double-time through the breach made in the Arab walls.

Cohorts of iron-clad cataphracts were already through the opening and wheeling on the open plain from left to right. Their lances were tipped with snapping guidons, making a brave show as they trotted past. A hundred yards ahead, to the right, the icon of the Emperor continued to glow and shine. A great red-cloaked block of the Faithful Guard was arrayed around the standard. Cohorts of Eastern legionaries swarmed past. At least four thousand men formed up into battle ranks between the icon and the Persian lines. Dwyrin laughed, then flipped back his hood. Rain seemed unlikely today, now that the fog was gone.

The sky was showing clear and blue, the sun a perfect white disk in the eastern sky.

"Take good care of me, Vlad." Dwyrin settled onto the ground, crossing his legs. He pressed his fingers into the loamy soil, feeling cold dampness in the ground. The first stanzas of the chant to calm his mind and bring forth the opening of Hermes was poised on his tongue.

"We will," the Walach grunted, squatting down between the boy and the enemy. From this height, Vladimir could see both swarms of Slavic spearmen advancing upon their right on the desolate ground between the Arab wall and the city ditch, and Persians off to the left. The Walach unslung his shield and grounded it, making a barrier in front of the lad. The two Faithful also parked themselves at his side, squatting behind their shields. There was more danger of stray arrows than anything else.

Dwyrin closed his eyes and the world of the unseen unfolded before him. A great shining eye swept out of the abyssal dark and over him, shedding radiance and warmth. When Uraeus had passed, he looked out upon the field of war. The shapes of soldiers hurrying forward writhed, filled with living flame, merging as they ran into a river of fire. The cold earth itself was dull and without light, but the massed ranks of the Persians and their allies were a brilliant beacon. The air distorted between Dwyrin and the distant enemy, subtly twisted by the patterns of defense summoned by the magi.

Be careful! Dwyrin thought to himself, struggling a little to keep the power hissing and sparking in his heart from bursting out in an uncontrolled flare. He had learned enough to keep from being overwhelmed, to guide the strength to strike at his command. The little tricks, like keeping himself warm or cool, or making the portrait of the Emperor blaze with light, were valuable tools. They bled off the strength and kept him aware and centered. The chants and symbolic patterns of the Roman wizards approached this understanding of the hidden world, but they did not get into the heart of the thing. Dwyrin knew, watching the Roman thaumaturges raise their wards and spheres of defense around the marching Legions, that he had—*somehow*—stepped past their limited wisdom. The foundation patterns of the world around him were so clear and obvious.

But that did not mean that he was invincible. The *mobehedan* of Persia were the last descendants of the ancient Chaldeans, the first men to harness the power of the hidden world. The priests in the temple of Pthames spoke of them in awe, for in legend the priests of lost Ur and Sanilurfa surpassed all others. Even now, as Dwyrin watched, he saw their skill was far beyond that of the Romans. In strength, each side seemed to draw even.

But Rome has me, he thought, letting perception expand. The Legions advanced at a walk, in a steady, measured tread, and the mustered will of the soldiers was influencing the hidden world. Their Legion standards carried power, invested by centuries of battle and worship. Ghosts of the Legion dead drifted around the signifer, calling in pale voices to the living men for blood and sacrifice. Even the lead javelins each man carried disturbed the forms and patterns around them, making dead spots in the bright firmament. *This will be my day,* Dwyrin thought, turning his attention inward. *I will prove myself worthy of my Legion.*

Whirling and hissing, shedding heat and light from myriad interlocking spheres, the core of fire within him sang with a clear voice. Dwyrin let the fire spring forth, dancing in the air around him. Swiftly he raised a sphere of defense, much has he had in the dawn attack. An orange glow spilled away from him, flooding over broken timbers and muddy ditches. Three, four and five layers he conjured up, setting the words of the ancient gods upon them, each moving in opposition to the layer without. Conscious of the violent effects his work engendered, he restrained the power in the shields from spilling over into physicality.

He began to sweat, his body feeling the strain of channeling such raw energies.

Across the field, behind a glittering shield of violet and blue, he felt perception shift. Someone looked upon him and thus, as such things were, he looked upon the other. A white-bearded elder peered across the distance, shape and will distorted behind a dozen wards. Dwyrin let the man see him, then struck out, the fire singing like a crystal glass.

The shock of his blow boomed through the patterns, a virulent burst of white leaving a jagged afterimage in the air. Darkness flashed, washing across the Persian wards like a stain of ink. The wards buckled, then shifted and held. Dwyrin laughed, seeing the wide-eyed surprise in the elder's face. *Now we will test each other.*

His fist clenched, drawing a blazing shape of lightning from the air. He cast, shouting a wild cry. Again the Persian shields flared and rippled, throwing thousands of distorted images of men and horses. The fire was in him now, hot as the sun, and he let it rush forth. A pitiful wailing rose up from the Roman mages, but he ignored their cries.

A Persian ward ruptured, shattering like crushed glass, smoke wicking away in all directions, though there was now no wind. Dwyrin pressed the attack, hammering at the enemy with blow after blow. A few weak bursts of yellow lightning leapt from behind the Persian lines, but too much of their strength was bent against his will, trying to deflect his attack.

A jagged white flare leapt from his hands, spinning out like a great wheel, flashing above the unknowing, unseeing heads of the Persian spearmen, who advanced across the grassy fields. Some of the soldiers ducked, though nothing visible made them flinch away from the sky. The Persian magi scrambled to match the wheel, throwing up a hazy blue wall of rotating dodecahedrons. The wheel smashed into the barrier, crumpling the twelve-sided structures like faceted eggshells. Dwyrin felt some of the Persian will falter, then suddenly go out. The blue wall splintered, each facet spinning away into smoke. Now he was at grips with the *mobehedan*.

The Hibernian's face was wreathed in a hot orange glow, but he grinned like a wolf, hurling bolt after bolt into the enemy.

Shahr-Baraz rode swiftly, pleased with the smooth, even gait of his warhorse. The *pushtigbahn* kept pace. The earth under their hooves trembled with motion. Shahr-Baraz lifted the visor of his helmet and craned his neck, looking to the right. His formation was moving swiftly at a diagonal behind the huge mass of his spearmen and archers.

A constant snapping sound filled the air, the effect of five thousand archers and slingers firing into the oncoming ranks of the Roman Legions. The Boar watched with a critical eye, seeing a dark cloud hissing into the morning sky. The archers—men in long woolen shirts, dark trousers and round leather caps, wooden quivers slung over their backs, long-staved bows in hand—were trying to keep up a steady rate of fire. Instead, clumps of arrows lofted skyward and fell in patchy rain, rather than a constant storm upon the enemy.

"Bah!" the King of Kings rumbled. He hoped they weren't hitting their own troops. Long lines of spearmen and some dismounted diquans in heavy armor fronted the archers. Ahead of the Boar, the left wing of the spearmen advanced slowly, urged forward by the horse archers anchoring the Persian left. While the Romans advanced across the whole length of the field in line, the Persians were only swinging their left out to meet them, making a long diagonal.

The Boar didn't know if the Romans would match his maneuver, but if they did, their far left flank would be exposed to the heavy Arab cavalry hidden on the hill, behind ranks of infantry and archers. Shahr-Baraz doubted if the Romans would be so rash. Of course, this left their right flank exposed to the weight of his attack.

He cantered forward, seeing bands of spearmen part before him. A clump of banners and flags lay ahead where a band of armored knights milled about on the field. Shahr-Baraz urged his mount forward and was quickly among them.

"Shahanshah!" General Khadames turned his horse towards Shahr-Baraz, gray beard jutting from his helmet. The older man looked grim, his face pinched. "We're moving, lord, but slowly."

The Boar nodded, raising his hand to signal *halt* to the Immortals trotting up behind. Off to his right, where Khadames' captains were driving the spearmen and archers forward, the body of a great host of *clibanarii* was waiting on muddy, churned ground. The diquans were moving restlessly, their horses eager, curved bows laid over their saddles, arrows already fitted to the string. "How long?"

"Only moments." Khadames shaded his eyes, rising up in his stirrups. "Here they come."

Shahr-Baraz nodded. He could see the Romans coming in great blocks, square shields forward, making a moving, solid wall. "Stand ready to loose arrows!" The deep-throated roar of trumpets and the flash of signal flags echoed his voice.

Ahead of the Boar, a space opened in the Persian line as it swung to his right. Only a mob of Slavic infantry were in the way, crowding towards the city, to his left, swarming up over the Arab ditch and rampart like dark blue ants. A trampled field of wheat stubble lay open before his Immortals, scattered with arrows, dropped weapons or shields and even a few corpses. A hundred yards away, a block of Romans advanced, standards and flags fluttering in the breeze. They were thickly packed in ranks, the bronze metal bosses on their painted shields catching the sun.

The Boar chopped his hand forward, a motion echoed by his bannermen, and the front ranks of the Immortals began to trot forward. Khadames and his horse archers peeled away to the right, but they did not go far. Shahr-Baraz and his officers remained behind while the pushtig-bahn flowed past in an armored stream of leather, iron and steel. As the lines of pushtigbahn trotted forward, the men unlimbered their long stabbing spears. Shahr-Baraz felt the earth tremble as six thousand men began to gallop, plunging towards the Roman line.

The King of Kings turned his horse, spurring back towards the center of his army. Though his heart yearned to rush forward, horse thundering over the grass, mighty sword in hand, to lose himself in the hot shock of combat, hewing down his enemies, duty commanded that he remain aloof from battle. Grains spilled away, and he watched the cloud of dust rising from the rushing mass of horses and men.

A dozen yards away, Khadames raised his hand and thousands of clibanarii arrayed around him lifted their bows as one. The old general waited a beat of his heart, then slashed his hand down. Eight thousand men loosed as one, the rippling *thwack* of strings on leather arm guards sharp in the air. A hissing moan rose up as a vast cloud of arrows leapt into the sky. Shahr-Baraz was pleased, seeing a second volley loosed within two grains of the first. The initial arrows had not even struck their targets.

The shahanshah wheeled his horse, waving at Khadames. "Close up behind the Immortals," he called. "Strike hard!" Then he galloped away, back along the long line of archers and spearmen holding the center of the field.

Cursing violently, Rufio crouched behind a heavy scutum, holding the shield at an angle. The sky darkened and a storm of arrows flashed down with a chilling hiss. Yard-long shafts ripped through the formation of Faithful, though the men stood rock solid, heavy round shields angled towards the sky. He staggered suddenly, one of the arrows crunching into the surface of the shield. The triangular iron head ripped through three layers of pine laminate and cracked out of the hide backing. Another shaft splintered violently on the metal boss. Rufio cursed again, shoulder sore from the impact. Only feet away, one of the burly Scandians holding up the Emperor's icon staggered, a gray-fletched shaft jutting from his upper chest. The man swayed, then caught himself, though blood leaked from the wound. He did not drop the pole gripped in his scarred hands.

Fifty feet away, Rufio saw the mass of Eastern legionaries stagger as well. The rain of arrows was fiercest there, in the rear ranks of the Twelfth Asiatica. Rufio knew most of the men were veterans, but they had been recently constituted from the remains of three other legions shattered at Yarmuk. Theodore's failure in Syria weighed heavily on the Eastern army.

A rumbling in the ground resolved itself into an onrushing mass of horsemen. Everyone tensed. The Persian cavalry slammed into the front ranks of the Twelfth with a huge *clang!* Rufio couldn't see the front rank, not through the black haze of falling arrows, but he saw the legionaries surge backwards. Their centurions and tribunes were screaming, trying to keep the men in ranks.

Suddenly, the armored heads of Persian diquans loomed up among the legionaries, laying about them in a frenzy with spears and heavy maces. Rufio leapt up, ignoring the arrows sleeting out of the sky. The shock of the Persian charge carried them deep into the lines of the Twelfth. The arrow storm slackened and the captain of the Faithful Guard turned, shouting in a bullhorn voice to his men, "Forward! The Guard, forward!"

With a great shout, the Scandians unlimbered axes and swords and charged forward, fur cloaks flying. The Persians drove hard, splitting the Legion line in two. A dozen of the diquans spurred their armored warhorses out of the melee, aiming for the Emperor's standard. Rufio hoisted his shield, running forward, a throwing spear gripped in his right hand. Around him, the Faithful swarmed forward in a forest of red beards and tall conical helms. Rufio hurled his pilum into the shield of one of the horsemen. The breach was sealed by the Faithful, axes blurring red in the air, forcing the diquans back. The pilum's lead point snagged in the Persian's shield, dangling, dragging the man's arm down. Enraged, the Persian shook his arm, trying to free the spear. One of the Faithful, bellowing a war cry, hacked at the diquan while he was distracted. The tempered edge of the ax bit into the man's neck, crunching through a chain-mail gorget, spewing blood. The Persian struck across his body with his sword, the blow ringing off the Scandian's helmet. Then another of the Faithful rushed up and two axes hewed into the diquan's legs, splintering his laminate armor. Blood gouted, and the knight fell from his horse, disappearing into the violent melee.

Rufio shouted, screaming at the legionaries from the Twelfth. They fell back all around the Emperor's standard in panic. The charge of the diquans shattered their first three ranks and threw the rest into confusion. Only the Faithful seemed to be holding, a thin line of red cloaks between the Persians and the icon.

"The Emperor! The Emperor! Stand and fight, you dogs!" Rufio bellowed.

Some of the legionaries rallied, taking heart from the towering, glowing image of Heraclius, but more fled past. A clump of men carrying the banners of the Twelfth stopped, seeing him. Their signifier and aquilifer stood out sharply against the midday sky. Rufio clenched his teeth and drew his gladius, running up to join the four men. Seeing their battle standards halt, more legionaries began to gather, shaken but regaining their nerve. The sun rose higher into the sky. It was getting hot. Rufio wondered if he would see Martina again. At least the Persian archery had stopped.

Heedless of arrows snapping past in the dusty air, Dagobert spurred his horse forward, plunging into the confused mass of Eastern light infantry. Men scattered away as he rode into their midst, followed by a wedge of his own household troops. The Western legate was furious. The Eastern troops, mostly archers and slingers, watched him pass, faces filled with puzzlement. They seemed directionless, standing about in disordered cohorts and maniples. Persian arrows flicked out the sky. One of Dagobert's aides suddenly cried out, then slumped forward over his saddle, a black-fletched shaft jutting from his neck.

"Turn and shoot back!" Dagobert cried, forcing his horse through a band of Eastern spearmen, long ashwood weapons waving about him like reeds. "Form a line!"

The Western commander had been pacing the Eastern troops' advance with his own reserve, a force of some six thousand Sarmatian lancers, following behind the veteran Third Augusta, which anchored the right wing of the Western line. He had seen the Persian heavy cavalry burst out from behind a screen of horse archers and crash into the main body of the Eastern troops. Despite a hurried search, he had not found Prince Theodore and his staff. Dagobert was sure the man was here *somewhere* but with the Eastern formations breaking apart in the face of the Persian attack, *he* had to do something.

The Sarmatians followed in two columns, pressing forward through the scattered Eastern infantry. Now the Western dux had a clear view of the melee. Persian diquans in their full armor, including even their horses, had shattered the Eastern infantry and had pressed them back into the side of the old Arab fortification. The glowing portrait of Heraclius still rose above the battle, now surrounded by dozens of other banners and standards and a ring of men in red cloaks, though they were hard-pressed, fighting on foot against the Persian horse.

"Columns! Deploy! Prepare to advance!" Dagobert pointed with his ivory baton and the Sarmatians spilled out from behind him, their heavily built chargers neighing and whinnying as they spread out into a line three deep. Between the Western troops and the Persians, the ground cleared as those few remaining Eastern spearmen and legionaries scattered to the south.

"Dux!" Dagobert turned, even as the Sarmatians formed up, their long, heavy lances swinging down into position to charge. "You must fall back!"

Dagobert scowled at his aide, one of the Latins in his service, rather than the Franks who were already drawing their weapons—long-hafted axes or heavy hand-and-a-half swords. The Roman officer was pointing back over his shoulder, at the main body of the Western army. The four legions arrayed across that front were continuing their steady advance, though the Third Augusta had begun to shift, refusing its right, so that the Persians did not turn its flank.

"Sergius, we have to break this Persian attack. Prince Theodore is nowhere to be seen. One swift charge will restore this position!"

"I know, dux, but these Sarmatians will do that. You are in command of the whole army!" Sergius leaned close, his whole posture intent on Dagobert. "You are responsible for everyone, not just this little battle. We must return to the center."

Dagobert almost struck the young man, but then restrained himself with an effort of will. His father and grandfather would not have paused for an instant before throwing themselves into the thick of battle. Their worth as men depended on courage and bravery and their public expression. Part of the Frank yearned for violent release, but he was more Roman now than barbarian. "Very well. Merovech! Take command of these Sarmatians and strike! The rest of us will return to the center and see about these other Persians."

Turning his face from Sergius, Dagobert wheeled his horse, then galloped off, back behind the Roman lines. The other Franks glared at the Latin officer, but they followed. Merovech spurred his horse forward, waving his sword, and the Sarmatians began to trot towards the Persians, slowly picking up speed.

"Ready!" Khadames raised his hand again, feeling the weight of the heavy laminated armor on his arm. Once he had born it without qualm or effort, but the last two years had leached his body of its old strength. The cold mornings in this rainy land pained him. Even now he felt a remnant of that chill in his bones. His horse was walking forward, guided by the pressure of his knees. His clibanarii had spread out a little as they advanced in the wake of the Immortals. Now they were four lines of men, rather than a thick block nine deep. Grass, mud and the bodies of dead Romans and Persians passed by, littering the ground. "Draw!"

The pushtigbahn had torn a huge hole in the Roman line, helped by a withering arrow storm laid down by Khadames' horse archers. But their advance seemed to have stalled, swirling in a roar of battle around the glowing shape of a man standing on a low hill. Now a great force of Roman *auxillia*—Huns or Sarmatians by the looks of their armor and horse barding—was preparing to counter-charge into the Immortals' flank. Khadames and his forces had begun the day hiding behind a screen of massed spearmen; now they were partly obscured by the dust kicked up from the melee. Too, they were the reserve behind the Immortals, hanging back, keeping out of the battle.

Two hundred yards away, the Roman horse began to wheel out, speeding up to a trot, their lances glittering in the sun. Khadames drew his own sword, a Damawand-forged blade that curved towards the tip, with a thick back and a single cutting edge. There was just enough time . . .

"Loose!" Eight thousand men released as one, their bows singing, and a black cloud leapt up, hung for a long, still moment in the air, and then plunged into the Sarmatians as they swept forward on the attack. Hundreds of men were knocked from their horses, the beasts pierced, screaming, thrashing on the ground. The momentum of the attack staggered, but then picked up to a gallop. "Loose!"

Shafts raked the flank of the charging Romans, pitching more men down. Khadames waved his sword in the air, letting it catch the sun. "Advance!" The Persian clibanarii stowed their bows in a smooth motion, sliding them down into the *gorytos*, then their horses were cantering forward, picking up speed. Khadames was in their midst, his horse rushing forward over the lumpy ground. Ahead, between the lurching bodies of his men, he could see the Sarmatians swinging out, away from the Immortals, to meet him. Their numbers were visibly depleted by the flights of arrows. Their lances dipped towards him, but the Persian charge was already at full speed, thundering across the field.

Shining figures stormed across the glittering field, rising as they ran forward until they towered higher than the ramparts of the city. Dwyrin was vaguely aware of the giants, though his concentration was focused on shattering the last of the matrices that protected the Persian magi. The Eastern savants were fighting hard, their wills compressed to diamond brilliance as they struggled against the Hibernian. Fantastic creatures boiled up out of the earth—titans and dragons and horned men—hurling themselves against Dwyrin, battering at his orange-red shields, stooping over the heads of the mortal men struggling and fighting on the broad field.

The phantasms might have distracted Dwyrin a month ago, but now he could see through them, though they were marvelously complex. Far below the earth, stone and rock groaned and shifted, yielding slow mottled power to him. Despite the fierce eagerness flowing through him, Dwyrin was tiring. His physical body suffered as the strength in the spark of fire rushed out. The mental effort of giving so much power, shape, purpose and form was terribly wearing.

Luckily, there seemed to be only a few Persian savants arrayed against him, and those whose wills battled his seemed to lack skill. Briefly, he wondered what had happened to their great _mobeds_ and _mobehedan. Where are the priests of their eternal fire? Dead,_ he supposed, _already stricken down in this endless war._ Azure lightning raged against his shields, splintering the first shell of defense. Dwyrin mentally shook himself, returning his attention to the struggle.

The Persians tried to attack on multiple levels at once; some sent phantoms against his mind, others tried to bull their way through his ethereal defense, still more were working a pattern that would cut him off from the power inherent in the earth and the air. For an instant, he let them come, ceasing his attacks. They raged against him, brilliant lightning bursting around him, the patterns of earth and air and stone ruptured in their fury. Giants assailed him, lashing down with enormous spiked clubs; fanged mouths opened in the earth—all these things were seen only by his eyes. The mobeds were not wasting their strength by assailing him in the physical world.

His strength gathered, Dwyrin's will rode stealthily along the backwash of their lightning and bolts of fire. The violence of their attack distorted the hidden world, making perception difficult. He was sweating now, his body strained to the breaking point. A particularly vicious pattern smashed against his rotating spheres, sending glowing orange fragments in all directions. A bloody cut suddenly opened on his cheek, leaking clear fluid. Dwyrin flinched but did not let it distract him. _Just a moment more . . ._

Heartened by the rupture of his defense, the magi redoubled their assault, lashing him with waves of carnelian and abyssal darkness. Another sphere shattered, leaving golden glyphs hanging in the air, then they were swept away. Dwyrin bent his head, enduring the attack. Each time that the Persians sent their power against him, a tenuous, flickering pattern linked him and they for the tinest of instants. Each blow echoed back in a swirling infinitesimal cloud of reaction. His will flashed along the path, following the burning paths cut in the air.

Suddenly, like the sun breaking from behind a dark cloud heavy with rain, he was within the Persian ward, standing in their camp, looking down upon them, a dozen boys and beardless men shuddering and sweating in the shade of their tents. Persian soldiers in long coats of mail watched over them, bared swords in their hands.

Why, he thought, looking upon them in horror, *they're only children!*

Behind him, the pattern of their defense sparkled like wet pearl, but it had been rendered useless. Dwyrin said a prayer, calling upon Badb Catha, the black crow, to carry their souls to the western islands, where these children might drink deep of green mead and sing in joy, sitting among the ancient heroes. Then his hands struck, palm to palm, and the air rumbled and shook. On the ground, the bodies of the twelve Persians stiffened, a single thin cry escaped one throat, and then they were dead.

Dwyrin leapt back, shuddering, to find himself in his body, eyes open, staring up at the sun, tears streaming down his face. The bearded faces of Vladimir and the Faithful loomed over him, enormous and dark against the radiance of the sun.

"Lad!" Vladimir was shaking his shoulders. "You're alive?"

"Yes," Dwyrin croaked, terribly thirsty. "Is there any water?"

Trumpets pealed, cutting the dusty air with their bright metallic sound. Dagobert scowled furiously, urging his warhorse forward through the serried ranks of Eastern cataphracts. The horsemen astride their thick-bodied chargers waited at ease, helmets riding on their saddle bows, short beards gleaming with sweat. The Eastern troops parted before the Western dux, letting him and his staff thunder past. Much like their Persian adversaries, the Eastern horsemen were armored from toe to crown in overlapping lozenges of iron, with heavy curved bows slotted behind their four-cornered saddles. Long spears rode close to each hand, joined by a profusion of maces and heavy swords. On his left, the easterners bore dark blue shields, tabards and banners worked with gryphons. To his right, a flame-vermilion predominated and bore a rampant dragon.

"Prince Theodore! What are you doing?" Dagobert's calm had frayed enough to let long-held anger spill out. He did not wait for the Eastern lord to reply before stabbing his armored finger sharply back at the clangor and din of battle that raged along the Arab wall. "Your men are hard pressed!"

"*My* men?" Theodore's eyes narrowed at the sharp words, his face cold. "My men are here, obeying my command. Those legionaries there—I do not know who they serve, but I am not responsible for them."

"What? Are you mad?" Dagobert nudged his horse alongside the Eastern prince's, reining over hard when the Frankish charger tried to nip the Eastern stallion. Despite the dustiness of the day, Theodore had managed to keep the glossy black hide of his mount sparkling clean. Further, the Prince and his staff were sitting a-horse, at ease, under a huge silk pavilion held up on five tall poles carried by servants. The opaque red silk allowed them to stay cool despite the sun high in the sky. "Your Twelfth Asiatica is getting ground to bits!"

Theodore shrugged, his gilded armor clinking gently at the movement. "As I said, barbarian, I do not command the Twelfth. Those men are mutinous, having marched out of the city without either my leave or command, following some trinket, some magicked-up picture of my esteemed noble brother. In fact, I am sure that *he* did not order them forth from the city, either!"

Dagobert shook his head, amazed and repulsed at the same time. "You'll not help them, then?"

"Why should I?" Bitter anger seeped into Theodore's words. "Their centurions swore to abide by my command not more than two days ago! Now they show themselves to be baseless, dishonorable men. Let them drink deep of treachery's wine. . . . No. I shall wait and see their punishment; then—perhaps—I will take a hand in this, to save you from your folly."

"Will you?" Dagobert felt uncontrollable fury mounting in him, but he sagely suppressed the urge to strike the Eastern lord. "You would take the field of battle, then stand aside while your countrymen, your fellow soldiers, were slaughtered before you? Take care, Prince, for your actions verge on cowardice and treachery!"

Theodore laughed, surprising the Frank, then leaned close, dropping his voice. "Barbarian, you struck a poor bargain. Your army is committed to battle, your allies weak, your enemies strong. I know that you have been conniving with that black-eyed whore son, but I do not hold it against you. Your plan was clever, bringing forth the Emperor's standard. You knew I would have to come forth out of the city or lose the confidence of my men— but hear this, I do not have to fight."

Dagobert ground his fist against his armored thigh, metal squeaking on metal. "We are Romans, we must stand together, fight together, or the Persians will brush us aside like gnats. The city will be besieged! What will you have then? Nothing."

Theodore smoothed his close-clipped beard down, smiling. "I will be rid of many traitors, barbarian. The Persians are the gnats buzzing about the walls of my city. They have tried twice before to take Constantinople and they have failed. This will be the third time. I say, let them come and bleed themselves to death on her walls."

"Fool!" Dagobert's temper snapped. "They have a fleet, you will be blockaded and starved out! We *must* defeat them in the field, then smash the remnants and drive off their ships. You must order your men into battle, restoring this flank and turning the Persian right wing."

"Must I?" Theodore rubbed his thumb and forefinger together. "Persuade me."

Dagobert heard a great rushing sound in his ears. He cast around, staring wildly at the long rows of Eastern cataphracts, at the small band of his own men, at the battle raging along the Arab wall. A great pall of dust spiraled up from the melee, broken by gusts of arrows flickering through the air. The Romans were falling back, fighting hard, anchored on the tight knot of red-cloaked guardsmen and the gleaming icon of the Emperor. The portrait was riddled with arrows, some of which were burning, adding trails of white smoke to the fume in the air. The Frank turned back to the Eastern prince, who was watching him and grinning.

"What . . . do . . . you . . . want?" Dagobert could barely make himself say the words. He felt dizzy, unable to grasp the incredible arrogance of the man. Who bartered for pigs on the battlefield? Where was this Eastern whelp's honor?

"My brother is very sick." Theodore straightened up, a sad look on his face. "He is not well enough to rule. His son, young Constantius, would make a fine emperor. Of course, he is not quite of his majority yet. He will need a regent."

Dagobert stared at the man's face, seeing the smile, the gleaming white teeth, the feral amusement dancing in his eyes. "That is monstrous."

"It is necessary!" Theodore snapped in a commanding voice. "The state is crippled. I will take command of these legions and crush the Persian wing. You and your master, the oh-so-noble Galen, Emperor of the West, will support me in placing Constantius on the throne under my regency for the next two years. Once this battle is done, you will also follow *my* command while we kennel these Persians and their Arab dogs."

"And your brother? What of him?" Dagobert felt a sickening gulf open under him.

"Our traditions hold," Theodore said in an offhand way, "a crippled man cannot be emperor. I am sure, after such a long sickness—my poor brother has lost a hand, a nose, some vital parts—he will be retired and can live out the rest of his unfortunately disease-ridden life on some quiet island, with his *wife*."

The Frank recoiled from the undisguised venom in the Prince's voice. *What do I do?* Dagobert cocked an ear, hearing the roar and clash of arms behind him. The Persians were pressing very hard against the Romans. Without the support of Theodore's heavy cavalry, the line might break, forcing the Romans away from the city and opening their right flank.

"Very well," Dagobert said, his heart sick. His face contorted, then settled into a frigid mask. "Constantius will be Emperor, and you his regent."

"Very wise." Theodore smiled genially. Then he raised his hand. For a hundred yards in every direction, thousands of armored men lifted their heads, seeing the signal flags rise up, echoing the Prince's motion. "Advance!"

Dagobert wheeled his horse away, cutting across the line of march. The Eastern cataphracts surged past, the earth rumbling with the trot of their horses. The Frank felt ill, but he had his own business to attend to.

Jusuf shaded his brown eyes with a hand, perplexed. "What *are* they doing now?"

Out on the plain, the regular blocks of the Roman line were shifting. The four Western Legions had advanced abreast across the irregular fields, then stopped. The main body of the Persians had matched their motion, leaving the two armies only a hundred feet or so apart. Clouds of arrows, sling-stones and javelins arched back and forth. Now—much to Jusuf's consternation—the Romans were angling away from the Khazar position, falling back on their right.

Dahvos, sitting astride his horse a few yards away, shrugged his shoulders, making his armor creak. "Their right wing must be falling back. Messenger!"

One of the courier riders scrambled up onto the crest of the hill. Both Khazars, as well as the coterie of staff and guardsmen that followed them, were standing on the eastern end of a low hill. The Khazar lines stretched off to their left, mostly arrayed across the slope and in the shallow valley between the Roman lines and the Arab position on the hill opposite. Down in the valley, there was a darting, swirling engagement between the Khazar light horse and their Arab counterparts. The main bodies of both armies remained in reserve, crouched on their respective hills. The Arabs seemed to have fielded a large army of heavily armored infantry, which stood in four deep ranks on the opposing slope, amid old fieldstone walls and abandoned vinyards. Their archers and slingers were busy sniping at the Khazar horse in the valley, or exchanging shots with the Khazar archers at the base of the hill.

"Lad, go find the Roman legate in command of the Tenth down there and find out what is going on." The courier dashed off, though he was not the first to speed between the two allied forces. Communication between the allies was poor. How many Romans spoke Turkish? How many Khazars could hold forth in Latin?

Dahvos bit his lip, eyeing the battle slowly unfolding before him. From this height, the scene took on a surreal quality, as if he were looking down from the heavens. Men were dying in droves down there, but here—in the slightly cooler breeze, among the softly rustling olive trees—there was a sensation of peace. "The Persians must be hammering the right, trying to break through to the road."

Jusuf nodded. "We shouldn't be here."

Dahvos sighed in agreement. Initially, putting the Khazar army on the left—all horsemen—had seemed like an excellent idea. *Put that down to bad scouting,* he thought ruefully. The Arabs crouched on the opposite hill had shown the fallacy of that. Dahvos was not willing to send his men across the soft ground in the shallow valley, then up a hill against massed infantry. "Truth. This is an infantry position. We're not going to be turning this flank."

"Your orders, khagan?" Jusuf smiled gently at his half-brother. "Do you want to try pushing the Arabs off their hill?"

"No!" Dahvos shook his head violently, pointing with his chin. "Not with half their line behind a stone wall and uphill, I won't."

"We could dismount our heavy horse, then strike down this slope on foot and into the Persian flank. The rest of the *umens* could cover the advance with archery." Jusuf motioned down the rolling slope below them. There were low walls here, too, the remains of old farms and houses, then the flats and the Roman line. Dahvos tapped his teeth with a thumb.

"No, we won't do that either. If we leave the hill our flank is exposed and we lose mobility. Jusuf, take all of the heavy horse back through the orchards, onto the road, and swing behind the Tenth Fretensis. Then the Legion can cover your flanks and you can get to grips with the Persians."

Startled, the older man shook his head in dismay. "Dahvos, are you sure? We'd have to back eight thousand men off this hill, march through those narrow lanes and hedgerows to get to the road. Let me take the heavy lancers straight ahead—our horse archers and light horse can cover the wing."

Jusuf half turned in his saddle, motioning with a gloved hand at the plain. "Look, the Persians have drawn off all their cavalry to the far end of their line. There's nothing down there but spearmen backed by archers and slingers! We can crack right through them!"

"And the Arab horse?" Dahvos slapped a hand against

his thigh with a *crack*. "They have a reserve, too, though we've not seen it. They must be hiding back behind their infantry, just like ours are hidden in these trees. They will countercharge into you and you'll be exposed and afoot. Get the lancers back off the hill and follow my orders!"

Jusuf met his brother's eyes, feeling a tension in the air between them. There was a fierce light in the younger man's blue eyes. Jusuf ran a hand back through his hair, feeling his scalp slick with sweat. *He is kagan,* thought the Khazar, *and he is probably right.*

"Yes, kagan," Jusuf barked, raising an arm in salute. "As you command."

He turned the horse and trotted off through the ragged lane of olive trees. He felt anxious, hurried, eager to be done with this thing. Jusuf shook his head as he rode, regretting the harsh tone in his parting words. *But there is no time to lose in argument or apology.*

"Tarkhans, attend me!" he shouted as he rode through the orchard, drawing the attention of his banner leaders. "Leave your men who are exposed on the crest; everyone else reverse and follow me. We're back to the road!"

Nearly seven thousand Khazar lancers swarmed onto their horses, slapping helmets on their heads, stowing waterskins. The orchard quickly filled with dust and a deafening racket as the tumen mounted up and then turned in place. Jusuf was quickly hoarse from shouting, trying to bully the men into order again and get them moving back down the hill. Thousands of men did not reverse direction easily.

Oh, he thought in disgust, watching a pall of white dust drift up above the trees, *this is secret, all right.*

A thicket of spears crashed into the shield wall. Rufio, standing shoulder to shoulder with the Faithful, felt the blow on his shoulder and hip. A wild screaming filled the air as the Slavs and their Avar masters stormed in again, slipping and sliding on ground thick with a slurry of blood, mud and entrails. Three times the Avars and their levies had rushed the Faithful, trying to break through the Roman line, and three times the staunch defense had thrown them back in bloody ruin. Bodies were heaped up on all sides, limbs hewn off, faces cut open, heads lolling at impossible angles. Rufio twisted his shield, slipping a spear point, though it ripped across the painted linen. The Greek stabbed out, his gladius licking against the arm of a Slav.

The black-bearded man shrieked like a harpy, stabbing wildly overhand, trying to strike Rufio's head or neck. He barely noticed the tempered steel of the sword sink into his bicep and then rip out again. Nerveless fingers slipped from the haft of the spear and it clattered away, disappearing among the sweaty, straining men on all sides. Rufio smashed out with his shield, cracking the iron-bound rim against the man's face. The Slav gasped, blood spattering from a ruined nose, then shuddered as Rufio's blade plunged into his armpit. He fell away.

The Greek had no respite. Two heavily armored Avars, their scale mail gleaming under fur cloaks and yellow-and-brown surcoats, pressed in behind the dying Slav. Both barbarians were fighting afoot, though Rufio glimpsed they were wearing the long split iron "skirt" favored by the Eastern nomads. A straight sword jabbed at the Greek's face, ringing off his helmet guard as he ducked aside at the last moment. Desperate, for both men were obviously veterans, Rufio jammed his scutum up, catching their swords as they lunged and knocking them away. Shouting for the Faithful on either side to follow, he rushed forward, slamming into the body of the first Avar.

The man's high-cheekboned face disappeared behind the heavy shield with a ringing *crack* as the wood hit his riveted helmet. Rufio slashed sideways at the other horseman, but the point of the gladius grated across the iron lozenges of his armor, then stuck between two of the palm-sized plates. The Avar's sword snapped back, biting into the edge of Rufio's shield. The soft iron squeaked as Eastern steel bit into it. Rufio kicked out, catching the man on his hip. The Avar grunted, then both rushed forward. The Greek's shield took the blow and he was knocked down, sliding back through the grayish-red slurry.

Rufio twisted, trying to rise, but the first Avar leapt in hacking and the long, straight blade rang off the shoulder plate of the Greek's lorica. Stunned, Rufio was thrown down again. Feet and legs flashed past his face, then the sun was blocked out. A great roaring sound erupted around the captain. The Faithful stormed forward over his body, their long axes hacking and spinning in the sunlight. One of the Avars fell, his shield cloven in half by a huge blow, arm shattered. Rufio staggered up, clutching at Olaf's arm. The old Scandian stood over the captain, protecting him with his body.

"Form shield wall!" He barely managed to gasp out the words, but the Faithful were already pressing forward, in a tight knot, shoulder to shoulder, their massive shields making a solid wall across the front. Arrows hissed past in the air. A dozen more Slav and Avar bodies lay crumpled on the ground. Rufio seated his helmet again, tightening the strap under his chin. The air seemed enormously hot and he was sweating rivers under his heavy armor, but he pushed up into the line of battle.

The hundred-and-twenty-yard front between the barrier of the Arab wall on the left and the ditch in front of the city wall was tightly compressed, but both Avar and Eastern troops continued to pour into the fray, fueling the ferocious struggle with more and more bodies.

Off to the west, beyond the ruined wall, Rufio was vaguely aware of a mounting roar of men and iron and the thunder of hooves shaking the earth.

"Cousin." Zoë held out her left hand, gloved in gleaming mail. Odenathus was astride his horse, close by, and the glossy brown mare stepped delicately forward, bringing her rider leg to leg with Zoë's. The young Palmyrene, his long, lean face filled with worry, reached out and clasped fingers with his cousin. "Are you ready?"

"I am." Odenathus' liquid brown eyes met hers, steady and unflinching. "Do you remember when he couldn't even keep a wagon wheel in the air?"

"Yes." A terrible sadness gripped Zoë, though she knew that Dwyrin had done nothing to bring about this day. He, of all their little five, had remained true to his oaths and sworn allegiance. Everyone else had lost faith, from emperors to queens. "I remember. But he is not a lost child anymore. We must be swift in action, relentless, like a striking hawk."

Odenathus nodded, but she could see her own despair mirrored in his expression. Even through his heavy glove and her armor, she could feel the heat in his hand.

"Meet my mind," she commanded, closing her eyes.

Zoë and Odenathus bent towards each other, putting away all thought of the horses under their thighs, the hot wind in their hair, the distant thunder of battle. Zoë felt the shell of her self slough away and she raised her eyes, looking out across the storm of light and shadow and fire that marked the battle. Men struggled and died, their tiny flames sputtering out, leaving a horde of ghosts raging in the air over the plain. The brittle patterns of the Roman thaumaturges remained as well, distorting the air over the battle lines of the Legions. But there on the ruined wall was a burning light like a sun rising through fog.

Dwyrin. Zoë flinched away from the glowing star, realizing that he could feel her touch, even through the storm of hate and fear and rage that billowed up from the battle, fouling the air and twisting the patterns of the world. A vision of his face—such a familiar, freckled, grinning face—all slick with sweat and haggard, drained, lingered with her.

There is no margin for friendship, she growled at herself, raising her arms. Odenathus moved with her, his thought entwined in hers, making them more than a single mage. With a full five in tandem, like a swift, skilled racing team, they could exert tremendous pressure upon the pattern of the world. Now, with only two of them, they would have to trade speed for power.

Zoë's will leapt across the embattled plain. Odenathus was with her, his strength hers, his will anchoring her like a mountain. Dwyrin's wards rose up, a burning sphere a hundred feet across, enclosing the boy and the frightful icon that blazed with such ferocity at the heart of the Roman army.

The Palmyrene Queen ignored the looming shape of the Emperor, his head wreathed in storm clouds, thunder on his brow, lightning leaping from gauntleted hands. The men fighting among the shadows of his feet might feel their hearts lifted, weary limbs given strength, fear banished, but she knew only a terrible burning hatred for the Empire that had betrayed her.

"The city and the Queen!" She punched at the wavering figure of the boy, hidden behind his swirling, inchoate shield of disks and signs. Lightning leapt at her touch, raging against the wards. Sigils burst into brilliant light, touched by her power. The whole sphere de-formed, spidering with cracks, as it shook from the blow.

Behind the ward, Dwyrin staggered as well, stunned by the fury in the stroke.

"The city!" Lightning burned, flooding the plain with an actinic white glare. The Hibernian was thrown down on the ground, his spirit form stunned. The outer surface of the ward splintered, shedding smoking flakes of orange light, then shattered along one of the cardinal points. Zoë's entire mind was engaged, letting the hate and fury that she had carried from the ruin of Palmyra flood forth. Her spirit arm slashed down again, wringing dark lightning from the sky.

The oblate sphere flattened, then cracked through. Dwyrin screamed, the side of his face burning with ultraviolet flames. His hand rose up, will rallying. The flames eating at his skin died. Power flooded from the sky and the earth to him, leaping like a wadi in storm flood, and a skein of light sprang up around him. Zoë staggered back, feeling the echo of that strength. Lightning leapt from her fingers again, playing across the glittering shield, but arced away uselessly.

Dwyrin's will turned upon her, focused like a Syracusian mirror, and he clenched his fists, then slammed them down. The earth buckled and shook, and a blast of flame leapt up, slashing across her. Zoë leapt to the side, feeling the heat of the bolt hiss past. Inwardly, she quailed, seeing his power rising like the sun, growing stronger and stronger.

O Dusarra, aid me! She dug deep into the earth, groping for strength in rock and stone and deeply hidden water, but there was nothing there. The land was already stripped bare, the *mana* in its heart swallowed up in this conflagration. A bare blue flicker of the Shield of Athena sprang up around her and she rushed through a mnemonic to reinforce the—

A pure white bolt exploded from Dwyrin's open hand, bursting through her shield with a hammer blow. Zoë screamed, her spirit shattering, burning blue shards ripping across her. Everything whirled down toward darkness, though she clung to consciousness with a grim effort. She fled, leaping across the field, rushing for the safety of physicality. Glowing white shapes rushed around her, snatching at her with burning teeth.

Dwyrin had grown huge, like a god himself, dwarfing even the figure of the spirit-emperor. His hand reached out for her, a ghostly shade lit from within by lightning. Zoë turned on the hilltop, her ghostly shape crouched over her own pale, sweating body. A ring of lightning blazed up around her, tearing the hounds of light into fragments. Her slim hand clutched at the sky, dragging down the thin power in the wind, then stabbed out at Dwyrin.

The Hibernian shrugged off the blow, though his shape

dwindled. He was rocked, staggered by the blast. Zoë smiled grimly, catching lightning in her fingers, twisting it into a new pattern of attack. Now his orange ward sprang up again, though it was patchy and weak. The enormous strength that had filled him only moments before was fading. She could feel his weariness.

Dwyrin! Her words leapt across the dark void between them and his head snapped up, blue eyes burning, a word forming on his lips.

Odenathus struck, bursting from hiding amongst the struggling shapes of men, green fire blazing from his brow, leaping from his striking hand. The bolt raged across Dwyrin, crumpling the pale orange shell around him. He cried out, stricken, and fell. Black flames licked up around him, and Odenathus struck again, his pattern grim and frightful, driving a blazing viridian spear into the boy's heart.

Zoë cried out, feeling an overwhelming burst of pain leap across the remnants of their old battle-meld. She staggered, clutching her chest. Breath failed in her throat.

Khadames, grunting with effort, parried the overhand blow of a Roman cataphract. His sword rang like a bell, then the old Persian went hilt to hilt with the Eastern soldier. Their horses jostled, each biting viciously at the other. Khadames punched the man in the face with his fist, the reinforced metal gauntlets cutting the Roman's cheek. Grappling, they struggled for a moment, but then another Persian clibanarus thrust a spear into the Roman's side. Metal links snapped and parted under the blow and then a trickle of blood appeared under the man's helmet.

Sweating and gasping for breath, Khadames pushed the dying Roman away, spurring at his horse, trying to break out of the press of men and horses all around him. The Sarmatian attack had broken on the Persian diquans, unable to build up the momentum to use their *kontos* effectively. In these close quarters the Persians' armored horses lent them the advantage. Most of the nomads were falling back, trying to break away from the clibanarii.

"Form diamond! Form diamond!" Khadames rode among his men, shouting and gesturing with his sword. Off to his left, towards the ruined Arab fortification, the Immortals were vigorously engaged in slaughtering the remainder of the Roman infantry holding them back from the road. Some of the pushtigbahn were already fighting on the metaled, stone surface of the highway. Two of the Roman Legion standards had fallen, hacked to bits by the Persians. The legionaries, disordered, were unable to hold back the heavily armored horsemen. "Bows! Ready bows!"

The old general pushed up his visor, letting a blessedly cool breeze wash over his face. His men were riding or running back towards his banners, forming up again. There was very little time. Another great mass of Romans—their heavy horse, the cataphractoi—were already surging forward, brushing the remnants of the Sarmatians aside. Like his own clibanarii, they were armed with horse bows and armored from head to toe. Khadames rose up in his stirrups, glancing left and right, gauging the order of his troops. Many men had lost their horses and were now fighting on foot.

"Bows!" he screamed, his voice thin and hoarse, but enough of his captains heard the call to pass the order on through the swelling ranks. Each regiment was clustering around their own banners, making a patchwork line three ranks deep. Across the field, now littered with dead and dying horses and men, the Romans were beginning to trot, gathering speed. Khadames watched them come, each grain passing with agonizing slowness, as his own men snatched bows from their *gorytos,* strung them in quick, assured motions, then drew arrows to the notch. The Romans were sweeping forward now, swords, maces and long spears in hand, rushing ahead.

"Loose!" Khadames slashed his sword down, feeling the air ripple with the singing *thwack* of massed bows firing.

At this range, barely a hundred feet, the shafts flicked across the distance in a heartbeat. "Loose!" The second rank of Persians shot through gaps in the first rank. The Roman charge staggered, slammed by a storm of arrows. Despite hundreds of men being hit, dark fletched shafts hanging from armor and shields, the Romans came on.

A thunder of hooves rolled before them and dust mounted into the sky behind. Khadames shook his head, surprised that their commander had ordered such a hasty charge. The old Persian would have chosen to rake the mass of the enemy with his archery first. "Loose!"

The third rank of Persians shot high, lofting their arrows over the heads of the first two lines of horse. Those di-quans had stowed their bows and closed up, forming a solid mass, bared long swords, lances and maces in hand. These Romans would not find a disordered foe! Khadames spurred his horse forward, galloping down the line of battle. Everywhere he saw his men standing firm and resolute. Now, he thought, they could advance again into the maw of battle. The stain of the defeat at Kerenos River was black on the honor of Persia. Khadames grinned wildly, seeing brave honor etched on the faces of his kinsmen.

"Advance!" Trumpets and horns echoed his call, and all three ranks of horsemen began to move forward. Better to be moving, when mass collided with mass!

Then, over the heads of his knights, Khadames saw the Romans burst forth from the cloud of dust, charging full speed into his line. At their center, three ranks back, also rushing forward, he saw a tall man in gleaming golden armor, surrounded by many cataphracts in silvered mail. The old general's eyes widened in surprise. What fool wore such gaudy armor in the middle of a battle? *The Emperor? Impossible!*

"Archers! Archers to me!" Khadames curveted his horse. Three men in the rear ranks of the nearest regiment turned towards him, black beards bristling from their helmets.

"Lord General! We are archers!" Their voices boomed with the accents of Balkh, that ancient Eastern city on the green waters of the Oxus. The middle one, a tall fellow with mighty arms, spurred his horse forward. A bow was already in his hands, wrapped on the upper stave with a length of black silk. "What is your command?"

"There, do you see the man in gold?" Khadames pointed urgently out over the field. The Romans were only an instant from collision with his forces rushing forward.

"I do!" shouted the archer, flipping up his visor. He was young but well made, with clear dark eyes and a classic Persian nose. "Like a king or a god!"

"Kill him," snapped Khadames, "kill him, and the shahanshah will give you great honor!"

"I do not want honor," shouted the man, bending his bow, a long gray-fletched arrow already on the notch. "I'd have his daughter's hand instead!"

Khadames laughed, for now he knew the man, Piruz of Balkh, Prince of the North. "Then shoot well, Prince, and you will have your heart's desire!"

Forty feet away, the charging Romans slammed into the trotting Persian line in a huge *crash* of metal on metal and the screaming of horses. Immediately, the front line was embroiled in a vicious hand-to-hand struggle. Though the Roman horses refused to charge pell-mell into the solid wall of Persians, the momentum of their attack staggered the diquans. Khadames almost immediately found himself surrounded by struggling, fighting men. His own blade licked out, clanging off an upraised Roman sword. The heat returned, descending upon him like a burning cloak.

Piruz, sweat running down his neck and into the felt undercoat of his armor, sighted across the field, seeing his enemy shouting commands, rising up above his men in a waving sanguine forest of swords and lances. The Prince breathed, letting his heart settle. The bow stave flexed away from him as his left hand pressed against the bone-

covered back. Goose feathers tickled his brow as he raised
the bow up, a hiss of air passing his clenched teeth. The
roar of battle receded from his thoughts. Everything was
silent.

The man in gold turned to face him, his face a graven-
steel mask. Piruz saw, in that frozen moment, that the Roman armor lapped over his enemies' shoulders and arms
in fitted bands of iron. Ribbons hung down from the
peaked helm and a maroon tabard lay over his shoulders.
The golden king's voice boomed, urging his men onward.
Piruz did not know this Western tongue, but he saw a
powerful man in the thick of battle.

This is an honorable death, thought the Persian and he
loosed, the arrow singing away from the stave, arcing up
into the air, only one of many that flashed across the sky.
The stillness remained, his breathing slow, the long moment passing so slowly . . . Piruz' hand moved of its own
accord, drawing another arrow from the wooden quiver,
the smooth ashwood sliding against the curve of the bow
stave.

The arrow fell, spiraling down out of the sky. The
golden man was looking away, his arm waving, gleaming
in the sun. The triangular iron head of the arrow struck his
gorget of flattened iron links, shattering on the metal
plates. Piruz could not hear the sound it made, but he could
see sparks leap from the armor.

Again the Persian raised his bow, his movement effortless, the wind catching the black silk and ruffling it back
and forth. He knew that a mighty tumult was all around
him, a roaring and a clashing of arms, a titanic noise, but
he heard nothing but the wind singing against the horsehair
string of his bow. He drew, sighted, loosed, all in one
breath.

Amid a roil of color and iron and banners and bloody
steel, the golden man was slumping into the arms of his
fellows, his hand rising up to clutch at the sky. Crimson
welled from beneath the gorget, spilling across the golden

breastplate. One of the other Romans unclasped the visor from his helmet, letting cool wind kiss the man's golden hair. Piruz saw the distant face turn up to the sun, to the blue bowl of the sky.

The second arrow fell from the sun, glittering, and plunged into the man's eye. A violent convulsion wracked his body, his guardsmen crying out, closing about him, their swords bare. Piruz lost sight of the golden armor and the dying man it held.

Sound and motion returned, washing over the Persian in a huge billowing roar. He blinked, then shouted in alarm, seeing three Romans spurring towards him.

"Balkh! Balkh and Purandokht!" he screamed, hastily stowing the bow in its fleece-lined case. His hand closed around the haft of a mace and Piruz turned his horse, shield rising between him and the first attacker. His household troops rushed towards him like hawks, coming at his call. "The Empress! The Empress!"

The air trembled, slow-rising pillars of dust twisting in the wind off the Propontis. Mohammed rode under a green banner, held high at his shoulder by that young scamp Khalid. Under the hooves of his flea-bitten mare, high grass bent and swayed in the wind. The *qalb* of the Sahaba rode on all sides, trotting down the long grassy slope of the hill. A gently waving forest of lances and helmets was opening out into a great wedge as they moved.

In his heart, Mohammed felt a great relief. Khalid's scouts had passed on word that the Emperor had come forth, battling alongside his Legions. *My journey is almost complete,* he thought. The Quraysh clucked at the horse and she pricked her ears up, then began to canter, moving faster and faster as they swept down the hill. The drumming of hooves rumbling all around him, the qalb began to pick up speed.

Khalid shouted in joy, raising the green banner, letting it stream in the wind of their passage. Mohammed grinned back, feeling a great and encompassing sense of camaraderie with the young captain, for the Sahaba who flowed so swiftly over the ground, for all of the men who had chosen to follow him. Heavily armored guardsmen rode around him in a constantly moving circle. Mohammed knew they were Khalid's men, carefully chosen to protect him in this brazen charge. For a moment, the Quraysh regretted that his own Tanukh had become scattered through the army, serving as captains, as banner leaders, even generals.

Where is Shadin now? he wondered. *Has he seen the green banks of the Nile?*

A great rolling shout suddenly erupted from the throats of the Sahaba, thundering across the fields. Ahead of them, across a wide swale of stumps and broken walls, the massed ranks of the Legion grew larger with each stride of the horses. Mohammed reached down and half drew the blade of night, letting the sun gleam in its inky depths, feeling a fierce joy rush up in him.

"Allau Akbar!" roared his men, spreading out, galloping forward, their lances dipping down, shining in the sun, the wind whipping their banners and plumes back. *"Allau Akbar!"*

Mohammed rose up in his stirrups, the black saber singing over his head, and his own voice joined the rolling, enormous shout. A madness filled the men, he could hear it hissing in his own blood, a reckless passion for battle. *"Allau Akbar!"*

Ahead of them, the Roman legionaries were grounding their shields, shifting into a tortoiselike formation, their golden and red standards waving at the center of each line. The rear ranks would be readying their javelins, waiting for their centurions' basso shout, waiting, waiting, watching the enemy hurtle closer.

Mohammed slashed down with the blade, feeling an electric shock run up his arm. The saber trembled in his hand like a live thing, eager for battle, straining to leap into the throats of his enemies. Everything was narrowing down to a hazy gray tunnel, focused solely on the faces of the Romans, sweating and pale, who stood before him.

"Allau Akbar!"

The Arab charge swept down into the shallow stream, water leaping up in white plumes from the hooves of the horses. In an instant they were past the barrier, surging up in an unending stream of leather and steel and screaming men, and crashed into the Roman ranks. Kontos, leveled in the charge, speared into the Roman shields, the horses, mad, shouldering into the mass of legionaries. Twelve-foot lances punched through armor and laminated wood alike, crushing the first rank of swordsmen with a rippling, unending *crash*.

"Allau Akbar!"

Mohammed slashed down, the edge of the black saber cleaving through the Roman soldier's shield, his arm and the leather straps that held the wooden *scuta* to his bicep. The young man shrieked in agony, feeling his arm tear away. The Quraysh was already past the beardless boy, his blade whipping around, splintering through the helmet of another Roman. Gray and red spurted from the side of the man's head and he too was down.

The Quraysh surged forward, slashing his way through two and then three ranks of Romans. The legionaries seemed stunned and filled with fear. The Arab charge, heedless and unstoppable, tore through their ranks. Legionaries fell on all sides, hewn down by the ferocity of the Arabs. A brief flurry of javelins arched up, falling into the ranks of the Sahaba. Horses screamed, their flanks pierced, but the faithful, gripped by blood fury, did not pause. Did not the faithful ascend to Paradise upon death, to sit at the right hand of the Lord of the World? Against such a reward, a brave death was little payment.

"Allau Akbar!"

Mohammed whirled the mare around in a half-circle, his powerful arm slashing the black saber down again and again. At his side, the massive guardsman that followed Khalid was also laying to with a will, a mace in either hand. The Romans began to break, faltering, some running, a few—older men, centurions—standing fast, stabbing at the horsemen around them with remorseless efficiency. Mohammed rushed one of them, a gray-bearded veteran crouching behind the square shelter of his shield. The fierce madness that howled in the Sahaba filled his sword arm with irresistible strength.

The Roman's gladius slashed at the red mare's face, but she danced aside, her hooves light on the ground. Mohammed let her take the lead, then leaned over, his right arm whipping down. The point of the black saber cracked through the shield like a lightning bolt, shattering wood and linen and hide. The centurion cried out in fear, then the sound was cut short by a harsh gargling. Mohammed wrenched the blade free, seeing it slide out of the shield slick with blood.

"Sahaba! Sahaba to me! On! On!"

A bellow answered him, the faithful swarming up on all sides, their armor streaked with blood, their horses' fetlocks red with gore. The Romans were running, some casting their swords and shields away, others wandering, stunned, on the field.

"Allau Akbar!"

Dwyrin gasped, his heart splintered by a blazing green dagger plunged into his chest. Above him, wreathed in smoke, silhouetted by the abyssal vastness of a black sky, Odenathus towered like a giant. The Palmyrene's face was contorted with rage and hate, his hands twisting the spirit weapon in the Hibernian's heart. Dwyrin felt the edges of his self shudder and dissolve, his essential being flaking away from the raging viridian fire.

Only the whirling interlocking spheres at his heart remained steadfast. Dwyrin gasped, his mind nearly paralyzed by agony. He knew that his physical body was contorted, thrashing on the cold ground, fingernails digging into the loamy earth. Dissolution beckoned, offering release from the waves of searing pain that swept through him, tearing at his concentration.

There is the spear of fire, which cannot be quenched by man, or undone, but lights the world.

A voice called to him from a great distance, speaking in an unknown tongue. Dwyrin heard it, blood leaking from his mouth, and resolve flooded into him, steeling his will. All these things—the fire, the burning dagger, pain— were illusion. On the bleak ground, his fist clenched and his eyes opened; he was free of pain.

Odenathus met his gaze, furious, then the rage and hatred cleared and Dwyrin saw his friend looking back at him. Tears were leaking from the corners of the Palmyrene's eyes.

They were sitting in the darkness, listening to men singing in the night, sharing an amphora of wine. They were tired from a long day of effort, moving the Legion carruca across a wooden bridge and into the great camp. Dwyrin had never felt such a weary, comfortable peace before. His heart was content, smelling the smoke of the cookfires, feeling the cool air of night on his face.

Dwyrin slashed his hand up, letting the power curling and smoking in his heart burst free. There was agonizing pain again, ripping through his brutalized, overextended body, but the blow shattered Odenathus' spirit form. A high-pitched wail grated against Dwyrin's nerves, but the Palmyrene youth's looming figure was suddenly and violently gone. The Hibernian surged up, the hissing point of light flooding his will and intellect with strength. He looked upon the distant hillside, covered with short brown grass, and saw his old companions slumped astride their horses. Zoë's spirit was dancing, weaving a pattern in the air, her fingers blurring in frantic motion.

Dwyrin leapt forward, his fists burning with power. With a swift motion, he drew a fist to his heart, then flashed it out, palm forward. A burning black mote snapped out from his hand, shrieking through the air. Millions of tiny burning sparks—the air itself in all its ceaseless motion—corkscrewed around the track of the black mote, which swelled enormously as it rushed forward.

Zoë's eyes widened and Dwyrin could feel her fear rush up like a whale breaching in the slate-gray sea off some Hibernian shore. Then the mote—swollen to an enormous black disk—struck her azure lattice and shattered it, a hammer plowing through a glass cup. Zoë screamed, a hopeless wail, and her spirit form dissolved. The mote exploded, blasting away the lattice and the scattered patterns still drifting around the crown of the hill.

Dwyrin sagged to his knees, the hill growing distant, shrouded by the haze of battle. Weariness washed up again, stronger than before, and he could barely concentrate. His will slipped, evaporating, and he was in his body again, drenched with sweat, still lying on the parapet of the old Arab fortification. The golden glow that had emanated from the Emperor's portrait was gone, leaving only clouds of dust drifting over Dwyrin's body. All around him, the roar of battle continued unabated. Vladimir had disappeared, leaving him alone.

The boy wept with exhaustion and grief, his face turned to the dusty white sky.

A rattle of drums echoed back from the towering walls of Constantinople. Rufio, leaning on his sword, exhausted, his face bleeding from a bad cut, raised his head. The Avars were falling back, their fourth attack on the battle line of the Faithful a corpse-laden failure. Fewer than five hundred of the original two thousand Scandians were still able to fight. Mismatched cohorts from the Sixth Ferrata and the Fourth Parthica formed most of the line. Their ranks were very thin. A wide swath of Avar and Slav bodies carpeted the ground in front of the shield wall. Flies were beginning to gather, drifting in huge clouds over the dead.

"Hold your positions!" Rufio barked, stilling a movement by the Faithful to advance. "Find your centurions and maniples, regroup!"

The Scandians milled about, their faces red and slick with sweat. Their shields were nicked and splintered. Some men had been fighting wounded and now they were culled from the front ranks by their centurions. Rufio climbed the side of the Arab rampart, Olaf and some of his kinsmen at his back. The golden glow from the Emperor's standard had died out. The captain of the Faithful was concerned. The effort of holding the Avar attack had consumed all of his attention, and it had left him on the city side of the Arab fortifications. A whole other battle was still raging out on the open plain.

When he reached the top of the wall, he cursed, seeing that the cohort of Faithful protecting the icon of the Emperor had been forced back through the double rampart and ditch and were engaged in a sharp melee with a group of Persian diquans. Rufio spun, then shouted down at the men on the city side of the rampart.

"Reserves, up here on the double! Fourth Parthica, forward!"

The cataphracts of the Fourth wheeled their horses around as soon as they heard his call and galloped up the road that cut through the ramparts. Rufio waved them on, then slid down the bank of loose earth himself. Nearly a hundred of the Faithful sprinted after him, a bellow of rage on their lips. No Scandian would fight alone today! Legionaries from the Sixth also scrambled up the rampart and began sliding down the inner slope.

Rufio ran forward, the soft ground yielding under his boots. Faced with Roman reinforcements, the Persians were beginning to fall back. Half of their number began shooting from horseback, black-feathered arrows winging over Rufio's head. He turned his shield and angled it towards them. The Emperor's icon was smoking from fire arrows that had been shot into it. Luckily, the heavy glass and gold was not flammable. Horns blew, summoning the Persian horsemen back beyond the outer rampart.

Reaching the side of the men holding up the icon, Rufio gasped for breath. "What has happened? Why did you fall back?"

The nearest of the men, his face running with blood, the stump of an arrow jutting from his shoulder, turned towards him. "Captain, the iron men broke, driven back onto the road. We barely escaped through the wall. Some men were shouting that Prince Theodore is dead."

"Dead?" Rufio's face split with a snarl. "The worthless bastard!"

A mounted cataphract of the Fourth rode up, his helmet plumes indicating that he was a cohort commander, or *ekatontarch*. He leaned down. "Captain, the Persians have fallen back, but I see fighting on the road ahead. What do we do?"

"Attack up the highway immediately," Rufio snapped, wishing he had a horse. He couldn't see very far from down on the ground. "We must not let the Persians break through. I will send the rest of the Parthica up to support you, and as many of the Sixth Ferrata as we can spare."

The ekatontarch sketched a salute, then galloped off. A column of his men hurried after, blowing their signal horns. Rufio turned back to the standard bearers. "You men," he shouted, pointing at the Faithful who had followed him over the wall, "take this icon. All these men are wounded, they must go back to the city immediately."

Grunting with effort, the Greek took the edge of the heavy platform himself, letting the Scandian with the bloody face fall to his knees. "Come on," Rufio shouted, "take up this burden." At his feet, the wounded man coughed blood, making a bright patch on the dark soil. Dozens of the Faithful crowded around, thick hands grasping the platform and helping their companions away. As soon as the icon was secure, Rufio let go.

"Take the standard to the top of that wall, so that all

might see the Emperor still stands!" The Faithful, voices raised in a marching chant, began to move away towards the inner wall of the fortification. Rufio, after taking a deep breath, ran in the other direction, towards the roar and clatter of battle on the other side of the outer rampart. Olaf and his kinsmen followed, though within moments one of them staggered, struck by a Persian arrow, and fell onto the loamy ground.

"Stand! Stand and fight!" Dagobert's throat was raw, burning with thirst. Despite the weakness in his left arm—badly bruised by a Persian mace—he urged his stallion forward through the ranks of the Third Augusta. Arrows whipped past him in both directions. The Western troops were faltering, trapped between the main body of the Persian army to their front, and now the Persian knights on their right. The remains of the Sarmatian lancers were fighting shoulder to shoulder with the Frankish dux and his household *fyrdmen*. Another Persian arrow smashed into his shield, the point burying itself in the thick wood. Dagobert felt sick.

His only consolation was the thought that no one would ever know of his foul bargain with Theodore. News of the death of the Prince, stricken by a stray arrow, flashed through the ranks of the Eastern Legions, reaching Dagobert only minutes after the man had gasped out his last breath in the mud. A great groan of fear went up from the Eastern troops, inspiring the Persians to redouble their attack.

The Persian clibanarii had broken through to the highway, but Dagobert and his Sarmatians had managed to stem the collapse of the Western right flank. The Easterners had flooded away, fleeing towards the city, but even that panicked motion seemed to have halted.

Perhaps we can still re-form our line . . . A wild blowing of bucinas and cornicens off to his left interrupted Dagobert's train of thought. The Frank wheeled his horse towards the sound, peering across the gleaming helmets of his troops. Far off to the left, where the Western line joined the Khazars on their hill, he could see a roil of dust and the signs of battle.

"Follow me!" Dagobert spurred his horse forward, swinging out of the melee. His mouth was dry with fear. The fighting was far in back of where the Roman front should have been. Darkness hung in the air over the ranks of men. The Sarmatians galloped after him, their lances swinging up. The Frank whipped his horse, sending it bolting forward. He was behind the Roman line now, racing past groups of wounded men trudging back towards the camp in the hills. They stared up at him as he thundered past.

Ahead, a sudden *crash* shook the air and the afternoon brightened with the flicker of lightning in the clear air. Dagobert felt his fear grow, clawing at his throat.

Boom! Fire leapt up on the plain and a roiling cloud of black smoke began to climb into the sky. More lightning flashed. Dagobert could see men running, throwing down their helmets and shields. Clouds of dark gray smoke drifted among the ranks.

Dwyrin's head jerked up, eyes smudged with fatigue. Something was moving in the hidden world: a shape, a presence like a mountain, a glowing, brilliant white star. He blinked furiously, trying to see. What he could hear, though, was a great moan of fear rising from the ranks of the Roman army. Dwyrin scrambled to his feet, head averted from the blinding light.

"Gods of my fathers . . ." Vladimir stood on the rampart, mouth open, a look of utter fear upon his face. Dwyrin grasped his shoulder, hiding his head behind the solid bulk of the Walach. The effort was fruitless; the sinew and bone of the Walach were translucent, incapable of shutting out the burning radiance.

"Vlad, what do you see?"

"A pillar of fire striding across the plain." Vladimir choked out the words. "It walks like a giant! Our men are running. They are being struck down by the lightning!"

Dwyrin's fingers dug into the Walach's fur cloak. He was so tired he could barely stand up. Both legs were trembling. "Vlad, you must take care of my body. I am going to . . . stop that thing. My spirit may not come back, but don't leave my body behind!"

"I understand." Vladimir couldn't tear his eyes away from the storm of lightning and roiling smoke darkening the plain, but his powerful arms hoisted the boy up onto his back, holding him as if he were a cub being carried across a rushing stream. "I won't leave you."

Dwyrin closed his eyes again, veins in his forehead throbbing, breath quick and shallow. Fire beckoned, the flame that burned at his heart.

Mohammed raised his hand, a booming roar of thunder echoing his motion. His eyes rolled up, spittle drooled from the side of his mouth. Lightning leapt from his fingers, ripping across the panicked mob of Roman legionaries. Hundreds of men were dying in the motion, shrieking in fear, their cloaks bursting into flame, skin charring. Arcs of violent purple light leapt from sword to cuirass to spear, setting cloth and leather afire. The sky darkened with swirling clouds, and fires raged across the plain, sending up pillars of white smoke. The sun faded, shrouded in fumes.

Under him, the mare trembled and shook from the tips of her ears to the end of her tail, unable to move. Thunder cracked and rolled in a constant shattering roar overhead. The Roman thaumaturges were stricken down in the first moment of the attack. Now the Western legionaries fled before him. The entire Legion facing the charge of the Arab *qalb* had been slammed aside by the weight of their arms, then scattered by this sudden apparition.

Bow down, idolators! Bow down before the true God!

The voice from the clear air made the earth shake, collapsing those few buildings still standing in the old suburbs of the city. Mohammed seemed to be at a great height, striding over the field, seeing the running men as tiny ants fleeing his shadow. He raised his other hand and winds lashed the plain, springing from boiling black clouds. Lightning stabbed down, leaving burning trails in the air, tearing great fiery craters in the ground.

Here is the wrath that was promised to the unbeliever!

Mohammed was distantly aware the horse under him was dying, her brave old heart suddenly failing. His physical self toppled to the ground, but he had no need of such a thing anymore. The power that spoke from the mountaintop, the Lord of the Wasteland, had entered him. He had no need of anything.

If you do not follow the righteous path, then the fires of Hell await. . . .

A blast of fire rocked Mohammed back. Orange and red flames raged around him, enveloping his towering body, fire eating away at his phantasmal limbs. In an instant he was no longer a giant figure of smoke and lightning, but a man lying on the ground, staring at the sky in a daze. Khalid and his guardsmen were huddled around him, trying to burrow into the earth. Mohammed staggered up, head ringing with the echo of that titanic voice.

"What . . . what was that?" He stared around, gaze suddenly settling on a point of brilliant orange light to the southeast, near the gates of the city. Great drifts of dark smoke blew across the field, driven by eddying winds. Everywhere before him there was the litter of war: spears, arrows sticking up from the ground, twisted bodies, the corpses of horses, smashed helmets, discarded shields and bits of armor. The Romans seemed to have disappeared, though scattered fires plumed up puffy white smoke, obscuring everything. "What happened?"

Something moved in the air, rushing towards him. Mohammed grasped for his sword, but the ebon blade was gone, lost among the tufted grass and wheat stubble. Shouting defiantly, he flung up his hand.

The air boomed like a great gong struck in the nave of some colossal temple. The clear air rippled and shook, wavering like the heat above a forge. Flame bloomed out of nothing, darting to the left and right. Mohammed stared in surprise, seeing the grass leap into flame in a half-circle before him. There was a power set against the Quraysh, something on the far hill. Steeds of flame rushed across the sky towards him, burning figures on their backs, hurling spears of light.

The air shook again as glowing bolts crashed into the invisible barrier around him. Mohammed staggered back, stunned, hands grasping at the air. He cried out, distraught, "Where is the blade of night?"

The sound fell flat on his ears. Khalid grasped his boot, shouting up at him. Mohammed could hear nothing. He was deaf. Flame washed over the clear dome and he could feel tremendous heat beating against his face.

"No," Mohammed said, stepping forward. The fire failed and died as he advanced, snuffed out by some invisible power radiating from him. "I will not yield to you."

The burning mote on the hill flashed again, and again. The air convulsed between them and Mohammed shouted in defiance, striking with his fist at the air. A thunderous *crack* answered his motion and black clouds swept forward across the sky. This time, he could feel the power in the air and the earth, he could feel the strength of the Merciful and Compassionate One in him, guiding his thoughts, bending its will upon this enemy.

The sky lit from horizon to horizon with a blast of light. Lightning jagged down from a dark and boiling sky. At Mohammed's feet, Khalid still clutched at his boot in desperation, stunned by a shattering sound rocking the world. Patik was clinging to the other boot, weeping mindlessly.

A burning indigo bolt leapt across the sky, high over Rufio's head. The Greek flinched and looked away, though the *boom* that followed nearly threw him to the ground. The searing afterimage of dark lightning etched across his vision, but he regained his feet.

"Fall back," he screamed into the howling wind. He turned, sword bare in his hand, and gestured violently at the Faithful. The Emperor's icon gleamed, reflecting odd lights and fires burning on the plain. "Fall back into the city!"

Rufio ran ahead, pushing and shoving at the men on the road, clearing a path for the standard. Thousands of men and horses blocked his way, stunned and paralyzed by the conflagration in the sky. The Greek pushed through them as fast as he could, fleeing the battle between gods.

"Retreat! Retreat!" Tears streamed down his face, lit by the staccato flare of lightning. "Fall back!" Around him, slowly at first, the Eastern troops began to move. Within moments a huge mob was pouring through the broken teeth of the Arab wall, flooding down the road leading to the massive shape of the Great Gate.

Among them, the red cloaks of the Faithful stood out like clots of blood in the darkness.

Near the middle of the plain, a half-mile from the conflagration of smoke and lightning and burning fields, Shahr-Baraz stood, helmet under one arm, the wind eddying around him. Bursts of light washed over him, throwing his hooked nose in sharp relief, shadowing his eyes. Black clouds blotted out the sun, throwing everything into a supernal gloom, but he remained, witness to the fury of the gods. His mailed hand slowly smoothed one jutting mustache, twisting the end to a point, then the other.

His army cowered, lines of spearmen and archers hugging the earth, wailing and weeping. Only a few of the officers even dared to crouch, staring up at the mammoth half-seen figures battling in the murky air. The clibanarii were already fleeing back to the north, their horses uncontrollable. Many of the diquans had been thrown to the ground and limped or crawled in search of some kind of safety. Even the King of Kings' officers were huddled in the lee of his blowing cloak, clutching the ground, their eyes averted from the dreadful sky.

But the Boar did not look away, though the air before him burned and curdled, distorted by the powers struggling in the ether. Fires reflected in his eyes, leaping up from the shattered land. He watched and waited, idly wondering who would triumph. Shahr-Baraz thought it very amusing his victory did not hinge on the success of either power.

Fire licked across the sky, silhouetting the clouds with a pulsing red glow. Mohammed flinched, taking a step back. None of the furious barrage of flame, smoke and shining bolts had broken through the clear shield protecting him. He felt the unseen power that shifted the tides in their courses moving in tandem, a strange partner in this struggle. Effortless strength seemed to fill his limbs, making his eyesight and hearing keen. Testing this power, Mohammed grasped at the sky, feeling storm and wind move at his command.

Thunder boomed in the clouds, presaging a brilliant *crack* of lightning leaping from earth to sky. Distantly, the Quraysh felt his enemy shudder, stricken by the blow. A flare of orange light lit up the walls of the city and the circumvallation. Mohammed smiled, feeling a giddy rush of pleasure. He could move his hand just *so* and . . .

Rain roared down out of the sky, mixed with hail and howling wind. The grassy fields flattened down before the gusts. Heavy droplets spattered on the broken walls of the old farmhouses. Mohammed stabbed out a hand, shouting. Lightning flickered, arcing from cloud to cloud, lighting them with a sullen yellow glow. A mammoth cyan bolt stabbed from the ground, enveloping the wavering orange sphere on the distant wall. Mohammed felt his enemies' defense crack, weakening. He could feel the terror of the Roman soldiers, struggling through the torrential downpour, the ground turning to queasy black mud with every step.

Rain fell around him, too, but here within the circle of this invisible protection it was a gentle cooling mist. The Quraysh laughed in delight, thinking of the summer storms of his homeland. "You are weakening, my enemy. I think you are nearly spent."

He clenched his fist, will pressing on the sky, the clouds, the earth. A rolling series of blasts shook the ground, a howling cauldron of fire and lightning and hail converging on the sphere of orange light. Abruptly, like a wick being pinched, the light went out. Across the distance, Mohammed could feel the struggling, fierce will that opposed him suddenly fail. There was a wink of orange flame and then only rain and darkness. The fires burning across the field sizzled down to smoke and ash, drenched by the towering thunderheads sweeping across the sky.

You are finished! Mohammed thought. *I will crush the last breath...*

Distantly, his physicality heard the words "Now! He's done it!"

Then a blinding crack of pain burst behind his eyes and Mohammed, lord of the Quraysh, master of the Sahaba, crumpled to the ground, blood seeping from a fierce purplish bruise behind his left ear. As he fell, there was a curious sensation of distance between his body and his mind. His spirit turned, looking down from a great height, and saw his body sprawled on the grass, the powerful figure of the man Patik looming over his body. Khalid was crouched over Mohammed, hands upon his face.

An arrow? Mohammed was confused. He reached out for his body, seeking to rise and stand and see the desolation of his enemies. There was nothing there. Darkness suddenly flooded from the ground, covering the earth. Mohammed cried out, reaching into the void.

O Lord of the World, where are you? Have you . . .
Then oblivion.

Khalid rolled back the white-bearded man's eyelid. Rain drummed down out of a black sky, coupled with gusts of wind blowing heavy drops at right angles to the ground. The young man grinned, his teeth white in the darkness.

"I could not have planned it better myself!" He stood, back to the wind, and gestured to Patik. His guardsmen rose, making a solid circle of bodies around them. "Quickly, now, before the Sahaba notice."

The Persian nodded, pulling a length of gleaming silk from his belt. Patik unfolded the cloth, then unfolded it again and then again. With each iteration, the size doubled until it easily covered the body lying sprawled on the ground. Deftly, Patik laid the silk on the ground, then rolled Mohammed's body onto the cloth.

"Hurry!" Khalid hissed, digging into a bag that he carried at his belt. "Faster!"

The stoic Persian ignored the younger man's command, making sure he tucked the Arab's hands and feet gently onto the rectangle. Once the body was suitably arranged, he folded half of the cloth over, completely covering Mohammed from head to toe. Then, working with precise, ordered motions, Patik folded the long length of silk over, then over again. In an instant, the cloth was once again a small square in his hand. This he put into the pouch at his belt. He was sweating heavily, though the driving rain washed the salt from his face and arms.

Khalid knelt on the muddy grass, his hands busy with a length of dark red twine coiled around a wooden spool. With one hand he drove the spool into the soft ground near where Mohammed's head had been. With the twine fixed, he spun off a long length of the cord and swiftly arranged the twine on the ground in the outline of a man. Bending close over the muddy grass, he blinked rain out of his eyes and twitched sections of the twine into a more accurate shape.

Patik stood over him, shielding Khalid from the worst of the rain and hail sputtering out of the dark clouds. Visibility across the plain was poor, now reduced to only a few hundred feet. Khalid rose up, still on his knees, and fumbled a stoppered steel bottle from his belt. Turning his head away and gritting his teeth, the young man sprinkled black dust on the muddy ground within the shape described by the twine.

Vapor boiled up out of the ground, writhing like a forest of snakes. An ominous groaning sound issued from the earth and Khalid backed away, making a sign of warning. The mud heaved, cracking open, fumes and smoke issuing forth. The young Arab made a horrible face at the foul odor. Then the clots of mud and broken earth and rainwater began to slide gelatinously together. Within the space of one or two grains, the mud and grass had congealed into the shape of a man. A tall man, broad shouldered, with a long white beard lying across his chest.

Tendrils of grass crawled across the face, slithering into eyes, nose and ears. Rain sluiced across the naked body, washing away the mud and dirt. Fumes and smoke settled on the cold dead flesh, seeping into the pores and crevices of the body. Blood congealed out of the air, marking a wound on the muscular chest.

Khalid stood, looking down, silhouetted against the storm-wracked sky. His face was impassive, shadowed against the darkness. "So are the Makzhum revenged upon the Quraysh. Put a cloak on him, then lift him up." The young Arab thought that he could feel his father and his grandfather looking over his shoulder, pleased.

Patik and the others crowded around the body, fitting boots on its feet, a tunic, lifting the cold heavy arms to slide on a cloak. Khalid saw his horse had fled in the face of the storm. Casting about in the grass, he found Mohammed's sword and gingerly lifted the weapon by the hilt, sliding the blade into his own sheath. He walked somberly forward, head bent in thought or grief. His men hoisted the body on their shoulders and followed, their passage lit by the rumble and crack of lightning in the clouds and gusts of rain. The day grew cold.

Khalid saw some of the Sahaba approaching, moving cautiously forward through the rain.

"Oh, my friends," he called to them, raising his hand, face a mask of grief. "I have sad tidings for you."

The Sahaba, seeing Patik and the others carrying a body on a bier of spears, stopped dead in their tracks. Their eyes grew huge, seeing the pain on Khalid's face.

"Who has been struck down?" one of them cried out in alarm, pushing forward through his fellows.

"God has fixed the length of Mohammed's life," Khalid answered. "Today was the last day."

The man who had spoken staggered as if struck by a heavy blow. "Mohammed, our teacher, is dead?"

"No!" Khalid shouted, voice rising above the rain and growling thunder. More Sahaba approached through the rain, drawn by the commotion. "He is not dead. He has gone to god, to the power speaking from the clear air, which sets the moon in its course, which directs the tides."

Some of the Sahaba fell to their knees, weeping, clutching their spears. Khalid looked out over their faces and saw desolation entering every heart. He did not intend to say more, but a great voice suddenly issued from behind him.

"You men," Patik boomed, head raised into the driving rain. "If anyone here worships Mohammed, let those men know Mohammed is dead. But if anyone worships Allah, let him know Allah is alive and immortal forever." The Persian paused, noble gaze passing over the great host of men gathering around him. He met every eye fiercely, and there was no sound on the field of war save the drumming of rain on the ground. "Mohammed," he said, powerful baritone rolling out, "is only a messenger, and all those messengers who came before him have also died. Now that your teacher has fallen, would you turn away from his path? Whoever turns back will do no injury to Allah, but Allah will reward those who are steadfast and follow the righteous and straight way."

Then even the Persian fell silent, though his companions stared at him in surprise, for they had never heard so many words from him at one time. Khalid stared hard at the man, but Patik ignored him and slowly, with measured steps, the litter bearers turned to the north, towards their camp and the black-hulled ships. The Sahaba turned as well, their heads bent against the cold wind and rain blowing into their faces, and followed, all in silence, each man alone with his grief.

Jusuf tilted back his broad leather hat, letting water pooling around the brim spill off onto the flagstones of the Roman highway. He and his lancers were arrayed on either side of the road, spears and swords laid across their saddles, bows carefully stowed in their wooden cases. Ahead of them, scattered across the edge of the plain, were perhaps a thousand Khazars on foot, a thin sentry line to watch for the enemy. Jusuf did not think the enemy was coming, though. Not today, not in this weather.

Long lines of Western legionaries trudged past, heads bent, many carrying wounded comrades, the standards and banners of each cohort hanging limply against their gilded poles. Even the faces of the men were gray. Jusuf watched grimly as they marched past. This was a defeated army.

As he had feared, his *tumens* had taken too long—almost two hours—to wind their way out of the orchards and off the hill. By the time he had come up on the rear ranks of the Eighth Gallica, the sky shook with awesome thunder and the tumult of wind spirits in combat. In the face of that raging storm and dreadful lightning, the horses refused to advance. The Khazars bided their time in the shelter of the hill. Now the best they could do was provide a safe haven for the retreating Western troops.

"Lord Jusuf!" One of the men on picket duty jogged up the road, long hair plastered against his head by the rain. "A band of horsemen are approaching!"

"Stand ready!" Jusuf waved at his tarkhans, drawing their attention. A ripple ran down the lines of horsemen as men shifted shields around and stirred themselves, ready for action. The Khazar lord nudged his horse forward. A last bedraggled cohort of Romans splashed past, the men leaning against one another. At their rear, a grizzled-looking centurion was walking backwards, shield still at the ready, a gladius bare in his hand. Jusuf nodded to the man as he passed. The Western officer said nothing, his eyes focused on the rain.

The mare clattered up onto the road, tossing her head, and Jusuf reined in, waiting in the middle of the road. After a moment, shapes appeared out of the rain, horsemen in scaled mail and conical helms. Rain-soaked plumes lay against their shoulders. Jusuf saw that they bore red shields blazoned with rampant dragons.

"Ho!" he called through the steady drumbeat of rain. "Who is your commander?"

A tall man in their midst looked up, then wiped water from his eyes. Jusuf spurred his horse forward, seeing that it was the Frankish legate, Dagobert. "My lord! Are there more men coming?"

Dagobert shook his head, eyes desolate. Jusuf caught his reins, halting the man's horse. The Khazar bent close, eyes intent on the face of the Roman officer. "What happened?"

"We are beaten." Dagobert's voice was barely audible. He leaned heavily on his saddle. "These are all the Sarmatians that escaped . . . the Third Augusta is gone, the Tenth Fretensis shattered. Did any man leave that terrible field alive?"

Jusuf leaned back, seeing that the Frank's will was broken. He had seen this before, where a strong man tasted defeat for the first time. His mind would be filled with terrors and doubt. "Many men have left the field, hale, unwounded." The Khazar projected certainty and confidence in his voice. The Frank only looked away, long blond hair lying in streaks across his noble brow and strong chin. "Your army remains, my lord."

"But so many are dead. . . ." Dagobert's voice died away. Jusuf turned his horse, clucking at the mare to walk. Together, the two men clopped up the road. In the mist around them, the Khazars, still alert, folded in behind the Sarmatians. The Khazar pickets loped in, long-tailed caps bouncing on their shoulders. They stopped to help the wounded and then faded into the gloom.

Torches guttered, hissing in the rain, throwing a fitful light on the walls of the Great Gate. A remnant of the Faithful Guard stood in the passage, one great iron-bound door already closed, the other pulled halfway shut. Their cloaks were stained and torn, heavy with clinging mud. Armor was twisted and bent, links missing, shields hacked and split. Most of the men leaned wearily against the stone walls, eyes bloodshot and heavy with fatigue.

Only one man showed any motion, a stocky, thick-built Greek pacing back and forth in front of the gate, just out of the rain. The moat running before the *prochtisma* sparkled with rain and hail pelting down out of the sky. The clouds overhead pressed close to the earth, heavy and dark, blotting out the sun. A gloom like twilight was upon the fields, even though Rufio guessed it was late afternoon.

He worried, staring out into the rain. He could barely make out the graveyards lining the highway. The long siege had destroyed all the trees within sight of the walls, but broken pillars still marked the fringe of the old burial places.

"My lord?" The *ekatontarch* in charge of the gate garrison approached. "We must close the gate. The army has entered . . ."

"Not all of them!" Rufio turned on the man, livid with

anger. "There is still one more soldier out there."

The Greek officer did not back away, his face rigid. "My lord, we *must* close the gate."

Rufio's eyes glinted, fury mounting. But the man was right. Emotion was clouding his judgment. The captain of the Faithful felt a familiar chill. He had seen so many men die. They would just be two more . . .

"Captain! Look . . ." The Faithful were pointing out into the darkness. "It's the Walach."

Rufio turned and saw a hunched figure stumbling down the road, half bent under some burden. The Faithful came forth from the gate, weapons ready, exhausted but still wary and game for one more struggle. Rufio walked forward, black eyes flitting from side to side, watching for an ambush. In this weather, a thousand Persians might be just out of sight, hidden in the gloom. The figure came closer, and Rufio saw it was Vladimir carrying a limp body on his back.

"I have him," the Walach gasped as he stumbled up. "I have him."

Rufio put his hand on the boy's face. His cloak and tunic were sodden with rain and Dwyrin's flesh was cold to the touch. "Inside! Everyone inside! Prepare to close the gate!"

Men crowded around them, taking Vladimir's burden. Dwyrin was lofted on their hands, his head lolling back, and they carried him into the gate on a bed of stout shoulders and brawny arms. Rufio was the last to enter the tunnel, still watching the rain-swept darkness.

Then the gate ground closed with a deep *boom* and the fitful light on the road went out.

)⚬(

Helena, Empress of the West, stood at a window, her face lit by flickering red light. Her hair was loose around her shoulders, her makeup reduced to smudged streaks. She seemed very tired. The Empress rocked gently from side to side, a young child curled against her shoulder. The little boy was drooling on her gown. Outside, under a night sky filled with smoke, fires were burning furiously in the ruins of the Subura district. The bitter smell of hot ash and cracked brick drifted in through the window. As she watched, a great tower of sparks roared up behind the firebreak dividing the Forum from the Subura tenements. Despite the massive brick wall blocking her view, Helena knew an apartment block had just collapsed in fiery ruin, tiled roof caving in, a jet of incandescent flames leaping up, roaring out the windows.

"They say, in Rome, fire is profit." Helena's tone was conversational.

The other figures in the dark room did not answer. There was a low bed, half surrounded by gauze drapes. The only illumination came from the window, a wavering hot red light. A young woman lay on the bed, her side and arm tightly bound in cotton bandages. She was sleeping, her breathing even and steady. A pattern of ugly bruises covered her face. Sitting beside her, hands clasped in her lap, Anastasia watched Thyatis sleep. The Duchess was still dressed in cerulean, though the sky-blue cape had been lost during the panic in the circus.

"She won't wake faster if you hover like that," the Empress said, turning away from the window. Her hair gleamed with the light of distant fires. "You should sleep."

"No. Not until she wakes." Anastasia did not look up.

Sighing, Helena settled gracefully into a plush upholstered chair. Her son, shifting, made a burbling sound then fell asleep again. Murmuring echoes filled the air. Occasionally, distant trumpets sounded over the rumble of the flames. "What then? Do you think she will forgive you?"

"I hope so." Anastasia's voice was hoarse with exhaustion, but since a priest of Asclepius had put his hands upon her, Thyatis' color improved and the Duchess's worry eased. "Her anger will fade."

"Really?" One of Helena's carefully plucked eyebrows arched in amusement. "She might take being shot with an arrow amiss. Some people dislike that."

Anastasia looked up, finally, and there was a hint of a glare in her look. "Not if no one tells her. Not if no one harps upon the event like a town crier . . . bringing it up again and again and *again*."

Helena laughed softly, trying not to disturb the baby. "I will say nothing. But what about the Gaul and his daughter, what about those mercenaries of yours?"

"They will say nothing." Anastasia flashed another glare, then settled back in her chair, hands covering her face. Her voice grew fainter. "I will send Vitellix and his little troupe away, laden with gold and gifts. They are going home, to Gaul. The men . . . they are circumspect. They can see what is happening in the streets—they will not brag of this!"

"No, I suppose not." Helena watched her friend closely. "How do you feel?"

"Empty." The Duchess stared out the window at drifting clouds lit from below by countless fires. "But my mind seems clear and I am not without hope."

"Because she is alive?" The Empress pointed her chin at the sleeping woman. "You're getting sentimental."

Anastasia just stared at Helena, her face entirely in shadow. "I have come to care for her."

"You once told me you could not afford to love anyone save the Duke. Do you remember that? You said that he was safe to love because he was dead. What hurt or betrayal could he offer? None! I thought that was very wise."

"Those were my words," Anastasia said peevishly. "Are you going to lecture me? Why do you care?"

"I care," Helena said in a serious tone, "because I have a son. An emperor's son. How can my child thrive and grow, live a long life, if his father is overthrown or defeated? No king's son is suffered to live by a conqueror or rebel! Galen must be emperor until my son comes of age, and you must help them both." As she spoke, a cold tone of command entered Helena's voice and Anastasia grew still. The Empress continued, her voice precise.

"With your help, Galen has prospered. Your illness has hurt him, weakening the state. You have been irresponsible. I cannot allow you these weaknesses."

The Duchess straightened up in her chair, her whole attention focused on the Empress. Despite the gusts of furnace-hot air that eddied around the window, a chill stole over her. Helena had never spoken to her this way before, not in all the years of their friendship. "My daughter is not a weakness."

"She is if her loss destroys you," Helena said in a clipped tone. "She is a weapon, one you used with abandon in the past. You cannot protect her or hide her from the world. *You* cannot hide from the world."

"I know this." The Duchess rubbed her eyes, getting sparkling white abalone dust on her knuckles. "I will help the Emperor, be he Galen or your son." Anastasia glared at Helena again, her full lips compressing in suppressed anger. "But I will not put aside my love for my daughter. Not for you or anyone."

"Then harden your heart to her death," Helena snapped, rising smoothly from the chair, still cradling the child against her shoulder. "You made her a soldier and she will die before her time."

"I know." Anastasia looked up, her face a controlled mask. "Why are you so afraid?"

Helena was at the window again, staring out over the rumpled hills of the city. The great burning in the Subura raged on, despite the efforts of the *vigiles* and the Legion troops that Galen had sent into the city. Other fires guttered amid ruins on the Cispian and Viminal hills. Everywhere members of the Green racing faction had lived, the mob had come, seeking vengeance for the "murder" of their favorite. The Empress put her hand on the cold marble windowsill.

"You are not blind! Look at the city—the mob is wild in the streets, barely restrained by the Praetorians and the Legion. Thousands are dead, entire blocks in flames, senators dragged from their homes and stoned to death or just torn apart. Madness infects everyone. Only the Emperor's swift denunciation of the act and the culpability of the Greens saved Galen's life, and ours. Do you think the Praetorians would raise a hand against the mob if they thought the Emperor were involved in this?"

The Empress gestured violently at the smoke-filled sky and seething red-lit clouds. She groped for words, but seemed to be gripped by fierce emotion. At last she said, "War threatens the northern borders; already it engulfs the East. The news from Constantinople is poor. Everywhere there is turmoil and trouble. Someone was waiting for this—for some spark to light in the tinder of Rome—and they grow fat from ruin. They want my son's patrimony!"

Anastasia rose, though she lingered for an instant by Thyatis' side, her fingertips gentle on the young woman's arm. "You think someone incited the mob?"

"Yes." Helena turned, silhouetted against the flame-shot skyline. "Was it you?"

"What?" Anastasia stepped back from the window, shocked. "What do you mean?"

"Did you order your archer to shoot Thyatis so she would lose the race?" Helena seemed to have grown taller.

A chill came over Anastasia again, raising goose bumps on her arms, making the fine hairs on the back of her sleek neck stand on end.

"No. I did not. I ordered him to shoot the Green driver, to save her life! His shot went astray. She leapt up on the back of the horse at just the wrong moment!"

"Perhaps." Helena stepped close, grim eyes searching Anastasia's face. "Do you know where your archer is?"

The Duchess shook her head, eyes wide with surprise at this turn in the conversation.

"He is dead," Helena bit out, furious. "The Praetorians found him in the river, missing his head. At first I thought you were playing a very bold game, running to me with your injured daughter, seeking shelter on the Palatine while the circus was engulfed in riot. That way you would be safe while the Greens and their ally, the lanista Narses, were destroyed. I wondered—did you already have a feud with the Greens? With Narses? Did you see a chance to clean house?"

The Empress cocked her head to one side, watching the play of stunned emotion on Anastasia's face. "But then I watched you while Thyatis slept, while the priest mended her broken bones and shattered ribs. Everything in you was concentrated upon her. This was not your plot. Someone else's, perhaps, but not yours. You did not even hear the sounds of battle in the streets, the roar of the flames, the panic in everyone's voice."

Helena's voice softened and she took Anastasia's head in her hands. Leaning close, the Empress pressed her brow against Anastasia's. "You watch her as I watch my son. I am sorry she was hurt."

Stepping away, Helena swung the shutters closed, plunging the room into darkness. "You must stay here until the city is quiet. There is no safety in the streets. I must take my son to see Galen and then to bed. You should sleep, if you can."

Anastasia found the wicker table by touch. She lit a

small gryphon-shaped lamp with a punk. Dim yellow flame licked up from the gryphon's nostrils. Thyatis' face was only half illuminated. Anastasia sat again, her arms clutched across her chest.

"Here." Helena bent down and lifted a blanket from the foot of the bed. "You're cold."

"Thank you." Anastasia pulled the dark blue quilt around her shoulders. Her voice was tinged with melancholy. "I will do what I can to help your son and your husband, Helena. I am afraid that events have moved beyond me. Many things have changed in my . . . absence. The world has passed me by."

"Huh." Helena grunted, the corners of her eyes crinkling up as she smiled. "The world always moves on, Anastasia. Our memories anchor us in the past. They will drown you, if you don't let go. Think about tomorrow instead."

When the Empress turned up the quilt to cover her friend's arm, the Duchess was sound asleep. The movement finally disturbed the little boy, whose eyes opened, and he made a face like a little monkey. Little fists batted at the air as he drew breath to wail.

"Oh, hush." Helena stood up, adjusting the baby and her gown. "Don't make such a racket. We'll go see your pater and annoy him with your squalling."

A withered hand entered the room first, clutching a trembling candlestick. Warm white light spilled over painted walls and a glossy wooden floor. A couch lay along one wall, covered with linen sheets and a blanket. Above the man lying on the bed, the gods upon Olympus looked down, hanging among the frozen birds and painted spirits of the air. In the flickering candlelight, their faces were filled with subtle life and motion.

"Troublesome child." The old man sat heavily in a curule chair. He was bent with age, the backs of his hands spotted and wrinkled. Leaning close, Gaius Julius squinted at the face of the Prince. It was pale and still, though breath escaped the parted lips. "You remain constant, at least. I win another day of life!"

The old Roman laughed, a guttural cackling sound. "You would laugh to see how fiercely I clutch to this shadow of existence. I treasure every moment, my lord, every moment." He frowned. "I wish that Alexandros were here . . . then we could be invalids together, comparing bedsores and the firmness of our stools . . ."

Maxian did not respond, lying still and cold under the sheets, his brow slightly furrowed. Gaius Julius had brought him here in secret, into one of the apartments the old Roman had recently acquired. This one was very small and very expensive. It was on the third floor of the last privately owned apartment building on the Palatine Hill. Gaius Julius found the investment now gave a rich return— the Praetorians and the Legion had sealed off the Palatine and the Forum, allowing no one through their barricades while the Blues and Yellows raged in the streets, slaughtering the Greens.

The thought brought a slow, blissful smile to Gaius' face. Unconsciously, his fingers moved jerkily, as if they were counting stacks of coins. His wagers on the outcome of the race had paid handsomely, filling his coffers with delightful gold. Even better, the mob's revenge on the Greens had relieved him of having to pay off his losses. And, of course, his agents were busy in the city tonight, as they had been for the past two days, acquiring properties that had been ravaged by the fires. Gaius had learned well, in his youth.

"I wonder," mused the old Roman, his wrinkled hand pressed against Maxian's cold skin, "if you will ever die? Will you just maintain, trapped in this half-life? Will I live on while you are sleeping? I'd think this a poor existence if I had not tasted true death."

The Prince had not taken food or water since his collapse on the roof of the Flavian. Gaius Julius had tried to moisten his lips, hoping to keep him alive, but the Prince simply did not change. The old Roman assumed that Maxian's sorcerous power sustained him. Shaking his head in wonder, Gaius turned away from the Prince and shuffled to his own couch, where he would lie down, eyes closed, thinking and waiting for the day to come again.

The candle burned down while the two men lay on opposite sides of the room, and finally flickered out as the last of the wax was consumed. In the darkness, the Prince stirred, his eyelids flickering open for a moment. Gaius Julius—despite his conceit—was unaware, his weakened body forced into a somnambulant state not unlike the sleep of living men. Sweat suddenly beaded on the Prince's forehead and he moaned, released from the odd stasis that had overcome him. His fingers clutched weakly at the sheets, then he subsided into a troubled sleep, filled with torments and phantoms.

Geminus jerked awake, flushed, his skin damp with sweat. He looked around, alarmed, his heart beating fiercely, and saw only quiet darkness. A light shone in the doorway from the hall. His fear began to fade when nothing horrific lunged out of the darkness at him, though he remained uneasy. Something was wrong. Thin lips pinched up as he rose from the cot. For a moment, standing in his sleeping robe, he dithered, trying to decide if he should call for servants to dress him.

The sense of unease grew, so he cast about and found a cloak. His feet bare on the cold floor, Geminus hurried out of his room, leaving behind even the ceremonial headdress and jeweled, heavy stole that he should wear to enter the fane of the Emperors. Thankfully, the slaves had made sure to keep the lamps in the tall hallway burning, allowing him to pad past their sleeping quarters and out through the stone partition into the main body of the temple of Venus and Rome.

He paused, standing in the middle of the massive floor. He looked towards the doors at the front of the temple but saw nothing amiss. They were closed, as the Emperor had ordered, for the duration of the "disturbance." A maniple of legionaries was camped outside on the marble steps. The entire Forum was closed off, sealed by barricades and guarded by hard-bitten veterans. Geminus tried not to think of what was happening outside of the Emperor's protection, in the narrow, crowded streets of the Aventine or the Subura. The smell of burning brick and wood was heavy in the air.

The seated statue of Venus, draped in frozen folds of marble cloth, was undisturbed, the holy flame burning before her as it had done for over a thousand years. Geminus bit his lip, his face screwed up into a grimace. *Something was wrong!*

His gaze lit on an alcove set off the main nave of the temple. A lamp burned there as well—not so large as the one before the Venus—set in a golden bowl and provided with only the finest-quality Egyptian oil. Geminus padded towards the little shrine. A wooden barrier kept the curious back from the shrine, but the priest pushed it roughly aside. The trouble in his heart peaked and he glanced around the alcove in alarm.

Everything was there. A Cassertan marble statue of the Emperor Galen stood on a plain white pedestal, the face holding a hint of his quick intelligence, the sculptor careful to suggest the wayward lock of hair that always seemed to fall over his high forehead. Offerings of fruit and corn and silver were still sitting in their porcelain bowls.

Geminus blinked, looking at the statue. There was something missing. There should be a second figure, smaller than the Emperor, but still honored and standing at his right hand. He could almost see it . . . *Was it Hermes? The figure was cloaked like a senator, like a patrician, but his feet were bare, with winged heels. A staff was in one hand, surmounted by a golden disk. His other hand was open, raised, and a pair of intertwined snakes crowned him, rising up in an entablature behind his head. It was a young*

*man, with an open, smiling face. But it was not Hermes
the god, the messenger.*

Geminus shook his head, trying to clear the vision away.
It persisted and the priest knew that in the morning, as
soon as gray light had broken in the east, he would hasten
to the sculptors and artisans who maintained the temples
and their statuary. A new figure must be put in place, and
quickly too. There could be no delay.

THE ROAD TO PERINTHUS

Bawling horns and shouting drew Jusuf's attention and
he urged his horse to greater speed. The midday sun
was hot, making him sweat freely under the iron and
leather and felt. The column of lancers following him
picked up the pace. Among these open fields and rolling
hills, two grassy riding paths paralleled the flagstoned
highway. Jusuf made swift time on the grass, his horse
flying along the cleared, level track. On the road, marching
legionaries slowed, staring back, their faces grim and
pinched under their helmets. Each man bent under heavy
bundles of equipment: spare armor, casks of water, twine
bags of bread. Within a few grains, Jusuf reached the rear
of the army.

In the chaos of their retreat, the Roman army had become thoroughly disordered. One entire legion, the Eighth
Gallica, had failed to stand fast, but had fled down the
highway towards the port of Perinthus. Many of the raw
recruits in the Western ranks had simply thrown aside their
arms and armor, bolting for the hills. During the first night,
as stray cohorts and maniples staggered in through the
Khazar pickets, Dahvos and Jusuf were informed that the

dux Dagobert had abandoned his Legions and fled with his household.

Dahvos and Jusuf shared a look, then the khagan said, "Whatever happened to falling on your sword?" A grim jest for a bleak night.

This news caused a fresh round of panic before Dahvos seized control of the camp and began executing deserters. The veterans of the Third Augusta argued for defending the camp. Dahvos agreed, but the other Western officers— fresh to command—demanded that the army fall back to Perinthus. Without the troops to compel their obedience, Dahvos had been forced to let them go. Two days later, a sharp Persian attack drove the Khazars and the remains of the Third out of the hills overlooking the city.

Now the Khazars and the Third retreated in good order west along the highway. As he rode up, Jusuf saw a force of Arab horsemen attacking the screen of Khazars covering the marching infantry. The rebels were not heavily armed or armored, but they showed a disconcerting, reckless ferocity. They did not fear death. The Khazar drew his sword and urged his horse forward. The mare clattered up onto the road. The Legion rear guard turned in place as the Arabs burst out of the trees. Even now, showing good discipline, they formed a double line, shields raised, the men in the second rank readying their javelins.

Jusuf nodded to the centurion at his end of the line of shields. "We'll drive them off."

"Maybe," the Roman grunted, "but we'll hold our position here for a bit and see how you do."

Jusuf laughed, though he saw the Arabs, shrieking war cries and a repeated chant of *Mohammed! Mohammed!* charging pell-mell into the Khazar skirmishers, scattering the lightly armed horsemen. Some of the attackers loosed arrows as they rode, showing great skill and horsemanship. The Khazar screen wheeled away, clods of earth flying up from their hooves, shooting half twisted in the saddle. Jusuf looked left and then right, checking the order of his men. The Khazar and Sarmatian cataphracts shook out into a line across the road, lances ready. The lighter horse archers thundered through their line and turned behind the legionaries. Jusuf shouted at them as they galloped past.

"Turn, form and fire! Bows!" The light horse began to regroup.

Arab arrows hissed through the air. Jusuf took hold of his shield, settling it on his arm, and gauged the distance between his *banda* and the oncoming Arabs. "Ready!" He raised his sword, signaling the lancers. "At a walk!"

The line of cataphracts began to walk forward, their lances couched and leveled. The horse archers behind them began to shoot overhead, lofting arrows into the rushing swarm of Arabs. Jusuf couldn't tell if they were hitting anyone; his attention was focused on the enemy that loomed rapidly before him.

"Charge!" He spurred the mare and she leapt forward, iron plates sewn to heavy leather barding rattling. On either side of him, the Khazars raised a great shout as they charged forward.

Ah-yah-yah-yah-yah! Jusuf felt the wind rush in his hair, keening in his helmet. Then the Khazars slammed into the Arab line with a *crash* and a *clang* of iron and steel and he was parrying an Arab sword, the bright blade flickering in the air. Sparks snapped away from the shock of contact and Jusuf felt his arm shudder, taking the blow. The Arab was screaming, raining blows on the Khazar. Jusuf blocked an overhand cut, then had to swing his horse around, interposing his shield. The wood splintered, ringing, as another Arab joined in, raining blows on his guard.

The Khazar charge faltered, locked in a fierce melee. The desert tribesmen were filled with an enormous mad strength. They were relentless, always pushing forward, ignoring wounds, cuts, even the slaughter of their fellows. Waves of chanting in their unknown tongue rolled over Jusuf. Each Arab seemed to live, fight and die with a prayer on his lips. Each time the Arabs attacked the rear guard, they suffered terrible losses, but they did not seem to care.

Jusuf took a blow on the side of his helmet and nearly fell out of his saddle, stunned.

"Strange . . ." Nicholas peered out at the fields before the city, his brown eyes narrowed. The sun was full in the sky, the day verging on hot, the usual northerly wind died down to a paltry zephyr. Even the huge granite slabs comprising the wall facing were beginning to warm. Despite the pleasant weather, a sick feeling of impending disaster curdled in his gut like rotten milk. The northerner leaned out, bracing one hand on the nearest merlon, and looked off to the south along the wall. "They've not buried the dead or taken them away."

Vladimir, also leaning on the embrasure, grunted. His nose wrinkled. "Perhaps they'll let the stink drive us out."

"It's very strange." Nicholas looked around again, then stepped down onto the stone walkway that ran just under the lip of the outer wall of the city. "The Persians are professionals—they should police up the field, finding their own dead for proper burial, throwing the corpses of their enemies into a burning pit. At least, they should gather up the arrows, spears, shields, all the useful things let fall in battle."

Vladimir nodded. He had lost his helmet in the bitter struggle between the Arab wall and the city moat. Luckily, the Imperial armory was well supplied. Some Persian out there, he supposed, might be wearing his helmet. "What do you think it means?"

Nicholas shook his head, puzzled. "Sometimes . . . if men die of plague or disease, a besieging army will fling the bodies into the town, hoping that the pest will spread . . . but we've had no rumors of plague or pox. There's no reason to just let them lie where they fell."

Vladimir leaned a mailed arm on the wall, scratching his nose. From their vantage on the Great Gate, he could see corpses scattered in clumps and bunches near the raised highway. The dead lay in drifts, like the wrack along the seashore after a storm. That tide had crested in the grave-yards that lined the highway, among the broken-down tombs and abandoned shrines. Sunlight glinted from abandoned helms and armor, making the muddy fields sparkle. "A pity we can't harvest them ourselves. . . ."

Nicholas grunted, arms folded over his chest. The Persians had occupied the Arab circumvallation after the big battle and passed the time sniping at Roman sentries on the walls and anyone that tried to leave the gates. "They dumped the bodies out of the Arab fortification, though . . . I guess they're happy to let them lie, but not lie with them!"

The northerner let his weary eyes rest on the looming gray mass of the second wall. Between the outer works and the inner was a fifty-foot section of cleared ground serving as a military road along the length of the city. Today it was deserted, with only a few men slouching about on errands between the massive towers of the inner wall and the outer. Everyone was exhausted, both in body and in spirit. Of all the Eastern troops that had rushed out of the city to support the Emperor's standard, only the Faithful Guard and the Sixth Ferrata could hold their heads high. They had smashed the Avar assault against the high-way, wreaking terrible losses on the nomads and their sub-ject tribes.

The same could not be said of the cataphracts of the Second Thracia or the legionaries of the Twelfth Asiatica. The Persians had soundly beaten both legions, inflicting heavy losses on their cohorts and capturing some of their banners and standards. Nicholas had seen their soldiers in the city, heads hung low, spiritless. Even the men who had stayed in the city, standing guard on the walls and towers, seemed disconsolate. Nicholas hated the thought, but the unexpected death of Prince Theodore had sapped the fighting spirit of the entire city. Who would command the defense of the city? The senators? Not likely!

Vladimir suddenly turned away from his idle observation of the plain, his ears pricking up.

"What is it?" Nicholas stood away from the wall, hand on Brunhilde's hilt.

"Men are shouting in the city." Vladimir strode away from the parapet, clattering down a narrow stairway leading into the bowels of the Great Gate. Nicholas hurried after his friend, fingers checking to see that he still had a helmet hung from a strap at his waist, that his armor was snug and tight across his chest, that nothing hung loose. *A riot?* He was worrying again.

They descended four flights of narrow spiral stairs, their boots squeaking on well-worn stone, and then they found a great crowd of soldiers in the courtyard at the center of the Gate. The red-cloaked Faithful were mixed with cataphracts in their white tunics and a motley lot of city militia. Everyone was making a great noise, shouting and laughing. Nicholas was surprised, even stunned, to see grim smiles and grins on the faces of these men. Only an hour before, when he had come down to join Vladimir, the courtyard had been a cold and dreary place, filled with spiritless men. Now their mood matched the faultless blue sky.

"What has happened?" Vladimir shouted over the din. His powerful arms plowed forward through the press of men. Nicholas squeezed through after him, buffeted by the soldiers talking loudly and slapping one another on the arm.

"The Emperor! The Emperor is coming!" One of the Faithful turned towards Nicholas, smiling hugely, his gap-toothed grin broad and yellow in the thicket of his dark brown beard. "He is coming!"

Nicholas was frozen for just an instant, digesting this news, and then he grabbed Vladimir by the shoulder. "Lift me up!" he barked. Vlad immediately turned, knocking down one of the city militiamen with his broad shoulder, and made a stirrup for Nicholas with his broad hands. Stepping into the rest, Nicholas found himself suddenly above the crowd, one hand on Vlad's shoulder for support. "Attention!" he bawled. "Form ranks! Form ranks! Faithful Guard to the front, everyone else behind. Right now, you loafers! Centurions! Find your men, parade order, now!"

The men, accustomed to the sound of command, immediately began to accrete in groups around their file leaders. Nicholas jumped down from Vladimir's shoulder. Already, as he ran, the bellow of centurions and under-officers was filling the air. More men were spilling out of the various barracks and chambers ringing the courtyard. Someone found a Legion standard and carried it out, the red flag dancing in the air, gold trim swinging. Nick felt himself smiling, though all this could be nothing but a market rumor.

He reached the inner gate and found the tunnel filled with curious soldiers and buskers selling bread rolls, rolled honey sweets and wine from bags slung around their waists.

"Clear the gate!" Nicholas' voice rang like a trumpet. "All civilians out of the gate! Form ranks!"

The merchants scattered like startled doves from the centurion's bellow. The soldiers darted to the walls, forming parade ranks in the vaulted tunnel. Nicholas stalked through the confusion, barking orders. Out on the street, in the warm afternoon sun, a crowd was beginning to gather. Excited children were running down the avenue that led into the heart of the city. Women were beginning to appear at the windows of the houses that leaned out over the street. Nicholas looked around, seeing many legionaries were craning their necks, staring out of the gate.

"You men, open that gate wide and form up in front of it, arms presented! Vladimir, you take the other side, make sure the tunnel stays clear!"

The sharp stamp of many booted feet moving in unison

caught his ear and Nicholas turned, squinting in the bright sun. People were clearing smartly from the avenue. Suddenly the citizens were gone and a phalanx of red-cloaked men, each at least six feet tall, filled the street from side to side, marching smartly forward, axes perfectly aligned on their shoulders, arms swinging. The Faithful Guard marched bareheaded, mustaches and beards sparkling with ribbons. At their center, on a litter of gold and pearl, a man rode in a silver chair. Nicholas felt shocked quiet fall over the crowd lining the street.

Even he felt a catch in his throat, seeing the pale figure riding above the heads of the Guard. Nicholas had only ever seen the Emperor once before, during the last siege, but his strikingly handsome face and curly golden hair could not be missed. The dark tan from years of campaigning was gone, replaced by a pale, sallow tinge to his skin, but Heraclius held his head high. His visage was composed, forbidding, but he raised his hand in greeting to the crowd as the litter entered the square before the Great Gate.

"Imperator!" Nicholas shouted, voice full and strong, ringing back from the towering walls of the gate. "Imperator! Thou conquerest! Thou conquerest!"

Heraclius' head came up at the sound of a single voice in the air. He smiled.

"Imperator!" boomed the ranks of the legionaries in the gate tunnel. "Imperator!" The sound echoed through the central courtyard. The Faithful continued to advance, their measured tread cracking on the flagstones of the street. Nicholas stepped back against the gate pillar and raised his right arm in the Western salute. At his side, Vladimir did the same. Heraclius passed, still staring straight ahead, but Nicholas thought he saw the man's eyes flicker sideways as the litter entered the gate.

"Imperator! Thou conquerest!" roared from the massed throats of nearly two thousand men. The sound rolled and boomed in the tunnel, sounding like tens of thousands. The crowd in the street, still amazed and stunned, began to cheer. Within moments, Nicholas was engulfed in a crowd of jubilant citizens, laughing and singing, their hearts suddenly light with relief.

Nicholas found himself embraced by a well-built woman with shoulder-length blond hair who gave him a big wet kiss on the mouth and then swung him around. He kissed her back, laughing, and then she was gone, swept away by the crowd. Hundreds of people were flooding into the square from the nearby buildings, cheering and passing out jugs of wine and beer.

Stone ground on stone, and a rectangular flagstone the size of a sleeping man levered up. Grit puffed away from the edges of the stone. Complete darkness was broken by a febrile green radiance seeping from the opening. A hunched, cloaked figure stepped up out of the hidden stairway, one pale, white hand holding up the stone block. The other hand clutched a crystal phial shedding sickly light. A small black shape darted between the woman's legs, sliding across the dusty floor, sending up puffs of dust. Sneezing, the little cat shook its head in disgust. The room had not been opened for a long time. Shelves lined the walls, filled with ancient bottles wrapped in straw.

The Dark Queen gently lowered the slab. It dropped into place with a heavy thud. She had shed the long gown, donning a plain black tunic, chiton and dark gray cloak. Her hair was bundled back behind her head, held in place by silver pins. She thought she would be inconspicuous in the palace. The cat sneezed again, then meowed imperiously, scratching at the door.

"Step lightly," the Queen muttered, taking care to leave the dusty floor undisturbed. Her hand pressed against the door, letting the sensation of ancient close-grained wood seep into her perception. After a moment, satisfied that no one was on the other side, she cracked the rusty bolt with her free hand and slipped out into the tunnel. The green light washed over casks and barrels, all heavy with dust and cobwebs. The Queen sniffed the air, then she turned left and moved off into the darkness. The green light seeped down the walls, puddling in the paw prints on the floor, then slowly faded away.

Men shouted, struggling across the flagstoned road, and the singing rage of iron on iron filled the air. Jusuf stared up at the blue sky, watching fluffy white clouds drift past. There had been a horse standing over him for a moment, nudging him with its soft warm nose, but another horse had come too close and the first mare had bolted off, whinnying. The Khazar's head seemed too large for his helmet. The metal dug painfully into his scalp. Weak fingers scrabbled at the strap under his chin, but the bronze clasp refused to budge.

A green-clad man on a horse blocked out the sun. His spear drew back, leaf-shaped blade flashing with sunlight. Jusuf stared up at the man, puzzled by the fury transforming the Arab's face, then blinked, blinded by the glare. Shadow covered the sun and there was violent motion. Two other men in leather kilts and fitted lamellar mail leapt over his body, stabbing at the first man with javelins. The horse reared back, its face pricked by one of the short spears. The green man lashed at them with his lance.

Jusuf felt hands dragging him back. A sharp pain in his side cut through the dull fog. The roaring in his ears faded and he could think again. He was sweating, the day hot, the riot of battle loud all around him.

"I'm fine," he gasped, trying to stand up. The Roman centurion commanding the rear guard dragged Jusuf to his feet. The Khazar felt his face, fingers coming away smeared with blood. "I'm fine."

The Arabs were still furiously engaged, trying to break through the Roman line by sheer ferocity. Arrows snapped among them, the Khazar riders shooting into the thick of the melee. The legionaries stood firm, holding off the Arab assault with spears and busy swords. Jusuf felt pain stab through his head. The side of his helmet had been crushed in, grinding against his skull, rasping away the skin.

"God above!" He managed to get the point of his belt knife worked under the chin strap and sawed away the thick leather. The helmet came off his head with a wet pop. Blood spilled out of the dented metal in a thin red stream. He felt sick.

THE PALATINE HILL, ROMA MATER

"**Y**ou stay away from her! Ow! Leave me . . . get off! Ow!"

Thyatis woke to the sound of a scuffle—someone was growling and shouting—and her eyes opened slowly. There was a beamed roof, dark wood against white plaster, overhead. Sharp words hung in the air like smoke. She blinked, realizing that her back and side were stiff with pain. A soft hiss escaped gritted teeth. *The mule kicked me again?* she thought curiously. *Who is making that racket?*

"Papa, help! Yeee-owch!"

Bracing for more pain, Thyatis turned her head and saw little Ila on the floor, her face pressed into glazed tile, one arm wrenched behind her back. A blond girl—a name trickled up from hazy, wobbly memory—*Betia*—was holding her down, knee pressed into Ila's back. Thyatis tried to grin, but that *was* painful and she realized that her face was throbbing and raw. Despite ferocious efforts on Ila's part, the Island-trained girl was easily restraining her.

"Let her up," Thyatis said, her words echoed by another's voice. Anastasia was standing in the doorway, her face a white oval in a sea of black cloak, chiton and stole. "Mouse, come here."

Looking smug, Betia let go and Ila, scowling furiously, retreated to the bed, legs planted firmly, her little brown body squarely between Thyatis and these invaders. Thyatis curled an arm around Ila, making her sit. Betia faded into the shadows by the door, smirking, and the Duchess slowly unwound her stole and veil.

"May I come in?" The older woman's voice was quiet and a little sad. Thyatis saw that she had dispensed with her usual powders and creams, leaving dark circles under her eyes and knife-thin wrinkles around her mouth. She seemed very old and careworn. Even her movements seemed slow, as if her limbs were heavy. Despite this, something in her face seemed hopeful.

"Where am I?" Thyatis gave Ila a squeeze and felt the little girl's fingers wrap around her own.

"You are in the Palatine," Anastasia said. "The Empress Helena is hiding us until the trouble in the city dies down."

"There's riots," Ila muttered out of the corner of her mouth. "They thought you were murdered by the Greens."

"I was . . ." Memory was a jumble of scenes and sensations. There was a momentary flash of brilliant pain. "I was shot from behind . . . an arrow as we came out of the turn?"

"Yes." Anastasia looked down at the floor. "One of . . . my archers shot you by mistake, trying to hit that accursed African."

Thyatis made a choking sound, then half crushed Ila trying to draw breath. The horse girl pounded her vigorously on the back and finally Thyatis was able to look up, tears streaming from her eyes. "I was shot with an arrow by accident?"

Anastasia nodded, her violet eyes smudged and pale. "I'm sorry."

Thyatis, exhausted by the coughing, lay back on the heavy pillows. "What do you want?"

"May I come in?"

Thyatis gestured weakly, and Anastasia came to the other side of the bed. Ila stiffened, then turned her back, pointedly, on the older woman. Betia remained, almost invisible, in the shadows by the door. Ila contented herself with glaring at the maid. The Duchess sat, fingers clutching a corner of the quilt.

"You'll be well," Anastasia said, trying to smile. "Helena's doctors are very good. They knitted up your ribs and drew down the swelling. Tomorrow, or the day after, you'll be up and around."

"And then?" Thyatis watched her patron curiously. She was too tired—drained, really—to muster anger. The Duchess seemed to have grown more solid, now that Thyatis looked at her closely. The glorious hair, the dazzling jewels and ornaments were gone, even her flashing eyes were dimmed. Lying in this quiet room, somewhere in the sprawl of the palace, Thyatis realized that Anastasia was just a woman, like herself, neither wiser nor more clever. Merely herself—tired, worn, disconsolate—and, perhaps for the first time, honest. *How strange,* she thought, *once I was more frightened of her than any man with a sword.*

"You can go where you please," Anastasia said, unable to meet the younger woman's eyes. "You are free of the arena, and free of Narses, and free of me."

The pale shadow of a grin lit Thyatis' eyes. Her right hand held Ila close. "What about the dreadful prince? Don't you need me to hunt him down? To murder him?"

"No." The Duchess' hand was plucking at the quilt, folding an edge over, then unfolding it, then folding the fabric again. "My spies cannot find him. He has vanished. Narses too, though he might have been killed in the riots."

"Are you going to stop looking?" Thyatis' eyes narrowed in puzzlement.

"Yes. What could I do if I found him? He is beyond my power."

Thyatis took Anastasia's hand in hers. The Duchess's fingers felt cold and frail.

"You're tired," Thyatis said. "You should rest."

Anastasia nodded, closing her hand over Thyatis'. "I will. I will. Soon."

"Now," Thyatis said, weariness leaching into her voice. "We'll both lie down and rest for a little while, and these two"—the younger woman motioned with her head at Ila and Betia—"will watch over us while we sleep."

"That sounds nice." Anastasia's voice was faint. Her hand felt light in Thyatis' grip, as if the woman had been reduced to shadows and air. "Sleep now, dear."

"I will." Thyatis closed her eyes, smiling. "You too, Momma."

Anastasia stood slowly, tears leaking from the corners of her eyes. She turned the edge of the coverlet over Thyatis' hands, hiding the thin glassy web of scars. Then she bent down and kissed Thyatis' cheek. The younger woman was already snoring softly.

Ila watched the Duchess go out with a narrow-eyed glare, but when the two invaders were gone, she curled up on the side of the bed and closed her eyes. Thyatis' muscular arm, browned by the sun, webbed with old cuts and bruises, held her close.

After a moment, the little girl's eyes opened, anger replaced by mournful sadness. "I never got to ride my horses. Dumb rules . . ."

THE ARAB ENCAMPMENTS BEFORE CONSTANTINOPLE

A warm yellow glow suffused the tent. Night wind luffed canvas, then a drape lifted away and Zoë entered, her face a cold mask. Odenathus followed, unwilling to continue their argument inside the meeting tent. The

Palmyrene woman stopped, staring around at the faces of the men gathered under the pavilion, then let Odenathus take a place beside her.

The oil lamps threw distorted shadows on the peaked roof. A low murmur of noise died down as Zoë entered, so she raised an eyebrow in question. It was clear that the lords of the Decapolis, the Mekkan chiefs, the Judeans, even the Yemenite ship captains had been deep in conversation for some time. Her face was tightly controlled, showing neither friendship nor rancor to the captains of the Sahaba. She waited, saying nothing.

"Lady Zoë, good evening." Zamanes, King of Jerash, stood up and made a deep bow to her. "I am sorry that you were not told of the meeting earlier. Please, take no offense from this. We are all struggling with the death of our leader, our teacher."

"King Zamanes." Zoë inclined her head in his direction. There was a frosty edge to her voice. She looked around the circle of men again, eyes glinting. Only Shadin and Khalid met her gaze, but they were straightforward men. "What are you discussing?"

"We debate who will lead us." Something in the King's tone made it clear the matter was still in dispute. "We wonder what we shall do, now that both Mohammed and the Emperor of the East are dead. A black day I had not thought to see."

Zoë bowed her head and slowly raised the hood of her white robe and settled it over raven-dark hair. Her people had different burial customs than did the Mekkans, but she had taken care to discover how a woman of the desert city dressed when a close relative had died. Odenathus began to fidget at her side, but she glared at him sidelong, eyes bare slits, and he became still. She looked back to Zamanes. "Have you chosen?"

"No, my lady. There is dispute. Mohammed never spoke

about such things, so we are without his guidance in this matter."

Zoë nodded, glancing at Shadin. The broad-shouldered general shook his head minutely. The old mercenary had tremendous experience in war, but he did not want the burden of rule. She pretended to consider the matter. "The Mekkans will not follow a king of the Decapolis or some other land."

A low mutter came from the collection of clansmen along the wall to her left. They were already glaring at the captains and chiefs of the old Greek cities. Zoë saw many had begun to wear their clan and city colors rather than Mohammed's simple green and tan.

She continued, her voice becoming wry. "The lords of Jerash, Petra and Judea will not follow the barbarians out of the desert. I imagine that the Palmyrenes will not follow anyone."

That brought a bark of laughter from Zamanes, then a chuckle from everyone else. The tension in the room lessened minutely. All of the men listened carefully.

"You will not," she said, "find anyone to replace the lord Mohammed. His gift will not pass on to another. No one can be anointed his successor. We cannot elect a new receptacle for the power of the Lord of the World. The power and the strength came into him alone. What came upon him in the wilderness was a miracle and such things are not repeated at the whim of men." She bowed her head, letting the hood fall over her face. She knelt gracefully, her hands clasped before her. "The lord Mohammed is dead."

There was a rustling in the tent as men knelt on the ground, knees pressing into the loamy soil. Zoë struggled for a moment with tears, her face hidden, then mastered herself. "What you must do, my friends, is to decide whether you will remain here, in this foreign land, or whether you will return to your homes."

"Return!" A bleat of outrage came from the back of the

pavilion and Zoë saw the young eagle Khalid al'Walid standing, staring around him in alarm. Her dark brown eyes narrowed, seeing that while nearly all of the men in the tent had bent their heads in memory of Mohammed, Khalid had not. "We cannot return! That dog Heraclius may be dead, but his city still stands!"

"What business is that of ours now?" Zoë stood again, facing the young man. It seemed strange for a moment that they were of an age. He seemed younger to her, but Zoë supposed the years lay heavier upon her than on this rascal and whelp of the desert. No suffering touched his handsome face. "We came here following and trusting in Mohammed. We intended to punish Rome for its treachery. Now the emperor who betrayed my city and the Decapolis is dead. The Roman army has been shattered. Even without our help, the Persians press the city hard. If it falls, then Rome will suffer a defeat like none in their history."

"Lady Zoë, once you swore in my hearing to see every last Roman dead." Khalid opened his hands, including the whole assembly. "We have thrown off the yoke of Rome for the first time in over five hundred years! Each city is free, each clan, each tribe. That freedom can be assured if we, with our allies, take Constantinople. The Empire will be stunned by such a defeat. We will have years to prepare for their counterattack."

There was a stir among the chiefs and kings and Khalid looked at them sharply. "Yes, there will be a counterattack. Rome will not abandon the riches of Syria and the Indian trade. They will invade our lands again. Decades may pass before we are safe from attack. We must drive them hard, punish them, slaughter their armies, burn their cities, scatter their fleets . . . each victory gains us another day of freedom. We dare not leave!"

Zoë nodded absently, watching fear and confusion war on the faces of these men. It was plain to her, like a minnow swimming in perfectly clear water, that they had already discussed her suitability to lead. With sidelong glances and muted laughter, these chieftains dismissed her. On another day, when she possessed an atom of strength to rouse fury in her heart, she would task them for such a slight. Right now, on this cool summer night, in this damp and humid country, she did not care about their child's games.

"My lords." Her voice was calm and broke across Khalid's impassioned speech like a knife. "Know this. Though my city is in ruins and Rome still stands, I am putting aside my revenge. It has cost too much—too many Palmyrenes lie dead, the lord Mohammed has fallen. There is nothing to be gained here but more death. That Heraclius has fallen is enough for me."

Khalid stepped back, letting her speak, and Zoë felt a curious acceptance from the young man. He seemed pleased by this turn of events. She did not smile at him, though she knew he thought he had won some obscure contest between them. Let him.

"I am going to take the body of the lord Mohammed," she continued, "and I am going back to Mekkah, where he will be laid to rest in the house of white stones, beside his wife. This is the proper thing, and I will see it done."

Shadin stood, towering over the men around him. His lean old face was pinched with concern, fists clenched at his sides. "My lady, you will need a proper escort! The lord Mohammed should not go to rest without brave men to carry his bier, to praise the days of his life, to extol his wisdom. I will come with you. All of the Tanukh will come with you."

"Shadin," she said, smiling, "I am touched by your concern. I think that I can find my way."

"No." Shadin shook his head slowly, neatly trimmed beard making a long shadow against the wall of the tent. "The lord Mohammed did mighty things, like one of the heroes of old. He deserves a hero's burial. Our numbers are not great, but if you will have us, we will ride with you to Mekkah." A low rumble of approval met Shadin's words. Many of the older men in the tent agreed. They did not like this crowded, damp land.

"I accept your offer, Shadin, because I know your heart is true." Zoë smiled at the old fighter and made a slight bow. "I will take a ship, a Palmyrene ship, and I will leave in the morning. These things said, there is no reason for me to be here, so I will leave."

Turning, Zoë stepped out of the tent. Odenathus made to call her back, but someone called his name and he turned away. A hubbub of voices rose behind her and she smiled, looking up at the drift of stars that filled the night sky. The tents glowed with lanterns and candles, making a pretty scene in the darkness. A great weight had risen from her. The thought of trying to wrangle all of those men and their pride and their ambitions had weighed on her. She hoped Khalid received a full measure of his victory! It was a relief to see that she did not have to pick up the mantle Mohammed had let fall.

A breeze came up off the Propontis, stirring the leaves in the trees. She turned away from the tents and began to walk, content to let her feet find their own way in the darkness.

Cloaked in shadow, Patik raised a hand and the two figures behind him became perfectly still. The big Persian could not match their complete lack of sound and motion, but he settled back, looking away from the slim figure of the woman passing them in the moonlight. Watching her out of the corner of his eye, he waited until she had descended the trail leading down through the Persian encampment to the beach. The Arab fleet was moored there, many of the galleys drawn up on the strand. After a little while, the crunch of gravel and twigs under her boots faded and he moved again.

Patik motioned the two figures ahead of him and waited while they slipped past. They carried a heavy cask between them on a pole, and the vessel sloshed quietly with liquid as they moved. Behind them, the noise from the big tent continued to seep out into the night air. Many men were arguing, without thought to what moved in darkness beyond the light of their fires.

Despite the gloom under the trees crowding the shore, Patik was able to follow the two dark figures through high brush and down into an inlet. The moon rose high enough to glitter on the water, letting him make out the sleek curved prow of a ship. Patik hurried, reaching the long gangplank as the two figures stepped onto the deck of the merchantman. The Persian stepped aboard only a grain later and sheathed the dagger. No one had seen them.

The deck of the ship was dark. There were no lanterns or lamps. Patik thought this wise, for the shoreline was well patrolled by both the Persians and the Arabs. The Romans had tried to send raiding parties across the Golden Horn in small boats. Many might question the presence of a hidden ship on the Galatan shore. The two dark figures moved carefully across the deck, the gurgling cask swinging between them. A patch of sable on indigo appeared, barely outlined by the gleam of the moon. They descended. Patik stopped at the top of the stairs, nostrils flaring at a subtle foul odor.

"Descend." The voice was hoarse and strange, filled with a metallic echo. Patik swallowed, suddenly nervous. He was afraid of the voice in the darkness. A stronger fear moved his feet and he climbed down into the hull of the ship. Invisible hands moved, closing the hatch over his head. Now the smell was stronger.

A black wagon sat in the hold, high round wheels touching the hull on either side. A shape moved in the darkness and a dim light sprang up, barely sufficient to illuminate the cloaked figures of the Shanzdah standing on either side of the cask, hoods thrown back, pale, leprous heads gleaming. Beside the wagon crouched a tall creature with the head of a black dog. It had the limbs of a man, smooth and muscular, but dark red outlined black pits serving as eyes. A rasping, metallic breath hissed from the iron mouth. Patik felt weak and put his hand on the wooden stairway for support.

The Shanzdah crouched down on either side of the cask, boots crunching in the layer of earth covering the floor. There was a sound of metal under great stress, then a *ping* as two bolts cracked in iron fingers. The two creatures moved in unison, lifting the cover of the cask. A strange light spilled out, a deep blue that made the darkness seem light. Patik blinked, eyes tearing up as if he had been blinded.

"Lift me up," gargled a terrible, inhuman voice. The Shanzdah rose, hands holding up a mottled, reptilian skull. Slow, thick liquid spilled away from fluted nostrils and a leering mouth lined with endless rows of tiny sharp teeth. "Ah. Now I can see. Turn me about."

The skull rotated as the Shanzdah moved, and Patik crumpled to the ground, consumed by overwhelming fear. Pale green points of light gleamed in deep-set eye sockets. Those eyes turned towards him and he felt the air turn cold. Ghastly laughter echoed in the black hold.

"Greetings, loyal Patik . . . or should I say the Great Prince Shahin, cousin of the late King of Kings, general of armies . . . The garb of a common soldier suits you. But here, you have done me such good service! You will be richly rewarded for your loyalty. Where is our prize?"

Shahin struggled to rise, arms weak as jelly. Despite clawing fear, the Persian managed to grope for his belt and draw forth a square of gleaming black cloth like a handkerchief tied up with a leaden cord. "Here," the Persian gasped. "He is here."

"Delightful!" The skull laughed, deep blue light growing stronger. Now some details of the hold could be made out, though everything was reversed, light for dark. The silent, immobile figures of two more of the Shanzdah became visible, standing against the sides of the wagon. "Give him to my beloved pet. They are old dear friends."

Patik crawled forward, unable to rise, and pressed the black cloth into the hands of the dog-headed man. That creature made no sound but took the cloth and then stepped back.

"Now, where is my body? Bring it here." The skull's voice tittered with laughter, though Patik thought it was the sound of crushed bone blown by a forge-hot wind. Averting his eyes, the Persian crawled back to the base of the stairs. Dreadful sounds began to issue forth from the wagon.

"Hello, auntie." Zoë ran her hands along the carved top of the sarcophagus. "I'm sorry you were lost in the sea for so long. I'm sorry I haven't come to see you." The rich dark wood was grainy with salt. Khalid's divers had removed the wrack and barnacles, but the original luster was gone. The Palmyrene woman sighed, her fingers tracing the inlaid figures of cloaked men and women, the camels and fine ships with triangular sails. By her command, the casket remained sealed.

Zoë sat down next to the sarcophagus, suddenly tired. She had put off this moment for days, hiding in her own tent. Zoë put her face in her hands, trying not to weep. The loss of Zenobia and the city forced her mind into something like madness, fueled by rage and a singular desire to destroy Rome. Then Mohammed and his gentle touch and kind words woke her from the dream of vengeance. Now he had been taken away and she felt empty. The vibrating fury sustaining her for so many months was just . . . gone. It felt very strange, her mind seemingly clear but purposeless.

What do I do now? In the pavilion, the desire to take the bodies of her aunt and her friend away had been very strong. That still felt like the proper and right thing to do. But after that? *Perhaps,* she thought, *I will leave all these lands. India is not far from Mekkah. There are many ships which ply those waters. They say the mountains looking*

down upon the golden cities of Mauryasana are the abode
of the gods. I could climb them and see.

Zoë was suddenly ashamed of dragging Zenobia from
her mountain tomb, desecrating her burial place. She stood,
lithe body rising gracefully, and turned, bowing to her
dead aunt.

"Auntie, I'm so sorry. I will take you home straightaway
and see that you rest among your fathers and grandfathers.
They will be missing you, I'm sure!" She turned, facing
the bier holding the body of Mohammed, wrapped in white
cloths. The spears had been lashed together with leather
cords, each man in the army of the Sahaba contributing
some portion. She supposed that, someday, men would say
the leather was washed in tears, the spears in blood. The
soldiers had been overcome, many falling to the ground,
distraught, when the body of the teacher had been carried
into the camp.

"Mohammed . . ." Zoë had to clear her throat. "I will
take you home, too. Shadin and I will carry you back to
the desert city. Khadijah is waiting for you, I know she is.
You will be happy there, lying beside her. . . ." Tears
flooded and Zoë could not continue, covering her face,
shuddering. "Oh. Oh, I'm so sorry. I'm so sorry. I should
have been there at your side. Damn that Khalid and his
thugs! They couldn't keep you safe. Not like I . . . should
have."

A thin tracery of fire appeared in the air, circling Zoë's
head. It rippled with white and blue, crawling through the
air. She was crying too hard to notice, but the glowing
worm spun out from her, encircling the sarcophagus, the
bier, then the whole tent. Outside, unheard, there was a
shout of alarm. "Why are you gone?" Zoë could barely
speak. "I just found you, my dear friend. Is this your God's
work? This cruelty? Does he love you more than I do? Is
he jealous?"

Fire burned in a trembling sheet, surrounding the tent,
lighting up the entire interior, glowing through the cloth

walls. Waves of heat washed over her, drying her tears. Zoë looked up, startled by the brilliant light, and stared at the wall of flame, puzzled by its unexpected appearance.

"Zoë!" Distantly, she heard Odenathus calling out to her. She turned around, seeing the wavering figure of her cousin through the leaping, silent flames. "Zoë!"

Scowling, wiping tears away from her eyes with the back of one hand, the Palmyrene woman préssed her other hand towards the ground. With the motion, the fire settled, sinking into the earth. The light dimmed, then went out, leaving the night darker than before. Outside the tent, some of the Sahaba gathered, gawking. Odenathus waited just outside the ring of smoking ground. He stepped into the tent, alarmed. Zoë made a face at him and turned away. The onlookers, seeing the look on her face, quietly slipped away.

"Zoë . . . what are you doing?" Odenathus leaned against the sarcophagus, trying to see her face. He sounded worried.

"Go away." Zoë wiped her eyes again. "I would like to be alone."

"No. You've been hiding in your tent for days. I wanted to talk to you."

"About what?" She turned again, keeping her face averted.

Odenathus sighed, sitting back on the edge of the sarcophagus. His foot tapped restlessly against the heavy wood. "Do you want me to come with you to Palmyra and Mekkah?"

Zoë faced him, her arms crossed. "You don't need my permission to stay here with Khalid and the army. They will need you, I suppose. The Romans still have some thaumaturges. You're pretty strong now . . . you could help them."

"Zoë, I do need your permission." Odenathus was very serious. Zoë lifted her head in question. "You are queen of the city. I am in your service. By your decree in the ruins, I command our paltry forces." He made a half-smile, long face brightening.

"Yes." Zoë sighed. "You are my subject. But I have already decided to set aside this crown, for all its riches and glory." A wry, deprecating tone crept into her voice. "Where is the empire of Palmyra? Where are the courtiers, the glorious city, the thousand maids and servants? I rule a ragged band of refugees, some ships, a great deal of broken shale and desert sand. I will not command any man or woman of the city to follow me. Shadin has volunteered, and his service I will accept."

Odenathus' expression changed subtly, growing sad. "You won't stay?"

"Here?" Zoë laughed, a silvery sound like icy water rushing over tumbled polished stone. "This is a dreadful country!" Something like a smile crept into her face, crinkling the corners of her dark brown eyes. "You have more here than I—Khalid and this band of brothers. The war."

Odenathus nodded, looking at the ground. "Do you remember when we reached Antioch after the Persian campaign? You were going to stay in the Legion—you thought it suited you. I was going to leave, to go home and get married! Now, everything is reversed."

"I'm not going to get married," Zoë said in a very dry tone. Then her voice softened. "Have you found what you were looking for?"

"Yes." Odenathus looked up, a plaintive expression on his face, half-confidence, half-remorse. "Do you suppose that our battle-meld will still hold, even with so many leagues between us?"

I think so, she thought, and he smiled, hearing her in his own mind. *You should go back. They are still arguing . . . I suppose Khalid will win in the end. He will be the kalif, the successor.*

Yes.

Zoë stepped close to her cousin, kissed his brow, then hugged him fiercely. After a long moment, they stood apart. Zoë did not watch him leave, turning instead to the cloth-wrapped body of Mohammed. Exhaustion crept upon her, making her arms and legs heavy as lead. She wanted to look upon his face, to see the proud brow, the noble nose, one last time. She yawned tremendously.

"It can't be that late," Zoë said crossly, raising a hand. The lamps died. Darkness folded around the tent. She could see the moon, a half-crescent dipping behind the pines. "Oh, it is late."

The thought of crossing the camp to her tent was too much for her. She laid down on the ground at the foot of Zenobia's sarcophagus, curling up, cloak laid on the ground as a bedcloth. Within a breath, she was sound asleep. A little time passed and then there was a clacking and a rustling in the casket. Something moved, sounding like a great number of crickets and beetles trapped in a stone bucket.

Sleep, daughter, sleep. All these foul dreams will soon pass away. Sleep and dream of delightful things. Dream of home.

NEAR THE CHARISIAN GATE, CONSTANTINOPLE

Shadows crept across broken earth, oozing among the fallen. Shade gathered in the moat, among rotted corpses and crumpled armor, until the ditch was brimming with night. Above, on the walls and towers around the gate, torches fluttered. Many eyes peered down from the battlements and from arrow slits. Despite weariness, the watch from the towers did not waver. The men of the city expected an attack.

Yet no one marked the appearance of a slim figure

among the pooling shadows. It came swiftly, drifting across the road, and stopped just outside the pale flicker of the torchlight. Subtly, night deepened around the figure. A soft rustling echoed back from the massive wall, but even that sound failed to reach the ears of the men watching above. The lord Dahak knelt, dark cape clinging to thin, bony shoulders. Here, hidden by the shroud of night, he did not bother to maintain even the simplest disguise. Fine scales glinted in the web of his fingers as they placed a stone box, only a few inches long, on the ground. The lord of the Ten Serpents grinned in the darkness, and he felt *strong*. His passage across the battlefield refreshed him, and his deft victory over the Voice of Heaven put chill joy in his heart. Tonight, with his armies everywhere victorious and his enemies in disarray, Dahak knelt on the cold earth and opened the stone box with anticipation. Before he had stepped beyond the threshold and looked upon the face of his master, the still-human sorcerer would have been paralyzed by fear. Even seeing such a box, looking upon such loathsome glyphs, holding such a foul object up to the sky would have been impossible.

In the box were two gleaming white pearls, each the size of a thumb. They nestled in silk within a cage of lead and gold. The inner surface of the box was etched with dozens of tiny, almost invisible signs. Dahak let the box lie open for a moment, long fingers pressed to his temples, his attention carefully directed elsewhere. Any adept would quail away from the vortex of forces rushing and rippling in the hidden world. Enormous pressures gathered, the warp and weft of the entire earth pressing against the box, trying to drive the twin spheres from existence. Shining gradients deepened, and Dahak felt his own power pressed aside by a deluge of singing threads eager to annihilate the pearls. The stone box began to sink into the earth.

The ground groaned, but the watchers ignored the slight rattle running the length and breadth of the city. Earthquakes were common along the Propontis. Dahak walked away from the gate and the box, which vanished beneath the loose soil. With each step he took away from the pearls, the pressure in the air lessened and his step was quicker. Curious, the sorcerer let his perception expand. After a moment, Dahak smiled. Far away and deep beneath the earth, something was stirring, uncoiling and rising from dark places. A thin, keening wail rippled through the ether, monstrous children crying out for an even more horrific parent.

The lord of the Ten Serpents looked over his shoulder at the looming walls of the city. He laughed softly at the impudence of the builders. Men thought they were lords of the world. They were wrong. The hidden masters, those like the abyssal shape Dahak served, truly moved the heavens in their courses. As he turned away he paused. At the edge of perception, something winked and flashed like a golden coin spinning in daylight.

Dahak's eyes, gleaming in the darkness, widened. His head came up sharply, as if he scented something in the air. There was a brief impression of spinning bronze and a lambent, cold green flame. A long, excited hiss whistled through the sorcerer's teeth.

An Eye of Shadow! he thought, avarice and delight stirring in his cold heart. *They were not all destroyed? Ahhhh* . . . Base thoughts stirred in the old, old brain of the creature. Clawlike fingers scratched restlessly at a glassy scar on his chest. The bite of the flint knife had been deep. *Perhaps . . . no, surely that door is closed! The Sisterhood would not be careless, leaving such a prize within reach.* . . . Lids dipped over his eyes, flicking open and closed, one by one. He rummaged through ancient memories, turning them this way and that like discarded trinkets found in a rubbish pit. Was there gold among the dross? *They sealed the land in water, to keep my hands from the burning stone,* Dahak remembered, even the language of his memories changing as he reached back across an abyss of time.

But with an Eye ... an Eye to sees all that is hidden, I might reach Atlas' drowned halls without danger.

Very deep in the mind of the sorcerer, far below any thought that he might allow himself to peruse, the thought of freedom kindled and a fingertip, sharp as knapped flint, scratched again at the glassy scar. Shadows folded around Dahak and he slipped away into the night.

THE PALATINE HILL, ROMA MATER

Late-afternoon sun gleamed from columns arrayed across the temple of the Divine Claudians. Atop the triangular pediment, dozens of brightly painted statues glowed in the direct light of the sun. Below the flight of white steps, a busy flood of humanity thronged the avenue separating the Palatine and its confusion of red-roofed palaces from the Caelian Hill and the temple. High on the side of the Palatine, below a monumental platform built by Emperor Septimus Severus to hold his new palace, the window of a third-floor apartment was open.

The reflected light made a bright rectangle on the wall opposite the window. The room was hot and dim. Maxian slept uneasily, his dreams troubled. His feet twitched and hands trembled, sometimes grasping at empty air. Linen sheets and a woolen blanket were scattered on the floor.

Across the little valley, a gong rang in the nave of the temple, signaling the end of the day. A reedy chorus of oboes followed and then the priests, their robes carefully arranged, tall hats on their heads, began to descend the steps, hands filled with offerings, with smoking incense on silver platters, with bundled rods and portraits of the great emperors. The procession turned upon reaching the avenue and walked north in a stately manner. The nine priests wound through the crowded avenues and into the Forum, where the temple of the Deified Caesar stood at the edge of the great public square.

In the dim room, Maxian's eyelids suddenly opened and he shuddered from the crown of his head to the soles of his feet. A wild look of rage and delight entered his face. With effort, he rose from the bed. The Prince cast about the room, legs weak. There were only two sleeping couches, an end table and a leather trunk. On the top of the trunk was a wooden tray with a strigil, a shaving razor, some soap and a basin for water.

Maxian crept towards the trunk, hand trembling, and seized the razor. He stood, swaying, and fumbled the bright metal to his neck. His fist clenched, tendons standing out, and the blade cut into his neck with a sharp, sawing motion.

"Here now!" Gaius Julius bustled into the room, then leapt to the Prince's side. His ancient hand, suddenly swift, seized Maxian's wrist. Gaius cried out, alarmed at the terrific strength in the Prince's grip, but managed to jam his own hand between the razor and Maxian's carotid. "Lord Prince! What . . . are . . . you doing?"

Maxian's face contorted into a terrible grimace, turning red, veins throbbing in his forehead. The razor bit deep into Gaius Julius' palm. Pale, thin blood bubbled out of the wound, but Gaius, his ancient frame filling with unexpected strength, pressed back, digging the fingers of his other hand into the Prince's wrist. For a moment, the two men swayed back and forth, struggling, and then the old Roman kicked the Prince's leg and Maxian was thrown to the floor.

The razor flew away, clattering off the wall. Gaius Julius tried to jam his elbow into the Prince's neck, pinning him, but the younger man twisted away, sending Gaius flying into the sleeping couch with a bang. The old Roman scrambled up, his toga completely awry, tensed for battle.

Maxian stared at him, his face blank. Then the Prince put a hand to his neck and it came away damp with blood. "Gaius? You cut me?"

"No." The old Roman breathed a sigh of relief, seeing Maxian's familiar expression in the younger man's face. "You were trying to cut your own throat."

"I was?" Maxian looked around the small, bare room. "What is this place?"

Gaius Julius laughed. "Some rooms of mine. Do you remember collapsing on the roof of the Flavian?"

"Yes . . ." The Prince stared at his hands, at the blood, then down at his naked body. "I was in the court of the dreadful king. His eyes struck me . . . I was destroyed, reduced to atoms." He laughed. "But I am alive. I am still alive!"

"Yes, you are." Gaius stood up. He stretched his arms and legs, bending his back. "Thankfully, you are alive and yourself again. Please, my lord, don't hurt yourself. I'm not sure if my social schedule can afford such a blow! Do you remember anything else?"

Maxian shook his head sharply, then brushed his ear with a hand. "There were many voices, like flies buzzing. I remember . . . they were trying to tell me something, something important. Ah, it is gone now."

"Good." Gaius Julius looked at the young man sharply, his high forehead wrinkling. "Did it work? Your ritual, your spell?"

Maxian grinned, brushing his long dark hair back out of his eyes. "I'm alive! That's enough for the . . . moment." The Prince suddenly swayed, his face growing pale. Gaius Julius caught him before he could fall, then eased him down on the couch. Beads of sweat had appeared on Maxian's face. "Gaius . . ."

"What is it?" The old Roman leaned close, trying to hear the Prince's faint voice.

"There is a great darkness in the East . . . I can feel it, like a cancer."

"A cancer?" Gaius Julius looked stricken. "In your body?"

"No." Maxian seemed to rally, gathering himself. He sat up, his face a grimace of pain. "There is something attacking the Empire itself. The Oath is not strong enough to hold it back."

"The Oath? You can feel what it feels?" Gaius Julius took a step back, astounded.

"Yes." Maxian gasped, standing, moving as though the air itself resisted him. "We've got to get into the palace. There is a device I need in the library there."

"Empress?" A polite knock echoed through the salon where Helena was sitting, writing at an elegant wooden table. At the sound, the murmur of conversation stopped. She looked up, putting down the snow-white quill in her hand on a holder of Cosian marble. A Praetorian centurion stood at the door, his helmet tucked under one arm, its stiff horsetail plume jutting up behind his elbow. The man looked more than usually stoic. Helena smiled brightly at him, catching his eye before it could wander.

"What is it, Salvius? Are you looking for my husband? He's in the Curia Julia, hobnobbing with the senators. He is in a taxing mood today."

"I know, Empress. A message has come from the thaumaturge watching the *telecast*. It is Empress Martina. There is a problem."

"Very well." Helena rose, smoothing down her cream-colored gown. "I will be there immediately. Return to your post."

The centurion saluted, then disappeared from the doorway. Helena rose, motioning to Anastasia and Thyatis to remain quiet, and went to the door. She looked outside and saw that only the usual guards were at the end of the hallway. She closed the door, then set the latch. Hopefully, no one would barge in unannounced.

"I must go," Helena said, turning back to her guests.

"Martina is a dizzy young thing. A problem for her may be of any measure, small or large—the slight offered by one of the *logothetes* or an invasion of titans. I will be back soon."

Anastasia rose from her chair, dark silk stola rustling like aspen leaves. "I don't understand. Martina is Empress of the East, she is a thousand miles away." One of the Duchess's eyebrows, recently restored to its usual glossy black shape, rose. The weariness that had afflicted her seemed to be gone, banished by Thyatis' recovery and their nominal reconciliation. Helena was not sure how reconciled Thyatis was, but they were on speaking terms at least. The little blond slave Betia rose in tandem with her mistress, like a pale shadow.

Helena nodded, distracted, as she gathered up her papers. News from the East had been worse and worse. Galen was working overtime, trying to adapt to the reported destruction of all four legions he had sent to raise the siege of Constantinople. "There is a device that lets us speak with her, if there is pressing need. Galen calls it a *telecast,* for it allows sight and sound to be sent far away. Come, if you wish to see it, you may, but we must hurry."

Anastasia and Betia stood, gathering up their palla cloaks. Thyatis stepped away from the wall, limping slightly, her bandages still visible under the tunic she wore. The younger woman's sea-gray eyes flicked from one woman to another, seeing deep concern on the Duchess's face. The Empress's mind was already far away. "Where is this device?"

"In a room off the small library. Quickly now, we will take a hidden passage. It would not do for you to be seen here, not with all these troubles in the streets."

Helena walked quickly, leading them through a series of interconnected rooms, across a hallway, and then up a narrow flight of stairs. At the end of the stairway, she put a heavy bronze key in a complicated-looking lock, turned it twice, then pushed the door open after a solid *click* was heard.

They stepped into a high-ceilinged room, the clerestory pierced by many arched windows. Small panes of glass filled diamond-shaped spaces in an iron grillwork. The walls of the room were covered with wooden racks pierced with storage slots. Everything had the peculiar musty smell of books and scrolls. At the center of the room, illuminated by slanting bars of late-afternoon light, was a granite block. On the top of the block, wreathed in sparking green fire, something was spinning with enormous speed.

Anastasia blanched, her hand going to her mouth. Helena strode forward, her head high, and gestured imperiously at the thaumaturge to step aside. The fat man was sweating, his face drawn and pale, but he moved aside, letting the Empress look into the burning disk.

Thyatis looked at Anastasia with concern. The Duchess had turned quite white and was only standing with the swift assistance of Betia, who was holding her up by main strength.

"What is it?" Thyatis leaned close, her fist groping at her waist for a sword that was not there. "You're trembling."

"That thing . . ." Anastasia could barely whisper. Her glorious violet eyes were huge, reflecting the dazzling green fire. "It should *not* be here. They should not use it in this way! O goddess, the danger . . ."

"What should we do?" Thyatis glanced over her shoulder. Helena was snapping questions at the image of a frightened young woman wavering in the middle of the spinning disk. "I can strike down the thaumaturge—that would break the spell."

"Yes," breathed Anastasia, pulling herself together. Terrible fear was still plain in her face. "We must get the device out of here, right away. No *man* should be allowed near the *inum da'umimtim armirtum nesi*! This is forbidden! Can you kill him quickly?"

Thyatis nodded, though she had no weapon save her bare hands. She shifted stance, rolling up on the balls of her feet as if she were floating. Helena had her hands on the granite block, listening intently to the phantasmal woman, her face growing more and more serious. At her side, the red-bearded thaumaturge was sweating heavily, his whole attention turned inward.

The main door to the room suddenly banged open, making everyone jump. The telecast's spin slackened markedly and the vision of Martina disappeared. Helena spun, a sharp word on her lips. She stopped cold and closed her mouth.

Maxian stood in the doorway, an old man holding the door open behind him. The Prince was wearing only a hastily thrown on cloak and a black unbelted tunic. He was barefoot. "Helena?" Maxian sounded surprised, brushing unruly hair back from his forehead. "Sister, what are you doing here?"

"Trying to learn what has happened at Constantinople," snapped the Empress. "Gart, get this thing working again. Now." Her cold tone brooked nothing but obedience.

"Yes, Empress." Gart swallowed, his round face almost as red as his beard. "I will try."

"You will do this thing." Helena's fierce look made the man start in surprise. "If you do not, you will be killed." Gart nodded, then pressed his hands together and closed his eyes, thick lips moving silently as he tried to center himself.

"Let me." Maxian pushed past the thaumaturge, breaking the German's concentration again, the Prince's attention fixed on the slowly spinning bronze disks. The outermost disk, carved with runes and symbols, had already clattered to the granite surface of the block "I know the necessary pattern. You were looking upon Constantinople?"

"Yes, before you barged in, giving everyone a fright." Helena stepped aside, motioning violently behind her back to the three women at the hidden doorway. "I had no idea you were in the city."

"I was ill." Maxian moved his right hand in a circling pattern. A sharp, metallic taste suffused the air. The bronze disks whipped up into the air, emitting a keening sound. The green fire licked from the edges of each segment as they spun faster and faster. In the blink of an eye, they were a solid blur and the sound had hissed down to a nearly inaudible hum. An image of a blue and white and brown sphere leapt into being, then was swiftly replaced by a rushing vision of clouds and sea, then twilight and a city. A great city. It was burning and covered by swiftly moving darkness.

"Ah!" Maxian shouted in dismay and stepped back. The blood drained from his face. "This is the enemy." He clenched his jaw, his body stiffening. The vision changed again, suddenly focusing on a dark room and the pale, frightened face of a young woman. A boy stood behind her, his face tight with concentration. This time the air did not waver or distort. The image of the Eastern Empress was clear and perfect, as if she were standing only feet away. "Empress Martina?"

"Yes," quavered the girl in the burning disk. "Who are you?"

"I am the Caesar Maxian, Prince of the Western Empire. Your city is under attack. Do you know what comes against you?"

"No!" Martina seemed on the edge of complete panic. A little boy, perhaps only two years old, was clutched in her arms. "There was this awful sound, like the earth itself groaning in pain, and the darkness came! I can hear sounds of battle. . . . What can we do?"

"Stand away from the disk," grated Maxian, raising his arm stiffly. There seemed to be a terrible resistance in the air around him, but the stone floor under his feet suddenly splintered and cracked. The edges of the granite block were shedding dust and small flakes in a drifting cloud.

The sound began to rise again, hurting Helena's ears.

The Empress had stepped back and now she felt something press against her face, pushing her away from the Prince. She stumbled, unprepared, and felt powerful hands catch her, lift her up and place her in Anastasia's arms. The Duchess clapped a hand over the Empress's mouth and together they slipped back into the dark opening of the hidden door. Betia drew the door almost closed behind them.

Thyatis was frozen by indecision. She was wounded, weaponless, her side and leg still throbbing with pain. The Prince had his back to her, power wicking up into the air around him in a thin shining cloud. His entire concentration was focused on the disk and the young woman on the other side.

"I am coming through," Thyatis heard him say, "stand well back."

Thyatis turned, casting about for a weapon, a quill knife, a candlestick, anything!

She met the eyes of the old man standing just inside the door. They were a keen dark brown, and she recognized him—the *editore* from the senator's party. There was a strange sense of familiarity, of recognition, but then her anger flooded up. Unconsciously, she snarled, her teeth bared in challenge. He smiled wistfully, then shook his head.

"Don't do it," he said in a soft voice, barely loud enough to carry over the grating hum issuing from the floor, the walls, the air. "You should go. Quickly!"

Thyatis stepped back into the hidden passage, her eyes locked with his, glittering with thwarted rage. Shadow fell over her, though the burning green light of the telecast gleamed in her eyes for a long moment. Then the door swung closed with a soft *click*.

In the room, the sound of the telecast grew to a howling roar and winds began to rise in the confined space, lashing at the books and scrolls, ripping them into the air, swirling in a tight cyclone around the man and the blazing-bright disk. The image of Martina had fled, and Maxian gathered himself, all of the strength and power at his command focused on this one thing.

Like begets like. Like is like. Two identical things are the same thing.

He sprang up onto the edge of the granite block, feeling the stone slough away under his foot, then leapt, leg and arm extended, into the furiously whirling disk, which had expanded enormously, now easily taller than a man.

The air shook with a tremendous *boom!* Gaius Julius was thrown back against the door, cracking his shoulder against the oaken panel. He turned his head away, blinded by a brilliant light. Tears streamed down his cheeks and he raised a hand, trying to block out the radiance.

═◎═◎═◎═◎═◎═◎═◎═◎═◎═◎═◎═◎═◎═◎═◎═◎═◎═◎═

CONSTANTINOPLE

)I(

A ceramic cup danced on the edge of a low wooden table. Dwyrin struggled awake, his mind dulled by exhaustion. It took him an endless moment to realize that the cup should not be spinning and bouncing from side to side. Then the table itself jumped up with a *bang* and the cup toppled over, crashing to the floor. The Hibernian, eyes wide, clung to his cot, feeling the entire building dance on its foundations. A long, slow, rumbling *crack-crack-crack* echoed out of the floor. Then there was silence. Dwyrin blinked. Dust was drifting down from the ceiling. He stared at the vaulted roof, watching in horror as cracks rippled across the plaster. There was a grinding sound.

He rolled out of bed, then jumped to the wall. Plaster cascaded down in a loud *boom* and threw up a huge cloud of choking white smoke. Coughing, Dwyrin scrambled to find his woolen trousers, pulled them on, grabbed a tunic and then bolted out of the room.

The hallway was filled with confused, frightened men. The Faithful Guard had taken a severe beating in the battle among the tombs, losing nearly half of their number. The survivors were a little jumpy. Dwyrin struggled to pull the tunic over his head, standing in the doorway of the room he shared with Nicholas and Vladimir. The Scandians were shouting, their voices hoarse as bears'. The air was filled with dust, making it difficult to see. Some of the lanterns had been knocked down by the shock. Luckily, they had guttered out on the tiled floor.

"Dwyrin!" Vladimir appeared out of the murk. His sweeping mane of dark hair was white with plaster dust and he had a cut alongside his nose. "Something is happening. You must come quickly."

"I can feel it." Dwyrin ran after the Walach, who had not waited for him to answer. He could feel something, a terrible heavy pressure in the air. There was something moving in the hidden world, something monstrous. Dwyrin's mouth felt dry and his limbs seemed to weaken, even as he ran, feeling the enormous power that had shaken the earth. Vlad led him out of the wing of the Bucoleon that housed the Guard and up a flight of stairs. The stairs were narrow and old, a tight spiral leading into a tower standing at the end of the palace wall.

Nicholas was waiting, his face drawn and grim, looking to the west. He did not turn when Vladimir, huffing and puffing, reached the platform. Dwyrin climbed up, breathing hard, and leaned with relief on the balustrade. "What is it?"

"There, you can see for yourself." Nicholas had Brunhilde bare in his arms, his fist wrapped around her hilt, the flat of the blade pressed against his shoulder. Faint lights

gleamed in her steel body. Dwyrin turned, staring out over
the gloomy roofs of the city. Lights burned in many windows, but the city huddled in darkness under a sky filled
with racing clouds. Far in the distance, up the long slope
of the city, past the towering pillar of Constantine in his
great forum, past the looming inner walls, he could see a
line of fire running from horizon to horizon, all along the
massive bulk of the outer, Theodosian walls.

Dwyrin began to chant under his breath, summoning the
focus to enter the hidden world. Then he stopped, for his
mortal vision saw something impossible. The sky in the
west darkened as if ink spilt into the air. A wave of ebon
swept across the sky, racing past the clouds, covering the
moon. A great shadow fell over the city, swallowing up
the towers, the houses, then the column of Constantine,
then lapping over the walls of the Hippodrome.

Vladimir snarled, growling at the sky, but then the
blackness engulfed their vantage and the palace below. The
air began to grow cold, and Dwyrin could feel the black
tide draining strength from the air. Nicholas cursed, then
held out Brunhilde at an angle from his body. The faint
lights in the steel brightened until a dim bluish glow illuminated their boots and the stone floor of the platform.
Dwyrin did not notice, for his attention was fixed, stunned,
on the western horizon.

Something was moving there, in the darkness, something enormous. With a trembling hand he made the seeing
square, and distant towers leapt into view. Flames roared
up around them, violent and red, silhouetting the gates
against a wall of fire. The whole wall of the city was lit
by the blaze. Then, even as Dwyrin gasped in horror, a
black forest of monstrous tentacles rose above the stone
battlements. Glistening in the firelight, writhing with impossible life, they curled around the massive towers. Stone
buckled and cracked under the pressure. Thousands more
tentacles surged up, clawing at the merlons, crushing the
tiled roofs, squirming into arrow slits.

Boom! Even at this distance, Dwyrin could hear the collapse of the towers athwart the Charisian Gates. The air trembled with the noise. Vladimir and Nicholas stared out into the darkness, but they could not see what he saw. Dwyrin looked away, his mind reeling. "We have to go."

"Where?" Nicholas bent down, eyes flint hard and intent on the boy. "Where do we go?"

"To the sound of battle," the Hibernian snapped. The thing attacking the wall had shaken the earth with its footsteps. A nightmare out of some hidden pit, long thought lost and dead. Such power. . . . Dwyrin quailed at the thought of facing such a thing in the hidden world, of seeing its true shape writhing in chaos. *I must fight this thing,* he resolved, remembering an old man in a ruined temple, crouched over a bundle of wet twigs. *There is a fire that lights the world. It cannot be extinguished!*

Without another word, the young man turned from his friends and raced down the stairway, his feet leaping from step to step, his hands sliding along the ancient walls, holding him up. Nicholas sheathed Brundhilde with a muttered curse, then followed as fast as he dared. Behind them, Vladimir snarled at the sky again, then stopped, smelling a loathsome taint in the night air. Whimpering, he descended, the fur on the back of his neck and his hands bristling.

"Wait for me!" he called out plaintively. Ancient things were loose in the night.

A queer, groaning sound filled the musty air, rolling slowly along the length of the corridor. Stone ground against stone. The Dark Queen sneezed, then hissed at the stone roof over her head. Dust was spilling down out of the cracks between the huge slabs. Irritably, she flipped her long hair, trying to get clinging gray powder out of the thick tresses. At her feet, the little black cat meowed imperiously, darting ahead, then turning to see if she was following.

The Queen suddenly paused, turning to the west. She could feel something moving in the earth, shaking the land. She tensed, perceiving the writhing chaos of darkness that was pressing against the ancient walls of the city. "Child, this is very bad. Our old enemy has grown reckless. He must think himself a great power to lure one of Shudde-M'ell's children here."

The Queen ran forward in silence, her feet light on the cracked stone floor, though she did not leave any tracks in the dust. There were plenty of other smudges and footprints to lead her. The little black cat's nose was keen, too, and it darted ahead, a shadow amongst deeper shadows. The Queen could smell a daywalker infant in the air, her elegant nose wrinkling at the pungent odor. Ahead of them, a strange humming roar could be heard.

A bar of green light cut across the corridor. The Queen slipped up to the portal, then eased the heavy oaken door open a finger's breadth. At her feet, the little cat wormed through the opening, padding boldly forward on soft feet. A huge whirling disk of viridian fire lit the room. The hum, even louder now, came from a set of bronze disks that spun in the air, forming a matrix for the strange vision that confronted her.

"I remember this place. . . ." The Queen whispered to herself, sliding through the opening into the room. She looked around, her face filled with sorrow. Once, long ago, she had spent many hours in this room—then it was new and filled with light and knowledge—with a dear friend. The memories brought a sharp pang with them. *But mortals pass, leaving only pain behind.*

The Queen found a patch of shadow on one wall where a wooden scroll case jutted out. The green refulgence made everything look strange, but she stepped into the alcove and all sight of her vanished, save for a pair of pale, white eyes. The two people in the room had not even noticed her. They were cowering away from the whirling, humming disk, watching the image of a man speaking sharply on the other side. The Queen's rich, dark lips quirked, seeing the face of the young man in the burning sphere. *Another circle closes . . .*

Ignoring her mistress's wishes, the little black cat crept across the floor, haunches in the air, green eyes reflecting the powerful glow of the disk. The woman was trembling, almost weeping, with a little boy clinging to her shoulder. The child was bawling, frightened by the strange lights and sounds. The little cat hopped up onto the table behind the woman and batted at the little boy's face with a soft paw.

The boy looked up, round red face streaked with tears, and caught sight of the fuzzy black creature. Blue eyes widened and it groped for the cat with both chubby hands. The little cat smiled, showing tiny white fangs, and let herself be picked up. Drool streaked her short-napped fur, but the cat did not seem to mind.

Dwyrin hobbled into the temple of Zeus Pankrator, right foot hurting from a stone he had stepped on in the courtyard. The vast domed room was filled with gathering men, most of them the Faithful Guard, but also legionaries barracked in the palace. Great chains hung down from the ceiling, holding iron wheels suspended in the air above everyone's heads. Cuplike receptacles holding candles in glass flutes ringed each wheel. Every candle was lit, shedding a warm white light on the faces of the soldiers. Far above, the dome gleamed and shimmered with a massive painting of Zeus himself, seated among the storm clouds, with gray-eyed Athena on one side and victorious Mars on the other. The images seemed to float in a shining sky, even in this dark night. Dwyrin grimaced, hopping along on one foot.

"Here, let me . . ." Chuckling, Vladimir scooped up Dwyrin and set the young man on his powerful shoulders.

"Vlad! I can walk, you know." Dwyrin felt absurd, perched above the crowd of men in plumed helmets and burnished, gleaming armor. The Scandians were gathering at the center of the room around an elevated block of stone. Nicholas was pushing through the ranks of legionaries. Vladimir followed, plowing through the sea of shorter men like a galley.

The block of stone, Dwyrin saw, was an altar. A corpse was lying on it, wrapped in grave cloth. A tall, golden-haired man was standing on the steps, speaking quickly to officers gathered below him. Rufio stood at the man's side, a bared gladius in his hand. More of the Faithful were also standing close by, helmets hiding their faces. Everyone was very grim. Dwyrin could feel an electric tension in the air.

"Runners have come," said the golden-haired man in a powerful voice. "The gate of Charisus and the Great Gate have both fallen. The earthquake toppled the gate and then something that cannot be described forced its way though. Our only hope is to hold the old walls of Constantine, halfway across the city. I will take the Guard and my household troops up the avenue of the Mese to hold the North Road gate. Gregorios, you will take the rest of the men, and anyone you can find in the city, to hold the entrance of the West Road."

Some of the officers shouted their understanding, then pushed away through the crowd. Vladimir worked his way around to the side of the altar, finding Nicholas in close conversation with Rufio. Dwyrin still felt very strange, seeing everything from above, but the Walach did not seem to notice the extra weight. The Hibernian ran his hands through his long red hair, quickly braiding it back behind his head.

"You're the firecaster?" Dwyrin looked down into the pale, haggard face of the golden-haired man. He was broad in the shoulder, though his skin seemed to sag on the bone. The blue eyes were haunted and shadowed. Despite the frailty of his body, the man was filled with nervous energy and he seemed to carry the heavy iron armor without complaint. A thin circlet of gold crowned him, holding back his stringy hair. "The witch-boy, Dwyrin?"

"Yes, lord. I am." Dwyrin bobbed his head, unable to make the proper *proskinesis*. "I mean no disrespect, but I hurt my foot."

"None taken." The Emperor smiled, showing uneven yellow teeth. "This is not a day for ritual. Rufio says you are very strong, as strong as any wizard he's ever seen. Can you stop this monstrous power that comes against us?"

"I don't know." Dwyrin shook his head, feeling queasy at the thought. "I will try."

"That will have to be enough, then." Heraclius reached up and clasped hands with the young sorcerer. A grim smile lighted on his lips, then disappeared. "I will do the same."

Dwyrin nodded again, feeling some spark of strength pass between them. The Emperor's eyes were bright and strong, even though his face was that of an ancient, sagging and wrinkled. There seemed to be no fear in him, even though the enemy had breached a wall that had never been overthrown in three hundred years. Heraclius turned away, raising his voice in a strong shout of command. "On the march, my friends! We go to battle!"

The Faithful were already tramping out of the huge room, their voices raised in a deep-throated chant. Dwyrin looked down at Rufio and Nicholas.

"We go with the Emperor," said the captain of the Faithful, squinting up at Dwyrin, his black eyes fathomless in this poor light. "Save your strength, boy, you look as poorly as he does!"

BOOM!

Green flame jetted away from the edge of the spinning disk, licking across rows and rows of bundled scrolls and leather-bound chapbooks. For a wonder, the ancient parchment and papyrus did not burst into flame. Maxian landed heavily on the floor, his knees bending, and he had to catch himself with his hands. Steam hissed from his body, curling up into the air. The center of the wheel of fire quivered, distorting the vision of the library on the Palatine, then steadied again.

The Prince stood, shaking his head and popping his ears. "Empress?"

Martina was on the floor, body curled around her son, who was peering up at Maxian with wide eyes. A little kitten was clutched tight in the boy's hands, mewing angrily. The Empress was shaking, but Maxian couldn't tell if it was from fear or shock. He reached down and lifted her up.

"Empress, everything is fine. Look at me."

The woman's eyes, screwed shut, slowly opened and she gulped. She seemed astonished that the Prince was actually before her, holding her up. "Caesar Maxian . . . you're real!"

Maxian laughed, then lifted her, her son and the cat up onto the table. "Quickly now, while the disk is perfectly clear, step through." He pointed into the library in distant Rome, where Gaius Julius was waiting, arms raised to catch her. Helena was standing right behind the old man, a thin hand raised to her lips, staring in astonishment. "Go on, just step through. There's only a momentary dizziness."

"I . . . I can't!" Martina wailed. "This is impossible!"

Maxian shook his head, irritated by the delay, and pushed the woman hard in the back, throwing her through the wheel of fire, which still hissed and spun and smoked, and flames licked away from the whirring edge, lighting the room with a sullen green glow. Martina squeaked, then fell through the clear air, her image distorting for a moment as she passed across the disk. Then she was on the other side, gasping, her child screaming, the little cat squirming free from its chubby hands. Maxian turned away, the woman forgotten.

A pale-faced young man, dressed in priestly robes, was staring at him in wonder.

"Do you know how to keep the device attuned?" Maxian's voice was sharp.

"Yes!" stammered the priest. "I do."

"Good, then keep it focused on Rome, on the library. A great power is attacking your city—I do not think that I can stop it, not here, not so far from Rome, but I will try. I will send anyone I meet to you. Pass them through the disk, but only while the air is clear within the circle!"

"I understand," the young priest said, his whole demeanor changing, becoming confident, his face grim. He caught Maxian's shoulder as the Prince strode towards the doorway. "I'll wait for you to come back."

Maxian glanced at him, saw the determination on the boy's face, then nodded. "Don't wait too long. You must not let the *telecast* remain open if the dark power comes upon you. If you fail, Rome will die as well."

Maxian bounded up the steps at the end of the corridor, taking them three and four at a time. The old marble was slippery, but his bare feet found good purchase on the stone. At the top of the steps, there was a crumbling, damp arch and corridors leading off to the left and right. A farther stair, narrower, led upwards. The Prince paused, staring around, and realized that he had no idea where to go. He had never been in the palace of the Eastern Emperor before, if that was where he was. The short time he had spent in Constantinople had been restricted to the racing district and the harbor.

"You must go outside to look upon the enemy, but those stairs only lead to a warren of tiny rooms, all alike." The voice was melodious but dry, like the autumn wind in trees almost bare of leaves. Maxian turned, feeling a familiar chill. There was a woman, stepping forth from the shadows, her face pale against the black stone. The Prince knew her, and felt a trickle of fear pass through him.

"Did you receive my token?" he said, sliding one foot back, turning to face her. In his mind, a pattern was already forming, expanding from a single bright point into a glittering sphere of pale blue. He had not expected the struggle to begin so quickly. Defenses began to rise, though the air seemed weak and lacking in strength, as if the brick and stone and water far beneath his feet were already drained of power.

"I did," she said, gliding forward, long dark red hair plaited back behind her head. In this poor light, her pale flesh seemed to glow and her eyes burn like stars on a moonless night. As before, she bore a tall staff of bone in one slim hand. The physical shock of her presence was muted but still present. "Nineteen of my children went away with you, but only two returned, wounded and limping. I looked upon your bauble but cast it away. My children will not be your slaves, Prince, nor will I."

"I did not offer slavery," Maxian snapped, angered by the implication. "That formula would free you and your kind from the pain which cripples you and binds you to the cities of men. You have skill—I can feel it. You could make the serum. You would be free."

"We would be slaves to a drug." The Dark Queen grinned mirthlessly, her fine white teeth gleaming in the darkness. "I have seen these things before. The body changes, adapts; soon the pain returns, worse than before. My children are as they are—in the way of the world, strength is balanced by weakness. They can run in the beautiful night, hunting, they are strong, fearless and quick. Against these things, your 'serum' is of little use. They do not want to be daywalker, they are K'shapâcara! They are the first people!"

"Are they?" The Prince was suddenly curious. "Why are you here? Are you in league with the thing that cracks the walls to gravel? That feasts upon the dead of the city?"

"No." The Queen drifted closer, her pale hand brushing his cheek. He could smell her now, a heady, rich odor like newly turned earth and the first green buds of spring pushing through the snow. The girl Alaïs had smelled a little like this, but had been only a pale imitation of her mistress. He shivered, feeling his body respond.

"The thing crouched outside the city, hiding from the sun and moon alike, is an old enemy. I have faced it before, long ago." The Queen smiled, leaning close, her lips parted. "You have grown strong, Prince. Very strong. I can smell your servants, hear them, all around us. It has been a long time since a daywalker child attained such strength." Her voice softened, caressing, and Maxian caught her hand, forcing the hot touch away from his neck.

"Can it be defeated?" His gaze was fierce and direct. "How do I fight this thing?"

"We fight it, Prince. Together. It is strong, but not invincible. Not yet." The Queen drew away, her hand lingering on his muscular arm. She seemed to condense, or focus, becoming diamond hard, even the air around her shrinking away. The bone staff moved, pointing down the left-most corridor. "This way leads outside. The enemy is close; are you ready?"

"I am." Maxian felt the last of his shields, pearlescent and gray, slide into place. For the moment, they were still invisible to the mundane eye, but the air trembled around him, subtly distorting his features. He could feel the dark woman summoning her own patterns into place as well, and he marveled at their intricacy and ancient strength. Here was a creature who far surpassed him in skill. *But I am the stronger,* he thought, feeling confidence flow into him. *Rome is with me, and the Empire.*

The Queen loped away down the corridor, a swift black shape against the dim walls. Maxian ran after her, his bare feet slapping on the marble tiles.

The *Empress Irene* pitched up, her curved prow breaking free of the waves, sending white spray flying away into the night. At her rear, on the steering deck, Dahvos held tight to one of the mast lines, feeling the deck yaw away from his feet. In the darkness, their way lit only by a red glow from the city, he couldn't see the waters of the Propontis, but he knew they must be heaving like a blown horse. The wave slid past and the *Irene* wallowed down into the trough. Black water surged up, spilling over the prow. Steam boiled from the sea, rising up in transparent clouds. The Roman captain was screaming at his men, the rowers and the steersmen both, and the galley began to swing into line. Dahvos squinted at the dark, seeing the crest of another huge roller coming at them, picked out by the light of the burning city.

Dahvos had set out from Perinthus in the morning, his fleet pulling hard to make time up the Propontis against the prevailing cold wind out of the northeast. Several chaotic, endless days had followed his arrival in the port city. The rebellious Eighth Legion refused him admittance at first, then relented after the centurions from the Third challenged their honor. The Western recruits and their officers were shamefaced, lining the streets as the battered remnants of the Third and the Khazars entered the city. Dahvos had treated the officers of the Eighth politely, but they no longer held any kind of command. The legionaries had been folded into the Third, returning it to full strength.

The banners and standards of the Eighth had been taken away and put into storage on one of the Western supply ships. Dahvos pretended not to notice, but the legate of the Eighth had been found dead, embracing his own sword, a day later. The Khazar prince prayed each night, thanking the good Lord that the mutinous Romans had not decided to hold the city against him. The men of the Third had pressed him to decimate the Eighth, but there was no time for the traditional punishment. What could he do? He needed the men.

The fleet captains, on the other hand, were eager to test themselves against the Arabs and Persians. Thus this sortie, to try the mettle of the blockade before Constantinople and see how these massive wooden horses performed on the water. Dahvos had never commanded at sea, but he trusted his captains and their crews. He hoped to get a feel for combat on the water. Salvaging this war seemed to hinge on victory over the enemy fleet.

Now, watching the walls of the city grow closer with each sweep of the oars, he wondered if there was any reason to dare battle. The sea was angry, filled with strange currents and these huge, almost invisible swells. The western half of Constantinople seemed to be aflame, with a muted crackling roar carrying across the water. As he watched, dread growing in him, he saw columns of fire leaping above the walls lining the harbor and the shore. The Arab fleet was nowhere to be seen. Had they fled the earthquake?

"Captain! Signal your ships—half of us will enter the harbor, slowly, the other half must stand to sea, watching for the enemy."

The Roman captain paused in his harangue and nodded. Then he started shouting again, even more loudly than before. Sailors scurried to either side of the ship, lanterns raised in their hands. Dahvos could feel the *Irene* shift as the steersmen bent their tall oars into the water. The galley swung to the left, heading for the breakwater protecting the military harbor.

The Prince of the Khazars leaned forward, hand still wrapped carefully around the rope, watching for the opening in the breakwater. There should be lights in the towers flanking the entrance, but against the fire in the sky, it was hard to see.

"There!" he shouted, pointing at a triangular sail catching the glare, and the steersmen changed their course again. The ship, a merchantman, was wallowing out of the harbor. The *Irene* surged forward, the flautists on the lower decks calling for a faster stroke. The Roman captain came to the rail, staring out over the dark and troubled sea.

"They are too low in the water," the captain said, pursing his lips. "Yes! There, do you see them? A heavy cargo."

Dahvos counted his eyesight keen, good enough to spot a ptarmigan in a willow break, but this lurid, shifting light reflecting from the sea confused the eye. The merchantman grew closer, its round hull rolling in the heavy waves. He hissed in surprise, but one look at the skyline of the city, all engulfed in flames, and he understood. The merchantman was crowded from railing to railing with people, packed as tight as salt herrings in a barrel. They made no sound, all white faces, though they stared across the water at the passing ship. Dahvos felt the hair on the back of his arms rise up, seeing the waves slap against the side of the ship, only inches from the gunnel. A thin red stream was spilling from the wash ports.

The Roman fleet parted, letting the merchantman pass through, and Dahvos turned back to the city, his face grim. "All hands to arms," he barked at the captain, startling the Roman from a dreadful reverie. "If you have spears, pass them out. Signal the other ships."

Nodding, the captain shouted for his officers to join him on the rear deck. The Khazar turned back to the ghastly scene. Now he could make out the breakwater, which was thick with men and women and children, some clinging to the rocks, the sea surging up around them. A wailing cry rose above the roar and crack of the burning city. The harbor would be madness, filled with thousands of desperate people. Dahvos swallowed, realizing that he was going to make a terrible decision. The night seemed to grow even darker.

The Faithful Guard marched into the square around the temple of Mithra Ascendant in a line fifty men across and ten deep. The arches of the Valentinian aqueduct vaulted overhead, glowing with the ruddy light of the burning districts. The temple itself rose in the middle of the square, a great merlot and cream confection of towering pillars, massive statues and three gilded domes. Before them, the square was filled with terrified people, all running from the west. At a barked command, the Faithful extended their line, covering almost half of the square. Men and women in their sleeping clothes, some carrying ragged bundles of belongings, others empty-handed, stopped, seeing the formidable wall of iron, steel and great oval shields. The citizens wept, then fled past on either side, rushing like a stream around a jutting boulder.

The sky above, beyond the black arches of the aqueduct, was glowing red and deep orange. The strange inky darkness that had passed over the city was now replaced by a surge of sooty clouds. Smoke billowed up from the burning city, filling the sky. It glowed and throbbed with sullen light and reflected fire. In the square, as the Faithful began a measured advance, axes and great swords at the ready, the glow cast long shadows on the ground and painted the shields red.

Dwyrin, now kitted out with a pair of borrowed *caligulae,* trotted along, flanked by Nicholas on one side and Vladimir on the other. Rufio was not far away, pacing the Emperor, who moved surrounded by a double row of the Faithful. Heraclius was wearing battered old armor, with only high red boots to mark him as Emperor.

"Hoi nekroi! Hoi nekroi erchesthe!" shouted a man as he stumbled past, his face mad with fear.

Dwyrin stared after him as he pushed his way through the line of soldiers, fell onto the stones, and then crawled away, weeping. The plaza was emptying, leaving only scattered bodies of those knocked down in the mad flight. A measured drumming paced the legionaries, the sound of their boots echoing back from the empty buildings surrounding the temple square.

"What was he saying?" Dwyrin whispered, looking over at Nicholas. The northerner shook his head; he hadn't understood the words either. Brunhilde trembled in his hand, quivering like a hunting hound. With each step, Nicholas' thin face grew grimmer. Strange winds were at play in the vast open space of the square, sending dust and grit into the faces of the Faithful.

"I don't know," Nicholas said, holding up a hand. "Something about the dead, I think. Captain Rufio!"

The black-eyed Greek looked over, seeing that Nicholas and the left wing had stopped. "What is it?"

"I see something, there beyond the temple. We should wait here, I think, where our flanks are protected by the buildings and the aqueduct footing."

Rufio was about to answer, but a stern voice cut him off. "No. We advance. I want to see the face of the enemy."

Dwyrin saw Nicholas start to protest, but the other speaker was the Emperor, glaring between the stoic faces of the Scandians. Nicholas backed down, saluting, his arm stiff. "All maniples, arms ready, advance at a walk!"

The Hibernian let his mind settle, trying to put the distant roar of flames, the tramp of hobnailed boots, the rattle of iron and leather, the harsh breathing of the men around him out of his mind. Tonight, under this dreadful sky, thinking of the vast crawling thing that he had seen, it was very easy. The fire leapt to his will, an eager lover, already pleading for release from the prison of flesh. He looked across the square, his mage-sight casting aside the darkness, the gloom, the odd gray fog that slowly oozed from the stones.

Dwyrin cursed, a lurid, harsh word he had learned from his thaumaturgic instructor. At the same time, a strange wild howling filled the air and the plaza reverberated with the vibration of thousands of running feet. The Hibernian lunged forward, pushing his way through the stolid ranks of the Faithful. Vladimir and Nicholas shouted after him, then Vladimir was close behind, shoving men out of his way. There were shouts from along the line of shields, some of alarm. Other men had caught sight of the enemy.

Dwyrin ducked under the shield of the man in front of

him, then stood up, tense. The entire square was suddenly filled with a surging, running, howling mob. Tens of thousands of figures lurched towards the shield wall, shrieking and screaming. Their numbers seemed limitless, filling the whole plaza from side to side. The red glare of the sky illuminated them fitfully, showing patches of white and black, empty eyes, missing limbs.

"The dead," Dwyrin hissed, raising his hand in a sharp, angry motion. "Stand back!"

Vladimir reached his side, saw the seething horde of corpses rushing towards them and blanched with fear. "The Draculis! The Draculis have come against us!"

Dwyrin snarled, his will intent, and fire blossomed in his heart and spoke from his hand. A hissing white bolt of flame leapt out and scythed across the shambling mob that was now only a hundred feet away. The creatures screeched, engulfed, thrashing wildly as white-hot fire burned into their eye sockets and burrowed into their withered chests. A hundred went down, incinerated, and a thousand poured into the gap, clawing their way forward, dead eyes fixed hungrily on the line of the Faithful.

"Stand! Stand!" Nicholas shouted, his voice a basso roar over the tumult. The dead stormed forward, some in rusted armor, some naked, some newly dead with their flesh still pink with the residue of life. Flame licked out from Dwyrin once and then twice, setting huge swaths of the mob alight. Even burning, wreathed in blue flame, they kept coming. "The Emperor! The Emperor!"

The dead slammed into the shield wall, mouths gaping black in the horrid red light, rotting hands clawing at the faces of the Scandians. The Faithful took the charge with a grunt, then fell back a step. Their axes slashed down, hewing heads from gangrenous necks, arms from pasty, white torsos fat with worms. The endless hollow shrieking of the dead rose and rose, rending the air, drowning out the bull roar of the centurions, hiding even the cries of the Faithful who fell, borne down by the pressing, irresistible weight of the living corpses. Even hewn to bits, lacking heads, legs, arms, the dead bit and humped forward, sliming the ground with black, rotting entrails. A vast, suffocating stench rolled before them.

Dwyrin was surrounded by an arc of desolation, clouded by a choking, bitter smoke of incinerated bone and charred flesh. Vladimir was at his back, hacking wildly at anything that lurched too close with his great ax. The blade was slick with noisome gray-green fluid that seeped from the wounds of the dead, or burst from their abdomens as they were cut down. The Hibernian's face was a tight mask of control, but fire lashed out again, ripping long burning avenues of destruction through the pressing tide. Despite this, the Faithful were forced back a yard, then another.

Nicholas, fighting in what was suddenly the front rank, stabbed Brunhilde into the chest of a corpse coming at him with a Legion pilum. The creature staggered, then clawed its way up the length of bright steel. Grunting, Nicholas slammed the thing's face, feeling bone crack under the impact of his armored elbow, then wrenched the long sword free. Undaunted, the creature clawed at his head, bony hands scraping across the cheek guard of his helmet. A fingertip, still sheathed in flesh, caught in his eye slit. Nicholas gasped at the stench, then slashed Brunhilde down, cleaving the arm from the body. The finger wiggled into his helmet, a sharp nail jabbing at his eyelid.

Nicholas staggered back, out of the line of battle, shouting with fear and grasping at his own helmet. Too late. The finger was already inside the close-fitting iron, squirming against his cheek. Frenzied, Nicholas tore at the strap under his chin, feeling the nail bite at the soft surface of his eye. There was a sudden, blinding pain and then he felt the helmet give way. Screaming in fury, Nicholas grasped the wiggling bony worm in both hands and it popped free with a wet sound. Blood slicked his face, spilling down his cheek. The vile thing squirmed in his gloves, still trying to kill. He threw it away, out over the heads of the corpses shambling towards him.

Nicholas blinked, half blinded, then wiped blood from his face. He gingerly touched his left eye and found a loose flap of skin over something squishy and moist. He felt faint, then he was on the ground, staring up at a burning sky. In his hand, Brunhilde was keening, a sharp, piercing note of dismay. "Vlad! Vlad! Help me!"

Dwyrin heard Nicholas cry out, then knelt swiftly, his mind speeding through ancient, half-heard chants and patterns. Everything was coming to him with dizzying speed, power wicking up out of the ground, flying down from the sky. He had wreaked enormous destruction on the surging mob of the dead, but there were still thousands coming on. Dwyrin knew, in some calm and observant corner of his mind, that these were not just the dead of the battle, so strangely left to lie on the field in the rain and mud, but the ancient dead of the city tombs and graveyards. Their numbers might be limitless.

The limestone flags of the plaza were ancient, long separated from their native hills and mountains. The fire in them was buried deep, hidden, barely an ember. Dwyrin touched it, feeling the quivering spark come to life in his presence. *Wake!* he called to the stones, moving his hand in a sharp arc that included the whole plaza. *Wake!*

"Fall back! Re-form shield wall!"

Rufio skipped aside, letting one of the living dead lunge past him. The captain's face was a grim mask under his helm, and he slashed down with his gladius, neatly severing the hamstrings on the back of the thing's legs. It toppled over, momentarily crippled. Despite their horrific, unnatural life, the corpses still had to use bone and muscle to move. The Faithful fell back, their axes and spears making a glittering hedge before them. Rufio was sweating heavily and his mouth was fouled with this stench that hung in the air like black fog.

He glanced to his left, looking for Nicholas, and saw to his horror the left wing had swept away from him. Hundreds of the things pushed into a gap in the shield wall, cutting the line of battle in twain. Rufio backed up hurriedly, seeing the gleaming iron helms of the left falling back towards one of the streets opening onto the square from the south. He reached his own line and looked sharply for the Emperor.

Heraclius was not far away, his armor dented and slick with gray-green ichor. The Emperor had a barbarian-style longsword in both hands. It was nicked and almost black with age. Only five or six of the Faithful were still with him, clustered at his back, watching in all directions. Their eyes met and Heraclius smiled, a half-grin. "Rufio! Where is the boy? The firecaster?"

The captain looked about, then he saw him, a hundred feet away, surrounded by a milling circle of the dead. Strangely, they were not attacking recklessly, but slowly edging their way forward. Heaps of burned, ashy corpses were strewn around the barbarian. The boy was kneeling on the ground, his face screwed up in concentration, his palms flat on the ground.

"I'll get him!" Rufio rushed forward, his sword licking out and cleaving the head from the nearest of the walking corpses. He smashed through the next two and was into the circle. Dwyrin looked up and Rufio skidded to a halt, ash puffing up around him in a cloud, his heart stricken with dread. The barbarian's eyes were burning, filled with leaping flame.

"Rufio!" Heraclius cursed, then dropped his hand. He turned, gesturing with the longsword he had torn from the rotting grip of the dead. "Come on, lads, we've got to—"

BOOM!

A vast blast of fire leapt from the stones, ripping from one end of the plaza to the other, shooting skyward in a flare of greenish white. Tens of thousands of the dead were caught in the explosion. Hundreds of tons of limestone slabs volatilized to an incandescent white-hot cloud in one stunning blast. Corpses and bits of corpses were flung skyward, each wrapped in clinging green fire. Heraclius was thrown back by the blast, into his bodyguards. They skidded backwards in a rattle of iron and wood, a tangle of arms and legs.

The Emperor was stunned, seeing only the shoulder vambrace of one of the guards and a sliver of red sky. At least two strong men were on top of him, crushing the breath from his chest. Cursing, he shoved at them, trying to lift away the mail pressing down on him. It was getting hard to breathe. Slowly, for his arms were far weaker than they once had been, he managed to shove the bodies aside and crawl out onto the stones. The sky was lit for miles in all directions by a hissing flare that consumed the center of the plaza. Everything was as bright as noon, tinged with strange green shadows. The roar of the combusting stone was so loud that Heraclius was deafened.

He managed to get to his knees. The guardsman on top of him seemed to be dead, his armor smoking and his beard alight. Heraclius batted at the smoldering hair with his glove, but it did no good. Acres of dead seemed to surround him, all thrown down by the blast. Many of the buildings fronting the square were now burning, smoke flooding from their windows. The temple of Mithra was a wavering vision, barely visible through the heat haze and smoke. He looked for a weapon, anything, and for any of his men who were still alive.

Something crashed into his back, throwing him down. The Emperor rolled weakly, swinging around. A figure dressed in scaled mail loomed over him, burning with clinging green fire. A spear was clutched in its bony hands, the wooden haft already smoking and charred. Heraclius groped for a sword, then screamed as the spear stabbed at him. There was a sharp grating sound, sparks flying as the spearhead cracked through a joint in his armor, and then a spreading coldness in his chest. The Emperor scrabbled at the spear, trying to pull it out.

The corpse ground the point around in his ribcage, grinning white bone in the ruin of its face. Heraclius struggled, kicking at the thing's leg, then his hands slipped weakly from the smoking wood and his head lolled back, blood spilling from his mouth. With a dry hiss, the corpse wrenched the spear from the man's chest, then crumpled to one side, the green fire eating through its legs and back. Smoke boiled up out of the breastplate, obscuring a stylized emblem of two palms decorating the back of the armor.

Dwyrin scuttled forward, his face averted from the wall of intensely hot flame that roared around the circumference of his little cleared circle. Grunting, the young man heaved Rufio onto his shoulder. "You're a heavy bastard," Dwyrin hissed between gritted teeth. The man seemed to be alive, though part of his face was badly burned. "Let's walk now!"

Rufio managed to get his legs under him and Dwyrin turned in the direction he thought Vladimir had run. The Walach had promised to come right back, but the Hibernian could not see him. Stray corpses staggered past, some burning, some not. There was the sound of battle off in the mouth of one of the streets. Dwyrin staggered that way, dragging Rufio. Behind him, the lime fire continued to hiss and burn, greedily feasting on tens of thousands of corpses.

As he ran, the Hibernian suddenly felt a dreadful chill and looked up in surprise. Something swept past, overhead, something winged like an enormous bat, and angry, speeding east towards the heart of the city. Dwyrin nearly tripped on a crawling arm, disturbed by the presence in the sky. He had felt the power once before, long ago. The memory was a scar, glassed over, buried but not healed.

He tried to run faster, hoping to find Nicholas and Vladimir somewhere ahead.

The *Irene* slid across the dark, oily harbor waters. The crew were silent, bent over their oars, the grate and rattle of the oarlocks muted. Fire burned all along the ramparts above the military harbor, lighting the sky. Huge clouds of smoke were mounting into the sky over the city, glowing orange and vermilion. There was no wind. Many galleys were splintered and broken on the stone piers, their hulls listing above the slick water. Everywhere that Dahvos looked, he saw close-packed masses of people. They filled the quays and the breakwater from side to side. Even the half-sunken ships were covered with huddled figures. The white faces, pale and silent, stared back at him as the ship sailed past.

"Lord General," the Roman captain whispered, "we're not going to land, are we?" His eyes were wide and filled with fear. The crowds had fallen silent when the first of the Western galleys had entered the harbor, though before that a tumult of prayers, screams and moaning wails had filled the air. "They'll swamp any boat putting ashore."

"I know," Dahvos said in a cold tone. "We are not going to take on any civilians."

"What?" The captain swallowed a curse, staring out at the nearest dock. Women were holding up their children, their eyes pleading. Some younger boys had leapt into the water and were swimming towards the passing ship. On the deck of the *Irene,* sailors were waiting with bill hooks and spears to drive them off if they tried to climb the railing. "There are thousands of people . . ."

"I can see." Dahvos faced the man, his face a rigid mask, half in shadow from the ruddy glare. "This city is doomed. The Persians will not sit idly by while the defenders are distracted by earthquake and fire. They are attacking the land walls at this moment. All we can do, with these ships, is take aboard every fighting man we can.

Then, perhaps, there will be a chance to recapture the city in the future."

"But . . . but the people!" The captain gestured wildly at the docks. "They'll all die!"

"No." Dahvos looked up, gauging the progress of the fire, seeing the towers and battlements of the seawall lit with a furious red glow. "The fire cannot burn stone. They will be safe here, if cold and wet. In a day, the fire will have died down and they will return to their homes. The Persians are not monsters—they will let them resume their daily routine."

"My lord, that is monstrous! How—"

"You will do what I command," Dahvos snapped, hand sliding around the hilt of his longsword. "We will put in there." The Khazar pointed ahead, across the water, to a long quay that jutted out into the middle of the harbor. It was thick with people crowding right up to the edge, but there was also the glint of armor and helmets among the crowd. At the end of the dock, the main road from the city descended on a causeway from the ramparts above to the harbor.

At the captain's command, the *Irene* swung towards the pier, her oars moving in swift unison. The ship crabbed around, then slipped forward in smooth, effortless motion. Dahvos saw, as their destination became clear, a surge in the people packed onto the dock. A wail rose up, pitiful and hopeless, from the other piers and people began to beg and scream. His jaw clenched and his lips thinned to a hard line. The soldiers on the main pier were fighting now, hacking at the mob pressing against them. People were toppling from the sides of the dock, shrieking, and hitting the water with a boil of white water. The *Irene* slid closer, her foredeck packed with marines, all in cork armor. A young man, still clad only in a nightshirt, swam out, clutching at the oars dipping from the water.

One of the marines, seeing him reach the prow and his hands grasp futilely at the smooth oak, leaned down. A hush fell over the crowd on the dock. The marine stabbed down with a long leaf-bladed spear, catching the boy in the chest. There was a thin scream, then a bubbling sound as the boy was pushed under the water. The ship swept on and the body was pulled under the dark water by the roil of its passage. The people moaned with fear, suddenly knowing that they were doomed.

Dahvos stared ahead, watching the pushing struggle on the dock become a battle. More soldiers were pushing through the crowd, throwing people into the water, striving to reach the end of the dock. The *Irene* was very close now, only a hundred feet away.

The sky lit suddenly, washed by a virulent white light. Dahvos hissed in surprise, flinching away from the city. The clouds, still boiling and thick, lit like a stained-glass goblet held up to a flame, showing ribbons of color and hidden plumes within glowing white columns of smoke. A sullen, drawn-out *boom* followed. Something had happened in the center of the city, throwing up a great radiance lighting the sky in all directions.

The Khazar khagan blinked, a trickle of fear in the back of his throat. Great powers were struggling in the city, as they had on the plain. He suddenly wished that he had remained at home, on the open grasslands of Sarai, with his family. *O God of Avrahan, watch over us tonight, let us come through this test. . . .*

The Dark Queen glided to a halt in a pool of shadow. Ahead of her, the street ended in the sweeping circle of the Forum of Constantine. A massive column rose from the center of the plaza, rising up a hundred feet, crowned in gold by a striking marble statue of the first Emperor of the East. The pale face stared west, down the arrow-straight avenue of the Mese. The Forum was surrounded by temples and imposing public buildings. Four centuries of construction had ornamented the center of Constantinople with graceful buildings and blocky monstrosities.

Maxian stopped as well. Her lithe speed had taken him by surprise, but then he had remembered what Alaïs had taught him, letting the night carry him forward.

He made to speak, but then felt the shudder of power in the hidden world. Something white hot, burning furiously, was suddenly unleashed a mile or more away. The sky flashed bright and then the afterimage reverberated in his mind and vision. The tall column threw an immense shadow across the plaza, silhouetting thousands of people milling about in fear. A rumbling crack and thunder followed, then a greenish-white flare leapt up into the sky. Maxian could not see the source, for there were many buildings in the way, but he could feel the intense heat on his face.

His shields rippled as outflung power washed over them, but it was not a directed attack. This was the flux from some massive burst of strength. He wondered what had been the focus, but knew that anything at the center of that maelstrom must be destroyed.

"What is—" Maxian stilled, the Queen having raised a thin hand. She turned, looking over her shoulder, pale eyes glittering against the white radiance flooding the sky. He half sensed her intricate layers of protection growing even stronger.

"Do you feel him?"

Maxian nodded, his skin going cold. Something rushed towards them in the night air, a heavy darkness distorting the hidden world with its very presence. The Oath was very weak here, in the East, but some fragments remained, clinging to the ancient monuments and the mile marker standing at the base of Constantine's pillar. The matrices shuddered at the touch of whirling chaos passing over them. "It is not alone."

"No." The Queen's voice was faint. "It has learned, I fear. Before, we fought many against one. Now it has gathered servants—Stand ready!"

The black point in the air suddenly swelled into a shape,

rushing through the sooty air. A figure like a man, but trailing a long obsidian cloak. Something like wings flared back from the body, but they folded away as it lit on the golden ring at the base of Constantine's statue. The servant came, too, sweeping out of the night sky, the firelight of the dying city gleaming on a head of iron. Maxian stiffened, recognizing the likeness of one of the dead gods of Egypt. Fear seemed to emanate as a physical force from the black shape clinging to the summit of the column.

The crowds of people in the plaza fled, wailing, running as fast as they could in all directions. Men trampled women, threw down children and babies. Blood spattered on the cobblestones. Maxian looked away from the grisly sight, but his resolve hardened. He felt weak without the comfortable embrace of the Oath, but he was still strong. Maxian stepped out into the plaza, the pulsing white light in the sky falling upon him. The air was thick with heat, ash and the bitter iron stink of blood and urine. As he did so, the Prince set his will to draw on the strength in the stones beneath his feet, in the air, even in the buildings surrounding him.

His shields and wards flashed a deep brilliant azure, swelling with strength. The thing on the column turned towards him. Maxian felt the gaze like a blow, and a faint wash of darkness lapped around his wards. The margin of his perception heard gibbering cries, smelled a charnel stink, felt the crack of bone and the bubbling gasp of a final breath. The Dark Queen was gone, disappeared into shadow.

Begone! he called across the empty air. Laughter answered him, foul and repellent. *You will not take this city. It is under my protection.*

There was no answer. Instead, the sky darkened with dizzying speed. An ebon tide spilled across the smoky air, coming from the west, blotting out the clouds, swallowing the greenish-white flare. Maxian felt power fade from the world around him, seeing even the hurried, busy motion of the tiny motes that made up the air slow and fade. A deep chill fell across him and his breath suddenly puffed white.

The iron-headed dog leapt down from the column, landing softly, though his booted feet cracked through newly formed ice on the flagstones. It advanced, a black staff crowned by a snake's head in hand. Maxian drew breath, feeling the chill sear his lungs, and stepped sideways. A whirling vortex of intent flashed to his right hand. The iron dog loped forward, staff cutting down. Maxian braced himself, then staggered back. Darkness licked against his ward, soundless, but the blow was heavy, splintering the outermost pattern into a dizzying spray of smoking fragments.

Maxian slashed his hand in a sharp arc. This time there was sound. A crackling thunderclap ripped across the plaza, trailing a burning, jagged bolt. The lightning washed over the iron dog, outlining its own wards and patterns, snapping and popping fiercely. The creature was thrown back, skidding across the ice. Maxian leapt ahead, rage boiling up, fueling his power. A forefinger stabbed out, lighting the darkness with a *crack!* of power.

Ultraviolet waves hissed, radiating out in a swift shock. The iron dog's pattern buckled, rippling like a sea in full storm, glyphs and symbols flashing in sudden brilliance, then fading to nothing. Smoke boiled up from the surface of the plaza, the frost exhaling in a white cloud. The thing was forced down to a crouch, iron head bent. Maxian could feel the presence of the dark figure in the dog, making an odd double echo in the thing's pattern. He struck again, lips pulling back in a grimace, and the plaza lit with an azure flash.

The clouds rippled away from the blast, swirling into cone-shaped vortices, and lightning cracked and raged around the figure on the ground. The iron mask began to glow a cherry red and there was an involuntary scream. The figure clawed at the mask, fingers smoking as they touched the hot metal. Maxian felt a fierce exultation, feeling his enemy's pattern suddenly waver and fade. His fist clenched, twisting in the air, pushing away from his body.

The air convulsed between them, twisting around a sizzling blue-white sphere that leapt from Maxian's hand. The flagstones of the plaza rumbled, cracking in line with the sphere, and then the iron dog was engulfed in a raging explosion of lightning, smoke and hissing fire. Struggling at the heart of the maelstrom, the iron dog groped for its fallen staff. Then the last pattern buckled, de-formed by enormous pressure, and there was a rumbling, echoing *crack*! as power flooded in, pinning the creature to the ground.

Maxian leapt back, soaring into the air, feeling the space around him twist and bend. The dark figure on the column at last entered the fight. Black fire shattered the cobblestones, flinging debris in all directions. At the same time, Maxian felt the ebon cloud converge on him. The temperature continued to drop and he was forced to divert some of his intent to keeping the air around him warm enough to breathe. Darkness lapped around him, sidling out of the sky in patchy sheets. The shadows sizzled against his ward, fragmenting, but draining the outer layers like a tap in a dam. Each whisper-soft blow leached more and more strength from the shield.

Cold laughter echoed from the pinnacle of the column. Maxian was assailed by visions and hideous sounds. Squirming mouths, studded with pinlike teeth, fastened to his flesh, sending jolts of agony through his limbs. Something monstrous swelled in the air, batrachian wings blocking out the sky, the outline of the pulsating form impossible to define. A forest of black tentacles squirmed over his body, digging at his eyes, sliding gelatinously into his mouth and nose.

Maxian struggled to keep his pattern solid, groped for the power to strike back. He felt himself falling, plummeting towards the cold, icy stone of the plaza, but ignored the sensation, thinking it was a hallucination.

The Prince hit the ground hard, cracking his leg, then feeling his ankle splinter with a *pop*. True pain coursed through him and he screamed. The shadows in the air had eaten away the pattern that had held him aloft. Tears smoked from his face, freezing in the incredible cold. He lost concentration, fingers digging into the ice, a long scream of pain rending his throat.

Get up, boy, get up now! A furious voice echoed in his mind and he felt his arms push him up from the ground. *We're all dead if you don't put that pain aside!*

Frightened, Maxian felt himself lurched up, most of his weight on one foot. His other ankle was like a red-hot ember shoved under the flesh, burning at his nerves.

Heal yourself, you bastard! You're a fucking priest of Asclepius!

Shadows crowded around, seeping through the remains of his shield. Maxian tried to breathe, but the air had frozen again. He gasped, choking. One of the shadows spilled through a crack in the pattern, touching his wounded foot. The skin froze, cracking away from the bone in thin, shell-like sheets. Maxian stared down in horror, watching black corruption creep up his leg.

Do it! The voice had a strange accent, and Maxian felt his arms twitch, wrenched from his control. *Columella! Show me how to do this! He's lost his fucking mind.* A babble of other voices answered, filling Maxian's head with chaos. He trembled, unable to move, his feet frozen to the ground.

Lord Prince, an urgent voice, elderly, Roman, with unmistakable traces of a patrician Latin accent, penetrated. *You must open yourself to the healing power. Now!*

Maxian responded to the snap of command in the elderly voice, his mind finding the pattern that restored flesh and bone and the vital humors. Health suddenly blossomed in his flesh and the pain stopped, cut off like a joint split by the butcher's cleaver. His mind was clear, even the strange voices fading away. The air warmed within his

compressed, almost destroyed shield. Ice melted away
from his feet. The crawling skin of shadow cracked, then
hissed to vapor. Bone knit in his shattered ankle, flesh
regrew at a phenomenal rate, strength returned to arm and
leg.

A sharp shout of command focused his mind, and pure
white light flooded from his upraised hand. The shadows
fled, shrieking, dissolving as the light touched them. Maxian stood, hale, upright, on the blocky flagstones of the
plaza, his shields restored, burning blue and white in the
darkness.

A scene of devastation greeted him. The column of Constantine had been shattered, leaving a concrete stump jutting into the air. The statue itself lay broken in pieces on
the far side of the plaza. Most of the buildings surrounding
the Forum were burning furiously, their marble facades
hissing with blue-white flame as the lime in the stone
cooked away. Great smoking pits belched flame, clouding
the air.

The Dark Queen was on the attack, her staff spinning
in the air, a flicker of standing lightning describing a wheel
of power. Her voice was roaring like a storm, calling
words of power, breaking the air with staggering bolts of
crimson lightning. The dark thing was wreathed in its own
brittle shell, horrific images flashing around it, describing
a faceted pattern. As Maxian watched, lightning licked
down from the sky, shaking the reptilian figure, burning
through two, three, four layers of its defense. It howled,
touched by the Queen's rage.

Maxian leapt into the air, wind rushing around him. He
crossed half of the massive plaza in a single bound, alighting on the ruined stump of the great column. Movement
caught his eye, something crawling in the ruins. It was the
iron dog, head low, still smoking with heat, but it crawled,
bloody fingers dragging the ruined body through the tumbled brick and concrete. Grimacing, the Prince focused his

will, feeling the reverberations of the Queen's attack shake the world. He chopped his hand down.

An ultramarine-blue flame leapt from his hand, tracing a sizzling arc through the air. It touched the iron dog, flinging it to the ground in a violent blast. Concrete piers, revealed under the shattered cobblestones, collapsed. A plume of dust and rock flew up, lit from within by flickering lightning. The iron dog gave a wail and vanished, smashed into the earth. Smoke billowed out of the collapsed area. Maxian grinned, his face feral, and turned away.

The thing in darkness had withstood the Queen's attack, shrugging off the hail of blasts and lightning strikes. Now the shadows scattered in the air swarmed around her, shrieking and dying in a blaze of crimson bolts. As fast as she struck them down, more flooded out of the night sky. Burning red motes joined them, hurling themselves against her pattern, destroying themselves in a mad rush to overwhelm her. Maxian saw his enemy clearly, for the first time.

It bore a human guise, tall and lean, with long dark hair falling over bony shoulders. Once the face had been noble and handsome, striking, with a powerful brow and sharp nose. Now a mottled darkness was on the skin, curling around the flat ears and deep-set eyes. Though the skin was pale, there was a rippling shimmer that made it seem dark. Maxian felt an instant and powerful revulsion. Here was a thing that was the enemy of Man. Something primordial in him howled in defiance, urging him to kill.

Maxian's hands blurred in a pattern, making the air around him groan. Power wicked up out of the earth, causing stone, concrete, marble, brick to quiver to dust all around him. There were hidden ways and adits under the city. They shook, roofs collapsing, supports crumbling away. Water poured from broken cisterns, flooding the tunnels before it froze. The nearest building, a four-story temple adorned with friezes of the ancient gods at the harvest and a dozen lithe statues of nymphs, shook and then fell, toppling into the square with a roar.

He struck, everything focused into a shining cyan mote that hissed across the space between the column and the dark man. The figure spun, feeling the world shift. Its thin red eyes widened in surprise, then it soared away, flashing into the sky. Maxian's orb ripped in pursuit, accelerating to enormous speed. The enemy twisted, flashing a clawlike hand in a matching pattern. A black lattice congealed out of the air. The cyan orb plowed into the center of the matrix.

Maxian was thrown down, smashing against the rubble-strewn ground. The sky split, filled with a ravening blue-black flare. All across the city, buildings crumpled, crushed by the blast of superheated air. Maxian rolled away, feeling his shields buckle, compressed down to within a finger's breadth of his skin by the shocking roar and burst of power. The remaining stump of the column shattered, flinging chunks of concrete, marble and brick across him.

Debris rained down, making his shield flare with each blow, but the Prince gritted his teeth and rode it out. An enormous thunderclap followed, blowing a fine rain of grit into his face. Shadows and clouds alike were blown back, leaving a great still space over the heart of the city.

Maxian scrambled to his feet, feeling his skin burning. He wiped a hand the length of his body and the dead, ruined flesh firmed, filling with life. His eyes, half seared away, quivered and vision was restored. The dark thing was gone. The sky empty, save for a distant boil of clouds.

But it is not dead. Maxian could feel the presence at a distance. The power had withdrawn, stymied for the moment. The prince looked around, suddenly sick. He could feel thousands of people, dead and dying, within his immediate vicinity. They had been hiding in the buildings, cowering in basements or inner rooms. The blast had thrown down every standing building within blocks, leaving only stray single pillars, jagged shells of houses, perhaps a lone wall standing alone, pierced by a window.

The Queen was gone. Maxian climbed across the wreckage, searching for her. He could not feel her anywhere. He hoped that she was not dead. The iron dog was gone, too, the collapsed section of plaza now filled with new rubble. The Prince felt desolate, alone. After a moment, he gave up the search.

It will be a long walk home, he thought, disheartened, *if the telecast is closed.*

The city seemed dead and Maxian was ashamed. This was no better than a draw. Worse, the enemy would hold these ruins once he was gone. But there was nothing he could do by himself. *I should not have come. . . .*

A hint of mocking laughter chased him as he jogged east towards the palace.

"Look out!" Rufio croaked, looking behind Dwyrin. They had staggered down a sloping avenue from the square of Mithra, stumbling over corpses both fresh and ancient. The Hibernian had lugged the heavy Greek, armor and all, nearly a block before Rufio managed to get on his own feet. Dwyrin thought the guard captain looked pretty bad, his face burned, most of his hair missing, one eye closed and bruised, yellow serum leaking from under the lid. He hoped he didn't look worse.

Dwyrin turned, exhausted. He felt weak. The fire in his heart still pulsed and burned, but everything else was stretched thin. Only the greenish-white flare in the north gave him heart, knowing he had struck a heavy blow against the enemy. The stuttering light helped them too, showing them the way down the avenue.

A yowl cut the air and the Hibernian grabbed Rufio's arm, pushing him away from the sound. A high-pitched yipping followed and then a pack of men rushed out of the shadows. Their long hair was greased into long spikes at the backs of their heads, their faces white with ash. They were lightly armored, with thick leather tunics stiffened by boiling. Most of them didn't even have metal helms, only caps of hide sewn with iron plates. Dwyrin crossed a fist before his body, his will struggling to call the fire.

A spear flicked out of the night and crashed into his shoulder. Gasping, Dwyrin was swung around. He fell back, barely catching himself. The tip had gouged into his shoulder, leaving a smear of blood. A cold sensation wicked down his arm. Struggling to ignore the pain, he turned back towards the enemy. One of the barbarians, whooping, lunged at him, hacking overhand with a long-hafted ax. Dwyrin ducked aside, feeling the blade hiss past, and then grabbed the man's face.

The Slav bit at him, still whooping a war cry, but Dwyrin's fingers dug in and there was a hot rush of flame. The man's shriek of agony was cut abruptly short and steam boiled out of his ears. Dwyrin pushed the corpse away, the head and shoulders wrapped in spitting flame. The rest of the Slavs drew back, sliding to a halt. The Hibernian snarled, flame spilling from his hand. Their eyes caught the glow and they began to back away.

Dwyrin stabbed out a hand, fingers stiff, and one of the Slavs at the end of their bunched line suddenly burst into flame, screaming hoarsely. The man writhed, bright blue tongues of fire rushing from his mouth. Smoking, he fell back. Dwyrin glanced over his shoulder, looking for Rufio. The Greek had found a sword, a heavy, thick-bladed barbarian weapon, and was holding it in both hands, half blinded but ready for battle.

"Run!" the Hibernian shouted, turning back to the enemy. He barely caught sight of a mass of rushing shapes and the fast patter of bare feet on stone. The Slavs had lunged forward, spears stiff in front of them. Dwyrin gargled in pain. Two of the leaf-shaped iron blades sank into his chest. Then a third pierced his neck and he went down.

Fire bloomed in his mind, though a swelling black tide filled his arms and legs with cold. Two of the Slavs incandesced, bursting apart in a brilliant white flare. The rest, blinded, staggered back, their clothes and armor smoking. Dwyrin tried to breathe, but there was only a horrible choking sensation. It was very cold. Very cold. The fire in his heart continued to spin, hissing and sparking, but now there was only darkness all around him.

The shape of an old man, his ancient face graven with dismay and pity, loomed over Dwyrin.

Rufio blinked, seeing sparkling motes fly across his vision. The boy had gone down under the rush. Shouting madly, the Greek stormed in, the heavy sword cutting sideways. There was a jolt as the blade bit into the neck of the nearest Slav. Blood jetted out, smearing the sword crimson. Most of the barbarians were still burning, though some of them were rolling on the ground, trying to snuff the flames. Rufio cut on a diagonal, the whole weight of his body behind the blow, and another Slav collapsed, his spine cut.

The boy was pinned on the ground under two bodies. Blood spilled from his mouth and nostrils. Rufio reached down, dragging a body away. The strange fire was still glowing in the Hibernian's eyes, like a distant lantern. He was convulsing, trying to breathe.

Rufio's fingers touched the iron spear point embedded in Dwyrin's throat. He swallowed a curse. There was nothing that could be done. Tears ran down the side of the Greek's nose, cutting a trail in the ash and soot. As he watched, the fire died in the boy's eyes and his body suddenly became still. "Good passage," Rufio whispered.

A shout roused him from his prayer, and the guard captain turned, his face bleak, the heavy sword raised in guard position. The street had filled with more Slavs and the stocky shapes of their Avar masters. High stiff plumes marked the officers. Thirty or forty of the spearmen, their faces painted with ash and woad, loped forward, yelping.

Rufio reached down and snatched up a spear, haft still smoking. He balanced it in his hand, then, as the Slavs sprinted to the attack, he hurled it, left-handed, with all his strength. The shaft transfixed one of the barbarians, throwing him back, blood spitting away in an arc. Then the others were on him, spears thrusting.

The Greek parried the first thrust, blocking it away with the flat of the sword. Then he rushed them, crashing into three of them, his elbow cracking across the nose of one. The others shouted, swirling around him. His blade hewed through another spear, cutting through the arm behind it. Rufio staggered, his armor grating as they stabbed at him from all sides.

"The Emperor! The Emperor!" he shouted, whirling, the long iron blade shearing through a bearded face, bone cracking, droplets of blood flying into the eyes of the next man. The air suddenly hissed with arrows and he staggered. A black-fletched shaft jutted from his arm, the triangular iron head punched straight through an iron ring. Rufio felt weak and knew that blood was seeping down his arm in a bright red stream. Another shaft plunged into his chest with a cold shock. His arm flew up, the blade rising. A Slav knocked it away with the haft of his ax.

They closed around him, eyes bright. The skyline of the city was glowing behind them, the sky a roiling mass of cloud and flame. Rufio coughed, his beard clotting with blood. Another of the barbarians raised an ax, the edge gleaming with red light. The Greek cursed under his breath.

This is going to hurt.

Brunhilde wailed, whipping around Nicholas' head. Her mirror-bright edge slashed through a man's back, cleaving metal, gristle, muscle like soft dough. The northerner, half mad with fear, choking in the tight air, shoved the corpse away with his boot. Behind him, Nicholas could hear Vladimir bellowing, his ax thunking into something heavy. The remaining Faithful, still chanting hoarsely, were on either side of them, pushing their way through the crowd.

Tens of thousands were packed onto the harbor docks,

weeping, crushed, pressing madly for the sea. Nicholas put his shoulder into the press, pushing past a dead woman, still held on her feet by the mob all around her. Brunhilde keened, blood soaking into her blade, and Nicholas stabbed forward, cutting down another man. He could hardly see, his left eye packed with cloth and a bandage.

Far ahead, across a sea of heads, tossing and crying out, he could see the end of the dock and the masts of an Imperial galley. The last hour had been a gruesome struggle, inching their way forward through the mob, finally reduced to chopping their way through the bodies of the citizens. From the height of the harbor causeway, the fleet had been in plain sight, standing off in the harbor waters, one ship at a time venturing to the end of the main pier, taking on the red-cloaked shapes of soldiers. Now it seemed impossibly far away through a dense thicket of weeping, crying people.

Nicholas felt heartsick, forced to kill fellow citizens, but he wanted to live more than he wanted to die. The sword licked out again, stabbing through the throat of an enormously fat man, his tunic blazoned with the crest of the bakers' guild. Nicholas crawled over his shuddering body, Vladimir and the others right behind him. Suddenly there was an empty space in front of him.

A line of soldiers, their shields overlapping, blocked the way. Grim eyes stared back at Nicholas over the top of the *scuta, pila* held at the ready to stab anyone that came too close.

"Nicholas of Roskilde, under-captain of the Faithful Guard," he gasped. Vladimir and the other Scandians were still pushing up behind him and Nicholas tried to hold them back. A thicket of spears was right in front of him, only inches from his abdomen. "We're Legion! We're Legion!"

The wailing around them changed in pitch. The galley at the end of the pier pulled away from the stone dock, oars flashing as they dug into the black water. The chorus

of despair changed, becoming even more hopeless, if that
were possible. The centurion in charge of the shield wall
shouted something and four of the men stepped back, making a narrow opening. Nicholas darted into it, sheathing
Brunhilde as he ran. Vladimir muttered some prayer behind him, holding his ax, still slick with blood, close to
his chest.

Slowly, in bunches, the Faithful filed through the opening in the shield wall. Nicholas looked around, utterly exhausted. Groups of other soldiers were standing or lying
in the open space. The surface of the dock was wet with
a slime of blood and urine and greasy fat. Gathering his
remaining strength, Nicholas turned back, catching Vladimir's eyes.

"Form everyone up and count off. I want to know who
lives and is with us. I'll report to the commander here and
get orders."

The Walach stared back with dead eyes, his face slack.
The last two hours seemed to have drained everything from
him. Nicholas turned away, shutting the ever-present sound
of the mob pleading for life from his mind. He caught sight
of the commander, a tall familiar-looking man in unfamiliar armor. Not a Roman, he thought dazedly, walking carefully, winding his way through men lying asleep on the
dock, their armor stained and pitted, their hands clutching
spears and swords. They did not seem to mind that they
lay in blood and offal.

The muted, crackling roar of the burning city continued
unabated.

In a black humor, Maxian pushed open the door to the
musty room deep beneath the palace. The shimmering
green light had faded in his absence, though the disks still
spun, hissing, in the air. The young priest was waiting,
facing the door, his hand raised in a sign. When he saw
that it was the Prince, he breathed a sigh of relief and
lowered his hand. Maxian slammed the door behind him,

then sketched a sign on the wooden panels. The oak shivered, growing out from the edges, filling the doorway from side to side. Leaves sprouted from the ancient surface and roots crawled across the floor, digging into the cracks between the flooring tiles.

"Go through," Maxian snapped, glaring at the priest for no good reason. The library on the other side of the ring of fire seemed crowded. There were Praetorians with drawn swords, the Empress, two more of the Western thaumaturges, even some Eastern officials. Everyone was staring back at him, dismay writ large on their features. "Go!"

The young priest clambered up onto the table, then stepped swiftly through the translucent disk. It shuddered, fracturing his image, and then he was through, stepping down into the hands of the legionaries. Maxian looked around the room, seeing row after row of ancient, moldy books, tattered parchments, rat-eaten scrolls. His anger shifted a little, away from his own recklessness to the poor treatment given these works.

Then he shook his head and sprang up onto the table. He paused, muttering, his head bent towards his chest. His left hand began to glow, shining with a deep reddish color. His fingers opened, revealing a shining glyph that shed a flickering radiance. The Prince bent, placing the sign on the tabletop. The glowing character faded into the stone. Then, without looking back, Maxian stepped through the wavering oval, feeling his hair rise and everything twist for an instant.

A dull crump shook the foundations of the temple of Hecate, rattling the statuary lining the roof and the triangular pediment. In the empty courtyard below, wind gusted between the pillars, blowing scraps of parchment across the tinted flagstones. Within the fane of the temple, the sacrificial fires were dead, the offerings covered with frost. The black sky had sapped the heat from everything within the walls.

The Dark Queen ghosted between the columns, her hood framing a pale, drawn face. She was exhausted, barely able to move, groping from shadow to shadow. A bitter taste of burning lime hung in the air, biting at her eyes and tongue. The violence in the ground beneath her feet faded away and she knew—even without casting her thought—that her old friend's library was buried under tons of rubble.

The whelp of a prince, she thought savagely. *What a fool. Like he can cover his tracks now ...*

The Queen reached a deep well that sheltered under the eaves of the temple. Thin steam rose from the black pit, warm air rising from the tunnels under the city and striking the frozen air. She swung her leg over the edge, then spidered down the sides. When only her head remained above the stone lip, she snarled at the west, thin arms trembling to hold her up. The dark power was still there, gloating outside the city.

Laugh, monster. This is my city. My *city! You will never have it.*

Then her pale eyes blinked and she was gone, vanished into the bosom of the earth.

***

PERINTHUS, ON THE THRACIAN COAST

***

Drums boomed, marking a slow, steady beat. Alexandros, one hand light on the reins of Bucephalas, trotted along the raised, metaled road that led into the city. The gates stood wide, the entrance tunnel through the walls bright with lanterns and torches. Bucephalas swung his head, tossing a thick black mane woven with ribbons, and snorted, smelling other horses. Lines of men in Western armor, legionaries, stood in ranks along the road. Their standards and banners fluttered in the light breeze off the sea. Alexandros raised a hand in salute, letting the sun sparkle from his mailed gauntlet.

Behind him, advancing at a steady, measured pace, marched thirty thousand Goths. Their long *sarissa* dipped and swung like a metronome, their booted feet crashing down as one. An impressive sight, thought the Macedonian, turning his horse in the shadow of the city gate. The first syntagma tramped past, entering the gate with a shout. Each man turned as he passed, their heads swinging in unison, their helmets gleaming with the afternoon sun.

"Alexandros!" they boomed, a thousand men with one voice. "Victory!"

Then they were past, and another regiment passed, and then another.

The Macedonian sat on his horse, smiling slightly, thinking of another day, long ago.

Men marched past, bearded men, with their helmets plumed with horsetails, their oval shields shining with the sunburst of Macedon. A great fleet waited on the shore, waiting to cross into Asia. Persia lay beyond, the mightiest empire in the world, endless, its armies without number. Waiting for him. As the gods had promised.

"Comes Alexandros?" A man with long blond hair rode up on a spirited gray horse. He looked tired, his face worn and shadowed by the fringe of a beard. He was not a Roman. "I am Dahvos, kagan of the Khazars. There are two legions here, the Third Augusta and another, which is currently nameless. I have letters for you, from Rome. They say that you are to take command of all of us—my men, the Legions, your own. Emperor Galen expresses great confidence in you."

Alexandros nodded, clasping hands with the man. The Khazar's eyes were haunted, as if he had looked upon an abyss. The Macedonian looked at him for a long moment, then smiled.

"Well met, kagan Dahvos. I have heard your nation is a brave and noble one."

Dahvos did not answer, turning away, his face stiff. "I will show you the city."

Alexandros nodded, then turned Bucephalas to follow. The Goths continued to march into the city, tramping through the tunnel. Within the stone walls, there seemed to be only soldiers. A city stripped for war, then. Alexandros grinned to himself, urging the stallion ahead. There was a heady smell in the air, a tension that spoke of battle and coming glory.

He could even see the Asian shore, if he climbed the walls.

And there are Persians! he exulted. *Within the reach of my lance, my eye, my spear!*

THE PERSIAN CAMP

Zoë yawned, waking from dreamless sleep. She felt blessedly relaxed, heavy quilts lying on top of her. She wiggled her toes, finding a cool spot under the covers. Her eyes opened, seeing the light of morning shining through the canvas of the tent above her. Distant, muted noise reached her ears, speaking of men moving about the camp. The bitter taste of burning pine and juniper logs was in the air. Satisfied that all was well, she turned over, reaching across the bed.

There was no one beside her, the space cold and empty.

"Ah, how late have I slept?" she wondered aloud, sitting up, stretching. The black mane of her hair fell in front of her eyes and she brushed it back behind her ears.

"Not too late," said a familiar voice. "There is still some breakfast left."

Zoë turned, smiling, and climbed out of bed. Her sleeping tunic was mussed, but she smoothed it down. "Auntie! I didn't know you were here."

Zenobia smiled back, her glorious blue-black hair sweeping over a pale shoulder. She was dressed as befitted a queen, in glowing white silk, with a collar of emerald and pearl around her elegant neck. The jewels nestled between the curves of her bosom, half hidden in shadow. Silver bracelets girdled her arms and there were rings of gold on her fingers.

"I'm always here for you, daughter. Where else would I be?"

Zoë laughed, perfectly happy, and reached down, taking her aunt's hand. It was warm and strong, exactly as she remembered.

To be concluded in *The Dark Lord*

Author's Note

During revisions of this work, a number of chapters were wholly removed from the text. The author bears every responsibility for exceeding the stipulated manuscript length. Those who are interested in the missing portions can find them on-line, at this URL:

(http://www.throneworld.com/oathofempire/en/storm_deletions.html.)

The marching song of the Gothic pikemen drilling in their camp at Aquincum is:

Around her hair she wore a yellow ribbon
She wore it in the springtime, in the early month of
    May
And if you asked her why the heck she wore it
She'd say she wore it for her soldier who was far,
    far away
Far away
Far away
She wore it for her soldier who was far, far away
Around the block she carried a baby swaddled
She carried it in the springtime, in the early month
    of May
And if you asked her why the heck she carried it
She'd say she pushed it for her soldier who was far,
    far away
Far away
Far away
She carried it for her soldier who was far, far away
Around his grave she laid the pretty flowers
She laid them in the springtime, in the early month
    of May

And if you asked her why the heck she laid them
She'd say she laid them for her soldier who was
   far, far away
Far away
Far away
She laid them for her soldier who was far, far away

The marching song of the Gothic troops on the Field of
Black Birds is:

The grand old dux of Eboracum,
He had ten thousand men;
He marched them up the hill,
And marched them down again.
Now when they were up they were up,
And when they were down they were down,
And when they were only half way up,
They were neither up nor down.

Look for

The DARK LORD

by Thomas Harlan

Now available in hardcover
from Tor Books

)H(

Grimacing, the Queen turned away from a casement window, sleek dark hair framing her elegant neck and shoulders. Outside, the roar of shouting men filled the air. Beneath her slippers, the floor trembled with the crash of a ram against the tower doors. The room was very hot and close. Swirls of incense and smoke puddled near the ceiling. For a moment the Queen was silent, considering the array of servants kneeling around her husband's funeral bier.

"Antonius Antyllus," she said, at last, as a fierce shout belled out from the courtyard below and the floor shook in response. "You must take my son."

The stocky Roman, clean-shaven face pinched in confusion, half turned towards the back of the room. At the Queen's arched eyebrow, a slim young man in a pleated kilt stepped forward. The boy was trembling, but he raised his head and met the Queen's eyes directly. Antyllus made a questioning motion with his hand, brow furrowed. "Pharaoh, I cannot take him away from you . . . where will he go? Where would he be safe from your enemies?"

"Home," the Queen said, stepping to a silk and linen-draped throne dominating the room. As she moved, her attendants drew a gown of shimmering black fabric from a chest. A blond handmaiden knelt and raised a headdress of gold and twin scepters. Beside her, a dusky maid bore a jeweled sun disk, ornamented with an eight-rayed star in bronze. "To your home, to Rome, as your son. His Latin is excellent. He has been raised, as his noble father wished, a Roman."

Antyllus shifted his feet, unsure, but finally nodded in surrender. There was a huge crash from below and the drapes swayed. The legionary tried to summon a smile, but there was only bleak agreement in his fair, open face. "Another cousin," he said, looking upon the young man, "among dozens of our riotous family. . . . " His eyes shifted to the corpse on its marble bier and grief welled up in his face like water rising in a sluice. "Father would wish this, my lady, so I will take your command, and his, to heart. Your son will find sanctuary in the bosom of my mother's family—they are a huge clan and filled with all sorts. . . . "

"Go." The Queen raised her chin, sharp sea-blue eyes meeting those of a man in desert robes, his lean, dark face half shrouded by a thin drape of muslin. "Asan, you must take Anytllus and Caesarion to safety—a ship is waiting, at the edge of the delta. Will you do this thing, for me?"

The Arab bowed elegantly and stepped away into the shadows along the inner wall of the room. Antyllus did not look back at the Queen, boots ringing as he strode to the hidden door. Caesarion did, looking to his mother with bleak eyes. His youth seemed to fade, as he ducked though the opening, a weight settling on him, and the Queen knew the boisterous child, all glad smiles and laughter, was gone forever.

Voices boomed in the corridors of the tower and the shouting outside dwindled, replaced by the clashing of spears on shields. The Queen did not look out, for she was well used to the sight of Roman legionaries. Instead, she settled on the throne, long fingers plucking at the rich fabric of her gown. Narrowed eyes surveyed her servants and councilors, a meager remnant of the multitude who once clung to the hem of her glory.

"Get out," she rasped, voice suddenly hoarse. Sitting so, facing the closed, barred door to the main hall, she could look upon the shrouded, still body of her last husband, laid out in state at the center of the chamber. "All of you, out!"

The Queen raised a hand imperiously, golden bracelets tinkling softly as they fell away from her wrist.

They fled, all save fair Charmian and dusky Iras. The Queen listened, hearing the tramp of booted feet in the hall, then the door—two thick valves of Tyrian cedar, bound with iron and gold and the sun disk of Royal Egypt—shuddered. A voice, deep and commanding, shouted outside.

The Queen ignored the noise, leaning back, letting her maids fix the heavy headdress—a thick wreath of fine golden leaves around an eight-rayed disk—upon her brow and place hooked scepters in either hand. The doors began to boom as spear butts slammed against the panels. She closed her eyes, crossing delicate fingers upon her chest, then took a deep breath.

"I am ready to receive our conqueror," she said quietly, looking sideways at the blond maid, who knelt, tears streaming down her face. "Where is the god?"

Iras lifted a wicker basket from the floor, then removed the fluted top. Something hissed within, thrashing, bulging against the sides of the basket. The dusky maid grasped the viper swiftly, just behind the mottled, scaled head. The snake's jaws yawned, revealing a pink mouth and pale white fangs. Iras worked quickly, squeezing the poison sac behind the muscular jaw with deft fingers. A milky drop oozed out into her hand. A brief spasm of pain crossed the Nubian's impassive face as poison burned into her flesh, then the maid tilted her hand and the droplet spilled onto the Queen's extended tongue.

Cleopatra closed her mouth, clear blue eyes staring straight ahead. The door splintered. Ruddy torchlight leaked through, sparkling in clouds of dust puffing away from the panels with each blow. Then she closed her eyes, long lashes drooping over a fine powder of pearl and gold and amethyst. At her side, Iras broke the snake's back with a twist, and then dropped the creature onto the floor, where the serpent twitched and writhed for a long moment.

The two maids knelt, bowing one last time before their Queen, and then they too tasted the god's blessed milk and lay still, as if asleep, at her feet.

The ruined door swung wide and the legionaries stepped back, tanned faces flushed, the chin straps of their helmets dark with sweat. For a moment, as they looked into the dark room, no one spoke. There was only the harsh breathing of exhausted men. The centurion in charge of the detail glanced over his shoulder, a question plain in his sunburned face.

"Stand aside," a quiet, measured voice said. "There is nothing to fear."

A young man, his hair a neat dark cap on a well-formed head, limped across the threshold. Like the soldiers crowding the hallway, he wore heavy banded mail, a red cloak, and leather boots strapped up to the knee. His sword was sheathed—indeed, the man claimed to have never drawn a blade in anger—and even on this day, he did not wear a helmet.

Gaius Octavius, defender of the Republic of Rome, the victor—now, today, in this singular moment—the master of Rome and Egypt, looked down upon his last enemy with a pensive face. Nostrils flared, catching the brittle smell of urine and blood, and he nudged one of the slaves sprawled below the throne with the tip of his boot. The girl's flesh was already growing cold.

For a moment, standing over the body of the Queen, the young man considered calling his physicians, or discovering if any Psyllian adepts were in the city. But then he saw the woman's cheeks turning slowly blue and knew he had been denied a great prize.

"Khamûn," Octavian said in a conversational voice, "come here."

There was movement in the doorway and without turning the Roman knew the frail, spidery shape of the Egyptian sorcerer knelt behind him, long white beard trailing on the mosaic floor. No one else entered the room.

"Royal Egypt is dead." Octavian stepped up to the throne itself, one foot dragging slightly. "She is beyond us, her flesh so swiftly cold, joining her Dionysus in death. . . ." Octavian barely spared a glance for the dead man in the center of the room. He was already quite familiar with the strong, handsome features—he had no need to look upon them ever again. "Your gift to me, as you have so often called it, has vanished like dew." Octavian turned, one eyebrow rising, his eyes cold. "Has it not?"

Khamûn bent his head to the floor. "Yes, my lord. Alive, alive she . . . "

Octavian turned away, back to the dead Queen, who sat upon her throne in the very semblance of life, save for the patent stillness of her breast and the inexplicable failure of the vibrant energy, wit and incandescent charm that marked her in life. The Roman bowed to the dead woman, acknowledging the end of their game. "Pharaoh is dead, Khamûn. But I am content. I will rule Egypt, even if I may not possess her."

The sorcerer nodded, though he did not look up. Octavian looked to the doorway, where his soldiers were waiting, afraid to enter. "Scarus—find those servants who remain and bring them to me. They have unfinished business to attend."

"Here is your queen," Octavian said, standing on the top step of the dais. He looked down upon a clutch of Egyptians the legionaries had dragged from the tower rooms. Others would have escaped, he was sure, but these slaves knew their mistress well. "She has joined her husband and sits among the gods. Look upon her and know Rome did not stoop to murder."

The servants, faces streaked with tears, looked up, then bent their heads again to the floor. Octavian stepped down, careful to lead with his good foot. A wreath of golden laurels crowned him, and his stained soldier's cloak had been replaced with a supple white robe, edged with maroon. The lamps were lit, joining the fading sunlight in illuminating the death chamber. Both maids had been carried away, but the man and the woman remained, each in their chosen place.

"Has a tomb been prepared for your mistress?" Octavian's voice rose, for more Egyptians stood outside, in the hall, the late Queen's ministers and councilors among them. "A place of honor for her and for her Dionysus?"

One of the slaves, a broad-shouldered man with a shaggy mane of blue-black hair, looked up. His limbs gleamed with sweat, as if he had run a great distance, and he spread his hands, indicating the room. "Yes, great lord, this tower is her chosen tomb."

The Roman pursed his lips and looked out through the tall window, across the rooftops of the houses and temples of Alexandria. Even here, within this great edifice, he could feel the mournful chanting of the crowds, the restless surge of the city. Alexandria was a live thing, filled with furious, fickle energy. Octavian swallowed a smile, acknowledging the Queen's foresight. *Let you sleep within the walls of your beloved Alexandria? That will not do!*

"This place will not suffice," he said, looking down upon the slave. "You must take her away—far away—into the desert. Prepare there a hidden tomb, safe from the eyes of men, where these two may lie in peace for all time. Let them have each other in death, for eternity, for their time together on earth was so short."

Many of the slaves looked up in wonder and Octavian saw the black-maned man's eyes narrow in suspicion. The young Roman raised a hand, stilling their questions. "Rome does not wish to know where you place her—nor should you tell another, for tomb-robbers will dream of Kleopatra's treasure with lust. Take her far from the dwellings of man. Let her find peace."

Octavian turned away, looking out upon the city again, and he waited, patient and still, until the slaves and servants bore away the two corpses. Then he smiled and laughed aloud, for he was alone. Fools! Let Rome be magnanimous in victory—it costs nothing—and the witch-queen will be well hidden, far from the thoughts and dreams of men.